George V. Higgins was … er columnist before becomin… h in 1999 he was a professor at Boston University, teaching creative writing. His previous novels – critically acclaimed volumes in what Lord Gowrie has called 'his unfolding masterpiece' of contemporary New England – include *The Friends of Eddie Coyle*, *Cogan's Trade*, *Penance for Jerry Kennedy*, *The Mandeville Talent*, *Swan Boats at Four* and, most recently, *Sandra Nichols Found Dead*.

ALSO BY GEORGE V. HIGGINS

The Friends of Eddie Coyle (1972)
The Digger's Game (1973)
Cogan's Trade (1974)
A City on a Hill (1975)
The Friends of Richard Nixon (1975)
The Judgment of Deke Hunter (1976)
Dreamland (1977)
A Year or So with Edgar (1979)
Kennedy for the Defense (1980)
The Rat on Fire (1981)
The Patriot Game (1982)
A Choice of Enemies (1984)
Style vs. Substance (1984)
Penance for Jerry Kennedy (1985)
Impostors (1986)
Outlaws (1987)
The Sins of the Fathers (1988)
Wonderful Years, Wonderful Years (1988)
The Progress of the Seasons (1989)
Trust (1989)
On Writing (1990)
Victories (1990)
The Mandeville Talent (1991)
Defending Billy Ryan (1992)
Bomber's Law (1993)
Swan Boats at Four (1995)
Sandra Nichols Found Dead (1996)

A Change of Gravity

George V. Higgins

A *Warner* Book

First published in the United States in 1997
by Henry Holt and Company, Inc.

First published in Great Britain in 1999
by Little, Brown and Company
This edition published by Warner Books in 2000

*All characters in this publication are fictitious
and any resemblance to real persons, living or dead,
is purely coincidental.*

A CIP catalogue record for this book
is available from the British Library.

ISBN 0 7515 2351 8

Typeset by Palimpsest Book Production Limited,
Polmont, Stirlingshire
Printed and bound in Great Britain by
Mackays of Chatham plc, Chatham, Kent

Warner Books
A Division of
Little, Brown and Company (UK)
Brettenham House
Lancaster Place
London WC2E 7EN

A Change of Gravity

1

On the afternoon of the second Thursday in November, US District Court Judge Barrie Foote as she preferred ate her lunch alone, reading her *New York Times*. She sat at the head of the long polished mahogany table in the library of her chambers in the courthouse on Main Street in Springfield, Massachusetts, luxuriating in her daily forty minutes of silence. When she had finished eating – tuna fish with fat-free mayonnaise, shredded lettuce and tomato chunks in a pita pocket; Diet Coke; large coffee, black – she picked up the telephone handset and said, 'Ask Sandy to come in, please.'

She gathered up the waxed paper, flimsy paper napkins and unused packets of salt and pepper that had come with the sandwich and stuffed them back into the bag – along with the hollow red plastic straw that Spiro, the counterman at Dino's Deli always included, so that she might stir into her coffee either the two packets of sugar or the two packets of Sweet 'n Low that she also never used – and lobbed the parcel with her left hand in a low arc over the table, applying a little backspin, faultlessly thunking it into the metal wastebasket in the corner. 'It's a *three*, my friends, an' nothin' but net,' she said softly. 'Crowd in this place's goin' *wild*.'

Two years before, during the interval between her appointment by President Clinton and congressional confirmation and her swearing-in, she had told an interviewer from the *Springfield Union News* that she thought 'nurture outweighs nature in the makeup of the adult animal – it's supposed to, anyway. If you're born lucky, and you pay attention, it does. Overlook either one, odds are you're dead meat.

'Nature first. We're born with what our parents' genes give us. They couldn't do much about what they gave us to inherit. So that made me then a light-skinned African-American female infant. But a lucky one. I came into the kind of upper-middle-class world that your daddy can afford to give you if he could bring the ball up on the right like nobody's business, back when he was in his prime. His best years out on the floor in the NBA were over before the big money really started raining down, but the front office always treated him well, before and after he retired. My father's had a good life. And my mom didn't do too bad either.'

The interviewer identified her parents: Reginald Carpenter, point guard for the Fort Wayne Pistons in the late '40s and early '50s, and Evelyn Field, the Northern Thrush, a regular headliner at the Drake, Palmer House, and Ambassador West grills well into the mid-to-late '60s, 'her signature song a slow, torchy arrangement of "You Belong to Me" done especially for her by Mel Torme.'

'Which in turn made the odds pretty good that if I didn't get sick, or hurt in a car crash or something, I *would* grow up, and if I did I'd be a light-skinned black *woman*, and in fact that's what I did.

'Because my father and my mother were comparatively well-off, in the course of growing up I got a good education, private schools, music lessons and so forth. Which meant that when I met my future first husband, we were both in college. Headed, we expected, for professional careers. When I graduated from Brown back in Nineteen-sixty-five – Ray was two years ahead of me; Providence, Sixty-three – if you had that respectable kind of life in mind you did things by the book. And that was especially true if your skin didn't happen to be white. If you knew what was good for you, anyway – and Ray and I both did. Fourteen years later when we parted company, I'd built my whole legal career and reputation as Barrie Foote, not Carpenter, so when we got divorced I was willing enough to let Raymond loose but not to let go my share of his name. I kept the education that my parents gave to me, and I kept Ray's last name as well, 'cause that's how and what I became what I am now.

'Professionally, that is, as a partner at Butler and Corey, first female black lawyer they ever hired. Also the first black to ever make partner. Both of those events in my life without doubt have left deep imprints on me. I'm certainly not the same woman I was when I came east to Brown; not the same as the one who came out of Georgetown Law so long ago, needing a job where her husband was, which happened to be here in Springfield.

'Ray'd gone to work at Valley Bank right out of the Wharton School. And I was able to get a very good job here, not only because Ray'd made his share of contacts around town but also because I had one of my own. I knew Bob Pooler from Georgetown. He laid the groundwork for me at Butler, Corey. The firm didn't hire me because I'd known Bob in law school – he was two years ahead of me – but the fact that I knew Bob had a lot to do with how I got the first interview.

'So that's what I mean about nurture. Everything that's happened to me's made an impact on me, made me a different person from the one I used to be. I *think* – at least I hope – I've become a better one. One who got that way because she learns from experience. What I've learned and the people I've known are parts of what I am today, because of the way I grew up.'

The interview had taken place in the dramatically modern soaring fieldstone-and-redwood home Foote shared with her second husband, the internationally known artist, Eric Hedges. It was set on a ledge off a private road off South Street near Tillotson Hill overlooking the Cobble Hill Reservoir in Blandford. 'Eric and I first met at a solo show of his at the Ainsworth Gallery in Boston, seems like it must've been a hundred years ago. Ray'd gotten involved with a group of businessmen and banking people here and down in Boston who were trying to buy a dilapidated old racetrack out in Hancock. There'd been a big scandal. Word went around the New York Mafia was behind the original deal. Some people went to jail, and those who didn't, the people who'd originally built the track, ended up going into bankruptcy. No one could find a buyer, so it ended up the town took the property for unpaid taxes. And there it sat, weeds growing all over, buildings falling apart.

'Ray and the people he was with were convinced it still could be a money-maker. So their idea was to buy it cheap, rebuild it, and then either sell it to someone else or else reopen it and run it themselves. Warren Corey, one of the senior partners at Butler, Corey, was involved with the group, and that year I was working for him. All of us were in Boston for something connected with it, licensing hearings or something, and after the hearing I went to the gallery. I'd always admired Eric's work, and that's how we met. I'm the only one who gained anything from that racetrack project. The deal itself fell through.

'Now Eric, he looks at things from the artist's perspective, and that's had an influence on me, affected how I see the world. And again, that's what I mean. About how we're the sum of our experience; what we are.'

The text of the interview was illustrated by several photographs, one of her in a judicial robe, another of her at her desk in her new chambers, three showing her at home, casually dressed in a tawny cowled sweater and fitted jeans, her black hair in a shiny page-boy framing her slightly feline face. Eric had said she'd done a good job and should be very pleased, and she had said: 'The *photographer* did a good job; I grant you that. But I don't think *I* did. Do I really talk like that, say fatuous things like that, to people I don't know? Cripes, I sound like such a phony there, like the way Ray used to, accepting one of his semi-annual awards for being such a *wonderful* house nigger.'

'It does the job, though,' Eric had said, and he had been correct. The profile made her seem to deserve the distinction she had achieved.

Sandy Robey opened the door and came in, a file folder in his hand, deducing from the thunk, the fact she was still seated at the table and the pleased expression on her face what she'd just done with the lunchbag. 'You know, Judge, you really should let us get you one of those wastebasket-backboards,' he said.

Robey tried hard to be cheerful; preparing to turn forty was a sour portion for him. He believed that at one-sixty-five he was about twelve or fifteen pounds overweight. His wife disagreed – much too gaily, he thought – saying he ought to lose closer to twenty. The Rogaine with minoxidil that Foote had encouraged him to obtain and apply two weeks before had not visibly arrested, much less reversed, the gradual but alarming recession of his coarse reddish hair. His dentist had admonished him to see a periodontist for attention to what he diagnosed as advancing gum disease that otherwise would leave him toothless before fifty, 'unless I have the good sense to die first.'

'Backboard, *huh*,' she said, 'what do *I* need with a backboard? Swishers're all I put up. Now what kind of nonsense you bringin' here that's gonna get us all distracted this fine autumn afternoon from already-pressin' business?'

Robey had put the folder on the table, sat down and tapped it once. 'Just one small matter, Your Honor,' he said. 'Shouldn't take much time at all. US Attorney's got a balky witness. This grand-jury, corruption investigation he's only been hinting at discreetly to the papers for about a year or so. Guy's lawyer says if they bring his client in, he's going to tell him to claim he'll incriminate himself if he talks. The US Attorney's granted him Use immunity but he says that isn't good enough. Says if it's not Transactional, the US Attorney'll use the testimony to get leads to other evidence, then turn around and use that to cut his client's head off. So the US Attorney – the assistant's Mister Warmth, Arnie Bissell – wants you to give him and his guy a hearing, tell them the USA doesn't lie to people and so Use is good enough and his guy has gotta talk.'

'Bissell wants *me* to tell this lawyer and his client that the US Attorney's office never fibs?' she said, widening her eyes. 'I do that and God'll surely strike me dead.'

Robey laughed. 'Bissell says it shouldn't take long – ten minutes at the most.'

'Ten *minutes*?' she said. 'Why should it take *any* minutes? Just do it like always. Have him send up a written order and I'll sign the thing on the spot. Then have him threaten the guy. If he stays coy, *then* we'll have a hearing. What you and I want to do here this afternoon is get back to the late Mister Nick Hardigrew's Really Lousy Last Weekend.'

'Mind telling me what you thought of what got put in this morning?' Robey said. 'When the girl said he had his hands folded in front of him, and his head down, like he's saying grace? And he stayed that way, all the way down?'

'I don't know,' the judge said. 'Either he was saying his prayers or else he'd gone into some kind of trance. Blissed-out completely. Or maybe he was paralyzed; panicked and froze when he realized what was happening. He had to've known it when his chute didn't open. And to've known what he had to do next. This wasn't his first jump. Why didn't he pop the back-up? I suppose at that velocity it's pretty hard to hear what somebody else's yelling at you, "*Pull the reserve chute, for God's sake.*" So maybe he couldn't hear the others. But she said that *she* could hear them yelling – that's why she didn't yell herself. Makes it seem as though he should've heard them too.'

'Unless he didn't want to,' Robey said. 'Maybe what happened was what he intended to have happen. Nobody we've heard yet seems to really want to come right out and *say* it, but isn't that where they're leading us? That the reason why the main chute didn't open when it should've, when he was clear of the plane, was that he'd made sure it wouldn't. That there wasn't anything wrong with the job the packers at the jump-center did. The reason it didn't open was that sometime between the time that they packed it and checked it and said it was fine was that he'd done something to it himself. Sabotaged it. So he *knew* it wasn't going to open. He'd made sure of it. All he had to do was just have the will-power to keep his hands together until the ground came up and hit him. Unless he'd sabotoged the reserve too, of course, but we've got no evidence of that either.'

'Suicide,' she said, reflectively. 'He meant it to happen. Not an accident at all. This whole on-and-off romance he'd been having with sky-diving, for how many years was it now, two or three? My notes're out on the bench.'

'I think it was three,' Robey said. 'Which was another thing that didn't add up. He seems to've been sort of casual about it. The testimony Tuesday, didn't one of the witnesses from the jump-center testify this would've been his eighth or ninth jump? Seven or eight of them uneventful, before the one that killed him. Not that many, really, considering how long he'd been at it. It wasn't an obsession with him, like it usually seems to be with people who come back after the first time they try it.'

'Yeah,' she said, 'the fellow did say that. The majority never jump twice. They're thrill-seekers, kind of people who dare each other to do things, usually while they're having several beers. Young, most of them. Try it once and say "Oh-kay, that's it; now I've been there and done that." And then never do it again. The real sky-divers're the ones that get hooked and stay with it, like skiers. Jump every chance they get, ten or twenty times a year. Our absent party doesn't fit either profile.

'But still, he's qualified; he's allowed to jump without a buddy close enough to try to save him in mid-air. Which he has to be able to do if he's going to be able to kill himself. The day the chute didn't open just happened to be the day that he picked to do what he had in mind all the time.

'All right, find me a motive. Why make it look like an accident? There was no incentive in his insurance. Million-dollar policy for accidental death; isn't small-change, no, but his coverage'd been in effect for over twenty years. Suicide-exemption clause expired eighteen years ago. No motive there to fake an accident.

'Did he have some kind of horrible disease? If he did he was the only one who knew about it. Family didn't; doctor didn't; none of his friends did either.

'A scandal about to break, he chooses death over disgrace? Possible, I suppose, but we've got no evidence of one.

'His business was in good shape. Nurserymen and people in the landscaping business probably felt it just about the same as everybody else does when the economy was flat, few years ago, but his seems to've come through it okay.

'So the only reason he could possibly've had to do it then would've been chronic, severe depression. Unipolar mental illness.

'You could infer that here, I guess. I suppose in any case of suicide, you almost have to think the poor bastard must've been miserably depressed. Literally out of his mind. But if Hardigrew was that far gone, wouldn't he've shown it in some way? Started drinking too much? Become withdrawn? You'd think so, but he didn't. He spent years in a bottomless Hell, getting ready to do this unspeakable thing, and during all that time none of the people who knew him and *had* known him for years: not a single *one* of them, had the slightest *hint* of what he was going through?

'It doesn't make sense. So depressed you want to kill yourself, and finally you do it, but *not* so depressed that anyone who loves you, or sees you every day, even *notices?*'

'I don't know,' Robey said, 'but it does seem like that's what the defense's driving at.'

'Well, they've still got a lot of work ahead of them,' she said. 'Far as I'm concerned anyway. There would've been a clue. Something you could look at now and say: "Hey that was kind of strange. Someone should've noticed that. Taken his car keys away from him. Had him put away, or at least put him to bed. Given him some mood-elevators; jacked him up on feel-good pills."

'There is no such clue. He got up that morning down in Suffield, self-destruction on his mind, showered and dressed like he always did; had a good breakfast after that. Again: *just like he always did.* Man's almost fifty, same age I am now. By the time you've reached this stage in life, made something of yourself – this is a successful man here, came from modest circumstances and did pretty well for himself – you've developed a full set of habits. A lot of the things that we do are repetitive, have to be done again every day, over and over again. Habits simplify your life. You *know* what to do, – it's automatic. Don't have to do so much thinking.

'That's what our Nicholas did that last day; he followed his regular habits. He *seemed* to be in good spirits. Showers and gets dressed and eats. He goes out of his ten-room house on an acre-plus of prime land, so we're told, got to be worth at least three or four hundred thousand dollars, in the neighborhood it's in. This looks like one happy guy. He gets into his bright-yellow Saab convertible, drives himself up to Barnes Airport in Westfield; he's signed up for a gorgeous summer Sunday of sky-diving. Several times before he's done this without any mishap whatsoever, not even a sprained ankle. But this time it's going to be different. Today he's going to kill himself.

'If you think that, then there wasn't any accident or any negligence involved here. When he stepped out of that airplane, in his mind he was doing a perfectly normal, rational thing.

'I can't believe it. Why go to all this trouble? There're plenty of places you can drive to and walk up to and jump off and kill yourself, if that's what you want to do. Don't need any training to do that. All the lessons; the classroom instruction; the tethered training jumps from that steel tower they've got up there: what is it, three or four hundred feet off the ground, and they take you up there and you *jump*? Forget it. I'm finished right there. I wouldn't dare to *climb* that high, never mind jump off. You want me to conclude he did it all in order to kill himself in style? All the supervised practice jumps with the instructors: everything was preliminary to the big day when Nick Hardigrew got himself killed? Nobody was negligent? No one failed to exercise due care? It wasn't anyone's fault?'

'Well, maybe,' she said. 'I suppose we never know what hell people could be going through behind their eyes where we can't see it. What they might do to stop the pain they're in.' She shook her head. 'I can tell you one thing though: The more I hear of this one, the gladder I am it didn't go jury-waived. Let those good people figure it out. I don't envy them for a minute.' Then she said: 'Well, 're we ready to go now? Tell them to bring down the jury.'

'I dunno,' Robey said. 'When do you want the immunity hearing? Four today or first thing in the morning? I need to know now, so I can have someone get word to the witness's lawyer so he'll know when he has to come down here.'

'Sandy,' she said. 'I already told you: we don't need a hearing. *May* need one, but don't need one yet. Tell whoever it is down there in the US Attorney's office to send up the order they want me to sign. *Then* if the witness still takes the Fifth, *then* we'll have him in and I'll put on my usual impressive performance, plant my brogan right on his *neck*. What's the matter with the government anyway? This isn't the first one of these things we've ever had here. They should know by now how we do them.'

'The *guy's* lawyer's the one that wants it,' Robey said. 'He's got some argument why he thinks the grant's improper, unenforceable, and therefore his client shouldn't be compelled to take the Fifth and make the grand jury think he's guilty of something, before he gets in to see you.'

'That's a new one,' the judge said. 'Who dreamed up this new way to waste time? Some jackass with his first federal case?'

'Could be, now that you mention it,' Robey said, grinning at her. 'I know I've never seen him in here. Heard of him though. Geoffrey Cohen's his name. People say he's not bad. Think his office's over South Hadley.'

The judge regarded Robey with mixed vexation and amusement. '*Shee-it*,' she said, 'you're not telling me that. The jackass lawyer's *my* lawyer? Was, anyway. Did a good job for me, too. What the heck is he doing down here, federal criminal case? He's not a criminal lawyer; Geoffrey's a *divorce* lawyer. He's always been that. Bob Pooler's the man for this kind of ugliness. People should stick to what they know.'

'In the first place,' Robey said, 'Cohen appears to be branching out. That drug case that you drew last Thursday there. Sanderson, I think it was? Golf pro; in the winter he tends bar in Vermont – moderate amount of coke; Bissell tells me Cohen represents the broad who turned him in. State plea-bargain of her own. Apparently in this corruption matter that we're talking about now, Bob Pooler already had a client. His client's the one they want Geoff's client to sink. Bob'd have a big conflict of interest.'

'Who's Bob's client?' the judge said. 'What poor devil're they after now?'

'From what Bissell told me,' Robey said, 'the lucky nominee's the ever-popular Daniel J. Hilliard. Former state rep from Holyoke? Chairman of House Ways and Means when he stopped running, Eighty-two, Eighty-four, I think it was. His pals on Beacon Hill gave him his very own college. Hampton Pond Community. Since then he's more or less faded out of sight.'

Judge Foote looked glum. 'Oh I hope that that isn't so,' she said, after a while. 'I hope that isn't true. And I hope if it *is* true that they don't decide to indict him. And if they do, then I hope they lose. Now I don't want you telling anybody else what I just said, but *goddamn*, I wish they wouldn't do that.'

'Oh God, I'm sorry,' Robey said, looking chagrined. 'I didn't realize you knew the guy, were close to him.'

'Oh I wasn't,' she said quickly, silently chastising herself for having spoken impulsively and hoping not to have to tell more lies than she'd be able to remember. 'Not the way you're thinking, at least. Keep in mind, Sandy: I can almost always tell what you're thinking. Shame on you.' Robey looked sheepish.

'It was nothing you could really call "personal,"' she said, thinking: *It was more what you'd call sexual.*

'I got to know him from when I was still married to Ray. Not *happily* married by then, anymore, but still, you know, under contract.' *For another eight or nine years or so, as a matter of fact – not that I let that stand in my way.* 'That racetrack deal I mentioned, 'Seventy-two or so, early in 'Seventy-three. One of the chores the Chief had me doing involved staying in touch making sure the local reps were up to speed on the project. Dan Hilliard naturally was one of them.' *Getting into bed with Dan Hilliard wasn't on the Chief's specs; that was extracurricular.*

'I saw him three or four times. Once I had to drive down to Boston, I recall.' *And a room in the Lenox Hotel.* 'And then the other times I went up to Holyoke, the huge second-floor office he used to have there. Unless it was crowded, your voice echoed in it. I thought he was a very *nice* man, a thoroughly, *truly*, *nice*, man. I suppose I have to say he was charming.' *He's buying it*, she thought, with a tincture of relief and shame. *What they say is true, I guess: Once you get the hang of it, you never lose the touch. Very nicely done, girl, very nicely done.*

'In fact I may've been a little bit too hard on you just then. Now that you've gotten me thinking about it, I remember having it go through my mind at the time that if I hadn't been still married to Ray and so forth, I could see myself getting very interested in this Hilliard guy. Although of course he was still married then, too.'

'Talk was he never let that interfere with his personal life,' Robey said, smirking. 'He is a charmer, no question. I remember when his wife was divorcing him; she alleged adultery. There was a *lot* of talk. That was a fairly unusual thing to do: meant someone was *really* pissed off. There was *considerable* speculation about whose names might get dragged into it, how many other divorces there'd be, if theirs ever came to a trial.'

'I recall that,' she said, a lot more calmly than she had lived through it.

'And then when it didn't,' Robey said, 'when it settled – word was she cleaned him out – then the word was that was the reason.

That he'd done the right thing and given her everything she asked for, so she wouldn't raise such a stink that he'd have to leave town – maybe along with a lot of other people. Bad enough he was washed-up in politics; if he let that stuff hit the fan he would've had to forget the college job, too.'

He paused. 'I think Geoff Cohen might've even had that case.'

'He did,' the judge said. 'Sam Evans from our shop represented Dan. Sam was the divorce specialist. He was extremely good at it. Up until that case, consensus was he was the very best around. He couldn't make divorce *fun*, but if you had to go through one and you could get Sam Evans, at least you could relax a little, knew you were in good hands. Top-notch negotiator; meticulous about details; scrupulously honest – and a complete gentleman to boot.

'After the Hilliard case was over, Sam was almost inconsolable. He said with all the sexual misconduct Hilliard had against him, there'd been nothing he could do; he'd never had a chance. The only hope that he'd had was that Geoff'd make the kind of dumb mistake young lawyers sometimes make out of inexperience, and give Sam something he could use.

'Didn't happen. Sam said Geoff'd known *exactly* what he had to work with; played his cards perfectly; made no mistakes at *all*; and as a result ended up cleaning Sam's clock for him. After that in this part of the world there were *two* "best divorce lawyers around." In fact what Sam said about Geoff was what made me hire him. Sam'd gotten close to Ray during that racetrack deal; I thought it'd be too hard for him.'

Then she frowned. 'Who's the poor guy they're trying to make sink Dancin' Dan? Anyone else I might know?'

'I don't know,' Robey said, 'you might. His name's Ambrose Merrion. Canterbury District Court clerk. Ever got a speeding ticket on the way north to ski on something steeper than you've got right where you live?'

'I don't ski,' she said. 'People fall down doing that. Break their legs and stuff.'

'Not if they know what they're doing,' Robey said. 'Anyway, that's how I met him. Trooper wrote me up for eighty on Route

Three-ninety-one in Cumberland. The other way to meet him's being active in politics. All the real Democratic insiders around here, all the way up to the state, even national, level: all of them would know him, know him very well. I doubt any one of them's ever paid a ticket in Amby's district.'

'Did you pay yours?' the judge said.

'Truthfully? No, I didn't,' Robey said. 'It *went, away*. But not because of my secret life as a Democratic honcho. And not because I *tried* to fix it, either. The time when I got stopped up there for being in a big hurry, Marie and I were on our way to Montreal. Some friends from when she was at McGill; she hadn't seen most of them since she'd graduated, so naturally she was all keyed up. But I was excited too. This was going to be the best vacation we'd ever had. Couldn't *wait* to get there's why I was driving so fast. I told the cop that in fact I *hadn't* realized how fast I had been going. Either he didn't believe me or that wasn't a good-enough excuse – he wrote me up.

'I probably put being stopped completely out of my mind before we even crossed the state line into Vermont. And when we got home from those two-glorious-weeks-of-packed-powder, I didn't have the ticket. It was gone. I don't know what I did with it. I may've figured I'd get a summons in the mail; when it came I'd pay the ticket. But the summons never came. And of course I didn't notice because who thinks about a bill that never came? Then about, I dunno, three or four years ago, 'fore I started working for you, I got stopped again. On the Mass Pike on the way to Worcester. Paul McCartney concert at the Centrum: Marie's a big fan of his. We're running late, as usual, so I was speeding, as usual. Got bagged for eighty-five. Suddenly it all comes back to me. Cop's back in the cruiser with my license, registration, punching his computer, and I'm thinking: 'Oh my God, I never paid the one I got going up to Montreal. This cop's going to see there's a warrant out on me and he's going to put me in jail.'

'But it didn't happen. Except for the fact I was getting another ticket costing me about a hundred-fifty bucks, and now we're *really* late for Paul McCartney, everything's perfectly fine.

'I couldn't understand it. The next day I called up the court in

Canterbury and asked about it. Not that I like paying speeding tickets so much I go out looking for 'em when they get lost, but I was worried. I didn't want it hanging over me.

'I gave my name, not what I do, and the woman asked me to wait while she got Mister Merrion. He came on and I told him the reason for my call, and he said: 'Oh, yeah, of course, Judge Folkard's clerk. Forget it. It went away.'

'"Went away?" I said. "What do you mean?"

'"I disappeared it," he said. He sounded like it was routine.

'"But why?" I said. "You don't know me. Did someone call you or something?" 'Cause Judge Folkard'd been known to do that a few times, when his daughter got caught flying low coming home from New York. He was from the Old School, back when people did those things and didn't think a thing about it. I thought I maybe mentioned it and he'd taken care of it for me, and then forgotten to tell me. He's just that kind of guy.'

'He'd better not be that kind of guy where people can see what he's doing nowadays,' she said. 'You can't *do* that stuff any more. People get angry. First thing you know, you're in disgrace.'

'I know,' Robey said, 'but that wasn't it. "Oh no," says Merrion, "nothing like that. Professional courtesy's all. I know that stretch of road where Trooper Dacey busted you, and I know Dacey pretty well too. I don't like him. He's tucked it to me more'n once onna road. My tickets I hafta pay or he'll raise some kinda stink. But other people, he can't connect to me, their tickets're different matters. I don't think eighty's too fast where you were, *when* you were there, and therefore I didn't think Dacey should've grabbed you for doing it. So I dismissed it. 'Substantial justice': that's our aim in this court."

'Naturally I thank him, but I'm also a little bit uncomfortable with all of this, so I say to him: "Well, I appreciate that. But you realize of course, it doesn't mean . . ."

'He cut me off. "Oh, calm down," he said, "for cryin' out loud. If I get a speeding ticket driving too fast onna federal reservation, I promise you I'll pay it. I won't call you up and say to you: 'Hey, you gotta fix this for me. On account of I dumped one for you.' This's between me and Dacey. It's a case of requited dislike. Every chance I get, I give him a shot. You're just an innocent bystander here. This isn't a serious matter."

'Year or so later I ran into him at a wedding. Bride's father's a honcho in the state Democratic party. He introduced us. Amby said the name was familiar, and I reminded him the reason. "I got a Dacey ticket, and you bagged it for me," I said. Offered to buy him a drink, which he accepted; said it'd probably get him indicted for taking a bribe for fixing tickets, but what the hell, he'd risk it. Joined us at our table. Got started telling stories and stayed for the rest of the day.

'Marie didn't like him; I did. Same with the other wives 'nd their husbands. Men liked him, women didn't. He used a lot of profanity, which I suppose was partly because we were all having lots to drink and everybody tends to cuss more when they're drinking. Marie and the other wives're dropping a few effs of their own every now and then, by the time we all called it a day, but . . . I don't know if you ever notice this, but women who hear every single cuss-word a man says, even if he says it under his breath, they never seem to be able to hear all the ones they use themselves.'

'Can't say as I have,' the judge said.

'Yeah,' Robey said, 'well anyway, I've run into him a few times since then, conferences and so forth; had a few drinks and some meals. I enjoy his company. We're not buddies, never will be; age difference's too big. But I like him. I like his attitude toward the poor bastards who go through his court. He seems like he really does all he can to help them. No bleeding heart, I don't mean that, but he seems like a compassionate guy. Like he'd give you a break if he thought you deserved one and no one'd know it'd happened. He seems like he cares what happens to people, and if a rule has to get bent or some facts get overlooked so things turn out better for some poor bastard who made a mistake, but nobody really got hurt, well, I think he would bend the rule.'

'The name's not familiar,' she said. 'Eric may've run into him, but I wouldn't know about that. He doesn't tell me anymore when he gets stopped. I give him too much grief. He's convinced his Range Rover's invisible; cops can't see it when it goes by at ninety. Pays all the tickets by mail. First I hear of it's when I get the insurance bill on my car and it's gone up again because he's a listed driver and he's gotten some more points. He says he likes to drive fast. If that's what it costs, so be it; he'll pay it. Says he doesn't want any redneck cop getting it into his head that his wife, the federal judge, fixes tickets for him.'

'Probably a good idea,' Robey said. 'But anyway, that's who Amby is. An all-right type of guy. Not a bad fella at all. Big, under six feet but fairly wide. White curly hair. Face's kind of red; he could lose a few pounds if he wanted, 'thout doing himself any harm. He looks like what he is: he's a pol. He's been a pol all of his life. Been pals with Dan Hilliard since I don't know when; thirty years, probably more. Danny's the guy that got him appointed. From what Bissell feels he can let me in on, apparently Merrion's been repaying Danny for the favor ever since. Not paying him kickbacks, anything like that – just giving him lots of nice presents.'

'*Gratitude?*' the judge said. 'They're indicting people for *gratitude* now? Do they think it does some kind of *damage* or something? When did they make *that* against the law? Not that I ever saw much evidence of it actually taking *place* around these parts. Matter of fact, I wouldn't think there's ever been enough of it to warrant prosecution.'

Robey laughed. 'Yeah,' he said, 'but apparently, what Bissell says, Amby's *really* grateful. This's the kind of appreciation that gives gratitude a bad name. What he did was he bought Hilliard a membership in the Grey Hills Country Club. Also bought himself one.'

'The Chief belonged to that,' she said. 'He used to talk about it, now and then, when I first joined the firm. Pooler's father, too, I think; Lee Pooler was a member, unless I'm mistaken. That's the high-rent district.'

'That it is,' Robey said. 'And they're the type of people Grey Hills used to be for. Very exclusive. But then about, oh I don't know, twenty-five, thirty years ago, the club ran into some kind of a financial emergency. What you and I would call "strapped for cash." Had to open up the membership and let some new blood in to fatten up the treasury. "New money" would've been more like it. Big rebuilding project or something. The very exclusive people like the Coreys and the Poolers couldn't see their way clear to footing the bill by their elegant selves, so the only alternative was to open the doors and let some of the better-heeled riffraff in.

'Most likely joining then didn't cost Merrion anywhere near what it'd cost today, if you could even get in – I don't think they're accepting new members now. But still, as you say, it wasn't small change. And on top of that, since then apparently what he's been doing is paying the dues for both of them, too. That isn't petty cash either. Bissell thinks maybe three-four grand a year. I bet it's more like eight thousand apiece. Split the difference and call it, six grand a year. Twenty years of that go by, it begins to mount up. Bissell thinks over a hundred and twenty thousand dollars by now, Merrion's paid in for his pal Danny. That's fairly serious money.'

'*Cowa-bunga*,' she said. 'On the salary a clerk makes? You've got to be kidding. How on earth could he possibly do that? How much are we paying district court clerks these days?'

'It depends on where you're the clerk,' Robey said. 'The statute doesn't actually come right out and give any specific numbers. It's this very complicated formula that of course the legislators made just as hard to figure out as they possibly could when they wrote the salary statute. Sixty or seventy grand, I would say, by and large. Some of them probably get around eighty. And since Merrion's Hilliard's pal, and Hilliard used to have *mucho* clout, Merrion's probably one of those. Say eighty thousand a year.'

'Well, that's not too shabby,' she said. 'But still, I wouldn't think it was country-club country for him and a friend. Not Grey Hills level, at least.'

'Well,' Robey said. 'Bissell sort of seems to think that what he gets for salary isn't all he makes, result of being clerk. Seems to think he's got some other source of income. I assume it isn't bribes – if it was, Bissell'd have him keeping his room tidy at Club Fed by now, down in Allentown PA. But what it could be I can't imagine. He didn't come from big money. His father was a car salesman up at Valley Ford in Holyoke. Nice guy. Everyone liked him, but he wasn't rich and he died young. His mother worked in a bakery. I don't think he's moonlighting at anything, either.

'Still, his overhead's always been low. He's never been married, so he's never been divorced. If he's had any children he's had to support and send to school, no one seems to know about it. His mother's in a nursing home; I assume she's on Medicare. I assume he supports her, whatever else she needs. When she had to go into the home, he sold his condo up at Hampton Pond and moved back to the house he grew up in. So really, I don't know how he could afford Grey Hills either, when he first did it or now. It's a mystery to me.'

'Maybe he's teaching law,' the judge said. 'Nights or something? At Western New England.'

'I don't think he's a lawyer,' Robey said. 'He may be, but I don't think he is. If he had've been, I don't think he'd be doing what he is now, being a district court clerk. I think Hilliard would've gotten him a judgeship.'

'Yeah,' she said, nodding, 'he probably would've at that. Well, I don't know Danny all that well, but what I know I've always liked. And now this pretty picture starts to unfold before us. I won't say I can hardly wait.'

'I can't say I'm looking forward to it much myself,' Robey said. 'My mother's father opened the Armstrong Tile store over in West Springfield after World War Two. Bigelow Carpet line was later. My father ran the business after Grumpy died, 'til it was *his* turn to retire. Your family's been living in an area, really not that large a one, doing business fifty years, going into people's homes, time and time again; whenever something like this happens you're bound to know some of the people affected by it. Not that they're friends of yours, exactly; they're just people you've been on good terms with, part of the landscape, the same social fabric. Hate to see them fall and get disgraced, get their lives destroyed like that, torn apart in public. In a way it's happening to you.'

'Although not saying that I think, for one instant, mind you,' the judge said, 'that Dan Hilliard never did anything wrong. Something most other people probably also would've done, but still very much against the law? Sure, of course he did. He had balls. He would've done *lots* of slightly illegal things; shady, questionable things. Probably hundreds of them, over the course of the years.'

She paused and then chuckled. 'Like everybody else in his line of work back then, when he was still in it. It was the custom and usage of the trade, the good old political trade. No one ever got *too* badly hurt.'

She reflected. 'Come right down to it,' she said, 'I guess what I'm really saying is that I don't want to see the guy *caught*. Must be about sixty by now; a small living legend around here by now – so I would think, anyway. Living legends should be more careful. Stay out of these little schemes and scrapes they always seem to be getting into, and then getting hurt by. Avoid doing things that'll wreck their careers, if they get caught doing them. And if they can't manage to do that for themselves, then we should look out for them, as though they were endangered species. Can't have our legends becoming extinct.'

She hesitated. 'Like you say, it's funny how it hits you. Almost like you were somehow involved in whatever they had going on up there in Canterbury, and now what's happening to them is also happening to you.'

'Yeah,' Robey said, 'but Cohen still wants his hearing, so I've got to call him and tell him: When do I tell him to come in?'

She sighed. 'Ahhh,' she said, 'tomorrow, I guess. Tomorrow afternoon. Quarter of two. And this one we'll do here, in chambers. If the US Attorney wants to showboat this thing now, making public speeches and calling for Dan's head, first let him get an indictment.'

2

From the very beginning Janet LeClerc, then twenty-nine, had felt threatened by Merrion. 'The guy,' she would say abruptly to the impersonally cheerful cashier at Dineen's Convenient where she bought her cigarettes and coffee, 'I forget his name. You know him, the one I mean; big white-haired guy down there, the courthouse; not the judge, the other one.' This happened Friday mornings following the third Thursday afternoons when Corinne (pronounced 'Kreen' by her fellow workers), 'the switchboard woman' called to remind Janet soothingly that she must report on Saturday for her monthly conference. 'Because we know that sometimes, you, well, sometimes people who're scheduled to report, forget. These things. Everybody does – they're not part of their routine.'

'I don't know what he wants me to say. And I need to do that, don't I, say what he wants me to say – he could have me put in jail.' Therefore every time she had to see him she told him she did her best 'to have a regular routine, you know. That's what I do.' Because from what Corinne said to her, that seemed to be what they wanted. But because it never seemed to satisfy him – 'It's like he don't believe me or he doesn't want to *listen*' – she felt anxious each time as she did it, wanting him to believe her. Then afterwards she wasn't sure she remembered doing it.

So at their eleventh conference in the clerk-magistrate's office of the saddeningly rundown Canterbury District Courthouse, on the morning of the third Saturday in August, she once more earnestly described to Merrion her trust in routine as a pathway to the virtuous life she believed he wanted her to lead. 'I think that's how I can do, you know, like you said for me to do: to see if I can just stay out of trouble. For a year. So that other thing I did there, you can make it disappear. You know: like you said you would.'

The courthouse, closed on Saturday, was quiet. 'Not so much distraction,' Merrion explained to Hilliard. 'Man can actually hear himself think in there if he wants to, on a Saturday. Not so many fuckin' people always callin' you, the phone, bumpin' into you and stoppin' you, askin' things and sayin' things, gettin' in your way. 'S why whenever me and Lennie decide we're gonna take on another one our projects – stay outta trouble a year and we drop the charges on 'em – I always see them Saturdays, when there's a chance I can think straight.'

Mornings Mondays through Fridays the beige rubber-tiled corridors and stairwells, eight feet wide, were fetidly overcrowded. The ventilation system became overloaded by nine-fifteen each day. Too little air rebreathed too often by too many nervous, sweating people became warm and moist.

Describing his work-day environment at the shag end of a winter day to Hilliard in the dark-panelled grill room of the clubhouse at Grey Hills, the room lightly touched with the aroma of maple logs burning on the hearth, Merrion said: 'When I first got into it, over Chicopee, I wasn't ready for it. Mobs of people, day after day, smelling like meat that went bad. When I was doing the substitute teaching; when I was with you and we're out campaigning, meetings and rallies, conventions and so forth: there were people around us, and they weren't all always our friends; sometimes they hated our guts. But at least you could go toe-to-toe with 'em, stand there and *fight* with the bastards, 'thout turnin' your stomach and suddenly thinkin': "Jesus, I'm gonna throw up."'

He stared morosely through the mullioned bay window at the orchard of fruit trees bare and black in snow behind the clubhouse at the base of Mount Wolf, the remaining blue light darkening into violet and black in the late afternoon. The maple wood snapped in the fire and the bartender made the bottles clink as he removed and replaced them one by one on the shelves, wiping dust from their collars and shoulders.

'Most of the people who come to the courthouse 'cause they're in trouble: The way they stink, they deserve it. You *should* get in trouble for smelling like they do. They don't wash themselves or brush their teeth or even use some mouthwash. They don't change their underwear and socks, or their other clothes either. And lots of times you'd swear the person that you're talking to's never figured out why the stalls in public toilets always seem to have those rolls of paper in them. So as a result they look dirty and they stink. Their breath's foul, and it seems like there's *armies* of the bastards. Day after day after day they keep comin', an ill wind that blows through the world.'

'When we talk about democracy,' Hilliard replied, 'they're who we mean. They're exercising the fifth freedom. Freedom of speech; freedom to worship; freedom from want; freedom from fear; freedom to smell like a wet bear.'

On the weekdays, worried-looking men between twenty-five and sixty, some heavily muscled, as many of them white as black or Hispanic, struggled frontally through the crowds of young people, using their shoulders and observably restraining strong impulses to shove others out of their way. They wore rumpled dusty suits that did not fit, under stained tan and gray raincoats with crumpled, button-tab collars that stood away from their necks at odd angles. Or they wore baseball caps and windbreakers or nylon parkas, open on plaid flannel shirts; plain tee-shirts; tee-shirts with messages extolling naked co-ed sports; chino pants or jeans or corduroys or warm-up pants; scuffed loafers broken-down at the counters, steel-toed yellowish-tan construction boots or heavily soiled white training shoes. They carried cardboard containers of coffee and folded newspapers, and if they were not on the way to report to Probation Intake, the room with the big gold-lettered brown sign on the right as they came in, they asked people in uniforms or men and women in civilian clothes who seemed to be at home in the surroundings how to find Room 7, 8 or 11.

Three assistant clerk-magistrates, two men and a woman, presided in those airless eight-by-twelve-foot rooms as though they had been built-in, permanent fixtures installed along with the electrical wiring and the brown vinyl mopboards during construction of the pitted ivory-painted cinder-block walls. The first assistant, Robert Cooke, nephew of the late Most Rev. Edmund Mackintosh, auxiliary bishop of the Roman Catholic diocese of Springfield, was a thin, dour white man in his early fifties who became hostile when he knew or suspected that the person talking to him favored legal access to abortion. His wife, Mimi, had at last convinced him after many years first not to start conversations on the subject, and second not to try to attempt subtly to ascertain how others viewed the matter, because when they differed with him he became either sullen or scornful, depending on whether he considered them his superiors or inferiors. 'And it *hurts* you, Bob, it really does. It hurts you at the courthouse and it's why almost no one wants to see us or be friends with us except people who agree with you, and so when we go out that's all we ever talk about, and that's no fun at all.'

Tyrone Thomas was the third assistant clerk, an amiable black man in his early thirties who wanted no trouble and tried to make none. In his teens he had become the protégé of a basketball coach at Cambridge Rindge & Latin School in Cambridge who'd gone on to a second career as a state senator. Thomas avoided prejudice by ignoring it if possible and by avoiding aggressive individuals who made ignorance impossible. People who knew him and his wife, Carol, a tall and beautiful light-skinned black woman who worked as a field-audit supervisor for the Internal Revenue Service, believed he had married well above his station and wondered what she saw in him. He tried not to share that puzzlement and pretended not to notice or be hurt when he sensed it unexpressed or inferred it when implied.

The second assistant was a somewhat-overweight thirty-eight-year-old white woman, Jeanne Flagg. Her father, Archie Oakschott, after eighteen years on the bench had taken senior status as a judge of the Norfolk County Probate Court in Dedham, near Westwood where she had grown up. She continued to wear the cotton and wool, light blue, light grey and light green suits she had purchased when she had gotten the job – four years before she became accustomed to the court-house-ritual morning coffee breaks with pastry in the snack bar. No longer somewhat underweight, she was therefore uncomfortable in her clothes, moving carefully and slowly, aware that each change of position tested the seams to the limits.

The assistant clerk-magistrates had to decide whether there were sufficient grounds to recommend to the judge that orders should be issued under Chapter 209A, Massachusetts General Laws, restraining the men who came before them from getting near enough to the people whom they had claimed to love, in order to harm them again. Usually the victims were their wives or girlfriends, but sometimes the men had beaten their children, or hurt their defenseless parents (men accused of sexually molesting children were processed differently). The assistant clerks grimly tried with squinting eyes to see things that could not be seen, hoping to reduce by means of narrow wariness the unreliability of the guesses that they made about whether the particular man under scrutiny was likely to lay rough hands – in most instances, again – on his female sexual partner; whether he would benefit from still another chance either to control his use of beverage alcohol or quit taking the illegal drugs that he thought licensed him to commit violence. Or whether instead he would soon steal away back into his addictions like a furtive animal skulking back to its kill to feed the rage that made him use his hands on her – and might some day if continued come to involve a gun or knife or club.

Each of the visitors knew what would happen to him if the clerk-magistrate decided that he was either unable or lying to conceal his refusal to stop hitting the woman who had angered him by attempting to influence some aspect of his behavior by means other than prompt oral, vaginal or anal attention to his sexual requirements. He would have to go before a judge who would reason that he must be put in jail. Otherwise the judge would think himself at risk that the man who this time had beaten the living shit out of the woman he considered his chattel would kill her the next time he got riled up. If he did that then the judge would get reamed out on TV and in the papers. The men knew: that judges did not feature getting reamed out; that they themselves did not want to go to jail; and that the clerk-magistrates could seldom be appeased more than once by signs of contrition and remorse. But they also knew that if they were placed under orders restraining them from having anything to do with their scared women, or put in jail for having violated such an order, the next chance they got to get drunk or stoned each of them would know first who was to blame for putting him into this desperate, humiliating, probably hopeless, situation: the woman who had either called the cops or made enough noise while he'd been hitting her so that a neighbor had called them. And that secondly in that red anger each of them would know uncontrollably that she must be punished for it, more severely than before, so that she would not do it again, not ever. And each of them also would know already and exactly what form the punishment must take. This gave them a dim sense of inexorably advancing doom that threatened them with despair so bleak their minds cried out for a drink or a dime bag that would make it go away.

So the men who had hit their women, filled with resentment as they were, did not try at all to hide the fact that they felt troubled and dejected – and very often severely hungover, as well. Trying to conceal the resentment, they exerted themselves to appear even sadder and more miserable than they felt, forcing themselves to grovel abjectly – thus making themselves feel even worse.

The clerk-magistrates and the other people who worked in the courthouse were well aware of this tactic and its practice, and the vengeful feelings it was meant, but failed, to conceal, so they treated the batterers differently from other defendants, discounting their displays of woe, sadness, regret and remorse by sixty to seventy percent. This made it difficult for the personnel to conduct themselves in their customary courteous professional manner, dealing with the men who had hit women. The only way they could do it was by acting as though they didn't know why it was the men had come before them. This was harder for the women workers in the courthouse than it was for the men, because they had to hide fear as well as anger and contempt for the defendants. The men who had hit women found the pretense unconvincing and knew very well that the courthouse people did know that was what they had done, and scorned and despised them for doing it. The men tended to be fairly quiet, but still visibly resentful of this additional injustice they perceived against them.

Most of the time most of the people who worked in the courthouse tried to seem sympathetic and be polite to everyone who was there because they had gotten in some kind of trouble. The defendants often found their professional solicitude condescending, and sneered at it to demonstrate contempt, but in that, too, they were mistaken; it was not feigned. The personnel felt real empathy with hard-working men and women who had never been in court until the morning after the night they had had too much to drink and had gotten stopped driving home at two in the morning, doing fifteen miles an hour in the middle of the road, steering by the yellow lines, had blown .18 on the Breathalyzer, ten points over the legal state of drunkenness, and had fallen down when ordered to stand on one foot. 'There but for the grace of God' was a phrase they often murmured as the Driving-Unders begged futilely to retain their licenses in disregard of punitive statutes mandating revocation. When they were convinced that an injured defendant, accused of resisting arrest, had in fact been unsuccessfully attempting to defend himself against a police officer gone out of control, they saw to it that the judge handling the case became aware of the relevant facts, even if no evidence of them was offered in open court. They also often felt real pity for aimless early teenagers from dysfunctional homes whose undifferentiated fear and pent-up hostility enabled them to commit their first serious criminal offenses on the apparent basis of mere evil impulse (new personnel speedily acquired and inexpertly used the diagnostic jargon of psychology as a handy means of mental self-defense, reflexively learning early that they needed it to explain behavior they would otherwise find frighteningly incomprehensible).

The majority of the young people crowding the stairwells and the hallways were repeat offenders, but experience did not enable them to foresee whether they would have to go into the courtroom, perhaps emerging from it with their wrists in manacles. They had been ordered to report for interviews with other courthouse personnel, either adult probation officers or Department of Youth Services caseworkers. Until the public address system raspily summoned them by name to report to Rooms 17, 18, 18A or 20, they beached themselves in the halls and clustered in the stairwells, obstructing the passageways. Some were morosely silent, but most talked, elliptically, ceaselessly asking each other for predictions that none of them could make, repeating questions none of them could answer, now and then casting wild glances outside the groups of people whom they knew, wishing to discover somewhere in the hallways someone their age who looked just like them – and who therefore could be trusted – but knew the answers to their questions; could tell them what was going to happen to them when the judge went on the bench.

Even those who had been most boisterously demonstrative in the corridors spoke cryptically and softly, never assertively, once alone in those conferences. Averting their eyes from the persons pressing questions on them, they shook their heads a lot, shrugging their shoulders and rolling their eyes; saying 'Myunoh' – for 'Mmm, I don't know' – to indicate they lacked sufficient information to say where they had gotten the narcotics or the stolen property the police had found on them, or when they were asked to account for the whereabouts of some fugitive habitual associate or the gunshot wound of some hostile competitor.

If the person talking to them was a probation officer they evaded answering because they believed their only hope of deliverance from jail lay in preservation of the officer's considerable ignorance of what they had been up to. The hazard for those under questioning by DYS caseworkers was similar: removal from the street and commitment to DYS custody. So they too were uncommunicative. The probation and DYS officers knew this and it frustrated them. When the recalcitrance of their clients prevented them from deciding with assurance whether the young person could be safely left at liberty or should be locked up – usually, *again* – their annoyance at being thwarted and the same perception of risk that made judges uneasy about letting batterers go free prejudiced the officers in favor of commitment.

Young offenders conferring with counsel appointed to defend them, mistrusting their free lawyers' willingness, ability and intention to do a good job for them, accordingly felt entirely free to mislead them or lie to them, as suited their moods. Knowing this, and having a great many cases, the Mass. Defenders therefore tried to ascertain as efficiently as possible whether this client like virtually all their others was unable or refusing to assist in his own defense, and therefore must be pleaded-out to the best deal the defender could get. The defenders customarily did not ask their clients to say whether they were innocent; attorneys and clients alike proceeded on the tacit understanding that the defendant in question, no matter how many times he might ritually, vehemently deny it, had in fact committed the offense alleged against him.

Most of the clients were black or Hispanic, either undersized, short and gaunt, or broad and grossly overweight, but of average height. The frowning or tearful brusied young mothers with pacifier-sucking infants in their arms or small children riding on their vast hips seldom seemed to be comforted by what went on in the courthouse, but the young males in unguarded moments often appeared at least cheerful, if not actually happy, at ease, hanging out among friends in familiar, shabby surroundings.

From time to time this insouciance bothered the judge. 'It's almost as though this's their real goddamn *home*,' Judge Leonard Cavanaugh mused one day to Merrion at the bench, having gavelled the courtroom quiet for the fourth time that morning. He was almost keening, cupping his left hand over the microphone that rose up on the flexible gooseneck to capture what he said for the recorder that preserved everything it was allowed to hear in the courtroom.

Later in the judge's chambers, Merrion demurred. 'More like their real *school*,' he said, 'not so much their real home. When we were about the same age as these little maggots are now, we weren't doing drugs and ambushing other kids we didn't like. We were driving *teachers* nuts; we were driving our *parents* nuts. The principals of our schools called us "You-again." But we were *not* bugging the *cops* all the time, and the people who worked in the courthouses then never laid their eyes on us. Most of us didn't know where it was.'

'Yeah, well, it's not that way any more,' Cavanaugh said. 'It's not as though it's someplace they should never have to come;

their parents're gonna kill 'em when they get home. They're not afraid or embarrassed. This's *normal* for them, just an ordinary thing; that's what's so frightening. Get collared selling drugs or breaking in or stealing cars; get yourself arrested; this's where you come. Routine. Just another stop on their regular routes, another place where they go. They actually live part of their lives here. Where they validate them, really – authenticate their existences. It's really frightening.'

The young people expanded, seeming somehow to take up more room than had been enclosed by the roof, cellar hole and exterior walls of the courthouse. On weekdays – especially Mondays, when the mornings yielded up the weekends' ripe harvests of police operations in Hampton Pond, Hampton Falls and Cumberland, the other towns within the Canterbury jurisdiction – they sat and stood along the walls, sat and crouched upon the stairs, hunkered in the corners and bunched up on all the maple benches. Endlessly but slowly they went into and came out of the elevator that plied up and down between the basement and the first and second floors, distributing them among the corridors leading to the offices and conference rooms and courtrooms; never coming to rest even when standing still or seated and admonished to be silent in one of the three trial sessions. As they moved about they had much to say to one another about the inexhaustible variety of things to do in the great tempting, *yielding*, wide world outside; before, after, during or instead of, days and weeks and months and years spent or to be spent in the other spacious world inside, in jail, together or with absent friends or strangers. They had so much to talk about that they never seemed to finish saying it, and so were never quiet. They held endless discussions at their normal outdoor-hailing conversational volumes that accumulated, reverberating and combining to make a ceaseless, unintelligible, unrelenting din like the noise of an assembly line building heavy machinery; noise that broke like surf against the walls and surged along the floors, echoing against the ceilings of the corridors and stairwells and restrooms, booming, wearing and abrading and eroding the tender surface of the mind and nerves.

Most of the young people left the courthouse each day before noon. Those not led away tearfully or broodingly in handcuffs trooped out the side door (the ceremonially wide front doors at the top of the broad crumbling concrete steps – Barrows Construction having used too much sand in the mix, sand being cheaper than calcined clay and limestone – being locked and blocked for reasons of security), shuckin' and jivin'; genially menacing; waiting for the twilight and the dark to come; untied black and white high-top basketball, cross-training and workout shoes flapping, a hundred, two hundred dollars a pair; oversized black pants billowing, unfastened and unzippered black sweatshirts and hooded jackets sliding off their shoulders, jostling and shoving one another as they passed the metal-detector archway that had screened their entrances.

But noon was too late to soothe Merrion's mind; by the end of each morning it had become raw and inflamed, so that by the middle of any weekday while he would have been willing to concede that calm reflection and assessment might once more be possible, he would be in no mood to attempt it. Once during his ninth or tenth year on the job, by then as first assistant, Richie Hammond had said to him after a brutal day: 'This's an awful job, you know, a really awful job.' And he had said to Richie, slowly and distinctly, meaning every single word: 'There are days when this can be the *worst* fucking job in the world.' It had passed into standard usage in the Canterbury courthouse. 'Okay, altogether now, kids: what kind of job is it today?' 'The worst fuckin' job in the world.' And then everybody would laugh, and think to themselves that this laugh in defiance of the fact that there was absolutely nothing to laugh about would be what would get them all through the day on the job.

Except when he was being truthful, as he did not often allow himself to be – once or twice with Cavanaugh, who looked incredulous, suspicious that Merrion was putting him on; several times with Hilliard after a good round of golf, a dinner and some drinks – Merrion always led that cheer and acted convincingly as though he believed it. But on those other occasions he said: 'But I guess in fact I *don't*, really, believe that. As silly as I know this sounds, Dan, except maybe to you, there have been times in that courthouse when I think I may've done someone some good.

I'm not saying now I think I've saved people. Nobody saves other people. Only idiots think they can do that; only bleeding-heart assholes'd even try. But maybe I've managed to actually grab some poor kid or some poor strugglin' bastard and help him pull himself up out of the mud. Give him a break, maybe first one he's had, see if he gets just that one break, maybe he can save himself.

'More'n a few of 'em have, Danny-boy, and that as you say, 's a true fact. Some nights I get reckless, I can't get to sleep, I got too many things on my mind, something I'm worried about. And then when that happens, that's when I start thinking: 'Hey, why can't I sleep? What the hell am I worried about? If I wake up tomorrow and I find out I'm dead, I did some good things, I was here. I figure I rescued a person a year, each year I been on the job; that's over eighteen people by now, otherwise might've ruined their lives. Not that these've been real dramatic cases; not saying that at all. Just saying that some fairly ordinary people that you've never even heard of managed to get themselves straightened out, so they've had quiet, ordinary, maybe even fairly happy, lives. Instead of the exciting kind you *would've* heard about if they *hadn't* turned themselves around, because they would've been in big trouble. They would've been making headlines.

'And that's what I've always figured's really been the kind of thing that down on the ground is what the two of us've been doing all these years in politics. What we've always thought the whole thing has been about, getting you elected, getting me into my job. Making it so that when something good needed doing down in Boston, or in the courthouse out here, there'd *be* someone there who would see the need and make sure it got done. And so that's what I think I can say I have done. So I usually sleep pretty good.'

Merrion required quiet to encourage contemplation and reflection. Then he could enjoy intellection, and think he did it well. Silently reveling therefore in the Saturday luxury of it, he pondered what Janet had said about routine. As he had on several previous occasions, he once again concluded he completely believed her, and knew her to be sincere.

Nevertheless, Merrion was not encouraged. He did not share Janet's confidence in routine as a safeguard of virtue, and he knew dolefully that Janet's best effort to do anything was unlikely to be very good. He gazed steadily at her but did not make any comment.

The quiet did not soothe Janet LeClerc as it comforted Merrion. So to fill it she told him again that she had devised her routine on the basis of deductions that she made from her observations that many of the other residents of the eighteen-unit building where she lived appeared to have routines. 'Not that I'm minding their business,' she said, 'or anything like that. I wouldn't do nothing like that. But you know how it is: When you're around all day long, you see things. Can't help it.'

She said that from what she had seen, most of them were single, as she was. She presented her data earnestly, as though she had been commissioned to carry out a poll producing the results. Merrion thought: *Survey figures released today show that fifty-nine percent of those living in the same building with Janet have daily routines. The remainder said either that they have no opinion or else they don't give a shit.* That was television; it had taught her that if she noticed something in her idleness it meant something – data *must* mean something; the mass had been collected, hadn't it? People wouldn't go to all the trouble of finding out all of this stuff and then putting it on TV if it wasn't important. Janet believed in TV. All the TV that she watched, day after day, when she'd had nothing to do: she didn't like many of the things she saw and heard on it, but TV itself as pure will and idea enjoyed her full and complete confidence.

'Sort of between marriages. It seems like they've probably *been* married, most of them, one time or another. They're all really that *young*, you know? Like most of the people are who've never been married, usually are. Just looking *around*, for somebody *else*, somebody else to be with. They're exactly like me, marking time. Except *they've* already all got their routines, the same ones they had back when they were married. It's not like they got divorced from their jobs, when they got divorced from their wives. Or their husbands, either. They just used to be married in the morning, when they went to work, but now they aren't that anymore.'

Janet had never been married. Merrion knew she wanted very much to be married, or at least to *get* married, so that then, if it didn't work out, then at least she would have *been* married. 'Because that way it would be better. It would seem more like normal, you know? Like everything was normal. Because lots of people've been married, and then they got divorced, and so people understand that. So they're used to that, and they don't think it's so strange.'

She had told him all about it the second or third time he'd called her in for a conference, back when they were first getting acquainted – back around the turn of the century, it seemed like, when he was still only just beginning to find out she was another one, still able to resist the unpleasant discovery that he'd gone and done it again, let himself in for it once more, in the early autumn of 1994. 'Always been a big ambition of mine, to get married,' she'd told him, looking down at the ring finger embarrassingly naked on her left hand in her lap, twisting the skin of the knuckle with her right thumb and first two fingers. 'I think most people do, expect it'll happen, think they'll get married some day. It wasn't the only thing that I thought I'd like to do, but it was the big one.'

He reported that conversation to Louella Daggett in the regional office of the Commonwealth's Department of Social Services. Daggett was a short stocky black woman in her early sixties. She had arthritis in her knees that made it very difficult for her to get around. She cited it to justify her irritable disposition, but Merrion had known her years before she'd ever mentioned arthritis and she'd always had a lousy disposition. Merrion thought it was probably attributable to the kind of people and problems she encountered in her work. But believing that frustration made her irascible did not impel him to tolerate her surliness; their discussions about individuals whose behavior had attracted the attention of the court as well as DSS tended to be acrimonious.

Louella had been Janet's caseworker since she had gone on welfare in 1986. She said 'when Janet first came on the reason that she gave us was that she'd had a husband and he'd left her, run away. We took it at face-value, we always do, their stories, but we also check them out. We couldn't find no husband. There'd never been one. The husband who'd left her, "Wayne" she said his name was: he'd never existed. "Harvey," we called him, "Harvey, the bastard." She was apparently the only living person who'd ever been able to see him. No one else ever had. Deserted by a phantom husband; can you beat it? Wish-fulfillment, but a lousy job of it. Here she'd gone and dreamed the guy up, gone to all that trouble, and then he turns out to be no good. You'd think if you made up your own husband, well, he might not be a good provider but at least you'd think he'd be a fairly faithful companion, at least around when you needed him. Not Janet's make-believe husband. Janet couldn't lay sod right-side up.

'Completely serious about it, though. Couldn't talk her out of it. Claimed she'd actually *been* married – not divorced, just married – and the only reason that she had to be on welfare was that her no-good husband'd run off someplace no one could find him and make him pay support. Fact there was no marriage license in the records in Springfield didn't faze her a bit; maybe it was Chicopee, or maybe Holyoke. Couldn't find a record of her marriage there, either. We checked with the State House, Secretary, State. No record there. We told her that.

'Didn't miss a beat. "Then it must've been somewhere else. Maybe we went to Vermont and got married. My memory's never been good. It was all quite a few years ago." Could *not* talk her out of it, no matter how you tried.

'This went on for two or three years. Then after a while she stopped remembering him. Harvey went off the screen, disappeared without leaving a trace. My guess is she thought she had to be a deserted wife in order to get a check and then someone convinced her she didn't. Or maybe she just finally forgot it. She's not all there, you know, poor thing. In addition to never having been what you'd call extremely bright, she does not have all her marbles.'

He could remember how Janet had looked when she had first talked about marriage. She had shaken her head, making the dark tendrils of the dull, dark-brown pageboy-haircut she was wearing then flick around her ears and the corners of her eyes. Daggett snickered at Merrion when he'd suggested that maybe she could persuade Janet to 'get herself cleaned up some, you know? Do something with herself? Wash her goddamned greasy *hair*, for starters. No one's going to hire her back, only thing she knows how to do, wipe tables up in restaurants, clean up the cafeteria in some hospital or school, if we send her up and she comes in looking like she does now, needs a wiping-down herself.'

'You're still sort of new at this, aren't you,' Louella'd said to him. 'Been at it now, what, only twenny, thirty years? And you still haven't quite got the hang of it. You courthouse guys, you make me laugh. You're all alike. You're all so cut-and-dried. You all think it's all so simple. All you political types. You trip over one of these people like Janet and you think the reason she's miserable's because no one else ever noticed her before, took a hand in her life. If you'd run into her six months or ten years ago you'd've gotten her all straightened out long before this – but never mind; you'll take care of it now.

'Nuts. You know why it says in the Bible that we'll always have the poor with us? Because it's true: we always have and we always will. You court guys don't seem to know this. You've all been spoiled rotten, is what. "Do this. Do that. Do it right now," is what you tell them. "That'll fix it." And then, of course, they do it, and it happens. It gets fixed. Until you turn around and they see you're not looking their direction anymore. Then it gets unfixed again, just like it was before.

'You guys got *jail* to offer. That's how come what you say goes. A person don't do what you tell him? *His* ass goes to *jail*. A person don't do what I tell her? Well, what'm I gonna do? Cut her money off? Sure, take her check away. And then you know what happens next? I'll tell you what happens, *aw-toh-mat-tick-lee*. *Her* ass goes right out on the *street*, because that's where she takes it, for sale for twenty dollars. And when she offers, suck off an undercover cop, and gets herself arrested, she tells the first judge she sees how it's all my fault. I cut her welfare off. What's a poor girl supposed to do? Is she supposed to *starve*? And when that shit makes the papers, boy, and gets on the TV, guess whose ass goes on the line. My ass goes in the deli slicer. *I* come out cold cuts.

'Now your Janet project, all right? I know you got a good heart, Amby, probably a generous one. But that don't make you smart. You just lemme tell you something, here, what you're up against. I told that girl, two hundred times, to get her *self* shaped *up*. And she tells me, two hundred times, she'll get to it right off. She will surely get to that. And the next time that I see her, what is it I see? Same old thing I saw before, looks just like she always did. Like she got left out in the rain all night or somethin'. Hell, not all *night* – all *year*. You haven't got a project here; you got a *career*.'

'And I don't see why I can't do it, do this thing.' Janet in the August morning was talking again about marriage. 'People do it every day. In the paper all the time, I used to see it there, when I got the Sunday paper. All these people, getting married. So then, why can't I? Look at my mother. Jesus, look what she did, what my damned mother did to me. Went off and left me by myself? Nobody to fall back on? All by myself in this thing. But that didn't stop her. No, not at all. She could still get married, damn her. Sure, *she* could get married, if she wanted to. And she was no good at all. Well, so, I don't see why then I can't.'

Merrion could not respond without giving her some kind of reaction, but he did not want to lie to her or tell her what he thought. He knew from years of dealing with people like Janet how important hope was to the hopeless. His experience came mostly from dealing with hapless men, usually between twenty-five and forty-five; generally still hungover, unshaven and dirty after still another night in the familiar surroundings of the holding tank. Disgusted cops wearing rubber gloves had thrown them in there bodily after they had pissed in the street in broad daylight. *again*: yelled something obscene at a cop, *again*; vomited on a display-window, *again*; slid their filthy hands under the sneeze-baffle to rummage in the lettuce-tray in the McDonald's salad-bar, *again*; or insulted some woman, *again*.

They weren't going to be improved much by the fresh thirty days in jail they now had to serve, *again*. He knew it and they knew it. But tradition nullified knowledge and established that they still must be exhorted, assured with ardent forcefulness that they *must* – and therefore *would* – emerge reformed. Almost all of them were traditionalists too, made so by repetition of the ritual. Just as drearily convinced by much experience as their exhorters were that miraculous transformation wasn't going to happen this time either, once again they summoned up the strength to reject the certainty, once more trying very hard to believe what they knew to be untrue.

The few who didn't make the effort were the ones who no longer gave a shit. In a way their resignation was a farewell present to Merrion, a kind of dreadful peace; once he could see that one of his regulars had given up hope entirely, he knew he was not going to have the sad duty of seeing him many more times. He resettled himself in his excellent chair and reminded himself that whatever the merits of the matter might be, he was still smarter than Janet. He did not say anything.

Satisfied by his silence that if she'd been in danger, she'd escaped from it, Janet veered back to the subject of routine. 'They live mostly by themselves, most of the time, you know? Like sometimes they might have someone stay over, a Friday night or for the weekend, or something. Sometimes for longer. But they live by themselves most of the time.'

She stopped again, craftily, and waited, to see if he would speak. She was still waiting, but now not very confidently, for Merrion to say something that would give her an idea about why he had asked her to come to his office in the courthouse at 9:15 on a Saturday in August, when she would have assumed it would be closed. When he didn't she talked some more, to fill up the dead air. When she was alone, she prepared for such occasions by talking to herself. Wherever she might be – on her way to the store every day; out taking a walk; sitting on a bench in the park; exploring the supermarket again – Janet talked to herself, a low, unceasing mutter – people did look at her funny sometimes, the bastards, but she tried to pay no attention to them. When she was by herself there were none of those official silences she really didn't like. She was nicer than most of the people who had called her in over the years: when she asked a question, she was polite enough to acknowledge it, at least with a shrug.

Merrion gazed at Janet and wondered idly where the two of them fitted among the planets and the stars onto the infinite curve of the universe, and why it had become necessary that from time to time they occupy adjoining places.

'My front window,' Janet said. 'You just can't help it, noticing things, you've got a window like that.' Her third-floor unit, number 14, sitting atop number 7 on the second floor, number 1 on the first – one bedroom, bathtub with shower, small kitchen, living-room/dining-room combo – had a picture window overlooking Eisenhower Boulevard. 'Sixteen-ninety-two Eisenhower Boulevard.'

She said it somewhat ruefully but defiantly, too, almost proudly, as though aware that the address conveyed a kind of raffish distinction Merrion would recognize. 'You must know something about where I live. You got me in there, didn't you? Right? I've got that part right, haven't I?'

She had it right. 'I got you in there,' he said. 'I called the super for you, what, almost a year ago now. Lucky for you, that one unit was open and the guy owed me a favor, something I did for his kid.'

That was all true. Merrion had sidetracked Steve Brody's damned kid safely away from a crack-cocaine prosecution into a private, long-term, residential drug-rehab program run under a state contract in Stowe, thus sparing the kid a criminal record (for the time being, anyway, Merrion'd thought, not expecting much more than that) and opening up the apartment where Mark'd been living with a girlfriend as useless as he was. But it wasn't all of the truth. Among the many other things Merrion knew about that building was the fact that the Town of Canterbury on the last business day of every month by check drawn on the Canterbury Trust Co. disbursed $385 in public funds payable to Valley Better Residences, c/o Canterbury Trust Co., Canterbury, Massachusetts, in full payment for the coming month's rental of that apartment to Janet LeClerc (until the town had changed over to direct deposit of payments to vendors via electronic transfer, the cancelled checks were returned to the town every month stamped on the back by the bank 'credit to account of Fourmen's Realty Trust – Valley Better Residences').

Merrion's familiarity with the location went back almost a quarter of the century. The building was still new when he first visited it late in 1970, completed earlier that year. F.D. Barrows Construction, the same low-bidding jerry-builders that had constructed the new district courthouse thirteen years before, had put it up. The low-grade bricks were unweathered. The cheap mortar of the pointing was neat, regular and even. The newness concealed the shabbiness for a while, but Merrion, cursorily inspecting it as he went in and out of it, once or twice a week – three or four times if Larry had been having a bad stretch – week after week, looked on as the weather wore the mask off.

Larry had gone to the cheap brand-new place to die. The whole world itself'd been pretty new then, as far as Merrion'd been concerned. He contemplated it and he saw that it was good. It looked to have been much better built than 1692 Ike, and at the age of thirty he had reason to believe he was soon going to have it on a string.

3

Merrion visited Lane the first time on Saturday, the day after Christmas, bringing a holiday fifth of Old Granddad. It was one of three Christmas bottles from lawyers allocated to each of the three assistants by Richie Hammond. He reserved both big baskets of fruit – from abstemious attorneys balancing their strong beliefs in temperance against their disinclination to lose their ready access to continuances of cases for which clients had not paid and forgiveness for late filings – and the other nine jugs for himself. Protesting the injustice to Hammond by reminding him that Lane had split the take evenly, Merrion had learned by chance that Larry was living alone. 'Yeah,' Hammond said with satisfaction, locking up the office at 2:00 P.M. on Christmas Eve and collecting the last of his gift parcels from the oak bench beside the door. 'Thought being generous one day a year'd make people forget what a bastard he was all the rest of it. And what did it get him? Not much. Now he's up there by himself on the boulevard, all by his lonesome, gone and forgotten as well.'

'What the hell're you talking about?' Merrion said. 'Larry's got a big family, six or eight kids. He lives with his wife down in Indian Orchard in the same little house they raised all those kids in. "One bathroom and ten people trying to get in it."'

'Well, his family got wise to him,' Hammond said gaily. 'Told him either he hadda lay offa the grog, or go live by himself somewhere else. Serves the prick right, you ask me.'

Merrion had felt sharply embarrassed not to have found out earlier. He had not made any effort to contact Lane in the month that had passed since Larry, having no choice in the face of Carnes family power, had turned the chief clerk's job over to Richie, going on what was called *terminal leave* the week after the four-day Thanksgiving break. He thought it strange that Larry had not telephoned him either, but knew guiltily that did not excuse his own omission. Initially suspicious, as he was of everyone, Larry after a year or two of daily scrutiny had accepted Merrion as 'a fairly decent guy, once you get to know the kid, make allowances for him,' and made him his office protégé, teaching him what the job really meant and entailed, grooming him someday to take it. To Hilliard Merrion admitted: 'I owe Larry. I should've shown more respect.'

When the court had opened with Larry as its first clerk, the title of *magistrate* was not included in the statutory definition of the office that he held. But that was in fact the job he had soon begun to do, years before the law was changed. He had started exercising magisterial powers when he and Charles Spring, the first judge to preside in Canterbury, soon after taking office deduced that Spring's job would become a lot simpler and less time-consuming if the judge informally ceded to his more-than-willing clerk and complicit fellow-investor enough actual power to decide *de facto* Small Claims civil matters – applications for summary process brought by landlords, tradesmen and public utilities against people who had failed to pay their bills. Lane began to hold what he and the judge called 'preliminary screening hearings,' putatively to enable the judge to conduct 'official sessions' more expeditiously, 'saving everybody's time.'

The bill-collectors immediately perceived that this procedure was by far the quickest, surest and most efficient way to get judgments against stubborn debtors. They learned to agree to allow 'Judge Spring to decide the case and sign the judgment on the basis of the memo I'll write up of this session, and then after you've seen his ruling, if you have no objection, he will sign a judgment. If you do have an objection, all you'll have to do is state it and he'll hear the case.' If within three days neither party entered an objection to Lane's memo, a judgment tracking the content of the memo was entered on the docket, carrying the 'Chas. Spring' signature Lane had expertly forged.

When there was an objection, experience soon demonstrated,

the judge, after rather brusquely holding the full hearing requested by a disappointed litigant tended to decide the case against that party, disappointing him again. As that understanding gained currency, the formal debt-collection process became even speedier in the Canterbury District Court. The grateful lawyers thought it fitting to be openly generous at Christmas and eager to pick up bar-tabs when they saw Lane in The Tavern after a hard day on the job.

From the beginning Lane was publicly forthright about the civil powers he'd annexed as well the power to dispose of minor criminal matters; experience on the civil side revealed to the legally savvy the meritorious economies of time and expense of the Lane approach and led to its adaptation for quick and quiet resolution of minor criminal matters – especially motor vehicle violations, but no one involved saw any need to publicize that. 'Phone bills; oil bills; light bills; gas bills: most people've got no idea what a mountain of chickenshit we get every day in this building,' Larry said. 'Until he took the judgeship, Chassy was one of them.'

Spring as a somewhat-affected teenager had formed the lifetime habit of abbreviating his given name as 'Chas.,' when he signed it in black ink with a gold-nibbed Waterman fountain pen, copying the steel-point signature reproduced as attestation of ironclad security on the cover of every policy issued by the company his namesake grandfather had founded in 1884, Pioneer Valley Insurance. His seventh-grade teacher, amused by the mannerism, had taken it at face-value, applying the durable nickname.

'Chassy'd always been a rich kid; what'd he know? Bills came into his house and went out the next day, paid. His daddy never had to go to court and have a judge yell at him, tell he'd better pay Ralph at the Gulf station down in Ingleside for the rebuilt engine in his car; fifteen bucks out of his paycheck every week until he paid the whole three hundred. Tell him if he didn't do it, Ralph was gonna get the car. If the engine in Chassy's father's car started burning oil, Chassy's daddy knew what to do. Nothing to it: he went down to DeSaulnier Chrysler-Plymouth, picked out a nice new Imperial hardtop and wrote out a company check. When Chassy finished law school and came home to practice law, he didn't have to run himself ragged, finding a job, get himself all tuckered out. He went to work where Dad worked, in the general counsel's office of the insurance company Dad'd inherited from Granddad.

'So, when Chassy became a district court judge he was shocked by what he discovered. Up 'til then he'd thought a civil matter was something that you did in superior or federal court. You hated to, but you had no choice. Major borrower'd begun defaulting on six-figure construction-bond payments. You had to protect your investors. It wasn't something that happened to *you*, because you'd gotten more than two months in arrears on your TV installment payments. 'And anyway, what the hell *are* these things, these "installment payments"? Don't people have to *pay* for what they get in your store before you let 'em take it home?'

'Chassy just had no idea how many people there were who didn't pay their bills for the plain and simple reason that they couldn't. They didn't make enough money to buy all the things they thought they really oughta have, but they'd gone out and bought them anyway. The first month or so we're in business here he thought the reason that we had such a volume of Small Claims business was that Arthur and Roy Carnes'd been telling the truth when they talked their buddies in the legislature into setting up this court for their very own. It was true: the four towns had really *needed* it. But since he thought it was all backlog, pent-up demand, he assumed in time we'd clear it up. Then when we didn't, because it wasn't, he didn't know which way was up.

'Instead of getting less, we got more. Once the plaintiffs and their lawyers finally found out we were here. It was like the tide coming in. Chassy finally realized something new hadda be done.

'It isn't easy to do something new in any courthouse, this one especially. A lot of the people in here: once they got to know Chassy a little, they decided they probably were never going to like him. There were days when I was one of 'em. He could be a fussy bastard, really get on your nerves. And he treated Lennie – Judge Cavanaugh, when he first came aboard, awful young but still and all, he *was* another judge – like he was shit. Naturally Lennie didn't like him very much, and he had company. That was why when Chassy wanted to get something done in *his* courthouse, it could take a pretty long time. Even when everybody else could see it was a good idea, as his ideas generally were, they were in no hurry to see it get done.

'So we had to fix the problem with Small Claims by ourselves – no help from anyone else. We decided that in the afternoons I'd become a junior judge. I'd hear all the petty civil cases. That'd free up about three or four hours every day for Chassy after lunch to do what he really liked to do, and was *good* at doing, too: watching the stock-ticker, following the market, picking out what stocks he thought we should be investing in with all this *money* we now had. Which me and Fiddle and Roy naturally *wanted* him to be doing with his time, just as much as he did. *Much* better having him out there making us richer'n to have him sittin' on his ass here in the court all afternoon, hollering at a buncha poor dead-beats whose chief money problem was they didn't make enough to pay their bills.

'So what we would do was have the normal sessions in the morning, until noon or as long's it took. Then unless we had a criminal matter go to trial, the afternoon – and we all tried very hard around here to make sure we *wouldn't*; we had those police prosecutors and the defense lawyers beltin' out plea-bargains left and right – as soon as we broke for lunch Chassy'd grab his coat-n'-hat and *run* out the door, *jump* in his Chrysler and high-tail it down to the brokers in Springfield. The rest of the day that's where he'd be, happy as a pig in shit at Tucker, Anthony and R. L. Day, down there on State Street; *in his element*. It was home to him there; he belonged. His daddy'd started taking him there when he was a little boy. And because *he* was happy, and also outta here, everybody in the courthouse who didn't like him was happy too. Me especially, of course, because he was making me money.'

'When Chassy called the Canterbury District Court "my court," he meant it,' Lane told Merrion. 'He acted like he owned the place and could do anything he liked. When people said he was arrogant, they were right. Whether he did it on purpose, to piss people off, or he never realized how people took it; that I really never knew. I didn't really mind it, myself. He was a smart son of a bitch and he treated me all right. He helped me make money. Naturally I'd think he was a pretty okay-type of guy.

'And anyway, the fact of the matter was that when he said "This is my courthouse," he had it about right.' Spring had grown up in Holyoke. He had gone to Deerfield Academy and then to Harvard ('46) and Harvard Law School ('49) with Roy Carnes. Carnes in 1952 had won the first of the five terms he would serve in the state House of Representatives, representing the easterly part of Holyoke along with the towns of Canterbury, Hampton Pond, Hampton Falls and Cumberland. In 1960, Holyoke voters approved his all-but-hereditary succession to the state Senate seat held by his uncle, Arthur, forced by failing health to retire.

Virtually by acclamation, Arthur had won what became known as 'the Carnes senate seat' when the death of the incumbent opened it in 1946. That had been less than a year after he was invalided home from World War II army service in Europe. He had lost his left arm during the drive for the Rhine. When he died in May of 1966, a fellow WW II veteran and friend of many years, *Holyoke Transcript Telegram* city editor and weekly columnist Reg Gault collected and published a full page of tributes to him, ending with his own: 'Arthur was entitled to wear the Distinguished Service Cross, the Silver Star, two Bronze Stars, and three Purple Hearts. He seldom did.

'He figured in many eyewitness stories of combat heroism. I didn't hear them from him; I heard them from other soldiers, who had fought alongside him. Arthur was born in this city in 1913. He went away to school, and then he spent those war years in Europe. He took his legislative work seriously, as he took everything except himself, and so until his health forced his retirement, he kept an apartment in Boston, where he spent much of his time. "Far too much of it," he would tell you, voicing just about the only complaint I ever heard him utter, "too far from my home, from my friends, and much too far from Grey Hills," the club he'd been instrumental in creating on the abandoned estate of Jesse Grey, and the golf game he'd astonishingly somehow learned to play again with one arm – "not quite as well, though," he would say – after his war wound.

'His home, then, always was here. Wherever his life and work and service to his country took him, he never really left. His heart and spirit remained in Holyoke and this valley along the Connecticut River, with the people that he knew and served so very well. He never forgot where he came from.

'He always knew who he was. He never lost sight of the job he had to do. He was a devoted son, husband and father, an honest and far-sighted public servant, the kind of candidate who gives meaning to the term "public service," a hero and the best friend a man could have. Raise a glass today to Arthur Carnes – *Ave atque vale*.'

The Carneses, Arthur in the Senate and Roy in the House, had first combined in 1954 to carve the Canterbury District Court jurisdiction out of the Holyoke, Chicopee, Palmer and Northampton Districts. There was merit to the rationale they publicized. The continuing escalation of the Cold War made it likely the civilian population around the US Air Force Strategic Air Command base at Westover Field would increase, as more and more Air Force dependents moved in. The Fisk Tire Company was working two shifts to meet the booming demand for real rubber tires to replace the synthetics rationed in wartime. The new Monsanto plant in Springfield was attracting young workers and their growing families. The University of Massachusetts at Amherst was expanding. And, as Larry Lane said, there didn't seem to be any reason to think business would be tailing off at the Tampax factory in Palmer.

'Like it or not,' Arthur said in the Senate, 'more people means more work for our court system, just as surely as it means more work for our school systems and our hospitals, more demands upon our water systems and our highways. Either we expand our facilities and agencies or we overcrowd and overload them to the point at which they simply cannot get their jobs done, and break down. If we expect and want the prosperity of our cities and towns to continue, with the population growth that good times economically attract, we have to be prepared to pay the price in necessary services. We need another court.'

The Carneses had intended that Arthur would become its first presiding justice, but by the time Chassy Spring's building committee – Chicopee assistant clerk of court Larry Lane served it as consultant – and Fiddle Barrows's construction people had the building ready for occupancy, early in 1957, Arthur's prostate cancer had been diagnosed. The prognosis was encouraging, Arthur's regular physician having digitally detected the growth early. But his cancer specialist said that in his view with radiation treatment and chemotherapy ahead of him, Arthur was probably going to find himself having to spend a lot of his time in a hospital johnny at Mass. General in Boston, and would most likely be more comfortable and have a better chance of recovery if he stayed close by. 'Particularly since you've already got your apartment in Charles River Park. Instead of getting yourself into a new situation where you have to travel a hundred miles every time you have to come in.'

'So there they were,' Larry Lane said. 'Arthur and Roy with their brand-new courthouse and nobody to put in it. Except me, of course, I was ready enough. Anything to get out of Chicopee and away from that bastard Popowski. Maurice was a son of a bitch. So they had a clerk. But they also needed a judge.

'Roy thought about it and decided he didn't want it. Too early for him to put himself out to pasture. He was still in his thirties, waiting to take Arthur's seat in the Senate, still thinking maybe some day he might make a run for Congress.' In 1962, when Roy moved up, Dan Hilliard, a Holyoke alderman because of strong though private Carnes support, won his first election to Roy's former seat in the House.

'It's hard for me to think now only fifteen years've gone by since we opened the place,' Larry said to Merrion. 'So much's happened since then. Take me for example, what's happened to me. You want the truth, I thought what happened to the Carneses was kind of funny. The two of them had it all planned out so neat, so firm, so fully packed, so quick and easy on the draw. Then the doctor sticks his finger up Arthur's ass, finds a little bulge up there that don't seem right to him, and "That's it. All bets're off. It's time to make new plans." Serves me right, I guess, that now it's happening to me. *I'm* on terminal leave.'

Bureaucratically *terminal* meant 'using up vacation time before formally commencing retirement,' but in Larry's case it carried another one of its meanings as well. He hadn't told anyone outside of his family. Until his mind was changed by Merrion's visit, he hadn't planned to tell anyone else.

His eyes had instantly filled up when he saw who was at his door. 'Where the hell've you been?' he said, his voice clogging up, grabbing the Christmas whiskey with his left hand, using his right to pull Merrion into the apartment.

'I just found out, Thursday,' Merrion said, shutting the door behind him. 'I would've come over yesterday but I hadda stay with my mother. My brother Chris didn't show up again, the shit, and she got all upset – I couldn't leave her on Christmas. But I didn't know, you're here by yourself. I just assumed you're okay. I know now I should've asked. But no one told me. I feel awful bad about this, Larry. Should've given you a call.'

'Ahh,' Lane said, shaking his head, clearing his throat, 'never mind the details, pal; stick to the important things. First thing is to get some ice here. Then we can figure out who's to blame, you for not calling or me. Not all *your* fault, you didn't know. Glad to see you's what's important. Kind of lonesome here. Not as tough as I thought.'

He put the bottle on the red Formica counter dividing the kitchen from the dining area and opened the refrigerator freezer door. He put the tray on the counter and then rested his hands on the surface and gazed at Merrion. In a flat voice he said: 'Doctor says I'm dying, Amby. He gives me a year to live and says it's not going to be fun. It's lung cancer, both of them. I'm too old for one of those new transplant-operations and it's too far along to stop. I'm numberin' out my days and as far's my family's concerned, I can do it by myself.'

His wife and his kids had made his choice clear: he'd 'either quit drinking, get a second opinion, maybe have surgery, radiation and the chemotherapy, and at least do my best to get better,' or else he would have to get out. 'They said she couldn't take it, watching me die, without at least tryin' to get better.'

He snorted. 'Which is never gonna happen, me get better, matter what I do, or don't.' Talking made him wheeze. 'Everybody knows it; nobody ever does. Doesn't matter what the hell I do to myself or let someone else do to me – better I'm not gonna get.

But that's the choice my family gives me. Get better or out of their lives.'

He told Merrion that he'd asked for time. 'I've *seen* what all that medical business does to a guy. It slows the dying down, I guess, lets him live a little longer. I don't argue with none of that. But what they do to you guarantees you're not gonna enjoy any life you get afterwards. If they'd drug you enough – morphine, maybe some of that heroin the cops've got in their evidence locker – make you happy no matter how shitty you felt or how much of you's even *left*, well then, that'd be a whole different thing. Something like that I might go for. But this *other* shit? I don't want it. When I go, what goes will be me. *Me*, pissin' and moanin' like always, not some dim bulb that finally burned out. That's all I was asking them for, time to die my own way.'

Describing the outrage to Merrion had made Lane indignant again, and therefore very emphatic. 'Not more time to *live*, you understand. I wasn't asking for that. Not looking for miracles here. Not from *that* bunch, at least, fuckin' damned ingrates they are. Just some time to *think*. Seemed reasonable to me. After all, I've supported the whole fuckin' raft of 'em,' Larry had eight children, 'all of these fuckin' years. Roof over their heads; warm dry place to sleep; pretty good food, by and large. Didn't cook it, no, but I paid for it – oughta get some credit for that. Court's indulgence, as we say? Couple of days, over the weekend, decide which life I'd like better, little short one I've got left. I *needed* some time to think. "Sunday night be all right, say? After the Celtics game? I'll give you my answer then.'

'They were pissed off. "In other words, Dad, you're gonna drink your way through another weekend, right? Just like you always've done. And then come Sunday night, when you're totally shitfaced, will've been for two whole days, *that's* when you make up your mind? Like your head'll be clearer then?'

'They actually had that much fucking nerve. "You bastards," I thought. "You bastards," I said, "you fuckin' bastards. So this then is what it comes down to. Forty-two fuckin' years I've been working, counting the service and all, and now I finally retire, don't have to work anymore. And what do I find out that makes me? Your prisoner. I gotta do what you say.

What an honor. Takes my breath away. Gimme the whiskey instead."

'Then I stomp out and go back down the courthouse. Gonna change my pension plan. None of them get any of it, all my years of damned hard work. Started six years before any of them came along. Eight of 'em didn't even *exist*. I created my own enemies. Am I feelin' sorry for myself, at this point? You betcher your ass I am, Amby.

'Now this stuff in here,' he'd gestured around, his one-bedroom apartment – number 11 at the rear, on the second floor, with its dreary-brown, early-winter view of Ransom's Brook flowing down the cement trench – 'this is what I've got left. But it's pretty grand, don't you think?'

Larry was beginning slyly to explain. The wind eddied groaning around the already-pitting aluminum sashes of the cheap double-glazed windows, ill-fitted into the brickwork, from the maker of the windows in the almost-new courthouse, the lower corners of the double glass already fogged in white crescent shapes with moisture condensed from vapor penetrating the thin rubber sealant. Merrion'd tried to look favorably impressed, but he wasn't. He thought it didn't look like much.

Larry hadn't been fooled. He'd grinned like a Doberman. 'Yeah, right, I know. It isn't. It's cheap shit, built to a price, all right? Building-to-price's the way you make money on an investment property like this. Cheap buildings bring in a real profit, even if they do look ten years old from the day when you first turn the key. It's a fat little pot fulla gold at the end of a rainbow; every month it gets fuller.'

'They don't know,' Larry said to Merrion. 'Not one of my family's got a clue. Never told Richie either. Decided a long time ago I don't like the guy. Chassy appointed him, favor to Roy Carnes, but Chassy never made me think I oughta trust the guy, or that he did, either. And anyway, the fewer people that know what you're really up to, better off everyone is.

'You get a family yourself some day? This dame of yours ever gets her thinking straight, two of you settle down an' have kids? Beautiful, good for you. Good health and prosperity; may there be many days in their lives, and the sun shine on every damned one. I hope they treat you lots better'n mine treated me. But the same advice holds, either way. Tell 'em nothin' beyond what they need to know, case tomorrow you're hit by a bus. The rest let 'em find out after you're dead, you're still on speaking terms then.

'That's what I always did. They didn't know what the stakes really were, how much they had riding on me. What keeping me happy was actually worth. How much effort they oughta put in. *That's* why they thought they could get so high and mighty with me. They had no idea what it'd really *cost* 'em, what they'd be losing, if they went and got me pissed off. The pension was all they knew about, see? Well, all of my kids now, they've done pretty well – thanks of course to the way that *I* brought them up, but you're not gonna hear that from *them*. They can take care of my wife, if they have to, without even breathing hard, right? So my pension for Ginny they're willing to risk, I guess, if they've even thought about that.

'So as a result, after what those pricks did to me, I'm on my way back down the office. The minute that I get there, the first thing I am gonna do is change that fuckin' pension. What they bet, they lost. Gonna screw them right out of it. Just like they all screwed me out of the rest of my life, right to die in my own fuckin' *house*, when they put me out in the street.

'But by the time I get down there, I've changed my mind. 'Fuck 'em 's what I've now decided. What'll I care, my wife gets the pension? I'll be dead and buried, six feet under 'fore they find out what I did to her, got even. And then they'll go out and start bad-mouthin' me. Make me look like shit, all over town: my poor widow, she ain't got a dime. What a bastard I was; I left her destitute, all the rest of that crap. Right here, in my very own town, which I've lived in all my life. And I won't be around to fight back. Tell all the people what *they* did to *me*, treatin' me like a sack-ah brown shit, I had the nerve to get sick. What good is that gonna do me?

'"No, better like this." That was what I decided. Better if they never know, the rotten bastards, about all the other stuff there was, they never dreamed of. The big boodle. *That's* where the real revenge is. Not takin' it with me, no, still can't do that, but I can keep it away from them. That's as good as you *can* do, at least. Almost as good in the end, Slick, wouldn't you say? Almost as good in the end.'

It'd taken Larry longer than his doctors and he had expected, dying at the pace set by the cancer, but doing it his way. He hadn't finished up until just before Columbus Day in 1972, twenty-one slow, hard months later. Merrion had visited him at least once during each of eighty-two of those eighty-seven weeks that Larry Lane lived at 1692 Ike.

During the first week of March in '72 Merrion had been pretty much recovered from the flu that had sent him to bed during four days of the last week of February, but still feared he might infect Larry. Each year he had taken the same nine days of vacation that he'd started taking in 1962, the first year he'd been on actual salary with Danny – the last week of June and the first week of July, combining vacation days with the holiday for the Fourth. Beginning in '66 he attended the annual clerks' conventions during his time away each June. The first week in July was his one-quarter share of the month's rental of the two-bedroom cottage he rented with Dan and Marcia Hilliard at Swift's Beach in Wareham, and he spent it there fucking Sunny Keller, when she came home on leave from the Air Force to him as the summer herself, even the July it rained.

Over twenty years later he still missed Sunny Keller, and every so often late at night in the card room at Grey Hills when he had had enough to drink, he would shake his head and say it again, right out loud but softly, that he still didn't see why she felt she had to volunteer to go and take a chance on getting herself killed, and then actually get killed, and then he would say 'fucking war,' even though it hadn't really been the war that killed her – just a heavy rain in Hawaii that could've fallen anywhere. But without the war it wouldn't've fallen onto her. One night Dan Hilliard'd had a few drinks too, and he'd begun to feel sad himself. 'You think, you silly bastard,' Danny had said, 'you think you were the only one.'

'You son of a bitch, I do not,' Merrion had said. 'I know very much better'n that, god damn it. I know she fucked other guys. Sunny always fucked other guys. But I couldn't help that, you know. There was nothin' I could do about that.'

'Not fucking, goddamnit,' Hilliard had said. 'Not fucking I'm

talking about. I meant it was you thinking you were the one, that you were the one that was crazy about Sunny. And you were jus' wrong about that. It was everyone, all of us, ever' damn body, always liked Sunny, right off. And more'n a few of us even got so we loved her. Not that we fucked her, I didn't mean that, but we also loved her. We did. So you shouldn't think that, that it was just you, that it was just you that loved Sunny. 'Cause it wasn't just you that loved Sunny. That was the way that she was.'

All the other weeks except for flu and his vacations, Merrion had gone to see Larry. Every time he'd gone there, he'd said the same thing. 'Just dropped by, see how you're doin'.'

'"Checkin' up on me," you mean,' Larry had replied every time, wheezing it out and then coughing deeply, moaning as he dredged another shallow air-passage through the viscous tide collecting in his lungs. 'See what progress I'm makin'.' Igniting another Lucky Strike; gradually devouring and dissolving himself from the inside out, the brown whiskey yellowing his skin; even using two reagents, the process still took its luxurious time.

'You got to be patient,' Larry had said. 'After all, it stands to reason, am I right? Takes seven years to make the stuff, age it – isn't that what they claim it takes? Bound to take it a while to work. But I don't mind. I'm in no real hurry here to clear out. But I got no desire to hang around, either. Either way, perfectly all right with me.'

Over the course of the twenty-one months the building had become etched in clear detail in Merrion's mind, the three-story, eighteen-unit rectangle squatting cramped on a mingy acre-and-an-eighth shelf of land ('being approximately 49,005 square feet, more or less,' the deed to the trust recited) filled and levelled with the wreckage of buildings demolished in Urban Renewal projects in Springfield, Holyoke and Chicopee, putting a questionably buildable site in place of the nine-percent grade of the natural ravine cut by Ransom's Brook. The fill – pulverized brick, thick greyish clay, mulched fibreboard, chunks of cement – glittered with shards of window-glass and china; bent steel spikes and rough zinced rods stuck up between dead blades of grass browned and flattened by the early frosts. Larry Lane and the other four men in the Fourmen's Realty Trust had gotten the fill free for their investment. 'Must've been damned near two hundred loads,' Larry said, confirming what Merrion's eyes told him. The place had been built on debris.

'Crap built on crap,' Larry said, laughing. 'Just like the people who live in it now – more stuff that nobody wanted. We got it for the cartage, for taking it away. Fiddle Barrow gave his drivers all the hours they could stand. When they finished his contract work for the day, had them go and get it, bring it over here. Eight, ten tons at a time, dumped it right down the slope of that ravine there, right to the edge of the cement trench. Lot of it didn't stop at the edge, went right along into the brook. But what the hell did we care, huh? Wasn't costing us anything. No one saw it go in. There was always plenty more.'

Number 14, Janet's unit, was at the front, on the third floor of the six-unit stack to the left of the entrance on the westerly end of the building. The other twelve, Numbers 2 through 19, skipping 13, were stacked on the easterly side of the door, four units on each of the floors. Janet knew the habits of others in the building, people whose names she didn't know; she'd deduced their business by watching them.

'From my fucking picture window,' she'd said once, matter-of-factly, mildly startling Merrion. 'Some fucking dumb pictures I get from it. Better stuff on stupid TV. OJ: I was watching that. More innaresting stuff'n people in my building've got going, onna TV there.' She attended the lives of the other tenants as though they had been staged for her, like the athletic events and movies she watched avidly. She preferred professional hockey, she told Merrion, ''specially when they have the fights,' seldom missing any game broadcast, no matter which teams were playing. Like the other people in her building they were features of the video in her life, silent players passing through it, their purposes unstated, their function as far as she was concerned being to entertain her. She thought that few of them tried hard enough, no matter what resentments she expressed by grumbling at them.

She did that a lot. She had plenty of time. Far too much of it, in Merrion's estimation; it allowed her the leisure to overheat her imagination, already running on more mood elevators than Merrion believed could possibly be good for her. Xanax, he thought it was, that Sammy Paradise'd said, assuming *his* own source was telling the truth. But that was not a safe assumption; Lowell Chappelle was the source, the probationer snooping around in his girlfriend's apartment for damaging information about her, who had heedlessly taken him in. Chappelle was assuming Janet hadn't substituted something else for what'd come in the Xanax-labelled bottle that he'd seen when he browsed her bathroom medicine cabinet. She'd mentioned Elavil at least once to Merrion. Janet knew her drugs.

Louella Daggett was no help. She wouldn't tell Merrion what elixirs Janet was on, beyond confirming she'd been given something that would make the world spin nice and slow and even, no bumps. Louella cited rules of confidentiality Merrion did not believe existed, or should not if they did.

Janet had nothing in her life but raw time. When she sat in her best chair to watch her shows all day on TV, and her hockey games at night – Boston and Providence Bruins; Hartford Whalers; Springfield Indians, Kings, Falcons; New York Islanders; Rangers; or New Jersey Devils; God only knows which teams or how many – after she got back from Dineen's convenience store each morning, that was all she had: time, nothing but time. She was waiting to die.

Sam Paradisio thought Chapelle could make it happen for her. He thought Chappelle *had* done it to others, committed murder. 'Just because nobody ever caught him at it, that doesn't mean the bastard hasn't done it. There was this one bank that got robbed, 'way the hell out in western New York State, Olean, during the time that he was out before he went in this last time that he got caught. All the earmarks of a Big Sid Charpinsky job – that was his neck of the woods, out that way, part of the world he come from. He was in the Rockingham County Jail up in New Hampshire, there, Exeter, same time Chappelle was in for an armored car thing he did. The two of them became asshole buddies.

'Bastards do not stay put any more. They refuse to just stay in one place nowadays, where a man can keep an eye on them. They're all over the place now like horseshit. Well, I saw the surveillance photos on that one, the New York job. The US

Attorney showed them to me, and they showed this one poor bastard gettin' mowed down. Just gettin' fuckin' *riddled* he was. And the guy that was doin' it looked an awful lot to me like my friend Lowell, guy who's usin' the Mac Ten. Wearin' a mask, but even so, more than a passin' resemblance. The same build, and the same way he's got of movin', way he carries himself. We know what Chappelle is capable of. Army trained him too good. He could be anyone's killer. Available, formal occasions. Weddings and funerals, bar mitzvahs. Bastard'd have to get his own eight-hundred number, there'd be so much demand for his work.'

Merrion rejected that notion at once. It alarmed him. He didn't like being alarmed. Larry'd said one day to him when he was still feeling really good, which usually meant savage and mean: 'I've reached that magic age where I only have to do the fuckin' things I want to *do*, and only think about the things I fuckin' *like* to think about. So, if I don't like to do it, it's a thing that I don't like, or I don't like to think it, well then, my friend, then I don't.' Merrion had agreed with Larry at the time, and now, approaching the same age, agreed with Larry even more, even though he was dead and had been dead for more than twenty years. *Another legacy from Larry: words to be dead by.*

Still the thought lingered, skulking around in the back of his head, bothering him with its shadow. 'I'm never gonna leave this place,' Larry Lane'd said to him. 'Well, I go out now and then, time to time, right now. And I'm gonna *leave*, of course – some day I'm gonna have to. But the only way I'm gonna do it is when the six guys bring the long black car around. *Then*, well, I'll have to leave.'

Somehow or other about a year or so into Larry's last mission Richie Hammond'd found out that Merrion had been going to visit him. 'Every week, is it?' Richie'd said to him. 'Every week you go up there, and stay about *two hours*? What the hell you do up there with him, up there in that place with that shrivelled-up old bastard he is, all that time alone with him? Guy's fuckin' dyin' – *isn't* he? That's what I hear, every place I go. Everyone says it, all over town. "Larry Lane isn't long for this world," 's what I hear. "Larry Lane's on his way out, this time." That's what everyone's sayin'.' Then he had paused and looked hopeful, waiting for confirmation.

Merrion had not said anything. He had shrugged, throwing in the eyebrow-raising. He did that whenever Richie started irritating him, which was fairly often. It wasn't insubordinate – not that Richie as a practical matter could harm him in any way at all. Even if he did start keeping a log and writing it up whenever Merrion yanked his chain; as long as Danny Hilliard had access to a telephone that worked and a friend alive on Beacon Hill, it would take St Michael the Archangel to lay a bad hand on Ambrose Merrion.

His silence pissed Richie off. That was another thing Richie didn't know how to do right, get pissed off properly. And *usefully*, so's to set a precedent, one that people would shudder to remember and try not to do again whatever it was that had set him off. He just got plaintive and made himself look ridiculous. 'Well answer me, for Christ sake, Amby. I asked you a fuckin' question.' That was why Merrion did it. 'What the hell do you do up there with him, for Christ sake? The man's a *dyin'*, *fuckin'*, *man*.'

Merrion had shrugged again, but this time as Riche'd begun to work up another pisspot eruption, he'd given him words to go with it. 'We tell each other stories,' he'd said blandly. 'Well, Larry tells *me* the stories, how things used to be. What went on, and what it all meant. History lessons of this place. I mostly just listen, nod now and then. Sometimes I ask him a question. But you know, there're days, when we had somethin' happen. Something's gone wrong down here. And as he knows and you know and I know myself, most days something generally has. And those weeks I have something to say. Stories to tell him, put some fun in his life.'

That had enraged Richie. He'd come out of his chair. He slammed both his fists knuckles-down on the top of the very desk Merrion now occupied, so hard that it had to've hurt, and then braced himself on his stiffened, locked arms. His face had gone crimson immediately, right up to the roots of his brown greying hair. His voice'd gone up along with the blood pressure. 'You son of a bitch you; you son of a bitch; you son of a goddamn-damned bitch. You're tellin' Larry Lane what we're doin' in here? You gettin' his input on stuff? You're gettin' his clearance on stuff? He hasn't got no more power in here. That bastard is retired, even if he isn't dyin' – like everyone else knows he is and they are glad. Once you are retired from here, that is the end of your power. Then you have got no more power in here and you might as well *be* dead, like you are gonna be. You cut that stuff out now, right now.'

4

According to Sam Paradisio's very best hearsay, Janet's most dangerous conduct was her smoking habit. 'And this is not because I think everyone should quit today and then if they won't do it on their own, the government should make them. I'm the only person whose smoking ever bothered me, and I am in favor of letting people kill themselves any way they like. What I am not in favor of is other people killing them, for any reason whatsoever, and this lady's smoking habit, about two packs a day, could be something that will do that, make that happen. For her this is high-risk behavior.

'What makes me say this is that's what my violent hardened felon tells me. He's pretty specific. When he was in jail, they put in that No Smoking rule, and he hadda cold-turkey the habit. He said it was a real bitch.

'"Way worse'n going off cocaine, or the booze or the pills. You can still get the butts, sure, but when you do you can't smoke 'em. Well, there're ways, but they're hard. How can you smoke without making smoke, which all the damned screws can then smell? If they don't actually see it. Pills and the other stuff: those you can do without anyone seeing you do it. But havin' a smoke: that's really hard. When they said you couldn't have any more of that, you really couldn't, just about, so that one's a real motherfucker."'

Sammy Paradise had reported his conversation with Chappelle to Merrion over lunch on Friday of the previous week, the second in August. They had occupied their usual dark-brown oak booth in The Tavern on the northerly side of the green opposite the

Strand Theater in the center of Canterbury, a block from the courthouse. Also as usual they could talk about confidential matters because they had the place pretty much to themselves; the restaurant workers paid no attention to their conversation and because they met at 1:15 when the court was in recess, there were no other customers.

Merrion was having a good sixteen-ounce strip sirloin steak broiled medium rare, a baked potato with sour cream and chives and a salad glistening with oil and vinegar dressing. He had nearly finished a pint of Löwenbräu dark beer and he planned to order another 'for dessert.' Paradisio was eating a chicken salad sandwich on dark bread and as customary nursing a twelve-ounce glass of Miller Lite that he did not intend to finish.

Paradisio said Chappelle told him Janet's smoking was 'the only thing about her he's got strong feelings about. He really doesn't like it. Because when she does it, it makes him want to smoke. And it was real hard for him to quit. He told her that and she said she can't stop. She used to smoke even more, she told him, but then a while back she cut down. And she's got it down now to the point where she can actually ration them.

'He tells me that drives him nuts. "I could never do that. And I am a guy that they made quit completely. I know what I'm talking about. Only smoke so many a day? Guarantee you, that'd drive me nuts.'

'He acts like he's got her on surveillance. This's obviously become an obsession with the guy, keepin' track how much she smokes. "When she goes to bed at night she's got about four or five, maybe half a dozen of them left. Just enough to get her through the morning, just 'til she goes out again. Sittin' onnie edge the bed, there, 'fore the shower an' shampoo. Then: after she gets dressed and puts the coffee-maker on, dries herself off, an' brushes her hair. To dry it in the air, before she uses the hair-dryer. 'Not as many split-ends,' she tells me," this's him, now, tellin' me, '"when you do it this way you don't get so many split-ends."

'"She says. Maybe that takes two butts. Mark down *two* for that, brings us up to three. Coffee's ready, ahh, then sugar, milk, have another one or two while she's drinkin' that. Now it's time to get dressed and go out the store, get ahold of a paper. Don't hafta actually go and buy it; just look up the page there where they print last night's number and see right there if you won. Scratch-ticket, large coffee. Use ten dollars' worth of food stamps, something costs about five bucks 'nd change. Leaves her enough to get change back to use for more smokes. Two more new fresh decks of butts. Something to look forward to, may turn out to be the only thing all day. Scratch the ticket. Have another one while you're doing that, or maybe on the way back. Six, I think, that makes it. Maybe seven, you lose count. Not that it really matters."

'That's how I get it from Lowell. "Smokin's the principal thing in her life, when she's all by herself. What she does when she's doin' everything else, or not doin' a damned thing at all. She's a real junkie on those things." For him, this is an obsession.

'Lowell with an obsession's an idea that bothers me,' Paradise said. 'It bothers me because I think he's tellin' me the truth when he says her smokin' gets to him. It makes him worry she might be the cause of *him* going back to smoking again. He's aware that it's possible he might get unlucky again, doing something that he knows he shouldn't do – like robbing another bank or something. And if he gets *caught* doing it, which he knows's always a risk in that line of work, that would mean that he'd end up going back inside again. If he ever gets lugged again – and almost anything'd do it, record like he's got; parking overtime'd be enough – that'll be all it'll take. Put him right back in the can, and this time it'll be for all day, the entire rest of his natural. Habitual criminal, multiple loser like he is, the new law could be "*Ten* strikes and you're out" – he would still qualify, easy.

'So, say he hasn't got anything in mind right now, any special thing he's got in mind to get a large amount of money fast. That's good, but with him it's always been kind of a temporary condition; he's always in it 'til he spots something that looks like prime pickings. "Candy," is what he calls it; a job that's too good to resist. Well, he's older now, lost a yard or two off his fastball, and he swears he's reformed. But in the back of his mind he still has to think it could happen again. Some big opportunity might turn up any day, and Lowell just wouldn't be able to pass it up. He knows himself pretty well by this time, what his limitations are. He gets hot pants when he sees a job he thinks he can knock over easy. Major temptations're hard for him to resist.

'This's a big country. When he's been able to, Lowell's always been footloose, but he's spent a lot of years inside and he hasn't seen all of it yet. He knows somewhere he hasn't been yet there's bound to be another temptation he couldn't bear to turn down. The only reason he hasn't gone for it yet is that he hasn't seen it. If he sees it, he knows he'll say *Yes*.

'So he might get caught again. If does, he's back inside. They're not going to let him smoke. He'll have to quit again. Lowell ain't sure he could do that. He's *dead sure* he doesn't want to.

'That's why I think he's tellin' the truth, that he's pokin' her all the time and he likes that all right, but it *bugs* him that she smokes. I don't think this's good news for this boneheaded broad that you've got on your hands here, wasn't too bright to begin with. This is a dangerous man.

'He's proven it, many times. The videos of him in banks when he's been robbing them show a very scary man in a state of cold homicidal rage, capable of doing anything. You would not want to've been in one of them, getting cash on your MasterCard, when Lowell and some friends stopped by to make a withdrawal. The people who've attended his robberies in person 've testified that he's frightening to behold. 'Terrifying' is a word they often use.

'This is the man whose woman's smoking truly infuriates him. He likes screwing her and having her blow him. For that he has to be around her, so he tries not to let her smoking make him mad. But self-control isn't Lowell's stock in trade. Self-restraint isn't something that he's good at, especially where sex's also involved.

'This guy is what teenage boys wish they were. He's a sex engine. In the place where you and I have got our penises, he's got a jack-hammer. He's what they call a paraphiliac. He's got an abnormally powerful sex drive. There really is such a thing as being sexually insatiable, and he is that. When he's been in the can, they've had to put him in solitary several times for sexually running amok, assaulting other inmates. Either he wants to bugger them and they don't want him to, or else he wants them to blow him and they're not keen on that either, so as a result he's going to beat on them until they see it his way.

'Keep in mind what kind of polished gentlemen make up our prison populations. These guys that he's threatening are thugs themselves, hardened criminals like him – and *they're* afraid of him.

'When he's been in solitary, locked up by himself; *knowing* there's a TV camera on him every minute; no access to any erotic material outside his own diseased imagination; he's been observed masturbating to orgasm eleven times in one twenty-four-hour period. In that same period he also had a wet dream. He'd been jerking off all day – that is what they had him doing; merrily watchin' dirty movies – every half hour or so. Then he went to sleep for a while, five or six hours, I guess and while he was asleep he got hard and came off again. And then when he woke up, the first thing he did was jack off.

'This was at one of the institutions where the psychologist got permission to test this new aversion-therapy on him. It sounds like some kind of a fantastic joke, but it's some starry-eyed nitwit's bright idea of a new treatment for sex offenders – child molesters; bell-ringers; guys who beat up prostitutes; rapists.'

'Every type of leading citizen,' Merrion said.

'Right,' Paradisio said. 'I guess no one's ever proven it works, but then no one's ever proven any of the standard, traditional approaches've worked either. I don't think anyone's ever come up with a cure for those guys they could demonstrate was reliable. So you could ever feel really comfortable letting them loose. Basically they show the dirty pervert all kinds of filthy stuff, find out what really turns him on. Then overpower him with it: Show him dirty movies and let him beat his meat until it's raw or it falls off, whichever comes first. It sounds to me almost as though it oughta be cruel and unusual punishment, stir the guy up into such a frenzy that he does that to himself; has so much fun he really hurts himself.'

'While the medics thoughtfully look on and take notes, I presume,' Merrion said. 'All in the interest of science, of course. Are we still sure we know which one of these people in the playroom's the guy who's got the problem? Or is it just possible that *both* of them're now upstanding – one from watching the movies, the other one from watching the watcher?'

'That was my first thought,' Paradisio said. 'Anyway, when they put Chappelle in the box and made him watch porn flicks all day, he took to it right off. He really seemed to like it.'

'Oh, I bet he did,' Merrion said. '*Much* better 'n reshelving the books in the prison library. *Much* more fun watching' 'Debbie do Dallas' ''n it is mopping down the dining hall. What'd he do, set a new record for the pony-lope?'

'They shut the VCR off after three hours,' Paradisio said. 'By then he'd finished off five erections.'

'Very impressive,' Merrion said. 'They should groom him for the Olympics. Maybe the way to rehab this guy is get him a movie tryout. If he doesn't get stage-fright, he could be worth a fortune. He's not a bad guy after all; just a poor unhappy kid who missed his true calling in life.'

'Yeah,' Paradise said, 'but they didn't do that, so as a result I've got him. What I'm afraid'll happen is that some night after he and Lady Janet've been drinking and he's been in her a couple or three times, he'll be ready again before she is. And she'll say "No, let's wait a minute, honey. Take a break and have a smoke, make ourselves another drink. We got all night to play." And he'll go berserk and either kill her for putting him off or else force her do it, and in the process be so rough he'll kill her without meaning to. Not that it'll matter much to her.'

'If he's telling the truth,' Merrion said. 'Dangerous guys don't always do that, as I'm sure you probably know.' He did not wish to believe that Chappelle was a threat. If he was then he would first have to think of something he could do that would keep Janet safe, and then he would have to do it. That would be more work for him. 'More work's against the chief clerk's religion,' Larry Lane had said.

'Well, yeah,' Paradisio said, 'but like I say: I don't think he's lying to me. He doesn't have anything to gain by doing it. Why lie if it doesn't get you anything? He doesn't give enough of a shit about me or the pathetic little things that I can do to him. Put him back in jail? It's practically his second home. I don't care, but it's still bad news for the broad. She's pissing him off. That's never a wise thing to do.

'I think you should at least tell her. He's not doing this 'cause he's in love. Because he likes her, even feels sorry for her. He's fucking her because she's got the equipment, what he prefers to get the job done. Brains're not included in that, so it's okay with him that she's not only stupid but probably not right in the head, talks ragtime or isn't all there. Dependable pussy is what he's after, and that's what she's offering this week. This week and the week after next. If her talk starts to distract, he just buys her another drink. And if one pop doesn't quite do the job, another one after it will. Sooner or later she'll pass out on him, and then he can go to sleep. Knowing he'll get back into her again two or three times in the morning.

'Lowell Chappelle is a practical man. Half-breeds're often that way, I've noticed. Used to working the fringes; they get pretty good at the game. You've got to find some way to warn her, and make her *understand* she's being warned.'

'If you just bought a carton of cigarettes, you mean,' Merrion said to Janet. 'If you bought a carton, say, every five days, then you wouldn't need to go down to Dineen's every morning, the way you do now. Then only every fifth day.'

'Well, maybe every three or four days,' she said. 'I've always been: "Have I got it?" Then I'll have it. The booze and the pills, and the cigarettes, too. Or if I had something to sniff.' She frowned. 'Which I haven't been doing for quite a long time. I wouldn't want you thinkin' that. But when I did, when I was doin' that, that was the way that I did it, all right? Just like with everything else. If I've got it, I'll use it. No matter how long it's supposed to last me, I'll use it if I got it around.'

'I wasn't suggesting . . .' Merrion said, 'anything like that. I didn't mean anything like that. That you might be back on the stuff. You gave me your word, you wouldn't do that – you were all finished with that stuff. And that was an important part of our deal, that you'd keep that promise to me. Because otherwise, you know, all bets were off. No help from me with the judge. Or with the people over at Welfare, or with the building super, either, up at the place you live. Well, so far as

I know, you have done that, stayed clean. So I'm still trying to help you.'

'Because those fuckin' neighbors of mine I've got up there,' she said, 'they are real nosy people, and *mean*. The people who were there when I moved in there, like you said, when you got me in, those were very nice people there then. I got along with them good. But then one at a time, they all seem to've moved out. Always just one at a time. Almost so you wouldn't notice. And then if you did, well, you'd just assume, the new ones'll be just like them.

'But it didn't turn out that way. These're not nice people there now. These're a very mean, *loud*, kind of people. I don't like them. I'd like to do something to them. Spray-paint their cars or something like that. Get back at them for how they act. But I don't. I don't do annathin', say nothin', to them. I just go along there, minding my business, not a care in the world. Don't give them no bullshit at all. I'm not that kind of person. But I'm not so sure about them. I think if they wanted, get rid of a person, you know? That they might start thinkin' how to do it, that would hurt their reputation. And if they couldn't find something out, well, it's not like I'm sayin' I know they've done this, they got you all concerned here like you are today, so you thought you had to see me.'

'I have to see you *every* month, Janet,' he said wearily. 'It's part of our arrangement, and by now I shouldn't have to tell you again, every month when you come in. When I have someone call you and remind you to come in, it doesn't necessarily mean I've heard something about you. Or that I haven't, either. It's just time for you to come and see me and let me see how you're doing.'

'I know, but I'm just sayin',' she said, 'that if they told you something then they must've made it up. 'Cause they didn't see *nothin'*. All I am sayin' here is that they could've, they *could've* done that, it's the kind of thing they might do.'

She looked anxious and wrung her hands. 'You see what I'm sayin' to you? They're the type of people that would, *would* do something like that, make up some bad things, just to get someone in trouble. These are very mean people. They would do that to me. They would do that to anyone, really. They wouldn't stop at annathin'. It wouldn't matter to them. Somebody really should do, you know, something about them. Someone really should. Before they go and hurt somebody else. They really don't care what they do, as long as they get their own way.'

She paused and thought, frowning, looking at the floor. She nodded, as though satisifed she had settled something in her mind that had troubled her. 'I could do it myself,' she said, looking up and nodding again. 'I could fix them myself if I hadda. I don't know if you know this, if this's something I told you, before, but I can take care of myself. A lot of people; all my life a lot of people've been always thinking I couldn't do that, take care of myself. And some of them thought, well, they tried to do things to me. And then they were very surprised. I gave them a big surprise. I can *do* things. So I could, if I hadda, do something. And I *would*, too. Except for this thing I got, that you got over me; maybe it'd be better this time if you did it instead. If you did something to them for me. That I shouldn't, you know, do anything? Might get me in more trouble here?'

'No, you shouldn't,' he said. 'You have to stay out of trouble. That's your most important job right now: you stay out of trouble for a year. You're almost home now; only one month more to go. Then you'll have done it, the year. You can do that, you'll be free. You won't have to come in and see me anymore, which I know you don't look forward to. Being on your own again, and we'll hafta see if we can get you 'nother job. So that's what you want to concentrate on. Just a little bit longer: proving that you can behave.'

Janet wasn't bright but she was clever. She was playing for time. Sooner or later he'd become tired or hungry; have to go to the bathroom; meet his next appointment; decide to go home. Then instead of it being necessary for her to plead fatigue, played-out memory, generalized confusion, or something else, *anything*, in order to escape, he would call it off and let her go.

Merrion had first encountered play-acting during his indoctrination as a rookie clerk working the juvenile court session under the carefully reserved supervision of Larry Lane: Brylcreemed upswept wave of hair and the heavily spiced Jade East after-shave lotion; flared trousers and the counterfeit Gucci loafers; bushy grey-black mutton-chop sideburns: Lawrence D. Lane, Clerk of the Court, acting monarch of every damned thing he surveyed. 'You're only young for a while.'

Larry did it with panache; he did not like training novices. 'No mercy,' he said, telling Merrion how to deal with beggars seeking undeserved favors – or asking them on days when Merrion did not feel like granting any, even to the worthy. 'For any damned reason at all, or for *no* reason at all. No quarter. Especially when they start in on you, giving you the old routine. They're trying to distract you. Get you to thinkin' about something else, and then actually discussin' it, talkin' about it with them, somethin' you weren't even thinkin' about when they came in.

'When they do that, you start saying 'Bullshit. Bullshit, bullshit, and *more* bullshit.' And you keep *on* sayin' it, all right? Until they get discouraged, go away, and stop trying to do it. I tell you, son, I tell you true: it's the only way.'

Merrion had been politically insinuated into Lane's office as a reward for more than six years of doglike devoted service, the first two as an unpaid volunteer, in behalf of the electoral ambitions of Assistant by *de facto* House Majority Leader Daniel Hilliard. Roger Hulsman of Wey-mouth retained his clawlike hold on the title, the perquisites and pay, for what he had announced would be his final term – thus 'laming his own fuckin' duck,' as Hilliard said.

That political experience had made Merrion mistrust any tactic of dismissing a voter or disappointing a potential ally except the familiar one getting rid of the petitioner by soothingly lulling him into the hopeful but mistaken belief that if at all possible his wishes would be granted; sending him away already softened up for the gradual accretion of the understanding that he wasn't going to get what his patron had already made painfully clear was going to be extremely hard to bring about. A neutral party seeking a favor was a loyal friend in prospect. If circumstances made it necessary to reject his proposal, the prudent politician tried to do it so that he did not go away an enemy.

Lane smelled Merrion's reservation. 'This isn't politics you're playing now, not while you're in here. Not when you're dealing with the scum that we have to deal with. These bastards can't do a thing *for* you or *to* you. What these bastards are's fuckin' *helpless*. In here you don't have to be nice, even *pretend* to be nice. You're *official*; you are *real*; and this's *the* real fuckin' world, where you are right now. They are the real people in it, the dirt off the street that's tracked in here.

'The outside where you used to be may've looked like the real world to you and Hilliard, but trust me, my friend, it was not. Out there you were dealing with other real people who wanted to be doing what they were doing, in the place where they were doing it. Sometimes it was the same thing you wanted, or Hilliard wanted, so you had to fight those other people to get it. Sometimes you beat them and sometimes they beat you, but most times either way, you could respect them.

'What you're doing in here is dealing with scum. They *don't* want to be in here. They don't *want* anything except Out, so they can go back to doing what they *did* want that got them hauled in here. They hate you but they respect you. You're *god* to them, at least for that day that they're here. But don't let it go to your head; every other day somebody else's money, somebody else's car, the booze or the white powder is their god. It's not like they're choosy. But just the same, that day when you're their god is a long one. It's the rest of their lives. That's what it looks like to them. That's as far as they can see; it's the way that they think and they live. The *only* way they *can* think, you see? *Because* that's the way that they live.

'They got a short attention span. A long weekend for them's as long as your whole baseball season. They think in terms of how long they've got left to be high on what they just smoked or injected or sniffed, before they have to go out and get some more money, one way or the other, to get stuff to get high again – before otherwise they crash and burn. Our week is a month in their lives, and six months in the County House for these bozos's the same as the rest of their lives. It's further'n their eyes can see.

'So that's the new power you got now. It's you who decides what it's gonna be for them. Whether they live or whether they die: doesn't matter. Good reason; bad reason; no reason at all, except you got a hair 'cross your ass. All totally up to you here.

'Most of them already know. They know if they don't like what you say you will do *for* them or *to* them, even if it's nothin', they're up shit creek. Nowhere else to go. Your bad mood is their tough shit. Any place else they go, over your head, upstairs: if they get anything at all they'll get less, or else so damned much more that when they leave this place they'll wish they'd known enough just to've stopped at you.

'You're thinkin': "What if one of these bozos gets mad, what if he gets really mad? What if he goes to his rep, to *my rabbi*? What'll happen to me if he does?"'

'I'll tell you what happens then, he tries to pull any that shit,' Lane said. 'Not one fuckin' thing's what happens. Not one fuckin' thing. Because you know what? There'll come a day, this year or next, when *his* rep or *your* rabbi's gonna need a big favor, and this'll be the only place in the whole fuckin' world he can get that favor done. His kid takes a bust or his wife's drivin' under; some guy he owes big takes a collar for askin' a lady cop in plain clothes if she'd like to give him a blow-job. Lemme tell you somethin', pal: When that day comes that this guy's rep or your rabbi has to make that phone call, here, to get it straightened out – as he knows it will – he doesn't want havin' you remember how he stuck it up your ass when some shitbird-civilian complained. As he knows you will if he ever does.

'He didn't put you in here so that you'd get mad at him, and then when he needed something, get even – tell him to go fuck himself. He put you in here so that some day when he absolutely has to get a favor done, you'll remember him kindly and be grateful to him – for that thing *he* did for *you*, so long ago.

'So, when the scumbag, any scumbag, goes and gripes to his rep about you, your rabbi won't do a damned thing to you; that's what he'll do. Why you think it is that the guys like Brother Hilliard put their friends in here? You ever think about that? It's because they know what we find out, just as soon's we get in here: We become bulletproof. Bulletproof even from *them*. In this job, we're immortal. If you're smart you only want your *friends* to be immortal, and to *stay* your friends after they do.

'Now, with the shitbirds that don't know this, you might as well teach 'em. Sooner they find out, the better. The way we do things in this place. We have to get rid of some bastard, which we have to do every day, well, that's what we do: We get rid of 'em, fast as we can. Sometimes we make mistakes, but that's all right. We back each other up. All the way up, and then back down the line. We make it stick. That way the thing works for *us*, instead of us workin' for *it*.'

Merrion had never uttered Lane's mantra, but he had applied the tactic, furtively at first; time and time again he had seen it work. It always worked.

He looked at his watch. It was coming up on 10:00 A.M., forty-five minutes to his regular tee-time at Grey Hills. Janet had taken enough of his morning. Saturday was his day off. He cleared his throat. 'Right,' he said. 'Well, there I can't help you. Help you get along with the other tenants. I don't run the building. You got a complaint there, you see Mister Brody. If he can, I'm sure he'll help you out. But that's not why I wanted you in here.

'The reason you're here is you're seeing a man name of Lowell Chappelle, and letting him stay overnight.' She opened her mouth and he held up his hand. 'Don't even bother,' he said on a rising inflection. 'I won't tell you who told me, I don't have to tell you, and I'm not going to tell you. If you try to tell me it isn't true, I'll call you a liar, which you will be. And it will upset me, Janet, if I find I have to do that. You haven't lied to me yet, that I know about – and if you ask around, people will tell you: I *always* know, when somebody tries to lie to me – as I didn't think that you would when I gave you a break. That's the reason why I've been able to try to help you out a little. Because I know you've always told me the truth. Just like I've always told you the truth. So, when I tell you that something about you's started to disturb me, as I'm telling you something is now, you know I'm telling the truth.

'What's disturbing me is that what I hear's been going on in your life is not good. It's a very bad thing in fact, what I hear, *and I know very well that it's true*. So, since the only thing that you can really say to me is that it's not true, and that will be a lie, which would be a very bad mistake, the best thing you can do right now is just shut up and listen to me.'

She closed her mouth and looked scared.

'Good,' he said, 'that's much better. Mister Chappelle is a convicted felon. Mister Chappelle's been convicted seven times. I've been around long enough to know what went on when he got sentenced. The first two or three times he was young and looked scared, just like you're looking right now, so the judges went easy on him. They were in hopes that he'd mend his ways. He didn't. So the judges started giving him time, in the hope *that* might straighten him out. His third or fourth trip on the merry-go-round, he got two years and did one. But that didn't do the trick either. Apparently he still wasn't convinced that the lawful life's the best one.

'When he came out, he stayed out for less'n two years, probably not being good, but being careful – or lucky. Doing bad things but not getting caught. Probably went to his head; maybe made him a little bit cocky. Alas and alack, his good luck ran out – as good luck has a way of doing. He slipped up and he got caught again, did another bad thing someone could prove.

'So this was his fifth trip, let's say. He still got off easy, considering his history. The judge gave him five in the jar. He came out after he'd done three, still having learned very little. People're starting to think: "He's had all these chances, all this instruction; and still he doesn't behave. Maybe he's not a good kid. Less'n a year and he's back in the gravy. Gets ten-to-twelve and does most of the ten.

'So when he came out, his next-to-last trip, he'd been in the courts on six offenses – fourteen years in the slammer. Even allowing for the fact that he got an early start – he was seventeen, he first made himself known to the authorities – after six convictions for doing bad stuff, he's no longer an innocent kid. He'd used up his slack. So when he got grabbed the seventh time, and he had a *machine gun* with him, people were convinced he was a bad actor, very bad boy indeed.

'So they said to him: "Okay, Mister Chappelle, *now* we get the idea. *You* don't seem to get the idea. Here's your program: Twenty years to be served, FCI McNeil Island, 'way out there in Washington State. This time you're doing hard time.'

'This gentleman caller of yours, Miss LeClerc: Leaving aside the obvious fact that at age fifty-seven he's kind of old for you, twice your age, he is not the kind of fellow we like to see refined young ladies under our care and supervision hanging out with all the time. Much less shacked up with in respectable apartment buildings we got them into, and which we've been paying the rent on. So we want you to break it off with him. *As of now*, this very minute, Mister Chappell is off-limits to you.'

'But I *like* him,' she whined, pouting her lower lip. 'I'm a normal woman, and I need a man, and he always treats me real good.' She paused and pouted, lowering her head so that when she looked at Merrion she had to look through her eyelashes. 'I like doing things for him,' she said, 'and he likes having me do them. He says that's the only reason he's ever had any trouble with a woman, was because she wouldn't do the things he wanted her to do. But I *like* to do them, and so therefore we're fine.'

Merrion sighed and stood up. 'Uh uh,' he said, 'I don't care to hear it. You've got the word. I just gave it to you. Quit entertaining Chappelle at your place, and don't see him any other place, either. You do, and I'll hear about it, and when I do, I'll do something about it. Furthermore, I will do it to you.

'You won't like it. The first thing I'll do, I'll pull your case out of the file – which I can do since I'm the one who put it in there – and I will tell the judge what you've been doing. Screwing Lowell Chappelle, a bad actor and known felon. Not at all the kind of person we want hanging around with defendants who've got cases on file here in this court. This to Judge Cavanaugh will mean the same thing it means to me: that the deal we made – I would place your case on file; you'd behave yourself and do as you're told – that deal isn't working out.

'I *know* what the judge'll do, just in case you don't. What he'll do is tell me to take your case *out* of the file and mark it up for hearing, any old day I like, and that's exactly what I'll do. Then, come next weekend, I'll send a couple of cops and a matron over to your place and catch you flopping around in bed with Mister Chappelle, as you've been told not to do. They'll put you in the lock-up for the rest of the weekend.

'On Monday the judge'll have me call your case, and before you can so much as catch your breath and call me even one bad name, he'll make a finding of guilty on that old charge of grand larceny. To which, you'll remember, you've already admitted facts sufficient to prove guilt. And then he will send you to jail. You'll do a year down in MCI Framingham, Janet, okay? Mister Chappelle won't be on your list of approved visitors, just like he isn't out here any more, now that we've had our nice little chat, but you'll hardly notice.

'There'll be so many other things for you to dislike, you'll probably forget all about Lowell. You'll lose your nice little apartment – we won't keep it vacant for you, while you're gone, and we won't get you a new one when you get out again. You won't have any privacy, or your freedom to do what you like, as little as that has been. No indeed, Janet, once you get down there, all day long you'll do just as you're told. And you'll be told plenty, my dear. Now, is that what you want me to do?'

She looked at the floor and shook her head No. 'Aloud,' Merrion said, 'answer me.'

She looked up with fear and shook her head again. 'No,' she said, 'please don't do that to me.'

'I don't want to,' he said, making statements. 'But I will, if you make me. You know that. You won't make me now, will you, Janet?'

'No, I won't,' Janet said. 'I'll be good.'

5

Three-eighths of a mile back from Route 9, facing southwest at the foot of Mount Wolf in Cumberland, the pale grey three-story clubhouse at Grey Hills that Saturday morning stood impeccably white-shuttered in green August shade, the lofty old maples and oaks flanking the drive bowing and rustling in a variable northwest breeze. Jesse Grey had started the sixteen-month process of building it in 1896 as the thirty-six room manor house and centerpiece of his 332-acre estate, suitable for the new life as a country gentleman he had in mind to crown his success in the paper-milling business on the Connecticut River.

'Success that came right out of the hides of the poor devils working for him. Drove his people unmercifully, full double-shifts, sixteen hours a day in the mill, five and a half days a week. For twenty or thirty cents a day,' Larry Lane said, recalling Grey with dutiful second-hand malice. 'They tended to die young – one of 'em was an uncle of mine, Uncle Eddie; was dead before I was born. Before they got to be twenty-five. Bastards like Jesse just worked them to death. What did they care? When the morning came someone didn't show up, or did but collapsed on the job, Jesse had 'em waiting in line to replace him.

'No one around here at the time really knew the whole extent of what Grey'd had done up there, woods he'd had cut down and the pasture he'd had turned into lawns,' Lane said. 'He brought in all his own foremen from outside. He hired local labor to improve Wolf River and the South Brook for trout fishing, make them run faster with deeper pools; clear the brush and put up the fences, white board like you see on TV, the horse farms in Kentucky on

Derby Day; lay out the bridle paths and build the tennis courts and pool. The house and barns and stable; the quarter-mile exercise track. But all anyone really knew enough to speak of was the part of the job that he did; that the bathrooms were all Italian marble; the size of the big crystal chandeliers. They knew it was grand and elegant, sure, but just how grand and how swell didn't come out 'til years later.

'Then when it did almost no one was interested. One of those WPA writers FDR put to work in the Depression went back and dug up the history of the old place, to go with some pictures they had taken of it for a book about the valley. They put copies in all the libraries around here. For all the good that did; nobody read the damned thing. Well, I did, but you never could go by what I did. Nobody else ever read it.

'What this WPA guy did was track down the ledgers with the accounts of the money Grey'd sunk into that place. It came to about nine hundred thousand dollars – and this was at the turn of the century. Be eight or ten million today.'

Thirty-five years later, two years into the Depression, Grey's heirs had found themselves too short of money to maintain the estate, and had been forced to put it up for sale. Lane had seen it as it was then. 'Still used to go and fish there. The fact the place was all neglected didn't mean the trout'd all packed up and gone away, or that Grey and his fine fancy friend's caught all of them before they faded away themselves. What'd always been there was still there; you could catch a nice fat two-or three-pound rainbow, or a good-sized brown down by the Ox Bow. The streams were still okay; just the place'd gone to hell.'

Lane had not been exaggerating. The photographs that the auctioneer had commissioned in the mid-Thirties for use in the brochure to advertise the property to potential bidders far away – without success, as it turned out – were on display in the card-room of the Grey Hills clubhouse. The sepia-toned eight-by-ten glossies showed the rolling lawns overgrown; the gardens gone to seed. The two-by-fours that had tautly framed the block-U-shaped chicken-wire enclosures at the ends of the two clay tennis courts had fallen down. Six deep slatted wooden lawn-chairs with arms broad enough to serve as trays stood bleached and rotten by the courts, four abandoned at odd angles along the sidelines of one, the others together near the westerly baseline of the second. Merrion imagined their occupants in better days rising slowly with tennis sweaters draped over their shoulders, the men in long white flannel pants, the women in long white tennis dresses going away from the chairs and up across the lawn toward the great house, the windows lighted golden in the blue twilight of some early autumn Sunday evening, '28, or '29, the future growing dark and closing in around them, the carefree people innocent, unaware it was one of the last weekend gatherings they would have together there, a rich contented family, with wealthy handsome friends.

In the old photographs weeds had reclaimed the playing surfaces. The buildings still barely standing then were dilapidated, all their window-glass long since shot out, needing much more than paint. The mews off behind the northeast corner of the house, where the pro shop now stood, had burned in lightning-started fires in the spring of 1930. They had never been rebuilt; in the pictures two charred vertical beams stood in the rubble. Most of the tiles – a watercolor done by some Grey family guest showed them to have been azure – had fallen into the vast swimming pool, exposing the white mastic that had dried on the cement underneath. The beams and the shingled roof of the four-room cabana and verandah lay collapsed on the edge of the apron on the southerly side. The house had tilted off at a slight angle to the east, its three massive chimneys leaning toward the center of its sagging rooftree, by then almost buckled. The barn, since demolished, in the photograph retained the double doors, large and small, up and down, each of them securely latched when Herbert Hoover was still in the White House, claiming to see better days just ahead for the nation. But the auctioneer's photographer had set up his view camera to take the picture from dead center at the front; Mount Wolf was clearly visible behind it through the gaps in its siding.

'The wonder was that *all* of it hadn't been torched, right to the ground,' Lane said. 'Only reason it wasn't was because by the time Grey's heirs sold it, they were just as down-and-out as everybody else. Not worth envying and hating any more. Besides, hardly anyone still alive by then ever knew them. Few oldtimers who were still around who hated Jesse couldn't do much to hurt him; he was long and safely dead. Got himself thrown by a horse, I recall, before FDR came in. You could call Jesse lots of names, but you couldn't fault his timing, came to knowing when to clear out.

'Anyway,' Larry Lane said, 'at that point taking pictures of it was a total waste of time, no matter if it was the WPA was throwing away taxpayers' money to make a book no one'd read or the auction house trying to see if they could scare up a buyer someplace in the world. They couldn't. The whole shebang was worthless, likely to stay that way. We look back now at the Depression and we nod to each other and say how bad it must've been then; took a world-war-economy boom to get us out of it, ten, eleven years of hopelessness and then five, six more of being afraid – no matter what the president said. But from here we can see that it come to an end. From there, the point of view of people living through it, out of work, no money to buy food, it looked different, like it'd never end.

'That's why Jesse Grey's estate was worthless; not because it wasn't still beautiful property but because no one had any money to buy it. So no matter what it'd cost to build it and equip it, it was worth nothing. And hopeless because there's no hope in this goddamned world for any *one* or any *thing* that isn't worth some kind of money.

'So, since it looked hopeless, just as you would've expected, if you'd thought about it at all, the Catholic fucking Church bought it. For chump change, of course, its usual price. What it generally pays if it doesn't get what it wants as a gift, absolutely for free. A hundred-ten-thousand dollars, all told, dirt-cheap even back then. Back taxes, of course, and about sixty grand in bank notes some overconfident Grey or other'd borrowed from some unusually stupid banker when the family fortune'd started to melt away meeting margin calls, month or so after the Crash. One cockeyed optimist going deeper into debt with another one, still convinced the rich kid's playground could be saved.

'A hundred-and-ten-thousand dollars. For three-hundred-and-thirty-two acres of prime land. Three-hundred-and-some bucks an acre. Bad news for the Grey family, of course, already up to its hips in bad news, but bad news too for the town of Cumberland, which didn't need any more either. That was the single most valuable parcel of property in the whole town, and just like that, it was off the assessment rolls, no longer a taxable asset. Even if and when the economy came back, as of course it did, that property wasn't going to be any use to anyone unless they had enough bucks not just to buy it but then spend rebuilding it. No one could afford to let an investment that big sit idle – unless you count the Catholic Church.

'God bless the Roman Catholic Church,' Larry Lane many times said, always seeming to marvel, laughing and shaking his head, as though he really had been at once utterly baffled and completely amused. 'As surely He must've, a great many times, to explain what it's gotten away with. Year after year; decade after decade; the century after the centuries before, the Catholic Church marches on.

'The bishop in the Thirties here – McLaughlin was his name, that much I *am* sure of; *Francis* McLaughlin, I think – apparently shared the predominant view of the men who run his church that a bishop can't have too much land. Or too many buildings, as far as that goes, even if they're all fallin' down. So when Jesse's remaining heirs – or their lawyers, *I* dunno, whoever all those people were down in *Phil*-la-*del*-*phy*-ay – when they put his great estate up for sale here, the only bidder in sight was the diocese of Springfield. One-hundred-and-ten-thousand American dollars. I've got no idea how or where his sacredness came up with the money. He never confided in me. Or what on earth he planned to do with the ramshackle place. Most people thought *he* didn't, either. Just get it first, and then, bye and bye, think about what you're gonna do with it. You've got plenty of time. 'Forever's a very long time'; that's the way the people think in Holy Mother Church. They've got the keys to forever.'

In 1948 eighteen wealthy men of the Pioneer Valley formed a real estate trust and negotiated the purchase of the property from the diocese. The deed recited that price for the transfer of the property to the Grey Hills Association, a non-profit organization newly-established by documents drawn up by one of their leaders,

Warren Corey, of Butler & Corey, was 'one dollar and other valuable consideration, receipt of which is hereby acknowledged.' The actual price was not disclosed. 'Three-hundred-odd-thousand was the price you heard quoted,' Lane said, 'just under a thousand an acre. But no one outside the deal knew.'

The architects the association hired to plan and oversee the beginnings of the four-year transformation shrewdly laid out the property so that the par 71, 7,241-yard championship golf course, designed by Robert Trent Jones, formed a natural tiara for the mansion. The country club opened in 1952, 'reinventing serenity in the beautiful valley of the Connecticut River,' *Life* said the following year in an October feature issue entitled '*Life* Goes to New England in the Fall.'

The architects and engineers curved the main entrance drive slightly, to preserve as many as possible of the tall oaks and broad maples forming a canopy over it, bordering the approach with low stone walls broken here and there for footpaths. Visitors approached the clubhouse among the undulating fairways and deceptively-beckoning greens of the most spectacular seven of the eighteen showcase holes, crossing the slightly arched stone bridge over South Brook into the circular drive at the main entrance hedged all around with rose, rhododendron, and lilac bushes.

A hexagonal brass lantern six feet long and two feet wide hung on a black chain under the porte cochère; except during high winds or snow-storms, an assistant steward brought a twelve-foot wooden stepladder from the equipment shack each Friday morning, set it up in front of the dark red front door and polished the lantern. Eight years away from celebration of its 50th anniversary season, what one columnist for *Golf* had called 'the crown jewel links of western New England' – to the considerable displeasure of notable members of several other equally exclusive clubs between Worcester and Albany – Grey Hills that August Saturday made the gritty vision of Janet LeClerc vanish from Merrion's mind like a dragon imagined in a cloud changing shape in the wind. He thought that if working Saturday morning meant you could drive your Eldorado down Valley Drive into Grey Hills and spend the rest of the day playing eighteen holes of golf and having lunch with your friend Danny Hilliard, only a fool would sleep late.

The brilliant white fine sand filling the traps was renewed every spring, trucked in from Eastham on the elbow of Cape Cod. Forty-two-hundred-dollar annual fees, rumored soon to be increased, six hundred dollars more, from three hundred and twenty-five members, covered that. In the summer the grass remained soft, emerald-jersey green, pampered early mornings and evenings with water from the cold streams Grey's laborers had improved, and whenever Merrion went there, he remembered what Dan Hilliard had said back in 1992 as they drank Dom Perignon to celebrate their twenty years of membership: 'It doesn't matter who you are, where you've been or what you've done, or how many times you've been here: Every time that you come back, drive down Valley Drive in the shade of those venerable trees; see the sunlight making the dew silver in the morning; feel the cool breeze slipping down from the hills in the summer; or smell the maple burning in the fireplace in the fall, that same sweet lovely hush still welcomes you. You can almost hear it whispering: "Peace now, the struggle's interrupted. You've come; you're here; everything's all right again."'

'I know you're always telling me I just don't understand what being members at Grey Hills means to you and Dan,' Diane said the next morning, towelling her hair as she emerged from her shower, 'but if that champagne toast he made last night wasn't the corniest thing I ever heard in my life, it's sure got to be well-up-there in the running.'

'It's simple,' Merrion said, baring his teeth for inspection in the mirror, 'Grey Hills is the only thing we've ever gotten, from doing what we've done all our lives, that was strictly for us, our reward. From the very beginning, everything that Danny's ever done in public life; everything that I've done, first when I was helping him run for office and then at the courthouse, has always been primarily for someone else's good. At least one somebody else; in Danny's case, down in the House, for all the people in his district, what he's thought would be best for them, his constituents. In my case, what would be the best thing to do in a given case that would make Cumberland or Hampton Falls or Hampton Pond or Canterbury a better place to live, either by helping to make sure that someone who's done something bad in one of the towns, violated social order, gets punished for it – so that he or she maybe won't do it again and also so that someone else who sees how they got punished for doing it won't do that same thing himself.'

'Yes,' she said, drying under her breasts, 'and if I'm not mistaken, you're both fairly well paid for your valuable services, and also get health-care and retirement plans.'

'Indeed we do,' Merrion said. 'We were never rich men. We'd've been awful fools to've done it for nothing.' He turned away from the mirror. She stepped away from the tub enclosure to make way for him, bending at the same time to dry her legs, and he patted her on the left buttock. 'Nice ass,' he said, 'very nice ass.'

'Animal,' she said, straightening up and out of his reach, 'sanctimonious do-gooder, claiming virtue for making a living.'

'Anyone else in my job or Danny's would've gotten the same money we do,' he said, one foot in the tub. 'But they might not've filled them like we have. That's where the virtue is: it's in how we've *done* those jobs. We really do think of them as public trusts. We really do work to make sure we deserve that trust. I know it sounds like campaign bullshit, but it's the truth.'

He took his foot out of the tub and stood contemplating her in her nakedness, glad explaining and pretending he was trying to convince her was giving him the excuse. 'Grey Hills is the indulgence we've permitted ourselves to get from doing that work. It's the only thing we've ever gotten that we said from the beginning we wanted purely for us. Knowing of course that we'd never really get it; as Danny said last night: "No question about it – it was totally presumptuous of us to even *think* it, think some day we might get in."

'This's one of the finest golf clubs in the world. For us to imagine we'd ever become members was silly. It was like some high-school second baseman making his league all-star team and thinking now he's got it wired, he is definitely on his way to the major leagues and a Hall of Fame career ending up in Cooperstown: a kid's golden dream and nothing more.

'And then son of a gun, we got in.

'In a way we still can't believe that we did it. When we were young men it looked way out of reach. We couldn't afford it, and not only that, if we'd *had* the money and tried to get in, they wouldn't've let us – we weren't well-bred enough for that bunch. So it was always something beyond our wildest dreams. And then all of a sudden, the planets align and we're in. There's only one possible explanation for this: it's what we got for being good men.'

He was tumescent and stepped back from the shower, starting toward her. She backed away holding the towel out in her left hand at arm's length and grabbing the other end with her right as though intending to snap him with it. She said smiling: 'No, no, Simba, not *play*time now; time to *wash*. *Coffee* first. Back off and get yourself into that shower. Tell yourself what a grand public servant you are while you're getting yourself clean. I've had enough of your pious guff.'

'The thing men always have to remember about women,' he said as though talking to himself, stepping into the shower, 'is the ones who're sexy lack soul.'

On a gray Saturday in Holyoke in the early spring of 1966, Dan Hilliard in his High Street office had invited Merrion to tell him what he wanted, nodding approvingly as he listened. 'Uh-huh,' Hilliard'd said, 'that *would* make a lot of sense, wouldn't it. Grab that clerkship for you now, while nobody's really mad at us. Oughta go through like grease through a goose. And it would too, if it weren't for just one thing, just one minor problem, standing between you and that job. Larry Lane. He has to clear it through Chassy, but he's the guy who appoints.'

'I don't even know him,' Merrion'd said. 'I don't even know who he is.'

'I know that,' Hilliard'd said, 'I realize that. That's a big part of this minor problem.'

6

Early in the spring of 1966, the second year of his third term in the House, State Rep. Daniel Hilliard, D., Holyoke, perceived that Merrion was getting restless serving as his chief assistant. Merrion was twenty-five. Hilliard, having turned thirty the year before, realized that Merrion's itchiness was appropriate.

He had logged more than six years in Hilliard's service. During the first two, unpaid, he had tailored his selection of courses and arranged his class schedules at UMass. to fit the demands of Hilliard's successful campaign in 1960 for a seat on the Holyoke Board of Aldermen. In '62, he had given up his part-time job at Valley Ford – and the assurance of a full-time position after he graduated; the idea didn't thrill him – in order to manage Hilliard's legislative candidacies and help him to deal with the responsibilities his victories imposed.

'The fact is,' Hilliard said to his wife, Mercy – during childhood her younger sister's approximation of 'Marcy' had become her family's name of choice – 'he's put his own life on Hold. He's subordinated his interests to mine for a very long time.'

'And it's worked like a charm,' Mercy said. She tried always to see clearly and be just. Where Merrion was concerned, that took effort. Some of his ideas and a good deal of his behaviour troubled her. For all his ferocious loyalty to Danny and hard work in his behalf, he was not the kind of decent, sober, principled man she would have chosen to be her husband's highly-influential right-hand man – if she'd been consulted about it.

'The reason it has is precisely because we *are* so close and work so well together,' Hilliard said.

'You're telling me,' Mercy said. 'If it weren't for me and the kids, most people'd assume the two of you're a pair of queers. As it is only some of them do.'

'They must not know about Sunny,' he said.

'Or if they do,' Mercy said, 'they don't know *enough*. With her clothes on she looks like a respectable woman.'

'Meow,' Hilliard said.

Mercy smiled demurely. 'Just stating the facts,' she said.

The Hilliard-Merrion partnership began on a snowy afternoon of the second Friday in January of 1959, at the counter in the parts and service department of Valley Ford at the corner of Lower Westfield and Holyoke Streets in Holyoke. Hilliard had come to pick up his black '56 two-door Victoria hardtop, having left it that morning to be serviced.

'The two of us already sort of knew each other some,' Merrion said later to curious people who'd seen them in action. Hilliard used his car a lot, which brought him often to the counter at the window in the service department where Merrion sat on his four-legged metal stool, the grey steel shelves of boxed small parts behind him. 'You couldn't say that we were buddies. We'd never had a beer. But we weren't total strangers when I first went to work for Dan.'

Hilliard had bought his car from Merrion's father. Pat Merrion had worked for twelve years as a salesman for John Casey, the last seven as sales manager, until his first stroke killed him – as he would have wished but not so early – at the age of forty-nine in February of the previous year, his oldest son's first year at UMass. Patrick Merrion's father, Seamus, had died at seventy-three in 1940, suffering his third and fatal stroke two years after his first. Pat, starting a new job at the Springfield Armory with a young wife and a new baby, Ambrose, at home, had also had to help his mother take care of Seamus. From that he had learned something he passed on to Ambrose. 'If you're determined to die of a stroke, do your best to die of the first one. Make it easier on your poor family.'

John Casey did what he could to help out Pat's family, and it was a lot. Remembering, Merrion said to Casey's widow at his wake: 'It was different in those days. People took care of each other. Their code was different. You looked out for your family and friends. They were all you had in the world. The same way you were all that they had.'

The younger boy, Chris, was ten when his father dropped dead. His mother, Polly, hadn't held a job since she stopped being a sales clerk at the Forbes & Wallace department store in Springfield to get married in a hurry in 1939. Casey had doubled the vacation pay Pat had accumulated; that was half of the $1,800 Bill Reed charged Polly for Pat's three-thousand-dollar funeral. 'Pat was always a favorite of mine,' Reed told her. 'If Ford made hearses and flower-cars, mine'd be Fords I bought from Pat.' Casey had expedited payment of the five-thousand-dollar group life-insurance policy Valley carried on each of its employees, close to two years' salary for a sales manager in those days. Mindful that base pay had represented less than half of Pat Merrion's average earnings and dead men earn few commissions and that a widow with a child at home could depend on less than $1,000 in Social Security benefits, Casey had also created the job for Amby as assistant service manager: twenty hours a week at $3.50 an hour.

'All I could work and stay in school at the same time, like my mother wanted. And health insurance for the three of us, too – we were very grateful for that,' Merrion said to Casey's widow in the fall of 1990. 'Your husband was a good man, Jo, a fine man. Everyone who knew him thought the world of John. He cared about what happened to the people who worked for him. He treated us as friends, not employees, and we've all lost one tonight.'

In those days the normal service interval between oil changes and lube jobs was every fifteen hundred miles. Hilliard was a careful owner. Merrion saw him frequently. 'This car's gotta outlive the payments. Oil's a lot cheaper'n new rings and valves,' Hilliard would say, every three weeks or so, writing a check for twenty-eight dollars and change for Marfak chassis lubrication, a new Motorcraft oil filter, and six quarts of crankcase oil as Amby stamped another service order PAID and punched the register.

'They'd love you in Texas,' Merrion said that winter day, having seen a *Transcript* column about the coming election that low-rated Hilliard's chances. 'You oughta go down there and run. If they only knew who you are, how *much* oil we got you buying from them, you wouldn't have to bother with alderman here – they'd make you the governor.'

'Hey, what can I tell you?' Hilliard said. 'The political bug is expensive. You run for office, you're out every night in your car. You gotta be; people expect it. Depend on a car like that, go through two sets of tires a year, you gotta take care of the thing. You better; otherwise some dark night you get stranded. Hafta walk home in the rain.'

'How's that thing look, anyway?' Merrion said, ringing up the payment and lifting the change tray out of the register to put the check in the empty drawer underneath it. It had been a quiet day, the weather keeping the customers away.

'Danny came in one day when I was bored out of my mind,' Merrion would say to people impressed with the depth of their friendship. 'I also was lonesome. No one to play with. The salesmen're all out in the front of the store; mechanics out back in the shop. They had each other to talk to. Also all had their own things to do. I was all by myself, without either. Only people I had to talk to onna job were the customers; that's how I come to know Danny.

'It's snowing: no customers. Everyone headed home early from work. I'm there by myself. Phone isn't ringing. I already finished the papers. Didn't have any my books with me; normal day, no time to study. No radio. And anyways, Friday afternoon in January: wasn't any game on. So I got nothing to do. Except now I got Danny. Naturally I don't want him to leave. Knew him well enough to know if I can just get him goin', he may not know it yet but he's gonna entertain me.

'That's an important thing, having someone else around you can talk to. People take it for granted, don't understand how important it can be until it's gone. My father died, I'd just started at UMass., but I wasn't going there because Harvard turned me down. I was going there because that was all my parents could afford. I was still living at home.

'So now he's dead. My little brother Chris's only ten and anyway, he's in school all day. My mother didn't have a job then. She's at home all by herself, like she always was, but now things're different. In a big way they are different. Nothin' to look forward to all day now anymore. My father comin' home at night: that'd been her big event. Hadn't been that big a deal for me and Chris. Lots of other people alla around us alla time. School all day; inna summer we're out playin' ball an' so forth. Goin' swimming. All that stuff, onna weekend with our friends. Didn't think about Dad comin' home at night like she did – but after he was *dead*, we did.

'My father loved to talk. "Talk your ear off if you let him," people used to say about him. "On any day I got nothin' to do; I'm just sorta killin' time, you know?" John Casey used to say, "those're the days I'm glad I got Pat. Never a dull day with Pat. Busy days, I'm still glad we got him. He's a large part of what makes our business successful – valuable employee. Best salesman we got, which's why he's the manager.

'"But say it's a brutally hot afternoon, July or August; nobody's around. You're open but you *know*: no one's ever comin' in. They're all at the beach, Mountain Park, on vacation. No one in the world's buyin' cars. We're all fallin' asleep at our desks.

'"*That* is a day when I'm glad we got Pat on the payroll. All I got do to get through a slow day like that – not makin' any money; can at least have a good time – is go down in the salesroom. Pull up a chair beside Pat's desk and say: 'Well, Pat, whatcha think's goin' on?' Anna next thing I know, my sides ache from laughin'. I mean it: they literally *hurt* – and it's time to close up for the night.

'"I'd rather all the days're busy, naturally – I wouldn't *think* of interrupting him. After all, havin' laughs ain't what we're in business for. Pat was on one of his patented rolls, there, he'd get onto sometimes, he'd have four sold by two the afternoon, when he'd finally break for lunch. And then two hours later, when he finally came back – he did *not* like to hurry his lunch – he'd have *another* prospect he picked up in the bar at Henry's Grist Mill. By five he'd have *him* sold – five inna day.

'"All you hadda do with Pat was leave the guy alone. When he was on a hot run, all you could see was *smoke*. So, it's more'n his talk that we're gonna miss; we're all sure gonna miss the man too.'

'He'd come home,' Merrion would say, 'and we'd have dinner and he'd tell us what he did. Who came in the dealership. What they had to say about what was going on. Talk and talk and talk. And most of what he talked about – I thought about it quite a bit since then, when he died – wasn't cars at all. Or baseball; wasn't golf. I don't think he ever *played* golf; don't think it ever crossed his mind. Basketball or football, anything like that; it was politics. When he picked the subject, as he could, at home, he picked politics.

'He *knew* about sports. He kept up with the games and the standings and so forth so he *could* talk about them – if that's what his customer had on his mind. He read quite a bit too – *Saturday Post*. *Collier's*. *Life*. *Time* 'nd *Sports Illustrated*. *Reader's* and *Catholic Digest*. Belonged the *Reader's Digest* book club. Every month unless you sent the card back, you got three or four books in one. Said he wished he could sell cars like that, send a card to people sayin' 'You don't mail this back to me, two weeks from today, you'll've bought a brand-new car.' They were mostly for my mother, but he generally tried to read at least one of them. Few of his customers taught up the road; hadda to talk to them too.

'He considered it part of his job, keeping the customers happy. You asked him how come he was so good at doing what he did, he made no secret of it: "The guy who buys a car from me today for the first time did not become my customer *today*. He became my customer three years ago, four years ago, whenever I first met him. Outside of church; having a few drinks. Rotary; Kiwanis; communion breakfast; town-committee meeting. Somebody's wake." Dad belonged to all the service clubs, went to all the wakes and breakfasts. But the one he liked the best was Democratic town committee. He always said he was glad he wasn't sellin' Cadillacs, "because then I would have to be on the Republican committee." Always hadda sense of humor.

'"That customer of mine didn't get to know me back then when he first did because he thought he might want to buy a Ford some day and I'be a good man to know. He bought the Ford from me today because he's gotten to know me as a man uses people all right doing business with them. So when he decided he needed a new car last night or the night before, he also decided he might as well come in and see me, and "maybe buy a Ford from Pat. Might as well, the price is right. Never put any pressure on me; always liked the guy for that." Really as simple as that.'

'He was always schmoozing people, not that he called it that. Their pal who talked baseball with them – or fishing, whatever they liked. But what he almost always talked about at home was politics, and then he died.

'At night after me and Chris and my mother got through having dinner, Chris'd go off to do his homework, watch TV or something 'til he hadda go to bed. And I'd be still sittin' there, at the kitchen table talkin' with her. What I should've been doing was studying. School wasn't easy for me. I was never what you'd've called a scholar, and with my job working for John Casey, and then on Danny's campaigns on top of *that*, I hadda lot on my mind. I should've been hittin' the books. But instead I am sittin' there, still in the kitchen, the this and the that, talking about what'd happened to us, my father dying like that.

'Not that we ever got anywhere, my mother and I, we had all those talks. Always the same thing, over and over again. What we'd done, to get through it; what we could've done instead of that, and whether that might've been better. Then what we thought we were gonna do next. It never changed. It didn't because it didn't have to. What we were doing was hangin' on there to each other, tryin' to get our heads straight. I was really worried about her.

'I remember saying to her one night – someone else'd dropped dead, someone else we knew; we'd just come from the wake; I've forgotten now who it was. She just seemed so *blue*, really *down*. She really had me worried. So I said to her: "*Hey*, look now, you, just in case you forgot: This dyin' business's a very bad habit. They say once you've got it, it's very hard to get over it. And the fact a lot of people that you really like, admire, and *never* expect to see them fall into it like Dad did, that doesn't make it any better. So I hope you're not thinkin' you might take it up. Me and Chris wouldn't like that at all.'

'None of it was easy. Then I didn't really think about it, but since then I've thought about it *very*, many times. The reason she was so glad to get her job at Slade's Bakery in the center, where the Video Image Store's now? She'd been pining. The job wasn't anything *big*; just working at the counter there, saying Hello, asking the people that came in what they had in mind that day. Putting up boxes of whatever they asked for. Brownies; éclairs; date squares; jelly doughnuts; cookies and cup-cakes; custard pies. Putting the bread through the slicer. All of that stuff. Everyone liked Mister Slade's custard pies, and he really made excellent bread. So he had a lot of business. That meant a lot of people coming in for Polly to wait on, pass the time of day with. Help her keep up with what was going on, make her feel like she's back in the world.

'That job did wonders for her. I think about that every time I hear somebody say there's such a thing as "natural adjusted rate inflation-unemployment," or "structural unemployment." That there's always gonna be five or six percent of the work force with no jobs. Nothin' the government can do about it. It's something can't be helped. Well *bullshit*; that's what I say. "*Find* something the poor bastards can do." Government has *got* to deal with it. That's what the government's *for*. It's a moral obligation, and I mean that. It's not just havin' no money that drags people down; it's feelin' like they don't *matter*, don't count any more. They lost the parts they had to play.

'I saw that with my mother. It was *having* that job that mattered to her. The sixty bucks a week she got: she found a way to use it, sure; it didn't go to waste. But basically the dough was gravy. That job kept her alive.

'After that it got a lot better at home, havin' dinner the nights I was there. The food wasn't as good 'cause she didn't have time to cook like she did when she was home all the time. And also, workin' in the bakery around food all day, she wouldn't be that hungry at night. But she'd bring home different things for dessert every night, and it was a *lot* better for her. You could see it. She was *much* happier. She had human contact again.

'You got to have that. We're natural herding animals. We're not supposed to be alone all the time, and when we are for too long, we don't like it. Don't handle it well. I think if you don't have that basic human contact, sooner or later you die.

'Anyway, that day Danny came in to pick up his car, I figured if I heckled him enough, he might hang around and entertain me. You get a guy who wants to be a politician like that, he's at your command. You even hint that you got something you'd like to talk about with him, *bang*, like that, you *own* him. His life is making people like him so they'll vote for him. Salesman like my father, only he's selling himself.

'He doesn't say he's doing that when he starts to talk to you. That would make you back away, think: "This guy's got something wrong with him. Don't wanna get too close." No, what he says is that if he gets elected he can do something for you – you'll have a better life. If he's good, he convinces you. You and a whole bunch of other people vote for him because he's made you think he can improve your life. All he needs to know is what you need, so he can then make the noises you will think mean that if you vote for him he'll get it for you.

'Of course by the time he gets through he's gonna have to promise a hell of a lot. Which means he's gonna have to be pretty nimble later on, it comes time explain to people in the *next* campaign how come they didn't get exactly what he said they would when they first elected him. But that's only if they remember. Most of them don't – unless the guy running against you reminds them. But even then, by the time they get to the polls they'll've probably forgotten the reminder. People don't forgive, matter what they say. But they do forget. Their attention span is short.

'That snowy day I figured if I heckled Danny enough I could get a few laughs out of him. My own dear mother, those nights we spent talking: she was always telling me I was a fresh kid; saying if I didn't watch it, some day somebody was gonna get sore, haul off and pop me one. All my friends'd too, same thing. You got a talent, you use it. So I shoved the stick in his cage and started pokin' him around, makin' trouble.'

Hilliard shrugged. 'It's still awful early,' he said. 'The only people thinkin' about elections this time of year 're the people runnin' in them. No one else's interested. They won't be 'til a month before. *Then* they'll all start lookin' at the candidates, decide what they're gonna do.'

'Think when they do that, they'll be lookin' at you?' Merrion said.

Hilliard grimaced. 'Ahh,' he said, 'you saw Dillinger's column. Boy has that guy ever got the right name, fuckin' assassin he is. FBI shot the wrong man, they plugged John – too bad they didn't get Fred.'

'Yeah, but is he right?' Merrion said. 'I know a lotta people don't like Freddie. My father couldn't stand him. Neither can Casey. My father used to come home nights and tell us something Casey said that day, something in Fred's column. Dad'd be roaring about it. But neither one of them could say it to anybody else; it might get back to Fred. Hadda keep their mouth shut. People read what Freddie writes and pay attention to it. He could wreck your business. And Freddie buys his cars here, too; don't want to lose his trade. People think he knows the stuff he writes about – it's inna paper, right? It must be true. And when he really nails somebody, pretty often he is right.

'So, if he is, today's column, and you're goin' down the toilet, why the hell wear out your car? Wear yourself out, too. What is it, you get your cookies this way? Gettin' your ass whipped in public?'

'*Jesus*,' Hilliard said, 'I need shit from you, too? You're as bad's your old man was. He gave me a ration every time I saw him; now he's dead, so I get it from you? You better not take too much for granted. Everyone loved Pat Merrion. They knew that's just how he was, always stirrin' everyone up. So they took stuff from him. You haven't got that record goin' for you. Your father was a good guy.'

'That's what everyone tells me,' Merrion said. 'But if he was such a good guy and all, then how come he named me "Ambrose"? That's a mean thing to do to a kid.'

'How do I know? Hilliard said. 'Maybe he was havin' a bad day. You may've been the cause of it, givin' him a lotta shit for no good reason. Decided he'd give you some back.'

'You still didn't answer my question,' Merrion said.

'I know I didn't,' Hilliard said. 'And you know why that is, you fresh prick? I don't know the answer myself, why I work my ass off and get nowhere. I did I'd give it to you. Why the hell not?

Dillinger's right, I've sure got nothing to lose. According to him, my second campaign isn't stirring up any more excitement than my first one, when I lost. That'll help me a lot. Even though this time I'm more mature, so people don't see me anymore as an upstart college kid trying to replace Roy Carnes, I'm still not getting anywhere. What if he's right? What the hell can I do?'

'You left out the part about how even though almost everybody now seems to think the guy who beat you the last time's turned out to be a real asshole,' Merrion said.

'Thank you very much,' Hilliard said. 'I'm really glad I decided to bring my car in today, so when I came to get it you'd be here to cheer me up. Instead of on some other day when you're up in Amherst there, taking Sandbox Two and Finger-painting One-oh-one, and old A.L. would've been here. No imagination, A.L. Never reads the papers.'

Merrion was laughing.

'Sure, go ahead, laugh your ass off,' Hilliard said. 'I now see I was wrong, I said you're as bad as your father, but your father had compassion. Now I not only get the pleasure of reading Dillinger's abuse myself; I get to enjoy it again when you quote it back to me. Not bad enough Fred says I'm already a loser; now I'm a *pathetic* loser; you're asking me how I like it.'

'You aren't yet, are you?' Merrion said. 'We haven't had this election. Nobody's beaten you yet.'

Hilliard stared at him. 'Yeah,' he said, 'that's right, they haven't. I'm just being *groomed* to lose. You got some idea, I might win?'

'I dunno,' Merrion said. 'I got this problem. My mind sometimes wanders. I don't always think about things that concern me. I think about whole bunches of other things, none of my business at all. Today I'm reading Dillinger and since I know you and I also know you're comin' in, don't have much on my mind . . .

'Well: two things. You're obviously gettin' nowhere kickin' the shit out of Gilson. As you've mainly been doin'.'

'It's like beatin' a pillow,' Hilliard said. 'You don't hurt your hands but you don't accomplish anything either. People don't even listen to me. It doesn't bother them that he's a dummy.

They're resigned to it. Maybe what this really is is a matter of equal representation: Gilson's the dummies' alderman.'

'So what I would do then,' Merrion said, 'is quit alienatin' the jerks. Stop even tryin' to talk to them. He's theirs and they're satisfied with him. Tell 'em you hope they'll be very happy. Leave them have him and go somewhere else.'

'Like where, maybe Hadley?' Hilliard said. 'This's where I live. Gilson's got the at-large seat that I'm running for.'

'But why is that?' Merrion said. 'Why does he have what you want? He's got that seat because two years ago young Roy Carnes decided he didn't want to be an alderman any more. He wanted to be a state rep, like his uncle Arthur used to be, before he moved up. There wasn't any new Carnes ready to step into his place. Open field. So you stood up and said you want the job, and the voters said: "No, you're too young." They voted for Gilson instead.

'We now know why they did it. It was not because he's smart. Anyone who voted for him thinking that now has to know he's not. He's proven that he's stupid. So Dillinger's got that part right. They thought you were too young, and he was the alternative and he was older.'

'Okay, but how does that help me?' Hilliard said. 'He still is, he's still older than I am, and now he's the incumbent.'

'He's still older'n you are,' Merrion said. 'But you are no longer so young. What are you now, twenty-six? Four years out of the Cross, 'stead of only two? You're an experienced teacher. You're familiar with the problems that face our public schools, 'stead of what you were back then: still feeling your way along, only your second year on the job. Not exactly elderly, but still more mature. Dillinger also said that.

'What you don't like's what he put with it, that you're not impressing the voters with it. Not convincing them you're not too young for the job anymore, so they don't need Gilson anymore to keep the seat warm. Now you're ready. Kick him out.'

'I start saying that,' Hilliard said, 'how do I avoid pissing off every voter over thirty? That'll make 'em elect him again.'

'Well, if I were you,' Merrion said, 'the first thing I'd do would be call up old Roy Carnes or Arthur and ask if you could come up to their office and discuss the next city election. Tell 'em young Roy can sit in too.'

'Why would the Carneses talk to me?' Hilliard said. 'I haven't got anything they want. They're through with the alderman seat, gone on to bigger and better things. I've got nothing to offer them.'

'My father started selling Fords here after World War Two because his boss down at the Armory was a nice guy and he liked him and he gave him some good advice. He told him once Japan surrendered the country wasn't going to need quite as many rifles as it did during the war. So there were going to be a lot of layoffs and my father was probably going to lose his job. Guy tells him: "You won't be the only one." Said lots of people were going to be out on the street, looking for work. Maybe for more work than there'd be for all of them right off. The ones who waited too long might wait a while before they found a new job 'til we got used to having peace again. Smart ones'd be the ones who looked for work before everyone else started looking for it.

'My father decided to be one of the smart ones. That's when he came to work here.

'Arthur Carnes before the war'd always driven a Chevrolet. But then he had two arms. After the war he only had one. He couldn't drive his old car anymore, because now he only had one hand, and in order to move the gear-shift lever he'd 've had to let go of the wheel. He was afraid to do that, so he had someone drive him down to Brel Chevrolet in Springfield in his car. He asked them if there was anything they could do so he could drive himself around again, 'thout risking killing people.

'When he came in here that same afternoon what he told my father was the people down at Brel didn't really seem interested in his problem, and he wondered if my father was. You bet he was. The first thing he did was see whether there was something Stuart Dean out in back could do to Arthur's Chevy, make it so that he could shift gears without letting go the wheel. Stuart said Yes, there was something. He could make a lever arrangement, like a bicycle handbrake, that'd make it so all Arthur had to do to shift the gears was reach his hand between the spokes and squeeze and that'd do it. He wouldn't have complete control but he'd have some, and it wouldn't take him but a second to do it and then grab the wheel again, so it ought to be okay. Stuart said it might be kind of awkward, but it'd work.

'Arthur said if it'd work until his new Ford convertible came in, he'd be more'n satisfied. My father said that was his first inkling he'd sold Arthur Carnes a car. After that when Roy Senior's father's old DeSoto wore out, Herb bought a Ford from Dad. And when they got rich enough so Roy's mother and Arthur's wife could have cars of their own, both of them got Fords. Roy drives a Ford, as you may've noticed, and so does Arthur, still. The one Arthur's driving now's the last car my father sold. Arthur ordered it from him the day before he died. That made eight he'd sold to the family, even though if they wanted to, they could all be driving Cadillacs by now.

'My father said what he admired about the Carneses was that they weren't the kind of people who just grab ahold of what they need or what they want, squeeze all the juice right out of it and throw the pulp away. He said Arthur and his brother acted like they were in it for the long haul. Kind of people who take an interest in what's going on around them today and try to make it better, because they plan to be here tomorrow and the day after that as well.

'That alderman seat was theirs for as long as they wanted it. It's out of their hands now because there's no new Carnes available right now to sit in it. Maybe there will be, eight or ten years from now, when Roy Junior's son's grown up, but right now there isn't. The man who's in it's a fool, and he probably isn't ever going to get any smarter. But he probably won't leave, either. He'll never try for anything higher, because dumb as he is, even he knows he'd probably lose.

'So what happens when Roy's kid is ready? By then Gilson'll've been there too long to throw him out. The Carnes kid'll have a fight on his hands.

'So then, why not save him the trouble? Go to the Carneses now and ask them if they'd like to help you change that. You'll knock Gilson off for them now, and then because you'll want to move on before too long, you'll leave it open again. As long as it keeps changing hands, when Roy Junior's kid's ready he'll have a chance. I bet Roy and Arthur would see your point. I bet they could help you a lot.'

'You old enough to have a beer?' Hilliard said.

'Have one, yeah,' Merrion said. 'Buy one? Not legally.'

Hilliard began to see the need for change around the end of March of '66, but he waited until evening of the third Friday in April to see if Merrion would raise the subject. He did not do so. After they parted that evening outside the office, Merrion declining to have a beer on the ground that if he did he'd flunk a quarterly in advanced psychology, Hilliard took inventory on the way home.

Things were unquestionably good. The black '65 Ford Falcon convertible with the red vinyl interior was hocked, but still nearly brand-new. Mercy's Country Squire wagon was only four years old. The pale-blue three-bedroom half-brick raised-ranch house, two-car garage under, where he lived with his family on the north slope of Ridge Street in Holyoke, was a better one than his parents owned. There was no primary opponent in sight and the few Republicans in the district – the southeastern part of Holyoke, Canterbury, Hampton Pond, parts of Cumberland and Hampton Falls – as usual were snarling at each other. His grip on the middle rungs of the House leadership ladder was secure enough to permit a swift lunge in the next term for the chairmanship of Ways and Means. 'Too good,' he thought. 'Must be time to fuck something up.'

Over dinner of fried filet of sole with Mercy and their three young children, Hilliard tried out his decision to address the subject when he and Merrion had their customary week-ending meeting at the office the next morning. '*Do* something about it. Get it over with once and for all.'

'Suspense getting to you?' she said. Marcia Hackett Hilliard had natural ash-blonde hair and blue eyes spaced wide apart, and she was a cheerful person. Even when she was obviously getting angry she looked like she still might laugh instead. She knew this and regretted it. She didn't like fights – 'unlike my dear husband, who goes around looking for them.' She was convinced that she had more of them than she would have had if people believed her when she said she was getting mad.

Timmy Hilliard, who was five, thrust out his lower lip and used his fork to push his fish around his plate. Mercy, not looking at him but at her husband, put her right hand out and took hold of Timmy's wrist. 'But I don't *like* fish,' he said, whining, trying to pull away. 'You *know* I don't like fish.'

'Tough darts, kid,' his mother said. 'I'm talking to your father. That's what the meal is tonight. Either you eat it or you go hungry.'

'Oh, partly the suspense, yeah,' Dan Hilliard said. 'Not wanting him to stew about it until Labor Day and then decide some crisp cool morning couple months before election he can't stay another year, doing what he's been doing since he was a teenager – he's *got* to do something grown-up. So then he tells me, and what shape am I in? No election fight, no, but I'll still have my hands full, back in session after the summer. All kinds of things I want to do there, but now I am distracted.

'Suddenly I'll now also have to do something for Amby, right off. And it'll really *have* to be good, owing the guy like I do. While I'm making plans at the same time to find somebody else to put in his place and then get him or her trained – while of course the new person trains me. Everybody who's good will've already signed up to run somebody else's operation. I'll have to settle for whoever's left.

'I'll be standing there sucking my thumb, marking time getting acquainted. Before I can even think about actually revving up what Amby and I've been planning to do since last Memorial Day. And anything that Amby'd like will've been filled since July Fourth, or promised anyway, people lining up support for the election. No, the time's come to deal with it; the time to do it is now.'

Timmy's sister Emily, nearly seven, ostentatiously used both hands, fork and spoon at the same time, to eat all of her fish, her mixed peas and carrots and her mashed potatoes too. The baby, Donna, eighteen months, sat in her high-chair with a small bowl of dry miniature shredded-wheat biscuits in front of her, staring vacantly at an invisible point midway between her father's left shoulder and the top of her brother's chair. Timmy sat far back in it, his shoulders hunched, and scowled at Emily, angry at himself now for giving her the brown-nosing opportunity she was exploiting. 'You're gonna be hungry later on, Tim,' Dan Hilliard said.

'I ate all *my* fish, daddy,' Emily said.

'I know you did, sweetie,' he said.

Timmy stuck out his tongue and said: 'Poop.'

'I mean it, Tim, really,' Hilliard said. 'You know we both want you to be healthy and strong.'

Timmy shook his head. 'Don't care,' he said. 'Don't *like* fish. Don't care.'

'Future office-holder,' Mercy said. 'Got the hang of it already. Rather be mad and go hungry 'n eat something he didn't think of to ask for.'

Her husband laughed. 'Uh uh,' he said, 'not quite right. Future office-*seeker*.'

'You're sure that's where Amby is now,' Mercy said. 'At the point where he has to move on?'

'Reasonably sure, yeah,' he said. 'And absolutely sure that if *he* isn't at that point yet, *I* am. It's what I think he oughta be doing. Getting started on making a life in the real world for himself. He's a talented lad. He works hard. He should have a good life. He should have a nice family, like I've got. Good wife, like mine; a few kids, even though they don't always eat what their pretty mother works so hard to make for dinner every night so they'll be healthy, grow up to be big and strong.'

Timmy reset his scowl and hugged himself. 'Don't *like* fish,' he said. Then he thought about it further and decided to speak louder. '*Hate* fish. Wanna leave the *table*.'

'Why, Timmy,' Mercy said, 'that's an *excellent* idea. You get out of your chair right this very minute and march yourself straight upstairs to your room. And get undressed and put your pajamas on and get into bed, and you know what you will've done then?'

'*No*,' Timmy said. Emily smirked delightedly. Donna gazed into space. Now and then she patted her right hand on the tray of her highchair.

'You will've put yourself to bed without any supper,' Mercy said. 'You'll've saved me and Daddy all the trouble of punishing you, which we really don't like to do. Only you don't behave.

But this time even though you're making us angry, acting like a perfect little wretch, you're also saving us the worry about what we're going to have to do with you. You've decided what the penalty should be for being a little stinker at the dinner table.'

'*No*,' Timmy said. '*Not* gonna do that.' Emily giggled a little.

'In fact,' Hilliard said, 'you'll've punished yourself *more*, I think, *harder*, than your mother and I were thinking would probably be enough to teach you a lesson we think you need to learn. What did you have in mind, Mercy, to make Tim see the error of his ways?'

'Well,' Mercy said, 'to tell you the truth, I hadn't decided. I was wavering between using the pliers to pull out his toenails and setting his hair on fire.'

Emily giggled exuberantly. 'You shut *up*, Emmy,' Timmy said.

'You know, Timmy,' Hilliard said, 'until you just made things worse by talking like that to your sister, I was about to say I thought what your mother just said sounded a little severe. But now you've made me unsure.' He sighed. 'I guess I really don't know what to do to you.'

Timmy looked apprehensive.

The transition from the stage of Timmy's disobedience to imminence of his actual punishment made Emily uneasy. She became solemn, pursing her lips as she began to pity Timmy. Donna began to shake her head slowly back and forth but her pupils remained fixed on the same point in space.

'How about,' Mercy said, 'how about we tell him that he has to do what he said he was going to do, put himself to bed without any supper. I thought that was pretty good. But so he doesn't get the idea he's going to be the one from now on who decides what it's going to cost him to misbehave, we also yank his TV privileges for, oh say, about two weeks?'

Emily looked both absorbed and horrified.

'Too much, I would say, to do both,' Hilliard said. 'But it wouldn't be enough if we just did one of them. What I would say I'm probably leaning to right now would be either no TV for a full month or else your no-TV-for-two-weeks plus no allowance, either.'

'Either of those sounds about right to me,' Mercy said. 'Why don't you decide?'

Emily had to squirm to deal with the suspense.

'Okay, I will,' Hilliard said. 'But it's going to be hard and take me awhile. You know how I hate to punish people. At least let me finish my dinner here, 'fore this excellent fish gets all cold.'

'Okay,' Mercy said, returning to her dinner, 'I may even finish my own. We've both been so busy here Emmy's really the only one who's had time enough to eat and had all her dinner. She's waiting on us for dessert. Which of course I'm assuming you agree there'll only be three of those at the table tonight.'

Timmy sank down still lower in his chair and looked morose. He sneaked glances at his father and looked like he might cry.

'Oh, that goes without saying,' Hilliard said.

'Unless, of course,' Mercy said, 'when you and I finish up here and I ask Emmy to help me take the dishes to the sink, it should turn out there were four clean plates to pick up, instead of only three and one still with food on it.'

'You mean then I might not have to do it?' Hilliard said. 'Not punish anybody? Well, that certainly would be better, lots more pleasant, if there were four clean plates. But there'd have to be an apology, too. I think. Two apologies in fact. One to you, for being naughty, and one to Emmy, for being rude. Then I'd probably go along.'

Timmy hesitated. He frowned deeply. Emily's face now displayed immense sympathy and hope. She urged him with her eyes. Timmy looked at her. Then he looked at his father. 'I'm sorry,' he said.

'Oh, not to me,' Hilliard said. 'You committed your offenses against your mother and sister. You have to make your apologies to them. And then you have to eat your fish.'

Timmy told his mother he was sorry, and obviously meant it. She smiled at him and tousled his hair. He told his sister he was sorry, less sincerely. She showed she felt much better by sticking out her tongue at him. '*Emmy*,' Hilliard said, 'don't think you need to start now.'

Emmy looked flustered and cast her eyes down. Timmy picked up his fork and began to eat his dinner. 'I still hate fish, though,' he said, thoughtfully. At first Mercy tried hard not to laugh, but Hilliard didn't and so she gave in.

'Let it then be spread upon the record of this House,' Hilliard said in a deep voice, 'that again-honorable Timothy Hilliard still hates fish.' Timmy laughed a little and Emily giggled too. Donna's eyelids began to droop.

'As I was saying,' Hilliard said, 'Amby should have a back-breaking mortgage to go with his school loans, just like everyone else. He should have worries. He looks and acts like he goes to bed at night and sleeps like a regular lamb. It's time he took on some adult obligations and responsibilities, keep him tossin' and turnin' all night like the rest of the grown-ups.

'I like the guy. I'd hate to see him just drift into one of those second-banana lives so many bright young guys settle for. Amby's got way too much on the ball. You see it happening around you all the time. They get involved in politics, not running for office, just helping out, but the stuff that they're doing's worthwhile. At first it's all right; it's perfectly fine. They meet some new people a lot like themselves and they have a good time. They get something done that they feel good about, and they manage to keep their perspective.

'But then the first thing you know, it starts to happen to them. You can see it happening, watch it right in front of you. They gradually start sliding into this sort of hip indolence. Get hooked on inside stuff; always in the know about what's going on before the dumb outside world gets a clue.

'They overlook the fact that all they ever are's privileged spectators. All they've really got's their own personal knothole. The reason that they always know exactly what's going on is they spend all their time at the fence, lookin' through that damn knothole. They begin to think it's a big deal: they can look through the fence and watch this whole game that almost everybody else only hears about on the radio, TV, or read about the next day in the paper. Not too many people have this kind of access; it must be a *distinction*, something special. They think it must mean *they're* pretty special. They start to act like jerks, swagger a little, feel *good*.

'They're partly right. The access, the entry, your own parking place: It's fun and it does mean something. It just isn't what they think it means. The reason there's the high board-fence around the game they're watching is the opposite of what they think it is. It's there to *hide* it. It's not there to keep the crowd *out*; it's there to keep the players *in*. The people without knotholes don't want 'em. They're the ones who put up the fence. They don't *want* to see the game. They think it's disgusting. If they had their way, they'd ban it like they do cockfights and bullfights and the dogfights in pits, and bear-baiting. Put in a king and then ignore *him*; that's what they'd choose to do, if you let 'em.

'Young guys don't seem to understand that. That once they settle for their knothole, that's all they'll ever have and that's all they'll ever be. Up against the fence all day, following a game that only matters to the players, watching a circus you gotta be in for it to count. Always at the carnival, best seats in the house, but all they're ever doin's lots of heavy lookin'-on.

'I delegate enough of my authority, give Amby enough responsibility, so that what his job amounts to is surrogate for me. An alter ego who works here while I'm on Beacon Hill. For a guy who's twenty-five, never ran for anything himself, most likely never will; knows he's better backstage than he could ever be out front: that's not bad at all. Very good, in fact. But it's not a career, or shouldn't be, for him. He's totally dependent on me. I lose, drop dead, or decide to be a judge? Amby's out of a job. But it'll become a career for him, though, by default, if he doesn't make a change pretty soon.'

After nine, when she had put the kids to bed and he had read the stories, they picked it up again in the living room. 'The years're going by,' Hilliard said. 'He keeps it up long enough and some morning he wakes up and it's his forty-seventh birthday, and he says to himself "Hey, I'm gettin' old here, just like everyone else always does, the ones that didn't die. What the hell've I become?"

'He'll know the answer. He won't like it: Not very much. Just another political hack, gotten as far as he's ever going to, just waitin' the string to run out.

'No, it's time he made plans to become an adult. Maybe about time even that he started giving some thought to gettin' married, setting up a home and family.'

'With Sunny Keller?' Mercy said. Her tone was not as innocent of judgment as she would have liked – if she had to speak at all and could not for once keep her mouth shut. Mercy had never wholly approved of the cottage arrangement at Swift's Beach. It bothered her, and Dan didn't make it any easier.

From the outset of it back in 1962, Dan while willing to concede that his approach to the landlady had been 'a little underhanded' – thinking each time he did so that it was a lucky thing for him Mercy didn't know about the deals made, actions taken and understandings acquiesced in during his average week on Beacon Hill – had dismissed her objections, saying it wasn't their job to elevate Sunny's or Merrion's morals. Mercy took a sterner view. She said they were 'deceiving' the woman who owned the house at the beach by encouraging her to think that they were renting it by themselves and the kids for the month, and that Amby and Sunny were merely friends who were guests, or related by blood to one or the other of them.

Nor was that the only thing that bothered her. Regardless of what Dan said about it, Mercy believed that good Catholics did not countenance or condone fornication, 'especially by renting the place we know he's going to be using to shack up. And that's what it is: shacking up.' She did not think she was being too strict; Merrion and Sunny had no intention to get married that she had heard about.

'If she had a ring, it'd be okay, then,' Dan had said.

'Not "okay,"' she said, 'but I wouldn't mind so much.'

'Be kind of hard for you to mind at all, wouldn't it?' he said.

'Maybe,' she said, 'but since they aren't engaged, it's very easy. Unpleasant, but easy.' As she saw it he was causing her to commit a venial sin by soft-soaping her into silent collusion, making her complicit in the cottage rental.

As he always did when she slipped up, Hilliard laughed that Friday night and said: '*That's* my little Emmanuel girl.' And she to her helpless irritation blushed and felt embarrassed, as she always did, even though she knew that she was absolutely right and there was no reason why she should.

'Should Amby marry Sunny?' he said. 'I'm not sure I'd go that far. Rather be a lonely bachelor all the solitary days of my life 'n be a worried husband all the time, any time I left the house. Sunny still looks kinda footloose to me.

'But then again, you never know. Maybe Sunny's the way she is right now because this's how she is right now. And when she's gotten it out of her system, maybe she'll be more like us. You can't be so hasty about people, you know, cookie. Just because when we were the same age that the two of them're now, we were already married and that was the right thing for us, with me runnin' for office and all that, that doesn't necessarily mean it's always gonna be the right thing for everybody else.

'But be that as it may, I still think it's time now Amby should get started on becoming an adult, makin' a real life for himself. So I'm gonna start kicking him out of the nest, see if I can shake him up a little. I owe it to him as a friend.'

7

In 1964, when he won his second term on Beacon Hill, Hilliard felt his political future was secure enough to warrant borrowing money for the long-term rental of good space for a district office. Merrion found space on the second floor of a three-story brick building on High Street in Holyoke, last occupied by a businesswoman named Condon. 'It's awful big, but except for that it looks good. I think it could work,' Merrion said. 'The Carneses own the building. They've had trouble rentin' it lately. The third floor's vacant, too. There's a tenant on the first floor but there might as well not be – Saint Vincent de Paul Society runs a second-hand store there. Old clothes and used furniture. Only open weekends. Otherwise nobody's down there, makin' noise and leavin' food around, draw the rats. It's a very nice building. Old but very solid. Well-built, you know?'

Hilliard was familiar with it. He had been there many times, he said, 'but never once willingly. Lillian Condon's dancing school. Or, to be more precise: "Miss Jocelyn's Studio of the Dance." Jocelyn was her maiden name. She called it' – he made his voice falsetto – '"my stage name. I went under it during my career in the theater." We all called her the Dance Lady. "Hafta go the Dance Lady tonight."

'She was kind of a pathetic case, not that I thought that when I was a kid. My father said in the Twenties she used to quit her job in Condon's Drugstore every spring, travel up to Maine and spend the summer working as a chorus girl in summer-stock in one of the resort towns up there along the coast. Bar Harbor, Boothbay; someplace like that. Did it for three or four years.

Hoping for an offer that'd get her to New York; either get a job in theater or some rich guy who'd keep her on the side. And every September, she came back to the drugstore. Finally she got discouraged. Gave up on the bright lights of Broadway and came home, convinced what God wanted her to do was spend her life with her legs together, standing behind the counter.

'After a couple years I guess she decided it'd be all right with God if she made a slight exception and married Condon's son, Jimmy. He took after his old man; he had a degree from the Mass. College of Pharmacy and his lower jaw receded. Maybe his thing did, too. He didn't give her any kids. Or else one of the stories about her was true: she couldn't have any kids. Rumor was that one of those summers she'd had to have an abortion. Not that anyone really ever knew it for sure, so far's I know – might've just been one of those nasty little secrets people like to make up about other people, put a little color in their own lives. No law says they have to be true.

'Anyway, Jimmy backed her financially when she started her dancing school. A couple years later he died. Maybe her being over there all the time giving lessons made him feel neglected or something.'

The space had been perfect for Miss Jocelyn's gatherings. In the early afternoons, little girls in leotards and pink satin slippers chewed their lips intently as they pirouetted, whirling dust motes through the sunlight slanting through the big two-paned windows looking west over High Street. Late afternoons and weekday evenings, passersby heard the clatter of high school girls learning to tap-dance, making them smile. Hilliard remembered the Friday evenings and Saturday nights: small crowds of older children ungainly and uneasy between the ages of seven and fourteen. The boys wore blue blazers and thin grey worsted trousers outgrown in the five or six weeks since their careful purchase one or two sizes too large, and ties clipped off-center to their collars. They huddled in a bunch and studied – some openly, and boldly; most furtively, surreptitiously and apprehensively – the girls across the room. Whispering excitedly and squealing in groups of five or six, in high-necked, short-skirted chiffon versions of long strapless gowns, the girls were learning to gossip. They were already covetous for future nights when they would have proms and – they desperately both hoped and feared – beautiful bodies and big swaggering boyfriends with half-curled upper lips and pants bulging at the crotch, begging urgently to feel them up; real adventures to tell and tell on one another.

'I guess the Dance Lady was fairly happy, though, with what she'd ended up with. She must've been; seemed like any time of day that you went by you could hear the music up there. She ran it about fifteen years. Not the brilliant career she'd originally had in mind, but still, that's what life's about: making the best deal you can. If you end up the widow of a sterile chinless husband, with nothing to look forward to but teaching sullen little kids how to dance, instead of as a rich man's plaything named "Mitzi," you live with it.

'My mother's idea was I needed a gentleman's polish and old Lil'd give it to me. It was my idea of torture. Once a week, every week, during the school year. Friday afternoons, when I was seven. Saturday nights when I turned eleven. Until I finally turned thirteen and got parole. Outlasted both of them, the one who made me go and the one who tried to teach me – I still couldn't dance.'

The space had stood vacant for three years since the dance lady's death at seventy-six. Hilliard remembered how she'd looked presiding over it: the brassy gold hair and the rail-thin body; the small breasts under the gold lamé bodice sometimes askew, and oddly-shaped – built-up, the girls reported knowingly, with wadded facial tissue – but as high as they had been when she was seventeen. Either her imperial bearing required accompaniment or she feared quiet; she kept the room echoing with music, pounding out tap-practice tunes on an out-of-tune Chickering upright piano; cranking up an old Victrola that used steel needles to scrape *Swan Lake*, *Les Sylphides*, *Tales of Vienna Woods* and vaudeville tunes from her extensive collection of scratchy shellacs, proudly turning up the suitcase-shaped, grey tweed Columbia portable record-player. It remained 'our *new, hi-fi, diamond-needle, record-player*' the six years he attended, groaning out ballads sung by Vaughn Monroe, Teresa Brewer, Vic Damone and Patti Page, the Singin' Rage, for ballroom instruction.

'It's a pretty big room, though,' Hilliard said. 'Do we really need all that space? And can we afford it?'

'It is a lot of space,' Merrion said, 'and we probably don't really need it. But we can afford it. It's not only more space'n we need; it's more space'n *anybody* in these parts right now seems to need. Carnes people aren't *giving* it away – that'd be against their religion. But they also know that if the dancing-school lady doesn't come back to life or they cough up what it'll cost to partition it, they might not *ever* find someone who'll rent it. The room is just too fuckin' big.'

'I wonder who it was originally built for,' Hilliard said. 'Wasn't for a dancing school, for sure. What'd someone want all that space *for*?'

'The agent said he thinks it was a meeting hall,' Merrion said. 'Catholic Order of Foresters, something like that; one of those fraternal groups the new immigrants used to join. Organized to sell themselves insurance. Hire someone to teach them all altogether how to learn English, take the exam for citizenship.' He snorted. 'Kind of newcomers we got comin' up now could use that kind of ambition, you ask me. But then of course they've already got the right to vote, not that they use it. And speaking English don't interest them a lot. Don't need to speak English, get welfare.'

'How much a foot?' Hilliard said. 'You'll notice how I tactfully pretend I didn't quite hear what you just got finished saying, toward the end there.'

'Yeah,' Merrion said, 'you may not hear it, and you'll never say it; but you think it, pal; I know that. You think the same way as I do on that. You keep it all to yourself all the time, and deny it when you're out in public.'

Hilliard sighed. 'Some day I've really got to set some time aside, close the door and figure out how we reform you,' he said. 'It's something that we got to do. Otherwise some night you'll start showin' up for one of my debates wearing a sheet and a hood, calling yourself the Grand Kleagle. People'll start thinking I must have something wrong with *me*, I've still got *you* around, killin' time between lynchings. Definitely have got to do that, and I will, too, some day, right after I finish rebuilding the Hanging Gardens of Babylon.

'But in the meantime, let's see if we can't talk about something less troublesome. How 'bout we start with the rent – what're they asking for this place?'

'The agent's saying two-fifty,' Merrion said. 'I know he'll take two-twenty-five.'

'What's that work out to, about?' Hilliard said. He liked strutting his mathematical skills. He had taught algebra, trigonometry and calculus during the six years preceding his election to the House. He looked forward to public budgetary debates; his calculating ability enabled him not only to show off but sometimes to intimidate his fellow aldermen and later on his colleagues in the House. 'About twenty-five hundred bucks a year?' In private he played down his talent a little, deliberately only coming close to exact answers.

'About that,' Merrion said, 'twenty-four-seventy-five.'

'Two hundred a month and change,' Hilliard said. 'Let's see how he likes the sound of one-seventy-five. That'd bring it in under two grand, nineteen-and-a-quarter, one-sixty a month – quite a bit closer our speed.

'In fact,' he said, 'more I think about this, what we ought to be saying's one-fifty. Sixteen-fifty a year, just under one-forty a month. We're going to be paying to heat the place. What do they burn there, anyway – oil or coal?'

'I think the agent said oil,' Merrion said.

'Good,' Hilliard said. 'Probably means the heating system's newer; won't be breaking down all the time. Tell him I'm terribly busy on the Hill and I won't have time enough to take a look at it until sometime next week. In the meantime, find out all you can, so when I do go over there, the two of us know more about the place 'n Carnes's fuckin' agent does.

'We're the ones doing the favor. Without us he's stuck with that space. Old Roy should be moistening his lips, getting set to pucker up and kiss me on the ass, I'm willing to be nice enough to take it off his hands.'

The landlord's agent, Brian Fontaine, looked to be in his late forties. He had reddish-blond hair that he combed back, and rather sharp features. He shifted a lot in his clothes, as though confined in them. He spoke softly and admiringly to Hilliard and Merrion about the building's many advantages, as though he had been calling their attention to subtleties of composition in a fine painting. Their conversation reverberated in the empty building.

Citing the fact that Hilliard's older or less able constituents would have only one flight of stairs to climb when they came for appointments, Fontaine pointed out that the broad wooden staircase was equipped with a pipe handrail in the middle as well as those fitted to the walls. He said the sturdy fixtures to hold onto with both hands would make older visitors feel secure while using the stairs. Hilliard remembered climbing those steps, treads worn even then, as slowly as he possibly could, and then after dancing school was over, vaulting down them two and three at a time, using the handrails as exercise bars. 'Yes,' Hilliard said, 'there's that. But they'd feel even better if there was an *elevator*, so they wouldn't *have* to lug their old bones up two flights, holding on for dear life with both hands.'

'*One* flight,' the agent said. 'You'd be on the second floor.'

'*Two* flights,' Hilliard said. '*One* flight up to the landing. Then, after you catch your breath, you've got to climb *another* flight – making *two* – to reach this level.'

'The staircase was built that way to save floor space in the building,' the agent said with weary testiness. 'It's one floor above the ground floor – only one flight of stairs.'

Merrion nodded. 'That sounds right to me, Mister Hilliard,' he said obsequiously, as though as anxious to ingratiate himself with Fontaine as he was to please Hilliard. 'It's a reasonable thing that he's saying. You could have two landings, three landings, four, you didn't mind how narrow and steep they hadda be. Still only the one flight of stairs.'

Fontaine took that as vindication. He let the reaction show on his face, sneaking a glance at Hilliard. Hilliard nodded and looked thoughtful.

'In fact,' Merrion said, the conciliatory tone vanishing, 'the only problem *I* still have is do you think your elderly constituents, the ones with the cardiac conditions, pains in their chest all the time; ones who're all crippled-up and lame, need to use a cane;

and in *wheelchairs*, even – do you think they're gonna find Mister Fontaine's explanation as reasonable as I do?

'Or are they maybe gonna say: "*Hilliard*? Second-floor Hilliard? He doesn't want to hear from me, what I need to have him hear. He *said* he did, when he was runnin', but that was to get elected. Now he's not *inna*rested anymore. Next election he's gonna find out something from *me*: I'm the one not innarested. I'm voting whoever the other guy happens to be.' I'm afraid that's what those voters'll do, Mister Hilliard. You know how demanding they are. They think *we* ought to cater to *them*.'

Fontaine had to work his facial muscles to dispel the expression of chagrin that displaced the look of victory on his face, but he did his best to agree smoothly, pointing out the availability of similar space on the second floor of another brick building nearby, owned and managed by the Carnes family. 'It's almost identical space, except that it's newly renovated and refurbished. Brand new Westinghouse elevator's just one of the many improvements. Best one they make, four-man car, top-of-the-line but very *compact*; so you don't lose that much of floor space where you put in your shaft. And at the same time it operates almost silently, *very nice*, and *quiet*. Most of the machinery's down in the basement. So that means you don't hear it start grinding and banging away up there over your head on the roof, every time someone enters the building or leaves. Be equally glad to show you that. Take you over right now, in fact. Got the key with me, right here.

'But I have to warn you: That machine wasn't cheap. Neither were the other renovations and improvements. We've had to raise the rent. It'll cost you a dollar a foot more for it'n Mister Merrion here told me you could afford – which as I'm sure you realize isn't that great a deal for us. If the figure that he gave me, around two dollars a foot or so's all you can see your way clear to paying, well, that *does* limit what I can show you. But now if what you're telling me's that you think you may be able to go a bit more to get what you've got to have, we've got what you want.'

Hilliard scowled and started to say something, but Merrion held up his hand. 'Danny,' he said, 'if I could get a word in here? I may be getting a little confused. It might help if I could get things cleared up here a little.'

Hilliard shrugged. 'Anything you think might help move this thing along.'

'I must've given you the wrong impression, Brian,' Merrion said. 'I never said two-bucks-a-foot was the most we could afford. I never gave you any dollar-figure. When you showed me this space last week I said it looked pretty big. Maybe double what we'd had in mind. And when I asked you how big it was, you said you'd have to check "but around a thousand feet, I think, eleven hundred feet." So I just did the easy thing, took the thousand-foot guess and multiplied it in my head, using two-bucks-a-foot as the number. Just trying to get some idea of what that would work out to be. Dollars-per-square-foot doesn't mean much to me; what I want is how-much-a-month.

'So when I said to you: "At two bucks a foot that'd work out, something in the neighborhood of two hundred bucks a month.' And then: "Who pays for the heat?" that really was all I was doing. Just getting an idea, you know? Then *you* said you thought Mister Carnes'd say you couldn't let it go for less'n two-fifty, as though I'd just offered two, which I hadn't. I never gave you any figure at all, or anyway, never meant to. I was just thinking out loud.'

The agent looked bored and annoyed.

'And wouldn't my friend Roy'd say that since it's me,' Hilliard said, 'who'd be renting this other space with the elevator, you should charge me the old rent? Roy's my campaign finance director. His office keeps my records. He knows how strapped for cash I am. Don't you think he'd want you to give me a break?'

'Mister Hilliard,' the agent said, grinning, 'I'm absolutely *sure* he wouldn't, and I'll tell you why that is. After Mister Merrion'd called and told me he was representing you, I decided maybe I'd better see Mister Carnes and fill him in. Because I know that Mister Carnes and Roy Junior, his son, and his brother, the Senator, all think very highly of you.

'I remember when you ran the second time for alderman Mister Carnes then told me when I went to vote for Roy Junior, for rep – his brother Arthur may've been running that year too, re-election to the senate – he hoped not only that I'd vote for them but also vote for *you*. He said you were a very nice guy, and an *excellent* candidate – all the Carneses were behind you.

'Well, if Mister Carnes says it, that's enough for me. I took his suggestion, and not only did I give you *my* vote but I made sure my wife, and my sister, and father and mother, I asked them to vote for you, too. And I think they all did it, too, and every time you've run since then too. Which would mean, if they have, you've gotten five votes from our family every time you've run, ever since Mister Carnes said that to me. Although maybe not from my father, the first time. He went to school with Mister Gilson – that may've swayed him the other way.

'So as soon as I found out who was interested in this space, I thought that maybe Mister Carnes'd want me to give you some sort of a discount – which in this case would mean taking a loss. But seeing as how it was you, he might want to give you special treatment.

'So I asked Mister Carnes how I was to treat you, and quick as a flash, Mister Carnes came right back at me, and he said to me: "Why, the same as anyone else. You treat my young friend Daniel just the same way as you'd treat any other tenant prospect. Show him what we've got available that you think might meet his needs and give him the best price we can. The same one we always charge everyone in our buildings: the fairest and lowest price possible."'

'That answers my question, I guess,' Hilliard said.

'And he went on to say,' the agent said, with delight, 'if you don't mind me saying this, also, that the Carnes family's already made quite a few large contributions to the various campaigns you've run. And to tell you he's got no intention throwing in the rent on top of that. He said: "Tell him we said we'd support him. We never said we'd adopt him."'

Hilliard looked at Merrion. Merrion shrugged. 'Hey,' he said, 'always said there's no harm in asking. And besides, since I'm gonna be the one in there most of the time, the more people those stairs keep from coming up to bother me, the more I like no elevator.'

The agent mentioned the amplitude of free parking on the steeply sloping lot out back: 'That's what makes it so well-drained, when it rains,' he said.

Merrion said: 'It's also what makes it so slippery it's useless half the year.' The agent looked perplexed. 'You tellin' us you never heard inna wintertime cars go sliding down it backwards, end up crashing into the ones parked onna street? Even with their brakes on and the transmissions in gear. Mountain goats'd slide down that hill, they're on it, we get ice. Which's most likely why you got those iron posts on both sides of the curb-cut, you pull in the lot. Anna chain there you can hitch across it, block the entrance inna winter anytime we got a storm. So people like you who don't know about ice, never dream a thing like that could happen, can't drive their cars in there and park them, and end up where they cause a lotta damage. Which the Carnes family might then wind up gettin' sued for, which is why there's no cars in it when we're gonna have a storm.

'Which is why it's most likely useless half of the year, when there's any chance of ice – and that's the fifty percent that you really need it, there's no place to park onna street. A selling point that back lot is not. In fact what it is is a *draw*back.'

The agent looked incredulous. 'Really?' he said. 'I never heard that before.'

'Then you must've never worked inna car dealership here where they had their own body shop,' Merrion said. 'I did. You'd've been the guy who ordered trim parts and glass and mirrors for cars that got hit, and the taillight lenses and chrome; and then you hadda sit there and take it when the parts didn't come and the car-owners didn't like it, and blamed *you* when it happened; then you would know that it prolly *did* happen. Any *number* of times.'

The agent looked chastened and said: 'Well, I stand corrected.' He called to Hilliard's attention the fact that the space was served by its own two separate restrooms. 'So your people who work here wouldn't have to share these with anybody else. The way that all people in the other offices in the halls here on this floor have to do.'

'*Would* have to,' Merrion said, 'if there was anyone in those offices, now. Which there hasn't been any since the S-and-H Green Stamp people moved all their operation here down to Springfield.'

'And I'll bet you a quarter,' Hilliard said, 'that if I go in what used to be the boy's room sixteen years or so ago when I was one of the poor boys Miss Jocelyn was making their lives miserable for here, I would find that the toilet nearest the door still doesn't flush all the way unless you hold the handle on the chain down – and then it sprays you so you look like you pissed your pants – and that it's still got the same old wooden seat it had then; never been replaced.'

'Mister Hilliard,' the agent said, 'I really don't know, I'm just the guy who does the rentals. I don't handle repairs or do maintenance, anything like that. They give me a list of the premises vacant. I rent them as best I can. You know more about toilets than I do.

'Now I have a question: How much're you willing to pay? 'Cause I know you've decided and you won't budge, and you know what Mister Carnes told me: I don't have much latitude either.'

'A buck anna half,' Merrion said.

'Your original two,' the agent said.

'We split the difference,' Hilliard said.

The agent looked sour. 'Good,' he said grimly, 'that was fun. Glad it's over.' He looked at his watch. 'I may even get lunch today.' They shook hands. 'I'll have the lease ready this afternoon. Otherwise tomorrow is fine. Just give me a call. Oh, and bring in the deposit and the first month's rent, too. That'll come to a total of three-twenty-eighty-two. We'll need to have that 'fore you get the keys.'

'I'll give it to you right now,' Hilliard said. He reached into the right inside pocket of his jacket and brought out a folding checkbook. He opened it and tore out the first check. Merrion positioned himself so that Hilliard could use the checkbook as a pad and Merrion's left shoulder as a desk. Hilliard made the check out to the Carnes Company for $320.82. On the back he wrote: 'First month's rent and security deposit/High St dist. off.'

The agent took it and gazed at him. 'Can I put this in the bank on my way back to the office?' he said.

Hilliard shrugged. 'Sure,' he said, 'Roy knows it's good.'

It was a bleak, painfully resonant room with varnished matched-board oak floors and oak wainscoating. Hilliard walked over to the left along the inside wall, passing the doors opened into the toilets and grabbed the ballet-practice bar still in place there. He tried to shake it. It was firm. 'Handy,' he said to Merrion. His voice boomed in the emptiness. 'We used to put our coats here in the winter. Fold 'em over it.'

Down below the front door slammed. Hilliard went to the window in the middle of the front wall. 'There . . . goes . . . *Brian*,' he said. 'First a stop at the bank and then off to enjoy his well-earned lunch. Brian's an unhappy man. He thinks he has a hard life.' He turned and looked at Merrion, still standing in the doorway. He grinned and said: 'Our first home, dear,' he said. 'Are you as excited as I am?'

Merrion laughed. 'I might say that to you,' he said. 'I don't think I'd say it to Brian.'

'You think Brian's a little light in his loafers?' Hilliard said. 'He did mention he has a wife.'

'He was *careful* to mention he had a wife,' Merrion said. 'He might even actually have one. Who's a woman, I mean – I understand some of them do. Wife is a perfect disguise.'

'Ever think about getting one for yourself?' Hilliard said, putting an arm around his shoulder as they left the big room. 'Not that I'm saying you need camouflage. Just a matter of: Wouldn't you like to? Maximum of temptation with a maximum of opportunity?'

Merrion shrugged. 'I brought it up a couple times with Sunny. The last time she was home, in fact. She told me she'd think about it. Said that the time before, too. I don't think she thinks she's ready. Maybe just not ready for me. I'm only twenny-three. Don't think I hafta worry that much yet.'

Hilliard followed Merrion down the stairs, their footfalls echoing. Three steps above the landing he paused and said: 'That stuff about cars sliding down the back lot – did all of that actually happen?'

Merrion stopped on the landing and turned around. 'You didn't believe me?'

Hilliard paused two steps up from the landing. 'No,' he said, 'I didn't mean that. It's just that I've lived in this town all my life, and I never heard that'd happened. I'd've thought I would've.'

Merrion turned back down the stairs. 'I would've too,' he said.

'Well, did it?' Hilliard said, crossing the landing and starting down the second flight behind Merrion.

'I dunno,' Merrion said. 'It could have.'

'You said it did,' Hilliard said.

At the foot of the stairs Merrion stood on the black-and-white tiled floor and smiled at Hilliard. 'Not exactly,' he said. 'You told me to go find out about this building, who built it and so forth, and why. Well, it turned out there wasn't much to find out. A guy named Reynolds built it, along with seven others, almost just like it, between Eighteen-seventy-nine and Nineteen-oh-one. Office space, for the people who managed the mills. And just like Brian told me, the dancing school was originally the Foresters' Hall. But I didn't find out anything, really, that would've helped us to drive down the rent.

'Therefore I asked him about ice. I don't think I ever actually said there was any. Or that any cars slid down the hill. All I said was I was surprised he hadn't heard about it. And I said I guessed *he* never worked in a car dealership ordering parts, because if he had've done that, then he might've heard about it. Then he'd know the reason for the two posts and the chain across.

'The chain and the posts're definitely there. I'm completely sure of that.'

'"But ice *could* be the reason,"' Hilliard said on the ground floor, laughing. He clapped Merrion on the back. 'What do you think's going to happen, when he tells Roy and asks him how come he never heard about the ice, and Roy tells him he never did, either?'

Merrion laughed. 'Well,' he said, 'nothing, as far's we're concerned. Brian's putting the check in the bank. Once he's done that, he can't back out. The deal's been cut.'

By the end of the next week the room was spaciously furnished, leaving plenty of standing-and-arguing room among four old wooden desks and a scuffed-up oaken conference table long and sturdy enough to accommodate ten telephone desksets on election nights and eight strong oak armchairs large enough for Hilliard and Merrion and six other robust adult males. Four of them came from the district and worked in it. The two who lived outside it were interested in doing business with the state.

They strenuously and passionately shared the purpose of making Hilliard look good, so that they would prosper along with him. But they didn't always agree on what ought to be done to achieve that. When they did agree they were often united in profane displeasure at some opponent's action or remark. So when they gathered at the table – Friday evenings during off-years; daily and nightly during election years – they often wound up shouting 'stupid bastard' and 'dumb fucking asshole' either at each other or in reference to rivals and opponents, pounding their fists as their faces grew red from exertion and anger.

At night the space that had been gently burnished in the evenings by the soft light from six floor lamps with golden-fringed red shades, when the lady with the brassy hair had held her Friday and Saturday evening waltz and fox-trot lessons for polite young girls and sullen little boys – 'one-two-three, *sly*-ud; one-two-three, *sly*-ud; *yay*-uss' – was now starkly lit by eight one-hundred-fifty-watt bulbs overhead, enclosed in white-frosted glass globes suspended from green-tarnished brass chains plaited with silk-covered power cords descending from white-spattered green-tarnished-brass ceiling fixtures. The fixtures were mounted flush against the chalky, white-washed, tobacco-browned, stamped-tin false ceiling, ornamentally filigreed at the corners with bas-relief representations of palm fronds.

It was a good location. High Street was busy then and the new office, three doors north of the *Transcript* office at its center, was close to the Sportsman's Cafe where the newspapermen went to pie their own type after work, filled with inside stuff they couldn't print but liked to trade with those they trusted. So a politician facing a late night in the office and a makeshift supper at nine, aware that his best asset is curiosity and a relaxed mind works better, could take a short break around five-thirty and run down to the cafe without coat or umbrella through a light rain for a couple quick beers without getting his clothes very wet, 'just to find out what's going on.' In the Sportsman's several of the men who sometimes shouted at each other and belabored the oak table in the second-floor office often met on better terms to drink Hampden Beer, CC or Dewar's and water, and denounced other men and each other in similar rough terms and the newspapermen laughed with them, feeling fortunate to be alive and important in exciting events, and to have such splendid tough friends.

Late that Saturday morning in the spring of '66, after the week's slate of routine but persisting annoyances had been discussed and new plans made to deal with them, perhaps even effectively 'this fuckin' time,' Hilliard had cleared his throat and asked Merrion what it was he wanted.

'Because whatever it is that you want, my friend,' Hilliard'd said, meaning every word of it, 'you'll have it. If I can get it for you, it's gonna be yours. You've earned it. If it's within my power, I'll do it, you know. I'll move heaven and earth if I have to. This you know's a true fact.'

8

'Oh Danny, up yours, for Christ sake,' Merrion said, discomforted and faintly embarrassed. He had cultivated the consensus about Hilliard: 'When Dan Hilliard says you're gettin' a pony, a pony's what you're gonna get. You can go out and get yourself a red-leather saddle; you're not gettin' a room full of shit.'

Merrion hadn't asked for anything because he'd been being practical. That was *his* policy. 'That is how we do things, me and Danny. He has all the great ideas. I'm in charge of making sure they really *are* great; won't cost more'n they're worth or get us two into trouble.

'Dan and I've always understood each other, right from the very first day. As long as we talk it over before anything gets promised, chances are what we say will get done. We've always dealt in the same line of goods: only in possible things.'

Hilliard used similar terms. 'We may not tell you what you'd like to hear, that we'll do what you want us to do. We'll only tell you what we think we can do, and then if you tell us you want us to do that, we'll do our best to get it done.' Neither of them mentioned the ballast to anyone else: 'Things that we *know*'re possible, because when we say we think we can do them, we've already gotten them done.

Merrion said he'd been thinking of appointment as an assistant clerk of a district court. 'Pretty much ruled out the chairmanship of the Turnpike Authority,' he'd said. 'Nice job, pay's good; hours're great, but I don't think you can pull that one off. Pope? I'm not really religious, and anyway, I ate meat on Fridays 'fore it was allowed. Chief justice? I'm not a lawyer.'

Hilliard was going to be. He'd earned his degree from Suffolk Law School, punishing himself in Boston night after night and days as well in the summers during his first four years in the legislature. Awaiting the results of the winter bar exam, he could admit 'it fuckin' near killed me. If I hadn't been young, it would've.' While still in law school he'd advised Merrion to drop his studies in education. 'You're not gonna teach school; you're too stupid to teach. I've *been* a teacher; I know. Go to law school instead. Make my life easy: no matter how bad you screw up, I can always make you a judge. Any asshole can be a judge.'

Merrion ignored him, getting his M.Ed. from Westfield State College. 'I got some *pride*: Never even been inside a goddamned law school. I got other good qualities too.

'Courts sit in the summer. Judges' robes look hot. I think a nice quiet district-court clerkship's what I'd like; bug no one and no one bugs me. File papers all day and look out the window; have coffee; read the papers, movin' my lips. Talk about sports and politics, right? Basically the same stuff I do here' in Hilliard's Holyoke office, when not working as a substitute teacher, pretending to wait for a job-opening in biology and freshman composition, in a public high school. 'If I don't find something pretty soon, I'm gonna hafta get serious about that. But it's not like I really wanna. What I want is something with the state or maybe feds. Pays at least nine grand a year and they can't kick your ass out in the street, next election goes the wrong way.'

Merrion said clerkships met those requirements. 'And your court job also pays better but that's not what makes it great – it's that no one's *after* you all the time like in this job, voters wanting something from you.

'See, the one thing I've found out from working in this job is that I don't want to spend my life doing it. I'm not knocking it now, understand me. I learned a helluva lot here, and I appreciate it. If it looked like you're headed for governor or US Senate, I'd have different stuff to do, manage a staff or something, like I do in a campaign – planning events, scheduling, bullshittin' the reporters – that'd be different. If you had a thing where I could be a chief of staff for you, like Larry O'Brien for JFK, or Leo Diehl for Tip O'Neill, that'd be a whole different thing – a ten-strike, right up my alley; I'd love it.

'But we both know there's no way that's gonna happen. It isn't you're not good enough, or smart enough, or anything like that; it's because you're not rich enough. You don't have the family connections. It's too far for us two to jump. And if I get a new job now, I still want to work with you, run your campaigns. I *love* doin' that shit, as you know.'

'I was hoping you'd say that,' Hilliard said. 'I think we're a good team.'

'Well, so do I,' Merrion said. 'And I'm glad we both understand that. Not going overboard here. But I don't want to deal directly with the public anymore, hand-to-hand stuff I do here. Since the civilians found out about we opened this office: people who want things from you now know they got a handy *local* place to go to, make their fuckin' demands. So they make more of them, save themselves a trip to Boston by buggin' me right here. I'm no good at dealin' with them: I don't like it and I don't like *them*, having to be polite to them.

'Sooner or later someone's gonna figure it out, and that'll be bad for you. So I should stop doing it, sooner.

'I am not the politician in this operation; you are. I am the mechanic. The world is full of assholes. I learned that by being your man in the district. I stay in this job for the rest of my life, I'll always be dealing with assholes. And I'll never get so I like 'em.

'I also realize no matter what I end up doing, I'm probably not gonna make a million dollars. So also for the rest of my life, while dodging assholes, I hafta think about making a living. Therefore what I have to do is find some kind of job that puts me in a different position. Where instead of *them* controlling *me*, *I'm* the one controlling *them*.

'These people, Danny,' Merrion said, 'I'm telling you, I don't know how you do it. The six years I've been working for you, I've paid attention, watched you. Seen you with them; talking to them, listening to them. Half the time they're not even making sense but you still listen to them, like they're making sense. Going to their functions it seems like they're always having – and you never get *tired* of it. Want to say to them: "For *God's* sake, will you shut *up*? Stop *talking* to me." Never lose your patience. I don't know how you stand it. If I knew that I'd have to do what you do for the rest of my life, I think I'd go out of my mind.

'I've gotten so I hate them. Always pestering people like me to get people like you to *get* something for them – cushy jobs and special treatment. When the truth is they don't even *like* us.

'You know what they're thinkin', they come in and see me? I don't think you do, and that's no reflection on you. When you're out campaigning, you're a candidate, sure, but also a celebrity. They want to be seen with you, maybe get their picture taken. Shows how important they are, the candidate knows them by name. So they're on their best behavior.

'You don't see the side they show me, swaggerin' in here to practically threaten me, try to order me around. They are fuckin' *insulting*. Act like they're *lowerin'* themselves, comin' in to ask for a favor. Way they see it, *they're* the ones doin' the favor, for *you*, asking you do something for them.

'It's all over them; you can *see* it. Thinking: "Who're these guys that we have to beg? They're *pols* – that's all they are. They don't deserve no respect. The only difference they see between politicians and the kid who pumps their gas and cleans their windshield down at Borromeo's Gulf is that you dropped into City Hall one day, maybe pay a water bill. And it so happened you hadda wait and a thought crossed your mind: "Hey, as long's I'm in the neighborhood, why not run for somethin', huh? Might be kind of fun." So you filled out some papers, and then next you got elected. Best day you ever had. You should be grateful to *them*.

'This is *all* of you guys now, I'm talkin' about here. *Alla* pols except Kennedy. He's got money. So he must've just needed something to do. Did everyone else a big favor, outta the goodness his heart. But all the rest of you ran for something one day on a whim, and then you won, no work involved. Except for that one lucky hunch, you're no different'n the guy snarling at me is. Prolly not even as good.

'I was not prepared for this. My father *envied* pols; he admired them. He wished he could be one himself. I used to think when I was younger, 'fore I went to work for you, it was too bad Pat didn't run for office. Even if he'd lost. At least he would've *tried*; gotten it out of his system.

'More'n just the town committee. Selectman, maybe, or town moderator. Or something part-time with the county. Because he loved the game so.

'He said the reason that he didn't, people sometimes told him he should run? If he announced for office, he'd offend people. Make a bunch of enemies just by doing that.

'"Just by *running*, you piss people off. Whadda you think you're doin', goin' after that job? You sure've got some kinda nerve.

'"They think they should be the ones to have the job, even though they never thought about it until they heard you wanted it. So therefore they're mad at you.

'"And if I lose, can I still do my job selling cars? People're now mad at me. For the rest of my life there'll be a group of people out there who'll never buy a car from me. Or from any other salesman who works for John Casey either, because I work for him and that means it's his fault too. Win or lose, I hurt John. I don't wanna do that. Create a group of people who if they still buy Fords will buy them in Springfield because I ran for something their kid brother Mikie wanted. If I beat him I'm a bastard, because I took what he wanted. If I lost, it doesn't matter; I'm *still* a bastard because I made Mikie *work* for it, made him spend a lot of money he could otherwise've kept.'

'Okay, that's what he said. But now that I've been in it like I have with you, I think he was pretty *smart*. He didn't come right out and say it, but he knew what politics made people think of you; hold you in contempt. Even when you're the guy they voted for, who won. You put yourself in their power, and therefore they despise you.

'Everybody liked Pat Merrion as long as he was a car salesman. They thought his friends got better deals than people he didn't know, so they wanted to be his friends. He *encouraged* them to think that. Then when it came time for them to buy their next car, they'd think if they bought it from someone else their old pal Pat would be sad. *They* wanted *him* to like *them*. He had the power. But if he ran for office he'd be asking them to like *him*. *They* would then have the power. They weren't as good and kind as he was, and he knew it. If one of them ran and won, Pat'd admire him. If Pat ran and won, they'd turn mean.'

Hilliard laughed. 'You do need a change,' he said.

'And the court job'd be a good one,' Merrion said. 'Unless people know someone when you're the clerk, you can say No – politely, but say it. And if you do they're shit outta luck. I could get used to that very fast.

'Then there's the nice steady paycheck. Once you start drawin' it, you're set for life. Until it comes time for you to retire, at which point you get a pension. It's not like you start hoping your friend who got you the job loses his next election; naturally you still want him to win. But if some guy comes outta nowhere and sandbags him, well, at least you've still got *your* job. And on top of that, I've heard reports: There're people who say it's not hard.'

'*No*,' Hilliard said.

'That's a rumor I heard,' Merrion said. 'I also heard you get vacation, and every year you stay there you earn more of it. I first heard that, I didn't believe it. But then I think about it. I can see why this would be. It's sort of like sex, I guess, little bit like gettin' laid? The more you like your work, the more of it you're naturally gonna do. And therefore the more rest you need from it. Or else your pecker falls off.'

'I suppose,' Hilliard said. 'But could anyone actually tell when you were takin' vacation? How would they know, if they looked around and couldn't find you, that you just didn't happen to come in yet this particular day? Isn't that you're on vacation; you just don't happen to be there, is all. Taking the morning or afternoon off, maybe even the whole entire *day*, to take care of a few things you know? Errands and stuff, we all have to do now and then. How would they know you were off on vacation?'

'They generally wouldn't,' Merrion said. 'The clerks're a lot like reps are, in that respect. Which is another feature of the job I really like; the fact that you can be at work and on the job without having to be actually present in the building. I always envied how you can do that.'

'It's pretty nice,' Hilliard said warmly. 'I've said that myself, many times. In fact yesterday, when I was in here, that thought crossed my mind. Technically I was in Boston, because we were in session. One-hundred-and-eleven-point-six miles away, two-hundred-and-twenty-three-point-two miles, round-trip. Eight cents a mile, couple dollars in tolls, Nineteen-dollars-and-eighty-four-cents – if memory serves, and it does.'

'And plus which,' Merrion had said, 'there's this other aspect of it: You associate with a much better class of people than you do playin' politics. Better'n I see in here, at least. You're now hangin' out with the criminal element. These're the guys alla liberals think so highly of, victims of society. Much classier type of person, by and large, 'n you're ever gonna run into in politics, people breakin' their word all the time.

'Job in a courthouse, you got some idea what you're dealin' with. Day in, day out, most the people you see're *common criminals*. And fully qualified, too, every last one of them, to be where they are. You know what to expect. Violators of by-laws, orders, ordinances and rules, regulations, all of those kinds of things, and all kinds, misdemeanors there, too. Your lower-grade felonies, less'n five years; malicious destruction of personal property; indecent assault on a child – takes a real classy guy to do that. Gettin' out of a jail before you're supposed to; or you tried and didn't make it, just for tryin'. Forgery, too, all that kind of stuff. Guys who unlimber their dicks at high noon and piss their brains out in the street. Right there in front of the church, Most Blessed Sacrament, say, up in Cumberland, just as the casket comes out. Beat up their kids. Slap their wives around. Swindle widows; cheat orphans; pick people's pockets. Bang into other guys' cars down the shoppin' mall, right? Without leavin' their name and address, so the poor bastard never knows who it was, put the dent in his car. Let their horny dogs loose with no collar and license. All of that kinda crap there.'

'You've done your homework,' Hilliard said.

'Damned right I have,' Merrion said. 'First thing I do, 'fore I ask for a job – now that I had this one, at least – is make sure it's a job that I want. This court job I'd fit right in. My kind of people. I'd get along with 'em fine. I'd doin' the same thing you're doin', the State House: fittin' right in with the crowd. Tellin' dirty jokes with the rest of the lads. Steppin' quickly aside but rememberin' to look sad, some pal of ours gets indicted.

'Always sayin' the right thing and so forth. "Tough thing they're doin' to old Magnus there. Trynah heave his ass inna jug; this's a serious thing. I hope it turns out all right for him. But do you think, just askin' here now, but in case it turns out they hook the poor bastard, I could have his parkin' space? Mine's awful far from the door. Rainy days I get all wet.' Takin' care at all times none of the shit spraying him spatters you.

'I've thought about it, all of that stuff,' Merrion said. 'I can handle that duty. The first thing you know, you're in your courthouse there, forty years've gone by like a shot. And you have not changed a bit. You don't look a day over forty yourself. No wrinkles, no lines – 'cept from Florida, maybe, goin' down inna winter so much, or playin' a game of golf up around here any time you can fit in a few holes. But no more'n, say, oh, three or four rounds a week. Wouldn't want to overdo it. How *would* you get wrinkles, livin' like that? What'd give them to you? Never a worry about anything; had a care on your mind.'

'Well, your waist might get a little bigger,' Hilliard said. 'Might find pants a size or two larger fit better. But that's only natural; get older, you slow down a little. Lose a few teeth and so forth. But still chewin' your food all right. Making your way through the prime rib at Henry's Grist Mill. Another night a couple monster baked-stuffed lobsters with the butter and the crumbs the Lobster Trap does up so good? Little light table wine, wash it down? Well, that's what you gotta expect then. You eat right: you put on some weight.'

'But that doesn't mean you ain't well,' Merrion said, 'or gettin' *old*. Just gettin' up there, is all. Need glasses all the time now? That's not age; it's all the readin' you have to do, papers and letters and stuff. You oughta get combat pay in that job, workmen's comp; all the eyestrain they put you under.

'No wonder you miss all those putts, can't see a bar-tab when you're out with a lawyer, another hard day on the job – a drunk-driving charge against one of his clients got mislaid, *again*; nobody could find it all day. So they hadda continue the case, and this's the third time it's happened. Chances are if a couple of fifties show up tomorrow that complaint'll *never* turn up.'

'Ahh,' Hilliard said, 'you're not thinking, I trust, of that kind of career. Guys who do that kind of thing have been known to go to jail. Guys who backed them for their jobs get most embarrassed. Reporters and voters are uncharitable; sometimes they think when a pol's friend gets caught dirty, that means the pol's a crook too. Can be a real handicap, next election. *I* sure wouldn't like to confront it.'

'Nah, I haven't got the balls to be crooked,' Merrion said. 'And I wouldn't do it to you if I did. I owe you more'n you owe me. But lots of guys did have the balls, Dan, a lot of guys who never went away. "Ain't it strange," they would say, "how things just disappear around here. Must be I'm becomin' forgetful."

'But you don't even have to do that. You're perfectly honest, do fine. I know if I get it, people will say that to me, don't seem to have as much respect as they used to. "Pilin' up the pension; got it made in the shade; without workin' a day in your life. At least since you left Hilliard's office, I mean. 'Til then you worked your ass off, doin' the guy's job for him."

'That's the whole secret of this thing, I think. The keys is that first you make sure that's what you do: you grow old. Don't do any of this *dyin'* shit they got there, no matter what anyone says. That, as they say, is a grave mistake. And then when you got that part down pat, no dyin' or gettin' real sick, then you make sure to live *well*. Live *gracefully*, know what I mean? So you get old, but you're still lookin' good. Like it was no trouble at all. That's how I want to go out. Lookin' good, like life was a cinch.'

'Yeah,' Hilliard said. 'Well, you sound like you got it planned out pretty good. But there may be one or two other things we oughta think about here, geography and stuff. Which one of these little dukedoms 've you got in mind? Where you come from can be important. You should really come from a town in the district you want to go into, if that wouldn't be too much trouble. Don't *have* to, of course, it's not in the *statute*, but it really helps if you do. Especially if you're a young guy, gonna tie up the slot a long time if you live, as you will – who ever heard a clerk dyin' in office? What the hell's gonna kill him? Overwork? Clerks don't *die*; they *retire*. Hometown boys have an easier time of it, when they gotta go through the hoops, gettin' their names approved. But you're from that backwater there.'

'"Backwater," nothin',' Merrion said. 'Canterbury's perfectly all right by me. I never hid it, I come from Canterbury. I grew up in Canterbury. My mother and brother're still there. He's got plans to leave, but she hasn't. I moved but I didn't go far, next town over. I'll take the district court of the Canterbury Division any day of the week. They've got a slot open there, too. That's another thing I checked; they're a three-assistant court but for some reason only two 've been appointed. Third-assistant clerk is vacant, ripe for plucking.

'Canterbury District Court, yes indeed. Pretty town, always liked it. Nice'n quiet; sort of country. Not too many girls there, but I drive; I got a car, not what you'd call a really nice new car, like some guys I know of, but still, I got a car, and it runs.' Merrion drove a maroon 1962 Oldsmobile Cutlass convertible with a white leather interior, white top and white sidewall tires, a cream-puff he'd grabbed the day it came in as a Valley Ford trade-in on a '64 Thunderbird.

'And you're sure you'll be happy there?' Hilliard said. 'You won't be coming to me in a year or so, saying to me: "You got to get me out of this? I know I asked you, do this for me, but I'm *losing* my mind in that fucking place"?

'I think the world of you, Ambrose my friend, but I know you, and you like action. And you know me and how I hate going back to the well. Doing things over I've already done, 'cause the guy didn't know what he wanted.'

'Remember what you told me years ago, Danny boy?' Merrion said. 'I first started working for you and we'd won, you were an alderman. And the papers said right off that wasn't what you wanted, even though you just won it. Saying you were aiming to be mayor. And you said: "Everyone assumes the job you go after can't be the job that you want. Doesn't matter whether it's the one you go after first or the one that you go after next, when you've started moving up. They never think you've gotten where you want to go; some bigger job must be the one you want.

'"The trick's to always keep 'em guessing, say nothing and sit tight. Don't rule anything out. While *you* decide, for *your* self, which job you want, and why you want it. Then go into high gear, do anything you have to, to get that fucking job. And after you've got it, fake 'em right out of their shorts. Stay as smart as you always were. *Keep* that lovely job you wanted, and *finally* quit doing all the shitty stuff you had to do to get it, now you got away with it.'

'Well, that's what I'm doing here now. I thought about it, and this's the job that I want. I can do something with it. I'm not lookin' for one I'll have to wait and wait to open up, and then when it does fifty other guys want it. I want to get in line now. I get this job I'll move up and retire as the chief clerk. This job's got my name on it.

'And if you can get it,' Hilliard said, because he liked to tease Merrion, 'then will you have any immediate plans to make an honest woman out of Keller?'

'I'd have to get her calmed down some first,' Merrion said. 'That could be a tall assignment.'

'You'd have fun trying though,' Hilliard said. 'All right, I'm in. I'll go to work. But you've got some work to do yourself, on Larry Lane. Get to know him and get permission. Kiss his ass if you have to; hold your nose, close your eyes tight and do it. Too bad Roy and Arthur made the new district and built the new courthouse before my time. Be nice if I could just phone Chassy Spring up now, and call the debt. Technically it's his appointment, presiding judge and all, but Lane's the guy you'll work for. Chassy'll probably do it if I ask him, but not without Lane signing off on it. I hope you can work with the guy. I hear he can be a real bastard.'

9

Hilliard's seven-year-old dark-green Mercedes Benz 300D sedan was not in the lot east of the clubhouse when Merrion parked his Eldorado coupe – metallic maroon; white leather-grained-vinyl tiara roof, gold nameplates and badges, and narrow-striped whitewall tires. He was nowhere to be seen around the locker room or the putting-practice green. *Running true to form: late.*

For him it was like having an irregular pulse: He recognized it as abnormal but lived comfortably with it, so it was all right. Aware that his attitude angered people who had business with other people as well as with him, he considered their reactions excessive and did not become upset. 'When I'm late I know sometimes people get pissed off,' he said to Rev Peter Healy, a friendly priest and Grey Hills member, irritated by his tardy arrival at a communion breakfast. 'I cram a lot into my life, much as I possibly can. Things sometimes take longer than I expect. Therefore I become late getting to the next thing. Welcome to reality. I can't do much about it, unless I'm ready to start saying No a lot. In this case that would've meant I couldn't come to this affair. You would've been mad at me. Thus proving that in politics saying No to people more'n you have to isn't a wise practice; therefore I'm not ready. So what *you* have to do, dealing with me, is master delayed gratification. You may find that also solves that problem you've been having with premature ejaculation.'

'You could call, though, once in a while,' Mercy would tell him. 'I don't like it, but I knew you had this problem and married you anyway. I have to live with it. Other people don't think they do. They think the least you could do is call up. Let someone know you're going to be late. You're inconsiderate. All that matters is when *you're* ready to get around to doing something; never when somebody else is.

'I know,' she'd say, 'I know I know I know. I met Danny when he came to a freshman mixer my first year at Emmanuel. The next week we went out. A month later we were going steady. I haven't seen the beginning of a movie since I was eighteen years old. The only times I've seen the priest come out onto the altar've been the times I went to Mass by myself. When I go with Danny I'm lucky to hear the epistle; he thinks if you hear the gospel, you've been. I pretended I liked baseball when he was courting me. I didn't, but it's easy when the ballgames you see start in the fourth inning. You'd like me to break him of this habit? Where do *you* live – Fantasy Island?'

Legislative colleagues criticized him as difficult to work with, saying his habitual tardiness had a domino effect on their schedules, making others angry at them. Friendly TV reporters allocating regional and statewide air-time became unfriendly as he failed repeatedly to show up for interviews on time. Commentators who differed with him ideologically found sinister implications, delivering commentaries suggesting that his chronic lateness betrayed deep-seated disdain for ordinary people, scorn he expressed more subtly and harmfully in the liberal and elitist legislation he proposed and sponsored. One *Globe* columnist who was black printed his deduction that Hilliard's failure to show up for an interview was proof of racism, prompting a colleague who was white to respond the next day: 'On the contrary, it proves his deep commitment to equal rights. Dan Hilliard runs his life like a no-appointments barber-shop; rich or poor, or black or white, everybody waits.'

In the fall of 1972 Hilliard arrived an hour and twenty minutes late for a George McGovern fund-raising dinner at the Park Plaza. 'No one in Boston last night probably would've minded much that the Democratic majority leader in the Massachusetts House decided to dine fashionably late,' Tom Brokaw said on NBC, smiling broadly, 'if Mister Hilliard hadn't been the person scheduled on the program to introduce the presidential candidate.' Brokaw's mischievous glee – designating 'Hilliard's gaffe' as 'one of many low-lights' in the chaotic state of McGovern's presidential campaign, 'reeling across the country from fiasco to debacle' – suggested to Merrion and others familiar with Hilliard's urges that the anchorman knew very well what had deflected Dan from the performance of his duty.

Fiercely chastising Hilliard by phone, as by then he had done many times face to face, Merrion said: 'Brokaw thinks you were off getting *laid*, for Christ sake. As I also think, and I'm not the only one, either. I think we're gonna have to get you operated on. Get you gelded like they have to do to horny race horses, get their minds off their cocks and make 'em behave, keep their minds on their business. You're makin' yourself into a laughing stock. Wreckin' your career with your dick. Pissin' yourself. I'm your friend and I'm fuckin' ashamed of you.'

Hilliard sounded miserably contrite. 'Mercy's mad at me, too,' he said.

'She oughta be,' Merrion said. 'Mercy's an intelligent woman. I'd be surprised if she wasn't. You think she believes you spend four nights a week in your Boston apartment watchin' TV and tattin' doilies? If she does, it's because she won't face the truth. And if that's it, it won't be for much longer – you're makin' it too hard for her. You're embarrassin' your friends, Dan, but you're making her life Hell on earth. Everyone laughin' at you. Brokaw, for Christ sake on national TV; he probably knows her name, for Christ sake, who the broad is you're fooling around with. And your office didn't help any either, some beauty in there tellin' the *Globe* "something suddenly came up." And if you try to tell me the *Globe* guy made it up, I'll tell you he should get an award. Next thing'll be Johnny Carson tellin' jokes about you inna monologue.'

Hilliard demurred, very feebly, saying Brokaw wouldn't have any way to find out the name of the woman 'I've been seeing.'

'Oh put a lid on it,' Merrion said, 'give me a load of that shit. What you're doing isn't "seeing." It's "fucking," "gettin' blow-jobs." Inna second place, everyone knows anything knows it's Stacy, and everyone who doesn't's going to pretty soon. Meat that fresh don't keep.'

Stacy Hawkes was a twenty-nine-year-old woman who preferred to work chiefly in the newsroom as a producer for the CBS Boston affiliate; a former Miss Connecticut during her junior year majoring in history at Yale, she had started out in the business as on-air talent. She said she did her occasional award-winning special reports on state politics to keep her teeth sharp and 'make sure I can still do it.'

Political reporters at competing Boston stations bitterly alleged she gained inside information by means that the males among them lacked. The females said they would not work the way she did.

Late for golf with Merrion that August Saturday, nearly a quarter-century later, Hilliard had logged more than ten years in what he called his 'public-educator suit' since his retirement in 1984 from what he described as 'the open and gross practice of politics.' *Hasn't changed him a bit.*

Merrion had not bothered checking the sign-up sheet on the wall of the pro shack to see whether they were still playing by themselves at 11:30 or if Dan, without telling him, had paired them with another twosome scheduled to start later. He sat contentedly in one of the puffy-cushioned light blue PVC-pipe armchairs in the dappled shade on the blue-grey flagstone terrace overlooking the first tee, at indolent peace with the summer-Saturday universe around him and all but one of the people within his field of vision in it. A mug of creamed hazlenut coffee cooled on the round white PVC table in front of him.

Over it he watched Julian Sanderson, Ralph Lauren golf ensemble artfully disheveled, set skillfully to work on the three new members. Not that he lacked talent; what he would be doing, lightly adjusting grips and forearms; tucking left elbows in; widening and narrowing; opening and closing stances, turning torsos ever so slightly – was overloading their minds, so that before they hit a ball that morning they would be focused upon doing their very best to hit it as he said.

During such engagements Julian talked only about golf and how to hit golf shots, the only subject – except perhaps, sex – he was really competent to talk about at all. It was therefore likely that his clients might play better golf that Saturday than they had on recent outings that had caused them to hire Julian – to teach what Dan Hilliard was fond of reminding himself and everyone within earshot when he put a tee-shot into the rough 'isn't about how to build a fucking rocket-ship to go to fucking Mars, just how to hit a fucking golf ball that sits perfectly still and says "Hit me."'

This would be a development so pleasant they would overlook its temporary nature and not only give Julian all the credit but kick in their respective shares of the one-hundred-fifty-dollar purse/fee he would be charging for playing a round with them. Merrion could see the basic fairness of this exchange, but he did not approve of it.

He did not like Julian. He believed that was not because Julian was good-looking. Merrion conceded the utility of good looks. Hilliard said that people often underestimated him because 'the choir-boy curls,' now white but still thick, 'and the cherub's face make 'em doubt you'd even *think* of pulling a fast one on them. So you can do it now and then, when you think you've got a good reason, and get away with it.'

Merrion regarded Julian as a nuisance. He thought that if Julian were to disappear suddenly it would be a good thing. Forty-two or so, a tanned and trim six-footer chiseled blond and handsome, with an athlete's languid ease of movement, Julian had six or seven years before accepted reality he'd resisted a long time: Contrary to his expectations, after much practice and success in prep school and college competitions he had turned out to be a considerably-better-than-average golfer.

Good enough to outclass all the other players in their age-group at their own clubs, such golfers can be worthy opponents in regional and state-wide pro-am tournaments. All they have to do is set their minds to it; short-change their responsibilities at work; slough their family obligations; get plenty of rest; go easy on the cocktails and watch what they eat – behave, in other words, as Dan Hilliard said, though only for a while, like people who get it into their heads to become candidates for major statewide office or national recognition – and then follow that regimen for two months every year. To be that good can be a dismal fate.

'Horseshoes and hand-grenades're the only sports where close is good enough,' Hilliard said, when he missed short putts. On their very best days they are not quite good enough to compete successfully on the Professional Golf Association circuit. For nearly eight years Julian had time after time come not-quite-close-enough to making second-round cuts at second-rate pro tournaments up and down the east coast. It depressed him to describe his travels to naive visiting players who assumed they must have seen this man, said to have been a touring pro, in the company of Greg Norman, Tom Kite and Chi-Chi Rodriguez hitting long drives, lofting beautiful wedge shots and sinking long putts across the screens of their game-room projection TVs. 'Oh, well, like the Nike Tour, out of Sawgrass?' Merrion had heard him say, elaborately nonchalant.

Having heard of the shoe manufacturer but not the golf circuit they'd look blank, saying, 'Gee, must've missed that one.' Their ignorance irked and embarrassed him; it did not surprise him.

Explaining, he would omit the fact that the Nike was a southern mini-tour, seldom televised beyond the reception area of the local cable-TV outlet with its headquarters office in the shopping mall on Route 1, or viewed anywhere except in the bar of the host country club. He also passed over the fact that 1993 had been his last year of touring, and left out the $100 entry fee he'd had to pay each of the fourteen Monday mornings that he'd tried to qualify for one of those 54-hole events. He passed over the additional $150 he paid to compete in the nine in which he'd made the cut, having managed to finish among the top eight players during one of those gut-checking Mondays. He did not mention what it had cost him – meaning: his father, Haskell; his friends knew him as Heck – to live downright crummy during his touring days, paying eighty-five or ninety bucks a night to scuff along in roach-infested motels at the height of the tourist season, the alternative being to bunk unwashed in his car. He sloughed all the dreariness with a sigh and admitted he hadn't really done 'all that well, my last year – only won about seven thousand or so,' sixty-eight-fifty, actually, if what Merrion had heard from Heck was the truth – in the fifteen seedy weeks he'd spent in Florida between New Year's and the end of March, the second-best season he'd had.

'Put it this way,' Julian would say, dolloping his rue with the lop-sided smile of charming chagrin that attracted females, 'I didn't play enough weekends.' The third and fourth rounds Saturdays and Sundays followed the second reduction of the fields after the second rounds played Fridays. Golfers ranked below the top 64, 96 or 128 were excluded. Those making the cut were paired up to compete for the prizes on Sunday.

When Julian was very young and still in school he'd been startled to discover, accidentally, the wonderfully seductive effect self-deprecation had on women. Gradually he'd come to understand that it would nearly always work, forever luring a gratifyingly regular number of solicitous women to tend gently to his needs. 'Lost boys,' he confided to male friends and occasionally to tolerant female friends as well, usually when he'd had too much to drink, 'get mucho ass.' Now, Merrion had observed, the angels ministering to Julian were of a certain age, but they still showed the old eagerness, flaring their nostrils and prancing around on the grass, their appetites and skills perhaps now even sharpened by practice, slightly improved by nostalgia.

Merrion recognized what he felt as envy, another reason for resenting Julian. In a few years, when the women in their early forties had finished with Julian, they'd be about the right age for him. But by then he'd have become a little too old to interest *them* – in the tinkling drinks, light conversations and ninety-minute dinners understood by both participants as preliminary to vigorous and protracted sexual intercourse. But then again, perhaps, on a cold winter's night, wind blowing past the window . . . *JFK? Sure, I knew him a little. One night down in West Virginia, back in Sixty, driving poor Humphrey nuts and . . .*'

'Sklaffed too many off the tees in sudden-death,' Julian said in the bar now, in the evenings to the visitors buying drinks, explaining his withdrawal from the tour. The kid was good in the clinches, no matter how he'd been out on the courses. And he looked as though he'd found a way to make up nicely for that deficit; for a player unsuccessfully seeking small jackpots – the best player late on a mini-tour late Sunday afternoon during Julian's years had usually pocketed about twenty thousand dollars.

But he had an impressive collection of multi-dialed watches, and heavy gold chains for all occasions.

'Birthday presents, he tells me,' Heck Sanderson said over beers one hot still late afternoon in the dark green shade. Merrion found that unconvincing but kept quiet, seeing Heck, though disapproving, believed it. 'Lots of people like him, I guess. Women-type people. Like to give him things. Don't like to live with him long, though, seem interested in having babies with him.' Julian was an only child. Heck had gone beyond the age at which his contemporaries had reported births of grandchildren.

Julian had been married and divorced once during the transition from his twenties to his thirties, but while he had had two or three steady ladies since then, the last had left him before George Bush lost in '92. Now he lived alone in a two-bedroom condo Heck had bought for him in a spartan half-shingled half-timbered white stucco housing complex on Route 2 west of Amherst. Most of the other tenants were young faculty from UMass. and Amherst College. Returning late at night in his monster-tired 4X4 Ford Bronco, he often had to clear his parking space of neon-pink and green plastic Big Wheels and small bicycles with training wheels. When cold weather closed the Grey Hills course for the winter, he commuted north six afternoons a week in the overcast darkness to tend bar at the Molly Stark Tavern, a rich skiers' hangout in southern Vermont. The previous May when he returned to Grey Hills to resume his summer career, he seemed to have what Merrion thought was a great deal of money for a barkeep, even a good one, generously tipped, but at least the job got him off Heck's list of dependents; Merrion kept his mouth shut.

Julian had played well enough and worked hard enough in the PGA Apprentice Program during the mid-through-late-Seventies to earn the card that qualified him to enter pro tournaments for the coming year, when he was twenty-four. He was coming off a record of having finished among the top ten in nineteen New England and Canadian pro-ams. According to Heck, Julian partially financed his first year on the road with $6,000 won from men whose professional success had made them overconfident. Mistakenly believing they'd become good golfers, too, they thought because Julian was a transient and they were scratch players on familiar home turf, they were each fifty or a hundred bucks a round better than he was. Because Julian was careful not to beat them too badly, many tried several times to disprove what was plainly so. Heck cheerfully provided the other $19,000.

From the outset Heck had agreed to provide $15,000. The additional $4,000 or so had gone to cover unexpected expenses: among them four new tires for Julian's Bronco, several disappointing pot-limit poker hands he'd drawn sitting in on a game down in Augusta, Georgia, the week before the Masters, and a flirtation with cocaine that for a few years scared the hell out of him – explaining his need for more money to Heck, he camouflaged it as a costly lesson learned in a high-stakes eight-ball showdown he'd lost in a billiard room in Baton Rouge. Heck guilelessly repeated that story to his friends.

Merrion had seen Julian playing poker and bridge at Grey Hills with some of the better-off but denser members. He had no trouble believing Julian had gotten hoovered in Augusta. Never having known Julian to wear out the felt practicing combinations in the hush of the mahogany billiard room at Grey Hills, Merrion disbelieved Heck's second-hand story of the embarrassment in Louisiana, but he didn't scoff.

When Steve Brody's kid, Mark, claimed to've seen Julian once or twice doing business with the dealer in Holyoke who had supplied Mark for about a year, until the night State Police dropped in on a buy, Merrion was not wholly convinced by Mark's story. He had no trouble believing Julian used coke, but doubted he'd use a local supplier – and if he had, it was probably Steve's rotten kid. Merrion believed Mark was setting the stage to retail Julian to the cops unless his father's clout with Merrion, earned by faithfully looking out for Larry Lane, was enough to save his ass from hard time. That made Merrion apprehensive that the time'd finally come when he'd have to say something to Heck, no matter how much it hurt him. After Mark's diversion into rehab, he braced the kid for the truth about Julian. Mark rubbed his red eyes, snuffled his corroded nose and said Heck's kid had been clean for a year. Merrion hadn't told Heck.

Heck Sanderson hadn't needed that. He owned the Mohawk

Printing Company on Route 2, a couple miles east of Greenfield. He claimed it was grossing $6.3 million a year, nearly double the amount it had been making in 1968 when his father left it to him, when Heck was thirty-seven. But for an unadventurous young man from a settled, comfortable family, prepared at Deerfield for Syracuse, a family tradition; excused by a heart murmur from military service; married to a childhood sweetheart from the family's Unitarian congregation in the town where he'd grown up, Heck had taken his share of punches.

His father, Haskell senior, had been a man of indisputably upright character, moral and honest to a fault. The fault was that he was a domineering, overbearing, parsimonious, 'general-purpose son of a bitch.' Heck had had to subordinate his own mind and spirit all the years he'd had to work for Haskell, grimly deferring to decisions that prevented the business from growing. When Haskell died of a stealthy brain tumor undetected until three weeks before he died – 'he got a headache so all-fired bad he was actually forced to spend the time and the money to go see a doctor' – Heck had managed the ceremonies of committal with spare, bleak, formal dignity, and that was all.

Having come into the life that his brains and hard work had earned for him, enjoying a few reasonable luxuries like membership in Grey Hills and a ski lodge in Vermont – 'if the old bastard wasn't dead, what I've spent would've killed him' – Heck's wife, Lisa, died at the age of forty-one.

She was felled by a cerebral aneurysm while standing in her back yard one sunny April morning, feeling very good indeed, a dark blue headband on her dirty-blonde hair, slim in her starched pale-blue man-tailored shirt, stone-washed blue jeans and white sneakers, her feet apart and her arms folded under her breasts, smiling in her certainty that she fairly sparkled.

When it hit she was talking animatedly with a handsome young nurseryman named Nick Hardigrew. He had blue eyes and wavy black hair, white teeth and the well-muscled body of a lifelong athlete, former lifeguard and outdoor worker. He had driven up from Suffield, Connecticut at her invitation to look at the property and prepare a bid on re-landscaping it, planting dogwood, cherry, silver birch and red maple trees. A certified arborist, he had earned his bachelor's degree in arboriculture at the University of Massachusetts in his mid-twenties after two years in the infantry. He had enlisted out of high school planning on a military career, but after washing out of airborne school at Fort Benning, had taken an honorable discharge. He had learned cardiopulmonary resuscitation so that he could support his family by moonlighting as an EMT while building his business.

When Lisa Sanderson collapsed he kept his head and used all of his skills on her, but nothing worked. When the Northampton Rescue Unit arrived he told the driver: 'That oxygen's not going to work. There was nothing I could do, that anyone could've done. She was dead before she hit the ground.'

She had died happy. When the stroke slammed her on her back, brain-dead, she'd been having considerable but very pleasant difficulty keeping her mind on trees and bushes. Having met him, she'd become convinced that her friend Nina Ealing from Longmeadow, another stylish lady on the board of trustees of the Springfield Symphony, was definitely having an affair with this young man. She had begun to suspect it when Nina blushed and became flustered, fluttering her hands as she *gushed* her recommendation of Hardigrew's work. And she'd become sure that he was now coming on to her, which she found charming and exciting. She had been consequently quite distracted by a fantasy in which she'd already given him the landscaping job in order to have sex with him on the green-and-white chaise lounge in the sunporch on some hot afternoon when he was sweaty and had removed his faded black tee-shirt and used it to mop his hairy chest, she having lightly and casually invited him inside with an offer of beer. She had also definitely resolved – simultaneously, it seemed, and perhaps more realistically, but ruling nothing out – to ask Nina wickedly over a drink after the next board meeting whether Hardigrew's bedding skills were limited to gardening. Then her happy world and her fine girlish plans and all her laughing dreams disappeared into the last darkness.

Devastated, Heck nonetheless seemed within a year or so to have recovered his equilibrium. The following winter, 1973–74, he'd remarried – quite suddenly, it'd seemed to his friends if not to his only child, then about twenty. Julian hadn't been noticeably affected by his mother's death. 'Hardly seemed to notice it,' Hilliard'd said to Merrion when Heck was not around. 'Not that it didn't *inconvenience* him; I heard him tell someone that the reason he didn't play in the Berkshire member-guest was the first round was the day of her funeral. But nothing serious.'

At first the new marriage seemed happy. The second wife was young enough but not *too* young, and that was good, such balances being important when a new woman moves into a small and settled community as the spouse of a prominent member. Not that anyone at the club was ever really sure of her exact age; she looked to be in her late thirties, a copper-haired and very pretty divorcée he'd met skiing, up at Killington. Some thought it ominous that while her name was Alicia, Heck called her 'Lisha' in their hearing, too close to his first wife's name to make them feel right about it – 'Lisa Two,' they called her, behind her back; suggesting Heck'd seized upon her mindlessly, as a replica.

In retrospect there seemed to have been no obvious reason why it shouldn't've worked out, anything that should have alerted Heck's friends to what was going to happen so they could have been ready to help him get through it. She was certainly pleasant enough when you met her, and by the look of it she seemed to be at least fairly well-off herself, so she didn't appear to be after Heck's money. She even took up golf, right after they were married. But then before anyone had really gotten to know her, Heck the following July put it around quietly that they'd been divorced and she'd moved back to Michigan, less than a year after they'd been married. He seemed to take it pretty well without the help of friends, though: 'Just one of those things, I guess,' was about all he had to say about it. 'I guess some things you just never know 'til you've tried 'em, and then when you find out they weren't what you thought you don't want them around anymore. That's the way it goes, some times; just the way it goes.' The consensus was that it couldn't've been Heck's fault – his business remained intact.

Heck made no secret of the pride he took in what he'd done to expand the firm, building much of it on major printing contracts he'd gone after and won from the Commonwealth. A year or so after Haskell's death, Heck had come down to Holyoke one Friday night with Carl Kuiper, a major electrical contractor from Deerfield. Carl was a big beefy man with a big stomach he shelved on the waistband of his trousers. He complained that he gained weight despite considerable exercise, snow-shoeing cross-country in the winter; in the summer rowing himself the 2.5 miles from his big stone house on Hampton Pond to his favorite fishing cove. His face was deeply red, partly from rosacea, a skin condition that his doctor said was aggravated in his case by reckless exposure to direct sunlight. 'But I always wear a hat,' he said, disregarding sunlight reflecting from the snow and water. His doctor also said the rosacea meant he should avoid drinking alcohol. 'Ahh, all I ever drink is beer,' he said. 'I sweat a lot when I work out and get dehyderated. I threw up and fainted once, I let that happen to me. Not going to again.'

Kuiper's place of business was outside Hilliard's district, but his voting residence was in it and he got a good amount of business from construction companies who had big and important projects in the region. He got more from the Commonwealth, and he considered those enough reason to warrant generous support of Dan Hilliard. He was one of the stalwarts, with a regular place at the big oak table for the 'dancing-school meetings' Hilliard and Merrion held in the second-floor office on High Street. Carl introduced Heck as a kindred spirit with some darned good ideas to expand the regional industrial base. Heck always kept his checkbook with him, too, Carl said.

In due course Hilliard led Heck by the hand through the whole rigamarole of negotiating State contracts, as he made a practice of doing with many businessmen he knew from his district and nearby – anywhere in the Commonwealth, really, if they came to him asking for help, because in those days he was keeping open the possibility he might want to run for Congress some day. Under Hilliard's guidance Heck tuned his pitch to the purchasing agent in the office of the Secretary of State and the Governor's commissioner of Administration and Finance. He emphasized the ripple effect that expanded light industry offering steady employment for skilled workers would have on the economy of the area, disproportionately and dangerously dependent on agriculture ever since the mills along the Connecticut River shut down.

Hilliard said he meant to make that the theme of his career. 'The way I see it, taking care of the voters in the district means working to improve their future,' he liked to say in the Grange and Legion halls out in the dark hills after summer had receded again, the fairs were over and the nights were starting to get cold. 'The future of the men and women who get up every morning and go out and do a job, come home tired at night, hoping they've done something that day that'll mean a better future for themselves and their children. A better day tomorrow, and then an even better one, the day after that. To do that we have to bring industry back here. That's the only way, and so I'm determined to do it, make this place prosper again.'

'What an utter and absolute load of shit that was,' Merrion said one night in Hampton Pond, fatigued and hungry but still an hour away from a drink and a meal, sliding into the driver's seat of Hilliard's car – he or another worker always drove between campaign stops, so that if the candidate's car hit someone or something, no one would be able to suggest it had happened because the candidate had been speeding to his next event, negligent or drunk. It had been maybe the second or the third time Merrion'd heard him unload that particular extravagance on an audience, but the first time he'd actually listened to it. Hilliard, also dead-tired, beat, had confounded him by snarling back: 'That "utter shit" I happen to *believe*, you fuckin' asshole. Every last fuckin' word of it. Don't you *ever* sneer at it again.'

Merrion had subsided, knowing Hilliard did not believe it, but *wanted* to, because after trying it out a few times, he knew it worked. '*Sings*,' was the way he put it: 'That stuff just sings to them.'

'The way I look at politics, and how it oughta work,' Hilliard would say thoughtfully when the mood washed over him again and he felt the time evangelically right, embellishing the theme that sang, 'it seems to me that it should be the man who gets the job in Boston should remember where he comes from, and he should make sure that when he gets there and while he's serving you down there, he's still listening to what's being said out here. Still listenin', and still talkin' to the people, the people who said to him: 'All right, now we've heard what you said, and we're sending you to Boston. Now let's see what you can do.'

'So here I am now and I'm sayin': "All right, now what else can I do? How can your government help you? And: How can you help, what can you do, to help me make our government work better?" See, we're just gettin' started here. We're not close to finished yet.'

'But Jesus Mary Joseph,' Hilliard would say, when they were in the office by themselves with no listeners around, when it was someone like Heck Sanderson he was teaching to dance, 'it's awful hard helping a black Protestant bastard like this. Haskell Senior was a Know Nothing. My father told me that. No Irish in *his* shop. "No Irish Need Apply." His son takes after him, too. I'd bet on it. You swallow that stuff with your mother's milk, you grow up a bigot.

'What we've always got to remember with Heck is we can't trust the son of a bitch. He didn't come down here with Kuiper that night because his heart'd leaped up when he heard me. He came down because Carl convinced him I'd be a good man for him to support, because if he did, he'd make money. And if somebody else comes along tomorrow afternoon and makes him a better offer to dump me and go with them, Heck'll drop me like hot iron. He's got harsh words to say about his old man, now that the old boy's in the ground, probably with a stake in his heart, but Heck'd join the Klan himself if they gave him sound business reasons.'

But Hilliard had done his best for Sanderson just the same and his efforts worked. Heck increased his financial backing. He described himself as 'one of Dan's oldest angels.' Publicly he said no one was happier than he was when the new campaign finance law went through, limiting each contributor to a maximum donation of $1,000 per candidate per primary and per general election campaign, 'Saved me a ton of money.' In practice Heck saw to it that each of his top ten or twelve employees – and their spouses – maxed out in all of Dan Hilliard's campaigns after that, at no cost to themselves. 'All open, perfectly above board. My shysters looked up the law. Perfectly legal, give my fine employees a nice raise if I want, so I did. What they do with it's their business. This *is* still America, right?'

In the same way, Heck at first took considerable pleasure as well not only in having a son good enough to play on the PGA tour but in financing him while he assaulted it. When asked, Heck said happily it had been worth the money. 'I'm glad he's got that talent. Kid's got absolutely no head for business. Don't want him around it. Golf keeps him off the street.' He confided to Rob Lewis – the funeral director in Amherst preferred by Protestants; a member of the state Republican committee who'd become Heck's 'best friend in the whole wide world, now that Carl Kuiper's dead' – that he'd bragged a little about Julian elsewhere that year he'd been married to Lisha. He said he'd mentioned his 'son on the pro tour' to other couples they'd met playing Indian Wells in Southern California and Dorado in Puerto Rico. Heck said he thought they'd envied him; at least the men did, anyway. When Rob said he thought they probably did, Heck repeated the story to Hilliard and Merrion the next time the four of them played, and they agreed with Rob.

After Heck and Rob had gone home Hilliard and Merrion had lingered over their beers and looked at each other, and finally Hilliard shook his head and snickered, saying: 'What a couple old whores we've become. "A little light hookin'? No problem." Get so you can do it 'thout thinkin' about it. Someone says "*bitch*," and you pucker up.' Merrion said heavily: '"*Sure* they did, Heck; they really envied you. Anything you say." Easy for them; they never met the kid.'

For six years Julian had been one of two assistant pros at Grey Hills, an independent contractor's slot that paid him $8,500 for part-time duties that were not clearly defined. It wasn't that he didn't have the credentials. He'd passed the playing and the membership interview, attended the PGA business schools and passed the written tests. His four years at Syracuse – 'majoring in pussy, best I can figure,' Heck'd said resentfully one night, after seeing some of the kid's grades – had given him eight of the thirty-six working credits that the PGA required. The senior pro at Grey Hills, Bolo Cormier, obliging as always, had signed off on the other twenty-eight for the work done around the club. Julian was qualified, but it was hard to see what he did.

He was supposed to be on duty in the pro shop between 7:30 and 10:30 A.M. Monday through Thursday, but often he closed the shop just before 9:30, hanging a sign in the door promising it would reopen at 11 – which it did unless the other assistant, Claire Hoxey, came in late for some reason or other. According to Hilliard, wearily serving out his third rotation of three years on the executive committee, Cormier had been repeatedly invited to explain exactly why it was Julian was worth his pay and what he did to earn it.

'Bolo has a little trouble with that,' Hilliard told Merrion. 'He says he's "real good" coaching juniors, on the ladders. Even though they generally lose. And even though most of us, every time we see the kids out practicing, it's usually Claire teaching them.

'Bolo says that Julian's also "real good" about teaching new members and members' spouses who're taking up the game,' Hilliard said. 'He can't actually *name* any duffers Julian's transformed into eight- or nine-handicappers, but he's sure it must've happened. Some time. Some day. To someone.

'I think Bolo's memory may be going. We may want to keep an eye on him. He could get lost out there in the bushes, one of those fenny dells out on the back nine where Bobby Clark always hooks a shot when he wants to get out of sight for a few minutes and have himself a drink from that flask of Bombay eighty-proof snakebite medicine none of us know he's got in the ball-pocket of his bag. Bolo ever got confused out there around nightfall, he could wander around until morning, die of exposure, hypothermia, we got a sudden cold snap or he fell into the pool, or one of the creeks. Wild animals out there too, you know; don't believe all this stuff they're always telling you about how all the catamounts an' pumas're extinct. They're still out there, waitin' for Bolo, gettin' ready to *pounce* on him, *WOOF*, turn him into quick nourishing snacks.

'Then again, of course, it could be all's the matter with Bolo is that he's got trouble remembering things that never happened. Could even be that's the cause of his trouble. I think a lot of us would have trouble, someone was to put us under a lot of pressure, situation it began to look like it could be important to remember several things, all at once, in detail, never happened at all. Test a fella's memory, you know?

'And I think – just throwing this out, not really saying it *happened* – but I think maybe that's what Bolo might be trying to do here, where Julian's performance is concerned. Remember things that never happened. That would be a very hard job. I'm not even sure *I* could do it.

'Because Bolo likes Heck, as we all do. He knows Heck's always been a bulwark for him when it's come to backing Bolo, like giving him more money. Naturally he's grateful, thinks highly of Heck. I myself personally remember several times that Bolo's gone after a salary increase, and a number of rude people on the board've gone so far as to suggest that maybe he isn't worth half what we're paying him now, let alone a nice raise on top of it. Heck's always stood *up* for Bolo, said: "No-no, no-no, no, *how* can you say such a thing? Bolo's salt of the earth, a gem of rare price; he deserves a big raise in pay."

'So Bolo – how would you put it here, huh? Bolo's "reluctant"? He certainly is; Bolo doesn't want to say anything mean about Heck's kid that might get back to Heck and hurt his feelings, maybe make him madder'n a hornet at Bolo. Who he's always taken such good care of around here with other people's money. So he sells him down the river, next time someone tries to tie the can to Bolo. That might explain this trouble Bolo has, every time we ask him what the fuck it is that Julian does.'

Dan Hilliard came up behind Merrion's chair and clasped his hands on Merrion's shoulders as Julian finished tinkering with the swings of each of his three pupils and one by one began to settle them into their stances on the tee. The first hole at Grey Hills is a par 4, 412 yards, nearly straightaway down an undulating fairway. The breeze was from the southwest, left to right, tending to push the ball toward the rough bordering the southerly bank of the Wolf River. Three bunkers surround the shaded, slightly elevated green. Julian stepped back. After a good deal of clubhead-waggling his first client hit a low drive that stayed under the breeze but hooked a little toward the low rough about 165 yards out. He stepped back and sighed theatrically, as though he had expected at least 210. Julian said: 'That'll play, Pete, that'll play. That's the worst shot you hit today, you'll go home a happy man.'

'Whatcha doin', Pilgrim?' Hilliard growled in his John Wayne imitation. 'Plottin' revenge on your friend for bein' *late?*'

'Contemplating what has to be one of the more baffling ideas of western man,' Merrion said in a low voice, so that it would not carry to the tee, 'Julian Sanderson in his colorful native garb. I spent the morning, good chunk of it, anyway, with a woman who's a borderline defective. Her I understand, why she may be needed in this universe of ours. Julian I don't.'

Between the beginning of 1967 and the middle of 1968, Merrion would not have told Hilliard about his morning chat with Janet LeClerc, not because Hilliard would not have been interested in what had happened to her, and what had brought it about, but because during that period he and Mercy had been coming sometimes violently to terms with the fact of Donna's severe mental retardation, and there had been no way to mention the subject around either one of them that was neutral enough so that it wouldn't freshen their pain. In July of 1968 the fear of hurting them had started slowly to subside.

Dan and Mercy had shown up for what turned out to be the last season at Swift's Beach. Merrion and Sunny had tidied the house and put all their gear into his Olds. Emily and Timmy were with Danny and Mercy. Donna was not. They were all subdued. Mercy took the kids quickly into the house before Sunny or Merrion could say much more than Hi. When the screen door on the porch had flapped slowly shut behind them and Dan was sure that they were out of earshot, he told Merrion and Sunny that he and Mercy had finally decided to do what both of them knew had to be done. He said that preceding Wednesday he had made a call to a man who owed him his job and continuing funding for several programs under his management at the State Department of Mental Health.

Hilliard took a deep breath and said he had told the man that regardless of how many there were on the waiting list for beds in the Walter Fernald School, or how important their names were, he and his wife would bring their daughter, Donna, almost four years, to the school on Saturday morning and say good-bye to her. He told the man it had to be that way; that he'd managed once more to make Mercy see it had to be done. The burden of having the child around and trying to take care of her was going to kill her if it didn't end their marriage first. He told the man he couldn't take a chance on waiting for their turn to come, lest she change her mind again. 'And Malcolm did the right thing,' Hilliard said.

That morning they had risen early, having packed the car the night before with what they would need on their vacation at the beach and all the things that Mercy, weeping, thought Donna might need to have around her at the Fernald School for the next several years that would most likely be the rest of her life. Hilliard had backed Mercy's green Ford Country Squire station wagon out of the garage and down the driveway of their home on Ridge Street in Holyoke; none of them spoke. He and Mercy sat stiffly in the front with their eyes filled with tears and Timmy and Emily sat silent in the back seat, each of them touching Donna wide-eyed in her car seat in the middle, knowing Donna wasn't 'right,' because they could see that, but also fearfully wondering if their daddy and their mummy some day would decide to do this to them. They had driven down to the Massachusetts Turnpike and taken that east to Route 128 in Weston, and from there they had driven north to Waltham to the state home for retarded children. 'And then we left her there,' Hilliard said.

'It wasn't quite the same as when I was a kid and we were going to see my grandmother up in Lewiston and we had to leave Comet at the kennel because the old bat hated dogs. But it wasn't all that different either.' He said it with his hands jammed in his chino pockets, his voice grinding flat and rough and low, his face desolate except for the tears in his eyes. 'For one thing, even though Comet didn't know it, in a couple weeks or so we were coming back for him. We at least knew we weren't abandoning him.

'And for another thing Comet was a *dog*, not my *kid*.' He sobbed and shook his head. Merrion went to him and put his hands on Hilliard's shoulders. Sunny inhaled sharply, spun around on the scrub and sand underfoot and started toward the house. Hilliard put his head down and shook it several times and wept. 'Isn't quite the same thing, I find,' he said. 'I wouldn't be a bit surprised if none of us ever really get over what we did today, no matter how many years we may be lucky enough or unlucky enough to have left to live, depending on how you look at it.'

Merrion hugged him and patted his back and crooned: 'Danny, Danny, Danny; oh my poor friend Danny.' Hilliard said he thought the best that he and Mercy could hope to do was to make it through what was left of the day before bedtime for the other two kids, 'who now for the rest of their lives of course will always wonder if there was something they could have done or should have done or tried to do that would've stopped their wicked parents from doing what they did to Donna, whether they want to or not.'

Merrion asked him if he wanted him and Sunny to get a room at a motel and stay up with them that night. Hilliard shook his head again and said No, taking out his handkerchief and wiping his face. He said: 'We have to get used to this. There's no way to do advance-work on sorrow. We have to get used to it ourselves, by ourselves. Might as well get started now.' He said he thought that it was likely that he and Mercy would get at least slightly drunk and go to bed and hope to Jesus they could sleep, but that at least they'd know in the morning it would no longer be the day that they had gone and done the thing, but the day that it would be beginning to recede into the past. 'One way or the other.'

'I spent this morning chatting with the borderline lady, part of my day-job,' Merrion said. 'A couple or three years ago the people who own the Burger Quik out on the pike, plus, I dunno, seven or eight others in the area, they dreamed up entirely on their own this very decent policy of reserving all the jobs they could for people like my kind-of-confused lady. Girl. People who are not super-bright but can learn to take directions, if there aren't too many of them and they aren't too complicated. That way they become reliable employees. This is a very fine thing for a person to be, no matter how bright he is. Doing simple but *real* jobs, not make-work which they spot *instantly* and know right off they're being patronized. Out of those basic jobs they can make something that looks like a real life for themselves – because that's what it actually is. They wipe off tables high-fliers like you and me slobber all over and then walk away from, never cleaning up the mess we made. They pick up trays and stack them and collect trash and throw it in the bins. And then they empty the bins and heave all the rubbish in the Dumpster out in back and soak a mop in clean hot water and mop the dirt up off the floor that we fine citizens tracked in. Not particularly *stimulating* work, but good honest toil all the same.

'Nobody *made* the franchise people do this. They had this bright idea all by themselves. It looks a hell of a lot like something you and I would've been real proud of, we'd been smart enough to think of it back when you were still up on the Hill showin' off. We could've passed a law to *make* 'em do it, hire the retards, ram it up their ass – or else we're gonna take their common victualler's licenses away and put 'em outta business. Or bribe 'em with a fat tax-break to do it. We'd've been real pleased with ourselves, if we'd've thought of that. But we didn't. Neither did any of the other public-spirited geniuses we hung around with all the time. This was purely a private idea. "Initiatives," I think they're called now.

'Unfortunately, the law of unintended consequences turns out to apply to private good ideas just like public ones. Full fucking force and effect. This humanitarian idea had something nasty in it nobody noticed. The franchise people were making these retards into targets for the predators. Someone's going to tell them if they're smart enough to do this donkey work and get four or five bucks an hour plus the benefits our nice franchise people also throw in, then it stands to reason they can also swindle people.

'Because that's the kind of company they start to keep, not meaning to, of course, as soon as they start getting actual paychecks. They may be small, but those paychecks represent *money*, and money draws serpents. First to see if they can get those checks away from those hardworking people who aren't terribly bright, and then see if they can't think up some way to use them, *manipulate* them, get even larger sums of money from other people. Some other innocent person who'd be on his guard against a crook, but who'd never suspect a poor retard.

'This case the predator snared first another lady who's also not stunningly bright and who also happens to work out on the pike at the Burger Quik with the lady who's now under my supervision. The plan was to cheat an old lady in Canterbury out of her savings account. The old con game; what Miss Iscariot did to make a living before she got distracted and found herself pregnant with Judas. The drill was that the two retarded ladies pretend that they found a bag of money which would be a flash-wad, couple fives and some ones and a wad of newspapers cut up the same size. They'd show the wad to the lady that the snake selected as the sucker. She was then supposed to agree to demonstrate that they could trust her to take the bag of money to the bank – which they're afraid to do themselves because they're not very bright and the banker might cheat *them*, and that's why they need her. But she has to prove they can trust her. This she's supposed to do by going to the bank and withdrawing all *her* money from it and then giving it to them to hold while she takes the paper bag to the bank and opens a new account in all their names, and deposits what's in the bag into that account. Which all of them will then share.

'While they of course in fact will be running like hell to join up with the boss crook – who, you can bank on it, has got no intention of splitting the take with them at all.

'Except that this time the Fagin picked the wrong old lady. She knows which end is up and her ass from third base. Instead of doing what they told her to do she tells the bank manager what's going on. He calls the cops.

'The cops grab the three of 'em, the two retarded ladies and the crook. Judge Cavanaugh does the right thing and tells the crook, who happens to be a broad herself, that she won't have to worry about board and room for the next five years 'cause the State's gonna take care of that for her. Both of the retarded ladies lose their jobs, though, since one of the job rules is you have to behave yourself.

'Still and all, it didn't seem to me or the judge it wouldn't do any good to send the retarded ladies to jail. So the one of the ladies who isn't my lady got sent back to her relative in Palmer who's her next friend, but since the one I've got doesn't *have* a relative like that, someone Lennie can appoint to act as her legal guardian, I win Miss Janet LeClerc.

'Now, all of this's all right. I know my role in this production. I know what Janet's role is. I'm the gruff but kindly public servant who's trying to do the right thing for the person who can't take proper care of herself. I also know what my part is in what's going on right here. You and I as gentlemen of very modest wealth but very considerable taste are going to play some golf and enjoy the rewards of long life in agreeable company, as is truly meet and just. These things I have got figured out.

'What I haven't figured out is the larger purpose Julian serves. As many years as I've known the kid and liked his daddy, better on some days'n others, I have never understood what Julian's function is in the cosmic scheme of things. I see that he defies the law of gravity, and most likely several others I'd rather not know about. Existing as he does without visible means of support – *sufficient* means of support, anyway – and I'm suitably impressed. But why is he on this planet? What the hell is he *for?*'

10

Julian's second student shanked his drive badly, high-hopping it off the turf into the grove of young maples down near the bend in the Wolf River to the right. Hilliard said he hit them intentionally because he enjoyed 'nature walks' along the riverbanks. Further down the river flowed placidly under a stone bridge set in the middle of the third fairway, just about a slightly duffed one-hundred-sixty-yard splasher from the tee. From there it proceeded through the maple groves left standing to separate the front nine from the back and out the other side, running along the fourteenth and fifteenth fairways and making a deep hazard behind the twelfth green. South Brook also meandered through the course, penalizing inaccurate irons on the eighteenth and sixteenth holes. Under Grey Hills proprietorship the streams that Jesse Grey and his friends had fished so avidly principally functioned as cold wet storage for slightly used two-dollar golf balls hit by players well-enough-off to call them lost and hit new ones for their mulligans rather than get their feet wet.

In the summer every two or three weeks, shortly after sunrise, teenagers from Hampton Pond and Cumberland sneaked onto the course and snorkeled the deeper pools where the currents deposited the lost balls, surfacing with thick-gauge wire baskets streaming water and brimming with a couple dozen Titlists, Pinnacles, Max-flis, Staffs and Spalding Dots; those uncut were unharmed by immersion. Then the kids pulled on their jeans and sneakers and disappeared into the woods.

The near-pristine balls they sold in furtive haste for six bucks a dozen, cash, to frugal and unprincipled golfers emerging from their cars in the parking lots or cursing hooks and slices while thrashing five and seven irons through the bushes along the fairways of public courses in Chicopee, Springfield and Holyoke. That phase of the trade was also clandestine; municipal course rules gave their pro-shop managers the same full-retail-price monopolies on sales of golf merchandise that Bolo Cormier enjoyed at Grey Hills. The public-course pros jealously guarded those rights, posting threatening signs condemning the ball-hawkers as trespassers and forbidding patronage of them – the kids often had to run from the cops.

Somewhat-nicked or badly grass-stained but still-usable balls went five-for-a-buck to the manager of the Maple Knoll Driving Range on Route 47 in Hampton Falls. It was his idea to retrieve the balls, knowing the practice to be illegal but confident that he could get away with it. He had provided the buckets the kids used in the expectation he would get *all* the balls retrieved, paying a quarter each for the unblemished ones and reselling them to his customers for the same price the kids charged for them at the public links. He was aware of their direct service of that thriving market, angered by their treachery, and powerless to do anything about it.

Some Grey Hills members fished the river and the brook early in the cold of April each year. By the end of May weekday traffic on the course, still moderate enough to permit play by twosomes and threesomes who could walk the course if they wished, towing their clubs, became nearly constant, and, afraid they would be hit by stray balls, few came to fish. On holidays and weekends in high season when the sign-up sheet filled early, club rules specified all must play in foursomes. Cormier claimed to take into account the ages, temperaments, mobility and skills of players when matching up single players or pairs of friends but admitted he was not always able to. Members who seldom purchased equipment in his shop or tipped him less than fifty dollars at Christmas often found their partners uncongenial, causing hard feelings. Cormier scheduled tee-times – electric carts required; no strolling allowed – every quarter-hour between 6:30 A.M. and 3:30 P.M. A sign in the office above the sign-up book stated that Grey Hills policy was to enable 288 players, about three-quarters of the membership, to play eighteen holes during prime time at least once each weekend if they wished, allowing 4.5 hours elasped time on the course for each full round.

Members of all ages denounced this practice as scandalously rushed. 'Might as well play public links and save the goddamn money; going to be this crowded here,' Rob Lewis said more than once.

Toward the end of Gerald Ford's term as president, a number of quieter members, original founders and their close friends approaching their eightieth birthdays, mostly retired, became morose as they learned one by one that age inexorably imparts greater inaccuracy and inconsistency to all aspects of most players' games. They began to play undistinguished golf. This not only made them unhappy but also prompted gloating, needling remarks by insensitive younger, newer members who observed their elders' difficulties when Bolo teamed them in foursomes. The older members found this taunting petty, but tried to pretend to be amused. Off by themselves they sulked and brooded, seething that the club had ever found it financially necessary eight or ten years before to admit the upstarts into what they still thought of as their club, forgetting they had angrily rejected the only alternative: to assess each of them a heavy dues surcharge to pay for needed improvements and repairs. At meetings of the executive committee they retaliated with barbed remarks of their own, disparaging the club's increasing emphasis on golf and allocation of resources to it as unwise neglect of its other recreational resources, such as fishing, that members of all ages could enjoy.

To rebut the younger crowd's assertion that so few members fished, they declared that they fished nearly every day each spring, when the more recent members, still with jobs to tend, were unable to use the club, and therefore were not around to see them. They said resentfully that they quit fishing in May only because forced to by the golfing traffic.

All of this was true. The fishermen – Rob Lewis and Heck Sanderson among them – would show up in cold grey April when the course was in poor shape, their faces and conversations severe. At that time of year they scoffed openly at golf, as inferior to fishing as a test, exercise and demonstration of intelligence, dexterity and skill. They said they stooped to golf themselves only because the other golfers made the nobler sport imprudent, lamenting their enforced neglect of a fine natural resource.

The considerable number and reasonable size of the fish that Lewis and Sanderson and the others caught from the two water-courses annually caused a small stir among Grey Hills golfing purists who saw them on cold weekends when they used the club for lunch and drinks and wistful conversation about great golf days soon to come. Finding the fishing outfits and the behavior of the people in them laughable, they had assumed that people who looked funny could not possibly catch fish. But the anglers had a point when they lamented the summer inaccessibility of the streams. They had plenty of fish, and members caught a good many.

There were some mature brown trout in the river, the largest of them – one or two three-pounders were caught each year and immediately declared lunkers – fattened by ten-inch rainbows stocked by the State Department of Fisheries and Wildlife each spring. The department estimated the cost of each hatchery trout at $1.50. Many of them perished soon after arrival, before fishing season opened, those that eluded the big wild browns caught and eaten by hawks, fishers and otters that had learned to gather in the shadow of Mount Wolf upstream of the club as soon as the state truck went back out to the paved road. The successful anglers were proud in the clubhouse when they returned with their creels and found someone who would incautiously ask to see their catches. They regularly had several good-sized trout to show. After the kitchen staff had cleaned and grilled the fish, the fishing members would eat them in the dining room with much boastfulness about their flavor and many foamy dark-beer toasts to each other's prowess.

They owed their fish to Hilliard. In 1975 when he was still a power broker in the House, one quiet afternoon in March he had idly fallen into reflecting about the previous Sunday afternoon and evening he had spent at Grey Hills, first at a quarrelsome meeting of the membership committee and then over dinner with Merrion. The night before he and Mercy had gone to a dinner party at Walter and Diane Fox's home on Pynchon Hill in Canterbury. Even though Merrion was also almost always there, at Walter's invitation, it was one of Mercy's favorite ways to spend an evening out.

'I don't know whether you noticed it,' Hilliard said to Merrion, cutting his cold roast beef, 'but when you suggested last night to Walter that he should join here, he just about laughed in your face. I don't think it was because he doesn't like *you*, or thought you were making fun of *him*. I think when you said you'd propose him and I'd second, he didn't believe you think anyone we sponsored would get in.'

'I guess I didn't get it,' Merrion said, eating lobster salad. 'I thought he just wasn't interested. Too rich for his blood, I assumed. Walter's fairly cheap, you know. "Throws nickels around like manhole covers," as Dad used to say.'

'That wasn't what he said,' Hilliard said. 'What he did was laugh and shake his head and say: 'I dunno, Amby. I don't think those folks're used to *you* yet, never mind bringing in your friends.' He especially mentioned Warren Corey's name, and Rob Lewis's. I think what he meant is that someone's said something makes him think we may be members, but we don't *belong* yet, and maybe never will. We didn't get in on our charm. Everyone knows we bought our way in – the club was desperate for money; we happened to have some, or you did; they held their noses and let us in. But they still resent the fact that they had to do it, and have to live with us now. *That* was what Walter was saying to you. *In* doesn't mean we've been accepted.'

Merrion shrugged. 'Fuck 'em,' he said, spearing claw meat, 'I like it here. I think it's a very nice place. Excellent golf course, very well run; I don't have to wait to tee off. Decent food and they serve a big drink. Expensive but I got the money; so, what? Me being here bothers someone else, that's their problem.'

'Yeah,' Hilliard said, 'but I was very conscious of it today at the meeting. What people said, how they acted, whenever a name would come up: I watched them to see how they'd react. I decided I think Walter's got something there. These bastards may like our money all right, but they're not very keen about us.'

'Ummm,' Merrion said, nodding and chewing. When he'd

swallowed he said: 'You prolly oughta stop goin' to dinner at the Foxes' house, is what I think. They're a bad influence on you. First you think Diane's trynah break up your marriage, giving Mercy dangerous notions, and now you're tellin' me what Walter said got you so edgy you're lookin' for insults today. You're becomin' a little hoopy, looking for conspiracies. You and fuckin' Jim Garrison. Next thing I know, I'll be in the audience, you're the speaker; I'm prolly dozin', waiting for the finish when I jump up from my chair, kick off the standing ovation – and all of a sudden I'll be hearing you tell the people it was Nixon who killed Kennedy.

'And anyway, if they are bigoted, whaddaya gonna do about it – call in the IRA to blow up the swimming pool?'

'Oh no, much worse'n that,' Hilliard said. 'I'm going to do is think of something I can do that'll make these bastards beholden. Something for them that they either never *thought* of doing or if they had, they couldn't've made it happen. But I'm not gonna *tell* 'em, right off, who did this wonderful thing. I'm gonna sit back and watch 'til they've gotten attached to it. Then I tell 'em they owe it to me, and if they want to *keep* it, they'd better kiss my ass.

'And I never said I think Diane Fox's a bad influence on Mercy or that she's trying to break up my marriage – where the hell did you get that idea?'

'It's obvious,' Merrion said, finishing his lobster and dabbing his lips with the napkin. 'You're paranoid about Diane. Many times I've heard you say you think Mercy's spending too much time with Diane; she gets all her ideas from Diane. One of them's that you're fucking around, which you are, and that's why Diane worries you. Meaning you think Diane's got it in for you.'

'Well,' Hilliard said, 'I'll admit I'd like it better if Mercy had other friends, too.'

Mercy had served on the Hampton Pond Community Service Center board of directors that had given Diane Crouse Whitney her first salaried job in counselling in 1970, when she got her master's in social work from UMass. They had taken to each other instantly. 'Now I think I finally understand how you and Amby became friends so fast,' Mercy said to Hilliard, the night she met

Diane. She was standing by the front-hall closet of the house on Ridge Road in Holyoke, whipping off her tan trench-coat and paisley scarf, swirling them like a matador's cape to put them on a hanger.

'I feel like I've known this kid we had in tonight for years and years and years. She's only twenty-seven, which I know we thought was pretty old then, back when we were, but now it seems pretty young.' She leaned against the frame of the hall doorway in her camel-colored short wool dress belted with red leather at the waist, her arms folded. He sat in his easy chair in the living room watching TV.

'Especially for family counselling. She's in the process of setting up a private practice, she told me afterwards. I held up a bit outside so I could talk to her a bit more; she told me Walter Fox's already showed her two offices in Hampton Pond. In that she'll be able pretty much to specialize in therapy for adolescents, young adults. She says she's just a grown-up kid herself, but one of the luckier ones. She made the dumb mistakes and did the stupid stunts that get kids in trouble, but came through them pretty much intact. Lots of kids don't, and those're the ones she can help.

'In the job we're offering, she won't be able to do that, concentrate on one age group. The referrals the center will get from the clinics and social agencies, the court will be people from every age group. She'd have to find a way to deal with *all* of them. A lot of the people needing help're going to be in their forties and fifties – parents who're screwing up because they grew up in troubled families; husbands and wives who aren't getting along; substance abusers. And elderly people; there's a real need for bereavement counselling. Her age could be a handicap. People tend to resist telling their problems and taking advice from someone who's younger than they are.

'So if we give her the job, will she be able to cope? She's confident she can, of course, but how can we be sure? She's just gotten her degree; her judgments can't be all that empirically *informed*; how does *she* know what she can do? What basis does she have? How can we be sure?'

'That's easy,' Hilliard said, nursing a Löwenbräu and watching

Karl Malden and Michael Douglas wrap up another case on *The Streets of San Francisco*, 'you can't.'

'But then I ask,' she said, 'does it *matter* how old someone happens to be? I'm really not sure. Anyone who wants this little part-time job, that doesn't pay much money, is either going to be young and inexperienced, like she is, or, if they're older, they're probably going to have something wrong with them. Either no experience, because they're career-changers, getting started late in counselling or else when we check their references we find out why they left or got fired from their previous place. I think we don't have much choice.'

'So do I,' he said, his eyes on the screen.

'*Ohhh*, you're not *listening* to me,' she said, stamping down the hallway into the kitchen. 'I don't know why I even *bother*, telling you anything. You never pay any attention.'

'I was paying attention, for Christ sake,' he said, his gaze still fixed on the screen. 'What is it: if I agree with you or I don't interrupt you; or I don't answer a question because you haven't *asked* me one – I must not be *listening*? I haven't been paying *attention*? For Christ sake, gimme a fuckin' break here.'

'Stop talking to me like you talk with Amby,' she said loudly. 'This's Thursday night and you're at home here with me. It's not Friday night and you're not down on High Street, talking big with the boys. Try showing some class for a change.'

'Jesus H. Christ,' Hilliard said, taking his gaze off the screen as the volume went up in a Sears tire store commercial, speaking louder so that she could hear him in the kitchen, 'first I tell you for once I've got the night off. I don't have to go anywhere.' He heard the cork come out of a wine bottle. 'This is good because you've got a meeting. This'll be one night when the kids won't have a sitter. So, I'm a good daddy. I help Emmy with her math and I flog Timmy into at least *starting* to read *Ivanhoe*. Then I even make them go to bed. Now you come home and you tell me, well, the substance of it anyway, that you're very impressed with this young woman who just got her master's, and even though she hasn't got any experience and you're afraid she might have trouble dealing with older patients, might not be her cup of tea, you're still very much leaning toward the idea that she's the one that you should hire, give her the job and get it over with. So you won't have to go out to meetings anymore on Thursday nights when you'd rather stay home after dinner with your family. And anyway: no matter who you end up hiring, anyone could present problems. That you'll always have that possibility.

'Not that you came right out and actually said all that stuff, but what you didn't say I could hear anyway. It was implied.' The titles began to roll for *Harry-O*, starring David Janssen.

She came into the living room with a goblet of white wine and sat down. 'Okay wise guy,' she said, 'so I guess you *were* listening. You're so smart, tell me what I do now.'

'Is that my good Muscadet you're drinking?' he said.

'No it's not,' she said. 'It's the cheap Almaden Mountain white, from the jug. Now answer my question.'

'Go through the rest of the interview process,' he said. 'Then when it's over, turn on the charm with the other committee members and hire her.'

'I don't *want* to go through it,' she said, pouting and sipping the wine. 'She's the fourth person we've interviewed now. That's six hours we've put in, listening to people tell us how much they want the job.'

'You sound like Emmy with her algebra,' he said. "Don't see why they make us *take* this. I don't *like* it."'

Mercy tossed her hair. 'I do *not*,' she said, 'and I don't care if I do – so there.' He laughed. 'Six others we didn't even grant interviews to, they were so obviously unqualified. We've got four more scheduled to come in. One's a forty-six-year-old psychology Ph.D. on the staff full-time at the Knox State Hospital. His letter says he wants to set up a private practice and he's decided Hampton Pond's where he wants to do it. He's making eighteen thousand dollars a year as a senior therapist and he's only got three more years to go at Knox – which he can't do and come here at the same time – before he qualifies for a pension. I'm not sure I believe him. It doesn't make sense to me. Either he's fooling himself or he's playing with us. He's not going to dump that fairly good salary now and take our little job, paying six thousand dollars a year; if all he has to do is tough it out at Knox three more years and retire. There'll be another little job around some other pretty little town three years from now; he can start his practice then.

'The others that we've said we'll talk to: there's something slightly wrong with them too. You look at the résumés and think to yourself: "Gee, I wish *that* wasn't there." "I'd feel better, she didn't have *that*."

'This other woman; she's forty-eight. That's a good age for our job; young enough to talk to the kids but still mature enough to be accepted by the older patients. She's had children, boy and a girl, both grown now, off on their own, apparently doing just fine. She's been divorced. Okay, nothing wrong with that anymore, having gone through a divorce; getting so more have 'n haven't.'

She paused and chewed her lower lip. 'Oh, must tell you this: this Diane also asked me, *very* casually, *just* by the way, out there in the parking lot, if Walter Fox might be getting a divorce. Well, I know from you that he is, but I'm not sure she should get it from me. So I said I didn't know. I think she might have her eye on him. Little old for her, you'd think, but still . . .'

'Oh, I'd think Walter can still probably get it up once a month or so, he gets proper rest and eats right,' Hilliard said.

'Pig,' she said. 'Anyway, this woman's divorced: how that gives me a small problem? It's because she's been divorced *three times*. Once, even twice: sure, I could understand, but is it likely this woman's had three marriages fail and every time it was the other person's *fault*? That's hard to believe. And even if that's the case, she *did* have that much bad luck, it would still bother me. One way or the other that has to say something about what kind of judgment she's got, picking *three* husbands she couldn't live with. I'm certainly not going to want to hire *her*. I don't think anyone else will, either. So I don't think we need to see her. We should cancel that interview.

'Am I being fair?' she said. 'Probably not. This younger woman's been through a divorce, and she isn't thirty yet. Plenty of time yet for her to rack up a couple more husbands, before she turns forty-eight. Would that make a difference to me? Could be. But she isn't forty-eight yet, she's twenty-seven, and her having the one marriage now behind her doesn't cause me the same concern.

'It's the same thing with the other two,' Mercy said. 'Something on their résumés that says regardless of how articulate, personable and compassionate they may turn out to be when they come in, we're not going to want to hire them. One's a man who admits that he's an alcoholic. He tries to make it into an advantage. Says he's been sober eight years – he's forty-two now – and he's counselled many other alcoholics who've told him he's got a special empathy for drunks. Maybe he has, but so've bartenders, and drunks aren't the only kind of patients we get. A lot of them, sure, but that's not enough, knowing how to get the boozers into AA and get themselves straightened out. I don't want him.

'The other one's another man who's also got something in his background that disturbs me: he got all his training from his church. It's one of those evangelical Protestant churches, and for all I know he's a very fine man. But what we're looking for here's a counselor, not a lay preacher, and I think if we hire him every priest and minister and rabbi for miles around'd be up in arms.'

'ACLU probably too,' Hilliard said. 'Public money funding private religion – paying for missionary work. Nothing like a good old little church-and-state dust-up, get everyone's bowels in an uproar. No, I think you're right about all – I doubt you'll hire any of them.'

'So then,' she said, 'I should call up the others and see if they agree that we should cancel the rest we've got scheduled? Say: "Let's hire this one we saw last night. I think she's great. She's smart and she's eager and with the alimony I assume she gets she can live on our salary. And call up the others and tell them we're sorry but we've filled the job, and we won't be talking to them."'

'Rotten idea,' he said. '*Please* don't do that.'

'Why?' she said. 'I'm sure it's what we should do.'

'*You* are,' he said. 'The other four people on the search committee may not be. One of them may be secretly backing one of those three or four candidates you now want to brush off – or one of the others you've already seen who didn't impress you as much. Don't forget that the committee called for these statements of interest, *invited* and *solicited* those applications. People go to infinite pains when they compose those things. Their lives and egos go on those sheets of paper. They're not going to be pleased if you now just go and dump them.

'And the instant that you try to do what you said, any member of the committee who's got a candidate's going to be dead-set against anything and everything you propose after that. No matter how great the new friend you met tonight seems to you, they'll never vote for her; you will've made her into "Mercy's candidate." Never mind how pissed-off the candidates you didn't have come in'll be, with some justification; the other people on the *committee*'ll start hollering bloody murder. "You're as bad's your husband, going outside the process, ramming stuff down people's throats. You're trying to railroad us; who the hell do you think you are?"

'Even though they pestered you to get involved because they know with Donna in the Fernald we're interested in mental health, and you might even *know* something about what a counsellor needs to be. And because they figure maybe you can sweet-talk me into getting state money for their center. And maybe you might be able to do that, if everybody plays nice. But that little scheme'll go right by the boards if they decide now you're trying to run the show for them. You try to bull something through on this, they'll turn on you like dogs. People who don't like *me* will oppose your choice for that reason, and people who oppose you will try to get back at you through me. Don't do it. Scuttle the statewide phase, sure, but honor the rest of the appointments.'

'I really liked her, though,' Mercy said.

'I understand that,' Hilliard said. 'You've made that very clear. Try not to do it again, with anybody else. Don't let on yet how impressed you were. Anyone asks, be open without telling them much. Be creative with the truth; if you have to, lie discreetly: misrepresent stuff they won't ever be able to prove. Say you're determined to keep an open mind. Give all the applicants fair, impartial hearings. You may've been more impressed with one or two than you were with a couple others, but that may be just the way you happened to feel the night they interviewed. May want to change your mind before you vote. You might let it slip out you think the best *so far* might be this – what'd you say her name is?'

'Diane Whitney,' Mercy said. 'Her maiden name was Crouse. She's originally a midwesterner. Came here when she was still married – her husband had a job at UMass., teaching economics. She's really quite pretty; sort of freckled, reddish hair, ties it back in a bun; might have a *slight* problem with her weight, I'd guess, but who hasn't. I can't imagine why any man who was married to her would ever want to divorce her.'

'Maybe he didn't,' Hilliard said. 'Sometimes it's the lady's idea.'

Walter Fox's divorce from Jackie had come through in the fall of 1970, a few months after Diane's appointment as the resident counselor at the Hampton Pond Community Service Center. Early in 1971 they married, Diane prevailing upon him to sell the massive white Victorian mansion in Hampton Falls left to him by his grandfather Phil and for their wedding present buy one of the properties his agency listed. It was a beautifully kept Federal Period two-story grey wooden house with white trim and a yellow door set among the oaks and maples on the rocky knob of Pynchon Hill. Her principal motive was the sunny new kitchen shrewdly installed at great but tax-deductible expense by the previous occupants, bent upon selling quickly at a good price. But they could afford it; Diane's practice had prospered nicely, and although Walter's extremely conservative management of the Fox Agency tended to keep profits small, they were steady.

Feeling herself unexpectedly settled and secure as she approached thirty, she began to develop an interest in what she called 'really serious cooking.' Sabatier knives protruded from the birch block next to the stainless-steel six-burner gas range. The Zero King refrigerator dispensed cubed and cracked ice. Diane's was the first Cuisinart Mercy Hilliard saw in someone else's home.

'And the nicest thing about all of the equipment,' Mercy said, 'is the absolute magic she does with it.' Mercy admired her new friend boundlessly. The nine-year difference in their ages bothered neither of them at all. They talked on the phone four or five times a week and lunched every Friday in the glass-enclosed Flower Room at Gino's Hearthside, ordering salads niçoise and drinking iced tea so as to avoid gaining weight, and also so that neither Diane's patients nor Mercy's classmates in the UMass. graduate school of education would detect alcohol on their breath Friday afternoons.

To Hilliard it seemed clear from the beginning that Diane dominated the friendship. He was uneasy about it. It was Diane's example, if not something she'd said – for all the difference that made – that had prompted Mercy to think about what she would do if he should decide to divorce her. Mercy admitted it to him. 'It happens,' she said, 'it does happen to people. People you'd never expect it to. Diane said when she married Tommy and left Wisconsin-Madison to go to London with him, she never dreamed they'd ever break up. But by the time they got to UMass. she'd decided she'd better get her degree. She'd seen a couple of their friends get divorced, so she knew it did happen, and when it did the woman was a lot better off if she had something she could do. She said that was what woke her up – she didn't have any job skills. And even then it was almost too late – he left for Chicago before she could finish up.

'If she hadn't been already enrolled in the program, so people knew her and got her financial help, she would've been *sunk*. She got enough alimony to live on, but not enough to pay tuition. Without the help she would've had to drop out. Or else take a lot longer getting her degree. So it's a lot better, safer, to make sure that you're prepared. It may never happen; it'll *probably* never happen. But it's good to be prepared all the same. And anyway, what'm I supposed to do when Emmy and Timmy've grown up and have their own lives? I need to have a life too. A real job to go to, which I've never had. So even though I know of course I'd never divorce you – I could never love anyone else – I still want to have something to do.

'And I also know even though I'd never leave *you*, divorce isn't out of the question. A lot of your time's spent away from home, with interesting, exciting people. Doing interesting, exciting things. And more and more of them these days, are interesting and exciting young *women*, in the careers they're in because they're very *good-looking* young women. And *smart*. I know you're always saying TV reporters are just pretty faces and hairdos, don't have a brain in their heads. Well excuse me, but I don't believe that. A lot of these women are smart. That's how they got those jobs, by being smart enough to know how to capitalize on their looks to get a job that pays them more in a year than I've earned in my whole entire life.

'Some day one of those little cuties could decide she'd like to be the wife of a bright young and handsome politician who might be going places. And decide to make a play for you. Get rid of the wife and move in. Think you'd fall for it, darling?' she said.

'No, of course not,' he said at once.

'Well that's nice to hear,' she said, 'but I'm not sure I can be sure of that. You may not know the answer yourself. How you'd react if some woman put an effort into it, tried to lure you out of our bed into hers. And if you *don't* know how you'd react, as I don't want to think you do, I don't know, either, do I?'

By afternoon on the quiet Tuesday after his rancorous allegation of anti-Catholic prejudice at Grey Hills Sunday night, Hilliard in his office at the State House had decided what to do to avenge it. He had called the Department of Fisheries and Wildlife and amiably suggested the first stocking of the brook and the river that ran through Grey Hills. The man who took the call and recognized the name of the chairman of Ways and Means had been prudently indifferent to the fact that the stretches of the streams the caller proposed for improvement at taxpayer expense were privately owned, posted off-limits to non-members of Grey Hills. The stocking had begun. Delight among the membership who chanced to catch the hatchery trout and deduced their origin was immediate and unfeigned. Hilliard was not allowed to lie in wait; Warren Corey identified him at once as the member deserving the thanks. For the next several years, until mortality put an end to it, the anglers at Grey Hills at Corey's instigation annually held 'The Fish Dinner,' honoring Dan Hilliard as their benefactor. If they were dissembling, they did it well enough so that he was never able to detect it.

In the years since Hilliard had left the House, no one in the legislature or the governor's cabinet had found the cost of the stocking in the budget for Fisheries and Wildlife, so no one had made a second call to Fisheries and Wildlife threatening public denunciation of the practice as unauthorized and corruptly wasteful. The stocking continued.

'Hit another one, Steve,' Julian Sanderson said in the August sunshine, too warmly and indulgently. 'Yeah, you're among *friends* here, Steverino,' Pete said heartily and expansively, 'mulligans all around, all day long.'

Asshole, Merrion thought disinterestedly. To Hilliard he said: 'There, see what I mean?'

Hilliard laughed, releasing his grip on Merrion's shoulders, along with a gust of Courvoisiered breath into the air around them, pulling a chair up at Merrion's left. He sat down: six-two, a hundred-and-eighty-or-ninety pounds, thickening softly around the middle; the black hair starting mostly grey over the ears; a grand smile on the slightly flushed face evincing years of practice – but because of the practice showing as well the warm heart behind it – and clasped his hands at his waist. 'Diversion, Amby,' he said. 'Julian is for diversion. His mission's to be a guide for the world at play time.'

11

In February of the 1982 election year Hilliard cheerfully endorsed Joseph Bryan, a House colleague, for the Democratic nomination for the largely ceremonial and thus lightly regarded office of lieutenant governor, then vacant. It was an automatic; Bryan had done many minor favors for Hilliard and was calling his chits.

In May the senior US senator with four years remaining on his term received bad news from his cardiologist: 'I'm afraid the results of the angiogram don't look good, and you're too old for a transplant. Without one at your present pace you may last three years. For your family's sake as well as your own, you ought to consider retirement.' Shaken, the senator had confided in his staff, and one of them, stupid or treacherous, had leaked it before the victim could collect his wits and plan his succession.

The governor, a shoo-in for re-election, had long coveted a senate seat. It was apparent that the senator would defer his resignation until after the general election so that the governor, a friend, could appoint himself to fill the vacancy. The next lieutenant governor would succeed him. Suddenly Bryan had two strong competitors. Each of them had done several very important favors for Hilliard. Each of them sought his support. Matters became complicated.

Merrion one night about a week before the '82 primaries was in a motel bar in Worcester with several reporters, among them Charlie Doyle. Charlie's facial skin had folds as deep as those in the hides of bulldogs, and the silver sweaty stubble in the crevices glistened in the light when he changed expression – as he did with admiration, talking about Hilliard. Charlie said that as long as he'd been around the game, 'and that is one long fuckin' time,' he'd never seen anyone who could duck a question better than Dan Hilliard.

'I collared him this afternoon and asked him how he stands now on the lieutenant governor thing: is he still with Bryan? If you'd been standing here beside me you'd've sworn he's answering it – I know I thought he was. He wasn't.

'He may be the best I've ever seen, it comes to slinging it. He will not lie to you – at least so you could prove it. He does not refuse to answer, and he doesn't whine and plead. "Oh gee, you can't ask me to do that." Stuff's beneath him. You stop him and you say: "Hey Dan." He says: "Hey Charlie," and that's how it begins. He stands there and talks to you, and twenty minutes go by in the twinkling of an eye – he doesn't seem to stop for *breath*.

'You just can't help but be *impressed*, even *thankful*, all this *time* he's giving you. And he's so *earnest* about it. When he gets through doing it, he's just as fresh as springtime, and you're totally worn out. And *furthermore*, what's more important, you don't know a single thing you didn't know before. You may know even less. At least until this afternoon, I knew he was still with Bryan.

'Now I'm not sure of *that*. I've had the Hilliard Treatment, and boy, do I feel good, like a million bucks, Dan Hilliard's been so good to me. When you feel like you've just had sex you've had the Hilliard Treatment. Yes, my child, you have been fucked, but it's really not so bad – you've been fucked so *very well*. That's why all us whores like Danny; he's what makes the job worthwhile. We let him have his way with us, anytime he likes, 'cause we have a good time too.'

Then Charlie Doyle had smiled. 'That's how he does the magic tricks. He gets you to help him. You don't even realize it. You went in as his adversary: this time you're gonna *smoke him out*, once and for fuckin' all. But before you even know it, you've become a volunteer from the audience, right beside him in the footlights, grinning like a fool.

'You know what I bet?' Charlie'd said. 'I bet he's always like this now, he's so good at it. He's with the wife and kids, and one of them says to him "Daddy, can I have an ice cream cone?" He does the same song-and-dance he does for you and me, everyone he deals with, face-to-face and day-to-day. By the time he's through, the little kid has either gone to sleep, or lost all interest in the fuckin' ice cream cone. Grown up, gone off to school.'

'Julian's one of those people,' Hilliard said on the patio, 'that you go to when you really don't have enough on your mind. You give him money to relax you. Julian's very relaxing. He's in charge of fixing things that don't *need* fixing, and really don't have to work right anyway. Like golf. You do not have to play golf, much less play golf well. Golf is an option, nothing more. The problems it creates for those who get problems from it are volitional. The only reason they exist is because we wish them to. Julian solves those problems.'

Julian's third client hit his drive straight down the fairway with a nice loft on it, but it traveled no more than 150 yards, down to the first little hollow. He appeared to have sacrificed distance for accuracy. Julian cleared his throat and said: 'Nice and true, Paul, nice and true. Need some more oomph on it, though. Little more meat in it.'

'Gotta get the old *ass* into it, Paul,' Julian's first client said, still gloating over his drive as he got into the cart with Steve. Merrion hoped idly the gods of golf would punish Pete severely for the rest of the day.

'*Julian's* optional, too,' Hilliard said.

'Yeah, yeah, where the hell've you been?' Merrion said, looking at his watch. 'It's twenty after and the message that you left on my machine yesterday said our tee-time was eleven-thirty. Fuck've you been all this time?'

'I was over at the house in Bell Woods,' Hilliard said.

'You were over the house in Bell Woods,' Merrion said. 'What the hell're you doing Bell Woods? Fourteen years, you haven't lived inna place? You forget all a sudden who owns it?'

'Mercy called up from the Vineyard this morning,' Hilliard said. Under the terms of the property settlement agreement Daniel and Marcia (Hackett) Hilliard had in his words 'fairly rationally reached, meaning not too much blood was let' negotiating their divorce, they retained joint ownership of the house at West Chop, the survivor of them to enjoy a tenancy for life, at his or her death the remainder of the estate to be sold and the proceeds evenly divided between Timothy and Emily Hilliard. Mercy got occupancy during August, which both of them preferred; he had the run of it from Memorial Day through the last Saturday in July.

'She gets the part she calls "the hurricane season, when it's so crowded you can't move, horribly crowded, and so hot you can't do anything." Says it proves she got screwed on the deal. I say what she got's "the best part of the summer, when it's nice and warm and everyone you want to see is there,"' he said. 'Of course it isn't crowded when I'm there; no one who's got any sense goes there in June. July; they wait – 'til August. The sun and the Gulf Stream don't warm up the water enough to swim in until around the end of July, so all of us who go there before that either stay out of the water or freeze our balls off.'

She had gotten the main house in Bell Woods estates in Hampton Pond. 'When Nick Hardigrew was still alive, he had a key to the house. I think he found out how to get into something else over there too, but who'm I to make remarks? Nobody is. Hell, one of our English teachers, queer as a green horse but funny as hell; three or four of us were talking the other day about how all of us like western movies and nobody makes them anymore, and he says *he* even likes westerns. And somebody said: "Really? You guys like westerns?" And he says: "Oh, *yes*, absolutely, faggots *love* westerns. Especially the Lone Ranger. Man with a *mask* on; so he goes on top. And *Tonto*: Such a *hunk*. If he'd only take his shirt off. *Really* he is such a *dream*. And once you know *Kemo sabe* means 'Snookums,' I mean, how could anyone ever resist?" Everyone's got something going.'

'Anyway, Mercy didn't give a key to this new lawn guy she's got now. Told me she hasn't known him long enough yet to be sure she can trust him. So he was over there this morning and he called her and said he thought he heard water running inside, sounded like down in the cellar. Somebody had to go over, go in and look at it, maybe get a repairman. Tim's in Singapore with his new bride, seems to have a little better disposition than his old one did; showing her the assembly plants he runs from his office in Stamford, twelve thousand miles away. Emily's teaching summer session down in Santa Fe.'

Hilliard had not lingered conversationally over his surviving daughter's living arrangements since she and a female collegue at Smith had purchased a showpiece antique farmhouse in Worthington. Since Merrion's policy was to welcome and honor personal confidences but never seek such information, he did not know whether they remained on the speaking but distant terms Hilliard had salvaged by groveling for his daughter during the publicly colorful passage of the break-up of his marriage.

In those days, to Emily's explicit disapproval, he had been frequently described in the papers as 'debonair chairman of Ways and Means' and 'man about Hill and town.' The *Herald* called him 'Dancing Dan' in the caption of a photo of him in swim trunks, surrounded by three smiling bimbos – each with 'more cleavage'n Grand Canyon,' Merrion told him dolefully by phone – reclining on a beach chair with the ocean in the foreground and St Thomas in the background, during a February blizzard in New England, Fred Dillinger in his *Transcript* column called him 'our own sunshine-lover, Dapper Dan Hilliard playing patty-cake while we all shovel.'

He seemed then to be determined the parade of young women he was photographed escorting through his life would never end, one after another lissome lady in her twenties smiling at the camera with many white teeth and displaying long shiny hair, generally blonde, their large bosoms and long legs exposed to vulgar eyes and lewd speculation by microscopic dresses and 'wide belts instead of skirts.' But in time the fun did end – when he resigned his seat in the House in '84, four months ahead of impending electoral disaster, to become at age fifty president at Hampton Pond Community College.

He told Merrion that Emily had congratulated him on his appointment, saying she was happy because she figured he was 'finally getting tired of acting like the biggest asshole in the world.' Because Hilliard was his best friend and Emily was not, Merrion did not say what he thought: that most people who knew and liked her father had for a while sadly and reluctantly shared her opinion.

All that had been several years before Emily at age thirty-one and her partner, Karen, thirty-eight, had decided to make public their commitment to each other in a meadow setting, inviting the papers. *The Pioneer Valley Record*, a weekly in Cumberland, ran two pictures; Hilliard did not appear in them because he had not attended the ceremony.

'I was not invited,' he told Merrion. 'I chose not to be. Emily called me up and told me what was going to happen. She said she'd invited her mother and Mercy'd gotten all bent out of shape and begged her not to go through with it. Pleaded with her to be satisfied with living openly with Karen, if that's what she was sure she wanted to do. No one was trying to stop them, so why go public and cause the rest of us all this pain and embarrassment. Emily said Mercy should have joy, not that negative reaction, that she's found her life's companion and partner, and celebrate their union, and that just shows how insensitive we are to her real needs.

'Emily told me her mother's reaction made her think she'd better call me up and ask me whether I wanted to come, or would I rather try to make her feel bad instead, like her mother had just done. So she was asking did I want to be invited, and she would like to have my true and honest answer.

'Remember the big kid in the sixth grade with you – he'd been kept back so many times they had to let him out of gym so he could go and vote? Used to stick his chin out and ask you if you were trying to start a fight at recess – poke you in the chest before he hit you in the guts? Same tone of voice.

'I thought about the way she acted when Mercy and I were having such a grand old time of it kicking the living shit out of each other when we were breaking up. Emmy's contribution then was to make it worse for both of us by acting like she's the one who's getting hurt, squawking at me about all the bad publicity I was getting – as though I'd been out there trying to get it.'

'I don't remember you working too hard to avoid it,' Merrion said.

'No,' Hilliard said, his voice roughening, 'I didn't. I stopped living a monk like Sam Evans said after Mercy alleged adultery. The hell was the point of celibacy after that? Sit around and beat my meat *after* I've been publicly accused of getting laid three times a day? But I didn't go out and *arrange* the damned press coverage, which is what Emily's doing. She's deliberately staging this sideshow so it'll be in all the papers that she's a lesbian. Part of my job's enforcing college rules that say no public sexual conduct or display. And I've actually got people on my campus who say that's violation of academic freedom. So now Emily's very sweetly asking me if I wouldn't love to be a part of her little pagan feast.

'I gave it some thought. "Which'd I rather do: what my dear daughter's offering here or jump into a live volcano?" I decided I'd prefer the volcano. This isn't a celebration she's planning; this is a counterattack. No reason to stand out in front of it. So I said: 'Uh uh, no thanks. Appreciate the call though. Lots of luck to you and Karen. Toodle-ooh.' And that's the way we left it.

'So, who did that leave with a key around here? You're looking at him. Hot-water heater tank blew a relief valve. I got Ralph Stallings to fix it this morning, actually come out on a Saturday, but I had to be there, let him in. Then wait around while he fixed it; lock up again after he left.'

'You still got a key?' Merrion said.

'Yeah,' Hilliard said. 'I didn't realize it either, not for quite a long time. I first found out I still had it – I dunno when it was, five, six years ago, same situation. Somebody was going to go there to do something, install something, I dunno, and that was the only day they could come and she'd been waiting a long time have it done. But it so happened she had to be someplace else that same day, so would I be a nice guy and do her a favor and go over there, let him in. I was kind of surprised myself. It wasn't like I minded or anything, I'm only just up the street and let's face it, I pretty much come and go as I like. So it was no big deal.

'But when she first called up and asked me, did I still have my key; I admit I was kind of surprised. I said: "Yeah, I think I might still have it around here someplace; I don't think I threw it away. Why?" And she told me, and I said: "Well, geez, you know, the reason I'm not sure I've got it is I assumed it wasn't any good anymore. Isn't it sort of traditional, part of the ritual, that when the wife winds up with the house, she gets all the locks changed?'

'And she said yeah, she guessed it was, but one thing and another, she never got around to it. The kids when we split up, they were still living there. Later on, they're in college, they still had to have a place to come back to. After that Tim's first marriage came apart; he lived here until he got resettled. Emmy was sort of between jobs and up in the air for a long time, figuring out what she was. So they both would've needed new keys if Mercy'd gotten the locks changed.

'"It just seemed simpler," she said to me, "if I left things the way they were. And it wasn't as though, you know, I was ever afraid of you. I never considered myself a prospect for one of those afternoon talk-shows: 'Women whose ex-husbands stalk them.' I never went to bed at night thinking maybe you might be looking in the windows; I never thought you'd ever want to *hurt* me. Not in *that* way, anyway."' Hilliard smirked. 'My little Mercy, just as sweet as ever – always gets her little dig in.

'"And anyway," she says, "everybody that I know who's got a house, ex-husband or no ex-husband around, they've all got someone who doesn't live there that's got a key to it. In case someone needs to get in while they're gone, the fire department or something. Someone they can trust. Well, you're ideal – far as that kind of trust's concerned anyway. You live right near me; I know if I fall down some night, break my leg or something and can't move, if I can call an ambulance I can get you up and you'll come over, let the paramedics in. And when I'm on the island, you're usually here. So I just never got around to it.'

'So anyway, that's where I was,' Hilliard said. 'Waiting for Ralph Stallings to come. And finish his work and then go. Sorry to've kept you waiting.'

'So, are we playing?' Merrion said, catching another whiff of cognac, thinking: *Mercy's still stocking the bar in the study with V.S.O.P.*

'I called Bolo up this morning,' Hilliard said, 'after I called your house first and I got your machine. That to me says you'd either left already to come here or were on the road to God-knows-where-else first, and then you're coming here. Or else that you got lucky last night and you haven't been home, and as soon as you two get through hiding the salami a few more times with last night's catch-of-the-day, you're coming directly here. I didn't have your car-phone. So I called Bolo and told him the situation. So when you got here and came looking for me, tell you what's going on, ask you to wait; I'm on my way. Bolo said when I got here to find him and he'd fit us in whenever we wanted. I take it you didn't bother, see Bolo.'

'No point in it,' Merrion said. 'Your car wasn't in the lot when I got here. Obviously you're not here. I changed my clothes and come out here. Obviously also, something's going on, which so far I don't know about, but probably will when you finally get here. So I'll sit here and wait, watch Heck's baffling kid for a while. You've known me a long time, Daniel my friend. I'm the patient sort, not a guy who craves excitement. I'm more the type who likes to sit back, take his time and see how things develop. Hell, I outwaited Larry Lane and Richie Hammond, both; so far that's worked out pretty well.'

Hilliard snickered. There was no happiness in it. 'Well, yeah, up 'til now it seems to've,' he said. 'Like the guy who fell off the roof forty stories up: when someone yelled from the twentieth floor he was gonna get killed, he said: "Oh I dunno; so far now it's been all right." I'm just not so sure how much longer.'

'"How much longer" what?' Merrion said.

'How much longer things stay okay,' Hilliard said. 'I'm beginning to think time isn't always on your side. You can't always count on it being that way, time's always working *for* you. Stands to reason that sometimes it has to work the other way, right, in favor of somebody else. And therefore work against you.

'You shouldn't let yourself become too sure of things. They've got a way of turning on you in a flash and taking a big bite out of you. Things don't always stay the same, the way we're used to and they've always been. At least that's what I'm starting to think. This could be a true fact; that we may be starting to find out what we've got on our hands now may not be something we're used to. And we'd be a whole lot better off if we came to grips with it right off, started dealing with it. Things may now be very different. I think maybe we have to realize that.'

He paused and moistened his lips, gazing at Merrion as though expecting him to say something. Merrion frowned and shook his head. He said nothing.

Hilliard cleared his throat. 'Well, ah,' he said 'one reason I'm late . . . well, the reason I'm late is the reason I told you. I hadda go over Bell Woods. But I wasn't sorry, it made me be late. It gave me some time to think. I'm seeing some stuff going on that I'm not sure I like. And I'm not sure what we do about it. I wanted to think, before I saw you, about what it is that we should do about this shit.'

'Dan,' Merrion said, 'you're making me nervous here. I'm starting to get very nervous.'

'Yeah, I know what you mean,' Hilliard said, looking worried and licking his lips. 'That's what I mean, I was trying to say. I'm a little uneasy myself.'

12

'I doubt Larry Lane'd recognize the clerk's job you described to me,' Hilliard said in the High Street office, a week deeper into the spring of '66. 'If he did, he'd never admit it. My guess is he'd tell you he's never seen one like it in Canterbury. Mere suggestion'd give him palpitations.'

'He's making trouble?' Merrion said. 'Who's he think he is, chief clerk or something?'

'I haven't talked to him directly,' Hilliard said. 'I saw Chassy Spring at the spring Hampden County Bar Association hoedown over at the old Worthy. I thought it might be a good chance to sort of sound him out about having you come in. He was not enthusiastic. He said he wouldn't stand in the way if I told him that's what I wanted, but he also said Lane hasn't given him any indication his two-man staff's overworked.'

'There's a job open, though,' Merrion said. 'Like I said: I already checked that out, *long* time ago. Canterbury's authorized for three, three assistant clerks, Chapter Two-eighteen, Section Ten. There's only two there now, two assistant clerks – so that means they need one more.'

'Well,' Hilliard said, 'I'm not sure that follows. They may have *room* for one more, but that doesn't mean they *need* one. Maybe Lane's a thrifty manager, conscientious public servant, saving a dollar or two the taxpayers' money here and there if he can, and he finds he can get by with two assistants. One of whom, incidentally, Spring says Lane doesn't like at all. Some protégé of Roy Carnes's; Hammond, I think his name is. But what if we brace Lane and he says two assistants're a quorum? What do we do then?'

'Since when did that ever matter?' Merrion said. 'When a chairman on Counties – not to mention mine's also on Ways and Means and Judiciary too – has a friend and the buddy wants a job and the job he wants is open, when did it ever matter whether anyone else wanted it filled? Even if the guy dragging his feet was the guy in charge the office – when did that start to matter?'

'Oh, I couldn't give you the original example,' Hilliard said, 'but I can tell you what the situation probably was. The guy in charge didn't *want* the vacancy filled. From the outside you never know what's going on inside courthouses. The people who're in them think of them as their private domains. Statute may say there's room for someone new, but that'll mean that someone they don't know'll then be learning all their business. Maybe they've got something going on they don't want publicized.

'Or someone in the courthouse, the judge or the clerk himself, is saving the slot until someone gets out of the army or finishes school. Or the clerk reaches retirement age, which'll mean the guy he's hand-picked to succeed him'll be free to hire *two* new assistants. One of them being actually qualified; the other one being the retiring guy's bastard child by the fence-viewer's wife.

'You get the idea: one of the new guys would be someone he could not appoint himself, because it might not've looked right. Might've smacked of nepotism, started no end of loose talk – but if the guy *succeeding* him's the guy making the appointment, then it'll be perfectly kosher. The incoming chief clerk signs the bastard's paper, in order to get his own job.

'That's very often what the situation is, we find,' Hilliard said. 'And as soon as the Counties chairman sees that's what it is, the maximum heat he or anybody else – outside the governor, of course – can put on the guy who's set up the swap drops about fifty degrees. Technically, yeah, the chairman could probably make a demand; plant his feet and say "I want this *done* and I want it done *now*, and until it is you get no funding." He could do it *once*. But he'd be a fool if he did. He'd have to know once he's thrown his weight around like that, he'll never get anything else. He represents a client there, he'll have to wear a bulletproof-vest to make a safe trip to the bathroom.

'People don't *like* guys who threaten them. You put yourself in a position where you've got to be able to get a guy's job if he doesn't do what you want, you're not going to get many things done. You think you can get a clerk fired if he won't lose a ticket for you? Not likely. And even if you could, there'd still be a limit on how many guys you could get fired before you made enough people mad enough at you to get together and see if *they* couldn't get *you*. People rebelling like that, pretty soon you can't get *any*thing done. All you've got're guys chasin' around, rantin' and ravin' all over the place, trying to pay off their grudges. That's counterproductive. You want things to be the way most people like them: everything *peaceful*, and *calm*.

'The system depends on nobody's toes getting stepped-on. Everyone gets what he wants. It begins to look like there may not be enough jobs to go so that everyone who *wants* someone to get one can get taken care of; well then, what we do is get together and we talk. See if maybe we can work something out. Chances are we can see our way clear to agree that the money can be found, if we all look hard enough, and therefore we can go ahead and create a few more of those very popular jobs.

'To be given, of course, only to people who'll be grateful after they get them: don't leave that out. Because in the future there's probably going to be a way for them to express their thanks that they are – *without* makin' a lot of fuckin' *noise* and commotion about doin' it. By maybe holding a slot for us when two or three open up in their office. It's more beneficial for everyone that way, everyone getting along.'

'Yeah,' Merrion said. 'Well, okay, but I don't think that's what's going on in the Canterbury court-clerk's office now, that's short one clerk. Judge Spring; you told me once he's got two kids, and both of them're now big high-powered lawyers someplace. One is down in Boston and the other's someplace else?'

'Right,' Hilliard said. 'One of Chassy's boys, I forget the kid's name now, but I know he's very large in one of the big firms in Boston. The other one, I think, went to New York – very high up in the financial world, some outfit that underwrites bonds. Both making about a ton of money; bucks coming in hand over fist.'

'So they're outta my picture,' Merrion said. 'They're not leavin' jobs like that to come back here and take this job I want – they're both fryin' much bigger fish.'

'That seems about right,' Hilliard said. He smiled. 'Be interesting to know how Chass really feels about that: both of his kids doing so well. Proud, of course, naturally; you'd assume that. But maybe kind of envious too? That maybe if he'd done something like that himself; gone out into the big world and made a huge mark of his own. Instead he plays it safe and comes back here; practices law, sends out calendars and Christmas cards every year, until the finale, he becomes the judge next town over. This's not what you call your big finish. Got to ask yourself: Is this guy content? Was this *really* what he wanted out of life? Maybe; wouldn't've been my choice.

'I think about that. People who catch my attention for some reason, I begin to wonder how they feel about the way their lives turned out. If they think they made the right decisions. How the bad ones hurt them. How far they've come; how far they could've gotten if they'd been a *little* smarter, had a *little* better luck. Are they happy now; or are they disappointed? How I'll feel some day when I'm their age and now I'm the one who's looking back and seeing how *my* decisions all turned out.'

'Well, he's made himself a bunch of money, hasn't he?' Merrion said. 'Didn't you also tell me Chassy plays the market like Chuck Berry plays guitar? That oughta happy him some.'

'Oh shit, yes,' Hilliard said. 'My father's the Spring family dentist. Taken care of their teeth for years. *Made* a good many of them in fact; Spring family's got very weak teeth. They've all needed bridgework and plates. He used to talk, they came in. He knew for a fact that Chassy'd made a huge amount of money, stocks and bonds and so forth. *That* didn't bother my father; what did was that the judge never gave him a hot tip.'

'Bastard,' Merrion said.

'You'd think that, wouldn't you,' Hilliard said. 'Least the cocksucker could do, knows what stock is going up, is tell the people that he knows, so they could make some money too. Not *everybody*, no, just people that he sees around a lot like my father, for example, for his teeth. Not *advising* them, so you'd expect him to be calling them up every day or so and saying: "*Psst*, buy GM;

sell Coca-Cola," anything like that. No, just that he'd at least have the common decency, he knows he's going to see them, like an appointment with my father, let them in on whatever he thinks might be looking especially good.

'Dad said it to him once when he had him in the chair. Said: "Tell me, Chassy, aren't you just the tiniest bit afraid now? Doesn't it make you nervous to be sitting helplessly here in the chair with a bib on, and me standing over you with this high-speed electric drill I'm about to shove into your mouth? I could hurt you with this thing, if I'm not careful. I should think you'd want to do everything within your power to make sure you're in my good graces – so I'm going to do my best not to hurt you.'

'Dad and Chassy were in high school together. Most of my father's patients're like that: people he's known all his life. So it's okay for him to talk to them that way, and they can talk that way to him.

'The judge opens his eyes – he's like most people, my father says, closes his eyes so he can't see the drill or the needle – sits up straight in the chair and he asks my father what the hell he's got on his mind. And Dad puts it to him: "People say you make a lot of money in the market. I believe them. Mind telling me how come you never see your way clear to letting me in on the deal?"

'Judge sits back and closes his eyes again. "Don't mind at all," he says. "I've made some money in the market, as have many. I've also *lost* some money in the market, as many others have as well. All of my profits have come from investing my own money – well, mine and Delia's. I've risked it to increase it. When my risks have paid off, I've had profits, been happy. And when they haven't, I've had losses. Then I've been unhappy. I always *try* to buy stocks that are going to go up; I can't claim I always succeed.

'If I recommend you buy a certain stock, and you do it and make money, you'll be happy. You may even call me up and thank me. But you'll expect to keep the profit – as you should; it was your money that you risked. If you *lose* money, though, as you very well might, then you'll be *un*happy. And even though of course I know you won't expect me to make good your loss, you certainly won't call me up and thank me. In fact you'll probably secretly blame me for your loss, because if I hadn't put it into your head to buy that stock, you wouldn't've lost your money.

'So, when I come in here for a filling after that, what you'll remember won't be that you *solicited* the recommendation that caused you to lose money – it will be that you lost your money because you did something that I told you to do. And therefore you might decide that instead of trying very hard not to hurt me, or hurt me as little as possible, you wouldn't mind hurting me at all, because I made you lose your money. So it would probably be best for me if I found another dentist.

'I don't want to do that. You've been a good dentist. I've been coming to you for years. I've got you all trained. I'm too old now to break in a new one. I think *much* too highly of your dental skills to risk having to do that, by giving you market advice that makes it so I don't dare to come in here anymore.

'Now having said that I must warn you: If you hurt me now, and I decide you did it on purpose because I refused to make you rich, I'll have to have you arrested and put in jail for battery.'

'My father told Chassy he thought his explanation sounded reasonable and he'd do his best not to hurt him with the drill. He said what he *should've* said at that point was that if Chassy didn't start paying his bills on time instead of making him wait ninety days, he'd have him arrested, judge or not, and thrown in jail as a deadbeat. Spring family always took their sweet time paying their dental bills. But he didn't. Basically my father likes Chassy all right; just doesn't like having to wait to get paid for fixing his teeth.'

'Okay then,' Merrion said, 'Spring hasn't got a horse in this race. Judge Cavanaugh: Has he got a family? I don't know.'

'"The Boy Judge,"' Hilliard said, chuckling. 'Fuckin' Freddie Dillinger? That's what he called Lennie Cavanaugh, his appointment was first announced – ever since then, too, every time he's been in the news. It's really a wonder, nobody's ever horsewhipped Fred; just beat the old-fashioned shit out of him, some of the things he's put in that column Nineteen-fifty-nine that was, when Lennie got that job; remember because that was the year Mercy and I got married. He *was* pretty young, though – not even thirty, I recall. So that'd make him now, what, thirty-five, thirty-six? Nah, no kid of his'd be old enough. Might have a relative out there someplace, though, who's had trouble dressing and feeding himself. We wouldn't know.'

'Yeah, he could,' Merrion said. 'He could also have trouble digesting fried fatty foods and we wouldn't know that either. Look, I don't want to sit around with you and do our damnedest to dream up a hundred good reasons why I *can't* get this job. What *I* want to do is figure out how we can do the same thing for *me* that the two of us've done for so many *other* people, nowhere as deserving as I am: figure out some way so that I *can* get this job – *that's* what *I* want to do.'

'I'm sorry,' Hilliard said. 'I'm so used to doing what we do when we get a job-hunter in here, I guess I must've forgotten who I was talking to.'

'Yeah,' Merrion said. 'Well, this one time I'll overlook it. I did what you said, got some background on Lane. Since according to you he seems to be the chief hurdle standing 'tween me and the job. He's got a whole bunch of kids, eight of them. But only two of them don't already have jobs, and both of them're married daughters that don't even live around here. One of them lives in Japan or some other place nobody ever heard of. Her husband's with the State Department. The other one's married to some guy who works for a paint company. All the others've got jobs.'

'How'd you get this?' Hilliard said.

'Turns out my mother knows him,' Merrion said. 'His wife I guess isn't a very good cook. He gets all their pies and cookies from Slade's Bakery. You know the one I mean. Used to also be a cafeteria, back when we still had the trains coming through. Ma says he's a regular bear for the cookies, oatmeal raisin, chocolate chip. Goes through couple dozen a week, half a dozen or so at a time. Monday nights, Wednesday nights, then a dozen he comes in on Friday. Plus a loaf of the brown bread, for Saturday night – I guess him and the wife have baked beans. He's never in a very big hurry, Ma says, always got plenty of time to chat. He calls her "Polly," like all her friends do, and she calls him "Mister Lane." Now.'

'What'd she used to call him?' Hilliard said. '"Franklin Delano Roosevelt"?'

'She called him "Judge,"' Merrion said. 'But then someone told her – it was Chris; he was still living at home then, after I'd moved out – that he's just the clerk. "He's not the judge. He doesn't decide anything."

'Her reaction was: "Well, what did I know, he was only the clerk? Someone told me he worked at the courthouse. Who works at the courthouse, huh? Judges. How'm I supposed to know he wasn't one? I was never inside it, thank God – none of my family was ever arrested. We always behaved ourselves. He certainly looked like a judge ought to look, always very well-dressed and so forth. Although come to think of it, kind of flashy, for a judge. But always a jacket and tie, winter, summer or fall; shoes always shined; a clean shirt – and a hat, always a hat. A felt hat in the winter, straw hat in the summer. Nice camel-hair overcoat in the cold weather. Mister Lane is a very sharp dresser.'

'"Well," Chris tells her, "how he dresses doesn't count. It's what he does that counts. And all he does is file papers no one ever looks at, and collect the money for tickets. It's not like he can send you to jail. He don't amount to a pisshole inna snow."'

'To your *mother* he said that?' Hilliard said. 'Did your father rise up out of the grave and belt him one? Pat might've said "pisshole" out in back at Valley Ford, but never in front of her.'

'Well, the general idea was all I meant,' Merrion said. 'I don't know what Chris actually said. He was just givin' the general idea. Which's what I'm trying to give to you here. I asked my mother about him. I think I can work for this guy. I think it'd work out all right. Not someone I would call, I was lookin' for a guy go out'n have a few with, no, but otherwise, I see no problem.

'And let's not get carried away with ourselves here, either, when we're discussing this thing. This job that Lane's got with nobody in it, it isn't that big a thing. "I get by on it": was what Dad used to call his job, and that's all this job is, too. I can get by on it. A steady check is what I want. I never had any ambition.

'My own mother'll tell you that, if I'm not careful. God knows she's told me enough – she's always giving me that. "Second prize, the small change, the leftovers. You poor kid, you've simply got no ambition at all."'

Merrion had listened many times while she low-rated him to

others. 'It just isn't in Ambrose's nature to put himself forward, you know? He's tall enough and strong enough – and fat enough, too, God knows he should be, see the way he eats all the time. His father used to say he wasn't a bad athlete. Not that he was ever a real *good* athlete either – that might've meant he'd stand out.

'Pat never seemed to mind, though. I think now it was because he never aimed too high himself. Pat was always careful not to make himself conspicuous. Get his name in the papers, so someone heard about him. I think he approved of that attitude Amby had. He said if Amby didn't watch out, wasn't careful, he'd get too good at something in school, and pretty soon he'd wind up going far away to some fine university or something. I used to think he didn't mean it; that was his way of pushing Amby, getting him to do something. But now I'm not so sure.

'He'd say Amby didn't want people to *think* he wanted something really good to happen: "Mustn't let 'em catch you aiming too high for anything in this world. You might get it. Then God only knows what could happen. People might not *like* you anymore. Say you went high-hat on them, something bad like that might happen. It's just not worth takin' the risk, you know?" After a while Pat had us all convinced, Chris and me and Amby both. "Chris's the one who's got his eye on the moon. What Ambrose wants is for people to like him, to be the hero's best friend, covers his backside for him. Never the hero himself."'

Thirty years later Polly (Flavin) Merrion late that benign Saturday afternoon in August lay *non compos mentis* at age seventy-nine in the bed in the bright sunny room with southwestern exposure on a small enclosed patio overlooking a round pool with a tulip-shaped recirculating fountain at St Mary's on the Hilltop in West Springfield, picking at the hem on the lightweight white wool blanket, her sparse white hair neatly trimmed, set and combed, her faultless white skin clear and softly lotioned, a hint of color on her lips, her blue eyes 'as clear as Gilbey's gin,' as her dear Pat had used to say, just to get her goat. It had been about three years since she'd heckled her oldest son.

'My own dear mother, Rose, now,' Polly usually began, when giving him a roasting – he understood it to be her way of bragging about him – running on the first part of a manhattan as she had been one day in March of 1973 at a small luncheon that he'd thrown in the private dining room at Henry's Grist Mill. He'd invited about thirty people to celebrate his official promotion to first assistant clerk of the District Court of Western Hampshire (meaning: Clerk of Court-designate).

Clerk of Court Richie Hammond after stalling six months had at last formally appointed Merrion to his old slot under Larry Lane. Hammond had instinctively disliked Merrion from the first time they met, knowing on first sight he was a smart-ass. Ever since Larry Lane had died he had been forlornly hoping either that someone with more clout would become interested in the job – Hammond knew that was unlikely; Dan Hilliard was in the most formidable years of his ascent – or failing that, perhaps God in His wisdom and goodness would strike Merrion dead. God had not.

Richie had stopped stalling after being credibly threatened with summary dismissal from his own place. The threat had come in the form of a menacing phone call placed by a deputy administrator in the Administrative Office of the District Court Department in Salem. He said that the chief judge had just gotten an upsetting call about the next year's judicial budget from the chairman of House Ways and Means. The administrator had reported grimly that the chairman of Ways and Means appeared to be not only very angry but 'a very close personal friend of this Ambrose Merrion,' as well, and asked Richie Hammond if he'd been aware of that fact. When Richie said he had been – 'Everybody out here knows they're asshole buddies; that's the only reason Merrion got the goddamned job he's got' – the chief administrative clerk had said in a soft savage voice: 'Then would you mind telling *me*, so I can tell the judge, who's practically *beside* himself with fucking curiosity – I *think* it's curiosity; it may be something else – exactly why the *fuck* it is he had to get the call he got and I have to make this call right now, to get you to do what any fucking asshole with the brain of a retarded pigeon would've known from on the first day what he'd better do right fucking off or get his fucking *balls* cut off? Or would you rather quit right now, and we'll give Merrion *your* job – would you like that better?'

Hammond had soberly accepted Merrion's solemn invitation to

attend the joyous luncheon, but to the surprise of neither of them suffered an attack of the Twenty-four-hour Convenient Grippe when the day for it arrived.

'When Rose was among us,' Polly said, 'she had designs on my poor little Ambrose, and selfish ones at that. She'd always had it in her mind that if she ever had any sons of her own it'd be a good thing for her if one of them went into the priesthood. You know what they used to tell all the good Catholic mothers: "If you've a son a priest, your place in heaven's guaranteed." But she didn't have any, so that was a bit of a handicap for her, you see? In that respect, at least, she'd left a stone unturned.

'That was not her way at all, neglecting things. Of course she hadn't had any *wayward* sons, either, which'd also been known to've happened to perfectly good church-going Catholic mothers. No naughty boys she would've had to pray for, make novenas to Saint Jude for, the patron saint of the Impossible, and go and visit Sunday mornings down at the lock-up, or on Tuesdays and the weekends at county jail or something, like some unfortunate women she knew – and don't think she ever let 'em forget it, either; not for one stinkin' minute did she ever do that. "Those poor unfortunate creatures with those terrible crosses to bear, the poor things."

'But that still didn't give her one to bake the cookies for, and send down to the seminary, either, and she couldn't let her*self* forget that. I don't think nuns counted in that bounty-hunt and they didn't take young ladies in the priesthood. If they had, I think she would've thought nothing of wrapping me up and sending me along, "see what you can do with this one. Not much to look at maybe, but good with pots and pans, and she knows how to do a wash. Send her back if it looks like she isn't going to work out for you." But the choice wasn't available.

'So you could see what she was thinking, the minute he was born and we knew he was a boy. She thought maybe Ambrose might become a priest, if she took a hand in it – as she generally did everything that happened within a mile or two of her, and played her cards right, of course. Wasn't his namesake a famous bishop? And a saint? The bishop who baptized Saint Augustine, by God? Well, didn't that tell you something? Meaning that if the vocation didn't come naturally to our little boy, if the Holy Ghost didn't give him a good bat on the head and tell him what he ought to do, well then, she might get involved herself in working out the matter. Since she was pretty sure she knew what would've been God's will, if He'd only just spent the time and taken the proper interest in it. If you know what I mean. Bashfulness was not a thing that troubled her.

'So for a while then, after Pat and I were first married and Amby'd come into the world after only the bare decent interval, there, I'm sure she had her eye on him. Not that I'd want you to think, for even one moment, that my dear mother Rose actually had a thing to be concerned about where getting into heaven was concerned. Far from it – butter wouldn't've melted in her mouth, not in that one's. No, it was just that she was always one to believe that where salvation was concerned, you couldn't be too careful. If now a grandson was the closest she could come to meeting the requirements, well, that was the best she could do. Couldn't ask for more than that. At least 'til I told her I didn't think grandsons counted, met the tariff for admission to Jerusalem, the holy city, the same way that sons do. And so that more or less cut down her zeal.

'It really was all for the best. If Ambrose'd gone into the church, you know, none of you here in this room or even at this table would've ever heard of him at all. He'd most likely be the curate in a small parish 'way up in the State of Maine someplace, up there on the forty-fifth parallel, on the Canadian border. And he'd be perfectly happy, you know? Completely at peace with the world. My boy's a humble man.'

'At least she didn't say the celibacy stuff would've been no trouble for you,' Mary Pat Sweeney had said to him that night in the apartment he'd been renting then in Hampton Pond. 'If she had then I'd've known for sure I'd come to the wrong funeral after all.' Mary Pat had kept about a hundred-fifteen pounds in what seemed like constant merry motion back in those days, and not just in her office down in Springfield at Massachusetts Mutual, or at the evening and weekend county Democratic meetings, either.

Mary Pat was well-known far and wide – 'Oh sure, both ways,

north and south, up and down the river,' as she used to say herself, 'good-time Mary Pat' – for being the one person that you had to sign up before you could be really sure that what you had in mind to do would be a success. Merrion admitted cheerfully that her reddish hair and greenish eyes were the sights he first looked for when he walked into a room, 'just like everybody else does. Everybody else.'

She believed in realism, just as he and Dan did. While Sunny was around but stationed far away from home, he 'always seemed to get along real good with Mary Pat,' as Polly said from time to time, with some insistent wistfulness, the closest that she ever came to declaring her preference for Mary Pat among his girlfriends that she'd met. That was fully close enough for him to implying her somewhat-less-than-full approval of then-Lieutenant – later Captain – Geraldine Keller, USAF. Mary Pat in those days without discussion understood and apparently accepted the fact that she was his second-best girl and probably always would be no more than that. She appeared to believe that the reason was timing: he'd met Sunny first, at UMass., and because he was a loyal man, Sunny would remain first as long as they lived. Many times without wishing Sunny any ill Mary Pat therefore sincerely and coolly wished her dead. She excused such thoughts to the accuser in her mind with the mitigation that she never actually prayed for Keller's death. That would have been deliberate; she wasn't willing anything; she simply couldn't help thinking that it would have been much more convenient for her and better for Ambrose as well, if Sunny were to die young without any pain at all, peacefully, in her sleep.

Mary Pat further understood without being told that Merrion could stand it if she should happen to run into someone else who would replace him as first in her love (although she hadn't wanted the assurance, and would have summarily rejected it if he'd offered it). So – except for that first fucking week in fucking July every god-*damned* fucking year, and all the other fucking times fucking Sunny came home on fucking leave *again*, goddamnit, always unexpectedly because unwanted by Mary Pat – she and Amby did have their good times.

It wasn't easy for her. Mary Pat said nothing to nobody about nothing, as she put it, but then she didn't have to; she turned up the volume on her desk radio whenever WHYN-AM played 'Time Is on My Side,' by the Rolling Stones, and everyone who knew and liked her – including all the men, and she knew a lot of them, from her interest in politics – also knew she played the waiting game. She was generally steadfast and obdurate, silent in receipt of truly well-meant good advice from friends – including her boss, Carol, a peach, who was really good to her and mentioned it only once – until they stopped giving it, content to eyebrow smart remarks. She did allow a rather dumpy woman in Agents Accounts named Priscilla, from Three Rivers, whom she didn't even *like*, to get away with saying one beautiful June day during lunch outside on the lawn that she was 'never sure if the reason Sweeney's cubicle's always filled with smoke's because of all those Winstons she smokes or if it's from that torch she carries.'

Knowing immediately from the laughter that self-restraint had been a mistake, Mary had rectified it early the next month – when Sunny's annual July visit, now two weeks at the place in Falmouth Heights that Amby rented – had her in an ugly mood anyway. During a lull in a department briefing about the company's upcoming autumn media campaign of suggestions for avoiding life-endangering, artery-clogging, sedentary obesity, Mary Pat murmured rather loudly to the person sitting next to her that the ads should feature Priscilla as national poster girl. 'Show Priscilla linin' up a chocolate-frosted jelly doughnut,' Mary Pat proposed, well aware that her husky voice carried, 'drawin' a bead on a cruller. *That'd* put the point across: Henry the *Eighth'd* slim down.'

Then everything'd gone all wrong and come apart in May of 1973, when Sunny died in a hospital in Honolulu. The cause was severe head-trauma she had suffered when the rented Jeep CJ that she was driving rolled over and down a cliff in the aftermath of a three-car accident that killed another woman and injured four other people on a mountain road switchback during a blinding downpour. Merrion at first did not believe it. Stunned in his grief, he was badly surprised as well that Sunny had returned to Hawaii and he hadn't known about it. He had met her at the Royal

Hawaiian – she'd called it 'the big pink hotel on the beach, the one where everyone always goes once' – for her previous energetic furlough four months before, and had assumed from its delights he'd be returning for the next one. The married major from Coronado, California, who'd flown from Tan Son Nhut to Hawaii with her for ten days of R&R, when he recovered consciousness gave police a statement proving conclusively the crash had not been Sunny's fault. Somehow that *post mortem* exoneration hadn't seemed to help Merrion feel better at all.

That fact had not been lost on Mary Pat. Heedlessly leaving her desk at mid-morning as soon as she'd heard the news, putting off the explanation to another day – no one in her office ever asked her for it later – she had gone at once to his place to make stiff drinks and get in bed to give him a lover's help. She had arrived there knowing – she thought: instinctively, without possibility of error – he needed to have that done. It had always seemed to him afterwards that both of them had realized about ten seconds before she'd really begun trying to console him, it was never going to work.

Neither one of them had ever gotten over it. After a few more perfunctory, good-buddy, make-believe tries at making him feel better she'd decided on her own to give it up. While in one corner of his mind he believed she'd never found it getting any easier to do, she'd started saying No without excuse or explanation every time he called, and she had stuck to it. After a while he'd given up too, and rather gratefully stopped making the calls.

That August Saturday waiting for Hilliard at Grey Hills the most recent time he'd seen her had been by chance at a dinner-dance at the Sheraton Hartford hotel in '92 or '93, benefit for the family of a high-spirited, hail-fellow lawyer they had known from Seventies-early-Eighties New England Democratic politics. Disbarred and disgraced after having lived very graciously for many years on money he had not, after all, earned from representing a few extremely wealthy and secretive clients, as he had always seemed to claim. Instead he had stolen systematically and routinely from a couple dozen estates left by fairly prosperous clients whose heirs had trusted him, taking what he'd wanted as boldly as if it had been his. Caught, he had avoided criminal prosecution, certain conviction and plenty of jail by stripping his own estate as ruthlessly as he'd plundered his late clients' accumulations. The sale of everything he owned at distress prices, beggaring his still-young family, combined with the proceeds of his malpractice insurance policy amounted to enough to constitute ostentatious restitution of eighty-four percent of what he had stolen. He was sentenced to five years in jail, two of them to be served, three suspended for ten years. Granted thirty days to finish putting his affairs in order before starting to serve his sentence, he had needed only two to complete his liquidation by shooting himself in the head.

'Well, no one ever said Mickey wasn't thorough,' Mary Pat said, encountering Merrion at the bar. She still smoked the Winstons and weighed around the same trim one-fifteen, but she was dressing and decorating it a lot better. Merrion told her she looked like a million bucks. 'Yeah,' she said, satisfaction in that smoky voice, 'and even nicer, now I've got it.'

'Hit the lottery?' he said. 'Lucky you.'

She grinned and shook her head. 'Can't count on luck,' she said. 'Luck's not dependable, and as you know, mine's never been all that good. Stock market's much more reliable. Skill and smarts still count there, which is good. Helps if you clank when you walk, but it's really not all that complicated. You quit spending all your time partying around; start staying home and paying attention to what the rich people say.'

'You have rich friends now?' Merrion said.

'Well,' she said, 'I have a rich *friend*. He takes me where rich people go; I get close enough to listen.'

He hadn't asked her the next question because he'd known the answer. She'd delivered it anyway, shaking her head. He played dumb, smiled back and said: 'I'm missing something here, am I?'

She'd shaken her head once more. 'Probably nothing that ever really interested you that much,' she said. 'Funny how things seem to change, after time's gone by.'

'What is it that seems to have changed on us here, all of a sudden and all?' Merrion said to Hilliard on the terrace at Grey Hills, that Saturday in August.

Hilliard frowned and leaned forward in his chair. He rested his elbows on its arms and scraped it on the flagstones up against the table. 'I think,' he said slowly, frowning, 'I think . . . well, lemme put it this way: what I think is, anyway . . . I . . .'

'Well, this is reassuring,' Merrion said. 'If you're doing that.'

'You had some doubt in your mind, maybe?' Hilliard said, looking up from under his eyebrows.

'I was beginning to get a little concerned, yeah,' Merrion said. 'I was beginning to wonder if maybe instead of asking you to explain Julian to me, I should ask Julian about you. Or maybe get Janet back in and put a different question to her. "What's the meaning of life, huh Janet? You got a handle on this?"'

'Yeah,' Hilliard said. 'Well, look, whyn't we do this now, then, all right? Let's you and me just go inside and get a bite to eat, cheeseburger, something, a bottle of beer, talk it over in there, and see what we do about this. Would that be all right with you? Then, after that, play a round. Or maybe just nine holes or something.'

'Fuck going inside,' Merrion said. 'Tell me here what you think's going on.'

'I don't know,' Hilliard said. 'I heard things I don't like, but I'm not sure . . . Look, you gotta remember Bob Pooler.'

'Remember and hate the fucker,' Merrion said.

'Yeah, well, still,' Hilliard said. 'I think you should go, you know, talk to the guy, and see what he thinks about this. See what he's got to say.'

'Hear what the little prick's got to say about what?' Merrion said. 'What could that little shit possibly have to say that could possibly interest me?'

'Well,' Hilliard said slowly, 'I'm not exactly sure myself yet what the broad outlines of this might be, but what it seems to be is this: he thinks they may be thinking, the federal boys in Boston, about maybe starting up grand jury hearings out this way, down in Springfield, I mean, and if they decide to do that then they might be . . . well, you know what I'm saying, right? Might be coming after me.'

'Which of course would have to mean, then,' Merrion said thoughtfully, 'also after me.'

Hilliard frowned and cleared his throat, 'Yeah,' he said. 'Well, after us. That would be the gist of it. After you and me.'

13

The police station in Canterbury was the second-largest structure to be built in the new municipal complex, four buildings clustered on Holyoke Street a block north of the green. The town offices opened in 1981. The police station was completed in February of 1982. The largest building, the new fire station, and the public library were finished in April of 1983, during Hilliard's eleventh and last term in the House. Because he had been instrumental in the enactment of 1980 legislation granting $6.7 million in state aid to the town for the construction, the selectmen felt they had no choice but to invite him to be the keynote speaker at the dedication of the buildings as the Veterans' Memorial Municipal Center on the afternoon of Memorial Day of 1983.

It was not a popular decision. Many who had voted for him several times now severely disapproved of him and said they would never support him again, generating considerable and vehement negative advance comment. He thought he heard someone boo when he took the lectern, but he soon made his audience feel better, using the occasion to announce to the audience of sixty-three seated on metal folding chairs before him on the broad front walk that he would not be a candidate for re-election in 1984. Several women applauded vigorously, nodding for emphasis, saying '*Good*,' and 'Well, you *shouldn't*,' giving their husbands meaningful looks; one or two even cried 'Yea,' in ladylike fashion.

He declined to divulge his plans. 'You do,' Merrion said, 'and all you do is egg them on, whet their appetites. All they want is to see you humiliated, punished for the way you treated Mercy.

Okay, let 'em have what they want. Put your tail between your legs and look sheepish; tell 'em you're not gonna run. Cringe like a dog that's been beaten a lot. Try to cower a little – I realize you're outta practice, but do the best you can. That'll make 'em all feel superior and virtuous; like they've upheld the sanctity of marriage and the family, driving you out of office. You do some public penance, it won't be as much as you deserve, but it'll be enough. They'll be satisfied, forget about you and go on; find some other poor bastard to make life miserable for.

'They start thinkin' you're gettin' away with something, pretendin' to be humble but sneakin' away to something even better – this soft job that *you* invented – they're liable say: "Oh no you don't; none of *that* shit, there. Givin' up the rep seat, pays fifty grand a year, 'cause he's been a naughty boy, and that gets him a *better* job, he pulls down *eighty* grand? Uh uh, we're not lettin' him do that."'

'They'll find out if I don't announce it,' Hilliard said. 'Someone will've leaked it, time I make the speech. If they want to raise a stink and try to block it, they will. It'll all amount to the same thing.'

'No, it won't,' Merrion said. 'If someone else tells 'em, that's all it'll be: something that someone else said. But if *you* announce it, they'll think you're laughing at them, gloating. To them it'll sound like this: "Okay, you hypocrites, I am convinced. If I run again you'll kick my ass. Well, up yours; I'm not giving you the chance. I'm not gonna let you dump me. *And*, I got something much better cooked up. Pays even more and you'll never be able to vote me out of it, no matter how much I get laid. Doesn't that frost your balls, folks?'

'You know what they'll do then?' Merrion said. 'They will lynch you. If they decide you're not repenting; that you're giving them the finger, they will hang you by your fuckin' neck. They'll come to your condo and they'll drag you out the cellar where you hid and they'll march you down to Holyoke – they'll have a band and everything, put on a torch-light parade. And when they get to Hampden Park they'll tie your hands behind you and rope your feet together and loop a noose around your neck. They'll make you stand on the roof of your Murr-say-deez-Benz and they'll throw the other end of the rope over the branch of a tree and tie it down good and tight to the tree trunk. And then before someone backs the car out from under you, they'll have a butcher climb up on the hood, yank your dick out of your pants and chop it off with his cleaver, and hold it up for all to see, while the bishop gives his blessing and leads the crowd singing "God Bless America."'

'So I gather you don't think it would be a good idea for me to say what my plans are,' Hilliard said.

'That would be the gist of it,' Merrion said.

Reports of the address at the dedication said 'Hilliard appeared subdued.' An editorial paragraph in the *Springfield Union* reported that 'to many there, the personable and forceful chairman seemed chastened, no doubt by the strong public reaction to recent disclosures of his untidy personal life, almost certainly the principal reason behind his prudent decision to leave elective office.' As Hilliard had predicted, the reports did include informed speculation that he expected to be 'appointed president of the community college in Hampton Pond, scheduled to formally open next year, although at first offering only night courses at the Pioneer Regional School during hours when it would normally be unused,' but Merrion had also been right: no public outcry followed.

Freddie Dillinger in his *Transcript* column seemed a bit subdued himself. He was content to sneer, writing that the scheduled summer '84 completion of construction of the first of three new buildings planned for the HPCC campus 'will make the Hilliard Hilton the most modern – shamelessly lavish, many have said – layout in the Commonwealth's entire community college system. The throne room, palmed-off in main-building blueprints as the presidential office suite, will be spacious enough for Dapper Dan to host a full-blown consistory, should the College of Cardinals ever stop by Hampton Pond and need a meeting-place. Assuming the prelates are on speaking terms with him after his pending divorce, seen by many as the catalyst for his career move.' But Dillinger also seemed saddened by the prospect of Hilliard's departure from active politics. 'I have no trouble saying that I've always liked Dan Hilliard. He's given us a lot of laughs, although not always intentionally, and in this often-gloomy world it's hard not to like a man who's so often brought you laughter.'

'Praise from Caesar is praise indeed,' Hilliard said to Merrion. 'Imagine the cocksucker getting emotional? Probably had to wipe away a tear. How insensitive I've been: All these years I've been reading the guy without ever guessing he liked me.' He snorted. 'Freddie must think the old saying's a commandment: Each man kills the thing he loves. Does his best to, anyway.'

'I think we should give him a present,' Merrion said. 'How about we make a blivit, nice big bag full of fresh, soft dogshit, with a brick in it, throw it through his window on his desk.'

The run-up to the withdrawal began in the spring of 1980. When Hilliard figured in newsworthy events, the identifier in the papers gradually changed; 'Powerful Ways and Means Chairman' became 'Embattled Chairman.'

'I used to love it when they did that,' he mourned to his friends, 'called me "powerful."' He had begun to depend on them heavily for companionship. Weekends bothered him badly; drinks and dinner among 'my pals' Sunday nights at Grey Hills took on extreme importance.

What he called: 'my well-known downfall' began semi-privately. Mercy, on her way home from drinks with Diane Fox at Gino's Hearthside one fine evening in the spring abruptly decided that she'd had enough and determined to kick him out of their lovely new home in Bell Woods. By noon on Tuesday word of what she'd done had reached Beacon Hill. 'Dja hear what happened Friday night, Danny Hilliard? His wife got home this class she's takin' up at UMass.? Threw him out. He wasn't even doin' nothing. Didn't have a fight with her or annathin' like that. Just sittin' there, havin' a beer, watchin' the TV or somethin'. Had no idea annathin's goin' on; just waitin' her to come home. Make him some dinner, you know? How'd he know what she's got on her mind? But she comes inna door, says: "Okay, I've had it. Get your ass *out*. I'm sick of lookin' at you. We're finished." Hear he begged and pleaded her, too; prackly got down on his knees, she'd give him just one more chance. Didn't do him no good. "Nothin' doin'," she says, "I said *out*, I mean *out*. Now leave or I calla cops." He couldn't budge her. She was stickin' to her guns, an' that was it. His ass went out on the street.'

The public humiliation immediately crippled him politically. Mercy's assertion of control and his submission to it emboldened people who until then had concealed their envy of the power that made them afraid to show him any disrespect. He initially resisted acknowledging the change.

'Not that it ever really meant anything, as you know. The adjective, I mean. The job hasn't changed any since I got it. It's still either the second or third in line: Speaker; Majority Leader; and then Ways and Means. Or Ways and Means before the floor leader. I never had any more actual *power*'n anyone else ever did in the job. It just became part of the title: "*Powerful.*" Like when we were growin' up, the baseball team that always stunk, where the Red Sox always went to buy the player that they needed, Vern Stephens, Ellis Kinder? No one never called them the plain old "Saint Louis Browns." Always "the *hapless* Saint Louis Browns.' So I was always "the powerful chairman." "A sobriquet"; it didn't mean shit, but I gotta admit I did love it.'

'It *did* mean something, though,' Merrion said to him later, after he had begun to recover. 'It meant a lot. It's okay to *claim* now that it never meant anything when they said you hadda lotta power, just's long's we don't forget it's not true. It meant a *lot*. It was what my father used to call "a very handy gadget." When the papers kept reminding people how much power you had, lots of people believed it. They didn't think about how or why this should be, you seemed to have so much power. They just thought it was true. They saw it right there inna paper.

'They thought it meant that you could *do* something to them, something nobody else would've even known how to do. They didn't know what it was, and they didn't know anybody else who did, either, but they also knew they sure didn't want to be the ones who pissed you off so they found out. So therefore when I call, once they hear who's onna line they know you want something done; they pay close attention. They may think I'm a dummy but they're scared of the ventriloquist. They know he can cut their balls off. So they want to please me, you know? Want me to be happy. Piss me off; they got *you* pissed off. That they do not want to happen.

'I don't know what it was that they thought you could do to them then that you couldn't've done to them before. Maybe they just never thought about it. All I know's that when they did, I could make good use of it. All I hadda do was ask politely; right off they would do what we wanted. I liked that. It made my life easy. It was a good way to do business.

'Now I can't do that anymore. You got people laughing at you, result of you bein' such an asshole Mercy finely kicked you out. People don't jump to please guys they're laughing at. I hafta frighten them now, apply actual muscle; tell them if they don't do what we want them to do, they may be out of a job. It seems wasteful, you know? Undignified, too, using your power every time, *making* people do what they should *want* to do, just to get little stuff done.'

Other things changed in subtle ways too. Over the years Hilliard had spent a sizeable number of quietly congenial Sunday evenings at Grey Hills, maybe ten or a dozen a year, having what he called ' a little dinner with the lads,' turning one corner of the sparsely populated dining room into a men's club for the night, washing down steaks, chops and roast beef with whatever the indifferent house-red wine was that year. Merrion could usually be counted on; a phone call to his home would fetch him if he hadn't spent the day at the club, playing golf in good weather or if rain was pouring down, unassumingly catching a few hands of modestly profitable quarter-half poker in the lounge with a ballgame in progress on the TV across the room. Usually when he stood up from his chair he was thirty or thirty-five bucks ahead. He seldom lost, and never more than ten dollars; he quit early when he encountered a run of second-best hands. He refused side-bets on the ballgames, saying: 'No, I play cards because I know what cards will do. I don't know what people will do.'

Rob Lewis's wife belonged to The Opera, Theater and Museum Society in Springfield; each year between Labor and Memorial Days it offered members eight completely-packaged long-weekend travel-tickets-meals-hotel excursions to New York. Indulging her passion for the visual and performing arts, all of which Rob detested, Lena took all of the trips – 'Four thousand bucks a year and worth every damned penny; I'd sooner rub shit in my hair'n sit through another damned opera.' He was around at least seven or eight Sundays a year.

Heck Sanderson and six or seven other male members, widowed or divorced themselves – both, in Heck's case – long before Hilliard's travails began had for years on and off been at loose ends around the club at dinnertime, much gladder of Hilliard's company than he'd ever dreamed until he learned the hard way how much he'd come to value theirs.

'Get a good close look at this guy, fellas,' Heck said one evening late in June of that year to Merrion, Ralph Flood and Bobby Clark – who was as usual quietly and purposefully drinking exactly as much Haig & Haig Pinch as he would need to stay moderately, comfortably drunk until it was time for the twenty-minute, three-mile drive home to bed – when Hilliard had become particularly lugubrious, 'this's a very rare bird we've got with us here tonight. This here's the first man in North America who's ever gone through a divorce. He was married for years and then all of a sudden, one sunny morning, he woke all by himself – first one in the entire history, this republic. We got us a real curiosity here: when he dies we're gonna get him stuffed and put him in a glass case in the lobby on display. Members'll be able to look at him free, charge the public a quarter to see him.'

Then he had clapped Hilliard on the shoulder, hard, and guffawed. 'Aww, maybe I'm being too hard on him here. Being as how he's a Catholic and all, he most likely wasn't prepared for it. Catholics're much better'n the rest of us. Catholics don't *get* divorced, see, so he thought he had a *guaranty*. Never could happen to him.'

Merrion made a mental note to lose any and all future requests Heck made to Hilliard through him, and to make sure that if Heck's kid ever did get in trouble in the Canterbury jurisdiction, the case would go to Lennie Cavanaugh. Cavanaugh would do whatever Merrion suggested; Heck would not get many laughs out of what he had in mind to do if the day ever came when he could do it. Once when asked what he did for Hilliard after he'd left the Holyoke office to become a court clerk, Merrion said: 'Well,

Danny's sort of kind-hearted. It's a weakness of his; he suffers from compassion. He also tends to forget things. So if somebody does something to him that they shouldn't do, sticks a shiv in his back, say, he's likely, you know, to *forgive* the treacherous bastard. Say "Oh, he didn't mean it. I'll give him another chance." Or else forget he even stuck him inna first place.

'Danny knows he's this way, and he knows he shouldn't be. But he also knows that I am not – I am not like that at all. I am different. I don't forgive and I *never* forget. So what I do for him, I'm in charge of grudges. I collect all his grudges for him, make sure they're put away in a safe place, water 'em and keep 'em fresh and moist. And then when payback day comes 'round, as we know it always does, I have the right grudge to settle, and *whammo*, we pop the guy. I'm the guy who makes sure that the guys who hurt Danny get *nailed*, big-time, paid back at least double for whatever they did to us.'

Hilliard had been too humbled to get mad at Sanderson. He conceded the point. 'You begin to see things a different way, once something like this happens to you, I guess, huh?' he said. Heck, perhaps finding something disturbing him in Merrion's expression, cleared his throat and said placatingly, somewhat nervously, that he knew he certainly had. Merrion, mindful he had trouble maneuvering Heck into bad bets for much money at cards, noted the hasty contrition but deferred judgment as to whether it was merely tactical or sufficiently sincere to save Julian from what he had in mind – some good wholesome time in jail.

For Hilliard until his own disaster those Sabbath dinners had been mere felicitous accidents, irregular pick-up things that just happened; low-key, casual occasions of camaraderie for him and therefore the other men who'd been around for dinner and sat down at tables with him, connoting no unhappiness, dislocation or decline. Without ever thinking about it, he'd assumed that the explanation for their presence was the same as his: they were temporarily on their own and did not choose to cook. Until the winter of 1980–81, he had been at the club on Sunday nights in the dead of winter because in '73 Mercy and the kids had started spending February school vacations with her folks at their new chalet at Bolton Valley, skiing every day. February was a busy month on Beacon Hill, and Hilliard, who'd never skied well and found time spent with Florence and Bud Hackett 'not a garden of earthly delights,' had long since given up on both the sport and his in-laws. Mondays through Fridays those weeks he'd stayed in Boston in the small one-bedroom apartment that he kept on Lindall Street on the back slope of Beacon Hill (paying the rent out of campaign contributions while continuing to collect tax-exempt reimbursements for daily mileage), usually screwing Stacy three or four times – until early '75, when she caught her network break and moved to New York.

He always fucked Stacy at her place. Mercy regularly came to Boston to see her friends from Emmanuel for Symphony, or to shop at Filene's Basement, staying over once or twice a month to make Dan take her to a play, or dinner with friends from the House whose wives she deemed acceptably smart and polished – she was pleasant to their 'somewhat-loutish' husbands.

Mercy'd never hidden her suspicion of his vulnerability to sexual temptation, or her apprehension that by leasing the apartment he was revealing his intention to surrender to it. Nights when he was staying in Boston he usually called her at home around ten, while she watched TV in bed; she often kept herself awake an extra hour in order to call him back after midnight, half an hour after Stacy would have finished her shift at the station, saying: 'Just checking up on you, sweetie. Making sure you're still there. Didn't suddenly decide to pop out for bread and milk right after we hung up. Also that I don't hear someone walking around barefoot on her tippy-*tippy*-toes, being very, very quiet, while we're talking now.' She called in the morning, too, inserting long pauses in their conversations to see whether she could hear his shower running. She had sharp eyes that she used boldly, forthrightly inspecting his pad for traces of trespassing female occupancy every time she visited. 'Ooh, and how *is* the FBI these days?' Stacy would coo sweetly, with wide eyes, when Mercy's name came up.

Saturdays and Sundays book-ending the family ski-vacations Hilliard had spent working Saturday forenoons at his Holyoke office, after 1978 luxuriating by himself in the ten-room home in Bell Woods, proprietorially watching basketball games on his forty-inch TV and snow accumulating on the field and in the pine woods behind the house where Emily rode her Morgan horse. Sunday evenings he pulled on a white wool turtleneck and a blazer before driving languidly over to Grey Hills to see who might be around for dinner.

That lazy and expansive attitude he'd had – and imputed to his friends – of purely optional self-indulgence had been dispelled in the days of depositions and preliminary hearings in *Hilliard* vs. *Hilliard*, Hampshire County Probate Court #82–268-D, the D denoting divorce proceedings. Living by himself in a condominium he'd sublet furnished at the splendidly refurbished Old Wisdom House overlooking Hampton Pond, he found the change of residence 'discombobulating,' his mind thrown off-balance by the unfamiliarity of living in someone else's luxury. He told Merrion it was like waking up in a rented room on the road morning after morning; 'It's a very nice hotel, but now I want to go home,' he said. 'I lie there as I'm waking up and I think: "This is really a beautiful place, but when do I get to go *home*?"'

He had chosen to live there as abruptly as Mercy had decided she'd had enough of him. Merrion lived there, having purchased a two-bedroom unit during the rehabilitation and conversion phase of the old inn into condominiums six years before. Because he knew and liked the woman who managed the place, Glenda Rice, he could get the rental set up for Hilliard fast.

The hurry had been Mercy's creation; having taken eight years to make up her mind what she wanted done, she wanted it done at once. The day after Tax Day, Friday the 16th, she had come home from her afternoon seminar in statistics at UMass. later than usual, delayed by the unusual length of the conversation she'd had with Diane.

She'd been troubled for a week by something she had overheard in the Grey Hills pro shop the previous Saturday. She had been sitting behind the sweaters racked on the chrome trolley in the women's clothing section, trying on new Foot-Joy spikes. She was trying to decide well before the golf season started whether to order a new pair, which would be a fresh nuisance to break in, or continue to put up with the existing nuisance: her shoes occasionally gave her blisters. A man whose face she could not see and whose voice she didn't recognize came up to the counter where Bolo Cormier sat on his stool at the register, moving his lips as he read his paper and drinking coffee as he did most days between golf seasons. They had some brief conversation to which she paid no attention, but then as she hunched over to lace up the brown-and-white saddle-shoe on her right foot, dropping her head below the sweaters, she heard the man say: 'Dan Hilliard been around today – or's he with his new girlfriend down in Boston? I called his house and office – didn't get an answer.'

She had turned her head quickly to peer under the sweaters as Bolo said 'Dunno, haven't seen him,' but had not had the presence of mind to part them before the grey flannel slacks and the dark-brown tasseled loafers turned away from the register and left the store.

'Well, but did you really need to?' Diane said over the salt-rimmed conical glasses of marguerites in the Flower Room at Gino's, water splashing from the fountain into the low-sided kidney-shaped fire-brick pool with the Trader Vic's-type tropical-rain machine showering softly down over it. The sound system played an instrumental version of "Jamaica Farewell." 'What difference would it've made if you *had* found out who it was? Or'd recognized the voice? The point is that it's common knowledge, out there at oh-aren't-we-elegant Grey Hills, that your husband's got a popsy on the side. It's not some chick who picked him up in a bar and he'd had a few too many drinks and he was lonely, so they had a one-night stand. This is an *ongoing* thing. He's having an *affair*, creating a new secret history with someone who lives in Boston. I mean, my *God*, Marcia, pardon me, but that's what *I* think should concern you. If you have any question here, it isn't who *said* he's got a girlfriend; it's: "Who *is* the little slut?" *That's* what you need to know, so you can find out where she lives, hunt her down and scratch her eyes out.

'Assuming of course, that's what you have in mind; otherwise you don't need to know anything more. Do you have any idea at all as to who it might be?'

Mercy shook her head and chewed her lip. 'No,' she said, 'not now, I don't. A few years ago I would've said Yes. I was *sure* he was having an affair with this TV reporter Stacy Hawkes. You may've seen her; I know I used to, a lot, by accident. It's very hard when your husband's honey's on network TV. You can't help it; every time you see her, even after it's over, you think: "There's the little tramp who stole my husband." I think she's still on NBC; I *know* I won't watch NBC news. She got married a year or two ago; a former congressman, I think, retired to become head of some foundation. She must go for older political types. I don't know how she looks now, but back then she was *very* attractive. Looked a lot like me, as a matter of fact, which didn't surprise me – they say men often pick girlfriends who look like their wives. Does the fondness for look-alikes mean they have no imagination? Or because that way it doesn't seem so much like cheating?'

Diane laughed. '"This's okay because it's the same, even though it's really different; and it's *better* because it's so different, but *okay* because it's the same." Maybe that *is* how it works.'

'Assuming, of course,' Mercy said, 'that didn't sound like boasting. I probably should've said she looked the way I like to think I *used* to look, when I was about twenty; before three pregnancies and about fifteen years. The only stretchmarks this kid would've known about would've been the ones she left on the truth.

'We met her – *I* met her – at an inauguration party. I didn't think they had it planned. Dan's not the type to do that, although I suppose she might've been: "Ought to meet the incumbent wife here, see what I'm up against." It seemed as though we'd just happened to bump into her, turned around and *poof*, there she was – like a genie; someone'd conjured her up. And the *instant* that I looked at her, before Dan'd even had a *chance* to introduce us or we'd even shaken hands or said Hello or anything, I had the strongest feeling we'd been sharing him. I just *knew* it. Her expression, you know? She *looked* like she was smiling – very *well*, of course, as you'd expect, all that training they get before they go on-air, so they smile perfectly. But there was something else in it. Smugness, you know? Something almost *gleeful*. "You may not know who I am, dear – I'm the competition."

'I looked at him, right off, but there was no sign of it on his face. Completely pure-innocent look. Of course he's a politician; no matter what mischief he's really been up to, he always looks like he's serving Mass. And at the same time I was watching her, to see if she was glancing at him for the same reason I'd been doing. If she was, I didn't catch her.'

Mercy frowned. 'Not too long after that I read in the papers she'd gone to New York. So I haven't a clue as to who the current girlfriend is. The recumbent mistress.'

'Even so,' Diane said, 'is that really so important anyway? That you don't know who the bimbo is – her name or where she comes from? You don't really care what her pedigree is; how big her boobs are; how she met him; or whether she's the same one he was fooling around with last year. Or even if she's the *only* one or just the main one he's screwing now. Why does that interest you? The important thing isn't who he does it with when he's not doing it with you; it's that he's doing it with someone else. And from what you've been telling me over the years, he's been doing it for a long time. You've told me several times that when you've confronted him, his stories didn't match up but you knew he had someone. You could tell he was lying.'

'I know,' Mercy said, 'I have told you that. I've told myself, too, many times. But I've never been able to prove it, actually prove he was lying. I've never been really sure.'

'Yes, you have,' Diane said calmly. 'Back when McGovern was running and they had that big fundraiser for him in Boston? Dan was supposed to introduce him and either he was about two hours late or else he never showed up at all? You told me then, what you heard people saying. Even your mother told you she'd heard rumors, where he'd been instead of where he should've been.'

'It was that he'd been with Stacy Hawkes,' Mercy said. 'I got very upset. I asked him about it and he assured me, he wasn't seeing her. He was very contrite. He said he knew it looked bad, but it really wasn't what happened. He said he got tied up in a very hush-hush leadership meeting in the Speaker's office after five, something about the strategy they were going to use to grease a tax bill through or something, and he got so involved he lost all track of time. Not only that but he also thought he probably might've *let* it happen, in a way; *allowed* it to happen, some kind of a Freudian slip, accidentally-on-purpose. Because he'd let himself get roped into making the introduction at the McGovern dinner by someone he couldn't say No to – he owed the guy a favor and might need him in the future. When he wasn't really *for* McGovern, anyway; he'd wanted Kennedy. He hadn't wanted to make the speech in the first place.

'I don't think I really believed him. But he said it'd also hurt him with the party bigwigs, his not showing up like that, and he knew it'd also hurt me, and he gave me his solemn promise he'd never let it happen again. He promised me he was going to shape up, stop getting himself into situations like that where that's what people thought he was doing. And I didn't say any more.'

'In other words, he admitted it,' Diane said. 'And he promised you he wouldn't do it again. Those weren't the words he spoke to you, but that was what he was saying, and it was what you heard. You let him get away with it because you didn't want to hear him say the words he actually meant. And then you quickly made a very clear but *unconscious* decision: you decided you'd be better off staying with him – even though you knew he'd been out fucking around on you – than you would be without him, as long as he didn't do it again. That was what you said to him; he'd hurt you but you forgave him and were going to believe he wouldn't do it again. And on the strength of that you were giving him another chance.

'Those weren't the words you used, because you didn't want to hear yourself saying them. But that was what the words you did say *meant*, and so that was what he heard. And that was how the two of you, by working very well and carefully together, got through a major crisis. Teamwork. If it'd been handled any differently – with any less delicacy; with brutal honesty, say – it would probably have meant the end of your marriage. The perfect, picture-book couple, working together to resolve the crisis but at the same time making absolutely sure neither one of you had to come to grips with what'd caused it; take a good hard look at how damage'd been done. That way *you* could pretend there hadn't *been* a crisis, or any damage. You could tell yourself your marriage was rock-solid; everything still A-okay. And *he* could tell himself you'd given him permission to fool around, if he'd only be discreet.

'So,' Diane said, 'McGovern, you said? That would've been ten years ago. Stacy's long gone, but things haven't changed. Since then there've been other times when you've told me other, but similar, stories. Not really that many, but I've never thought that was because there weren't many to tell – you just preferred to keep them to yourself; that way they wouldn't seem so real.'

'Oh, gee, yeah, I guess,' Mercy said, shaking her head. 'Sometimes it's been pretty hard.'

'Hey,' Diane said, 'you two did a very impressive job that night, shadow-boxing with each other. Textbook example of how two people whose marriage is in deep trouble can keep it together if they both really want to, provided they're willing to compromise and then both work really hard. You both wanted to, had a lot to lose. You, the marriage, and Dan his political career. So you reached a *modus vivendi*, a way to live with each other.'

Mercy held the stem of her marguerita glass between the tips of the fingers of both hands and impassively met Diane's gaze with dry eyes.

'Happy?' Diane said.

Mercy snickered. '*No,*' she said, drawing it out. Then she said: 'That surprise you?'

'Yeah, sort of,' Diane said, 'if you *were* happy living this way, I'd say the accommodation you and Dan arranged was a very good one. Excellent, in fact. After all, the truce's held. It's worked for eight fairly peaceful years. You could even call them "contented." You've gotten along without any major blow-outs, far as I know. Your kids've turned out well; they seem to be in good shape. Peaceful two-parent families're good for small persons; the two of you're good parents.

'Dan's been successful. He doesn't drink any more than most of the men his age that I know, including my own dear husband. That's far too much, of course, but this isn't a perfect world. He doesn't gamble and he doesn't hit you. You may not think you still look as good as you did in your twenties, and you're probably right about that – so, say you now only look like about nine-hundred-thousand bucks. That still ain't chopped liver, dearie. You've got a lovely new home. You're making good progress toward an interesting career of your own.

'This's not a bad life that you two've made, not a bad little life at all. You're what, forty-two? And he's forty-six? You've been married about twenty years? Somebody did something right. Many people would look at what you and Dan have and say it looks pretty damned good. Dan's habitual and persistent infidelity's just about the only flaw in it, at least that I can see. If he did decide now that he wanted to change, for whatever reason – some philandering close friend of his were to die of AIDS and throw a big scare into him – he probably couldn't do it. He's priapic. By now he most likely can't help it.'

Mercy sighed.

'It isn't an uncommon problem, Marcy,' Diane said. 'Several of the Kennedy men seem to've suffered from it. Lots of marriages that have it survive forever, and I don't mean just royalty, either. Far more couples than most people think stay together despite incorrigible infidelity – or at least until one of the spouses dies, as close to forever as *we* get. If you're able to be happy even though it means you'll always have to overlook his one shortcoming – maybe that isn't the right word – my advice would be: Leave it alone.

'But if you *were* happy, or could convince yourself you were, you and I wouldn't be having this conversation. Or any of the others we've had about essentially the same subject through the years. So then, if all of that means that you haven't been happy, just *unhappily* sort of *inert*; that you're not happy now and don't really see much chance you ever will be, as long as you stay with him, *for the rest of this one life you have left*, then I would say: "It's over; it's dead and ain't gonna get better – pronounce it. Call it quits. Kick him out."'

Then the Sunday night dinners suddenly became very important to Hilliard, taking on an aspect of poignant urgency.

Merrion was compassionate. He had watched a number of people whom he knew reasonably well as they stumbled and staggered emotionally and mentally through divorces, and he was satisfied that the days and nights that they exhausted invariably brought demoralizing anguish under the best of circumstances. 'But yours is going to be worse'n the usual mean pissing contest, and God knows those're bad enough. This one I'm braced for.'

'Oh, she's going to crucify me,' Hilliard said, sharing a six-pack of Heinekens one night in the office on High Street.

'I reckon she'll try to,' Merrion said.

'And you don't blame her,' Hilliard said.

Merrion had prepared for that question. 'Danny,' he said, 'I didn't say anything, you start having the one-night stands while you're staying in Boston. I think it was prolly quite a while before I begin to know about them. Mercy knew as much as I did, I think, and what I knew was nothin'. You were bein' very careful then.

'But then around me – this's just around me; I don't think you've gone completely out of your mind so that you've started tippin' off Mercy – it seems like you maybe start gettin' a little careless. Droppin' a few hints here and there; sort of letting things slip out. I was stunned. It was so outta character for you. Adultery wasn't like you, Dan. "Cheating? On his wife? Danny Hilliard doesn't cheat, not on anybody. He doesn't break his word. Dan Hilliard told you something? It's gold; you can take it to the bank." I think that's how you got away with it so long. People who'd known you a long time, including me and Mercy, we never dreamed you'd ever do a thing like that to her. We weren't looking for the signs and so we didn't see them.

'So you start givin' clues. I do my best to ignore them. If you're getting laid in Boston, well, I didn't think it was the best idea you ever had – maybe get yourself a little herpes you then bring home to the bride; might be tough, explain that – but then I'm not your chaperone, tell you to keep your pants zipped. You didn't hire me for that. I'm your, what, "close advisor"?'

'"Confidante,"' Hilliard said. 'That's what they call you. They think I confide in you. We've heard the chimes at midnight. Tell you what it is I've got on my mind; ask you what you think I should do.'

'Okay,' Merrion said, 'so I'm your "confidante" then. "Friend" would've been what I would've said, somebody asked me what I was, I was trynah be anyway, but "confidante" 's okay. Lemme see if I got this straight now: this would then mean that when you started dropping the hints you'd been fucking your brains out – and I mean that here, literally – you were meaning to do it. You weren't being careless at all: You were *confiding* in me that you were getting a lot of out-of-town pussy while you're far from your happy home, and asking me for my advice.

'Geez, I'm really sorry, Dan; I blew it. Really let you down;

didn't realize that's what you wanted. If I had've, my advice would've been I didn't think it was very damned smart, fucking around on the side. In fact I thought it was fucking *stupid*, that is what I thought it was.

'Then I would've told you what you should've already known: "Seeing how I'm getting laid now and then, not as often's I'd like, but not bad, I know I'm not being a good example for you; *but I'm not trying to be one*. Being a good example's never been part of my job. If it had been, I wouldn't've taken it.

'"And furthermore," I now see I should've said – when what you were after was advice about extra-curricular fucking, but I was too stupid to see it – I should've reminded you of something that I would've thought you already *knew*, *without* me reminding you; I should've said: "*I am not married*. This is a very important distinction when what we're talking about's getting laid. I know there're people, still lots of people, who don't approve of getting laid unless the person who's in bed with you's your wife. Or if you're a woman, your husband. But nobody seems to think you should be punished for it if she isn't – unless she's someone *else's* wife, or you've also *got* a wife. Then they think you should be at *very* least admonished heavily, like we sometimes say in the court. Some would even go so far as to say you should be booted out on your lying ass and see how you like *that*.' And as of course we – and the rest of the population of the entire Commonwealth of Massachusetts – now know, Mercy belongs to that group.

'But that stands to reason. She's a wife. Wives're especially prone to this kind of thinking, or so I've been told. I do not have a wife. Once I thought I probably would, some day, if Sunny ever decided she oughta maybe come home and slow down a little, but as you know she died first – still goin' strong. Too bad. But the result is I not only don't *have* a wife; I never *did* have a wife – *and I never ran for office, so what I do is nobody's business*. It's *always* been okay for me to get laid. Not always *easy*, but if I got lucky, *okay*.

'"Since you *do* have a wife," as you did, back then, when I wasn't giving you the advice you wanted; pretty soon I now think you're not gonna, "getting laid *isn't* okay, no matter how big the young lady's tits are, or how hot she is for your rod. So my advice to you is "Cut it out."'

'But you wouldn't've,' Merrion said. 'If I'd advised you to stop fucking around, you wouldn't've done it – you would not've stopped fucking around.'

'Probably not,' Hilliard said, looking gloomy.

Merrion laughed. '"*Absolutely not*," you mean,' he said. 'Never in one million years. Because when you started letting me know you had all these gorgeous women coming onto you down there, you weren't being *careless* – you were doing it *on purpose*. And you weren't doing it so I would then clear my throat and give you lots of good advice you wouldn't take. You were doing it to let me know I wasn't the only guy who could get a piece of ass; even you, a married guy, were getting more, and better. What you were doing was bragging, old chum, just plain old locker-room bragging.'

Hilliard looked miserable. He rubbed the knuckles of the fingers on his left hand with his right thumb, and pursed his lips. He mumbled something to himself.

'I know, Danny, and I'm really sorry,' Merrion said, 'but I think you oughta hear this. You fuckin' earned it. When you were hurting Mercy, you were also putting me in a box, you started letting me know what you'd been doing. You hadda know it, too; that you were putting me in an awful position with Mercy.

'You and I both know she's never been that keen on me,' Merrion said, 'not from the very beginning, I first started working for you. What I was then, and what I'll always be, at least to a certain degree, is someone who Mercy put up with. But since then as the years'd gone by, when you first started letting me know you'd been out getting strange, things'd gotten so they'd started improve a little. She still wouldn't've picked me as her sponsor for Confirmation, but now and then, I said something, she laughed. It wasn't much, but it was progress. In this world you take what you can get.

'So this is where we are, Mercy and me, you decide things're too quiet. It's starting to get a little better with us, between me and her. I no longer have to wear a coat indoors if she's around, so I don't get a stiff neck from the chill. She still didn't like me; I'm not saying that. But I think she got to the point where she decided that you hadda have someone who can do my kind of work, cutting the balls offa guys; and who also knows what certain kinds of people aren't refined like you two are, think about what's going on. As I do, being one. And she sees that the reason that you have to have someone like me's because there's more people like me'n there are of you two, you want me to put it bluntly. So if you wanna run for something, what we roughnecks think is important, and you'd better have someone who can tell you. And once Mercy'd realized that, that was when things between us got better. She still thinks I'm a bad influence on you; and I know she'll never change that; but I think she's decided there has to be one, and I'm about the best one you could find.

'So at that point what we were, Mercy and me, we're partners in a small business. The plant and the product is you. Dan Hilliard Political Futures. Way she sees it – or used to at least, 'fore you got your thing caught inna zipper – her job is to keep you in good shape: physically, mentally, husbandly, fatherly – throw in morally, too. My job's to look after the other stuff you do; make sure you're in good shape politically and publicly. We don't have regular meetings, her and I, every month or two, but both of us know what we're supposed to do. What areas we're supposed to take care of. We've both got an interest in you.

'Then, thanks to you, several years ago I begin to realize we have got a malfunction-red light flashing in the morality area. Alarms going off in the husband and father sections too. The product looks like it may be onna way to destroying itself. Something needs to be done. I know this. But I'm not in charge of those sections. I have got no jurisdiction. I'm not even supposed to go into those areas; they're off-limits to me. And I can't report the malfunction to the person in charge of those sections because while I'm very sure she'll want to make the necessary repairs, *immediately*, I'm afraid she'll react in a way that'll damage the product's condition politically and publicly, by taking a hammer to it – making a big fuckin' stink. And when she does that, the product'll get mad at *me*, because the way he's gonna look at it, I damaged him confidentially and I abused his trust.

'So there I am now, right where you put me, spang in the middle: I'm fuckin' *stuck*; I'm helpless. All I can do is keep my mouth shut, and just hope an' pray you get over this hot spell of yours – before Mercy finds out what's now become *two* things: one being that you've been runnin' around, which I know'll destroy you with her; and two that I knew and I didn't tell her, which'll finish *me* off with her, too.'

Hilliard shook his head and cleared his throat, but he kept his eyes downcast and did not say anything.

'Those hopes and prayers did not quite work out as I wanted. I could see this. So when you stopped bein' coy, droppin' hints, come right out and told me you were fucking Stacy – you're like a little kid with a new electric train; you're fucking Stacy Hawkes, and you two just invented sex – I figured that was it; the shit was in the fan. You weren't coming to your senses; there was nothing I could do. Well, that was when I finally said I certainly hoped that you knew what an awful chance you were taking. And furthermore, I also said I'd seen some self-destructive assholes in my time but you took the cake. And you know what you said to me? Do you remember, Dan?'

Hilliard remained downcast and shook his head. He mumbled something. Then he gulped. Merrion said: 'What?'

Hilliard did not look up, but did manage to nod. 'Yeah,' he said, 'yeah I remember. I know what I said.'

'You laughed at me,' Merrion said. 'Then you told me to go fuck myself. And then a week or two after that chat, you missed the McGovern dinner.' He paused. 'I figured that was the end of you. I had you down as totaled. History. I thought you'd never survive it. So there I am, I'm all prepared for the bomb to go off – thanking God that at least I'd been smart enough to get my court job before you decide to commit suicide. And then weeks went by and no bomb went off. Nothing happened, so I never asked you. What the hell did you do? How the hell did you pull that one off?'

Hilliard shrugged. 'It took a while before it got back to her,' he said. 'The kids were still at home and in school, keeping her busy. She wasn't out that much with other people, especially people who knew what was going on. And when she was out with those kind of people, she was out with them with me. We tend to forget this, guys like you and me, but you have to be pretty deep on the inside to know most of the stuff that goes on. Not too many people are. Those who do know don't tend to tell their wives too much of it; they got secrets of their own they don't want me telling *my* wife, 'cause the next time she sees *their* wife she might tell her a thing or two. So they don't tell *their* wives I've got something on the side, and I don't tell *my* wife what they're up to. No one ever tells you this; you figure it out on your own. It's something we all understand.

'So even though everybody on the Hill's giving me the business, the story didn't make it out this way until Mercy's fuckin' mother picked up something in the wind, she's out flyin' around Weston on her broom, and then I had myself a problem.'

'I'm curious,' Merrion said. 'What'd you do?'

Hilliard shrugged. 'I saw it as a political challenge. If I'd never gone into politics, I never would've fucked Stacy. I never would've seen her, not in person anyway, and if I ever had've somehow, well, she wouldn't've looked twice at me. So I treated it as a political problem. I resorted to time-honored tactics: I stood up like a man and I lied.'

'And Mercy believed you?' Merrion said. 'Amazing. I never would've.'

Hilliard bloused his cheeks out. 'Of course you wouldn't've,' he said. 'The Charlie Doyles of this world wouldn't've. None of you would've *had* to. So therefore I wouldn't've told you that story; you would've laughed in my face. But she had a weakness, so she couldn't laugh; she had to believe me. And so she made herself do it.' He shook his head. 'If your next question's whether I'm disgusted with myself, the answer is: I am now, but I wasn't then. Then I was proud of myself, and that makes me feel even more disgusted.'

'And maybe even more ashamed?' Merrion said.

Hilliard looked at him. He pursed his lips and swallowed. 'Goin' for the full skin, huh, Amby? Not just for the scalp?' Merrion nodded. Hilliard said: 'Well yeah, that too then, pal of mine: even more ashamed.'

14

As Merrion had foreseen, once Mercy decided to act she came on like a locomotive. Urged on by Diane Fox, she convinced herself that even though she had collaborated in her own deception and assisted at her own resulting martyrdom, the humiliating pain her husband had caused her warranted retribution along with divorce.

For some reason of random malevolence, those days for Hilliard were also a season of especially fierce battles on the Hill. Hilliard summarized it as a period of 'hand-to-hand politics, but I was grateful for it. The war in the House was child's play, comic relief, compared to the one that was going on in my private life.'

At last angry enough to file – Hilliard was impressed, describing her admiringly to Merrion as 'madder than a hornet' – Mercy categorically refused sound advice from her lawyer, Geoffrey Cohen, to cite 'cruel and abusive treatment' as her seemly choice of grounds for seeking the divorce. 'No, Mister Cohen,' she said, deferring acceptance of his invitation to address him as 'Geoff' until she was certain that he fully understood whose wishes were to govern their dealings, 'I've already spent far too many years of my life living in the land of make-believe. I'm going to spend the rest in the real world, calling things by their right names. Adultery's the reason I told him to get out. Separation hasn't changed it. Adultery's the reason that I'm going to give the judge.'

Geoffrey Cohen liked to describe the four-lawyer practice that he ran from the second floor of the restored two-story white-shuttered brick building he owned on North Main Street in South Hadley as 'just an ordinary, quiet little country law firm with a rather boring probate practice' leaving it to clients and their chastened former spouses to promote his reputation as one of the most relentless advocates anyone could ever hope to find to extract money and exact revenge, 'which in most cases where you represent the wife amounts to the same thing.'

He deliberately did not look the part. He kept his chestnut-brown beard carefully trimmed van Dyke style, and with studied nonchalance subtly adapted the New England college-town uniform: good tweeds (lapels rolled, not pressed) and flannels (never baggy, rumpled or frayed, always sharply creased), with lightly starched (custom) shirts, striped or neatly patterned ties woven of heavy gauge silk, and highly polished leathers. This made it possible for him to commute with faultless ease among his appearances in the courthouses; his regular engagements as adjunct professor and guest lecturer on regional colonial history at the several colleges in the area; and his performance as the cellist of the Sebastian Quartet of Amherst, giving evening concerts of music of the Renaissance in the tidy small Congregational and Unitarian-Universalist churches of Western Massachusetts. 'It really would be more discreet, you know, if you did it the way I'm suggesting,' he demurred, not giving up, when Mercy first wearily rejected his suggested neutral phrasing of the divorce libel.

'I'm sure it would be,' she said. 'But I still want to do it my way. I don't have much appetite for discretion these days. Dan's discretion's what enabled him to make a plain fool out of me all these years, and my sense of propriety, along with my cowardice, enabled me to help him do it. It was supposed to make me feel good, but it hasn't, so now I've reached the point where I want to try something else. I want to go ahead and tell the actual truth, see how that makes me feel.'

'Yes, but this would be *judicious* discretion,' Cohen murmured. 'In court you can gain valuable brownie-points for it. Voluntary self-restraint. When you have this kind of case: parties well-known; the name is familiar, prominent, even; judges get nervous. They get jittery before anyone utters a word in court. They see potential for big trouble in a case like this. So some obvious self-restraint can pay big dividends. If they see you're doing everything you can to make it as quick and painless as possible for everyone else who doesn't necessarily want to be involved but has to be, they appreciate it.'

'Cruel and abusive' was the customary summarizing euphemism collusively employed in those days, before 'irretrievable breakdown' or 'irreconcilable differences' were officially recognized as serviceably sufficient grounds for legal, collusive termination of marriage. It indicated that each of the parties had become completely fed up with the other one, usually with more than adequate reason on both sides.

'C and A-T' meant there would be minimal public indignity. In fifteen minutes or less the wife and a relative or friend could provide all of the evidence needed. The wife would be sworn to tell the truth. She would duly – falsely – say that her husband had once thrown an ashtray at her, missing her by several feet but frightening her and causing her to become sad, so that she had cried. The corroborating witness would testify that while she had not observed the actual trajectory of the ashtray, the wife had called her immediately after the incident and between sobs told her that the husband had thrown an ashtray at her. The defense would waive cross-examination. The court would accept the plaintiff's evidence as prima facie proof that the marriage should be dissolved. The defense would not offer any evidence. The prima facie proof would become conclusive.

To insure that everything would go smoothly and the bland but arrant falsehoods would go uncontradicted by the husband, his counsel would have strongly advised him that since his presence would add little to the charade, everyone would be more comfortable if he did not attend it. Consequently he would be nowhere near the courthouse the day the case was heard, thus avoiding even the possibility that he would become noisily incensed upon hearing practical lies told about him – in a good cause which he supported when calm – and throw some kind of a fit, disrupting arrangements.

'So, why do that, drag it all out in the open?' Cohen said soothingly to Mercy. 'The sentiment's already solidly in your favor. Everyone already knows why you're making it official now, why you threw the guy out. It's not as though you really need to spread the dirty linen on the public record for everyone to know how he's mistreated you.

'The judges feel ever so much more comfortable when you leave that stuff out, so they don't have to see themselves as somehow getting involved in the messy business. It's almost as though they seem to think that when sexual misconduct's alleged, *their* fingers get sticky, too, handling the case. They're kindlier toward plaintiffs who spare the sexual details. Especially when they can imagine very well indeed, as you can bet they do in your case, all the juicy things you could've said, but didn't. How thoughtful and discreet you are. It makes you look good.'

'Mister Cohen,' Mercy said. 'As my dear husband likes to say: "Spare me all that stuff," only *stuff*'s not what he calls it. What you're telling me is that if I downplay to *my* judge why I put him out, *you'll* make brownie-points with *all* the judges – because they're scared of my big bad husband. They think he'll bury their next pay-increase bill if any one of them does anything that makes him mad. But here you come now, looking out for them: You persuaded his wife to be good.

'Danny's always said you're one slick little bugger.' When he heard the adjective *slick* Cohen wrongly jumped to the conclusion that Mercy was sanitizing Hilliard's characterization for his benefit, and that *bugger* had not been the noun that Hilliard had used. Cohen began to feel a bit of bloodlust for the fray. 'That's the reason I'm hiring you. But so you'll be slick *for* me, not *on* me. So, forget it. I won't play nice. If they're too dainty to read the word *adultery* on a piece of paper, they should try being the innocent victim. Try living with the reality of it for a while. See how it makes *them* feel, having people pity them; laughing at them behind their backs when they go down the street. Or else find another line of work.

'No, now it's Danny's turn. Let's see how he runs for re-election with his behavior out in public. If this doesn't get him at least a Republican opponent, if not a primary challenge, then we'll know the opportunists must've become extinct. "How can you believe this guy? He's an adulterer. He didn't keep his promises to his own wife. She found out she couldn't trust him. Finally she reached the point where she went to court and *proved* she couldn't trust him. What makes you think *you* can?"'

'The man I was married to made a fool of me. Let's see how he likes hearing that on the late news, what he did to me.'

Therefore the libel in *Hilliard* vs. *Hilliard* alleged 'open and gross adultery.' Most of the male reporters who covered the State House, having made compassionate sounds within earshot of Hilliard, once out of his hearing licked their chops and hoped cooler heads would not prevail before the case came to trial. Like Mercy, they had a beef with him. It had festered all the years it had taken Mercy to overcome her disinclination to believe that Dan away from home had trouble remembering his marriage vows. Long before she reached full boil, most of the reporters had known he was playing road games; many of them disapproved.

Their motives were professional, not moral. Soon after Hilliard's meanderings had commenced – around Labor Day in 1971, green-eyed, blonde-haired, petite Stacy Hawkes of Channel 3, then twenty-six, coming up with time-dishonored but mutually pleasurable ways to celebrate Hilliard's ascent in the House hierarchy – her professional rivals on the State House beat had begun to get heavy pressure from their editorial desks. The incidental time she and Hilliard spent with their clothes on, before and after the time they spent in her bed in her Beacon Street apartment, gave her many more quiet opportunities than her competitors enjoyed to talk informatively with him about newsworthy developments in Massachusetts politics. Stacy's reports from the Hill therefore regularly scooped those that her competition filed, and they did not like it. Several whose sexual advances she'd coolly rebuffed – one of them another woman – were also fiercely jealous of Hilliard, correctly perceiving the reason she granted him privileges denied to them. They alternated between smouldering anger and bitter laughter, calling her a whore behind her back and coming close to it face-to-face by curling their lips and sneering 'Yeah, and how'd you get *that* little tidbit?' when she goaded them delightedly with allusions to developments that she'd predicted on the air two nights before.

Their subtle inflation of Hilliard's public importance reflected their impotent envy. Unable to publish what they knew to be the actual reason why she would fuck him, and not one of them, they employed the word *powerful* as code for their perception that Hilliard's legislative authority unjustly comported a *droit de seigneur* to bed the fairest female among them. Wishing to see him rebuked, they exaggerated the extent and rancor of his opposition on the Hill, hoping each new challenger would manage to stymie him, casting so much doubt upon his abilities and fitness for authority that his steady progress toward becoming Speaker would be impeded if not halted. And if that happened it might do more than just rebuke what they perceived as his excessive ambition; it might prompt Stacy to reappraise his value to her and stop fucking him.

Long after Stacy Hawkes had departed for New York, their envy and resentment persisted, kept alive in part by their observation of Hilliard's effortlessly insulting ease in replacing her – repeatedly. Without really having fully thought it out, they continued to enlarge his public image in order to magnify the story of his ignominious demolition later. They had not necessarily contemplated the collapse of his marriage in their wistful projections of potential causes of his eventual downfall, but when it occurred they hoped it would serve the purpose. They would see to it, in fact, if Mercy would be good enough to make the details of his sexual shenanigans publishable by proving them to make her divorce case. They sat poised at their keyboards wearing the happy expressions of dogs hearing the grinding sound of the electric can-opener; even those who liked Hilliard had to agree that life in the news business now and then could be good.

Banished from his home; under seige where he worked, Hilliard was under orders also not to seek the kind of solace that had gotten him in trouble, the kind he had reasonably come to expect to find without much difficulty evenings after work in Boston. His lawyer, Sam Evans, had forbidden it. The joke in Franklin, Hampshire and Hampden County Probate Courts was that any divorce involving a well-known person or marriage property in excess of one hundred thousand dollars was not valid unless Sam Evans, the Butler, Corey partner specializing in divorce, had represented one of the unhappy parties.

Evans had assessed Mercy's allegation of adultery as true and accurate, but flimsy, perfectly fine and entirely understandable as an expression of rage but wildly out of proportion to the little circumstantial evidence she had to prove it.

'Gossip,' Evans told Hilliard, 'as I'm sure you learned in law school, isn't evidence. Not unless what you propose to prove is that people gossip. Which if that's their purpose, we will stipulate: "Indeed people do," will be our reply, and a lot of it's been about you. But sheer quantity of rumor does not make it into proof. Innuendo and insinuation don't amount to evidence.

'Now, that doesn't mean I doubt for one moment that you've been a bounder, a cad and a tosspot, and treated your good wife very badly. The judge isn't going to doubt it either, because when Geoff Cohen takes your deposition, he's going to ask you if you misbehaved, and since perjury isn't a tactic that prudent men use, you're going to admit that you did. And then if he makes you take the stand you're going to repeat it, and say that you're sorry, and try as hard as you possibly can to look like you really mean it. Be contrite, and confess you're a bastard, *and give him no names at all.*'

'Can I do that,' Hilliard said, 'refuse to tell him the names of my girlfriends?'

'Yup,' Evans said. 'Judge Hadavas's a bit of a prude. If I know him he's already displeased with Geoff for letting your wife charge adultery. He's also not the brightest flame in the candelabra. He probably shouldn't be on any bench, but if he has to be some kind of judge, he certainly ought not to be in probate. He doesn't belong there. He's not really in favor of divorce. He'd much rather married couples tried a little harder to get along with each other, like he and Vera always have, instead of coming into his court all the time on what he sees as the slightest provocation, whining and complaining how unhappy they all are. Those of us who've seen how Vera treats him when they're out and can imagine what a royal pain she must be at home, well, we're inclined to think James must try very hard indeed, if he gets along with her.

'I was in his session one day, waiting to argue a motion, and this poor woman was on the stand. She'd brought a motion for an order to increase her alimony and child-support payments. Apparently this'd become something of a hobby of hers – it wasn't the first time she done it. So she was being cross-examined, and her husband's lawyer was showing her no mercy, really bearing down on her. Finally he came right out and challenged her, dared her to admit that she was doing this again because she'd found out her ex-husband and his new girlfriend were going to get married, and she was bound and determined to do everything she possibly could to stick a wrench in the gears, disrupt their plans as much as she could – and if possible of course get all his money. He said: "This's *fun* for you, isn't it, Mrs So-and-so. This isn't a matter of *need* we've got here; this is a case of *revenge*. You *enjoy* doing this to my client, don't you – you're having one whale of a time.'

'And she just *wailed* at him; I thought sure she was going to break down and bawl: "No, I am *not*. I'm *not* having fun. I'm unhappy all of the time." And Judge Hadavas said: "*Huh*, so's everyone else who comes in here. What makes you think you're so special? Think maybe you can tell me that? Spend all your time thinking up ways, come in here and call attention to yourself. What you ought to's go out and find yourself a steady job, support your *self*. Get something on your mind besides yourself. That's all you ever think about, *of course* you're going to be miserable; just stands to reason. Deserve it, too, you ask me." Then she really did cry.'

'Did he give her the money that she wanted?' Hilliard said.

'I don't know,' Evans said. 'He took it under advisement. That's another thing James likes to do: keep everybody in suspense a while. Never decide a motion the same day it's heard. Always says he'll render his decision in writing in a week. That means: when he gets around to it. James's week's longer than yours and mine are; his runs about ten or twelve days. I think it's so the party he decides against won't be in the courtroom to holler at him when he finds out he got screwed.

'Point is, your wife's charged you with adultery. From the instant James Hadavas laid his eyes on the libel, which would've been about a minute after it was filed, he's been very uneasy. People will be watching this case, following it very closely. There'll be interest in how it comes out. There would've been some no matter what the grounds were, just because of who you are. But "adultery" gets everybody's interest. Judge Hadavas doesn't like being watched. So we know he's already anxious. The only reason he's got to be pleased at all with Geoff is that apparently he was able to persuade your wife at least not to name a co-respondent. If she had, Judge Hadavas'd then have a genuine circus on his hands. A circus he does not want.

'So, once you've admitted that you were unfaithful, I think he'll say that that's enough. There's no reason to identify your partner or partners, as the case may be, and declare Hadavas Day in the media. If Geoff tries to make you do that, which I doubt he will, I'm going to advise you not to answer and then if Geoff still insists, he'll have to go before Hadavas and see if he can get an order compelling you to answer. I doubt he'll want to do that, but if he does he'll just compound what I'm sure is already Hadavas's private disapproval of his choice of grounds. I don't think he'll get his order.

'Now this's important, Dan,' Evans said, 'and not just because I assume you feel the same way as I do about publicly naming everyone who for whatever reason agreed to go to bed with you.'

'Well,' Hilliard said, 'I like to think my natural charm and boyish good looks were at least part of the reason.'

'Yes,' Evans said, 'no doubt. All of us have our illusions. But still, if we can present you to Judge Hadavas as an honest penitent who regrets his sins and wicked deeds and the sorrow that he's caused his wife, instead of allowing Geoff to portray you as the unrepentant Casanova and lascivious rascal that we both know you really are . . .'

'Hey, take it easy,' Hilliard said, 'I've got a sense of humor, Sam, but I've never been that bad. All I ever did was take advantage of some situations I got into when my wife wasn't with me; that's all. It wasn't like I was ever on some kind of a campaign or something, see how many women I could go to bed with if I tried.'

'I'm not joking,' Evans said. 'I'm trying to get you to see how Judge Hadavas will look at you, if we give Geoff half a chance to paint that kind of portrait. Because if Casanova is the portrait Judge Hadavas sees of you, it will cost you dearly, my friend. And by the way here, another thing I should ask you: Your wife's health and well-being were also involved here, along with her pride and dignity. When you were running around on her, did you always use a condom?'

'Yeah, that much I did do,' Hilliard said. 'It wasn't like I thought I was the first one that any of my ladies ever took a liking to. I didn't know what they might've gotten from someone they'd been with before. They probably didn't know either, as far as that goes, that AIDS stuff takes as long to develop as they're now saying it does.'

'Every time?' Evans said. 'Invariably?'

'What?' Hilliard said. 'Yeah, I just told you that. For sure I didn't wanna bring *anything* home, give Mercy VD. I always used condoms, *religiously*. Even though I must say, I still don't like 'em.'

'Yes,' Evans said. 'That's what prompts my next question. That matter of your religion. Did you actually have a condom available *the very first time* you found yourself in one of those sexual situations you mentioned? Good Catholic guy like you are? That would have been keen foresight on your part – admirable or deplorable depending on your point of view. Either that or else finding yourself in that set of tempting circumstances wasn't entirely accidental. Mind telling me which one it was? Not to mention the practical aspect of where you could have kept your condom supply? Certainly not in your wallet, or at your apartment.'

Hilliard sighed. 'Look,' he said, 'the first time I stepped off the reservation, it was with this woman who's in television news. She was young, still in her twenties, but she'd been around. And I had my eyes open too; the reason she came on to me was only partly because she had hot pants for me – it was also partly, maybe even mostly, because she thought if she put out for me I'd tell her things the other reps who knew about them wouldn't tell to the other reporters. We fell in lust. It wasn't ever love. It was sex, for both of us, along with ambition, on her part, and it was extremely *good* sex. And thrills, very good thrills, not cheap ones: this was a fine-looking woman who really liked being in bed with a man and would've found a man to do it with even if it wouldn't help her career. I had a good time with Stacy. I was with her for over three years.'

'So?' Evans said. 'Why're you telling me this?'

'Well,' Hilliard said, 'because it seems to me that you've let yourself get a little behind the times about the dating game these days. I didn't have to go against my religion buying condoms before I went against it to have sex with Stacy the first time. Stacy had the condoms. Like I said, she was experienced. She got laid a lot, and she was prepared. She had a supply at her place.'

'And I take it that you don't claim,' Evans said, 'that your liaison with this woman, or any of the other women, however many there may have been . . .'

'So far, only eighteen,' Hilliard said.

'"Only eighteen,"' Evans said. 'You're quite sure of that.'

'Oh yeah,' Hilliard said. 'I know most of us always say that there haven't been very many, or "one or two," something like that, so that we don't look like we're bragging. But we all know *exactly* how many – and the women keep track, same as we do. If you count Mercy, I've fucked nineteen women.'

'Really,' Evans said drily.

'I realize that's not much of a total,' Hilliard said. 'I plan to add to it as soon as possible. Put my best efforts forward, you know? I've always had this tendency to fall in love, where I only have one woman at a time – besides my wife, I mean. I know it's held me back. There've been times when I've actually walked away from a chance to go to bed with a woman I was strongly attracted to, because I didn't think it would be fair to my girlfriend if I did. Not because most people'd look at it as being that I would've been cheating on Mercy with both of them, then; because the way I looked at it I'd've been cheating on the woman I was cheating with on Mercy. I've been doing my best to overcome that.'

'I can see where it's been complicated for you,' Evans said, laughing. 'Keeping nineteen women straight. Must be quite a challenge.'

'Well, but not all at once,' Hilliard said. 'And Mercy was sort of a constant, you know. It was her plus somebody else. So it was eighteen besides her, but usually only one of them at a time.' He paused. 'I'd have to say also, she was as good as most of them were, better'n several I had.'

'That was what I was getting at,' Evans said, 'as delicately as possible; not very. You didn't start compiling a fairly impressive life-list of sexual partners because of deprivation at home, I take it?'

'Nope,' Hilliard said. 'Mercy was always willing, God love her. She was a virgin when we got engaged – that was a big reason why we *got* engaged; it was the only way I could get her pants off. But after that she was as ready as I was. Sometimes in fact, she was readier. More'n once I drove home early Friday after having nooners with Stacy, wasn't feeling all that eager, but an hour or so later, there I am, having to get it up again to give Mercy a dash in the bloomers 'fore the kids came home from school.'

He chuckled. 'I was younger then. Good thing for me, I guess – kind of tough to explain to your wife she'll have to wait 'til bedtime 'cause you're not up to it; just finished banging your girlfriend in Boston.'

Evans furrowed his brow. 'And I can take it all of these eighteen women were unmarried?'

'Four of them had husbands,' Hilliard said. 'One of them was separated, in the process of getting divorced, so I'm not sure she really counted as married. But the other three married ones were cheating, same as I was.'

'Oh, wonderful,' Evans said. 'That means one of the imponderables we'll have to think about here is the possibility that one of their spouses will decide to divorce *them*, and name you.'

Hilliard shrugged. 'I realize it wasn't smart,' he said. 'But at the time I was not engaged in *being* smart. I was letting my dick do the thinking. Here I've got this good-looking woman practically throwing herself at me, and I know she's married, and she knows I'm married, and this obviously makes no difference to her, so then why should it to me? "Well, it shouldn't," says my cock, and therefore it doesn't, and the next thing I know, we're in bed. I don't know whether you've ever had that happen to you.'

'Can't say as I have,' Evans said. 'Probably wouldn't let it anyway, even if I had the chance.'

'Well, I have,' Hilliard said, 'and I am here to tell you: you missed something. It's *exhilarating* when that happens to you. When you've just been introduced to someone that you didn't even *know* an hour ago, and she looks like a movie star, and you can tell right off that she's so hot to trot you could probably fuck her right there on the rug, in front of all the people, if you wanted to. All you have to do is say the word and take her by the elbow, and she'll go *anywhere you want*, up on the roof, if that's what you want, and help you get her clothes off and then give you the ride of your life.

'When that happens you don't think about how smart or stupid or risky it is, or how you've got a wife and kids at home, or anything else in the world; all you think about is that all you have to do is ask and you can have her. It'd be a *crime* not to do it. So the decision's easy: you do it.

'At least that's the way I saw it. I was never that good an athlete. I wasn't an A student either. I had no talent for music. I wasn't especially funny. My father wasn't a major-league ballplayer. My mother was a housewife. Girls never paid much attention to me. I was who they went to the prom with when they'd begun to think no one was going to ask them. They were not on the cheerleading squad. I wasn't especially attracted to them. They weren't attracted to me. We were both involved in fulfilling a ritual. It was sort of like valet-parking. We both had to Go to The Dance or Be Weird; that was all. We didn't have very much fun.

'I was astonished when Mercy came on to me, very first time that I saw her. Absolutely knocked off of my feet. Here was this really cute girl who liked *me*, was all over me; didn't *let* me feel her up, *made* me. And could not keep her hands off of *me*. It was truly extraordinary. The first night I met her we both came in our pants, rubbing up against each other. I knew then we were going to get married. We had to – we had no choice.'

'Mutual hormone storm,' Evans said.

'Uh uh,' Hilliard said. 'I'd had those before and I've had them since. It was a lot more'n that. This was beyond *horny*, this was *mating*.'

'Well then,' Evans said, 'if that was the way that you felt about her, how could you do what you did? Did the feeling you had for her change?'

'No, it didn't,' Hilliard said. 'I still feel about her the same way today that I did back when we got engaged, and *finally* we could do what a man and woman're supposed to do when they're by themselves with their clothes off. When it was finally okay. Well, not okay, really, but close enough; the Church didn't allow it, but she did. If she called me up tonight and asked me to come over and put it to her, no promises to drop this case, nothing, I would do it. I'd be over there like a shot. She won't, of course, because "What would Diane say," and of course I'm now kind of pissed-off at her so I'd probably try to make her beg for it. But if she did call and ask me, I know I would do it. I always liked screwing my own wife. In fact thinking about it, I will go further: she may be the best lay I've ever had.'

'Then why all the others?' Evans said. 'The other eighteen: I don't see the logic to it.'

'That's because there isn't any logic to it,' Hilliard said. 'Or else it's because it's the same. I didn't go into politics because I wanted to be a politician any more than I went to law school because I wanted to be a lawyer. All I knew when I ran for alderman the first time and lost and then the second time and won was that even though I was a pretty *good* high-school teacher and I kind of liked it, and saw that if I stayed with it I'd do all right, it was not going to be enough, ever. There'd never be enough excitement for me. Never enough thrills and chills. I certainly didn't want the life my father had; fingers in other peoples' mouths all the time, smelling their terrible breath, looking over what's still left of what they had for dinner the past couple weeks. That's why I'd gone into teaching. I guess you could say I was restless. The only thing I could see being still left open to me was politics, running for office.

'It turned out to be the right answer. I really *liked* politics. I liked running for office a lot. I didn't like getting my brains beaten out, but I liked what I'd seen the first time out well enough to risk having it happen again. And then I got help, from the Carneses and Amby, and the second time I *didn't* get beat.'

'It wasn't because you had some idea that if you put yourself into that milieu you might be able to pattern your life on what you saw the Kennedys doing,' Evans said.

Hilliard snorted. 'Back then almost nobody knew how much ass those guys were getting. No, I didn't run for office because I thought if I won, I'd get laid a lot. I ran for office because I thought I could be better as a politician, make better use of my intelligence and my skills doing that than I'd ever be able to if I stayed a teacher. I looked at the people I saw ten or twenty years older than I was who were running for office and having a high old time for themselves, showing off and making lots of noise and so forth, and then I looked at the future that I'd probably have if I kept on doing the same thing that I'd been doing. By the time I was forty-five or so I'd have a pretty good chance of being a superintendent, or else fairly high up either in the Mass. Teachers' Association or the NEA. Not a bad life at all.

'But if I was going to do what amounted to getting out of teaching in order to boss teachers, or get them to elect me to help run their union for them, then why not make a run in honest politics? See if I was any good at that, and then if it turned out I was, then get out of teaching and go at *that* full-bore. So that was what I did.

'I didn't find out about the pussy until later.'

To preserve what meagre strength Evans saw in Hilliard's case, he had 'strongly recommended' that his client suspend his efforts to add to the number of women he'd bedded and 'avoid being seen in public unofficially with any attractive woman, *pendente lite*.' 'Meaning,' as Hilliard ruefully translated it to Merrion, 'that I'm not to get laid, except very discreetly, until the divorce case is over. This's all Diane Fox's fault, I have to go through this at my age, beating my meat by myself. Once I get this divorce shit out of the way I may have a law passed against her. Have her declared a toxic-waste dump and appropriate funds to dispose of her.

'It's surprising how hard it is to do that, get laid without anyone seeing. I never would've guessed. I'm not really sure I can do it. You say to a grown-up woman, would she like to have some dinner, maybe relax, have a few drinks, listen to some music. She's in the mood, agreeable, she's liable to say Yes, and come along with you, good time to be had by all. Of course anyone who sees you and knows you, knows that you're not married to each other, so they also now know what it is you're leading up to. The two of you're planning to get laid. So for me, for now, that's out. I've always been discreet, which's why Mercy hasn't really got any concrete evidence she can use to bean me, but now I've got to be *discreetly* discreet.

'I don't know how to do that. What do I do, I see a lady I might like to jump? Slip her a note that says that I'm in room two-ten, and would she like to join me there and have some food sent up, maybe have a glass of wine and watch the ballgame on TV? Oh, *very* smooth. She's not gonna go for that. She's gonna laugh in my face. The best you can hope for, you pull that stunt, you don't get a kick in the balls.

'Sam says the way to look at it is that I'm being punished. The punishment for getting laid with too many women is not getting laid with any women at all for a while. He's got that part right. This gettin' separated and divorced is no day at the beach. Makes it *lots* harder to get laid'n it is when you're still all safely married, got the wife at home and all, like all the other guys I know are who're always gettin' laid all around me, left and right. I don't recommend it at all.'

Merrion suspected that Hilliard had eased his loneliness by making it his business to become somewhat better acquainted with Mary Pat Sweeney, but never made any effort to find out if he was right. He did make it a point to hang around for what Hilliard had come to call the *après*-golf dinners at Grey Hills on Sunday evenings; as far as Merrion could tell, they were about the only interludes of peace and relaxation – 'fun,' Danny called it – that his best friend had all week.

But Merrion would not have chosen that word. Hilliard gave the meals an air of almost frantic desperation, trying to wring more happiness out of the hours than Merrion believed they actually contained, extending the evening with booze and then talking too loudly, too much. 'Those new buildings going up in Canterbury there? I'm the guy that built those, got the money for them. Almost seven million dollars. And what thanks I get for that? "That was two, three years ago. Whatchou doin' now?" I tell you, you get no thanks in this business.'

The chief of police in Canterbury in those days was Salvatore Paradisio, the formidable uncle of self-effacing Samuel Paradisio, the federal probation officer who had come to mistrust Lowell Chappelle's intentions toward Janet LeClerc. For Salvatore

Paradisio life was a serious business, always to be soberly conducted. To his ex-officio service as a member of the police station building committee named by the selectmen, he brought strong views tenaciously held on the subject of the proper design of police stations in general and what specific modifications would be appropriate for the one to be built in Canterbury by the F.D. Barrows Construction Co., the contract having been awarded as expected as soon as the tedious business of inviting, receiving, opening and considering competitive sealed bids had been gotten out of the way.

Merrion was a member of the five-person Building Committee. By then Deputy Clerk of Court, he had been appointed without his prior knowledge or permission – and when he was informed, against his wishes – at the suggestion of Richard Hammond, Clerk of Courts. Hammond knew Chief Paradisio just as well as anyone else outside his family did, and therefore while he agreed with the selectmen that someone from the courthouse ought to serve on the committee, he did not agree that he should be the one.

'After all,' Hammond told them, 'I've got a growing family. Demands on my time. Responsibilities. I've been planning to see as much as I can of my children in the next eight or ten years the two youngest've got left before they get all grown up. If I let you talk me into serving on a committee with Sal Paradise, I won't be able to do that. They'll be planning their weddings by the time I get home from the first meeting. I'll be tied up every night until I'm sixty-five.

'No, Amby Merrion's your choice. Bachelor like he is, he's got lots of time. Besides, he's pals with Hilliard. These're Hilliard's buildings, right? Way he tells it, anyway, he's the guy that got the money. So put his sidekick on the panel. Pretty soon the chief'll start to drive him 'round the bend, like he does everybody else who has to listen to him, and then Amby'll go to Hilliard and say: "Hey, for the luvva Christ, help me out here a little bit, willya? Get me some more State dough for Canterbury – make yourself look good and at the same time, help me make the chief shut up." And Hilliard'll do it for him, contradict alla mean things that his wife's sayin' about him, 'cause he still wants to look good, 'case he decides to run again.'

Chief Paradisio grounded his views of police station design, as he did his many other views, on his painstakingly careful and extensive study of human nature. 'Basically what I am is a professional scientist. My field is the continuing study of human nature,' he would say. 'All law enforcement officers are engaged in such studies. Or we ought to be at least: it's the essence of our work.' Because he habitually delivered his observations and findings in detail and at length whenever he believed that he had been invited to state and then defend any given premise – 'and has such *stamina*,' Dan Hilliard said, 'guy's a one-man filibuster; he can stay awake for days' – he generally prevailed against all who initially opposed any premise he happened to advance.

'It's a universal tendency,' Chief Paradisio said, 'to want to get away.' He was describing without having been asked how people reacted when placed under arrest, believing he saw the inquiry implied in a statement made by someone else at an early meeting of the Building Committee.

'I think it was, Diane, Diane Fox who was to blame,' Merrion told Hilliard over drinks at Henry's Grist Mill two or three nights later. Diane's practice as a Licensed Social Worker counseling troubled young people in Hampton Pond was established and thriving. She was on the building committee as an ex-officio member of the board of selectmen, having been elected to serve out the unexpired three-year portion of her late husband's term after Walter's sudden death at the age of forty-two. He had had a heart attack while jogging.

'I got to the library and went into the trustees' room,' where the police station building committee had agreed to meet, 'and I was hanging up my coat. The rest of them – the chief, Diane, Maurice Belding and Gerry Porter – they'd already gotten there ahead of me, and so they all were sitting down, and Diane, while they're waiting for me to join them at the table just by way of no harm sort of threw it out that she'd been afraid she was going to be late because the cat'd gotten out. And she'd thought – at least 'til she found it sleeping on the hood, her car, which I guess was nice and warm, this being a cold night, because she'd just gotten home to feed the cat and let it out, expecting it'd come right back in; that was the reason she'd stopped off there – that it'd run away.

'And that was what set Sal off about how come *people* run away. I pity people who have to deal with him every day. The guy is unbelievable.'

The chief said the desire to run away was the reason behind his desire for an internal receiving area for prisoners in the new police station. 'It's just a normal human thing, I guess,' the chief said, 'that when someone has you restrained; you're under his control; he's bigger, stronger, younger'n you are, most likely, and he's armed, to boot; plus there may be more'n one of him so that you're outnumbered too, and all of them're authorized to use deadly force, *on you*; well, it's naturally upsetting. You're probably not used to this, in all likelihood, and so it would be perfectly natural then that you would feel confined. Being as you are. And since you have been brought up in this country of ours here, as most of us have been, you have always had the notion that you are – well, what else? – *free*. And you are used to that. So now this guy in uniform, or maybe it's two guys, or one or two guys in plainclothes, could be that as well, whatever, but what you know is that they're cops, he has you in custody, and you are not free to go. And why would this be, then? Well, unless someone made a mistake – which we don't make a habit of doing and I want to assure everybody here of that right now on that point – normally it's going to be because you did something.

'It don't matter, really, does it, though, what it was. Because the overall effect's always the same. If you're drunk or operating under, you had a fight or something, or you're beating up the wife. Or you're breaking in a building. Or maybe you had drugs in your possession that you're selling someone, right? And you know you're not supposed to do that. But you're always on the lookout, aren'tcha, for the easy buck, and now it turns out, joke's on you, guy you're selling to's a *cop*, badge and everything. And he placed you under arrest. So here you are now; you've been arrested. Now you're going to the lock-up.

'Now at the present time if you would like to come down to the station as it is configured, the one on Lannan Street there, any night you care to come, although there'll generally be more to see on a weekend night – as Mister Merrion can tell you, having been there setting bail a good many weekend nights for people we've arrested, Friday or a Saturday. Unless it's one of those three-day holidays it seems like we're always getting now, at least one a month, in which case Sunday night as well we will have a lot of traffic – usually, that is. And the first thing you will see down there, and I will show you this myself or have a sergeant escort you, because sometimes one of these guys that we've got arrested will decide, you know, because he's drunk, he'll decide he wants to fight.

'This is also very common. A big part of our job as law enforcement officers involves fighting with drunks. If you want to be a police officer, you have to face that. It's reality. And when we arrest a guy for that, he's quite often going to get unruly with us, and we have to subdue him there, show him what the Mace is like, blast of that stuff in the face, get his mind off fighting us. And what you will then see is that when the cruisers pull up at the back door of the station, right on Lannan Street, with everybody passing by, you will have both your pedestrian and your vehicular traffic there as well. And this is where my men have to come to discharge their passengers, and not only the officers of the police department but also the State Police if this happens to be one of *their* arrests that they have made and they are bringing him to us. Or her, could be a woman; we do have to arrest the women sometimes too, although nowhere near as many. To be secured in our lock-up until someone can come and get this man or woman out.

'And the very first thing that you will instantly observe in virtually every single case, and virtually without exception, is that every suspect who gets out, he's got his hands behind his back account of how he's cuffed and all, the first thing that he always does, and I don't care he's drunk or sober, or he's on some controlled substance and he's higher'n a kite, but the first thing he does before he does another thing is: He takes a look around. And we all *know* what he is thinkin', every single time, no matter who it is. He's thinkin': "How can I get out of here?" How can he escape?'

The chief always stressed the sibilance of the initial syllable of the verb, relentlessly telling officers who mispronounced the word that 'when people hear you sayin' *ex*-cape like there was an X in it, which there is not, and which you just did, they think you are stupid or else ignorant, which you do not want. So therefore don't let me hear you doing it around here.'

'Now of course this makes no sense at all, no question about that. Usually the charge that we have got against you, when we bring you in, well, the fact is that you may've gotten everybody good and mad at you, doing what you did, may've even hurt some-one, but the fact is still that usually it's a fairly minor charge.

'Now when I say that I don't mean *you* think that it's minor, that it's a minor thing. That if it's operatin' under for example, so you stand to lose your license, sixty, ninety days, a year, whatever it may be; or this time you're gonna have to take that course they give you if you've been caught for doing this, and it's therefore gonna cost you. You not only have to go to all those lecture-sessions that they have – so there goes your evenings free and you are gonna have to sit now with a bunchah *drunks* that you now belong with; which you don't like thinkin' either, but you haven't got no choice now; you have proved it, you belong – and look at all those awful bloody pictures that they show. As many nights as that takes, and you're gonna have to pay for them, the cost of going to them, and that's no small amount, you find. Four, five hundred bucks I guess, is what they're getting for it now. You don't like that at all.

'And we don't blame you. But just the same, it isn't like this has to be the end of the whole world for you now. You're embarrassed, sure you are, and you ought to be, whatever it is you've done. But you're not the first one, done it. You're not gonna be the last. So what you want to do is take your medicine and learn from it, learn something from this bad event. Then put it all behind you and act like a normal person, and see that from now on you behave yourself so that you don't have no more trouble, which of course is what you want. That's what we all want, all of us, just to be left alone. And if you do like you're supposed to, chances are, that's how this will all turn out.

'But if you actually do it, if you actually try to escape, get away from the officers there that've gone to all the trouble of arresting you – and don't think they like doin' that, all the paperwork that that entails, and the court appearances and everything like that; they're not gonna do this unless they think they have to – but now they've done all that and brought you in, and now you're gonna try to *escape*? Well now if you do that, you're gonna be in one big peck of . . . well, a lot of trouble, anyway, and I trust you all know what it is that I'm talkin' about here.

'*Big* trouble. Resistin' arrest. A and B on an officer. Attempted escape, and on and on. No jokes here now. These're all felonies, and we're not gonna show you any mercy. We're just gonna multiply charges up on you; cut you no slack; give you no breaks: that's what we're gonna do. Because you went and acted stupid, and you made us take a chance of where somebody could've gotten really hurt, and we hadda go and stop you, and this always involves risk. That we do not want to have to be taking. If it turns out that nobody got hurt bad, well then, everybody was lucky, that's all. It wasn't no fault of yours. And so now we're gonna throw the book at you and you are goin' to jail. *You* didn't want that to happen and *we* didn't want it to happen. Nobody wanted it to happen, but you went and did what you did, and we can't have you doing that, so now you go to jail.

'You see what I'm getting at here. What I'm telling you is that now that we have got the opportunity here to design this new facility to meet the needs that we have got in a growing, modern community police department here. 'Cause that is what we've got now: a community that's growing, and it's getting bigger all the time, whether we like it or not. And with all the problems that all growing towns everywhere've all got these days, people movin' to the suburbs and it's only gonna just get worse, matter what we do because that's the way it is. And I don't care where you look, we've all got the same kind of problems. We're all doin' our best, lookin' for some way to get out of them. And that's why we need to look very carefully at this thing that we're doin' here and make absolutely sure we know exactly what we're doin'. And one thing I am tellin' you is that from my point of view as a professional law enforcement officer, lookin' at this thing here, one thing we absolutely positively have to build into this new police facility from the start is an internal reception area for receiving prisoners and any other people that we may be bringing in who're in custody. That we have found it necessary to take into custody, danger of harm to themselves or to others, whatever the reason may be. So that the cruiser car or the wagon, whatever it is there, it just arrives from the scene and what it does then is it pulls right in, right inside the building, and the door shuts, *boom*, down behind it, just like *that*.' He clapped his hands once.

'And then we open up the car doors there and we get them unloaded, and march 'em right into the bookin' desk-area there, and advise 'em and mug 'em and print 'em. And from there they go right into the cell. Then there they have been at all times since we pulled them out the cruiser: inside of the building, in the lock-up. So they haven't had another *look* at being outdoors again since they got arrested, because they've never *been* outdoors again once they got put in the car, the official vehicle there. And they won't be outside again until they've been bailed and discharged and allowed to go free, on their way, with the date set for them to be in court. So once you've done that, see, put the reception area physically inside of the building like I said, you have now just practically eliminated here that completely human tendency and temptation they all always have now, to try to get away and escape, and with all that that entails there, and that's a completely essential thing, I think here, myself.'

Shortly after 9:30 that Saturday evening in August Merrion's beeper went off while he sat cramped in a wicker chair too small for him in the now-glass-enclosed sunporch of the house in Canterbury where he had grown up, watching a taped rerun of final night of a big dog-show that had taken place six months or so earlier in Madison Square Garden in New York, trying idly once more to think of some way he could have a dog again without complicating his life beyond endurance, knowing that there was none. The number that came up on the beeper screen in faint light-emitting-diode grey was for the administrative line at the Canterbury police station. He lifted the wireless remote telephone handset from the wicker table next to his chair and punched the number in, and when he recognized the answering voice he said: 'Hiya, Everett, what we got?' He listened and then he said: 'My, my, that's unusual. How many involved here?'

Once more he listened and then said: 'Okay, I guess I'd better come down then. Gimme fifteen minutes. Oh, and better give Social Services a call. They may wanna take a hand in this. On second thought, no, make it half an hour. I've got the Westchester Kennel Club show on and we're judging the collies here now. I wanna wait and see who's gets the Best Bitch.' He laughed. 'Yeah, if it was the courthouse, it'd be no contest at all. *Biggest* Bitch, anyway – Joanie in Probation, win that one hands-down. Anyway, just tell 'em I'm putting my pants on and they keep their shirts on and I'm on my way; I'll be there, half an hour. Have 'em get their money ready, and if they haven't got any, tell 'em they better either use their call to get someone who's got cash to spare, or else make friends fast with somebody else in the cell-block who's got some. 'Cause this clerk makes no exceptions; otherwise it's Sunday in the slammer.' He paused. 'Yeah, see you at Sal's motor entrance in about a half an hour.'

He hung up grateful for the call. He had hoped for it. He intended to be generous when he rotated the weekend bail-setting watch (required when the court would not sit the next day because by law no one could be held more than twenty-four hours without bail having been set) among his three assistant clerks. He told them he meant it when he said that it was only because he was being a nice guy that he was offering them the option. He said that if they chose to tie themselves down one or two weekend nights in order to augment their statutory salaries with the magistrate's bail-setting fee of $25 in each case, that would be fine with him. On the other hand, any time that it happened that all three of them preferred to have both weekend evenings free, and forgo the extra money, that would also be all right.

He had a reason. Richie Hammond had hogged the detail, seldom permitting Merrion or the second and third assistant clerks, Bobby Cooke and Jeanne Flagg, to share the extra money. That had led to some resentment and hard feelings which in turn explained why it was Richie had so much trouble finding anyone who'd pinch-hit for him when he wanted to spend an occasional weekend away. Merrion wanted no such dissension. 'And besides,' as he told Hilliard, 'I'm single, and with what Larry left me, I don't need the fuckin' money. I just put it in my pocket until I get to the bank, put it into my account I'm saving up for when I have to buy my next car. Keep a record every dime, fuckin' IRS thinks they're gonna grab me puttin' cash into my pocket without payin' taxes on it, they can go and think again. That's the first place that the bastards look. I'd be stupid if I did that, and I'd be just as stupid, too, I didn't, let the kids take what they want.'

The weekend totals varied with the seasons. There were almost always at least four or five unlucky drivers whose dead headlights, faulty brake-lights or imperfect recognition of passing zones or stop signs justified a roving cop's decision to pull them over and require them to show their licenses and registrations, leading to arrests for suspended or missing documents, or operating under the influence of alcohol or narcotics. Documentation of their releases on personal recognizance in the amount of $100, promises of payment that would come due if they failed to appear the next day court was open to be processed and enter pleas, would yield a total of at least a hundred bucks a night. More often than not a Friday evening would produce an angrily baffled male whose frustrating week at work or out of it had convinced him that the only cure for his malaise was more beer than his ordinarily peaceful disposition could tolerate without becoming profane and noisy, frightening his wife into believing that violence would be next and causing her to call the cops. That would add another twenty-five dollars to the magistrate's net pay. Sometimes around graduation time or during the football season the State cops would break up an off-campus keg-party at a summer cottage on one of the lakes or a skinny-dipping outing at the reservoir, bagging a small herd of underage drinkers and public urinators whose releases from the lock-up in Hampton Pond would bring two or three hundred dollars. In the late Eighties the increasing traffic in crack cocaine had spawned an increase as well in the number of magistrate's fees, arrests for dealing it adding fifty to a hundred dollars a night.

It seemed to Merrion that that kind of money ought to be hard for a young parent to turn down, but surprisingly more often than he would have thought, both of the two young fathers and the young wife on his staff as well regularly passed it up, saying they wanted time with their families. And during the summer the absences of vacationing assistants usually put him on duty at least one night every week.

This night he was glad of it. On the way home from visiting his mother he had perceived himself to be in a familiar, dangerously barren mood. Polly had not recognized him, gazing into space and glancing at him only when it registered on her that there was something else alive and breathing in her room, the evidence being bright and cheerful sounds he made when he tried to talk to her. At least she hadn't mistaken him for Chris, which still occasionally happened 'and never fails to piss me off,' as he told Hilliard. 'Puts me right into a fuckin' rage, even though of course I know she's got no idea what she's saying. I dunno what I want from her, expect her to do, where that no-good bastard's concerned. Fifty, sixty miles away, maybe an hour's drive? If it's even that, and he hasn't been to see her since I can't remember when. Before she got really sick, I know, the bastard, been at least that long.

'I can't figure the little shit out. It's almost as though he holds me and her responsible for Dad dying like he did when he was still so young. Like he got gypped out of something or something, and we helped whoever did it. When he had much more of Dad's time'n I ever did because by the time he came along Dad'd made sales manager and didn't have to work so many hours – had more time to take Chris to ballgames and places by then I was too old to go with them. And who the hell does he think helped Ma pay his tuition, he went to Cathedral? Helped out with his living expenses or he couldn't've gone to BU like he did, even if with his scholarship. That all seems to've slipped his mind now. She still remembers his name, though. It's *my* name she always forgets.

'Jesus, though, doesn't he know? You got to take care of your own. All you and I've been trynah do, all these years, the things we ever done, it's always come down to steppin' in and takin' care of other people when their own people either didn't care about them enough so *they* would do it, or were so totally messed-up themselves they *couldn't* do it, but the need was still there. Somebody had to take care of it. And that was the way that we *always* saw it; that was the way we looked at it. Our job was to make sure the government picked up the slack. That's why the damned jobs *exist*; that's what they're *for*. You always take care of your own. Like I always looked out for your best interest, and you always looked out for mine. And we're not even related. We always took care of our own.

'Chris's never done that at all. It's like he's oblivious to the fact that he should; like the shit doesn't see his obligation. He doesn't take care of his own. But it's *his* name she still remembers.'

She seldom understood anything he said to her any more, but on good days she seemed to be pleasantly diverted by the noise he made, and liked it, the way she seemed to like the radio that the nuns had set to play soft-rock music at low volume on the table beside her bed, smiling absently and briefly from the distant world nearby where she had gone to live, if living was still what she did. He thought perhaps she had found his father, Pat, and perhaps her mother, Rose, there for company, and that maybe Rose was being nice, happier with them in that new world than she had ever been with them in the one where the three of them had lived before. He surmised that when she was off in that place she liked the sounds he made, not for their content, or the effort the producer of them made, but for what they were themselves, as a kitten likes and is amused by squeaking sounds emitted by a rubber mouse.

On not-so-good days, perhaps when she and Pat had quarreled, as they sometimes had when he had still been present where she used to live, and physically remained, or Rose was being cranky, the sounds that Ambrose made seemed to vex her, and when she verged on lucidity – as she generally did, once or twice an hour, regardless of her inner state – she would irritably make small, tidy brushing motions. He was fairly certain that she meant them to dismiss the noise-maker. On those days he subsided, and sat silently with her for as long as he could stand it, half an hour more or so, departing with the excuse in his head that the length of his stay no longer mattered, and the fact of it might not, either, except to the good nuns who observed in passing with approval his filial devotions.

This Saturday had been an in-between day. She hadn't really taken any notice of him or what he said. Her entertainment offering to him had been to look over vacantly and then pick tremulously at her third meal of the day – sections of pink grapefruit and a small dish of canned beef soup, accompanied by a half-pint container of skimmed milk and a slice of whole wheat bread with a pat of margarine, a dixie cup of peppermint-stick ice cream, served to her on the narrow telescoping bed-table, usable when she was in the wheelchair, as she had been that afternoon. Then she had placidly looked on while it was taken away, mostly undisturbed, and a short while after that he had gone away himself.

He thought that on Monday he might call her doctor again, for no good reason except his own need to feel that he had at least tried to do something, even though he knew before he made the effort that there was nothing to be done and it would do no good to try.

The doctor – he prefaced his answer to every question with 'As your mother's primary-care physician' – was a large slow-moving red-haired man named Carlson, in his early forties. He seemed always to be working out a complicated mathematical problem in his head. Most likely it was always the same one, Merrion believed, relating to the possibility of obtaining additional money for his services from the family estates or the insurers of the patients, without any additional or more effective effort on his part; endless, useless calculations of no possible use to anyone except him, conducted visibly so that it would always be clear to everyone that he did not and would not ever wish to be interrupted, and would regard any attempt to do so as an imposition, punishable by neglect of the patient.

That evident desire of his cut no ice with Merrion. He received regular quarterly statements from the Hightower Mutual Life Assurance Society in Fort Recovery, Ohio, reporting benefits it had paid to James N. Carlson, M.D. under Pauline Merrion's Medicare Supplement Extended Benefits Policy. If each of the forty-one other patients occupying all but three of the extended-care beds available at St Mary's on the Hilltop had a policy or other resource remitting to Dr Carlson, attending house physician, the same amount that he was getting from Hightower for Polly, that stolid man was pulling down $2,730 every week, $141,960 every year, for what appeared to Merrion to consist chiefly of saying over and over again that just as Merrion had thought 'there's been no change in the past um week, um um, no change that I see, at least. But her heart still seems to be very strong. Doesn't seem to be much more we can do that we're not doing already. She's, yes, she's still holding her own.'

On the television screen the beautifully silky, streaming tawny and white long-haired regal dogs trotted beautifully in turn around the ring on the leashes that their nondescriptly dressed diligently trotting handlers pretended that they did not need, and Ambrose Merrion on Saturday night sat depleted by his caring, watching them compete without ever knowing why, except that they existed, and that was what they had been bred to do.

15

Sergeant Everett Whalen emerged from the lockup into the ivory-painted cinderblock-walled corridor outside the lieutenant's office before Merrion finished removing his supply of bail forms from his beaten-up tan leather briefcase and getting himself settled at the bare old wooden desk against the wall. 'Amby, how they hangin',' he said. It was not an inquiry; Whalen walked soundlessly in his crepe-soled black uniform shoes and spoke as a courtesy, so that Merrion would not be startled to turn and find him standing there.

'Ah, two inna bunch, Ev, same as always,' Merrion said absently, without looking at him, flopping the sheaf of multicopy bail forms onto the desk, the top copy, white, blocked off and printed in rust-colored ink. He snapped the briefcase shut and tossed it onto the top of the desk against the wall, turning to face Whalen and resting his buttocks on the edge of the desk so that his left foot touched the floor and his right foot dangled above it. 'Our happy campers ready?'

'Thompson'll start bringin' 'em out to see you in a couple minutes,' Whalen said. He stood slumped with his hands in his pockets. In his late forties he had prematurely acquired the sallow skin, the shameful little paunch and the doleful, dismayed look of a careless man nearing sixty and discovering that the penalties of failure to eat properly, get sufficient exercise and moderate his intake of alcohol – plenty of cheap beer, generic six-packs, in Ev's case – are just about as disagreeable as medically predicted. He looked as though he had realized some time ago what was going to happen to him, sooner than it should, and had resigned himself to it. The dismissive scuttlebutt that Merrion indifferently remembered from a casual courthouse conversation was that Ev Whalen never had any good luck at all.

Apparently well before he'd been close to old enough to have learned very much about women or know anything at all about marriage, he'd made the bad mistake of marrying a somewhat older woman who'd had her heart set on having a husband and had pretty much settled for him as the best she was going to get. She had borne him two children, but then after those experiences and some further consideration decided that on the whole she wished she hadn't married him. While she still believed he had probably been the best she could ever have done, he didn't make much money; he bored her, and she didn't like him very much.

One night with four rum-and-Cokes in her she had disconsolately given him that news, confessing her realization that she would have been better off alone. Staggered, he said he wished she were. In his bleak grief he told her since she felt that way to get out of his house and he would raise the kids himself. She said she would like to do that and appreciated his offer, but they both knew he couldn't do it alone, not the way things had become. They were stuck with each other, fused by a bad event that wouldn't've happened if she hadn't grown impatient and they hadn't gotten together.

Merrion wasn't exactly sure what it had been. One of the children had some kind of serious disability, caused either by a birth defect that she could have prevented with better prenatal care or more prudent behavior, or else by a very bad accident during infancy. The calamity had occurred while Everett and his wife were still fairly young, ruining whatever slim chance they, with little else to hope for, had ever had of at least moving up a notch or two in the world on a policeman's pay.

When no-end-in-sight expenses threatened to destroy them, some of their friends and neighbors organized a ten-kilometer fund-raising walk around the Cumberland Reservoir. Disc jockeys at WMAS in Chicopee exhorted listeners to volunteer and sell sponsorships of themselves to relatives and friends for contributions of a buck per kilometer to 'this very worthy cause.' The week before the 10K walk, volunteers impeded shoppers leaving stores and markets at the local strip-malls by stepping into their paths and shaking white cardboard metal-bottomed canisters containing coins in their faces, demanding that they 'Please Help the Whalen Family.' Friends and neighbors staged a couple of dinner-dances at the VFW Hall in Hampton Pond, 'Benefit of the Whalen Fund.' They charged couples $25 per ticket for access to a cash bar and Music By The Muscle-Tones, a four-piece amateur Sixties Oldies band formed by two firemen, a high-school teacher and a lab technician who worked out together at the Canterbury Spa and Health Club, playing and singing together for the bright-eyed pleasure that it gave them.

Too indolent to change the local-access channel after the conclusion of an entertainingly contentious budget-meeting of the Canterbury selectmen, Merrion had watched the climax of one of those dances on television. The Whalens were standing awkwardly side-by-side like 4H livestock, a team of farm animals being auctioned off at the Big E Eastern States Exposition. Obviously not used to his clothing, Whalen wore a white shirt and narrow dark-red tie with a dark suit. His wife, whose name Merrion did not remember, wore a black dress with a high collar and long sleeves. They were standing on a low stage next to the 'MAS morning disc jockey, a laboriously jovial, heavyset young man with a microphone, doing their best to look humble and grateful while the fat kid boastfully announced that a measly 'three or four thousand dollars have been collected, from hundreds and hundreds of people throughout the Pioneer Valley, reaching out to help the Whalen Family.' He did not say that ninety percent of it had been five and ten-dollar bills donated by people who knew the Whalens only slightly but really did feel sorry for them, or else had been asked by one of Whalen's fellow cops to make a donation and thought it might be provident to do so. The DJ did not say the rest was small change badgered out of contemptuous strangers who didn't know a thing or give one good shit about the Whalens and resented being forced to use their pocket change – for once glad to have pennies – to ransom themselves from the can-rattling solicitors they deemed fucking goddamned nuisances. 'Wonderful, wonderful people, every one of you,' the DJ declaimed, extending his arms in symbolic embrace of people sitting at tables and standing in groups on the dance-floor under the balloons and crepe-paper festoons decorating the dimly lighted hall, staring incuriously – some blearily – at the Whalens. Because he knew Ev, Merrion had avidly watched the mortification, ashamed that he felt such fascination.

Then it had been time for Everett to grovel. He had taken the microphone and held it clumsily too close to his mouth so that it muffled his words, abjectly whinnying mandatory thanks to all the wonderful people who had worked on the great events and given money and helped out in any way at all; promising them that he and his wife – he grasped her hand desperately, as though reasonably apprehensive she might come to her senses and bolt, try to get away while he was occupied – and their healthy child, as well as the one being helped, would never forget their wonderful kindness and generosity. He did not quite promise to reciprocate on demand by donating one of his kidneys – or a lung, his heart or liver, for that matter – to any fundraiser who might ever need one and match his tissues, but he came pretty close.

As Merrion watched the event he'd begun to feel astonishment and wonder. He did not recall having given to the fund drive. He was reasonably sure that he had somehow inadvertently escaped every dragnet bagging all those niggardly donors. To the best of his recollection, it was the only such shakedown he had managed to elude since he'd first gotten into politics, forty years and more before. This amazed him. He calculated that in the course of his twenty-two-year career he had solicited campaign contributions for Dan Hilliard and other Democratic candidates and causes at least sixty times. The people on his trusty donor-list remembered him, with vengeance, when it came time for them to raise money for their candidates, colleges, church schools, drum-and-bugle corps, their children's teams and their favorite diseases, knowing he could not refuse. But somehow he'd escaped the posses of the Whalen Fund. He could not for the life of him explain how he'd done it, imagine what on earth he'd done or failed to do that had delivered him. Thereafter each time he saw Whalen at the station, he marveled silently once more.

'We got a couple more guests in since I called you,' Whalen said. He leaned his right shoulder against the corridor wall and folded his arms. 'Lady barkeep, good-lookin' head, from up Cannonball's, and we assume it's her gentleman friend that was with her. Routine coke buy. He was scoutin' up the customers; she was keepin' the stash under the service bar.

'Staties got a new choir-boy for undercover narc. He's the one who popped 'em. Looks like he's about sixteen. I guess he's actually twenny-three or four. They're workin' him out around here day and night this weekend without stoppin', seems like. Showin' him around like a new movie; anywhere you go you got a chance to see him. Hittin' every place they can. Settin' guys up left and right. Marijuana, cocaine, you-name-it; sellin' booze without askin' ID; solicitin' him for blow jobs; firearms; anything they can.

'Corporal Baker told me you can never tell what the hell is gonna happen, you drop a new young pretty boy into a hard guys' bar. Baker told me they got one guy down in Blackstone last week, had their Little Boy Blue workin' down the Worcester area, guy sold him a fuckin' recurve-crossbow. Looked like the antlers of a goddamned Texas Longhorn, mounted onna fuckin'-*gorgeous*, *inlaid*, *checkered*, big-game rifle stock. Fuckin' thing had to've been custom-made, some guy, most likely, use it to kill silent with. 'Magine havin' that around, fuckin' thing like that? Someone must've stolen it somewhere from someone else – down in Texas, prolly. Some rich oilman's killer weapon, kindah guy he must've been, and still some guy has got the balls go in and steal it from him.

'You beat that, fuckin' luxury crossbow? Whole buncha those bolts had for it, too, stubby iron arrows they use inna thing there; don't make any noise 'cept this sort of *whoosh* you let 'em go, but the guy saysah fuckin' thing'll go right through an *engine block*; right through a Ford engine block. What's this country comin' to, you wanna try an' tell me *that*? Guys sellin' things like that, people they don't even *know*, total *strangers*, even? Someone could wind up gettin' killed, that kind of shit goin' on.

'Anyway, they've got him going non-stop, the fake teenager, I mean. Just as fast as he can move, 'fore his cases start comin' up in court next week and some shyster-lawyer finally gets smart, asks for a hearin' on probable cause; kid hastah come in, testify.

Everyone gets to see what he looks like, he is no good anymore. Party's over.

'But inna meantime they're sure gettin' their money's worth. Corporal Baker, down the Monson station, used to be up in Northampton, brought in the last two the kid bagged. He told me kid made seven buys in *nine* bars down in Chicopee and Springfield just last night alone, three or four more in Holyoke tonight 'fore they hustle him up here.

'Grabbed one guy, parkin' lot at Donatello's, sellin' crack outta his car. Fuckin' two-year-old Isuzu, whadda they call it, Rodeo, Trooper, something. Trooper, I think it is. Anyway, it looks brand-new. They bust him, he's got two-and-a-half kilos. Run him and they find out that he's also got a couple priors. So they cuff him and they seize his fuckin' *truck*, all right? On top of charging him. Baker said they thought they could've had another guy that was there, too, in this blue Bronco.' *Julian*, Merrion thought. 'Forfeit his fuckin' car too. But before they could get him, they're so busy the guy with the Trooper, guy inna Bronco sees what's goin' down, and peels off. Outta there. Didn't even get a plate on him. They're pissed; fact he ran, you know he's dirty – could've taken his ride too.

'What the hell, huh? I suppose they figure as long's they're already out there, why the hell not? Not gonna do any harm; might just as well go ahead, do it. "Oh, nice car you got there. Sellin' contraband out of it? Sellin' illegal drugs, is that what it's gonna be? Naughty-*naugh*-ty." Take his car. He's a big boy, isn't he? Shouldah known better.

'I guess that's the way they look at it, anyway. You want my opinion, though, I would say the guy's been fucked. Serves the bastard right, I guess, peddlin' that shit. He don't care then why should I? Guy he picked to sell's a cop. People sell this guy anything. Then the next thing they know, they're up to their ears in the shit. Well, that's the chance that they took.

'I don't know, though, you come down to it, what difference it really makes, they do find out he looks like. This's the young trooper I mean. Half these people that're sellin', either so stoned themselves alla time, or else they're always loaded, out of their minds; they dunno the fuck they're doin' anyway. Or else they're just naturally fuckin' stupid. You know what I bet you could do? Could go right up to them and tell 'em, face to face, every single other person inna fuckin' gin-mill with them is an undercover cop, and have it be the fuckin' *truth*, and you know somethin'? It wouldn't make any difference; wouldn't make any difference at all. They'd still be there, sellin' stuff an' lettin' the people buy it from them, whether they know them or not, got any *idea* who it is. It's as simple as that.

'They think it's all a fuckin' *joke*; a laugh, is what they think. They think that that's all it is. You know, no big deal, they get caught sellin' coke. Year in the can, mandatory? Yeah, sure; tell me another one, willya? Half the time their lawyer's even got a fuckin' *clue* what he's doin' alla time, he's gonna get a *deal*, put 'em right back onna street. They get so they know the routine there, you know? You do this; you do that; you get busted; so what? That's what it is. You should know that.

'So, *good*, they get so they're part of it there. They get into the system, they fin'ly become part of it themselves. 'Til their faces start gettin' to where they're becomin' familiar, you know? To the people down at Probation; start to get so sick of seeing these bums they can't stand it anymore. "What's this? You back here again, you asshole?" 'Til it gets to the point someone goes to the DA and says: "*Hey*, get this jerk some *time*, willya, Christ sake for a change? Sick of lookin' at him every week." And then maybe they go away. Then maybe they do do some time. But then again, maybe they don't. It all sort of just *depends*, you know? It always all depends.' He shrugged. 'Okay with me, I guess.'

He snuffled. 'So, but what's been goin' on with you, then, huh Amby? Last time we see you, I mean. That new black kid, Tyrone, he was in here last night with us, you no doubt probably know.'

Whalen had continued to practice the nosiness that had made him a good beat-cop after he had his chevrons sewn on and gone indoors to work. It was what he had been trained to do, and therefore what he did. 'He can't help himself,' he told Hilliard, telling him about Whalen's latest probe. 'I don't know what it is he thinks he's doing. "Investigating," I guess. Keeping an eye out. That's what kept him alive when he was out on the street. Now he can't help doing it. I don't know *what* he's investigating or who he's investigating for doing it, and neither does he. But that doesn't make any difference. He's *interested.* He pigeon-holes people for ready reference – "there's Bob the fireman, front of the firehouse, right where he oughta be; check" – like he did keeping order on his beat. Even though there's no reason for it anymore.

'It isn't that he doesn't *like* Tyrone or that he treats him badly when Tyrone goes down there. The fact Tyrone's been a clerk here now for over six years probably means he's not "a *new* black kid" any more, but that's Ev's label for him. When he calls Tyrone "the new black kid" he means that Tyrone is black and still relatively young, and the rest of us clerks are not. He says "new" and "black" when he means "different." It sounds like something's wrong but there isn't.

'I know because I asked Tyrone, came right out and asked him. Made a big fool of myself doing it, too. At first I'm going to be, you know, *diplomatic*; I'm gonna be suave. Try to dance around it there, like I'm not after anything. I'm just making *small-talk*, Monday morning, after his first night down there by himself: "So, how was it down there? Everything go okay?" Like it'd been his first date. "Well, ah, you didn't try to feel her up did you, son?" Very casual and everything, that's what I am; store the extra butter in my mouth, I am so cool. Mister fucking Smooth.

'He thought I was asking him if he had any trouble makin' out the forms and stuff, and of course he thought that must mean that secretly I really think that he's kind of stupid. Because a moderately smart housecat could fill out those forms if it could figure out how to hold a ballpoint pen in one of its front paws and press down good and hard because it's making several copies.

'Tyrone tries to keep his face straight. "Oh, fine-fine, no problem, fine." Like: "What the *hell* is the matter with you?"

'So that made me get right to the point. I haven't got any choice now. I have to come right out and ask him.

''Cause I don't want that happening, any racial shit, which these cops, some of them I know are capable of that. Even though some of the other cops they work with and get along with perfectly fine, no problems at all, they *also* happen to be black; makes absolutely no difference at all, they still are *capable* of this shit and there's no use pretending otherwise, and . . . and

I just don't want any of it happening, any way at all. And if it is I want to know about it, and I'll do something about it. We got enough problems in this line of work without havin' any *that* shit goin' down. And we're not *gonna* have it, as long's I'm around in charge of things, and that's all there fuckin' is *to* it.'

'"Tyrone," I said, "here is what it is: the guy is not a bigot. Ev Whalen's not a bigot and he's not a racist either. But if he said something, or did something, maybe acted a certain way that made you feel like he is, all you've got to do is tell me what it was that made you uncomfortable, and I'll put an end to it. Once I talk to him, he'll be just as upset as I am, you took it that way. Because he isn't that way. He's not that type of guy."

'And Tyrone, Tyrone he just look at me and shake his head, and he be *laffin*' at me? He do, and then he say to me: "You really somethin', Amby, yes, you really, truly are." Then he clapped me on the back and said: "But you can put your mind at ease here, because everything is cool. Nothin' to concern yourself, not a thing at all. Everyone was very nice. Everything is cool."

'I am never sure whether Tyrone's playin' straight with me or givin' me the leg, and I will admit that. He's been workin' for me in the same office with me for several years and they have been happy years. I think we like each other fine. But every now and then I get the feeling that my friend Tyrone may be funnin' with me some, you know? Just a little bit; keep his hand in and all, givin' me the leg when I think he's bein' straight.'

Tyrone Thomas, thirty-eight, formerly of Cambridge, had become the third assistant clerk of the Canterbury District Court when Merrion had plucked him out of the lower third of the civil service list and appointed him in 1989 at the suggestion of State Sen. William Gallagher of Hingham, Chairman of the Senate Committee on Post Audit and Oversight. Merrion did not know or have any occasion to speak to Gallagher. Gallagher had never laid eyes on Thomas. Gallagher's suggestion had been relayed to Merrion by Dan Hilliard, president of Hampton Pond Community College.

Hilliard's request for a special supplemental appropriation of $3.9 million to finance construction of a new HPCC building incorporating a student union and computer center along with 'much-needed faculty offices and expanded vocational counseling facilities' was short one vote for inclusion in the consensus budget under review by the Senate Committee on Ways and Means. Sen. Tobias Green of Boston controlled that vote.

'I can't budge him, Dan,' Gallagher told Hilliard. 'You know I love you dearly and I want you to have your game room and your bar-and-grill and pool hall, jai-alai court and rumpus room. Everything you say you've got to have or else the students starved for knowledge'll burn down the entire campus and put you out of work. But Green's the swing-vote, and he's not gonna budge until he gets what he wants, which is a court clerkship for this Thomas kid. Not later; right now. Green has checked and he knows there's one open out at your end of the world, in Canterbury. If it's promised to someone else and you can't pry it loose, that's all right. At least it's all right with me. It won't be all right with Tobias; he'll call you a racist and say now he knows you're in the Klan. He thinks that, you don't get your building.'

Hilliard said he'd make the call and get back to Gallagher. Merrion said to Hilliard: 'Good. Send that darky out here on the next stage. This's the best news I've had since my no-good fucking brother Chris swore to me for I think it was the fourth time that he'll never speak to me again. This time I think he means it. Now you come along and tell me that this means that fucking vacancy – more like an open sore – is finally going to be filled.

'My Christian heart is filled with joy. Now I know Larry was telling the truth when he said he was happy when I got the job. He told me when Chassy Spring he was appointing me, 'cause you had hammered Chassy, he'd never been so damned relieved in all of his born days. "You getting it meant I was free. Free of all the nagging bastards who been after that damned job. 'Sorry,' I could then tell them, 'Dan Hilliard's man's the winner. You gotta beef, it's with him. I can't help you one bit.'"

'I didn't believe him then, but now I do, I do. It's the exact same thing with me. Now I can finally tell the late Richie Hammond's favorite nephew – and also the late Larry Lane's grandson – that the fucking job is *filled* and they are *out* of fucking luck, "So stop pestering me and beat it."

'The Lane grandson especially. His mother came from miles

away – she was in Japan, the time – to help boot Grampa Larry out of his own house and make him go somewhere else to die. But her kid is *delicate*; he told me he suffers from chronic depression and can't leave his bedroom about ninety-eight days a year. I told him this makes it hard for me and Lennie Cavanaugh to see how he could possibly hold down a job in the courthouse. I told him having to go to the courthouse every day makes even perfectly normal and stable people like me, haven't got a thing wrong with them, feel pretty depressed quite a lot.

'He thinks that shouldn't matter. He thinks the fact his gallant unsung dad singlehandedly resolved some trade dispute with Taiwan should make everything all right for him, always, in perpetuity. In other words, what I think doesn't matter. He wants the job and therefore I should give it to him.

'*Now* I can tell him he's probably right, but I can't do it for him. And: "If you're down in Hell listenin', Larry, understand that this one's for you." I can tell the same thing to the Hammond kid, too, who obviously doesn't know his late Uncle Richie hated me and did everything he could think of to fuck me over, or what warm feelings I still have for the bastard. "And Larry, if you're still listenin', if you should run into Richie down there, tell him this one's also for me."

'I will say to those two fresh kids: "Hate to tell you this, guys, but the both of you seem to've lost out. To a nigger, can you beat it? Hey, it's Affirmative Action – what can I tell you? I've been neutered, made to sing soprano and rendered powerless; also my hands have been tied. But I want you to know, I'll always have you in my heart."

'Same for the other four hundred and thirty-two people who've also let it be known that they'd like the job. Not a bunch of fireballs; most of them look to me like they need their rest and generally manage to get it. I will tell them you got me in a hammerlock, ignored my piteous cries, and ordered me like the Nazi you are to give it to this fine young gentleman of color. So now they can stop calling me and start calling *you* day and night to threaten you with death for giving it to Amos. Or was it Andy you just said? Whichever, doesn't matter; I can't wait 'til he gets here.'

Senator Green until his entry into politics in 1981 had for several years taught social studies and coached the jayvee football and basketball teams at Cambridge Ridge and Latin High School, where he had encountered Tyrone Thomas. Thomas had been the youngest son of a single mother whose two elder boys, by different footloose fathers, had both been in trouble with the law before apparently getting themselves straightened out as US Army volunteers. Tyrone had not been a standout as student or athlete, but he was a genuinely nice kid, and he had become one of Green's favorites, using his average intelligence as diligently in the classroom as he did his body and his average skills when playing sports, cheerfully doing what Green, his mentor – and after a while his surrogate father – told him to do. He earned a B+ average and varsity letters as a second-stringer in football, basketball and track, and received a need-based scholarship from the College of the Holy Cross in Worcester.

Correctly assessing as poor his prospects of even a brief career in professional sports, and believing that the practices and games took too much time away from his studies, Thomas dropped football midway through his first season and basketball after his sophomore year at the Cross, slightly disappointing one of the basketball coaches who had hoped he might develop into a capable substitute small forward, but gratifying Green. Green said Thomas's decision was a mature judgment, confirmed by his subsequent graduation with a 2.7 grade-point – low B – average in sociology, and his subsequent admission to the New England School of Law in Boston.

Thomas earned his J.D. while partially supporting himself and two children – his wife, Carol, also worked, as a $17,000-a-year clerk-typist in the State Department of Revenue – as a $24,000-a-year assistant manager of the Great American Inn motel on Fresh Pond Parkway in Arlington. When he graduated he had firm assurances from GAI upper management that his record in Arlington coupled with his college and law degrees put him on the fast track for early promotion to the national executive offices in Alexandria. He was flattered and inclined to stay with the company.

Senator Green told him not to do it. He said: 'If you do that,

Tyrone, if you sell yourself to them, you will be a big fool. Because that is how they do it now. They don't sell us in the markets any more to white planters who will own us 'til they decide it's time to sell us again. What they show us now is this tinhorn fantasy of a great career so that we will sell our*self* on it; do it to ourselves. What they will do with you is they will take you down there to Virginia, and give you some hocus-pocus about how grand you're going to be, if you stay with Good Kind Massa Company.

'What that grandness will be, Tyrone, when you finally achieve it and your head has cleared enough so that you can see what you have got, will be a desk and a chair outside of the office where the white boys go inside and shut the door to run the store, and that is where you'll always be, no matter where they send you. And send you they will. They will make you move and move, and then they'll make you move again, all around this great big country, anywhere they need to put a black man's face where folks can see it. No matter what they call it, that will be your purpose. That's what you'll be for. A mannequin, store-window dummy, nothing more 'n that; and you and Carol and your kids will have one lousy life. You won't ever *be*, *any*where, son.

'You'll always be where you happen to be now, on the way to someplace else. Not where you were before and not where you're going next, never anywhere. And then one day you'll get old and be retired, and you won't know where you want to be, or even where you've been. That's what they've always done to us, kept us on the move. "Noplace" will be your home. And that's no way to live.

'No, you listen to me, Tyrone. I've never let you down. I will find something for you. I will find you a good place.'

'What was the other one's name there again now?' Whalen said. 'The woman, I mean, not the new black kid. Jeannie, Jeannie Flagg there, 'm I right? Now there is a very nice broad. All of us like her a lot. Not much to look at, I grant you that, she should lose a few pounds, but still, a very nice broad. Very businesslike woman. Knows what her job is and does it. Very professional person. Last week there we had her in here both nights. Didn't see you at all.

'Anyway, it's been a while we seen you in here. Nice to have you back. Got something goin' on, have you, gettin' too good for us here? You been very busy or something?'

'Not particularly, no,' Merrion said, feeling easy and relaxed and in command. 'No busier'n usual, for the summer months, at least. I hadda have a woman we've got under more or less loose supervision come and see me in the office this morning. We've been hearin' some things that we didn't like, kind of thing she might be doin'. Kind of a sad case, really. Isn't what you'd call too sharp. Doesn't have a steady job; lost the one she had. No one to watch out for her, take care of her. Not much you can really do. So I made her come in today. Give her another talkin'-to, see if maybe that'll do a little good, get her straightened out again. Though of course it's hard to say. You know how it is, you guys: want to help the people that you come in contact with, but whether what you do does help, you never really know.'

Whalen showed no sign of interest in the woman's problem or identity. That indicated either that he already knew all he felt he needed to know about Janet LeClerc, or else that he knew nothing and was relying on his good and well-informed friend Ambrose Merrion to bring him up to speed if there was anything about her that he ought to know. All right, then, nothing to be concerned about; it was always hard to know what detail in any offering would capture Whalen's magpie attention as the jewel to be seized, and often necessary to offer several choices.

'Got in a round of golf with Danny after lunch this afternoon. Went down to West Springfield, saw my mother in the home. Geez, those nuns're awful good. They really do good work. All those poor people in there half-gaga, two-thirds of them out of their gourds, no idea which end is up, and those nuns're with them all the time. Don't get any relief. It must be an awful strain on them, hard life to hoe. Makes you kinda think twice, all this stuff we keep hearin' all the time, cuttin' back on Medicare. Nuns look to me as though they're gettin' pretty old themselves, gettin' right up there. And no young ones comin' up, young girls goin' inna convents, you believe what you read inna paper. Makes you wonder a little, you know? "Well, what's gonna happen, we get old and so forth, take care of us?" Kind of makes you stop and think: "Whoa, what we doin' to ourselves here?"'

'Danny's still doin' good, is he?' Merrion wasn't sure but Whalen seemed to be showing more interest.

'Oh yeah, Danny's always doin' great,' Merrion said, dialing up his alertness a notch or two. 'Doin' very well, he is. *Extremely* well, in fact. Kicked the shit out of me again out on the course today, for one example – cost me the usual twenny bucks. So yeah, I'd say he's doin' all right. Danny's lookin' good.'

'This'd be out at Grey Hills there, wouldn't it?' Whalen said, slightly disconcerting Merrion by seeming to act as though he, not Merrion, had been the fisherman feeling the soft tenative strike and Merrion, not he, was going to be the fish. 'You and him, Danny Hilliard: this'd be the spot there where you two guys always play?'

'Well, ah, yeah,' Merrion said, thrilling slightly, finding himself either playing or being played in a game he didn't fully understand but which seemed as though it could be dangerous, 'that's where we belong. So that's where we generally play. Pay all that money, you know, to belong, get so you know the course pretty good – doesn't hardly seem to make much sense, really, you then go and play somewhere else.'

'I heard that's a pretty hard place to get into,' Whalen said, musing. 'Heard it costs a lot of money, too. Arm and your other fuckin' leg to go with it, as the fella likes to say. 'Course Danny and you, you can prolly afford it. Danny really must've done awful good in that job, what I hear, when he was bein' a rep. House in Bell Woods anna one onna Cape, Martha's Vineyard, wherever it was.'

'Well,' Merrion said, 'he doesn't . . .'

'You know I never been on Martha's Vineyard?' Whalen said it with a note of surprise. 'Never went there in my life. Always thought I'd like to some day. People say it's so nice.' He paused and considered. 'Lots of things I haven't done,' he said, and frowned. Then he shook his head once, as though clearing it.

'An' thenna divorce; he had that too, diddun he, few years ago?' Whalen said. Merrion nodded. 'Sure, that's what I thought,' Whalen said. 'And they can be very expensive. Have to figure that cost him some dough. So I wouldn't know how much he's got left, probably not very much. But still, like I say, must've done awful good, for a guy that was just a state rep. You, you been single, all of your life, so prolly you could afford it.' He paused again, as though expecting a comment, but Merrion's mouth had become dry and he did not know what to say. He said nothing.

'But I never could, alla rich guys; I could never belong to no club like that. I know that without even askin'. Hell, I never even been *in* one. Only golf course I ever even *been* to was the Veterans', anyone can get in down in Springfield. I went there once with Billy, my wife's kid brother, Billy. He always used to play a lot there, back when he was still alive. He was on total disability, the full one-hundred fuckin' percent. So he always had plenty of time. Money, too. Plenty of time and plenty of money. Guess it ought be that way, though, you got hit with something means you're gonna die *that* young. He got sprayed with Agent Orange, Vietnam. So there wasn't any question it was *honest*; he was sick. You couldn't really begrudge him. He was always onna lookout for company, someone to go with him when he played. He played every chance he got, every day the weather let him. I was workin' mostly nights then, so he asked me once did I think I'd like to try it, maybe even take it up.

'I said: "Shit, I dunno. How'd I know? I diddun know the first thing about it." And he said: "Well, that's how you find out. Otherwise you never know. You should come with me, some time, and find out how you like it." Well, I didn't really wanna, but his sister, who's my wife, she was always after me, be nice to Billy. "He is dyin' and we have to treat him nice." So we made a date and the next time he was going he came over and he picked me up and I went with him. To the Veterans', like I said; that was where he always played.

'I didn't actually play, myself. What I did was, I just walked around with him. But I didn't think I'd like it. It seemed like it was awful complicated, before you even got so you were learnin' how to go about it. And you hadda have an awful lot of stuff there, that equipment, which I then had to figure . . . well, Billy, he said you could rent it if you didn't have it yourself and you weren't sure that you wanted to go out and buy it. Special shoes and everything, which I guess you have to wear. Not that I did, just had sneakers, but of course I wasn't playin'.

'I figured even that it'd have to cost a lot of money, and Christina and me, we sure didn't have much of that stuff lying around loose at that time – or any other time I can recall, the kid and all. I never came right out and told him that I wasn't gonna do it. We just sort of left it hanging up in the air there, the way you'll do when you don't really want to decide about something but you sort of know you have.

'Then he died. I never did find out what happened to his clubs. They were nice. He told me that they cost four hundred dollars. I don't think I ever saw them after that, when he was dead. Maybe one his buddies must've took 'em. Had to've been that – he didn't have no kids to take 'em so it wouldn't've been them. Friend of his must've come and took 'em.

'You two, though, I guess you and Hilliard there, you've belonged up Grey Hills there a pretty long time, right? So you two must've played a lot.'

'Over twenty years,' Merrion said. 'Joined there back in the Seventies. 'Way back, turn of the century, it was a big private estate. Belonged to a guy named Jesse Grey. Big mill-owner, Holyoke. Went to hell in the Depression. Then the bishop bought it, diocese of Springfield. After the war a group of wealthy people from around here got together and bought it from *him*, from the diocese: Warren Corey, all his pals. They thought they were *aristocrats*, *elite*. Very snobby and selective. Had to know who your grandparents were – and more'n that, had to've *liked* 'em; didn't count if they'd been the servants – 'fore they'd let your ass in the front door. Not all that keen on Catholics, either, unless they're from '*way* out of town – hadda be New York, London or Paris. Or Nazareth, maybe; that might've done it.'

He hesitated but Whalen's face showed no sign of amusement. 'Anyway, hadda be famous places like that. Very picky, back in those days, about who they'd let in. But then after a while, the snobs reached the point where they were beginning to run out of money. Gave them a whole different attitude, new outlook on the Great Unwashed. They decided they needed new blood, or at least new bank accounts. So they announced that they were expanding; that was when me and Danny joined up.'

'Pretty expensive, I suppose?' Whalen said.

'Well, it certainly wasn't cheap,' Merrion said. 'Not by my standards, at least. It's been so long ago I forget what it was, but I know it sure wasn't cheap.

'We thought long and hard about it 'fore we did it, Dan and I did,' Merrion said, feeling he was talking too much and too nervously, giving away more information than he wanted to, but hoping to create some harmless tangent that would divert Whalen from the topic of Dan Hilliard's finances. 'We talked it over quite a bit, thought about it a hell of a lot. Our feeling then was that Yeah, it was too expensive, but this might be the only opening we'd ever get. And even if it wasn't, we knew we'd never see a better price. Financially, no, it wasn't the best time in the world for us, either one of us, no, but the way we looked at it, we had to move. The chance probably wouldn't come along again. They got enough other new members to get them over the hump, they'd close the membership again. So we said: "What the hell, only go around once," and went ahead and signed up.'

'How much did it cost you, don't mind me asking,' Whalen said.

'Hell no, I don't mind,' Merrion said, minding a great deal indeed and silently cursing the man. 'I'd tell you if I knew, but that was a long time ago. It was no small amount, I can tell you that much, but exactly, I don't remember.'

'Tell me about, then,' Whalen said, 'about how much do you think it was? A thousand or two thousand bucks?'

'Oh no,' Merrion said, thinking *Fuck*, hoping he was still speaking calmly, 'I know it was more'n that. I remember saying to Danny back then: 'I must be nuts. I could trade in my car on a new one for this, get a brand new Olds for myself.' So it must've been two or three grand.' Whalen's eyes widened and he looked like he might be going to say something, so Merrion hurried on. 'But we went through with it anyway. One way or the other we scraped up the dough. I ended up driving the same car for about nine years, I think it was, and the cars they built then didn't last as long as the ones they're building today. It was always breaking down on me, really a pain in the ass.

'But now I'm glad I did it. Now I think it was worth it. You need something like that to stay sane.'

'Maybe that's why the wife's always saying that I'm nuts,' Whalen said mildly, his voice carrying no hint of sarcasm. 'I never had nothing like that at all. No way to stay sane. Couldn't afford one. Not if it cost as much as a new Oldsmobile. Heck, I never even had a new *Studebaker* or something; I never had a new *car*.'

'We always have a good time,' Merrion said, beginning to feel some hope that if he could just keep talking, scattering shiny conversational chaff in the air between them until the prisoners started to come out, he would be safe. 'Well, Danny usually has a better time'n I do, 'cause he usually beats me. I have fun, he wins the bets. Always gets me on the back nine. We come into the turn, I'm usually doin' all right, you don't know what always happens next. I usually got at least a couple, maybe three or four strokes onna guy. This time comin' outta the turn, I'm up four.

'Okay then, boys and girls, here we go, then, into the vicious back nine. Both of us double-bogey the tenth, as usual. The booby trap. I can never play that hole, but Dan can't play it either. Over twenny years we've been playin' that damned hole, and for alla those years it's been beatin' us silly, poundin' the shit out of us. I dunno why it is. It looks so goddamned *easy*. Deceptive, is what it is. Looks like you could get your par you played it half-asleep.

'Straightaway, par four, little over four hundred yards, four-oh-five's what the book says: Nothin' tricky, piece of cake. Nice wide fairway, all you gotta do's hit it straight and you'll be havin' candy. Theoretically you want your second shot to be up onto the green, but for most of us ordinary mortals that's gonna be your third shot you'll be tryin' to lay up there nice and soft. But be reasonable here: I'll take a bogey-five on a four-hundred-yarder any day. Eighteen bogeys and what've I done? I've shot a ninety, is what; I never did that in my life.

'Well, a couple times, yeah, I did, but that was a long time ago. My hand-eye thing was much better then. Bound to slip some, you get older. I didn't think about things so much then; I just went ahead and I did them, and that's always the way to play golf. You get old, you get so you start thinkin' too much.'

Whalen evidently wasn't interested in discussing the ravages of age; he said nothing. 'But anyway, the green's uphill, and not only that but it's *tiered*, and the upshot of it anyway's we both take fuckin' sevens. The tenth hole's beat us again.

'But that's all right. I'm still okay, still up by the four. But not for long. We're swappin' strokes alla way to fifteen. Wolf River runs along the left there; you got a hook like I do, you got that to think about. Which I of course do, think about it, and like I said, that's not a good thing to do. So as usual Danny tucks it to me. Par four, three-fifty-nine, and what do I take? A nine, a big fat nine. Splashed one, of course, so busy tryin' not to do that that I naturally do it – two strokes right there. And then got inna bunker; for good measure; dub my wedge 'fore I can get out. And then after I'm out, what do I do? Over the green and into the opposite sandtrap. One beach is nice, try the other.

'And what's Danny doing, I am having all this fun? He's parring the thing, naturally, like he pretty nearly always does. He's got the Indian sign, some kind of hex thing on that fifteen hole. He owns it. I don't know why that should be; it just is. Always been that way, too.'

Whalen shifted his weight from his right foot to his left and moved his upper body away from the wall. Merrion hoped that indicated he was growing restless. 'But then anyway, there we both are, playin' sixteen, even again like we started. We got three holes left. Theoretically I should be able, get a stroke or two of my lead back. Right. Both of us bogey the sixteenth, which I have had days, I could play that. This just didn't happen to be one of them. But then it all becomes academic, because I double-bogey the seventeenth and he comes away with a bogey. Danny's the one who picks up the stroke, and that'll be it for the day. The last one, the eighteenth we both take a seven. He ends up, he beats me by one. So it's me payin' him twenty bucks.'

Whalen stood and looked at Merrion as though he had been led to expect that Merrion had an act that would entertain him, and while he had enjoyed what he had seen up to that point, he wasn't sure whether there might still be some more to come. Not wishing to offend Merrion by seeming to presume the performance was over, he would therefore wait quietly until he got some kind of signal. He did not say anything.

'So I would say: Yeah, Danny looked all right to me,' Merrion said, moistening his lips. 'Looked okay to me there, at least, he was taking my money. Of course his busy season's comin' up here pretty soon, all the kids come back and so forth. So he's got that on his mind. Gettin' ready for the fall. But he's used to that, of course. That's a normal thing for him; happens every year.'

'Because I did hear,' Whalen said, now apparently satisfied Merrion had finished his presentation, 'I heard things maybe might not be, you know, goin' so good for him. And I figured if that was the case, well, you know him. You would know. But you didn't hear nothin', I guess? You didn't hear nothin' like that?'

'I don't, ah, follow,' Merrion said, feeling sudden tightness cramp his chest and thinking if it was a heart attack it would just have to wait; the business at hand was not to panic. He decided it would get him time and seem appropriate to frown and look mildly concerned. 'What kind of things, exactly?'

Whalen dropped his hands, hunched his shoulders, shrugged, purged his face of expression, refolded his arms and leaned his right shoulder back against the cinderblock. 'I dunno,' he said. 'I dunno what it was. You know how it is, you hear something. Don't always pay that good attention, when somebody's sayin' it. Then later on you see someone, maybe see somebody else, and that reminds you of it, you know?'

Merrion cleared his throat and said 'Gee,' but to his enormous relief Whalen seemed to believe they had had enough conversation and to expect no answer. He turned his head slightly away from the wall and turned it back over his left shoulder, contorting his face so that when he raised his voice instead of actually yelling down the hall behind him he was hollering at the pocked surface of the opposite wall. 'Hey Thompson, for Christ sake, hell's holdin' you up? Got Mister Merrion sittin' around here like he's got nothin' better to do. I got him down here 'cause you told me you got work for him. Now you got him coolin' his heels. Get the lead out, willya Christ sakes? Move things along for a change.' Then he looked at Merrion and grinned.

16

Shortly after 1:30 A.M., Merrion emerged into the parking lot behind the Canterbury Police Station, richer by $350 in bail fees but feeling no satisfaction. He was burdened in his spirit by grim inferences he drew from Whalen's ominous inquiries. The night air was pleasantly cool on his face. The mosquitoes had all gone to bed. *This'd be a nice time to sit out.* He had to sidle between the pair of black-and-white police-model Chevy Blazers parked too close together at the back door of the station. *Ah yes, the celebrated Blazers. The most expensive Blazers in the history of the world. Sixty-eight-thousand bucks, and only the beginning. A cop on lifetime disability; a career-ending criminal conviction; a million-dollar lawsuit; the lengths we go to in this town to support our local police chief.*

The four-wheel-drive vehicles had been added to the fleet the previous year after the selectmen, their skepticism worn down by three years of relentless lobbying by Chief Paradisio, had included an item appropriating funds for their purchase in the warrant for town meeting, at last accepting his strenuous argument that the two specially equipped vehicles were needed to pursue and capture what he foresaw as a growing host of similarly outfitted law-breakers seeking to escape detection and arrest 'merely by going in the woods to commit their crimes, or else committing them where they always have, and then getting away by driving off into the woods, where we can't go after them.' There was some opposition but the item passed by voice vote.

Iris Blanchard, thirty-two, was a member of the ad hoc Canterbury School Citizens Advisory Committee. Petite but muscularly athletic – at sixteen she had been a state champion gymnast; later she had graduated from Springfield College with a degree in phys ed and a certificate to teach it – she was the fierce single mother of four daughters, all enrolled in Canterbury public schools. Their father, Dave, a heavy equipment operator, had found winter work in Louisiana two years before but failed to return from it in the spring as promised, or remit any money for support. His whereabouts remained unknown. Unable to secure a position as a gym teacher, she kept the mortgage current on the house resentfully using money she'd inherited from a grandmother and earmarked for the girls' education, supporting them meagerly with her earnings as an instructor in aerobics in the Canterbury Spa and Health Club. Earlier that evening she had angrily expressed her considerable fury at rejection of a school budget item of $113,000 earmarked to restore art, music and drama to the curricula in all grades and establish a full varsity athletic program, including gymnastics, for girls at Canterbury High. When Sal's Blazer item passed she came to her feet enraged and shouting: 'Oh you filthy rotten bastards.'

Ruled out of order by the moderator, Mason Turner, the forbidding grey-haired senior loan officer at the Pioneer Trust Co., she ignored repeated blows of the gavel and refused to sit down. She called the selectmen 'nothing but a bunch of lowdown dirty cop-suckers,' bringing some startled laughter and scattered applause, 'approving extravagant new toys for the Paradise gestapo – instead of doing what's right by the kids.'

Scattered cheering broke out, countered at once by booing and shouts of 'Ah siddown, ya big-mouth bitch.' When she again failed to heed the gavel – declaring 'I'll talk as much as I want, assholes' – and the moderator's fourth order to be silent, calling him 'a damned lickspittle for that gang of spineless clowns,' Turner ordered the policeman on duty, Ptl. Greg Morrison, to escort her from the building.

She at first ignored Morrison's purposive approach and his gently regretful statement, ''Fraid I'll have to ask you to come along now, Ma'am,' instead yelling: 'Oh sure, Turner, pompous old fart, calling Sal's goons to the rescue.' Then she turned and snarled at Morrison: 'Get *away* from me, you jerk.'

He extended his left hand toward her. 'Intending,' as he

testified before Judge Cavanaugh a month later in *Commonwealth v. Blanchard*, 'since she had indicated that she would not come with me voluntarily, to place it firmly on her right shoulder, in order to lead her away.'

She grabbed his wrist with both hands and bit him on the joint of the thumb and the fold of flesh between it and the forefinger, chomping down so that she broke the skin, tore the flesh and drew blood. After Morrison had subdued her – with the help of an off-duty policewoman, Ptl. Connie Foley, a recreational boxer, who piston-punched Blanchard hard three times in the solar plexus – and placed her under arrest to be transported to the station and locked up, he was driven to the emergency room at Holyoke Hospital for nine stitches and a painful series of precautionary shots to guard against blood poisoning and infection.

'Not that we think she's rabid,' the nurse with the big needle told him, 'but human bites're the worst kind, when it comes to infection.'

'I've heard that,' the cop said, 'heard that many times. I don't need to be convinced *JesusmotherfuckingChrist!* – you hit the goddamn bone *again*. Is this your first time doing this or is it you don't like my looks?'

At trial, Officer Morrison further testified that doctors had told him he would have to wear the white plastic prosthetic device specially moulded to immobilize his left hand for at least six more weeks, in order to allow damaged cartilage to heal and see whether a torn tendon would mend without surgery. If x-rays showed that the tendon had mended, he could expect to spend between one and two months in rehabilitation. If the x-rays showed the tendon had not repaired itself, he would require surgery and rehabilitation and about a year to recover full use of his left hand.

Officer Morrison testified that since he was left-handed, the prosthesis prevented him from gripping his sidearm or baton, writing incident reports or using the two-way radio in his patrol car while underway, since to do so would require him to depend upon his unusable left hand to steer while operating the radio with his right. He said that as a result he had been on total disability ever since the incident and expected to remain off-duty for at least three more months.

After the trial, jury-waived, on a pretty afternoon in April, Iris Blanchard was found guilty by Judge Leonard Cavanaugh on charges of disrupting a public meeting; disorderly conduct; making an affray; assault on a police officer; assault and battery with a deadly weapon – to wit: teeth; resisting arrest; and mayhem.

'These are very serious charges, Mrs Blanchard,' the judge said, Merrion having briefed him about what the cops were saying at the station and around the courthouse about noisy female politicians who bit cops to dramatize their advocacy of children's issues – and their own obvious interest in creating new teaching jobs. 'If you think there's something funny or endearing in what your lawyer's tried to minimize as this "*feistiness*" of yours, I assure you I do not. And if you should appeal this verdict, as you certainly have every right to do, my guess is any judge and jury you may get in the superior court will agree with me – not you. Or your lawyer, either. Same when it comes to sentencing: You've given any judge deciding what to do with you several excellent reasons to do as the police prosecutor here's suggested: send you down to Framingham for a year or so, to reflect on what you did.

'And in fact I *am* going to sentence you to the women's correctional institution,' the judge said, 'not for a year and a day, as the prosecutor's recommended, but for *five full years*.' Iris Blanchard had been striving to hide signs of secret amusement, trying to appear contrite; now she flinched visibly and gasped. Her lawyer, Maxine Golden from the Mass. Defenders, moved closer beside her and put a reassuring hand on her arm.

'What you did wasn't funny. And I've been very much concerned by your debonair demeanor, the way you've behaved in this court. Also by some rather light-hearted statements that your lawyer's made in questioning the witness,' Golden's eyebrows lifted, 'suggesting to me that deep down inside you believe it was mischief you did, some sort of amusing *prank*.

'It was *not*. This was a bad and serious thing that you did. It was also extremely dangerous. For someone serving on a school committee, supposedly concerned with the education and development of children, you set one lousy example. You have to pay for your actions. Not literally, of course: there isn't any point in fining you a substantial amount, say several thousand dollars, as the statues would allow me; that would only be another way of sending you to jail, because you clearly couldn't pay.'

Blanchard gasped again and then began to sob, putting her hands to her face. Golden put her arm around her. 'So I'm in a dilemma, Mrs Blanchard, which I do not like, and I blame you for putting me in it. I think you need a severe lesson, but at the same time I'm aware you have young children and appear to be their only source of parental support. So I know you've been under a lot of pressure, and I'm willing to take that into account.

'*You* have to understand that you've put someone *else* now under pressure, terrible pressure. Officer Morrison's also a young parent. He and his wife have a new baby, who of course they both love very much. Just as much as you do your kids. And after what you did to him, to Officer Morrison, breaking the skin and causing him to bleed as you did, they both have to be very concerned of the possibility of very serious consequences.

'I'm talking about the HIV virus, the possibility that you may have given him AIDS.'

Now thoroughly alarmed, Golden stared at the judge, then she looked at her client and mouthed the words: 'Do you know if you have AIDS?'

Blanchard sobbed and shook her head, moaning: 'No, of course I don't. How could he *say* that to me? How could I have AIDS?'

Golden wheeled to face the judge. 'I have to object most strongly to the court making that statement,' she said loudly and as gruffly as she could. 'Without any grounds whatever to make that allegation? That's an *awful* thing to do, in a public forum, absolutely *shocking*. My client *doesn't* have AIDS. How could you even *suggest* such a thing.'

'Contain yourself, counsellor,' the judge said. 'Taking your client at her word, the most she can possibly say is that she doesn't *think* she has AIDS. As I understand it, when her no-good husband went to Louisiana and deserted her and their children two years ago, once and for all, it wasn't his first defection, just his last. He'd wandered off repeatedly before that, picking up women in bars. There'd been several previous separations, each followed by another unsuccessful attempt at reconciliation, during which she said he was always loving and tender. I assume that means they had sex.

'She doesn't know whether those other women, however many there may have been, were free of AIDS. Or whether one or more of those "women" might've been a man. All she knows is what her rotten ex-husband told her, and as we all know now, he was not to be trusted.

'So unless she's been tested, she doesn't really know whether he contracted the disease and passed it on to her during one of their lovey-dovey reconciliations, before he left her the last time and vanished into the mist. Therefore, Ms Golden, my question to you is: Has your client been tested since her husband lit out for the territories, and if so what were the results?'

Golden conferred urgently with Blanchard, pulling her loose to whisper and cupping her hand over the side of her face otherwise visible from the bench. Blanchard shook her head and said audibly: 'No, I never have been.'

Golden sighed. She lowered her hand and faced the bench. 'She says she's never been tested, your Honor.'

The judge sighed and shook his head. 'Oh dear,' he said, 'I was afraid of that.

'Well, no help for it; this is what I'm going to do here. Having in mind the very real anxiety that Officer Morrison and his wife have to feel here, Mrs Blanchard, and also the fact that – as I'm sure Attorney Golden can tell you – I have no power to *order* you to do this; there's a law against it and anyway, as I see it, you could invoke the Fifth Amendment: I am going to put over for one week formal imposition of the sentence in this case. During that time I want you to consult with your attorney and decide, *of your own free will*, whether you should have a blood test to determine whether you carry the virus that causes AIDS. If you do that *you'll* be able to say whether you would have tested positive when you attacked Officer Morrison last month. *And*, if you instruct the testing lab to deliver a copy of the results to Mister Merrion, my clerk, for the court's information and that of Officer Morrison, we will then know that too.

'Now, if all that should take place, this is what I will do here when I review the case next week:

'I'll suspend imposition of the sentence to MCI Framingham for a period of two years, provided you agree to resign immediately from the School Advisory Committee, making a public statement you now understand that your conduct at the town meeting was an outrageous, shameful, reckless, and dangerous act for which you are deeply, deeply sorry. And ashamed. And that even though you have expressed your deep regret to Officer Morrison and are keeping him in your prayers for his full recovery of the use of his left hand, you agree your actions mean that you're unfit to serve on the committee. And so you must step down.

'Assuming you decide that it's in everyone's best interest for you to do that, and the test results turn out to be negative – as I'm sure you hope they do as fervently as everyone else involved – you will further agree that at the end of that two-year period you will voluntarily submit to testing again. And if those results also prove to be negative for the HIV virus, and you have not been in any other trouble between now and then, I will reconsider, revise and revoke the jail sentence and you will be free to go.'

Blanchard's first blood test had been negative. In the fourteen months since then the x-rays had shown that Morrison's tendon had failed to repair itself. Surgery had been performed. The doctors had found greater damage to the thumb joint than the x-rays had led them to expect, and now believed the operation should have been performed the night of the attack. They predicted Morrison would never regain more than sixty percent use of his left hand – probably less, around forty.

Morrison two days later received a letter from Sidney Ferris, P.C., A Legal Corporation, doing business at 16 Amherst St in Hampton Falls, expressing his belief that the officer had grounds for a medical malpractice suit which could be brought on a contingent-fee basis at absolutely no cost or expense to him unless the suit was successful, in which case the fee would be one-third of the damages collected. Morrison had retained Ferris as his lawyer, authorizing him to file suit against Holyoke Hospital and the attending physician on duty in the emergency room town-meeting night, claiming actual damages for lost career earnings of $625,000 and an additional $600,000 for mental anguish, pain and suffering.

Ferris also handled Morrison's case before the Board of Workmen's Compensation, which awarded a tax-exempt permanent disability pension equal to fifty percent of his patrolman's pay. Ferris on behalf of Morrison had filed an appeal, saying that, as a matter of law, since Morrison had been injured in the line of duty, he was entitled either to a pension equal to one hundred percent of his pay, or else a fifty-percent pension calculated on the basis of the wages that he would have earned, given his likely prospects of rapid promotion to higher ranks during the additional thirty-three years he had expected to serve on the force.

Purely for amusement one night in the bar at Grey Hills, Merrion one night while having drinks with Hilliard had used drink-napkins to estimate the probable total cost of Iris Blanchard's tantrum, not only to the taxpayers of the town of Canterbury but also to the hospital and the doctor and their insurance carriers as well. Hilliard worked the figures faster in his head than Merrion could write them down on the napkins.

'With interest compounded at six percent, by the time they get the malpractice case tried, and figuring Morrison lives another fifty years, which at twenty-eight he should, collecting his pension all that time, I figure a little over seven million bucks. Seven million, seventy-thousand, you throw in the cost of Sally's two Blazers, the most expensive trucks built since the world began. And a good thing for all involved old Iris wasn't bred for the work, like a pit bull or something, take a man's arm off at the elbow; have to deed the cop the town if she had been.'

When Merrion got to his car, alert for sounds of stealthy scuffling in the dark – as he always was such nights, even though he was at the police station, lest some disgruntled defendant after being released had waited in the shadows to conk him when he came out and swipe his wallet and his car. Hearing nothing, he unlocked the Caddy quickly, tossing the portfolio in the back seat, sliding in and closing up all in one swift motion, re-locking the doors as he turned on the engine, the carphone keypad glowing green and chirping readiness on the center console.

At the next corner he had made up his mind and said loudly and roundly: '*Call . . . Danny*.' As he took the turn the voice-activated dialer started booping digits to reach Hilliard at his condo at the Wisdom House in Hampton Pond (to call Hilliard at his office Merrion would have said: '*Call . . . Hilliard*'; in his Mercedes '*Call . . . Daniel*'). Moving north on Truman Boulevard under the blacker shadows cast by the oaks along the edges, he listened to the phone ring eleven times before Hilliard answered thickly through the phlegm of sleep: 'This'd better be important.' Then he coughed.

'It is,' Merrion said. 'Put some coffee on for yourself and pour me a serious drink. No traffic, this hour. I'll be there in ten or twelve minutes.'

'*Minutes?*' Hilliard said, 'what *minutes*. Whaddaya talkin'. You muss be drunk or you're nuts. You got any idea what time . . .'

'Yeah, one-forty-one,' Merrion said, glancing at the digital clock on the dash. 'I'm coming from the Canterbury cophouse and I'm *not* drunk – although I must be about the only one who's still awake in town and isn't. Very drunk out tonight. Every time I thought we must be finished, they'd bring in another indigene, tanked to the gills, singin' and talkin', *all* kinds of ragtime. *Disgusting* how they carry on.'

During the late Seventies, Sal Paradisio had returned from a convention of the International Association of Chiefs of Police in Montreal smitten by the lingo in a lecture given by an Indiana University criminologist from Bloomington. He had started referring to locally resident groups as 'the indigenous population' and to individual residents as 'indigenes.' The usage had become a Canterbury PD inside joke. Richie Hammond and Merrion – when Richie for some reason wasn't hogging the bail fees as usual – had gotten used to being summoned by solemn cops on busy weekends to 'come down and handle a whole *herd-ah* misbehavin' indigenes.' Two decades later Merrion still heard older officers say 'the fuckin' indigenes're gettin' outta hand again.'

'I was *asleep*,' Hilliard said.

'Figured you would be,' Merrion said. 'Most people are at this hour.' The big car went through the night like a luxury liner on the surface of a calm sea, the moon blinking on and off among the branches of the trees like the dot-dash of a signalman's light.

'So why're you bothering me like this then?' Hilliard said, whining, 'I never did nothing to you.'

'I'm lonesome,' Merrion said. 'I've been working all night like a very good boy. Now I'm tired; I want to relax. Want to be with a friend, talk about the old days, when I sang in my chains like the sea.'

'Huh?' Hilliard said. 'What the hell does that mean?'

'I dunno,' Merrion said. 'I heard you say it a long time ago. I'm not sure but I think you said it to a woman. I meant to ask you what the hell you meant, besides wantin' to get her pants off. But then I decided you probably didn't know either. It just sounded good at the time.'

'Look, Amby,' Hilliard said, 'I'm waking up. You can't come up here right now. It's the middle the night and I got sleep to get and I'm going to go back to bed.'

'Don't hang up on me, Dan,' Merrion said. 'You'll just be wasting your time. I need to talk to you, and I need to talk to you tonight, and so that's what I'm going to do. I'll put you on auto re-dial if you hang up, which'll mean that you'll have to leave your phone off the hook, and it'll hum at you all night. So you still won't be able to get any sleep, or emergency calls from anyone else, and I know how you hate both those things. Now throw some clothes on and go out inna kitchen and put coffee on, and make me a Jack Daniel's and water, some ice. I'll be there in eight minutes and you'll let me in or I'll sit on the stoop and I'll cry. And when all the neighbors wake up and say what's the matter, I'll say I'm an orphan got left on your doorstep and you're too mean to take me in, and can someone take me to the rectory.'

'Tell me onna phone, Amby,' Hilliard said. 'Turn around and go back to your own house and bed, and tell me on the phone on the way. It's almost two in the morning for Christ sake. There's nothing that can't wait 'til morning.'

'Yes there is,' Merrion said, 'me.'

Hilliard groaned. 'Amby,' he said, 'I can't let you come up here tonight. I got someone here with me and, well, I just can't. I can't let you in if you come here. Tell me what it is on the phone.'

'Danny,' Merrion said, 'listen up now, friend of my youth: You have got to let me come in. Tell her to stay in the bedroom and sleep. Or him, if you now go both ways. You can say I insist if you want, 'cause I do. I don't want him or her to hear what I'm saying to you. This is strictly between you and me. That's why I've got to come up. This isn't something I'd say on a phone, anyway, but especially not on a car-phone. They don't need a wireman to sit in on car-phones; they don't even have to be cops – anyone with an eighty-buck scanner can pick up what you say, just by purest accident. That give you any inkling of why I am coming?'

There was an extended silence. The Cadillac rushed quietly up the boulevard under the bright moon and dark trees. 'I'll wake her up and send her home and make the coffee,' Hilliard said. 'Jack Daniel's, you said you wanted?'

'You got it, pal,' Merrion said. 'And don't bother sending her home. Just tell her to stay inna bedroom and sleep. This's not something we want to share.'

In a tee-shirt and grey drawstring sweatpants, clumps of his hair standing up and a look of deep concern on his face, Hilliard with a cup of tea in his hand met Merrion at the door and said: 'Will you tell me what the . . . ?'

Merrion shook his head and put his right forefinger to his lips. Then he pointed at the kitchen softly lit by one ceiling fixture over the sliding glass door leading outdoors and nodded. 'That my drink I see on the counter there? That's what I need. Let's you and me go and get it.' With his drink in hand Merrion took Hilliard's right elbow, steering him toward the door opening onto the townhouse patio. 'Mawn now,' he said, 'nice out tonight. Let's you and me go outside and chat.' He slid the glass door open.

'I think you're gettin' paranoid,' Hilliard said, hanging back.

'That could be,' Merrion said, 'I got every reason to be. Anyway, there's no question I'm spooked. I prefer to talk out of doors.'

Hilliard grabbed a dish-towel from the rack over the sink and led the way, Merrion sliding the glass door shut quietly behind them, Hilliard mopping the dew off the puffy green and yellow cushions of the lawn chairs. Seated so that he faced Hilliard and the glass door, Merrion said: 'The first thing to keep in mind when you deal with fuckin' cops is that you want to keep them friendly if you can – at almost any cost. So that when you have to tell them No, you can't do what they want – like on a warrant application, when they just don't have enough PC to let you let them go in and make a search some place – they understand you really can't give them one. They don't think you're a prick who's just giving them a hard time, just to be a prick, because they think of you as a friend of theirs, and they know you would give them the paper if you could. And that way they don't get mad at you so they all start giving you all kinds of fuckin' grief alla time. Which as you know, that group can do.'

Hilliard was still shaking off the dullness of sleep. 'Absolutely,' he said, 'because the last thing you want to have on your mind, and especially in a job like the one you've got, dealing with cops every day, you don't want to get them pissed off. But in any job, really, that'll always hold true: you don't want to get a cop mad at you. You get *one* cop mad at you, before you even know it, *all* the cops're mad at you. Because all the cops talk to each other, and they can make life miserable for you.'

'Right,' Merrion said. 'Now the reason why I woke you up to talk is Sergeant Whalen. Where Ev Whalen is concerned, and he *is* the one concerns me, the stakes're even higher. The guy's a human vacuum cleaner, a rug-beatin', shampooin', Hooverin' machine with a bright white light onna front when it comes to diggin' up dirt. He knows stuff nobody knows. Half the time he doesn't know himself he knows it, the dirt that nobody else knows. But that changes nothing; it's still vintage dirt, and all you've got to do to get it out of him is two basic things.

'The first thing's to make sure you stay friends with him. This isn't hard because he wants to be friends with you, even more than you do with him. He's very insecure, I think. He's always afraid that nobody will like him. So he's got enough motivation for both of you. He thinks *you're* the one who's being nice. By talking to him now and then, sure, but even more by *listening* to him, spillin' his guts out to you.

'So that's the second thing you do: You make it very clear to him that not only are you always glad to see him but you really *appreciate* the things he has to tell you. You aren't just humoring him; you're *interested.*

'That's the only two things you hafta do. He likes you; he'll talk. You say: "Hey Ev, how's it goin', huh, kid? What's goin' on; whaddaya hear?' And woof-woof; here it comes, you got it. Immediately the guy is telling you every damned thing he knows. Without even knowing, most of the time, what the hell most of it means, the *significance* of what he's sayin'. It's like you struck up a friendship at the track with a talking horse who tells you which one of his friends is gonna win that day – because he likes you. And when you mention one day you're startin' to feel guilty, you've been gettin' rich on him and you feel like you oughta share your winnings, he just shrugs it off and says: "Hey, great; I'm happy for you. But what good is money to me? I'm a horse. Bring me an apple sometime."

'Ev Whalen's info is that good and he's got no idea how valuable it can be to you. He would've made a hell of a newspaperman. He works a lot harder'n most of them do, and he finds out a whole lot more stuff. But he doesn't know what news is. He thinks if he recognizes the subject everyone else must already know it. He thinks he's always the last kid onna block to find something out. Oh, and he doesn't question anything. He assumes whatever he knows must be the Gospel truth.

'He doesn't interpret anything, either, tell you what to think about it. He tells you what he thinks but he's not real confident about it, so you can overlook it. And so those're the things I'm trying to remember all the time tonight when he comes outta left field and absolutely stuns me, we're out there inna back waitin' for the prisoners to come out.

'I forget how it came up, but it seemed like before I knew it we're talking how he's sort of vaguely heard you're in some sort of trouble, and do I have any idea what it is. At first I figured maybe he was just fishing around, but every time I tried to change the subject, which I must've, three or four times, he came right back to it. The gist of it seemed to be the Grey Hills memberships. He suspects they were fairly expensive, and he knows it costs a lot to play golf on the public courses so it must take one *shitload* of money at Grey Hills. He knows we've been playing there a long time, so we must've paid a lot of money, and he's really curious about where we got it. And also where you got the money for the Bell Woods house and the summer house, as well, which for all he knows is onna Cape but he did throw in that it might be onna Vineyard. He didn't mention under-the-table campaign funds or kickbacks, or maybe bribes, but I felt pretty sure if I asked him how it was he thought you got it, that is what he would've said.

'He had me close to panic. He kept pushing me on how much it cost to join Grey Hills and of course I didn't wanna tell him, so I keep saying I forget and trynah get him interested in something else, almost anything. I start tellin' him, what golf's about, and how you're always beatin' me – and he wouldn't buy it. It was like he had a bone in his teeth: he kept comin' back to how much it costs for Grey Hills. So finally I just gave up and fell back on the standard strategy of what to do when you're trapped: I made something up.'

'In other words, you lied,' Hilliard said, 'and hoped that he'd believe it.'

'You could put it that way, yeah,' Merrion said. 'I didn't actually come right out and say it cost between two and three grand. I said I remembered when we were doing it saying to you that if I put the price of the membership with what my car was worth, I could've had a brand-new Oldsmobile, which was true. And that as I recall it now, the amount of money that it would've taken me to make a deal trading my car on a new Eighty-eight then would've been two or three grand. Which is also the truth, or very close to it, but not close to the truth he was after.'

'Did he buy it?' Hilliard said. 'First, though, you tell me now, because now I don't remember. What was it, about double that? Six grand or so, apiece?'

'It was eighty-four hundred,' Merrion said, 'which I was *not* about to tell Whalen. I couldah had *three* Oldsmobiles, *six* if I'd spent your piece of the action. Four thousand for the equity share, three thousand initiation. Fourteen hundred down-payment on the annual dues. You're the math genius but I could do that one: times two, sixteen-thousand-eight-hundred American dollars. Not cheap.

'Did he buy what I tried to make him think it was? Probably. Two or three grand's still big money to Ev Whalen today. In fact I think if I'd told him the truth, and said sixteen-eight, he probably would *not* have believed me. That price to play golf would've boggled his mind, would've made him faint dead away. I doubt Whalen's *house* cost him that – if he owns one now, after his kid. One of his kids, I think he's got two, had something terrible happen. So as a result the kid's helpless. Ev has not had a good time in this world; I try to cut him some slack.'

'Sixteen-thousand, eight-hundred dollars,' Hilliard said musingly. 'Jesus, that *was* expensive. Seven percent compound interest, more than twenty years: fifty grand, about, by now, if you'd left it in the bank.'

'Yeah, right,' Merrion said, 'if you don't deduct the taxes that you hadda pay every April on the interest that it earned from year to year. Which you would've, of course, so that you'd now have a lot less. With inflation, you'd have nothin'. Less'n nothing, actually. Plus which the last time they talked about maybe re-opening membership, so they could put a dome over the pool and people could swim inna winter? They ended up not doin' it, of course, but before that the talk was they'd be asking thirty-five K for the equity ante alone. Which I think was most likely what killed it: not the prospect of the course gettin' too crowded, but the fact that the only people who would've had that kind of loose change to spend on playin' golf'd be pro athletes and major drug-dealers, and havin' them as members scared the power elite.

'So you could say that we got a bargain. I think it's been a damned good investment. It's hard to play golf and have drinks inna bank, and anyway, over the years I've dropped a lot of dollars doing stuff and buying things that weren't worth what I paid, and I've had my regrets. But I never regretted Grey Hills. That was a damned smart investment. I've been having a wonderful time for over twenty years now with my high-priced toy, and I'm not even close to bein' through havin' fun with it yet.

'But tonight I was not havin' fun. Tonight I am a worried man. Whalen has heard something about you and me, and that means it's out on the street. What it is specifically I could not get out of him. I suspect he doesn't know either, exactly what the feds're doing. But they're doing something, he knows, and that means this will not go away. So that's why I hadda see you tonight. I was hoping that maybe you could make me feel better. At least tell me what's going on, which you did not this afternoon; what they're after you for, and therefore why they're after me.'

Hilliard's face was grey in the moonlight. He licked his lips. He shook his head. 'I want to say I know, and of course I'll tell you, but I can't because I don't,' he said miserably, looking down and studying his hands. He stopped and shook his head. 'Pooler isn't sure either. Or he wasn't when he called me, late Friday afternoon.' His voice trailed away and stopped. He coughed a couple of times and changed his position, as though that would help to dislodge some foreign substance that had accumulated in his throat. He covered his mouth and coughed several times.

Over his right shoulder Merrion saw a robed figure come out of the shadows into the dim light at the front of the kitchen. It was a woman. He could not make out her features but could see that her hair was blonde and that the robe was too big for her. She went to the refrigerator and opened it, taking out a quart carton of milk. She put it on the counter and opened the cupboard above it, removing a glass. She poured the glass half full. She put the carton back into the refrigerator and closed it. She picked up the glass and turned toward the glass door, advancing into the soft light so he could see her clearly, looking straight into his eyes. Then Mercy Hilliard smiled complicitly at her ex-husband's best friend, so that he could not help but smile back. Then she raised her milk in a silent toast before giving him a small fluttery wave and disappearing back into the shadows.

Hilliard, still looking down on his hands folded in his lap, said: 'All Bob knew on Friday was that he couldn't see how the heck they could do anything to either of us on campaign funds or anything else. I haven't run now for over ten years. The federal statute of limitations is five. So I said: "Well, then there's nothing to get, and they've got their heads up their asses. I have to be in the clear."

'And he said, "Well, that's what you'd *like* to think, naturally, and not knowing exactly what their approach is, that is of course what you *would* think. But this's no ghost-image we're looking at here, something that will just go away. It's too substantial to be a mirage; the rumbling's just too distinct. It must be that they think they've found a way, to get around the time problem. Now our job's to find out just what that way is, and find a way to block them if we can. I'm on the case; I am actively on it. By Monday I should know what it is that they're after. Have Merrion come in to see me then, late in the afternoon. Then I'll be back to you."'

Hilliard looked up. 'And that's really all that I know, Amby,' he said earnestly. 'I know you don't like Bob, but at least after you see him, you'll probably know what it is we have to contend with. And that will be before I do.' Then he registered Merrion's expression of beguiled surprise. He spun in his chair and looked back into the kitchen, now unoccupied once more. He turned back and looked at Merrion. 'What's with you?' he said. 'Are you all right?'

Realizing he'd been holding his breath, Merrion exhaled heavily and smiled at Hilliard. 'I *think* I am,' he said. 'I'm still worried, of course, but for now that's secondary. You said something about ghosts just then: I could swear I just saw one right there in your kitchen. Has to be since it was the spitting image of your ex-wife, and I know she's on Martha's Vineyard so that couldn't be.' Hilliard's face reddened. 'Barged in on reunion night, did I?' Merrion said, grinning now. 'Little duet of "Auld Lang Syne," I take it?'

Hilliard squirmed in the chair. He found his practiced sheepish grin and turned it on. 'I've discovered that I may be getting old, Amby,' he said. 'And this world isn't getting any warmer. I find I still need all the friends I can get, even if only occasionally.'

Merrion finished his drink and stood up. 'Can't argue with you there, pal,' he said. 'Can't argue with you there at all.'

17

Leaving his house late in the morning of the third Sunday in August, Merrion was mildly pleased to register another day of sunshine. He began to feel actual cheer. The change surprised him; he'd been resigned to plodding through the day as best he could, resisting anxiety. He went to the grey and white house with the pale yellow front door on Pynchon Hill where Diane Fox had lived with Walter amid much laughter – and not just when they had friends over for dinner, either, although there had been a lot of that.

Merrion had always liked Walter Fox, 'always' having commenced in 1972 when he had first begun to get to know the red-haired ruddy-faced man with the bristling red handlebar mustache. Succeeding to the seat Larry Lane had occupied and left to him along with his ownership interest in the Fourmen's Realty Trust he found he had inherited Walter Fox along with the wealth. Fox's place had belonged to his late grandfather, Phil, who had died in '68.

The trust had been set up in September of 1956. The original investors were Charles Spring, Roy Carnes, Larry Lane and Finnis D.L. 'Fiddle' Barrow. Spring did the legal work, drawing up the declaration of trust, originally making his son, Edmund, practicing law in Boston, the nominal administrator, unpaid, omitting the names of the beneficiaries who were the actual trustees. The document made each interest in the trust indivisible in itself, inseparable from the remainder of the corpus, and non-transferable by conveyance or special mention in a will, except by express statement, oral or in writing, addressed to the other trustees, of testamentary intent to make a gift, or by testamentary deed of trust, to take effect in the event of disabling incompetence or death of the beneficiary.

At the initial meeting of the trustees, held on the second Sunday in November at the headquarters of the Barrows Construction Co. at the sandpits in Hampton Falls, Spring had described the trust agreement to the others as a *cordon sanitaire*. 'Discretion is important to us. If one of us dies, as all of us someday surely will, we do *not* want estate appraisers rummaging around in this operation, asking awkward questions. That's why we're making it a lock-box: very hard to get into; you had to be there. Almost impossible to get out of by yourself – unless you're literally willing to die in the attempt.'

The instrument provided that in such event, or upon application by a beneficiary or his attorney-in-fact for liquidation of his interest, the value of the interest would be determined by appraisal, and the surviving beneficiaries at their sole option and discretion choose either to admit the decedent's designee to his vacant place, or if for reasons of uncertainty or reservations about his suitability they chose not to, thereupon either by additional capital infusion or by sale of trust assets redeem the interest of the late beneficiary by payment to his successor in interest an amount equal to the value of his pro rata share.

The original arrangement soon proved to be geographically unwieldy. For that and other reasons, including perceived risk, in 1961, five years before the statute of limitations would bar state prosecution of any criminal offense possibly committed in connection with construction of the courthouse, Spring had thought it best to suggest to Edmund that he draw up the document substituting Philip Fox of Hampton Pond as the managing trustee of record.

Fox owned and operated the Fox Agency, Real Estate & Insurance. Fox's firm had handled the bonds underwriting the courthouse construction, so he had followed the project attentively and was keenly aware of its many ramifications. His agreement to serve as trustee specified that at the end of his first year he would be credited with a management fee of a ten percent ownership of the Fourmen's Trust fund, subject to divestment should he fail for any reason to serve for a total of at least five years. For the next four years thereafter he would annually receive a further interest amounting to two-and-one-half percent of the value of the fund that year, also subject to divestment if he failed to complete the specified term of five years. Thereafter he would participate in gains and losses on equal terms with the original four holders. While his duties as managing trustee would continue, he would cease to receive any additional compensation. Everyone involved in his admission to membership understood the interest he received to be hush money, although Lane was the only one who called it by that name at meetings, causing the others to wince.

Lane though blunt was right. Fox's addition to the trust served prudence as well as managerial efficiency. From his bonding work he knew that the original monies constituting the corpus of the trust consisted entirely of kickbacks from rigged-bid contracts and subcontracts for materials involved in the project, completed in 1957. The total came to about $135,000, slightly over eleven percent of the total cost of the building and grounds.

Spring conservatively oversaw its enlargement in the bond market. Nine years later he had more than doubled it, to approximately $315,000. On his advice the trustees then voted to begin gradual diversification of their holdings, transferring some of the profits from the bond accounts into common stocks and investing the rest in real estate, both by purchasing undeveloped land and by buying up mortgages insured by the government. In 1970, Barrows had commenced construction of the trust's first cautious venture in long-term ownership of residential real estate, the sixteen-unit apartment building at 1692 Eisenhower Boulevard, at a rock-bottom cost of $7,100 per unit – $113,600. The trustees also accepted Spring's recommendation that the trust become more aggressive in the stock market, using about seventy percent of their remaining capital to purchase common stocks issued by companies among the 500 indexed by Standard & Poor.

At the close of the 1968 spring meeting, Philip Fox had reported having been badly frightened by a premonition, and to be on the safe side wished to vouch for his grandson's bona fides and ability to keep his mouth shut; in the event of his death, he said, it would be his wish that the surviving original trustees/beneficiaries allow Walter to succeed him as both trustee and beneficiary. The other trustees dutifully scoffed at his superstitiousness, but agreed. In November they carried out his wishes, voting to admit Walter, not so incidentally carrying out their preference not to disturb the corpus of the trust – as would have been necessary if they had chosen to buy him out.

In 1972, the members convened for the regular spring meeting on the second Sunday in May at Larry Lane's apartment at 1692 Eisenhower Boulevard, he having become too infirm to travel to the Fox Agency offices in Hampton Pond, for more than ten years the customary venue for the semi-annual gatherings. With great difficulty Larry had made a statement. He had written it out on six sheets of paper. Interrupted by coughing, wheezing, choking and gagging, he had needed nearly eleven minutes to deliver it. To his old henchmen it seemed like eleven hours.

'It's no more obvious to you guys now than it's been to me for a long time that this'll be the last meeting I'll attend, and I thank you for coming here so I could do it. When November rolls around, I'll be gone, and damned glad of it, too. I hope I won't have to, but if I do, the pain gets so bad I can't stand it, I'll see to the end of it myself. I've been on the brink of that many times as it is, and I can see myself making that choice. And if I'm too far gone to do what needs doing, I've got a friend I can count on to help me. My family would too, in a jiffy, you bet, if I ever asked them, but I'd never let the bastards have the satisfaction.

'I recommend, if the Man gives you a choice, take the heart attack, or the stroke. Either one's got to be better'n this. The drawback of going that way is it's too sudden to make any plans; tell your friends how you want things done. Way I'm going, I do have some time. 'S the only good thing about it. I can tell you I'd like my place to go to Amby Merrion. I realize he's a good deal younger than everyone but you, Walter, but you'll all get along fine with him, I promise you.

'I recall being in the same position with all of you except Walter in April, Sixty-eight, when Phil Fox told us he'd had some kind of waking-dream or something, terrible premonition. He said he'd never put much stock in them before, but he'd never had one this powerful, and it'd really rattled him. He said he hoped, naturally, it'd turn out to be dead wrong, and that come November we'd be making fun of him, laughing how foolish he'd been. But if it turned out this one was right, and he did pass away before then – that was how he said it; he said "passed away," and then he gave a little shudder, like he'd had a sudden chill; I can *see* him, plain as day – his wish would be that we let Walter take his place. And then he spoke very highly of you, Walter, and so when it turned out that Phil's awful hunch'd been right, we naturally honored his wishes. And we've found out that his judgment was correct.

'Now since I'm having all this trouble talking to you, I'm going to cut it a little short here. I'd like it if you'd all consider that I've now said about Amby all the same good things that Phil had to say about Walter. He's a good guy. You can trust him. He keeps his word. He's gone out of his way to be a friend to me, faithful as could be, making sure I'm as comfortable as possible, doing everything he can. And he did it almost a year before he had any idea that there might be something pretty good in it for him. He's a decent man. He's got good character: by that I mean he's loyal, and if you tell him something's confidential, he keeps it that way. And that's about all that I've got to say. Except to say, Fiddle, that this's probably the last time I'll piss you off at a meeting, by calling our little arrangement 'the Foreskin fucking Trust' – as I've tried to do at least once, each time we've met, to see how mad you always get. Oh, and ask you all to join me for a few drinks – farewell drinks I guess they'd be. And thank you for how you've always treated me, for being my good friends.'

When Merrion succeeded to Larry's place in the fall of 1972, the value of the trust had more than doubled again. Walter Fox, having inherited not only his grandfather's interest but also his managerial responsibilities, conservatively estimated that each of the five shares was worth about $143,000. The corpus then consisted of the apartment building, each month grossing $6,160 in rental income – Larry had insisted that his share of trust income be debited $308.00 each month he lived in number 11, eighty percent of the rent anyone else would have had to pay.

By then Big Roy Carnes was dead. His son, Roy Junior,

Hilliard's predecessor in the House, had retired from the State Senate as chairman of the Committee on Post Audit and Oversight to become chief executive officer for financial operations of The Buehler Corporation, a New England textile company then completing its changeover from manufacturing to importing fabrics, mostly from the Far East, and beginning its relocation to Anderson, South Carolina. Two of the original trustee/beneficiaries, Chassy Spring and Fiddle Barrow, still survived, but Spring was in ill health in a rest home in Gloucester, near his son's home in Marblehead. Spring did not attend Merrion's inaugural, and would die within the year.

There had been three purposes for that meeting, held in Fox's main office in the white six-room bungalow with green shutters and a white picket fence that the Fox Agency occupied in the center of Hampton Pond (in Canterbury, Hampton Falls and Cumberland, the Fox Agency operated storefront satellite offices providing coverage extending into Holyoke, Springfield, Chicopee and Amherst and Northampton). Carnes, citing the demands his new position made on his time and energies, and the imminence of his permanent departure from New England, had invoked the buy-out clause. Stating in his letter to Walter Fox his confidence that Fox and the others would give him 'honest weight,' he had waived his right to demand appointment of a disinterested appraiser, noting in passing that he had 'often wondered why the hell Chassy ever thought it would *ever* be a good idea to give an outsider access to the books; what if he got curious and decided he wanted to know where the dough'd originally come from?'

Fiddle Barrow offered two proposals, prompted in part by his own increasing frailty but precipitated by Spring's incapacitation. The first had been to convert the securities into shares of a moderately aggressive mutual fund, Spring no longer being able to supervise the trust's investments and no one else among the trustee-beneficiaries appearing to have either the time to assume his oversight of market investments or the acumen to do it with confidence. The second had been to cede the management of the property at 1692 Eisenhower Boulevard to Valley Better Residences, Inc., so that thereafter the only task remaining to the trustees would be negotiation and deposit of the checks representing their profits.

Merrion, Fox and Barrow voted unanimously to convert the stock into shares of the Dreyfus Fund. Conformably to Edmund Spring's written statement of his father's wishes – 'he said to have him vote the same way as everyone else does, whatever they want to do' – Barrow cast Spring's vote as his proxy. They further voted to direct the Dreyfus Fund to transfer shares in the account to be established in the name of the trust in the amount of $143,000 to Roy Carnes, Jr., and to put the apartment building under Valley Better management.

Neither Merrion nor Fox then or later had perceived any need to divulge their common interest to outsiders. But each time Merrion after that went into any kind of community meeting or social occasion not knowing in advance exactly what he was in for, and found that Walter Fox was also involved, he was glad. Because they had that one financial thing in common, and treated it as clandestine, to Merrion it seemed they had a bond of secret knowledge. Fox seemed to share that belief. Each of them knew that the other possessed a reserve capability – 'Fuck you' money – hidden from the world, and hoarded the knowledge along with his own treasure.

As Merrion's business to the casual observer would have seemed to consist principally if not entirely of his job at the courthouse, so Walter's had appeared to be the Fox Agency, the insurance and real estate brokerage he'd inherited at the age of twenty-nine from his grandfather, Philip, in 1968.

On July 18th, 1968, the day of Philip Fox's funeral in the Episcopal Church of St John in Hampton Pond, government offices and small businesses there and in Hampton Falls, Canterbury, Cumberland and neighboring sections of Holyoke, Chicopee, Northampton and Springfield displayed hand-lettered signs in their windows and on their doors: 'Closed 11–1, in Memory of Phil Fox.' Or just: 'Philip Fox. 1882–1968.' A columnist for the *Springfield Union* wrote: 'Phil Fox died having spent a lifetime demonstrating, not declaiming, to all who knew him his unshakable belief that faith without good works is useless.'

Even Fred Dillinger eulogized him. In his *Transcript* column he described Fox as 'the man who singled himself out – if he was not first recruited, as he usually was – to lead the area when it was time to solicit donations. It didn't seem to matter to him what the cause was. To renew hope for a family burned-out of its home or a shopowner out of his business; to rally support for a fund-raising drive to send the Canterbury All Stars to Williamsport, Pa., for the Little League World Series; the Hampton Pond High School band to Washington for the Cherry Blossom Festival, or to New York for the St Paddy's Day Parade. And when someone said to him, "Phil, you're not a Catholic, and you're not Irish, either," he said, "You're mistaken, my friend. On Saint Patrick's Day I'm Irish – everybody is." He acted on his own each year to see to it that every hard-luck family had a turkey on Thanksgiving and Christmas, and a ham for Easter, too. Phil Fox may not have been a saint in Heaven's eyes, but to those of us on earth, he looked a lot like one. Phil Fox will be missed.'

That column ran the day before the funeral. Reporting 'the enormous turnout to bid good-bye to Phil,' the *Transcript* story said: 'He did not confine his good works to his home town of Hampton Pond. He considered himself a local resident of every community where the Fox Agency did business. Whenever Canterbury or 'the Falls' or Cumberland had a question whether there'd be cash enough to help the poor or the unfortunate, or achieve a common civic goal, Canterbury and the other towns always knew they really had no question – Canterbury had Phil Fox. His grandson, Walter, will have giant shoes to fill, and as we express our sympathy, all of us will wish him well.'

Walter was the successor because his father, Andy, had been among Marines killed at the Chosin Reservoir during the Korean Conflict. Phil's other son, Walter's Uncle Cameron, was an episcopal priest, vicar of a well-to-do parish in Litchfield, Connecticut; he had never had any interest in the family business, 'anything involving actual work,' Phil sometimes mildly said.

The consensus of the business community at the time of Phil's death was that Walter was a mere untested kid, too callow to take on the enterprise. His alternative was to sell the agency; there were aggressive bidders. He was aware of the consensus and it made him timid, but the operation of the agency was the only work he knew. At twenty-nine he felt too old to start a new career. Since he was the sole heir, it was his call to make. Nagged and hindered by his fear that the elders were right and he would make a disastrous mistake, he decided nonetheless to proceed.

The agency had rewarded his cautious management, perking along nicely and continuing to return decent profits, growing at a steady rate of two to three percent a year, just about keeping pace with inflation or staying a bit ahead of it. At first that gave him quiet satisfaction. Then after a few more years he became somewhat more assertive. He began to think his instincts might in fact be fairly good, well worth relying on.

His first wife, Jacqueline, was the first to discover he had changed. Having become 'terminally bored' in Canterbury, she had decided to unload her life with him there for a more stimulating career in TV production at station WTIC in Hartford. She was perfectly astonished when he hired Sam Evans to counter her libel for divorce with a vigorous one of his own. First he alleged desertion, claiming that her twelve-hour daily absence commuting to a ten-hour workday at Independence Plaza constructively amounted to desertion of his bed and board. Then he flabbergasted her by seeking custody of their child, and undisputed ownership and occupation of the marital domicile in Hampton Pond – alleging she had proved herself an unfit mother by constructively leaving him to raise their daughter by himself.

Then he really stunned her: he won, on both prayers for relief (Jacqueline had made the right career choice for herself, though; in the three years she spent in Hartford, she displayed an affinity for her new work that made her professional catnip to the people building CNN in Atlanta; lured to Peachtree Plaza, she vanished into Georgia, never to be seen again north of Washington, D.C.).

Apparently emboldened by results, Walter as Merrion saw it began to act 'like a guy who's discovered that he doesn't really have to give a shit.' He developed the confidence to admit freely he'd not only started out but remained 'wishy-washy, scared to death of making some dumb-ass greenhorn mistake that'll wreck the business' and that 'about the biggest change' he'd 'ever dared to make was adding on the logo,' the red brush-stroke profile of a fox that now adorned the agency's For Sale signs and stationery. While he freely confessed his opinion that its modest improvement in prosperity under his direction probably had more to do with regional population increases and his grandfather's reputation than with anything he had done, he began to think and soon after that to say that still he must deserve at least some credit for having been smart enough to leave a good thing alone.

One night at the house on Pynchon Hill, after everyone else had gone home and Diane was in the pantry cleaning up, he had poured 'one last nightcap' of Old Smuggler for himself and a Jack Daniel's for Merrion – 'Meaning this'll make the third, for each of you,' Diane said, from the kitchen – and said that 'of course the thing that no one ever seems to notice, when they talk about your business and how it doesn't seem to've gotten much bigger, sort of sneering at you, is at least that little business that you got *is* still *there*, still chugging along, going strong, just like it always has been.

'It may've been a *little* engine, when you took control of it, and that may still be all it is, but when you got your grubby little paws on it, back then, it was the little engine that *could*, and by Jesus it still *can*. A lot of others like it, owners had the big ambitious plans: well, where're they today? Not around any more – where could they've all gone? Gone belly-up, is where, not in business anymore. I think survival counts for something. I'll take it any day.'

When Walter died, at the age of forty-two, Diane knew there was more to his estate than the house and the insurance agency, but she wasn't sure what it was or how much it was worth. He had told her something about a twenty-percent interest in some sort of a real estate and stock investment partnership, not itemized but left to her under the residuary clause of his will, along with the house on Pynchon Hill and two-thirds of the value of the Fox Agency. She had realized her understanding was imperfect, but left it that way because she hadn't wanted to seem to be too interested in what her prospects were if her robust husband died young. It seemed so very unlikely. Therefore about all she knew about the trust was that some time ago his grandfather had somehow acquired an interest in an investment consortium that continued to yield steady income, and that Merrion was in it too.

Once or twice when she had rebuked Walter for regularly having more to drink than was good for him, whenever Merrion was among the people they'd had over for the evening, he had tried to excuse it by telling her that he and Merrion were 'more'n just ordinary business associates. We're also pals, we get a kick outta each other. A man *should* have pals; a man's *gotta* have pals. And even though I know you don't care much for Amby, pals're what we're gonna stay.'

She said she knew he needed to have friends and if he wanted to consider Amby one of them, that was fine by her. She said whether she liked Amby or not had nothing to do with what she was talking about, which was his 'habit of getting absolutely *sloshed* every time Amby comes here to dinner. Every single time he comes, you two wind up getting plastered. Don't you worry about him driving home when you've gotten yourselves in that condition, you say you're such friends. Aren't you afraid something'll happen to him? That he'll get hurt or maybe arrested?'

Walter had laughed. 'How many cops around here you think're gonna go and arrest the clerk of court? They know him too well. They'd never do that to him, never charge him with drunk driving. They did pull him over, they wouldn't arrest him. All they'd do's make him move over and let one of them drive him home, and the other one follow, the cruiser.'

'He still could get hurt, though,' she said. 'Or he could hurt somebody else. He shouldn't be driving that way. If you think I don't want him around, well, I'm telling you, that's the reason. It's because of the drinking you two seem to do whenever you get together. I get so I don't want to invite him, even though you like him, he's your friend. 'Cause I know what'll happen: You'll both get rip-roaring drunk.'

Walter refused to concede her point. He said. 'Amby and I have a good time together. That's what friends're for. Having fun with them, the short time we're all on the earth. One of the things, anyway. If anything ever happened to me, even though I'm sure he knows you don't like him all that much, if something ever happened to me, other guys we know'd forget all about you, but Amby'd take care of you.'

Walter seemed very certain when he said that and it stuck in her mind. So after Walter died, even though she believed his long uproarious evenings with Merrion had hastened his death, she went to Merrion and asked him what he knew.

He told her she would most likely be surprised when she fully understood what Walter had been up to, as in fact she was. She'd been startled to begin with when an appraiser pegged the market value of the Fox Agency at $830,000, about $200,000 more than Walter several years before had casually guessed it might be worth, but the price had been duly and unhesitatingly paid by the real estate subsidiary of a nationally advertised real estate conglomerate making it the western Massachusetts satellite in its linkage coast-to-coast. Her share of that sale was a little over $556,000, good for an annual income of slightly over $50,000. To her that was a lot of money and it made her feel a little guilty for having yelled at Walter what she now recalled as 'a few times' when he'd gotten on her nerves.

When she learned that those mixed stock and realty trust investments Walter had airily described amounted to just under another $192,000, she was mortified. Combined with the interest from investment of her two-thirds share of the proceeds from the sale of the agency, it would give her an income of nearly $73,000 a year before she brought home any pay from her practice. She had lived with Walter only for about eleven years and she was beginning to fear that soon people would find out she really hadn't known him very well at all. But then, as Merrion had reminded her, they couldn't very well say she'd married Walter for his money; she'd never dreamed he had it.

'Or his cockeyed politics, either,' she said.

Merrion laughed and told her Walter's conservative politics had been 'irrelevant. Walter always made me laugh.' He said that Dan Hilliard really had hated Walter's views and meant it when he sometimes said he couldn't stand the man. 'Some of the things that Walter said absolutely *infuriated* him. If he was pissed off when he left your house Saturday night, he'd still be pissed off when I saw him on Monday. Took me *days* to calm him down.'

He said that if Diane 'hadn't become such a wonderful cook you never would've seen Dan. Never would've laid eyes on the man. And he would never've put up with Walter. Of course Dan can be a major toothache too, he gets started on something. There were lots of times I thought that if Walter didn't finally say something that'd make Danny haul off and hit him, then what'd happen'd be Danny'd do it, say something that'd get Walter so mad he'd hit *Danny* in the mouth.'

He said he had told Hilliard many times that he habitually carried his insistence on political orthodoxy too far, especially when the cost of it would have been good times and laughs. Merrion told her Hilliard said this attitude proved Merrion lacked principle. 'Politically speaking, Danny says, I'm an easy lay. He's probably right. Compared to him, at least. But when he let Walter get on his nerves, Walter took it as a challenge. They deserved each other.'

Walter often said he had voted five times 'enthusiastically' for Richard M. Nixon, three of them as president of the United States. One night he said Nixon had been one of the two best American presidents to serve in the 20th century. Hilliard said he assumed Walter's other favorite was Herbert Hoover. Walter had blinked and said, actually, no, his other nominee was FDR. 'The litmus isn't which party the guy belongs to; it's how he reacts to the problems that the country faces while he's president. The third best may've been Gerry Ford. He gave us rest when we needed it.'

'That happened at your house,' Merrion said to Diane. 'You were feeding us this gorgeous fillet of beef. I forgot what the wine was Walter opened. It was red and I had a lot of it; that much I know. When Walter said that, Danny was astounded. The idea that Walter might actually have something serious and reasonable to say about politics astonished him.'

Walter also knew lots of local gossip and had a fund of dirty, racial, ethnic and religious jokes that he told with practiced élan. He followed and discussed professional and collegiate sports with discernment; ate and drank hospitably; and was as ready to denounce a blowhard on his own side as he was to ridicule a fake on the other. Those assets, together with his regular and unabashed reports of fresh misfortunes and new humiliations he had suffered on the golf course, had twice inspired Merrion to suggest that he allow Merrion to sponsor him to fill a vacancy left at Grey Hills by the death of a member (Hilliard, getting wind of Merrion's first offer, said he'd blackball Fox if it came to that, and Merrion had been concerned enough to remind Hilliard how *he'd* gotten into Grey Hills, and tell him if he did spike Fox, 'I'll get even with you'). But each time Walter after giving the invitation some thought had declined, citing the comfort-level of his second-generation old-shoe status at the Holyoke Country Club, and his 'pagan's apprehension that taking a dead man's place could be dangerous, just asking for trouble. Might tempt the ever-present faraway fellow in the bright nightgown, you know? "Goddamnit, if I'd've wanted that slot occupied, I wouldn't've snuffed Harold now, would I?"'

So Merrion had been genuinely saddened when he heard of Walter's death, and had meant it when he told Diane that he was sorry. She had patted his hand and said she knew he had been one of Walter's favorite bad companions, and expressed her opinion 'that if he only hadn't had quite so many friends like you, or enjoyed them quite so much, he might still be alive today.' But she said she didn't bear Merrion any grudge: 'He was a big boy, after all. He knew what he was doing.'

In her reconfiguration of herself after Walter's death, Diane became convinced the house provided spiritual strength. That was definitely something new for her. Walter at her urging had acquired it, a Fox Agency exclusive listing, as their wedding present to each other. He was quite aware its splendid kitchen was not the only reason why she preferred it to the house in Hampton Pond he had inherited from Phil. The other was the fact that that house had been tainted by his first wife's occupancy. He did not say that to Diane (he told Merrion once with some rueful nostalgia that he thought the principal reason he'd 'married Jaquie was she had these big dreamy bedroom eyes.' When Merrion said that was probably as good a reason as any for a first marriage, Walter said it probably was not, 'but it was as good a one as I needed at the time. Then I found out that what I thought was sexiness was just astigmatism, very easily corrected. As soon as she got her glasses and saw what I was up to, she turned on me, got *mean*'). As Diane had come to see it, the two of them – by having raised in the new house his daughter, Rachel, by his first marriage along with their two sons, with no more numerous losses of temper and exchanges of sharp remarks, soon regretted, than most hard-working, reasonably fortunate families manage to survive without permanent harm – had in the process made a kind of emotional investment in the building, and so had acquired spiritual equity in the very lumber, lathing, plaster and cement of it.

She had needed time to steady herself after Walter's inconsiderately sudden departure (Dan Hilliard, putting aside her part in the disruption of his personal life and therefore his political career, cheered her a little at the wake by muttering that while of course he was sorry, 'Republicans're like that, you know; always afraid if they hang around too long they'll get stuck with the check; so they duck out of everything early'). To go with the time she had required as well a good deal of help and support from longtime friends.

In that gathering of wits she had found herself to her surprise depending upon Ambrose Merrion emotionally. Walter had had many more secrets than she had suspected, and Amby was the only man she knew herself who also knew the secrets. 'It was insidious,' she said, when she realized later what had happened to her while she was engaged in doing something else. Coming over time to believe gratefully that the history she had in the house on Pynchon Hill would be a major source of strength, as long as she stayed put, she had also gotten used to seeing Merrion around in it a lot. When she had finished remaking her life to accommodate Walter's abrupt withdrawal from it, a little over a year later, she found Merrion had worked his way into it ('wormed,' she said once, to him, but he looked a little hurt so she didn't use that term again). Not into the place in her life that had been Walter's, not by any means – she had closed that off – but still in it, just the same, with a new place of his own.

'Animism, I know,' she said of her new attitude toward the house, preferring to keep conversations light until she had become sure enough of what she thought of Merrion's new importance to want to talk about it. 'Early symptom of the onset of feeble-mindedness. Or reversion to the primitive state. Next thing you know, I'll be painting myself blue and running around out in the woods with no clothes on, worshiping resonant trees, talismanic squirrels and sacred rocks. But a good house or any other place does have power to comfort, the solace of familiarity. It doesn't have to have a real soul of its own to do that, but it has to have some special something most houses don't seem to have – character. Most of them're just buildings, frames with walls and roof sections hung on them. When you get one that's more than that, you shouldn't part with it. It would be a sin against the Great Spirit.'

Merrion during the same period had been getting used to being around Diane a lot. In the course of helping her to master the financial matters that Walter had covertly managed out of her sight (as he had prudently kept them from Jaquie's view as well, thus saving more than a few dollars in the divorce settlement, obeying Larry Lane's rule against confiding financial data to possibly treacherous kinfolk with no honest need to know it), he grew accustomed to spending time with her, several hours during the weekend or an evening or two during the week. He enjoyed his new habit of her company, and saw no reason to discontinue seeing her after they had rearranged her assets under her control.

By then he had long since recovered very nicely and completely from the real but transient sorrow he had felt at Walter's death. He had not become happy that Walter had died, but he admitted to himself that he would have been seriously inconvenienced if Walter, as much fun as he'd always been in life, had somehow managed to come back. *Life goes on*, Merrion reminded himself firmly, when he felt his first and only feathery twinge of guilt after an evening of enjoying the company of Walter's widow. *Walter knew that and he left it just the same, and it went on without him. Poor judgment on his part; probably wishes now he hadn't done it. Tough shit for him.*

Once a week, most often Thursdays because he seldom could be absolutely sure until late Friday afternoon that he wouldn't have to be available Friday and Saturday evenings for bail hearings, he invited Diane to join him after work for drinks and dinner, usually at the Old Post Road Tavern – his established familiarity there had bred superior service and access to special dishes off the menu. When she resumed entertaining two years after Walter's death, it was assumed Merrion would act as host. From time to time she cooked for him on winter weekend evenings. Once or twice each summer, as he was going to do on that third Sunday in August, he drove her out to Tanglewood to hear the concerts her stepdaughter had selected as her birthday gift each March, and she made dinner reservations for them afterwards at the Red Lion Inn in Stockbridge.

Merrion more or less assumed that she would be available for any outings, the regular Thursday dinners or movies on the spur-of-the-moment. He would have been disappointed if she had said she had another commitment, but she never did. She would have been at least irked had he pleaded a prior social engagement made it impossible for him to bring over a bottle of red wine and share a pheasant she had bought on a whim and just finished roasting, but every time she had an impulse and called to invite him to do some such thing, he was always ready to do it. 'We do pretty well for each other, don't we, Amby?' she said to him very early one morning, kissing him safe-home just inside the half-opened door. 'Not badly at all,' he replied.

Hilliard, meddling in his business as usual, asked him one evening idly in the bar at Grey Hills – showing off for other people standing around within earshot having drinks after a budget committee meeting – if he was 'still at it, keeping company with the Widow Fox,' knowing the answer. When Merrion said that he was, adding that Hilliard damned right well knew it, he was vexed to feel his ears and cheeks getting hot. Thus rewarded, Hilliard prying further had asked him why he kept on seeing her. 'An excellent cook,' Hilliard said, 'but she can be a controlling woman.'

Merrion said irritably that he guessed it was something that he did, not something he had thought about doing, so therefore he supposed the reason that he did it was because he wanted to. Hilliard had nodded and said grandly that his many years of extensive experience and close personal observation enabled him to state unequivocally and without fear of contradiction that

that was indisputably the very best reason, bar none, that Amby Merrion had ever given for going out with a woman. That brought a little polite applause and a 'hear, hear' or two.

Merrion thought about it for a moment and said that the reason he had tolerated Hilliard for so many years was that from time to time – not very often, but still, now and then – he showed absolutely brilliant insight into human nature, and this was one of those times.

Merrion in the course of helping Diane through her sorrow had found her opinions to be based upon good instincts, and he got into the habit of seeking them when confronting important decisions of his own. It was natural enough, he supposed; after all, she was used to considering other people's situations and giving her advice, that being the way she'd made her living and career for a good many years. And she was obviously pleased, quietly flattered, when he consulted her. Once, more or less in obedience to some shabby impulse learned in politics, he supposed – no point in having an advantage if you're not going to try to use it – he tried to subvert her good will and affection. One evening late in 1992, over dinner at the Tavern, he had asked her advice about what he ought to do with Polly's house.

By then eleven years had passed since Walter's death, so there had been no question that Diane had recovered from the loss. The shattering decline into silence that would necessitate Polly's admission to St Mary's on the Hilltop had set in, rendering progressively more irrelevant his extreme reluctance 'to put her in the home'; he had reached a sort of marker in his life. But depressing as it was, the event had nonetheless been predictable for a long time; he had seen it coming much as Dan and Mercy Hilliard had known despairingly long before the day arrived that sooner or later they would have to put their daughter Donna in an institution providing long-term care. So he did not have the excuse that he had been dazed in shock that evening when he said what he should not have, asking Diane what he should do.

'You should move right back into it,' Diane said immediately. 'That's a good house, just like my house is a good house. That place you're living in right now,' a large garden court apartment in the Old Wisdom House overlooking Hampton Pond, 'may be where the swells all want to go when they retire, half the year playing golf and shuffleboard in Florida, the other half back here playing golf and lying about their grandchildren. But you'll never be one of those silly men in colored pants with white belts and shoes. Besides, you're not old enough.'

'Well,' he said, 'the golf I could handle with pleasure, but it looks like I probably won't have the grandchildren.'

'Looking for sympathy?' she said. 'Won't get it from me. Rachel's always apologizing for not bringing her two back here more often, "so they can get to know you." Uh huh. "Perfectly all right," I always say. "Time enough for us to become dear friends when they go to Harvard. *Then* they can drive out and see me."

'Nothing *wrong* with where you live now, it's a very stylish place. But no matter what you have somebody do to it, it'll never be a good house, the kind of place you hang onto and go back to, because it's where you *live*, and belong. What you need's the sort of place that hangs onto *you*; that's what I really mean. *It* keeps *you*, not you, it, and that's what keeps you going strong.'

'And you think I'm going to need one of those of my own,' he said. He had been ashamed of himself even as he said it. It was arguably excusable – 'never any harm in asking' – but just the same it had also been a cheap dodge to take advantage of her compassionate mood in order to wheedle something out of her, something that she didn't want to give him.

She'd raised both eyebrows and gazed at him over the big white plate of veal scallops in cream sauce, and then after a brief but unmistakably reproving silence, she had snickered. '*Amby*,' she had said, 'really now, of course you will. Of course you'll need your place to live. Of course you need a house.'

So the terms of their non-aggression pact, 'our treaty,' she called it, after that little stutter had resumed evolution along the lines they had begun to take, arriving at it fairly soon after Walter's death. 'Look, Amby,' she had said to him – she was a practical woman – making coffee in her kitchen, using her foot to steer her possessive grey-and-black striped tiger-cat along the mopboard under the sink so that she wouldn't step on it; she had called Merrion Saturday morning and asked him to come over two days after they had gone to bed together the first time because that seemed to her what should be done next.

'This sex business: we've got to talk about it. Come to some kind of agreement we both understand. Or else it's going to get out of control and cause all kinds of problems, maybe end up ruining us. I don't want that to happen. I don't think you do, either. Tell me you don't either, all right? Humor me, at least, and say it, even if you're not really sure yet. This is important to me. I'm surprised how important it is.'

'It's important to me, too,' he had said, sitting down at her kitchen table, and it was. Having left her very early Friday morning in the still darkness – so as to spare her attentive early-rising neighbors the effort they surely would have made to deduce the implications of the presence of what she called his 'flashy car' in her driveway in the sunrise – on his way home he had gradually begun to understand that he didn't know what he ought to do next, how to act or what to say the next time he saw her; arrive with an armload of roses or act as though nothing remarkable had taken place. He was slightly flustered to find that mattered to him. As it hadn't mattered, he realized, in the aftermath of what had become a fair number of other sexual friendships he had enjoyed over the course of what he was now somewhat startled to notice had somehow turned into quite a number of years.

'Thirty of 'em, in fact, give or take,' he said to Hilliard. 'And I have to say it's been quite a while since I can remember being actually concerned the next day about how the lady actually felt about the fun we had last night. Not since Sunny went and died on me, I guess. What was there to get all concerned about? All it was was just getting laid now and then. That's how the grown-ups have fun. And if we should run into each other again, or maybe call up and make sure we did that, well, maybe we'd fuck again. Or then again, maybe not. If the time ever came then when we hadda new chance, we'd see how we felt. "Inna meantime, many thanks, I hadda good time. Appreciate you lookin' out for me like that.'

'That was the way that it worked. There was this one woman I got so I knew pretty well at the New England Regional Meetings one year, and she was just real hot to trot. So we connected, and for the whole three days of that conference there up at Wentworth-by-the-Sea, that is what we did: we fucked our brains out. She had her regular steady boyfriend back home in Portland. He was a lawyer and she had no complaints at all; he took as good care of her as he possibly could – good swift dash inna bloomers two or three times a week. Regular as he could be, but that hadda be his limit. He was married, and either his wife wasn't dumb enough so she would actually let him pack a change of clothes and get out of her sight for an overnight trip – for fear he might not come back at all – or else he didn't feel he could neglect his practice for three days at a stretch, I'm not really sure. Whatever it was, I wasn't complaining. She wanted her cookies and I wanted mine and we found we could make a deal. A loose woman at loose ends: I take her as a gift from God.

'She was back the next year, and the year after that, and so was I, naturally, and both times we picked up like we'd never left off. The year in-between conferences, there's been nothin', no phone calls, no letters, no nothing; it's like for each other we don't exist except up in New Hampshire in June. But that once a year when we came back for the meetings, we came back all of the way. It was just the goddamnedest thing.

'The fourth year she didn't come back. I don't know what happened to her. Maybe the lawyer's wife finally found out and shot her or something like that. Or he divorced the bride and they got together. I was kind of afraid to start askin' around; thought it might look funny, you know? But it seems kind of strange, when you think about it: During those three years inna course of nine days I prolly fucked her thirty times. We were young; we did it like there was no tomorrow. And today I don't know if she's alive or dead, and she's the same way about me, and I bet she's no more upset than I am. It was straight sex, no more'n that.

'Well except for Sunny, that's how all of them were for me; that's how I looked at it, and I've been happy. I've been a contented man. Now it seems like I'm not looking at it that way any more. Something here seems to've changed.'

'See, I don't belong here, like you do,' Diane said. 'In this town. In this valley. Even though I've been here, more'n quite a while, it's not like I belong here. Or I *didn't* belong here, at least, when

I first came. I just sort of settled in for a while, and at some point after that discovered I had stayed. As though I'd gone to sleep and when I woke up, here's where I was. Where else would I open my practice? And after that Walter was here. So when I decided that I was with Walter, I also realized that I'd probably be here for the rest of my life. I was at rest; where I belong became irrelevant.

'Now I'm not at rest anymore. I'm not saying I don't like it, not that, but I am confused. When I started thinking Friday morning about what we did Thursday night, I had kind of a hard time keeping my mind on my patients' problems – which is what they're paying me for.'

'Wait a minute,' Merrion said. 'What is this you "don't belong here"?' Merrion said. 'Sure you do. You've been here for a long time. Close to thirty years by now, or so, pretty close to it. If you and Walter weren't together when I first came to the court here, I know he was, and you must've gotten here pretty soon after that. Because I've been in that courthouse now for about thirty years, and, I'm not saying that you're old, now, but you've been here a long time.'

She laughed. 'It's just dawned on you, hasn't it?' she said. 'Just hitting you now. I can see you thinking it. "My God, what the hell've I done? I've been to bed with an older woman. She's practically old enough to be my mother.'

'Oh boy,' he said. 'Diane, I hate to tell you this, but the fact of the matter is: you're wrong, very wrong. Women that I've always hung around with've generally been about my age, within three or four years of how old I am. Don't get me mixed up with my friend. I haven't hung around the schoolyard since I got out of school. I'm actually a very nice guy.'

She said 'Oh.' She sat down at the table in the kitchen opposite him and gazed at him for a while and then she frowned and looked at her hands and said: 'No, I know that. Or else I don't know that. Oh, I don't know what I know.' She looked up at him again. 'I didn't mean for this to happen,' she said.

'But you just said . . .' he said.

'I know what I said,' she said.

'Well, now *I'm* confused,' he said. 'First you said it was important to you and that now we've slept together, we have to get things straight and have some rules, and that was fine with me. And now you're telling me instead it's something else. A mistake or something.'

'Amby,' she said, 'before Walter died, I'd seen you a lot but I didn't really know you very well. I'd never really thought about you as *my* friend; whether you were someone I knew and trusted, and wanted to have as my friend; only about you as one of Walter's friends. When Walter died; after the shock wore off and I'd started to get my bearings and so forth, well, I certainly hoped sex would be a part of my life again – I'm a normal, healthy, adult woman – but I didn't really expect . . . I didn't know, I didn't have anyone in mind. I didn't have any idea, who it would be with. That I'd be with in this new part of my life.

'But I have to be honest with you: I didn't think it would be you. Now don't be hurt; I didn't think it *wouldn't* be you, either. You were never; it was never part of my plan, not that I had any plan, really, but . . . I don't know what I mean here. To get involved with you. As lovers, I mean.'

'Why not?' he said.

'Now you *are* hurt,' she said, 'and I didn't mean that to happen either. It's just that you and the people you know and the life you've always led, you were someone who was completely different from Walter. Whether you knew it or not, you were sort of a romantic hero to Walter. Do you understand what I'm saying? Walter was exactly what he looked like: a small-town, small-business, family man. His whole world was family, and the business that his family'd started, and the small towns where the family lived and knew the people, ran the business. His whole life was in the Four Towns; it always had been – he liked it that way.

'It was how I liked it, too. I'd grown up in a settled environment in Minneapolis, a very conventional family. But once I went to Madison to go to college that phase for me was over. I became rootless. I had adventures, I guess you could say, and I enjoyed them. But after some years I began to worry. I didn't have any base of my own. So Walter's Four Towns were nice for me to come back to, an orderly world where people stayed in the same place and you could depend on them. Not the *same* world but the *kind* of world

I'd grown up in. I don't think I'd ever been really *afraid* before that, uneasy, maybe, but with Walter I felt safe again. He was an utterly settled man. When I was with him I knew everything was going to be all right. I never dreamed he'd die so soon.

'He admired you. You, and as much as he fought with him all the time, Danny. When Mercy kicked him out last year, he was the only person I know, man or woman – except, I'm assuming, you – who was on Danny's side. The two of us had some sharp words over that. In a way you two were Walter's imaginary friends. You and Danny lived around here just like he did; you moved in the same world and you acted like everyone else, but you were also *different*. You were *pirates*. He liked his life all right, but it was quiet; there was *action* in the lives you two were living – they were *exciting*: You were in *politics*.

'In a way he wanted to be like you, or thought he did anyway, and because you let him be friends with you, he could feel he *was* like you, a little bit. He thought you brought a touch of glamor to his life. He was absolutely *fascinated* by the people that you know, all the rogues and rascals you and Dan did battle with, in your daily life. He envied you. I didn't mind that, as long as he didn't actually try to *be* like you; he couldn't've done it. He wasn't cut out for the rough and tumble, and deep down inside he knew it. But when he had too much to drink and started talking big; that pose he liked to put on, pretending he was part of your life, the *turmoil*, and the *drama*, and the *thrills*, well, he just loved doing that. For a while he forgot who he really was.'

'But you didn't,' Merrion said, 'you didn't love having him do it.'

'I didn't encourage it, no,' she said. 'But I didn't try to *dis*courage it, either. I don't think I could've, if I'd tried, but I didn't really try. He had a great time, a wonderful time, pretending he was one of you. But then you all went home. The next day he was back here with me, hung-over but with me, the solid Walter I'd liked the minute that I met him, and grew to love, and married. Of course I was glad he'd had fun. But I hoped he'd never change.

'And so when he died, well, I had no idea of winding up with you. When I felt it starting to happen, felt myself getting attached to you, I hoped I was getting it wrong. But I wasn't. I did become attached to you. Wanting to or not. And so now I have to deal with it, that's all. *We* have to deal with it now.'

'Yes,' he said.

'Be patient with me, Amby,' she said. 'I do have a good heart, you know.'

The young man she had met and started living with during her second year at the University of Wisconsin at Madison in the spring of 1963 had been a graduate assistant in the department of economics assigned to teach a basic survey course to freshmen, 'very bright and very intense, and very Marxist, too.' She said his name was 'Tommy.'

In February of that year he learned that he had won a fellowship to study for a year at the London School of Economics, 'which sort of disappointed him, because he'd wanted Cambridge. But I thought it was wonderful, and I thought *he* was wonderful and *we* were wonderful, and when it was time for him to go I went right along with him. Maybe I was right – who knows? Maybe the two of us actually were wonderful, just like I thought, and therefore when we lived in Saint John's Wood, flat broke, it wasn't really cold and dreary, like it began to seem half an hour or so after we got there. Maybe it *was* magical, *whee*, just like I pretended.

'Tommy couldn't pull it off, believing it was magic. I suppose it's just possible he was right, and I was silly. That fellowship was for one, not two, and my stuffy, settled Three-M parents – my father was a scientist for Three-M – back home in strait-laced old Minneapolis had cut off my allowance when I dropped out of school.

'They really took a very narrow view of things. They said they didn't recall seeing anything in the Wisconsin catalogue that described a year of shacking up in London as the third year of what they'd agreed to pay for me to get, a four-year, liberal arts education.

'They'd thought of that as their biggest present to me, the foundation of the rest of my life. After I graduated if I still really wanted to apply to Juilliard and see if I was a good enough oboeist to become a professional musician, I could do that. And if I didn't want to do that, or did but didn't get in, then I'd be able to teach music in high school somewhere, because I'd have that solid college education. I'd be able to make a living for myself like a responsible adult. But I'd only completed half of the bargain. Now I was living in sin and being free in London. So therefore no more money.

'I don't know – or maybe I just don't remember – what it was exactly that I was going to do after that, after Tommy's year in London. Live happily ever after, maybe. But it was okay, just the same. We had a year like every girl and boy should have, one of wretched, grinding poverty, but unlike a lot of traveling scholars, he actually did study, and he did get his master's degree. And then we came back to Amerika with a K instead of a C and were against the war and stuff, and Tommy taught at MIT and got his Ph.D. You had to give that boy credit. He looked like a dope-smokin' hippie; he talked like a refusenik draft-resister, and he really didn't have a single stinkin' capitalist-running-dog bone in his whole body. But he loved his economics and he worked his *butt* off, and whatever you thought about how he looked or how he talked, you had to admit he knew his stuff. The kid was *good*, clearly headed for stardom.

'So I dumped him, naturally,' she said. 'Couldn't have that now, could we, being married to a star? Absolutely not. I think I dumped him, anyway; it's possible he may've dumped me. Probably depends on who's telling the story. But that was all after a while, not right off. First he got a job teaching at UMass., and something studious and academic began stirring around again, deep down inside my fevered brain.'

She held her hands aloft as though to indicate she was having a vision. 'I perceive that I am getting on in years. By this time I am almost twenty-four, *ancient*, and I suppose I am beginning at long last to grow up. As the hot-shot young professor's, ah, demure young wife, I was able to get free tuition. Then I was able to talk the proper authorities first into accepting the credits I'd sort of left behind at Wisconsin, and also some I'd sort of picked up while I wasn't doing much of anything else besides sleeping with Tommy in England, kind of studying at the University of London. After that, talking *very* fast, into letting me switch my major to psychology.'

'Wow,' Merrion said, 'I'm impressed. They always made *me* give *them* money.'

She smiled. 'You probably weren't demure,' she said. 'I was, I was very demure. And academics're suckers for that. As a teacher's wife I was entitled to the undergrad free tuition anyway, and when they let me transfer credits like that, they were being maybe more than just a little bit crafty. They wanted Tommy to stay at UMass. Didn't want him flying off to some other place, better-known for its economics. So I'm sure it was at the back of their minds to use me to tie him down a little more securely, get his wife involved with a UMass. program of her own.

'So they let me study psych for free, being as how by then I was more interested in that than I was in music. I got so I enjoyed it. I was having fun. So naturally since fun isn't supposed to last very long, it seemed to go fast. It was kind of surprising how fast; what with summer-school and all, and no horsing around, everything fell into place. In just over a year I had enough credits to graduate.

'I'd barely started the grad program for master's in psychiatric social work when Tommy's comet ignited in the heavens of economics and he got precisely what everyone'd been expecting him to get all along: an invitation to join the faculty at the University of Chicago. Muslims have always had Mecca; Tommy in those days had Chicago.

'"I don't think I want to come with you," I told him. "I think I found out where it was that I've always been going. It was here. I want to stay here. You go if you want. I think you should." "So do I," Tommy said, and he did.

'When he left, me and UMass. both, I think they felt a little guilty, too, somehow responsible. After all, they'd lured my young husband to Amherst and what'd he done but go off and leave me there all by myself. Like it was partly their fault. I didn't discourage that. Whatever they wanted to think that helped me was perfectly all right with me. I'd finally begun to come down to earth and realize I was never going to be the first-chair oboe in the Cleveland Orchestra and have a torrid affair with George Szell. He was getting a little old for me by then anyway, and since I didn't have a husband anymore I decided the first thing I'd better do was find a way to make a living. And that's why I stayed.

'You see what I mean?' Diane said. 'I don't really belong here? This is just where I washed ashore? You and everybody else I've met and gotten to know well here all seem to have some kind of inner gyro that controls you, determines how you rotate. It may be a little out of kilter, so sometimes you spin off-center; quite a few of you're like that. But I've never seen you go *completely* out of whack. You may teeter and wobble around, but generally you regain control and keep on spinning. And it looks to me as though you can do this without having to think about what you're doing.

'I'm not like that. If something's important to me, I have to have a program, how I'm going to handle it – so it doesn't handle me. You're important to me now; we're important to me, so I have to have a program on how I'm going to handle us.'

'Why not just make it up as we go along?' Merrion said. 'That's what we've been doing up 'til now, isn't it? Worked out okay up to this point, or so I'd say anyway.'

'Because up 'til now it didn't involve sex,' she said. 'For you that apparently doesn't amount to a major change, but to me it does. I don't mean I'm a retroactive virgin here now. That's not what I'm trying to say. Sex is important to me and I've missed it since Walter died, and I have to tell you honestly that if you hadn't been around here the other night to do what you did so nicely; or if you'd made some excuse that made me think sex wasn't going to be a part of our nice friendship, pretty soon I would've had to start looking around for some other man who might be willing to devote some of his time and energy to keeping a refined lady comfortable.

'I've had the project in the back of my mind ever since a few days after Walter's funeral. Not that there was any emergency involved; I didn't have to restrain myself around the funeral director or anything like that. I just had it in my mind that sooner or later I'd have to start thinking about reaching an understanding with a discreet gentleman.

'And now that I've apparently done that, well, now I have to get everything all orderly and tidy, and settled in my mind.

Because I have to warn you, Amby, I've always been the kind of girl who's reasonably easy, but I tend to get attached to someone I'm having sex with. One-night stands're not my bag. So you have to be on your guard about that. I'm really asking quite a lot of you, I know. You have to provide me with sex and you have to be discreet and you have to be a gentleman about it. You may not want this job.'

'Lemme think,' Merrion said. 'The gentleman-part I think I can handle. I've had experience with that. The attachment part, too. I was attached to someone once, and I liked it, but that was before I found out I was lots more attached to her than she was to me. When I found out I didn't like it, but it didn't matter much by then because she'd done what Walter did, only a lot sooner. Inna meantime someone else got attached to me, and a very nice someone else she was, and still is, but I didn't get attached to her. She didn't like that a whole lot. But in this case, if you're telling me it's mutual, as you seem to be, then that shouldn't be that much of a problem.

'The discretion I may have some trouble with. The women I've known've been single like me. What we did was our business. I haven't had a lot of call for that particular specialty.'

'Well, you'll want to get to work on it, then,' she said. 'For the boys' sake, I mean. Rachel I'm not concerned about. Rachel, if I don't do something silly and get her all stirred up, will happily stay right where she is, down there in Washington; contentedly doing just what she does, "working far too many hours" in the office of counsel of the National Association of Broadcasters; "and spending far too little time with her husband and her kids. Not that Terry's liable to notice, since he's as bad as she is and works far too hard himself," in the legal office of the International Brotherhood of Teamsters.

'The boys're a different matter.' They were both still at Mount Hermon then. Phil, nine when his father died, had taken it hard and was still recovering, very slowly. Diane, when she and Merrion had become lovers, was not confident that the boy, 'so much like his father,' had yet completely regained his equilibrium, and would not do so until Christmas, 1990, when he came home during his freshman year at Connecticut Wesleyan and announced he had joined the Army, signing up for a four-year program offering training in electronics, and wasn't going back to college, 'probably ever.'

'Walter made no secret of it, how he'd hated college,' Diane, much relieved, told Merrion then. 'Many times he told me how unhappy he'd been when he was away at school, and how wrong his grandfather'd been to've sent him, made him go. "All I ever wanted to do when I grew up and came home from Mount Hermon was *stay* home from Mount Hermon and go to work in the agency and learn how to run the business, and then spend the rest of my life doing that."'

Her second son, Ben, four years younger, had been at Deerfield only a year when Walter died. He was a strange and solemn kid who seemed puzzled by his father's death, as though feeling he had never known his father well enough to miss him too much when he went away. He had already somehow begun to assemble what amounted to a new life for himself, using what Deerfield had given him to work with, spending all but his shortest vacations with a roommate whose family had a cattle ranch in British Columbia, putting so much emotional as well as geographical distance between himself and the house with the yellow door in Canterbury that he had in effect resigned from the family before his father's death.

'But that doesn't mean I think he needs to know that his mother's having sexual relations with the guy from the courthouse his old man used to have too much to drink with. I don't mind if he *does* know, if either one of them, Phil or Ben, starts to think about it, figures it out, and draws the obvious conclusion. As I'm sure in time they will – they're not stupid kids, after all. But I want them to have the option: either of thinking about it, and figuring out that their mother's having sex again, or of *not* thinking about it, if that suits them, drawing no conclusion at all. So that's why you have to be discreet.'

What they had done was work out an arrangement that looked to Merrion as though it might last him, at least, for as many years as he had left – 'maybe thirty or so,' he said one winter Saturday at Grey Hills when he'd had a game of racquetball with Heck Sanderson and then done ten laps in the indoor pool, 'if I keep this up,' as of course he had not. The substance of it was what Hilliard had been looking to find out when he poked around, and what Merrion would not disclose. They had promised to take care of each other.

'You certainly look like hell this morning,' she said affectionately after he had parked in her driveway and come into her house through the back door without knocking.

'Thank you very much,' he said, getting a mug from the cupboard and filling it from the coffee pot on the counter next to the sink, 'so nice of you to notice. I suppose I probably do. I've fucking well come by it honest, up 'til all hours with a pack of criminals. What the hell else can you expect?' He drank some of the coffee. 'Actually, though, I *feel* pretty good. And you look perfectly great.'

The cat rubbed against her shins and she nudged it away with her foot, hard. 'Oh no, you don't, you no-good bastard,' she said. 'Think you're getting back in my good graces that easy, you miserable son of a bitch.'

'Peter been a bad boy?' Merrion said. In order to afflict the man he called his sometimes 'oh-so-solemnly-religious, always-no-help uncle,' Walter had named the cat *Simon* and called him *Peter*.

'Peter shat in the bathtub again last night,' she said. 'Peter's landlady damned near stepped in Peter's shit barefoot this morning when she went to take her shower, which would've made her good and mad at Peter if she had. Peter would've been lucky if he hadn't ended up in the pound. Not that Peter's landlady enjoyed having to wash the crap down the drain and then scrub the goddamned tub before she could wash her body.'

'I told you when you did it,' Merrion said. 'I warned you when you had him fixed, you and Walter both: "You have that poor cat's nuts cut off, he's not gonna like it. He'll never forgive you, and he'll find some way to get even." And that's what he's been doin', ever since – what is it? Fourteen years now? Gettin' even with you. Just like I would've and just like Walter would've, too, if you'd done it to either one of us.'

'Finish your coffee,' Diane said, picking up the cat and heading for the door. 'Let me put this offender out and you can tell me all the way to the two fatsos all about the human desperadoes.'

18

'So you had a long night at the lock-up?' Diane said. They were traveling south on Route 91 toward Holyoke.

'Yeah,' Merrion said, moving out to pass a grey Ford Windstar minivan rocking erratically from side to side; the middle and rear seats were occupied by several sturdy children who seemed to be engaged in a tag-team wrestling match. 'Fourteen of them I hadda process. Doesn't take that long, each one, maybe ten-twelve minutes. Unless it's a Two-oh-nine-A, guy's been whacking the bride around. Those take a little longer 'cause I don't let them out and they don't like hearing they're staying in. Stand there with the cuffs on and give me a lotta argument, cuts no ice at all. Last night's most popular offense was drivin'-under, Staties're roundin' 'em up left and right, very big night for the troopers. But last night they're not collaring them in bunches, like they usually do, 'round when the bars close down. Last night it was one at a time. Every time I think I'm free, call comes in the radio they're bringin' in another one – so I hafta wait around.

'So for quite a while while I am there, I'm listening to Sergeant Whalen's ragtime. Everything that goes into Everett Whalen's ears comes out Ev Whalen's mouth. It's guaranteed. May not come out in the same order, or in the same condition. It may go in on Monday and then not come out 'til next Sunday, after all the stuff that went in Tuesday and Thursday. Everett ain't neat in his mind. But it'll come out; you can bet on it. So Everett's regaling me there, for what seemed like a long weekend. But finally Frankie Thompson – big black guy that runs the lock-up, really handsome guy, looks like O.J. Simpson, only bigger an' meaner, started bringing out the guests.

'The first six or eight of them weren't anything you'd really call unusual. The first one was this little black guy. Looked like a jockey, so help me; same size and build. Like a jockey you'd see at the track.'

'Or maybe on somebody's lawn,' Diane said. 'You know, one of those charming little iron lawn jockeys about three feet high that all the most elegant white folks used to have beside their driveways, holding out the hitching rings? They always had shiny black faces. Really, extremely attractive; lent such a *festive* note to the grounds.'

'Nah, bigger'n that,' Merrion said, purposefully ignoring her tone. 'Ottawa, he be *small*, but much bigger'n dat, and naturally not quite so well-dressed. He maybe would've qualified on size for a jockey job, but he looked really sloppy. Black sweatshirt with a hood, just the ticket for a seventy-six-degree night, seventy-percent humidity, after an eighty-four-degree day. That's the uniform shirt now. Teamed up with your truly-*huge*, baggy black sweatpants, and naturally your two-hundred-buck, National-Basketball-Association, stick-out-player-approved sneakers. Excuse me: *shoes*.

'These are his *work*-clothes; what the well-dressed young crack gourment with serious fashion jones wears to go out after dark breakin' and enterin' people's homes. The cops have suspicious minds. They see him scuttlin' 'round the back of the house, they're pretty confident the people who live there didn't invite him, tell him to drop by for a drink at any time, even if they didn't happen to be home. And when the cops find him actually *inside* the house, they believe he got into it – this may shock you – with intent to commit a felony therein. To wit, larceny of more than two hundred and fifty dollars, and he isn't picky; anything portable he can lift and carry by himself, and sell without too much trouble to a fence for about a hundred bucks, maybe a third what it's worth.

'Or maybe direct to upstanding, law-abiding folks like you and me, no more honest'n we should be. He runs into us in a bar where it's known you can often get a bargain and finds out we'd like to have an eight-hundred-dollar video-cam, but don't have quite that much cash on hand. Slightly-used'd be okay, if it was cheaper. Just by coincidence an hour later he's back with one a friend asked him to sell; he can let go for much less. This way we get a *twelve*-hundred dollar video-cam for the low-low price of two hundred bucks, and Ottawa gets himself enough money to score some dope and feel real nice for a couple of days. Everybody's happy.

'Except there *is* some risk involved, and this time, as will happen, he got caught goin' in for the merchandise. So now he hasn't got any laces in these state-of-the-art sneaks. For wear in the lock-up, the dress code that cops enforce is the floppy look. Take their laces away from them when they're checkin' 'em in at the desk, so they can't get really nasty and vindictive, make a noose and hang themselves in the cell. Everyone gets all bent outta shape at the cops when prisoners do that. Next thing you know, you got one of those pain-in-the-ass civil-rights cases on your hands; poverty-pimp lawyers on television every couple nights for the next four years, beatin' their chests and hollering how this's typical; the cops so down on po' niggers that the first thing they do when they lock them up is torture their black asses. Made this poor boy feel so depressed, locked up in Whitey's jail with no crack to be had, he took the laces off his shoes and *hanged* himself, an' went home to be with *Jesus*.'

Diane sighed and fidgeted ostentatiously in the passenger seat; Merrion elaborately failed to notice. 'Uh uh,' he said, 'cops want none of that shit at all. And they're heavy enough to make sure they don't get it – they take the laces away. Of course you won't be surprised to learn that this *humiliates* the prisoners, and therefore *also* is a violation of their many civil rights, of which they have got *hundreds*, it seems like: another cruel and unusual punishment inflicted only on black guys, because of their race. By other black guys like Frank Thompson.'

'Amby,' she said, and then let her voice trail off.

'What?' he said.

'Oh,' she said, exhaling loudly again, 'never mind, go ahead. I was going to say I wish you wouldn't talk like this, but it wouldn't do any good. Go ahead, get it out of your system.'

'The reason I think the way I do,' he said, 'is because I *see* the people up close that you're always feeling sorry for, but only see from a safe distance. So you assume they're the same kind of troubled kids you see up close every day, who're screwed up and have problems. But very few of the kids you see have criminal records, and there's a world of difference, Diane. The troubled kids the cops and therefore I have to deal with're not the same class of trade. Maybe they *used* to be once, and nobody helped them, and that's why they're the way they are now, but the reason doesn't matter. By the time I first see them, they've made the transition; they're criminal types. I know them better'n you, and it irritates me that even though we've been together a while, and you should know me pretty well, you still think on this point you know more than I do, and you *don't*.'

She frowned but said nothing.

'This fine young gentleman's print-out said his name was Ottawa Johnson. Now I didn't have any trouble with that; the name, I mean. I got over being surprised with the monickers these guys come up with a long time ago, back when I first found out one of them was actually the kid's real name, given to him by his momma – "I um-no, how come she done it; guess she jes' like the soun' of it." Alceedee Lincoln. I didn't believe him, but I was busy and didn't pursue it. Even though that was taking a chance, because if I don't get the kid's real name when they bring him in, and then he jumps bail, how the hell're we going to find him? We don't know who he is.

'Anyway, while after that I got another one. Adidas Busby. It was a slow night, or maybe I was just fed up with these people always giving me a lot of jive all the time, figure they can and why not. I went right to town on the little turd. "You listen to me, you little creep. You cut that crap out here right now. You clear on that? I'm not down here on my night off to take shit from you, tellin' me you're named after a fuckin' *sneaker*. The way you behavin' ain't cool."

'But he had been; he finally convinced me his real name was Adidas. Cops told me it wasn't even that unusual; I just hadn't happened to run into it before. Those people really do that. There're kids named "Reebok" and "Nike" around, too,

"Lawyer" "Colonel" and "Duke." Those're their actual names. I just wasn't aware of the style. Hell, I didn't know *annathin'*; instead of ranting and raving at a kid named after a sneaker, I should've been getting ready for prisoners named after nothing I ever heard of: Rajahlakah Muhammad and Buforce Elijah. I get a guy named after a *city* these days, and I *recognize it*, I can actually *spell* it, I tell you, I'm almost grateful.

'So I wrote it down on the form and gave Ottawa Johnson the once-over. He didn't look dangerous to me. So that's one thing out of the way, before I decide on his bail. I held my usual chat with him while I was fillin' out the papers; I'm telling him as he doesn't know that he's charged with B and E in the night-time and he has to show up in court tomorrow morning early if not bright and tell the judge whether he plans to get his own attorney or wants one appointed for him.

'"One appointed," says Ottawa right off, very sure of himself. He knows the drill pretty good, as you would expect from glancing at his papers. Six-page print-out suggests to the casual eye he's not a newcomer to the criminal justice system. They get that rap-sheet now at the station the minute the guy comes in. If it's not waiting for him when he gets there, logged-in by the arresting cop in the prowl car at the crime-scene. Name, date of birth, Social Security; in six or eight minutes his whole history prints out nice and neat any time of day or night. Prior offenses; outstanding warrants; bingety-bangety-boom.

'"You still gotta come to court and tell the judge that," I say.

'"I know dat," Ottawa says, very matter-of-fact. I'm sure he does. Ottawa turned eighteen on June fourth, and here we are now, less'n three months later, writing up his third adult encounter with the law. No rest for the wicked; Ottawa keeps busy. But no surprise there; Ottawa was precocious. Sixteen juvenile matters on his sheet. Some of them involved the unauthorized use of other people's motor vehicles. Others the unauthorized removal of stereo-tape decks and custom nag-wheels from other people's motor vehicles; the removal of stereos, TVs, silverware and jewelry from other people's dwelling places; and just about everything you can do with controlled substances – buying, selling, possessing.

'"Ottawa," I say to him, "I don't see no occupation, job, here on this printout. Whatchou do fo' a livin'?"

'"Yeah there is, it say right there," Ottawa he say to me. Points it out to me with his finger, there. "See? Says it right there: I'm Essesseye."

'Supplemental Security Income – S, S, I. In their eyes that's a recognized trade or profession. Like licensed barber or plumbing inspector. Or at least the Ottawas of our world think it should be. It's the occupation of choice among the majority of folks who visit the lockup and the courthouse. They be *disabled*, and can't *work*, so the Commonwealth gives them one-hundred-and-twelve dollars a month and the federal government kicks in four-hundred-seventy more. Meaning you and I and everybody else who's working for a living, and has taxes withheld from it, is making it possible for our governments to give every single shiftless bum who asks for it six-thousand-nine-hundred-and-eighty-four American dollars each year. They don't have to do a fuckin' thing but cash their checks – which is good 'cause they don't *feel* like doin' anything legal just now; what they want to do is *hang out*.'

'Oh, Amby,' Diane said, hopelessly.

He ignored her. '"Essesseye," I say to Ottawa, "now what inna world're you gettin' that for? You look pretty healthy to me. Why is it that you can't work?"

'"Well, 'cause I'm *nervous*." Ottawa says, and he grins. "I always been very nervous. So I never could hold a job down."

'"Maybe it's always doin' things that get you arrested that's making you so nervous," I said. "Havin' cops after you most of the time. 'Cause you been arrested a *lot*."

'"You know, that could be," Ottawa says to me. "I never did think of that."

'So,' Merrion said, maneuvering around an old brown pick-up truck doing sixty-five, towing a wire-fenced trailer overloaded with power tools – four lawnmowers; a wheeled leaf-blower; a large roto-tiller – and racks of untethered rakes and hoes and shovels banging around with each bump and curve, 'Ottawa seemed pretty familiar with what can be done to him at a trial in a court of law, so that advice didn't take long. Of course he's never really *had* a trial yet; his cases all plea-bargained, but he knows the warnings by heart. Along with the rest of his several rights and responsibilities as an accused. I didn't see any reason to make Ottawa stay overnight – make the taxpayers give him board and room, three hots anna cot, on top of everything else – so us two old hands had him on his way in a New-York-minute or so.'

'And now what'll happen to him, tomorrow?' Diane said. 'Is it even possible that this time somebody might finally take a look at this kid, take an interest in him, maybe even try to find a way to help him?'

'Ottawa asked me something like that. I did not say to him, as I will to you now, that he oughta know that by now, all the experience he's had. In the past there've been complaints from some visitors that such comments suggest to them we're "prejudice"; because the cops've lugged 'em, we believe they're guilty. I said "the judge'll appoint Mass Defenders to represent you. Trial in a month unless you plead before that."

'"M I gonna jail this time, you figure?" he says.

'"I'm not a lawyer, Ottawa," I tell him, as of course I'm not, "and if I were I couldn't give you any legal advice. You get that from your lawyer. You know all of this stuff."'

'In other words,' Diane said, 'the answer to the question I just asked you would be No. The answer's No.'

'"Yah," he says,' Merrion said, disregarding her remark. 'He agrees.' '"Judge'll continue the same bail," I tell him. "You don't show up; you'll owe the court another hundred. Next time the cops run you, you'll stay in jail 'til you see the judge."

'Ottawa's already coughed up his twenty-five-buck bail fee, two tens and a five. Your seasoned old pros prepare for another night in the life of crime by setting their bail money aside. Fold it up and put it in their sock or in their shoe. So if they get to drinkin' or stoned on crack or something, they won't be tempted to invest their gettin'-out dough in more happiness. Of course when they get well-wired, they pull off the shoe and spend the dough. But the principle is there. Anyway, Ottawa's money's still lying there on the desk. I haven't picked it up yet.

'"That goes toward it," he says, meaning the hundred for bail if he scoots and then gets caught. His tone of voice gives me my choice. I can take it as a statement or a question. In all the times that Ottawa's made bail before, it happens that he's either never gotten grabbed in Canterbury or else he's come in on a night when someone else had the detail. So he doesn't know me. He's trying me out. "Nice try, pal," I say, and I pick up the cash. "This's my fee, not your bail." "Just askin'," he says, and he grins. Just a couple old hands, like I said.

'Then I have a couple more kids who aren't as personable as Ottawa and're facing different charges, but basically got nabbed at later stages of doing the same thing: Being someplace where they shouldn't be, using stolen money to buy illegal stuff, and *not* being able to give the cops who happened by and caught them a satisfying explanation of why they were there and what their plans'd been. And so they got arrested.

'One of them said he actually has a steady job at United Parcel in Wilbraham. He said he was afraid being busted for buyin' crack might make him lose it. He looked very worried, so he might actually've been telling me the truth.

'One of the other two was on Essesseye. He has a physical problem: "Bad back. Chronic," he said to me. Put his right hand back on it right above his belt, so I'd know where it hurts. I didn't believe him, but I do believe his claim that a doctor and a caseworker believed him in the past – doctors and caseworkers believe many things the average person would strongly doubt and the average cop would laugh at.

'"The third one was kind of vague. He said he's on workman's comp. He had a bandage on his left hand. Said he sliced it twenty-stitches' worth cutting pipe on a construction job. Could be, but he looked shifty. He had almost four hundred bucks on him, though, so it's possible he was telling the truth. Also possible he isn't, and that he got the cash from selling something that he stole, or else from selling dope. Leave that one for Probation to sort out Monday.

'Then comes my next customer. She's a young-lady barkeep at Cannonball's on the road up by the pond. She sold – she's *alleged* to have sold, excuse me – a gram of coke to a State cop. He was in civvies and he looks like a Cub Scout. She's maybe about twenty-six, twenty-seven years old. Five-five, zaftig, very blonde, long pony-tail. Unusual for a defendant in that she is Jewish.

Rosenbaum. Leah Suzanne Rosenbaum. I suppose this's going to qualify me as an anti-Semite, go along with my well-documented racist tendencies, but the fact is we don't get much weekend trade from the Chosen People in my line of work.'

'They're not doing their part?' Diane said.

'Not even close to it,' Merrion said. 'Oh, now and then we'll get a stray, some Jewish college kid who went out partyin' with the hard-drinkin' goyim, or a middle-aged businessman who knew but forgot that Jews aren't supposed to be big drinkers and there's a good reason for that. The kid gets bagged in an underaged-drinking round-up, he's out drinkin' with his pals, not as drunk but just as under-twenty-one as they are, and therefore just as illegal, so he gets busted with them. His older landsmen: it's so unusual for him to have more than a drink or two that he doesn't realize when he's had too much, not being that familiar with the symptoms, so he tries to drive himself home. If you or I're in that same condition, we'd probably make it. We really shouldn't, we know, but because we've had some practice we'd probably make it all right. The Jewish guy's all over the road and promptly gets busted.'

'You can leave me out of that speculation, if you wouldn't mind,' she said.

'Sorry,' Merrion said. 'You idealistic grass-and-magic-mushroom people don't know about intoxication like we evil drinkers do. Forgive me for suggesting it. *I'd* make it home all right. *You* should stay where you are and sleep it off.

'This young lady's got a lot bigger problem,' he said.

'Selling a gram of coke?' Diane said. 'How big a problem is that?'

'Not big at all,' Merrion said, 'if that was the full extent of it. First offense, as this is, suspended for sure, with stern lecture. Cavanaugh yells at her for five or six minutes, "serious offense; mighty big risk you're taking, young lady; ruin your life," so on and so forth, "go forth and sin no more. Don't let me see you in here again." Her problem's not just what she *sold* to the cop after her boyfriend gave him the sales pitch that got him to the bar; it's what the cops *found*, *under* the bar, where she got the toot that she'd sold: thirty-four more grams, give or take.'

'I can never remember . . .' Diane said.

'A little over an ounce,' Merrion said. 'Twenty-eight grams to the ounce. That tips you off something's wrong here. It's unusual to find someone in her position with that much stuff within her reach. That's the second tier of the statute. Anything between twenty-eight and a hundred grams wins you a full five years as a guest of the Commonwealth. Mandatory minimum: they prove you had that much, you go. If she's the retailer, and the boyfriend's her floor-walker, then the dealer that they're working for's been kind of careless, exposin' his loyal employees like that. Leavin' the help to twist in the wind.

'That's dangerous. When employees start to shiver, they usually decide to clear their throats and see if the cops wanna patch the thing up and be friends. Case like this, the guy they have to talk about usually turns out to be the guy that owns the bar. If he isn't, he's the night manager and the guy who owns the joint's either stupid or partners with him. If the cops can prove the owner let that stuff go on, his liquor license is history. He may beat a criminal charge, if he can convince a judge he wasn't smart enough to know what was going on and get a piece of the action, but that won't save his license. He's supposed to know if there's something like that goin' on in his place, and get rid of anyone doin' it. Not do nothing and let it go on. The only hope he's got is that his people go through for him, swear he didn't have a clue.

'Over twenty-eight grams though, what Leah Suzanne's got this morning, that hope becomes kinda slim. That much makes her look like a kingpin herself. *Very* tough for a prosecutor to make more than an ounce of the stuff into less 'n fourteen grams, half an ounce, a mandatory three, and *then* shrink it even more so a judge can put her on the street. This child is in serious trouble.

'She's gotta know this,' Merrion said. 'She oughta be in tears, out of her mind. She's not, she's as calm as an angel. She's fixing her *hair*. Combing and primping, you know? I'm talkin' to her; I'm explaining the charges. She's nodding, not really listenin'. I guess it must be a lotta work, long hair like that, steady part-time job. Got this elastic ruffled thingie that she's gonna put around to hold it – that is in her teeth. She needs both her hands, work on her hair. One to hold it; one to brush it, really hard, *yankin'* it between strokes. So, she's got it all pulled around in front of her, over her shoulder there, all nice and brushed out. Looks at it; it's okay. All right: takes the elastic thingie outta her mouth, spreads it open with her left hand, pulls it on over the hair, all the way up the back her head, and then tosses her head alla way back, an' *flips* the hair back over her shoulder.

'By now I've finished with what the offense is. She's heard me say she's facing five years inna can. She gives me this big lovely smile, like I'd just told her: "You won the lottery, Cupcake." And then what she starts doin' is countin' out twenty-five more bucks from her bra, which's got a whole lot more'n just money in it. My own guess is that all that this young lady does *extremely* well on tips, tending bar at Cannonball's by making sure she always leans '*way* over the counter when she serves the drinks. And my guess would also be that whenever she's had a major purchase in mind, like a car or a high-priced vacation, she knows a reliable way to pick up a little extra money on the side. Prolly has to take her gum out for that, though – she took some out and started chewin' the instant I said she was free.

'I tell her about her right to an attorney and she says: "Get my own." I start to warn her what'll happen if she doesn't show up eight-thirty tomorrow, report to Probation. She says, really bored: "Yeah yeah, I know, a hundred bucks." Like it's all she can do not to say: "Get real – I spill more'n that."

'I begin to think I must've gotten the wrong lady's rapsheet. Accordin' to the one the sergeant gives me, this's her first arrest. "This your real name I got here?" I say to her. '"Leah Suzanne Rosenbaum?"'

'"*Yeah*," she says, very nasal voice, "that's who I am – don't I look it?" She laughs. "Have tah tell my mother that. She's always after me. '*Leah, Leah, heaven's sake, whyncha get your nose fixed.* They say there's nothin' *to it* no more; I'd do it myself, I was your age. You really should give it some *thought*."'

'"You ever go by any other names?" I say to her.

'"You *serious?*" she says to me. Thompson's bringing her boyfriend out. "I do not *believe* this," she says to him. "Can you believe this, Felipe, what this guy is doing? He's asking me if my name is my real name. You tell him, Felipe, all right? Tell him who I am here."

'Felipe's ambition in this life's to be a comedian. He sees this as the chance he's been waiting for, goes right into his shtick. The lockup's on network TV. "He don't believe you're who you are? Of course you're who you are. I take care of this for you. This's the guy here I tell?" And Felipe points to me.

'"Yeah, him," she says. She thinks Felipe is hilarious. "He's the one, thinks I'm not me."

'"Certainly," says Felipe. He clears his throat and stands up straight. "This young lady here I know most of my life to be Candida Rivera, right? Candida Rivera. She is Geraldo's top woman assistant, all right? That's probably where you seen her. Onna TV all the time. Candida Rivera." He looks her up and down. "Nice lookin' woman, don't you think? Very shapely, nice and plump." "*Hey*," she says, sticks her elbow in his ribs, "I'm not *plump*. What is this, *plump*?" Meanwhile he's looking innocent. "That what you want me to tell him, Candy? Everything *ho*-kay now, little one?"

'This cracks her up completely,' Merrion said, taking the ramp south of Holyoke connecting Route 91 with the Massachusetts Turnpike, in West Springfield. 'This is the most fun I have ever seen two people having who've just been arrested on a serious charge and aren't so drunk I can't let them out for fear they might fall inna river. They are perfectly sober, deep in the shit, and happy as larks.

'Well, nothing off mine. I give *him* the speech. Like her, although he's a spic and has a record, minor stuff, he's got what we call "ties to the area." Family lives here. Owns a house in East Longmeadow, with a mortgage. Wife and kids. He's also got a little something going with the barmaid; nothing says that means the wife an' kiddies're no longer local ties. And a bank account, as well, he says. I've got no reason not to grant him bail. She makes his bail fee. And that's where we stand, they're just leaving, when the woman trespasser comes out. The woman they arrested inna woods.

'The name she gave is Linda, Linda Shepard. She's in her early thirties, thirty-two, the sheet said, but she looks a lot older; maybe forty or so. She's got her three kids with her. Cops've got 'em back in the conference room the lawyers use, they come in to talk to their clients. Giving them tonic and something to eat, and they put a TV in there, too. Still, they got no place else to go so they're taking part in this "life experience," finding out what it's like to get arrested, put in jail. Great for "show-and-tell," their next foster parents ever get them back to school. One of them's eleven, other two're nine and six; Sylvester and Bruce and Demi.

'Mom's new boyfriend's also joining us tonight. Ronald Bennett, early twenties, looks like he had an IQ of maybe ninety, ninety-one, last time he was sober enough so that someone could sit him down and test him. His father most likely was his grandfather, and his mother's father too. The five of them, him and her and the kids, all of them living in a cabin up there in the State Forest.

'I'm getting all of this outta the report the Park Rangers leave off when they delivered this human trash. The Department of Natural Resources guys, the ones inna green four-wheel-drive pick-up trucks always bangin' around inna bushes, the State reservations, like they're chasin' rustlers or something.

'Their guess is these people've probably been living inna woods there since around the end of June. They are not really sure. One of them thinks that's the first time he recalls seeing them. But he didn't make out a report, not having any complaint to act on, any reason to do so. So there's really no way to find out, exactly. Probably don't know themselves, these people, how long they've actually been there. All you can do is ask them, knowin' if they do know they're gonna lie to you. It's their reflex by now, tellin' lies. And for Christ sake, why shouldn't they? What've they got left to lose?

'And anyway, doesn't matter what they tell you. All it takes is two weeks. Technically they're trespassing once they're living there more'n two consecutive weeks, fourteen days the same cabin, not paying their six bucks a day.

'Rangers say this isn't unusual, homeless people living in there, not this time of year. Rangers know they're there, see them all the time. They don't try to hide or stay out of sight. But generally they keep moving around. Cabin to cabin, three or four of them, pathetic dirty little groups, generally a woman and her kids.

Sometimes they'll have a rat-ass sorry excuse for a man along, like this one did, and after they've been there a while, they get so they know each other. They organize, set up a system. Rotate themselves around the camps. So none of them're ever staying more'n two weeks, the fourteen days, in any one of them. But all of 'em're always there, in one camp or the other. They're not *paying*, of course, but the way the Rangers look at it, if no one wants to rent the cabin, why not let someone who needs it but can't pay for it go ahead and use it? 'Stead of having it sit vacant anna homeless people out inna rain? Makes sense, 'less you figure the bums bein' in there means the people who *can* pay won't wanna come and use it.

'Anyway, you almost have to give them credit. They may be the castaways of our society, but they know the rules, and they do do their best to keep them. It's not enough, but they do try. The Rangers told the cops they generally don't bother them unless the squatters practically force them to. Like if the legitimate people payin' rent onna cabins start making complaints about their stuff bein' missin', they come back from swimming or fishing, out inna woods for the day. It's pretty hard to lock the cabins, no one can get in. Food gets stolen, which upsets them. Get even more pissed off if their cigarettes and beer disappear – although I'm not all that sure you're even technically supposed to *have* any beer when you're camping State property like that. Or if you can smoke inna woods; Smokey the Bear might not like it. But people do, I guess; pretty hard to stop them. Rangers probably do the same thing as with the squatters; only go in, enforce the rules, somebody gets drunk or something, makes an issue of it. Otherwise leave 'em alone.

'But anyway, stealing. If the squatters get to doing that, stuff starts being missing, then the Rangers wouldn't have any choice but to go in and throw 'em out and make 'em leave. But not unless they have to; that'd be what it amounts to. It's not something they like to do.

'Seven cabins out there. No heat, light or running water, anything; and people're s'posed to use the latrines. Never very far from one; four three-stall portable toilets and a trailer with four showers, two for men and two for women. But they don't go to all that trouble. They do it in the woods, wipe their asses off with leaves; it's easier. Messier, too, of course, and very unsanitary; little of that old *E. coli* bacteria in the drinking water; make a lot of people sick. But it's easier – easier rules.

'The only reason Rangers finally went in last night and arrested this group was because some legitimate workin' people who don't have any too much money of their own, spend onna two-week vacation that they earned by their hard work, they picked out one of those cabins back last spring, and reserved it. Now it's comin' up on their turn and they want it. They've been looking forward to it ever since they put their name on the list. So, they don't live that far away, and I guess they must've gotten wind of what was goin' on, homeless squattin' in the cabins. You're liable to get up here with all of your equipment and stuff, lookin' forward to your two weeks in the woods, and there's already someone sleepin' in your house. Never heard of Goldilocks but prolly wouldn't mind getting their paws on your porridge – even better, some of your beer.

'So yesterday, the husband of this family that reserved the cabin back in April, he goes to the trouble of taking a ride up there into the woods to make sure him and his family're actually going to get what they signed up for back then and've been looking forward to ever since, he starts his two weeks off with pay tomorrow. And what he finds roostin' in it is that woman and her three kids and her dirtbag boyfriend. And I guess it was perfectly obvious to him that they'd been in it a good long time, not just a week or so, and they had absolutely no intention of clearing out on his say-so when he shows up there with his wife and kids tomorrow.

'He didn't like it. I don't blame him. He got back in his car and drove back out to the office that they've got there and he bitched to the Park Rangers. Put it that way and they didn't have much choice. They saw the guy's point and arrested the squatters. Also hadda have someone go in and then clean the place up.

'Now, I feel sorry for everybody who's down on their luck, but feelin' sorry isn't my job. My job's to bail people charged with a crime. So I look at them, this woman and her scumbag of a man, charged with trespassin.' But the poor bastards've got no place to go, really. They're livin' on food stamps, bummin' cigarettes off each other. They're not denning up out in the woods because they're relivin' "Davy Crockett."

'These people're destitute. Kids're in rags. Mother's to blame for the squalor, of course, usin' her welfare, most likely includin' the kids' clothes-allotment checks, to buy booze for herself an' her fuckin' boyfriend, this Ronald shitbird. He's also on Essesseye. I didn't see much evidence he might be in danger of getting a job.

'This means I'm now in the same box as the Rangers were. I'm sittin' in the back room of the PD lockup around ten-thirty on a Saturday night and I'm a court clerk. What the hell am I supposed to do about this fuckin' mess? By that time I wasn't exactly myself anyway, either. What you'd say was on top of my game; I wouldn't've told you I was.'

'Why? What was the matter with you?' Diane said.

'Oh I don't want to bore you with all the details of it,' Merrion said. 'The day I'd been having yesterday up until then was bad enough without reliving it again today. We seem to be pretty well on our way here to having a nice day for ourselves, and I'd just as soon have it and leave yesterday back where it belongs: behind me.'

'Well, you will tell me, though, you know,' she said. 'I always tell you, when I've had a bad day. And you're the same way: You tell me. So you might as well just get started. And that way maybe by the time we get to Tanglewood and it's time to hear the Brahms, you'll have it off your chest and we can just enjoy ourselves.'

19

There was a fair amount of Sunday traffic westbound on the turnpike where it begins the gradual ascent from the valley of the Connecticut River into the foothills of the Berkshires, enough to keep all but the most intractable lane-weavers respectably in line, peaceably exceeding the posted speed limit by ten miles an hour, just under seventy-five. The heavy coupe was quiet and cool, going fast in a reasonably straight line, as it had been engineered and built to do, and Merrion had Diane's listening preference, WFCR-FM, Five College Public Radio, audible but just below normal conversational level – the announcer, displaying his erudition, was voluptuously saying '*Bayed*-rish *Schmet*-nah' to identify Bedrich Smetana as 'the Czech composer' of the selection just concluded, the overture to *The Bartered Bride*. Merrion frowned, repressing an urge to say 'Shaper.'

Diane misinterpreted both his expression and the reason for his silence. 'Come on, Amby,' she said, coaxing, 'tell me what's on your mind. That's what we do for each other.'

It was the kind of unpressured relationship she meant to have with him, one in which she intended that he would feel free to behave pretty much as he would have if he had been 'off-duty' with his friends and she had not been present. So far as she knew, he did, but she didn't have it quite right.

He believed he was making more of an effort to please her than he had made for any woman except Sunny Keller. When he was with her he was always on his better if not his best behavior; or intended to be, anyway. His effort was apparent to people who had known him a long time and seen them together. Dan Hilliard warned him he was 'getting somewhat pussy-whipped, you know.' He shrugged it off by saying that he supposed he was, 'a little, but Jesus, a man's gotta calm down some time, hasn't he? I mean, I may say that I'm not getting old here, but I have to admit I've been getting a little winded. Not tuckered out, no; a little *tired*. It hadda happen, sooner, later, I suppose; I been out raising hell a long time. Takes it out of a man.

'Plus which, even though you won't wanna, I think you gotta admit I could've made a much worse choice to slow down with, you know? I realize she's not your favorite person, and I can't say I blame you. But what happened between you and Mercy, and how much Diane had to do with it; well, that's something that Diane and I leave strictly out of what goes on between the two of us. I try not to talk much about you when I'm around her – not that she would mind because she's told me she likes you okay; she's got nothing against you.'

'Well, for Christ sake,' Hilliard said, 'how the hell could she, have something against me? I never did anything to *her*; she did something to *me*. I'm not saying she *set out* to do it, ruin my marriage, or that Mercy all by herself'd never've decided she'd had enough of me, but Diane had a lot to do with what finally happened – and *when* it happened, too, worst possible timing for me. Regardless of whether she meant to or not, everything she did had the result of turning my wife against me. I don't thank her for it.'

'Yeah, I know,' Merrion said. 'But I still do it, just the same, leave your name out of what we talk about. I just think it's better. And I never bring up Mercy's name and Diane doesn't either, much, although I know they're still very thick, very good friends themselves. And as a result, I think Diane and I get along pretty well. She's a real good woman. I like her. She's funny; she makes me laugh, and then she doesn't get mad when I do it. And she's not always trying all the time to reform me, or corner me, either, into getting married. Measuring me all the time.

'I had that happen to me once or twice, Mary Pat would get like that sometimes, and it made me nervous. I didn't like it. And've you got any idea how hard it is to *find* a woman our age who *won't* treat a man like that? Who'll just leave him alone and enjoy life, have fun? No, of course you don't. How could you? Your idea of a woman the right age is a thirty-six-C Wonderbra on a setta jugs that haven't even been inside a polling place yet; they don't turn eighteen until next year.

'I dunno, Danny; *you*, runnin' a *college*, all that firm young flesh bouncin' around all over the place? All that scary stuff we're always hearing all the time now, sex harassment cases? I worry, something might happen. Yeah, I realize you're an old hand, you could say, been doin' it quite a while now, and so far as we know, at least, you haven't been in trouble yet. But it worries me, Danny; I worry 'bout you all the time.'

He was right in his perception that Diane did not have matrimony in mind. She consciously tolerated more from him than she would have from a man she had been inspecting as a prospective husband. 'Gentleman friends are different from husbands,' she told Sally Davidson, a friend since their freshman year at Wisconsin. 'They don't have to meet the same requirements. The standards're nowhere near high. Be honest: the first thing to look for in husbands is whether they can make sure there'll be a roof over your head and you'll have enough to eat, be taken care of financially, if the day ever comes when they can't continue to provide those things. Walter was a very good husband. He left me very well-off, much better off than I ever dreamed of being. Even if something should happen to my practice, if I got sick and could no longer work, I'd be quite comfortable. So there's no pressure on me, no reason why I *need* to find another husband. Furthermore, I don't think I want one. Two weddings ought to be enough for a respectable woman. More'n that and you start to run the risk of looking *showy*, don't you think?'

'Always wanting to be the center of attention all the time,' Sally said. She laughed.

That delighted Diane; she deliberately tried to say things that would make Sally laugh because the sound she made reminded Diane of the noise made by agitated poultry. 'Uh huh, there they are again. I just heard a bunch of turkeys.' Sally laughed again. Diane said: 'You're not kidding me, you know. You've closed the gallery and started farming turkeys. Don't the neighbors complain?'

Sally laughed again. 'Not a *bunch* of turkeys,' she said.

'Well, what then?' Diane said. 'What are lots of turkeys? "Flocks," like lots of chickens? Crows? Doesn't seem as though they should be, being so much bigger and all.'

'"Gaggle,"' Sally said, clucking away as she said it. 'My father said a fair number of turkeys was a gaggle. Or was that for geese, and a "gobble," that was his collective noun for turkeys – I forget.'

Sally had stayed on to finish her degree in fine arts, marrying one of their classmates and supporting him by teaching drawing at Laydon Art School while he went to law school. Both becoming disappointed by the complete departure of excitement from their marriage, they had divorced after two years without rancor, thankful they had not had any children. With her lump-sum cash settlement, reimbursing her for his keep while in law school, she had purchased a small dark-green wooden building near the campus in Madison and opened a small art gallery: 'Atelier Sally.'

Four years later, while working toward her MFA, she had met and married an industrial designer older than she, also divorced, who'd returned to Madison for a doctorate. They had divorced after eight years; he had been unable to reject an offer of an executive vice presidency with an internationally known firm in San Francisco; she could not bear to sell her business, by then thriving.

Now she was 'semi-living with' an oral surgeon named Tony who was thirteen years younger than she was and did as he was told. She spent almost every night at his house except when he went to conventions, and during school vacations when his two daughters came to stay for visitation. During those periods she lived in her three-room apartment on the third floor of her gallery. 'Yes, I hadn't thought of it that way, but I think you're right. Tony's been after me again lately to get married. For the sake of his daughters, he says. He says even though I move out while they're here, they still know we're having sex.

'I'm sure they do. It doesn't seem to bother them. I don't really think it'd bother them if I *didn't* move out when they come here; it's his ex-wife who'd be bothered. Might haul him back into divorce court again – it's what she does instead of jogging. Six years they've been divorced, and *still* she's got her hooks in him. "So why get married?" I say. "What's the percentage?"

'"Well, but on that same reasoning, why not?" he says. "Then you wouldn't *have* to move out, even if she still was disturbed by the idea of us screwing. Then how she felt about it wouldn't make any difference."

'Well of course what I've wanted to say to that is that how his ex-wife feels about our activities doesn't make any difference *now*, but that wouldn't be true. *I* don't care how she feels but it *does* matter to Tony. So I haven't known what to tell him, but now I think I do. He's at a convention in Chicago this weekend. Wall-to-wall Porsches, I'm sure. You're the shrink; you explain it: what is it about dentists and Porsches? Suppose they feel safer and more comfortable driving if they're enclosed in small spaces, 'cause that's what they work in all day?'

'I don't know,' Diane said. 'Do we know what the gynecologists drive? That might give us some help here.'

She was rewarded with the gobbling sound again. Sally said: 'When he gets back I'm going to tell him what you said. If he starts in on me again, I'll tell him we can't because Diane says it's showy to get married three times, and I agree with her. Diane isn't getting married a third time; until she changes her mind, I'm not going to either. So there.'

'And if things *should* ever change,' Diane said, 'if I ever did decide I was looking for another husband, I don't honestly think Amby'd be someone I'd consider. I'm not sure, though, which seems to be a hallmark of the way I am with this guy – not being really sure. Now I know at first-hand what "ambivalence" is.

'I like him. I spend time with him. I don't mean we're always very sweet and kind, and loving, kitchy-koo. We disagree about things. We argue a lot. We quarrel. We're both adults. Sometimes you could say we even have fights. But they don't stop us from liking each other. He's caring and I find him interesting. I think he finds me interesting too.

'I like the things he likes to do – movies and going out to dinner. He takes me to Tanglewood in the summer, even though he'd probably rather go to a ballgame. He really does his best to be agreeable. I wouldn't think of asking him to take me dancing, but

I'm sure he would if I did. He probably wouldn't be very *good* at it – I doubt he had lessons when he was a kid. But he *is* good about doing things he isn't really all that keen about – because they're things that I want to do. He's considerate of me when we're in bed, too, very gentle. He knows how to show a girl a good time, so that part's all taken care of. I tell myself I don't know how lucky I am; a lot of women'd kill for this guy.

'But he's oh, I don't know; he's still sort of a lout. I'm not sure how to describe him to you. He isn't like any of the boyfriends either of us had, when we saw each other all the time.

'He's a court clerk. Clerk magistrate. It sounds like less than it is. He's got three assistants under him, and there're over thirty people in the office where they work. It's really a medium-sized legal business. File clerks, bookkeepers; and about a dozen or so more who work out of it, constables, deputy sheriffs and so forth. So what it amounts to is that he's sort of a cross between the CEO and CFO of the Canterbury District Court, and he reports to the presiding judge, who's the chairman of the board of this little company.

'But what he really is, is a pol. That's how he thinks of himself and how he got his official title, when he was still in his twenties. He's never changed. I suppose that's to his credit. He doesn't pretend to be anything he isn't. Or not to be anything he is. Been a pol all his life and makes no bones about it. He's good at it. The proof is that he got this prize. He isn't a pol because he's the boss; he's the boss because he's a good politician. He's proud of it.

'If you met him he'd remind you of those men you used to tell me that your uncles hung out with all the time down in Chicago. Smoking cigars and drinking whiskey; telling dirty jokes and laughing all the time, except when they were snarling; talking about all the mean and nasty, awful things that they were going to do to people. Or'd just finished doing, croaked someone good. Probably not people that you'd want to spend all of your time with; every so often you'd hear that one of them'd gone to jail. But still and all, fun to be around them; they were raffish. You could tell yourself you didn't have much choice. It was your family duty. "Crude as they are, they're also entertaining." That meant you could let yourself go and have a good time without feeling guilty about it. They made you laugh – that made them pretty nice guys, all in all, if you could overlook their rougher edges. "Rough but good-hearted." Amby's like that.

'He's certainly not someone you'd expect to find *me* consorting with now, at my age, and in my widow's weeds. Nor would I. When Walter was alive I thought he was rather vulgar. Poor dear Walter just adored him, so it seemed as though we had to have him every time we had a dinner party, and I used to have to remind myself I had some friends I always asked that Walter wasn't fond of, and he never complained. So if he wanted to have Amby, and the guy that Amby worked for, *with*, he would say, Dan Hilliard, well, grin and bear it.

'You would not believe this Hilliard. He's a college president now. It sounds like more than it is: just a dinky little community college. But that's what he does in *retirement*. He used to be chairman of Ways and Means in the state legislature. A very powerful man, and that's what he still looks like now. The way he moves, how he dresses and talks; he shows you he's used to power. He would've become Speaker one day, if he'd been able to control his sex drive. I'm best friends with his ex-wife, Marcy Hilliard. I'm as close to her now as I was to you. He thinks I'm the *reason* she's his ex-wife. All those chesty young bimbos that he ran around with had nothing to do with it. But the memory of power's still there; if you tried to imagine what the president of a tin-pot community college would look like; what he'd act like; what he'd *be* like; well, you would not imagine him.

'So anyway, there I would be, having the three of them over for dinner; Amby and Danny and Marcy; being the dutiful wife. Plus one or two other couples we know. I really don't know how I did it. I'd tell Walter to invite them, and sometimes they'd show up and Amby'd have a date with him, some woman who they'd both met in politics – either their husbands weren't interested in politics, or they didn't have husbands; they weren't really old enough yet. That was the explanation anyway; one didn't ask too many questions. And Marcy would be with Dan, and we'd all act like of course this new woman was with Amby. When it looked to me at least a couple times as though she could've been with either of them – and most likely had been, too, one time or another. We were never completely sure.

'I never knew what to expect from Dan or Amby, what either one of them would do or say, so I sort of just learned that the best thing to do where they were concerned was just go with the flow. Whatever they did was all right. And keep telling myself all the time they were there: "This's for Walter, this's for him. Walter's my husband and Walter's okay, and Walter likes these two guys. Walter thinks these two guys're *neat*. My dear husband is probably nuts."

'Then Walter died. And both of them were *so* kind, and *so* good to me, so, well, *sweet*, to me, really. I couldn't get over it. The last people I would've expected. And then, Amby, he knew all about this complicated investment trust that Walter had, that I didn't really know *anything* about: he was a big help to me there. And so, well, what can I tell you? One thing just led to another, as it usually does. You know how it can be. Suddenly there you are in bed with some man and you're not really certain who he is, or if you *were* sure that you wanted to be naked in bed with him. But then figured: Oh, what the heck, kinda late now. Might as well see what he's like.'

'That's how it was between David and me,' Sally said. 'That's just how I felt the first time I slept with him: "I'm very uncertain about this. Not sure at all that I want to be with him, I even like him enough." And then he turned out to be good in bed. Not that I had that much to compare him with, only two or three guys, but I certainly wasn't a virgin. He made my lights blink on and off. He said I was the best that he'd ever had – I *think* he was telling the truth. But we were healthy young horny kids; what the hell did we know? We thought great sex was all it took. Trouble was that it isn't, and that was all we had.'

'I think that's a good part of what I've got with Amby,' Diane said. 'But at my age, that may be enough. It's sort of like finding this great big dog around, when all I've ever been used to is cats; never had any interest in dogs. Never asked for a big friendly, clumsy dog, but now suddenly I seem to have one. And he gets into things all the time.'

She heard Sally laughing.

'Yes,' she said, 'well, all right. But that's what I'm saying: that may be why I keep him around. Sometimes I get impatient with him. Sometimes I'd like to *kick* him, give him a good swift kick in the pants and see if that might shape him up. But I don't, or I haven't so far, at least. And I must say most of the time I do *like* having him around. Even though I'm never really sure, from one moment to the next, what he's going to do, and sometimes it turns out to be something I don't like.'

'*Amby*,' she said, in the car again, 'come on now, let it out. That's what friends're for.'

'Okay,' Merrion said, exhaling heavily, 'sorry that I brought it up and it's against my better judgment, but okay, here we go. Yesterday morning, my day off, I start off by going to the office. This's because the judge and I, as I think I may've already told you, we've got one of our projects going on, only it's not going on exactly the way we had in mind when we started it, all right? So we've been getting a little concerned about it lately, some of the reports we've been getting.'

'This would be one of those jazz improvisations with the law you two enjoy so much?' Diane said. 'With absolutely no authority to do them?'

'Yeah,' Merrion said, 'a diversion. What we had in mind when we decide to do this one – and having in mind like you just said: we don't have to do them – was to see if maybe we can save this woman. She's basically retarded. Mildly, but retarded. If somebody doesn't at least *try* to do something for her, she's going to get so deeply involved in the criminal justice system – where we're both convinced she does *not* belong – that she's going to get hurt. And Lenny and I just decided we don't want that to happen.'

'Yes,' Diane said. 'This would be the woman that got involved with the evil gypsy. And I told you at the time I didn't see how you had any power to do this, and I thought it was a *rotten* idea. The woman who worked at the pizza parlor and she got herself mixed up in the swindle with the shrewd old lady and the bank account.'

'Well, the Burger Quik onna pike, but yeah,' Merrion said, 'that's the one I mean. And the judge and I know very well, going into this, what people would think of what we're trying to do here. We're not under the impression that the vast majority of people would necessarily *approve*, wholly – if they knew what we were doing, completely on our own. If someone was to tell them what it is we're doing and then ask them what they thought of it, a lot of them would then say: No. We're under no illusions here. We know what we're doing goes totally against the grain, *completely* against the grain, of the attitude that the majority of people today have toward the criminal justice system. What it should be doing and what direction it should be taking. What it ought to be accomplishing; the kind of results it should be getting, what we've got a right to expect.

'That's what they *think*, and that's the end of it. No matter what you tell them, you're not gonna change their mind. Inna popular mind now, the purpose of the justice system is *punishment*. "No, no more talkin' here. Get 'em offa the *streets*; we're *afraid* of them. Lock'em *up* an' then get rid of the *key*."

'We know this. People who're involved inna system like Judge Cavanaugh and I, who actually *know* how it works and what it does to people, we're not supposed to say: "Well, yeah, we hear what you're saying. But we still think what may be called for here, *in this particular case, involving this particular person*, is something slightly different. Instead of assuming that the best thing we can hope for is what you *know* you'll get, if we just let the system work the way it normally does, let's see if maybe we can *adapt* the system a little.

'"See, the system assumes that offenders're fungible; every one is the same. What works for one'll work for all the others. That's why the system doesn't always work very well. Offenders're people, and people *aren't* fungible. And Judge Cavanaugh and I think when you get a case like this one, what you oughta do is individualize the approach. See if something a little different might not work a little better."'

'You mean you've aborted another prosecution,' Diane said. 'That's what it amounts to, isn't it? Just sort of *noodged* it off to one side where the two of you can play with it for a while. With no idea at all what the outcome of this little game will be. That's why you're so bothered; something's gone wrong: just like I told you it would when you were so excited telling me a year ago about it. I knew right off it was dangerous. I told you. You wouldn't listen. You reacted the way you always do when you've asked me what I think about something you propose to do and I tell you "Not much." You got huffy and said: "Well, I'm the expert. You don't know what you're talking about."

'You did it *today*, not fifteen minutes ago, when I asked you a harmless question about how much hope some young kid has of ever getting help. I can't *imagine* why you're telling me about this poor woman again, this case that you've been screwing up, when we're trying to have a nice day.'

'Well, if that's what you want to call it,' he said, 'you could call it "screwing up," yeah. But if you're asking *me* for the term that *I* would use, I would say her case has been continued. Looks like just every other continuance we got, and there're dozens of 'em, literally, more'n you could shake a stick at. Technically that's what it is.

'But I would call it more of a suspension. We've continued the case, but we really don't expect . . . it isn't like we think there's going to come a day when this case's called for trial. No witnesses, for one thing; the old lady who's the victim was sharp but she wasn't in good health back when the incident occurred. And my understanding even *then* was that if much more'n another month went by before the matter came to trial, it'd be touch-and-go whether she could testify. And that was a year ago. So no, a trial in this case isn't out of the question; it's not very likely, is all. But we haven't screwed anything up.'

'You're gambling,' she said. 'She doesn't know it, but this woman that you're trying to control . . . what was her name again? I can almost see it in my mind.'

'LeClerc,' he said. 'Janet LeClerc.'

'Yes,' Diane said, 'Janet. Poor little Janet LeClerc, getting bossed around by you, who've got absolutely no authority to make her do anything, no case against her at all. But *she* doesn't *know* this, and wouldn't know what to do about it if she did – she isn't bright enough. The only reason that she's trying to do what you tell her is because you've tricked her, you and Cavanaugh. Lied to her, deceived her, conned her – just like the gypsy who was conning her and the other woman to cheat the sick old lady. The sheer moral arrogance: breath-taking.'

'Well, Jesus Christ, Diane,' he said, 'this's for her own good. It isn't like we're doing this because we want to *hurt* the woman, here, you know. That's what I'm trying to tell you. That this's something that we decided we would try to do, thought it would be a good thing for us to try to do, and now it turns out, like I said, that there was a catch.'

She overrode what he was saying before he could finish. 'No,' she said, shaking her head. 'Don't make it what it isn't. You're taking an awful chance here, and a stupid one to boot. The papers get ahold of this, they'll ruin both of you, you and the judge both. And you'll deserve it. You have no authority to do what you're doing and you know it. You've told me that yourself. Place the case on file, as you put it, and then make the defendant accountable to you. Set yourself up over this unfortunate creature as though you were her keeper. Rule her life.

'It's *okay*. The two of you've decided in your wisdom that what's legally available, the agencies and so forth, aren't effective enough for you. They don't do things the way you'd like to see them done. So the hell with the legislature and the laws and all of that stuff. You and Danny Hilliard; that's where this got started. The two of you spent so much time thinking up ways to manipulate people to get him elected, and then when he was elected, using every bit of power he could get, any way that he could get it, to do what you two wanted done, you lost sight of everything else.

'Something happened to you. You've got this disdain for the whole process. For you it's become a charade. Everything official's a show you put on for the dummies out front, to distract them while you do what was best for them. What the law says is not important; what matters is who's got the fix in. The law's what you *want* the law to be, and never mind what it says; *you'll* decide what matters.

'Who the *hell* do you think you are? Barging into her life, like you own it? Who on earth gave you that right?

'No one did. You've got no right. And in the second place, just what *are* you going to do, to punish her, if she doesn't do what you tell her, or does what you tell her not to do? Have you given *that* any thought? What are you going to do to her if she decides to call your bluff, get into trouble knowing you will help her? You create a dependency when you inveigle a person into reposing her trust entirely in you, *knowing* she's not bright or strong-willed – that's what enabled you to do it. A low-affect personality you've compelled to abdicate responsibility – that for all you know she might've been able to handle – for what happens in her life. Instead you make all her decisions. Amby, this is a dangerous game. Therapists who play it often find themselves wishing they hadn't.'

'I know it,' he said. 'That's what I've been trying to tell you. I really wish now that the judge and I hadn't taken this thing on. Basically what I had on my mind when I told her to come in and see me yesterday was what Sam Paradisio told me. I told you about him, my friend in federal Probation. He called me last week, said he's got information Janet's shacking up with this bank robber – most likely a stone killer, too, 'cept nobody's proved that yet. And *his* concern in my place would be that this vicious bastard'll decide it's time for Janet to disappear.

'Sammy thinks he's the type of guy who solves problems that way. When someone complicates his life, homicide is a thing he can do to simplify it. Sammy's afraid his guy'll kill this woman we've been trying to help.'

'Marvelous,' Diane said. 'Perfectly wonderful. He kills her and then of course there's an investigation, and that's when it comes out that she shouldn't even've been in the situation where someone could get at her to kill her. When she got in trouble, a year ago, she should've been sent to an institution, a supervised, structured, protected environment. Either getting punished or else getting some help. And that's where she *would've* been, if the judge and his clerk had enforced the laws. But instead they decided to take the law into their own hands. 'Cause they knew better.'

'Well, naturally this worries me,' Merrion said.

'I should think it would,' she said. 'It would certainly worry me.'

'But I talk to her,' Merrion said. 'I have a heart-to-heart talk with her, and I tell her to stay away from this guy, have nothing more to do with him, and she assures me she will not. She'll stay away from him.'

'Amby, you're a dear man,' Diane said, 'but how is she going to do that? How on earth . . . if the reason you don't want her seeing this man is that someone who knows him thinks that he might kill her, how do you think your Sad Sack of a woman's going to make him leave her alone? Isn't it more likely she'll set him off completely if she tries to do that? Provoke him into doing the very thing that you're afraid he'll do?'

'I don't think so,' he said. 'Or at least this morning, down at the station, I didn't think so. From what Sammy told me – and you understand this's confidential stuff that he's only telling it to me because he has to, do his job and I need him to, to do mine, so I shouldn't really be telling it to you – this's all very hush-hush and so forth.'

'Right,' she said. 'At least 'til they find the body. But once that happens, I think you'll find it becoming general knowledge fairly quickly.'

'Yeah,' he said. 'Well, I'm sorry I brought it up. But this squatter-lady last night, Linda Shepard, with her three kids named after movie stars and her dog-ass boyfriend, of course, to go with her and the kids: I had no idea at all *what* the hell to do with the five of them.

'So I say to Ev Whalen, I said: "Ev, 've you by any chance got any ideas here, what I can do with these folks? Assuming as I am of course that you don't want to keep 'em here, locked up in the jail overnight and tomorrow until Social Services opens up again Monday? I never run into anything like this before, where I couldn't release somebody when there wasn't any reason why they should be locked up, because they didn't have a place to go when they got out. Something you can do to just get these people under cover for a while, a day or two. You know?" And he just looks at me. Then he says: "*No*, not really, no. They don't pay me here to have ideas."

'"Well, you're a big help," I say to him. He gets kind of pissed off at me. "Hey," he says, "don't look at me. You've got these people here charged with a crime and you don't know what to do with them. I'm not in charge of homeless."'

'Well, he's right, isn't he?' Diane said. 'It isn't a crime to be homeless. The police aren't supposed to do anything except call the proper authorities when it looks like otherwise they might freeze to death, starve, or die without immediate medical care. Back when we were building the new station, I don't recall making any provision for that kind of problem, facilities for short-term family shelter.'

'We didn't,' Merrion said. 'There aren't any.'

'Well, doesn't that tell you something?' she said. 'The sergeant was right.'

'Well, that's what I'm trying to *tell* you, for Christ sake,' Merrion said. 'If you'd just . . . you know what it is about you people all the time, that gets on people's nerves? It's that it's always so important to you, matter what the situation is, to never get excited. Act like anything ever really mattered to you. You've always got to be completely in control. Always superior, cool, calm and collected, never upset about anything. That and the fact that you just *will not* listen. When somebody tries to tell you something that you may not understand, maybe don't know all the facts about – even though you always *think* you do; always sure of that – well, you got no time to hear it.

'You're always sort of lookin' down your nose all the time, at people like me who look to you as though we're gettin' so riled up and everything, like I guess I am right now; doing things you look at, and then sit back and say: "Well, *that's* a stupid idea." The reason you can do that and the reason we can't, and that we do what we do, is because we're *in* the situation. *We* don't have your luxury, being able to stand back and shake our heads and say: "No, I don't like the looks of that one. I won't take that case. That problem don't appeal to me. Not my specialty at all. Take it away. Find someone else. Don't leave it for me to get rid of."

'We're the people running the places where those people and problems you don't want get taken away *to*. We are the last fuckin' stop. After us there ain't nobody else. Every day we're in situations where it's pretty clear someone'd *better* do something, someone's *got* to do something, and *fast*, or something bad is gonna happen and we'll *all* be in the shit. The wheels'll come offa the world.

'To deal with this kind of problem day after day, we have to have *passion*. You can't do the hopeless work that we have to do every day without taking risks, and you can't take those risks without *passion*. Without *believing* . . . not that you're *better'n* anybody else, or that someone else couldn't do it better . . . just *believing* that you can do something that will make things better, because you *know* that you are *it*: there *is* nobody else. Behind you is the edge; people who get past you fall off. There is nobody behind you. Better, worse, almost as good: doesn't matter, they're not *there* – there *is* nobody else.

'I know I'm not saying this's right. I can't help it. I'm doing it like I always try to do everything else: the best way I can in the time that I got. That is the best I can do. Me and Danny're the kind of people who believe that people have to be taken care of; the work *has* to get done, any which way you can do it. And if this means you have to *get* excited, and *take* some risks, that's what you do: you get excited and you take them. So you can get something done. Because that is a *damned sight* more important than just making sure that you're not losing your cool all the time, and *that's* why we're doing what we are doing to poor little Janet LeClerc.'

She did not reply but reached her left hand forward and turned up the volume of the music. The traffic remained heavy but well-behaved all the way to the Route 20 exit in Lee and he took that west to Route 7 north up to West Street in Lenox. They talked about a movie that had cost more than 100 million dollars to produce and was doing almost no business, and how long it had been since there had been any new movie that either of them or anyone they knew had been eager to see.

The seats that Rachel had given to Diane for the concert were in the center of the shed twenty-two rows back from the stage, close enough so that they could see that the musicians in their shirt-sleeves in the orchestra were sweating at their work, and that both the piano soloist and the guest conductor had put on even more weight than their newspaper pictures and preview stories had suggested. The conductor had evidently taken no pains to moderate the volume and the tone of the orchestra so that the pianist's work on Brahms's second concerto would be presented to best advantage, but the soloist's work was perfunctory so that no real harm was done when the orchestra submerged it by playing too loudly.

At dinner at the Red Lion they were seated next to a table of six hosted by a red-faced man in his seventies who provided the entertainment for everyone at their end of the dining room by indignantly relating how he had lost a great deal of money at Saratoga the preceding day, more than he cared to say, betting on horses he had carefully selected from records he had spent many winter-evening hours systematically compiling and analyzing on his computer.

He said he believed the horses had 'lost on purpose. I'm convinced of it. It wasn't the jockeys – it was the goddamned horses. They were doing it deliberately. Stumbling, bearing out. All sorts of stupid mistakes. Any fool could've seen it. It was a conspiracy, a conspiracy of horses. They'd gotten together in the barns or in the paddock or someplace or other and cooked it up. Just to make me lose all my money and feel bad and look like a damned fool in front of my friends.'

Then leaving the track, chagrined and downhearted, 'what did I do but run into Dorothy,' one of his ex-wives, 'just what I needed.' She had insulted him loudly in front of a great many strangers. 'She disparaged my sexual prowess, can you believe it? Asked me if I could get it up "even once a year now." The nerve of the damned stupid cow. When the reason she gave all the papers when she left me eighteen years ago was that I wouldn't leave her alone for a minute. I couldn't deny it, it was true. But I should've anyway. I must've been out of my mind.' Diane and Merrion listened and then laughed along with all the other eavesdroppers, and the red-faced man beamed at all of them.

When they got back to the grey house with the yellow door on Pynchon Hill a little before 10:00, Diane invited him to come in for coffee, which in their code was her way of informing him that she would make love if he really wanted to, but he said he had a full day ahead of him and thought he better head home, and she was not displeased when they lightly kissed good-night.

20

On the job that Monday morning, Judge Leonard Cavanaugh at sixty-eight was the senior justice in terms of years of service in all the seventy-one district courts of Massachusetts, 'in my thirty-seventh year of presiding over routine arraignments and other foolishness.' Taking no pains to conceal the immensity of his accumulated weariness even on the morning of the first day of the week, sometime around 10:00 when he was 'good and ready,' he would take his place in his tall black chair behind the bench in Canterbury Courtroom 1. There as usual he would regard Merrion, whatever news that he came bearing, and the world and his own place in it the same way he had gradually come to view nearly everything: disapprovingly, usually powerlessly, with what he intended to convey as quiet resignation bordering on noble endurance.

'If you saw him you'd have no trouble believing he's the judge who's been sitting the longest. He looks it,' Merrion would say, when Cavanaugh's occasionally-puzzling, sometimes-intemperate behavior on the bench came up in conversation. 'He looks like it's been damned hard work, too; like it hasn't been easy for him. He doesn't look as though what he's been doing all these years's been a job that involved the use of his brain – which a lot of times, he'll tell you, it hasn't. "That's just the way they write it up." He looks like it's been heavy lifting. Hods of brick. Or he had to wear a wooden yoke, like they put on oxen, throw his shoulders into it all day, move a lot of heavy weights from here to over there. And then come in tomorrow and drag 'em back again. But he says he won't retire until they make him.'

Cavanaugh had been appointed an associate justice of the Canterbury District Court in 1958 at the age of twenty-nine. Like many lawyers he had in his student days begun to harbor an ambition to become a judge, seeing the judicial selection as official validation of professional distinction. But in 1958 his career history although bright was rather short. His student days were not yet six years behind him. His résumé recorded two years in the army's Judge Advocate General's corps – discharging the ROTC obligation he had undertaken both to avoid the draft during his years at the College of the Holy Cross and then at Fordham Law School and for the Army Reserve pay that helped to subsidize the education – and four years teaching commercial law at Northeastern Law School. He had also begun to lay the foundation of a money-making outside practice; he was Of Counsel to a seven-lawyer Boston firm specializing in corporate law. He had published two ponderous scholarly articles in the *Hastings Law Journal* on provisions proposed for inclusion in Article 9 of the Uniform Commercial Code: Secured Transactions. They had been cited favorably by two obscure commissions established by state legislatures considering the UCC; the Maryland commission had invited him to contribute two days of expert testimony, paying his expenses and a consulting fee of $1,200.

He had thus positioned himself nicely to make a lot of money when the day at last arrived – as it did, a decade later – when the UCC governed almost all business transacted in the United States; all he had to do was persist in the same fashion and his measured opinions about what the new law really meant and actually allowed 'would carry considerable weight,' a euphemism lawyers use for 'worth big money.'

In those days when he now and then allowed his mind to stray from productive thought and muse about his career, he usually thought ruefully about the time, energy and passion that his work was taking from his days and many nights, and wondered guiltily whether what was left for his wife, Julia, and their three young children was truly adequate. They were building a good life for themselves in their new Royal Barry Wills-designed colonial-reproduction home in Sudbury – the Maryland consulting fee had really boosted their hopes that soon they'd actually be able to afford it – and he was quite content with the progress he had made, reasonably sure that he had made full use of his time, intelligence, education and good fortune. His only real uneasiness came from his awareness that he was selfish, neglecting his family by working too hard, too many hours, as much because he revelled in it, knowing that he did it well, as because it was a dead-certain lock to lead to his advancement and the enrichment they would share. He soothed his conscience by telling himself that a young matron who insisted on a custom home in a wealthy suburb and started making Ivy League plans for her children before delivering them assumed the risk of spousal inattention.

So, unlike most prospective judges inwardly rejoicing but striving mightily to blush when their appointments are at last announced, Leonard Cavanaugh when singled out had not considered, wanted, sought or anticipated nomination to the bench in Canterbury, a town that he had never visited – or any other judicial nomination for that matter, that soon. Consequently he was not prepared to evaluate the development carefully, in order to decide calmly what he ought to do.

His surprise designation had been an exaction made upon a Republican governor by Cavanaugh's doting bachelor uncle, Andrew Finn, June Finn Cavanaugh's elder brother. He lived in West Boylston and owned and operated a Pontiac dealership in Worcester. He was short, five-six or so, barrel-chested and bow-legged; he had a seaman's rolling gait. 'People think that I look funny. My own dear sister says that, so I guess it must be true. I think it gives me an advantage when I deal with people. While they laugh at me, I take their money.'

In the late 1940s, like many other dealers in the car-starved, newly prosperous postwar United States, Finn without making any significant changes in the way that he'd been doing business since 1937 had suddenly started making lots of money, selling every new Pontiac and second-hand car he could get his hands on. He was delighted with the new prosperity, but he was not deluded by it into thinking that the Pontiac Division of GM had stumbled upon a secret formula that forever would sell cars to people who didn't need them.

Privately he believed that the product he was selling 'costs too much. It's nice to have, but isn't necessary. You can get along without what I have to sell. Your life won't be as easy or convenient, or anywhere near as much fun – but it'll be a helluva lot cheaper. The chief reason that most people have for buying cars, Pontiacs or any other kind, is because they want them and they're not thinking straight. Their ego's gotten the better of 'em. Otherwise they'd never take on the debt like most of 'em have to, buying something they don't actually *need*. Like they do milk and bread, a place to live, electric light and so forth.'

He believed further that the only way to sell more of his particular brand of the product than other dealers sold of theirs was by selling himself. He did that first by making himself well-known in the community where he had his place of business, and secondly by doing everything he could to ensure that its most prominent and respected leaders were seen smugly driving his product. 'So the other people seeing them get the fool idea that the way to get prestige – which I guess means looking like you've got a lot of power and money – is by giving me most of your money to get yourself a Pontiac.'

He had therefore commenced to use his new riches partly to support substantial and successful-looking candidates for national and statewide elective public office who shared at least some of his political views. They appreciated his generosity and happily agreed to be transported – and thus seen and photographed – during their campaigns and subsequent official duties arriving and departing from widely publicized events and riding in parades in highly polished red-and-white Bonneville convertibles, glossy ivory-on-russet Star Chief hardtop coupes and shiny dark blue Catalina sedans from Finn Pontiac in Worcester, 'The Friendliest Pontiac Dealer in Central Massachusetts – At Finn Pontiac, Everyone Wins.'

All of Uncle Andy's choices were Republicans. Except for his three congressmen, from the 1st, 10th and 12th districts, his state senator and his district attorney, most of his winners – three mayors, a governor's councillor, a secretary of state, one attorney general, and his biggest prize, this governor – had been electral long-shots coat-tailed into office during the

Eisenhower years, doomed on arrival by overwhelmingly Democratic voter-registration figures to be losers the first time they sought re-election without Ike at the top of the ticket, meaning: after 1956. When he wanted something from them that he thought his proven friendship entitled him to ask, Uncle Andy frankly and mercilessly reminded them that he had not become well-fixed in the automobile business 'by believing in the fuckin' Easter Bunny.'

Finn's governor – he called him that: 'My governor' – was no exception. He had told the candidate before he was elected that he would most likely win, but that his prospects for re-election would not be promising. After the election Finn did not shilly-shally. He made it clear to his governor early in his term that what he wanted in exchange for his support was 'a little present for my kid sister, June. She's married to a jerk, a failure, never liked the guy. But her son, my nephew Leonard, Lennie's a good kid. Worked his way through college, Holy Cross. Good school, everything I hear, at least, nothin' wrong with that; and then Fordham Law School. He's teaching law now, at Northeastern. And not only that, he's got some *sense*. Unlike most of the assholes you're gonna find you hafta appoint alla time. So I want you to make Lennie a judge. This'll make June happy, and she's a good kid herself, even if she does say that I'm funny-lookin'. It's the least I can do, my kid sister.'

The governor at first resisted, saying that although Leonard was obviously smart and able, he was too young. His nomination would become a cudgel that the governor's next opponent would use to 'beat me over the head with,' denouncing him for cronyism. Finn said that unless the governor somehow changed 'Boston Harbor into beer with a good creamy head, and make sure you get the credit, you know just as well as I do you're not going to have a chance against any Democrat two years from now. All he'll have to do to win is stay alive 'til the votes're cast and counted.'

Therefore, Finn told the governor, what was important was not whether the appointment of Finn's nephew to the bench would bring resounding cheers from the public. 'It's whether you remember who your friends've been, and do the right thing here, nominate my sister's fuckin' kid while you still got the power to do it, 'fore you get booted out on your ass. I don't ask for much from anybody, Eddie, even when I've got every right to ask. But this one I am asking; this one I want from you. So don't go making it hard for me here, all right now? He'll be an excellent judge, and his mother'll be proud of him. *I'll* even be happy – *I'll* be the one who's grateful to you, 'stead of you being grateful to me. All you got to do here is just get him appointed, while the appointing's good. It's simple; even you can do it without breaking a sweat. And it's not only something I want from you here; it's also the right thing to do. God'll reward you in heaven.'

When the governor came back and said his legal counsel told him that the Canterbury District Court judgeship was the best that he could do 'without having them get up a mob to tar and feather me,' Finn believed him and told his favorite nephew that if he knew what was good for him he'd 'grab it while I still got it within reach. I dunno how many other sponsors you've got that hang around with guys who want to be governor, or what *their* chances are, but Eddie is the very first one I've ever had, in my life – and I been tryin' a long time, at no small expense to me. Which is why I'm as sorry for my own sake as I am for you to tell you it don't look to me as though he's gonna *last*, you know? Looks like a one-termer, I'm sorry to say, once Ike retires and plays golf full-time. And I can't promise you I'm gonna have a replacement for him real soon. It doesn't look good at all.'

Leonard was filled with consternation. Until then a registered but politically inactive Democrat, he had in his four years of teaching acquired three close friends among the faculty. Two of them were slightly older; the third was nearly twice his age. He asked them for advice. They told him unanimously, earnestly and truly, that they were prescinding from their pronounced Democratic loyalties as they advised him not to accept the nomination. They said that while they fully understood that the temptation to embark upon a judicial career at such an early age was very strong, if he was as smart as they knew him to be he would resist it. They said that while his considerable intellectual powers, maturity of judgment and evenness of disposition satisfied them that his youthfulness was irrelevant to the issue of fitness and judicial temperament, his possession of those qualities at so early an age established him as 'a bright and rising star.'

They said it would be only a matter of time, and not very much of that, either, before someone tapped him 'as a non-political prestige appointment. Every politician needs one now and then, to take the stink off the cat and dogs he has to appoint – so the public doesn't gag on the payoffs.' They predicted confidently that patience would be rewarded within ten years 'at the outside' with a nomination either to an appellate court, 'where by rights you ought to be, with your writing ability and all,' or, failing that, 'an important position in Washington.

'What you've got to do is wait,' they said. 'Don't be in a hurry. Then when you die, you'll be famous, which's really the only way to be dead. Everyone says so. You won't have all that good a view of it yourself, but everyone who's still alive and knew you will sincerely wish you were also still alive, so you could be around to see it. "What a turnout, my God. What a shame Lennie's dead. Can't you just see him, if he could be here and see *this*, am I right? What a kick he'd get out of it."

'And these people won't be just *saying* they're sorry; they'll really *mean* it. Even if they did think sometimes while you were still alive you seemed pretty full of yourself. Once you're safely dead, they'll stop thinking like that. They'll be in *awe*, you were so famous. How many people get that kind of tribute, huh? How many people can actually say that, that people were actually sorry when they died.

'Except your family, maybe. When they see the big turn-out and hear all the fine speeches, they'll be so proud of what you were when you were alive they'll almost be *glad* you're finally dead. Now without having your big ego around, your grieving heirs'll finally get some real enjoyment out of your career. Even if they do find out later you weren't carrying quite as much insurance as they would've thought you might've, man of your prominence.'

Leonard demurred. He said it seemed to him that judicial service while still fairly young would enhance his résumé and therefore – as his hair began to turn grey, as theirs had, and he had to start buying pants in larger sizes and pills to treat various ailments, as they had told him they had been obliged to – mandate regular promotions to higher and higher courts, 'like they had to do with Ben Cardozo, until you finally get to the level where the only higher court is the one where Moses sits.'

His colleagues said that would probably be so if the appointment were at least to the *superior* court, extended as a prophylactic early coronation – preferably by a Democratic governor compelled to make and thus to disinfect a couple other highly unsanitary nominations, 'maybe a whole string of out-and-out stinkers. Then your precocity would count, and in your favor. Then you'd be getting the nod because you're a legal Mozart, you're so bright, and just like it didn't matter he was only four when he was writing symphonies and stuff because the music was so good, it wouldn't matter with you that you're such a young lawyer, because you're such a *brilliant* young lawyer.

'*But*,' they said, 'since it's to the district court and it's being offered by a practicing Republican, it'll be the kiss of death. If you take this thing, you'll regret it the rest of your life.' They said it would be deemed, correctly, a patronage bonbon, paying off his uncle. 'So although your precocity still *counts*, now it counts *against* you. Now you're not getting the job even *though* you're young, *because* you're so bright; you're getting this job because of uncle's pull, *even though* you're still wet behind the ears.'

They said acceptance of the Canterbury nomination would forever nullify Leonard's potential usefulness as a high-class nominee. 'Doesn't matter, he's your uncle; that he's family and he loves you very much. It's a hard world. You let somebody pimp you, fact he's kinfolk doesn't matter; still makes you a common whore.'

Leonard agonized. He said: 'But look, it's not that easy. If my uncle hadn't gone ahead and done this so I got this nomination, that'd be a different thing. Then of course I'd wait; I'd have to. I'd have no choice. I'd be just another meek and blushing virgin, hoping to be kissed some day – if not by an ugly governor looking for an appellate judge or a senator with warts but a prime federal vacancy, then at least by a handsome prince dangling a powerhouse deanship. But now that Andy's gone and done this, other people *know*, how shameless I am. No more playing hard to get: "Oh gee, I don't know. I'm not really sure." They *know* Andy didn't do this because what I really wanted was a

Raleigh ten-speed bike; I really do want a judgeship. Trouble is the Canterbury slot was all the governor had in stock the day that Andy went shopping.

'Well, too bad for me, that's how it turned out, but it *is* the way it turned out. I want to be a judge, and I've got this bird in hand. Not the best judgeship in the world, no, not one I ever wanted. But still, an honest-to-God judgeship. One more than most guys who want a robe 're ever going to see or have, mine to accept or reject.

'What if I turn it down and never see another one? It could happen. Say No, and bide my time, wait for a better one. People aren't stupid; they'll know what I'm up to. They'll say: "This young man does not suffer from lack of self-esteem."

'Suppose they then decide: "Okay, so that's how he feels, little prick: wants to start off at the top. Holdin' out for First Circuit Court of Appeals. Fine. Best of luck to him." And then I never get another one. What do I do then? I'll regret it all my life.'

His friends said that was the sort of anguish that generally made it much easier to give sound advice than to take it. Julia said his friends were right and he should heed what they told him, even if it did mean that Uncle Andy, who'd been known to be vindictive, would be very angry at him.

'Forget about him, Len,' she said. 'You can't make your decisions on the basis of how you think Andy Finn's going to react. It's your life, not his; you're the one who has to live it – even though he'd like to run it. There's a way to tell him nicely. You don't have to come right out and *say* it, that it's a third-rate judgeship and it isn't good enough for you – even though that *is* the reason. And if Andy still gets mad, so he never tries to get you another nomination, well, that's the way it goes.'

Julia also said that she was prepared to face the probability – Leonard had seen no reason to mention it to his friends – that if he turned down Canterbury Andy would probably cut him out of his will. 'My mother and I're the only kinfolk he's got. This isn't small change that we're talking here; this's serious money. Outside of what he spends on politicians, Andy's very frugal; he's really got no vices. He could pay off our mortgage tomorrow out of petty cash.

'Well, that'd also be too bad, if he disinherited you,' Julia said, 'although I doubt he would. Because as you say, who else's he got? And if he leaves it all to your mother, you'll get it anyway – just have to wait a little longer.'

'Unless my father spends it first,' Cavanaugh had said.

'She won't let him,' Julia said. 'She's got him well in hand. Look, this's being silly. Even if you never get another offer, you'll be better off. We'll have each other, our life together; you'll be *happy*, knowing what you did was right.'

Leonard had reluctantly rejected everybody's counsel and called his Uncle Andy. Choking back his misgivings, he expressed deep gratitude for the appointment, and with much fanfare became Associate Justice Leonard B. Cavanaugh. In the *Transcript* Freddie Dillinger called him 'the Boy Judge of Canterbury,' reapplying the label every time Cavanaugh was in the news until his own retirement, thirty-two years later.

The faculty colleague twice Cavanaugh's age in 1961 took a leave of absence to become special counsel to the US Senate Commerce Committee investigating price-fixing in the sugar industry. Not wanting to leave Boston and her friends, his wife opposed the move but went along when he made it, becoming sad and bitter. Three years later when his leave was about to expire, he notified the law school that with his wife terminally ill in Georgetown Hospital he could not return to Boston. A year and a half after that, widowed and then newly remarried to Sen. Harriet Fathergood, D., Ore., he resigned at seventy-two as chief counsel to become 'rich in my old age; now that I've found out what they mean by "better late than never."' He became chief of legislative liaison for Coldhammer Industries, an international conglomerate concentrating on the manufacture of packaged foods – the fourth-largest consumer of raw sugar in the world.

The second of Leonard's colleagues went on to become general counsel to the New England Council, serving eight years until appointment as Under Secretary of Commerce and later his selection as head of the Latin American Affairs desk of the World Bank.

The third became an associate justice of the superior court. Later he gracefully declined a federal district court judgeship, confident that he would be elevated – as he was, six years later – to associate justice of the Supreme Judicial Court of Massachusetts. In that capacity he wrote a majority opinion breaking new ground in the resolution of conflicts between the laws of privacy and those of creditor's rights. Soon after the SJC decision, his book-length treatise on effective legal protection of privacy in the computer age was published, immediately becoming the bible of the telecommunications industry. Relinquishing his SJC seat at sixty-five, five years before mandatory retirement age, he became Of Counsel to Magruder, Magrid and Locksley, P.C., at 1334 Connecticut Ave., N.W., Washington counsel to MarSat Corp., a leading manufacturer of satellite communications equipment.

From time to time Leonard found their names in the newspaper, or inadvertently saw them interviewed on television. He mentioned those sightings when he encountered the SJC judge at Massachusetts bench and bar events. He supposed his efforts not to sound wistful were not entirely successful, but even though his old friend was invariably warm and cordial, and tried hard to pretend that one judgeship was much like any other, they found as the years went by that they had less and less to talk about. Many times in the course of many evenings, in conversations that seemed to him, in the comfort of good food and wine, to merit some reflection on his long career in Canterbury; each time what he said, after shaking his head once, was: 'Well, it's simple, isn't it? I made a big mistake.'

'Then everybody's supposed to feel sorry for him,' Merrion perceived, and reported to Hilliard, back when Cavanaugh at fifty-four was dourly observing his 25th anniversary on the bench, Reagan was approaching the end of his first term as president, and the old dancing school on the second floor above High Street in Holyoke was still available for private conversations late in the evening. 'And I did, I used to feel sorry for him, I first went in there, heard him say something like that. One of his old pals'd gotten some great new job and his name in the paper, and Lennie was all depressed.'

Merrion snuffled, thickening his voice into the *On the Waterfront* pug's clot: '"I tell yuh, Charlie, I couldah been a contendah."

Well maybe – but then again, maybe not. What if that's all nothin' but the good old stuff? Maybe if he'd turned it down, never become the Boy Judge, famous from border to border – border of Holyoke, border of Ludlow – maybe he never would've gotten another bite of the apple.

'Maybe . . . ah yes, that sad word *maybe*. He wants is you to tell him you think if he *hadn't* taken Canterbury, that instead of everybody saying now that some guy he used to teach with has a mortal lock on the next Supreme Court vacancy, it'd be him; it'd be Lenny. He *waits* for you to do that, say that, grease up his ego for him – like a dog waits for you to finish doing whatever you're doing to that prime-rib bone with those pathetic little teeth of yours, and give it to *him*, who *needs* it; can *handle* it; *knows* what to do with the thing. Well, boo-fuckin'-hoo; you don't feel sorry for him and so you don't say it. And then when you don't suck it up and lie to him, tell him what he wants to hear, he sulks for the rest of the day.

'He's got no idea how he tempts me when he does that. He's got a question? I got a question as well. Does he know why his job was created? Arthur and young Roy Carnes did it for their pal, Judge Spring. Lennie was the jayvee team. The reason for his job was to free up Chassy's afternoons. This was years before I got my job, but according to Larry Lane courthouse people used to feel sorry for Lennie then. Chass treated him like a servant. Made it very clear to him and everybody else the only use that he had for him was to do the scut-work, clean up all the messy cases he left behind when he snuck out at lunchtime to play the market.

'Havin' heard what the guy hadda take, now and then I used to feel sorry for him. But now I don't, anymore. It's not a bad job that he's got. It's taken good care of him, all of these years. He didn't come from big money – although until a few years ago he expected to have a lot some day; he thought he was gonna come into a bundle, this uncle of his went to Jesus. Then Unk died and someone else got it. Too bad for Lennie. But just the same, since before he turned thirty he's never had to worry once about a paycheck. No one's gonna lay him off. If he gets hurt on the job, or him and the beautiful Julia get sick, the doctor bills're paid. And when the day finally comes, he decides he'll retire, state pays him a pension and covers her, too, long as they're still alive.

'You know what? He's got a real beef about that, lifetime-security deal. He hasta *contribute* to his pension fund, deductions from his paycheck. "Federal judges don't have to do that," is what he says. "While they're still sitting they get all they earn, after the taxes, of course, and then they retire on full pay."

'Okay, juicy deal, but so what? He isn't a federal judge. Most of the rest of us aren't either, and we have to contribute don't we? I said that to him once, he's pissin' and moanin', there isn't much left of his check by the time he gets it: "Hey," I say, like I just thought of it, "*I* have to contribute to *my* pension plan. What're *you* gripin' about?"

'I almost had him. He almost said what he would've regretted; had it right onna tip of his tongue. "You're not a judge; you're a clerk."

'He could see me thinkin': "Come on, come on, say it." He caught himself just barely in time. If he says it then I'm gonna say it: "And I'm not a federal judge, either, your Honor. *No* one in this courthouse is." He din't say annathin'.

'So okay, maybe he's right: His job's not the best deal inna world. But still, you come right down to it, it isn't a *bad* deal at all. Twenny-five years ago, he knew, didn't he, what it was he could expect? Sure he did. It was all laid out plain for anyone to see, even way back then. He wasn't stupid, was he? He didn't first learn to read *after* he took the job; he isn't saying *that*, now. So he knew what the deal was, and *he accepted it*. Hell is he bitchin' 'bout now?'

On Monday morning at 10:10 Cavanaugh buzzed Merrion in his office and Merrion without needing to answer the phone picked up his portfolio and his brown-enameled metal box of files, the paint worn away from the lower back corners by his thumbs over the years, and headed up the private east corridor to the door to the hallway that led from Cavanaugh's chambers directly onto the bench in Courtroom 1.

The eight rows of benches behind the bar enclosure were overcrowded, usual on Monday mornings, filled with the weekend yield of State and local police activities in the Four Towns and on the turnpike. Most of the people had been in the courthouse since it opened at 8:30. They were restless. There was a lot of traffic back and forth through the brass-studded, coarse-grained, green-leather-padded swinging doors that opened into the main corridor and foyer outside the rear of the courtroom.

Those who were defendants had reported to the probation office in the basement of the courthouse for intake processing. Many had accompanied defendants, in order to provide moral support, additional bail money or legal advice – or because they were small children of defendants who had no one to babysit and would have risked additional charges of child neglect if the kids had been left alone and a DSS caseworker dropped by to make one of the periodic unannounced supervisory visits required by regulations. The children cried and squirmed and fidgeted and dropped their plastic nursing bottles on the floor, so that their mothers had to grope around under the benches and pick up the bottles and wipe the non-spill mouthpieces on their sleeves. They slapped the children and hissed at them angrily, several of them in Spanish. Then they looked around anxiously in case someone official might have seen and recognized them as they hit their children, and had taken out a spiral notebook to write down details of their unfitness as parents.

There were thirty-four matters on the criminal list. Judge Cavanaugh was seated behind his desk. He cupped his hand over the microphone on the bench that fed the tape machines recording all public utterances at every session, and leaned forward so that his face and Merrion's were barely a foot apart. 'Hate to tell you this, Judge,' Merrion said in a low voice as soon as he had reached the clerk's desk, one step down in front of the judge's, and turned his back on the crowd, 'but as soon's you get through arraignments today, we got four domestic violence cases onna list I gotta ask you to hear. We got these two women comin' in, new, but the usual thing – say they want restraining orders, husbands battin' them around. And there's a *guy* today, too, little change of pace – Ellsworth Ryan's his name – wants one. I told him he hadda come in frontah you.

'I dunno what to make of this bird. He looks like he should be able to take care of himself all right, but he says she's always telling him he's got to sleep *some*time. That's all she says, nothin' else, but that's enough for him: he thinks that means that when he sleeps she's gonna get him. So, what do I know, huh? Ellsworth says he hasn't been able to get any rest. He's afraid to go to sleep. Says he's afraid if he does, his devoted wife Sheila, she gets a few too many drinks in her, she'll come and stick a bread knife in him while he's got his eyes closed and he can't defend himself.

'And then we got the Federico matter comin' up again, for your listening pleasure. Johnny Federico. His wife's name is Tishie, you recall. You oughta be pretty close to being on a first-name basis now. You put the paper on him, week ago, and far as we know, until yesterday he's okay, left her alone. Now she says she wants him violated. Had him picked up on the restraining order early last night. Cops held him overnight in the lock-up up the Pond, meditate upon his sins.

'She says he come home Sunday evening; he'd been to the ballgame, Sons of Italy from Holyoke hired a bus, took it down to Fenway Park, an' he had too much beer to drink. Must've got it onna bus. That horse-piss they sell at the ball-park now hasn't got enough kick in it give a young nun half a charge. Got back to Holyoke all fulla beer, and he decided: "Well, this'd be an *awful* good time, go back home and violate the order." Which he *knows* perfectly well he's not supposed to do, since you told him to stay the hell away from her and leave her alone. But he went there and started whalin' the shit outta her again. Neighbors called the cops but he either heard 'em comin' or else he got tired and left – when they got there he was gone. She makes out a complaint though, so they're onna lookout for him, and they grab him six this morning, someone spots him sleepin' it off inna park. So that's what *he* did last night. And if he tries to tell you that it wasn't him, ask him who it was; we gotta find him, 'cause he's mean. Her face's all bruised. He kicked her a couple times too, for good measure. Good thing for her he's not a soccer fan, he does this after a baseball game.

'Says she wants him put away this time. Ludlow, Lancaster; anywhere they got a bed – anna lock onna door he can't open from the inside. Not changin' her mind this time, backin' down from this man any more.'

'Uh huh,' the judge said, 'well, we'll see about that, won't we? She has before, I recall.'

'Twice,' Merrion said. 'Twice she's done it to us. Come in and said "This time he's got to go." And then when you tell him he's gonna do six months, she's starts to scream and holler, "No, no, you can't do that. How'm I gonna pay the rent, you put my Johnny in jail? Never see my man again."'

'Ain't love grand,' Cavanaugh said.

Four of the matters on the docket that Monday were bail revocations; the defendants had attracted attention to themselves by doing something sufficiently annoying to interest cops. The cops instead of immediately arresting them had detained them long enough to type their names into the computer. There without surprise they had found there was no need to make a new arrest of the annoying person, necessitating another paperwork-hassle to take him out of circulation; he'd already failed to show up to answer charges lodged against him by other cops on one or more previous occasions. Therefore he could be rousted on the basis of the existing paperwork and taken off the street.

Three were hearings on probation-office motions for orders to commit probationers who had exceeded the considerable patience of their supervising officers, usually first by not bothering to show up for their appointments and then making it worse by disappearing when the probation officers went looking for them.

One case was a State Police turnpike speeding ticket charging the defendant with operating his motor vehicle in excess of 90 miles an hour, but not with operating so that the lives and safety of the public might have been endangered. This meant that after an exhilarating pursuit with whooping siren and flashing multi-colored strobe-lights through early-morning thin or non-existent other traffic the cop had arrested him for doing triple digits but otherwise driving competently, and that the driver once pulled-over had been sober and polite, with all his papers in good order, and had not insulted the cop's intelligence by trying to lie his way out of it. The cop had given him a break, so now the guy was going to see whether being sober and polite – maybe even contrite – in the courtroom would get him found Not Guilty, thus rescuing him from a fine, surfine and costs that would set him back just under $400, and guarantee a surcharge on his car insurance every year for the next five that would make him feel like he was bleeding from the ears each time he paid it. If the cop showed up to give evidence, the gambit wouldn't work, but neither Merrion nor Cavanaugh ever blamed a guy for trying.

There were four drunk-and-disorderlies, two of them combined with charges of making an affray, the arrests having been made in bars in Hampton Pond and Cumberland after the managers carried out threats to call the cops if noisily quarrelsome patrons refused to quiet down. There were two cases of driving under the influence of alcohol. There were three narcotics cases, two of them the people Merrion had met in the Canterbury lock-up Saturday night.

'On the Rosenbaum matter,' Merrion whispered to Cavanaugh, 'the Rosenbaum and also the Fernandez matter, Leah Rosenbaum and Felipe Fernandez, his goes with hers. She's the barmaid up at Cannonball's. You can see her sittin' back there in the third row, over to the left beside the wall, young broad with big tits and a long blondish ponytail, see her over there?'

'Sleeveless red blouse, tight white jeans?' Cavanaugh whispered. 'She the one that just stood up there?'

Merrion turned enough so that he could sneak a glance over his right shoulder. Leah Rosenbaum had inflated her chest and was tucking her shirt in, looking toward the bench; she saw him peeking. She smirked. He felt his neck getting red. 'That's her,' he said, turning back. Cavanaugh concealed a smile from everyone in the courtroom but Merrion. Merrion tried to ignore him. 'Fernandez's the movie-star dude with the black hairdo sittin' next to her there. He's her foot-soldier, go-fer, delivery boy.

'Cocaine charge. Fairly heavy one, about thirty-five grams, time you get through. State Police matter. We've had a call from Mister Cohen's office this morning, and they say he'll be representing Miss Rosenbaum, and maybe – well, make that "probably" – Fernandez as well. But he's engaged before Judge Segal in the probate court up in Northampton this morning, will be all day, and so he asks at least that both these matters be held for second call, so they can get somebody here to enter pleas for them. But preferably just go off the calendar, put over for a week, if that would be okay with you here, until he's had a chance to have a talk with the DA. Let it go off the list 'til a week from Tuesday. See whether they can work something out, maybe avoid a trial here.'

'Geoffrey Cohen's handling drug cases now?' Cavanaugh murmured, raising his right eyebrow. 'My my. Music of the Renaissance and crack cocaine. "Tonight my friends, for you we have: concerti by Corelli and Scarlatti, and a gram or two." Quite a combination. Branching out a bit, is he?'

'Looks like,' Merrion said. 'Hard even for him, I guess, as much as he must be makin,' all of those domestic cases, resist the kind of retainers dopers offer these days.'

'Continuance look all right to you on it?' Cavanaugh whispered. 'Look, I know if Geoffrey's on it, oughta be okay, his word's usually good. But you hadda close look at these two birds: think there's any chance they'll flee?'

'Aww, I'd doubt it,' Merrion said. 'You always got that chance, of course, maybe the bastards bolt. But they had since Saddy-night to run and here they are today. I'd say "No, I don't think so." They look all right to me.'

Cavanaugh nodded. 'Off the list then,' he said. 'Give Geoff his week, which as usual with him's gonna come to about nine days. Like they say about his divorces: when he represents the wife, he thinks her half a hundred grand oughta work out to about seventy-five thousand bucks. But what the hell; like you say: anything to avoid a trial here.'

Other cases were: one larceny by check; one grand larceny, motor vehicle; one petty larceny, shoplifting; one failure to heed a Stop sign, Canterbury; four attaching plates, uninsured and unregistered motor vehicle; and eleven cruelty to animals. 'Guy had fourteen dogs penned up in his garage, Judge,' Merrion said. 'Hadda car in there with them too. Old Packard, hadn't driven it for years. Nobody knows why he had them, the dogs. They weren't pedigreed, reported stolen or anything. Seemed all right, they talked to him; perfectly-normal old guy. Told the cops all it was was he liked dogs. But he hadn't been feeding them, giving them any water, which seemed kind of strange, guy who liked dogs as much as he did. Or letting them go out, either. Dog officer said the garage was filthy, stunk like hell – overpowering. That was why the neighbors finally complained. But then it took her over a week to get out there. By then three dogs were dead. Those animal officers: male or female, doesn't make any difference. They all scream and holler how they want the job, and then when they get it none of 'em give a good shit about doin' it. Don't care about the animals at all. All they want's to get off the clock and have no one over them, no one they gotta report to. Then they can goof off the whole live-long day, and no one even misses them. They're always saying how overworked they are, and the towns don't give them enough money. But why should we? They do such a lousy job. But so anyway, we got the old guy. Dunno what the hell you do with him. He's too old to put him in jail. Fine him? Just come out of his Social Security; that's all he's got to live on. He doesn't have any dough.'

'Oh shit, I dunno,' Cavanaugh said. 'Put it down at the end of the list. Maybe by then I'll think of something. Or he'll do the right thing and die.'

There were three breaking and entering charges, one of them Ottawa Johnson's. There were the two trespassing cases brought against the woman and the man arrested by the Rangers in the Canterbury State Forest. 'That'd be the Shepard and the Bennett matters, Judge,' Merrion whispered.

'Trespassing,' Cavanaugh murmured, even though he still had his hand over the mouthpiece of the microphone. 'How the hell can somebody trespass in a State Forest? Thought that was the whole idea the damned thing: Nobody owns it; we all do. Supposed to be open to the public.'

'Yeah, but with some limitations, your honor,' Merrion whispered. 'Two weeks, six bucks a night. Your time limit's up, you go home. This woman, she's the Shepard, here, and her three kids and her shit-bum boyfriend, he's the Bennett, Robert,' checking papers, 'no, sorry, *Ronald*, Ronald Bennett: all of them, the five of them, what they've been doin's they've been been livin' there since June. Best anyone can tell. They all look like it's been at *least* since June, they hadda bath. Mean to tell you, these folks *stink*. Rangers go up there, gonna bring 'em all in? Before they could do it, take 'em out the cabin, they hadda go and get a buncha cardboard boxes, liquor cases, you know? Down at Wheeler's package store out on Route Five there. And then go back and help her pack up all her household goods and all their clothes and stuff. Pots and pans, everything. Blankets, and these thick quilts and pillows, filthy dirty, all of them – all kinds of shit. Whalen told me Rangers said they hadda put the rubber gloves on; God knows what was livin' in that shit. Campin' wasn't what you had these people doin' there; what they were up to was settling-in the place. Gettin' themselves all dug in to stay a while, ready for winter, looked like. Like they're woodchucks diggin' a hole for themselves in your lawn. See 'em doing that, they're not plannin' on leavin' right off – anytime soon anyway.'

'Holy shit,' the judge said. 'It's hard to believe, you know, Amby? As long as I been here, hearing this stuff, day after day after day, I get so I think: "I heard all of it, now. I must've heard all of it now." And then something else comes along. It gets so you just can't *believe* half of it, your mind just rejects it, it boggles, the things people dream up to do.'

'Yeah,' Merrion said, 'and I got to tell you, where this one's concerned, the camping's not all of it either. This Shepard matter, it's more complicated'n you might think. From what little I could get outta her there, other night up at the station, she may be tied up with our little friend Janet LeClerc.'

The defendants and their families and the witnesses and cops stood and sat and talked and sighed and shrugged. Some of them made faces of disgust. They asked each other questions and ignored those who asked them, and when they were jabbed or poked and asked again, looked annoyed and said that they did not know either. Information about what time it was was popularly sought and repeatedly given. The people moved around with their shoulders hunched as though there might be snipers watching the room. They went from row to row and bench to bench and crowded in, getting angry looks from those they displaced to sit beside people they wanted to talk to; they talked urgently in low voices, glancing furtively every so often up toward the judge's bench, as though plotting against him and Merrion and making sure they would recognize them when the time came to harm them. They took careful note of everyone inside the bar enclosure. People came and went constantly outside the rail. They got up abruptly as though they had just remembered something that they should have done before they entered the courtroom and went out hurriedly through the swinging doors into the main foyer. Right away, as though they had been waiting for the chance, people came from the main foyer through the swinging doors into the courtroom and looked around at the seats vacated by the people who had just gone out. Finding none they liked, the new arrivals leaned against the wall and put their hands in their pockets and sighed.

Inside the bar enclosure were the prosecutors, cops and lawyers both, and probation officers, two of them plus a third one who came and went with papers. Two lawyers from the Mass. Defenders huddled together, riffling absently through their files. They talked about the Red Sox and how erratically they'd been playing, considering what a bunch of overpaid rich bums they were.

'For Christ sake, how?' Cavanaugh said. 'How the hell can that all be connected with her? Didn't you have her in? Tell her to stay away from undesirable companions? Didn't you talk to her like we agreed and you were going to there?'

'I had her in,' Merrion whispered urgently. 'I had her in Saturday morning. I gave her a good talking-to. I told her she hadda, well, *you* know what I told her. I told her what we said I hadda tell her and make sure she understood. I told her to stop doing what she was doing. I told her to cut it the hell out.'

'Well, what did she tell you she'd do then?' Cavanaugh whispered. 'Tell me what she said to you. Did she tell you she'd do it or not?'

'I'm *trying* to,' Merrion said. 'That's what I'm trying to do here, for Christ sake. If you'd just let me, here, damnit, let me get the words out of my mouth.'

'Well then, *do* it,' Cavanaugh said. 'Tell me what she said to you.'

'Look,' Merrion said, 'what I did here, I think the best way that we go about this's just let this case of trespassing here that we've got, let it come forward, it's eleventh on the list, and appoint the Mass. Defenders on this, and continue it a week. Because this Shepard woman doesn't know and neither does her boyfriend, this Bennett character either; neither one of them has any inkling about the connection that I think we've got here with Janet. Because I don't think Janet's talked to them since I had her in here Saturday. They wouldn't've had any way of knowin' what I said to her then, unless she did. They didn't have no phone or anything, livin' up at the campground. In the State Forest's what I'm saying.

'And then, what I already did this morning was, I called Sammy Paradise and I asked him, is he free for lunch today. And he said yes, he is, he could do that if we wanted, and so what I thought the best thing we all could do here is if we just get together here, you know, and see if we can get something worked out. Have some sandwiches sent in and we just have them in your office after we recess at One today. Put our heads together here and think about this thing, talk the whole thing over and see what we have got here. What we ought to do. That sound good to you?'

'If I tell you there are times when I wish I had never been born,' Cavanaugh said, 'and you believe that I'm sincere, I really truly mean it, is there any way you know of they can make it retroactive? Anyway you ever heard of it?'

'Well,' Merrion said, becoming more offended, 'all I was just trying to do here was . . .' when there was a sound almost like someone with a chest-cold coughing during a lull in conversation and then someone with a deep baritone voice who was outside in the main corridor made a loud noise combining a scream of pain with a roar of outrage that stopped all the conversations in mouths-open progress in the courtroom. Everyone turned to look at the green-padded swinging doors. Both of them swung open very slowly, tumbling a short, stocky woman with swarthy skin and short black hair, wearing a red, white and green flowered blouse and a short red skirt and red high-heeled shoes off-balance backwards perhaps two feet in the air into the room and then hard onto the floor, so that she landed crashing seated on her large buttocks with her arms outstretched and her feet in the red shoes sticking up in the air. She wore eyeglasses with red frames and her face was contorted, and she had a small silver automatic pistol in her right hand, pointed at the ceiling.

21

Cavanaugh left hurriedly right after the gunshot. Following several minutes later, Merrion found him, sitting at his desk, still wearing his robe, his hands loosely clenched on the blotter, looking like a man recovering slowly from a sharp, unexpected blow.

'He looked the way he looked the day he got the million-dollar letter from his Uncle Andy,' Merrion said. He and Hilliard were having a late dinner that evening at Grey Hills. 'One that said he's giving up the lonely bachelor's life. The old boy – over ninety now, still going strong – has got a bale of money, and Lennie's more'n just his favorite nephew; since his mother died he's the old guy's only living blood-relative. Ever since I'd first known him, Lennie's been genuflecting to him on the phone at least once a week, goin' down to see him at least once a year. He pretended Red Sox spring training was the reason for the trip, but it wasn't. It really was to keep in touch with Andy. And it was sincere; he wanted his uncle's money, sure, but that wasn't all of it; he really does like the old gent. Even now, Lennie still calls, and goes to see him every year. But you can see the thrill is gone; *mostly* he was doing it for the money. Before he got that letter, when he was going down there to take a view, his uncle, try to check his vital signs without him noticin', you could see he was lookin' forward to the mission. Now it's obviously a chore, but he still hasta do it; otherwise Andy'll *know* he never really meant it, all those other years, when he thought he was gonna get alla dough. Andy gets that idea, he's liable, cut out Lennie entirely. Can't have that happenin'.

'Although my guess is it already did. The uncle made a good

part his bundle selling *used cars*, for Christ sake. You know he had to've seen right through Lennie. Probably tickled him. No matter where the Red Sox moved their training camp – Sarasota, Winter Haven, now Fort Myers – Lennie always got to Clearwater, where Andy lives. "I always make it a point to spend a few days with him, long's I'm in the area." There was one stretch when the Sox trained in Arizona, Scottsdale, I think it was, so that's where Lennie took Julia on their winter trip. But they still got to Clearwater to visit his uncle. I guess Clearwater was in the Arizona area those years.

'The rest of the year he's callin' every week at least, listenin' for wheezin', any shortness of breath, hopin' maybe to hear about a few chest pains; wishin' there's a way to take his pulse and get a urine sample by phone, fifteen hundred miles away. For *years* he's been doin' this, and all the time he's thinkin': "How much longer can he *last*? This *must* be the year I get rich."

'Then when Andy's eighty-eight, he sends his happy tidings, not by phone, by letter. He's gettin' married. He's fallen in love with this forty-year-old broad – "Elaine the fair," Lennie calls her – who comes in every day and does his cookin' and his cleaning. Lennie thinks she probably performs other services of a more personal nature that a lonesome old bachelor'd enjoy, "like makin' sure he gets his *cookies* every now and then." Lennie's still very bitter. The letter said they were gonna get married that spring, asked Lennie to be his best man. That day Lennie looked like someone dropped an anvil on his head, and that's exactly how he looked today.'

The judge had stood up at 10:43 and hurriedly retreated from the bench into his office, moving clumsily but quickly, making quite a bit of noise and plainly not caring that he did so, as though he had been suddenly awakened from a sound sleep by a strong smell of smoke and discovered the building on fire around him.

'By then it seemed like a good ten, eleven minutes've gone by after we first heard the shot,' Merrion said. 'I know it couldn't possibly've been that long, really, probably less'n a minute, but it seemed like a lot longer. We'd just been *suspended* by that sound, like a thunderclap so *close* the lightning had to've hit your house, right beside it anyway. It froze you. Everything just *stopped*, including time. My thinking did, anyway; I went into a *trance*; sittin' there totally *stunned*. Lennie came back to life first.

'By then I was facin' the courtroom. I'd been talkin' to him when the gun went off. That made me turn around. Now I hear this second sound behind me. I turn around again. It was Lennie, *jumpin'* out his chair, hightailing it off the bench. They must teach you that in Judge School. "A gun goes off in your courtroom, fuck everybody else; save your own ass first. Run like hell and find yourself a place where you can hide until it's over." No hero medal for Lennie.

'When he jumped up the chair banged on the Lucite pad it rolls around on. Everyone inna courtroom starts duckin' down. "Another shot" – hadn't done that with the first bang; they didn't have the time. Lennie woke me up. "*Hey*, maybe I should get outta here. There could be more shooting anna next one might hit *me*.' But I didn't; I just stood there. I was frozen.

'Then time started up again. It was like I hadda catch up on what'd gone on right in front of me. "Let's see now I was looking at him when the gun went off so my back was to the lobby doors. I turned around and this woman came *flying* through them, hit the floor, ka-*boom*.' Merrion clapped his hands. 'Like that. She was lucky that was all the distance her husband got when he picked her up and threw her – as we later find out he did – after she shot him. Pissed him off somewhat, I guess. He'd gotten another foot or so on her, gone to a little more club, say, a seven iron, no question she would've banged her head on the end of one of those solid oak benches. Would've at least knocked her out, given all of us more time to figure out what she had in her hand and what we should do about it. Because as it was I didn't realize at first what it was.

'Then I think: "My God, that woman's got a *gun*. That's a *fuckin'* gun, her hand. She could shoot someone. That must be the sound I just heard."'

'They never could fool you, Amby,' Hilliard said, digging into a large mound of chicken salad on a bed of lettuce, flanked by three small bunches of fat tawny grapes. Merrion had sent his steak back as over-cooked and was waiting for a plate of chicken salad.

'Not a chance,' Merrion said. 'I know what's goin' on, 'specially when I've got my eyes open and it's happening right in front of me. So I grab the phone on the desk and punch in 0, and, wonder of wonders, *someone was actually there, and picked up, on the other end of the line.*

'Inna courthouse, this is *astonishing*, much more unusal'n having someone shoot a gun off. But there she was; Corinne was *on the case*. I could hear her breathing. I couldn't believe it. She must've also been in a state of suspended animation. That's the only way, account for her being there and picking up and breathing loud enough for me to hear her. The switchboard's right there inna cubicle right off the main foyer; shot must've been even louder – she may even've seen the shot fired. But I'm givin' her the news just the same, I am makin' it *official*; I say "Corinne, calla cops up in here quick, annie EMTs too. Got a *shootin'* on our hands here."

'And she said: "*Huh*? Who *is* this?" Like she's gonna hafta think about this; decide whether she oughta do it. Not someone in authority, she won't. I say: "Never mind who it is, Kreen, this's Amby." I'm not making any more sense'n absolutely necessary either. "Calla fuckin' cops annie EMTs, for Christ sake. You wanna just do that for me?" And I guess she decides I am okay. She said, "All right, I'll do that right now."

'Then I put the phone down and it dawns on me we gotta whole buncha cops right inna courtroom. I see one of the locals, some case onna list, is usin' his handheld radio. It's not close to lunch yet, so I assume he's not orderin' pizza from Domino's; he's callinah station to tell 'em what happened. So I didn't need to get Corinne involved in this at all. That's when I realized I'd been in some kind of funk. Just standin' there, lookin' stupid, and the woman on the floor with the gun starts rollin' over now, on her right side. She's checking to see if she's hurt. Had all the wind knocked out of her, most likely, but now she's startin' to think about possibly getting up on her feet. Still got the gun in her hand, so if gettin' off another shot or two is something she'd like to do now, that is a viable option. Assuming it's still got some bullets in it, but one shot's all we've heard so the chances are it has – all the equipment she needs.

'At this point I notice two Staties who're also most likely also in for cases have come to their senses. Prolly only a few seconds've gone by since Sheila came flyin' in the courtroom, just *seemed* like a year or two. The two Staties're sittin' onna left inna rowah chairs just inside the railing. Now they're outta their chairs, bustin' their way through the people inna room. And they *land* on her like a big pair of bears and take the gun away from her. Those guys knew what they were doing. One of them held his gun on her, stomped on her right wrist on the floor so she couldn't move it, and the other one bent over and pried the gun out of it.

'You can see that I am finding it very hard to do serious thinking at this point, even though as a general rule I'm not bad at it. But I'm gradually gettin' the hang of it back. I first see her start scrabblin' around onna floor, I don't like the looks of it. I know there is some reason why I do not want this woman getting up from off the floor with that pistol in her hand. Now I'm figuring it out. She may be a perfectly nice lady, neighbors all speak well of her; but she also may decide to shoot me, and I don't want that to happen. I am now very clear on that.

'What I'm *not* clear on yet is what I should do so that won't happen. And I *know* that if you're not an expert, trained to handle the kind of dangerous situation you're in, you shouldn't do *anything*. Otherwise you're liable to do more harm'n good. Everybody knows that. Moving an accident victim: they've been tellin' us since grade school that unless you're an expert, never move an injured person 'less you gotta: if you don't he'll burn to death, or there'll be an explosion that'll blow him all to bits. You move him when you don't hafta and you paralyze his back. He will sue your sorry ass to Jerusalem, and you'll wish you'd stood back and watched the fucking bastard die. Maybe tossed a match or something. So, knowing that, I just stood there, deer-in-the-headlights.'

The waiter, an unfamiliar elderly man, delivered Merrion's chicken salad. Hilliard ordered a second glass of the house red. Merrion said: 'No, make that a bottle. I'll need at least two glasses to go with this.' The waiter nodded gravely and departed.

'I hope he can get back to us by midnight,' Hilliard said.

'He's in the same condition I was in this morning,' Merrion said. 'The way I felt after the gun went off.'

'Yeah, but yours was apparently temporary,' Hilliard said. 'His looks permanent.'

'It's a very strange feeling,' Merrion said. 'Out-of-the-body experience. Other people're waking up. Running around all over the place, whooping an' hollering, bloody murder, which for at least a while it looked like. Murder was certainly what the crazy bitch had in mind when she took the pistol out and let her husband have one in the brisket in the lobby.

'We're not used to this kind of event. On a Monday in the courthouse the routine is: we do the best we can, knowing it won't be enough. See if we can maybe make some sense out of what is basically an impossible situation *every* day, come right down to it, but especially impossible on Mondays. It looks like business as usual, and it is, but nothing actually makes any sense. The reason that it *looks* like it's making sense is that by now we're all so used to it being that way, chaos doesn't scare us anymore. We *oughta* be beside ourselves, frantic, but we're not; we're used to it. What we'd all been doing there was coping, same as always, when she opened fire.

'"We never hear that sound here, that we've all just heard." This's what I told the investigating cop. And this's an example, what I mean, about things not making any sense in that place. We had all kinds of cops, State and local both, right there in the courtroom with us when we heard the shot. But for some reason I'm not clear on it seems this disqualifies them from taking charge of the investigation. Being there makes them *witnesses*, apparently an entirely different kind of being.

'It's like the cops've got union rules for this kind of situation. Jurisdictional rules like the unions at the light company and the gas company and the phone company and the water department guys've got, who can open manholes, climb up poles, work on pipes and cables. Every crime's a new manhole to be opened. In this case, now I think of it, the crime that was committed was trying to open a hole in a man.'

'Jesus,' Hilliard said.

'Aw come on, I hadda hard day,' Merrion said. 'Apparently the rule is that nobody can have more'n one job on any given crime. Either you can *be* there, so you *see* it and *hear* it, in which case you are a *witness*; or else when the crime took place, you were *not* there; you got *called* to the scene. Then you *respond*, and *investigate*.

Take statements; collect evidence; put it into nice little plastic baggies with dainty little white labels you put your initials on. Make arrests and tidy up. So that then when this particular crime comes up to be replayed in *court*, you will be a *cop*, okay? Have to get all of this straight.

'It's kind of confusing until everybody finally gets their parts assigned. By now there's quite a few more people've come to join those of us who attended the shooting. It's becoming sort of a weird party-atmosphere now. People're all milling around all over the place, shoving each other, uttering warlike cries – "Get *outta* the *way*; I *tole* you to *move*' – so as you can imagine this takes a while. Have to make absolutely sure everybody's happy, no one's nose is out of joint, before we can get to work on this. "Now, now, Billy, play nice. Can't have any pouting. I promise if you do real good as a policeman this time, you can be a witness in the next one, okay Billy?"

'The strange thing is that if no woman'd come flying through the air through the swinging doors backwards with a pistol in her hand, I don't think any one of us in that room who heard the noise when the gun went off would've been able to say: "Well, that was a shot that I just heard. Someone just shot a gun off." It didn't sound like what we think of as a gunshot.

'I was thinking about that,' Merrion said. 'After the EMTs'd come and the doors're open now, I could see them out there in the foyer, attending to the victim. I recognize him from the jacket he had on. It was like a short white Eisenhower jacket, had his name on it in red over the pocket, "Ellie." Like the one John Casey made me wear at Valley Ford, I was a kid. He was this Ellsworth Ryan guy I just met, the way my office. Talked to him maybe two-three minutes, no more'n that. I think at this point I am practically the only guy in the courthouse who *has* met him at all, and knows who he is. Except for his loving wife Sheila, of course, his *devoted* wife, Sheila, who's just finished shootin' at him. That is what made him really mad at her, made him pick her up off her feet and fling her like a shotput bass-ackwards through the doors.

'He is one strong dude, this guy. Just been shot in the right side of his tummy, it looks like, and he can still do something like that. Pick up a hundred-and-fifty, hundred-and-sixty-pound woman and pitch her about nine-ten feet through a pairah swingin' doors. Of course the reason that he could was that he *was* strong and he was *not* disabled. It was a popgun twenny-two, not a grown-up gun like a forty-five or a nine millimeter, lot of stopping power. One them hits you, I don't care how strong you are, you would not feel like picking anybody up and flinging them through the air. You'd be feeling like somebody threw a bowling ball into your guts at couple hundred miles an hour.'

'And then also there was the fact that the slug didn't actually *hit* his stomach. What it hit was his call-book, and that took the impact, or a lot of it at least. Cops told me later when emergency room people got his shirt entirely off him, they confirmed what the EMTs'd told them to expect: the bullet never penetrated. Never broke the skin. Just an enormous bruise, I guess, so he's a lucky bastard, too, addition to being a strong one.'

The waiter reappeared soundlessly with a bottle of red wine, already opened, and two more glasses. He set the glasses down and poured the wine. Hilliard said 'Thank you.' The waiter nodded. Then he drifted away.

'I don't like it when they bring the bottle already open,' Merrion said. 'I always suspect it isn't a fresh bottle; that they're refilling old Côtes du Rhone bottles over and over out in the kitchen from a vat of cheap jug-wine from Outer Mongolia, someplace like that. Wine made from yak fat; there's a tank of the stuff in the basement.'

'I doubt it,' Hilliard said. 'I think in this case the explanation is the waiter's too feeble to get the cork out at the table, so he has some muscular pot-walloper out back use the corkscrew for him.'

'I think I saw the guy in a movie once,' Merrion said, 'a small supporting part. I forget the name of it. Boris Karloff was the star.'

'Now this would be your victim,' Hilliard said, 'or is it our waiter we're still talking about?'

'Could be either one, I suppose,' Merrion said. 'Except I don't think Karloff was also in the movie where I might've seen the victim. In that one I think the star was Peter Boyle.

'Anyway, today he was being an appliance repairman: refrigerators, washing machines, dryers, and when he came into the courthouse he forgot to leave his call-book in his truck. Good thing for him. It's one of those thick black leather ledger-things they make out of punched forms, two hard covers and a couple of steel bolts. He carries it hooked over his belt, back cover inside his pants.

'His adoring wife, Sheila, thinks when he keeps those appointments he meets lots of horny young housewives that he's bangin' all the time. For all I know, he is. So she gave him the idea first chance she gets she's gonna stick a blade in him. He got sick of it and told her he was comin' in today to file a complaint against her, for saying that, and ask for a restraining order, and so she decided it'd be fun if she also came in today and plugged him. Dovetailed very nicely.

'If he hadn't had that book in his pants he would've had a hole in a bad place, lower abdomen. You gotta take a bullet, you do not want it there. The bullet mushroomed in the book instead of in his bowels. EMTs told me later alla time he's inna hospital, they're making sure there's no traumatic internal damage, his beeper's goin' off like there's a prison break in progress. His office is goin' nuts, all these housewives callin': "Where the hell is Ellsworth? He's supposed to be here now. I can't get my washing done, he fixes my machine."

'The gun was a Jennings J-22, chrome-plated pistol. I never heard that particular make, and by now I thought I'd had, most of them. Dave Fisher, State Police lieutenant, first responded when the call went out for someone to take charge at the scene, he says it's a six-shot, throwaway, fifty-buck cheapie. I am fascinated.

'Sunny said to me one night after we finished going at it, I got up to get a beer or something, must've turned the ballgame on, my way back to bed, and she got annoyed. There we were, we'd just made love, and now I went to get a beer and turned the ballgame on. She said: "Men do not know what to do with women, really. That's where all the problems start. You like us for the sex part, like that fine. But after you've gotten laid, *immediately*, you start getting bored.

'I think it's because we don't have any moving parts, like machinery does. Planes and cars and boats and guns. No pieces that you can take apart and look at carefully, clean and oil, and then put back together, or maybe modify. See if they won't run a little better now, faster, smoother, quieter. Guys like things you can *adjust*. "Now, we fit 'er back together, snick-snick, click-click, *snap*, like *that*, *right*. Okay now, start 'er up. See how much better she runs now? Told you that'd do it."

'And she slapped her hands together, like she was dusting them off. "You can't do that with us. Women aren't *adjustable*. Well, okay, you understand that; you're resigned to it. There's nothing you can do to improve performance. It's *okay*; this's something you can *live* with. The standard way we work is pretty good. It just doesn't take a lot of *attention*, so you don't see any need to give us any more than absolutely necessary. Like: "dinner and drinks oughta do it." Low *maintenance*. Once you've used us there's nothing that needs doing for a while. "Might's well have a beer and catch a little of the ballgame." That's why you *irritate* us so much. You start *out* interested, sure, *very* interested, but then when it's all over, boom, on to something else."

'Maybe she was right,' Merrion said. 'Cars: she's got me here, I guess. Golf: keep my clubs clean, of course. Not much else I can do to make them work better; the punk results I get're my fault. I dunno dogshit about guns. Never paid any attention to them. I don't hunt. I don't shoot at targets. I was never inna service and I'm not a cop. I've never any reason to become interested in guns. But now I'm *fascinated* by what Fisher's telling me about this fuckin' pistol and how people use their guns.

'"Saturday-night special: for non-professionals. We're not talkin' robbers here, drug enforcers, nutbags here; guys who shoot up grade schools, fast-food joints, disgruntled postal workers. They want something heavier, more capacity. This item's made for your impulsive casual shooter, doesn't expect to use it very often; perfect for important family occasions. Although it is kind of unusual to hold the celebration at the courthouse, in the morning.

'"Non-profit shootings're generally night-work. Daytimes most people work, haven't got time to shoot people. Nights and weekends're when the amateurs take care of that stuff – that's when they've got the time. Passion-shootings, spousal matter like this, most people prefer the privacy of the home, they can relax and be themselves. Those who want an audience, though, maybe the third party to a three-cornered romance, like bars and the parking lots outside them – much more popular'n government buildings.

'"But *hey*, there're no flies on *this* little lady – I'm not sayin' that. Wherever you happen to be when your fuse finally burns all the way down, this cheap handgun is a perfectly proper utensil. Most women use knives; shooters're generally men. But that's okay; nothing in the rules says women can't shoot people too.

'"And contrary to what you may've heard, shooting isn't difficult, doesn't require great physical strength. Women can easily do it. You're a woman with a point to make, all you got to do is point one of these things at the person you're mad at, in this case your husband but could be your boyfriend, or your husband's girlfriend or boyfriend – any number of possible combinations. And *you* make the choice, you cute little dickens, because *you* are the one with the sidearm. Simple to use. Load it and point it and pull the trigger; that's all there is to it. If it's your lucky day, or night, and it isn't his, or hers, the gun goes off like it's supposed to and then there's this loud noise, like in the movies, and the bullet comes out the front of the barrel.

'"This is good news when that happens, good news for you anyway. Bad news for the guy in front of you, unless you didn't aim right. But good news for you because it means the weapon didn't jam. When you get a jam it gives the guy you aimed at time to express his feelings, how he felt when he saw you point a firearm at him and then pull the trigger. A lot of people take this sort of thing very personally, and quite often if the gun misfires they will take the opportunity to share their feelings with the person with the gun. If they don't have their own gun with them, they do this by taking his away from him and then beating the shit out of him. As the lady now leaving with the officers can tell you, this also applies when the shooter is a woman.

'"So if the gun went off and you're the guy holding it, that is good news. And if the bullet hits the guy you're angry at, well, that's even better news. It means the gun didn't blow up in your hand, which these cheapies sometimes do. That could spoil your plans for the rest of the evening. But it's bad news for the person you're mad at because he has a hole in him, probably not exactly what he had in mind when he set out for *his* night on the town. But what the hell, life's full of disappointments.

'"You now get the hell out of wherever it is that you both were when you shot him and dump the gun down the first storm-drain you come across. Then you start praying either that you *killed* the bastard, clean, so he doesn't get himself patched up through some goddamn miracle of modern medicine, and then get his *own* gun and start looking for *you*; or else that you *didn't* kill him, even though you did your best to, because now you are filled with remorse. Because that way you may've lost yourself a friend but you won't be facing a murder charge."

'Anyway,' Merrion said, 'I said to him that even though everybody who was in that room heard that sound the shot made, I doubt very much that any one of us could've said for sure afterwards that it was a shot we'd heard, unless someone told us or we saw the gun. I think we've all seen and heard so many shots on television, movies, we've reached the point now when we see someone with a gun, we expect it to go off and someone to get shot. Not really get hurt, of course; it's only TV, and we know that. And if the gun doesn't go off, we're kind of disappointed.

'But as a result, the opposite is also true. When we *haven't* seen a gun, then when we hear something that sounds like a gunshot we don't think it is. We think it's just "a loud noise" we can't identify. Or maybe "it's a backfire." We explain it away. But cars don't backfire anymore, but we still say they do. That way what we heard *wasn't* a shot, we've said it was something else. For us to know for a fact there was a shot, someone has to show us a gun.

'And Dave said to me that he thought that's very likely, may explain a lot of things that he's run into that sort of puzzle you at first, taking witness statements. "They're not telling you what they actually heard. They're telling you what they think they *must've* heard."

'So the two of us're having this fine philosophical discussion there about the gun that the two uniform Staties took away from our Sheila, and that's when I remember old Lennie's hunkered down out in back. "Excuse me," I say to Dave, my new friend,

"I better go see how the judge is doin' here. Handlin' all this excitement."

'So,' Merrion said, 'I went in there and I told him all the things that'd been happening out front while he's been in his hiding place and everybody else who was there except Sheila Ryan and her husband was touching themselves all over to make sure they didn't have any holes in them spurting blood or anything. He looked me right in the eye and said to me that he thought "it would be best if we didn't try to go back out there today and try to pick up where we left off before all of this happened and disrupted everything.

'"Just go back out there and make a general announcement," this's what he said to me, patient and serene as he could be, as though *I'm* the one who panicked out there, ran for his fucking life, and *he's* the one who's calming *me* down now, in the sanctuary. "Just tell them that everything that was on the calendar for today, for Monday's continued until tomorrow. Tomorrow at ten A.M. Tuesday." In case I might've gotten the idea that because of all the uproar Tuesday might've been *moved*, not come after Monday this week. Maybe after Friday instead.

'I felt like saying: "Judge, you *jumped* clear into Tuesday a while ago, you're already there. We'd better tell people to 'come back on Wednesday.' Give them time to catch up to you. You to fall back to the rest of us."

'But I didn't. I said: "Judge, does that mean you want me to call up Sammy Paradise and cancel that meeting, too, what I was telling you about out there before the gun went off?" Because now I don't know what the hell the man wants. I don't think he's too sure of it either.

'He looks at me like I have lost my mind. "Of course not, Amby, for God's sake. What gave you that idea? But what you can do, after you've gone out and told everybody court'll be suspended for the rest of the day here, you can use the time we'll have before this Federal Probation, Paradisio guy arrives to fill me in on him. So I'll have some idea of what I should expect from him."'

'"That I can do," I said,' Merrion said. 'What the hell kindah grapes're these? They made of iron or something? Fuckin' things look like they're rusty.'

'They're Furmint grapes,' Hilliard said. 'They originally came from Tokay, in Hungary. Years ago, I'm on the Hill, we had some hearings on a health bill to declare alcoholism a disease, make insurers pay to treat it. We had the usual parade of experts come in, and one of them got all wound up on what the stew-bums like to drink. They just love white Tokay wine, it's so sweet and strong. And cheap. I'd never had the wine and I made up my mind to avoid it. Don't want people thinkin' I'm a wino, too, along with my other hobby. I find the grapes cloying, don't eat them.'

'Jesus H. Christ,' Merrion said, 'is there anything you don't know?'

'Well, twenty years ago,' Hilliard said, 'I would've said: "No, not a hell of a lot." But more recent events've made me question my confidence on that point. I'd have to say now: "Quite a lot. Much more than I ever thought. And I didn't like learning it at all."'

22

'It's a very common tendency,' Sammy Paradise said earnestly over the submarine sandwiches from the Canterbury Village Sub Shop. 'Many of them do it.' Merrion had asked the court officer to get two Cokes, two Pepsis and two ginger ales as well. Paradisio when he saw the beverage selection said he 'should've asked for a can of canned iced tea, but it's probably too late for that now.'

Merrion had predicted it. 'Sammy's very serious about what he eats,' he told Cavanaugh. 'Whatever we get will have something slightly wrong with it. He will mention it. He won't want anything to be actually done about it; he just likes to keep the record straight. Sammy's very serious about everything, keeps close tabs on everything at all times. He lives as though he's been warned that his life's being taken down and may be used in evidence against him at a trial in a court of law. Basically a very nice guy, but for him everything in life is business. So life becomes business for everyone else who gets involved with him, like it or not.

'He looks ten years older'n he is. At least. He's got a few years left now before he retires, three or four, I think. But he looks like he's seventy right now. I doubt he ever looked like a kid, even when he was one.'

Cavanaugh did not react. 'I do have to give Lennie that,' Merrion often said. 'He isn't one of those silly bastards who're sensitive about their age. Maybe he got so much shit for bein' young when he was appointed 'fore he's thirty, must be his Confirmation picture inna paper, he thinks he must still look young. He doesn't, but that may not be what he thinks. He looks as young as most people do when they aren't, anymore.'

Paradisio was five-eight or five-nine; a soft, unassertive, hundred-fifty pounds or so. 'His idea of a good strenuous workout's making sure it's all right with the wife if he takes the car Wednesday night. Sammy will not use "my OGV," Official Government Vehicle, on personal business. She won't mind; she's known for months he's going to want the car that night, ever since he got the tickets in December. He put the dates on this year's calendar before he hung it up in the kitchen.

'He picks up their son, Jeff, and takes the turnpike to Boston. The daughters aren't interested in baseball. He thinks it's probably because they think they weren't supposed to. "They never really tried to play baseball, gave it half a chance. Naturally now they don't like it."

'Sammy doesn't have that much to say about the girls. I get the impression he thinks how they're doing now is their husbands' business. If they're doing okay, their husbands get the credit. If they're not doing okay then their husbands're to blame. Jeff is different. Apparently sons, married or not, remain their fathers' responsibility. Sam's very pleased with the way that Jeff turned out. I think this means he thinks he gets the credit. "Jeff's all right," Sam says, "Jeff's doing very good. He's a hard-working kid and a good family man and I'm very proud of him. He started in fish and he did his job and worked hard and proved he was reliable, and so now he's in meat. That's a solid job to have and it's a good strong company he's got it with, too, the Big Y. In that business you're not gonna wake up some fine morning and find out you lost your job; people stopped buying what you sell. All a sudden what you were trained to do and've been doing all your life, for years and years, is now obsolete. You're outta work; there's nothing you can do. *Terrifying*, but it won't happen to Jeff; it *can't*. People'll always have to eat so they're always gonna need food. What he's in is secure.

'"But Jeff's also got a growing family, four kids, and you know what that means: Gotta be thinking now about tuitions down the line, all that kind of thing. And I'm through that; I don't anymore. And I'm one of the few guys I know who when the time came, didn't get hit as hard as I expected we was gonna. I actually made out a little.

'"See, Jeff got outta Cathedral, he went the Navy. Now you did have tuition, Cathedral. It's a parochial school. But his mother wanted it, thought it was better, and so what the hell, I went along. 'This's something that she wants for the kid, might as well let him do it.' But it wasn't very much, couple grand or so a year back then. Nothing compared to college, which'd been what I was getting ready for. But then he ended up not going. When he came out the service he said he was too old, go back to school, and besides, him and Carol wanted to get married. Start a family.

'"His mother was kind of disappointed, thought he should get his degree, but I supported him in that decision. Couldn't've done much else, said anything much against it – not and been consistent, dropping out of AIC like I did. But also I agreed with him. I didn't think he needed it. I thought he could get along without it and if he didn't want to do it then he probably shouldn't – he wouldn't get nothin' out of it. And on the basis of the way that things seem to've worked out, I think you'd have to say that both of us were right.

'"And then his two sisters. Well, Deb just did the two years to get her nurse's thing there; the associate degree. The bachelor's which was two more years, she didn't do 'til later – and she paid for that herself. So it was just Marie Louise that actually went and stayed the whole entire four years. Not that that was not expensive, having her down New Rochelle there – Jesus, checks I used to write. But still, it wasn't that bad. Her being the only one of the three of them that really *went*, the whole four years. The way it worked out, me and Lois hadda pay for just the six years of college, not the twelve like we'd been planning.

'"So okay, now I buy the tickets, Jeff and I go to the ballgame, and that's sort of my present to him. His coming to the games with me, that's his present to me."'

'It's like it's some kind of a sacrament,' Merrion said to Cavanaugh, 'going to the fucking ballgames. He exaggerates the meaning out of all proportion. Once he said to me that I must know what he was talking about, how much he gets out of it, because I probably did the same thing with my father, and I said Not really – we only went once. Why, I couldn't tell you;

it just wasn't a big deal for us. Sammy didn't know what to say. I hadda try to help him out.

'"Look," I said, "Pat was just never that much of a sports fan, is all. He could talk sports with the customers and *sound* like he liked sports; he didn't *mind* them. He'd watch a game, TV. But going to the games, all that kind of thing? Didn't interest him. He was a nice guy and a good father and he took us fishing, me and Chris, the Connecticut shore, Long Island Sound. But only once or twice. I don't know what made him do it. He must've gotten the idea from someone at work, so when he got a day off, he took us and we rented the equipment and we fished. Caught something too, I remember. I forget exactly what. It was okay, but no regular thing. It was a pretty long drive.

'"We never had things that we did on a regular basis with him. But it was all right, you know? It really was. He worked hard, six days a week, and when he got a day off he worked around the house, cut the lawn, I dunno – painted the hallway. He's been dead forty years. I don't recall now exactly what he did with his spare time. But I know he didn't collar me and Chris and tell us that we couldn't play baseball with our friends over Curtis School field, or go swimming up the pond, because he had a day off and we hadda spend it with him. Pat just wasn't like that, and I guess neither was I. So it was really okay."

'Sammy looked very confused. Flustered. Like he'd said something that he shouldn't've. He said: "And of course, you couldn't after that. You never had a son." And then he got even more upset and looked at me and said: "Amby, you know, I didn't mean to say that. I'm sorry. It came out."

'And I said to him: "Didn't mean to say what, Sam? That I never had any kids? Well, so far's I know, at least. But I knew that. And yeah, sure, now I sort of envy you, all my friends with grown-up kids. Envy you *now* – I didn't used to, when you've got the heartache of bringing them up. Naturally, you do that; you get to be my age and you think it must be nice to have the kids. *After* it's too late for it: *that's* when it crosses your mind, like *lots* of things, everything else you missed out on. 'I should've gone to Rio. Would've been nice, to see Rio. Should've done that, I was younger.'

'"It's just cheap regret, tinsel. Fact is, I didn't. And it wasn't that the right girl never came along, so I never hadda chance. Even back when I was going around with this woman I thought I was probably gonna marry, kids were not on my mind. I don't think they were on hers, either. I don't think she ever mentioned the subject. I think I *could've* been a father; far's I know I wasn't shooting blanks. One time, kindah scary, I was still in school, it looked as though I might gonna be one, but it turned out she was just late. After that I always took the precautions.

'"So I never made an actual *decision*, I wasn't gonna get married and have kids. I just never got around to it. But I knew it. You didn't hurt my feelings, saying it."

'I'm not sure he believed me,' Merrion said to Cavanaugh. 'He looked awful contrite. But anyway, that's what it is: to Sam what him and Jeff do with the Red Sox every summer is a holy thing.

'Six times a season,' Merrion told Cavanaugh. 'I used to think they must go at least once every week that the Red Sox were home. Every time the two of us met for lunch during the baseball season, it seemed like they'd gone to the game the night before. Not that we started meeting to talk about baseball; it was for business, a pleasanter way to discuss things we needed to talk about anyway, in the course of doing our jobs. So you and I know what we're doing here. Larry never did that, and Richie didn't, either. But I think they should've. A certain amount of regular, ongoing coordination between the state and the federal systems: I think it's essential these days. There's so much overlap now, especially with all the drug stuff. I know: Probation. But the state probation guys don't do it enough, at least in my estimation. Maybe the ones in Superior do it, but on the District level, they don't.

'Anyway, we both just figured that since we gotta do this, and since, you know, you're both gonna have lunch anyway, well then, why not meet and have something to eat the same time? Made sense.'

'And you're good at having lunch, aren't you, Amby?' Cavanaugh said.

'Hey,' Merrion said, 'you're tellin' me I'm fat, is that it? Jesus, what I have to take in this job – anna pay's not all that good either.'

'But by judicious use of the expense account,' Cavanaugh said, 'you're able to make the ends meet.'

'Oh, what's this we got now?' Merrion said. 'Now I got *you* also gettin' on me, claimin' I cheat onna gyp sheet?'

'I don't know,' Cavanaugh said, waving his hand. 'I also don't care. That's between you and your God. Or Theresa in the treasurer's office. Whoever it is, it's not me.'

'Well, okay, then,' Merrion said. 'Anyway, now you're gonna meet Sam and see for yourself. He's a little like his uncle, the chief: he's got *enthusiasm*. He's really into his work.'

'As many times as I've seen them do it, your Honor,' Paradisio said over the sandwiches, 'and it must be hundreds now, it never ceases to amaze me. They try to make me think they've become attached to me. And therefore I've become attached to them.

'It's ridiculous. It should be pretty clear, no matter how stupid you are, how much you wanna believe what you gotta know just isn't so, it isn't gonna *matter* if I like you; I think you caught a bad break or you're a nice guy, or if you make me laugh. I imagine you also run into this yourself, Judge, now and then, this same phenomenon: sometimes it just about drives me crazy. The law's put someone in your power, and he knows it, but he seems to have the idea that if he can ingratiate himself with you, you won't exercise it.

'Well as we all know, it *isn't* that way and it *can't* be that way. You can't allow it. Instead what the situation is is this: "If you give me a reason, so I have no choice, what I'm gonna do, my friend, is violate your sorry ass. Callin' me your buddy, or any of that shit, just won't do the job for you. Cryin' won't help either, do you any good at all. Get your mind clear on this: If you violate the terms of your release, and I find out, as soon as we catch up with you you're goin' away again. And nothin's gonna change that."'

He wore, as usual, a frayed and starched long-collared broadcloth shirt that had taken on a greyish cast, frayed at the cuffs and collar, and one of what must have been a large collection of flimsy neckties, modestly patterned and shy, that made tiny knots when tied.

Merrion found them embarrassing. To Hilliard: 'I hate those

neckties of his. They're offensive. It's so hard to remember what they even look like, five minutes after you've left him. Almost like he's daring you, you know? He's gonna call you up later and test you. "See? I knew it: You don't remember what color tie I've got on. That's how much attention you pay me." The only other time you see ties like his is when you're in a Filene's Basement or some charity thrift shop and they're hanging up in bunches, wooden pegs. They should stay there. He buys his pants out of catalogues and they come with Ban-roll waistbands – I don't know that but I'd bet.'

In cold weather Paradisio wore tweed sport coats that lacked heft, and in warm seasons he wore shapeless hopsack blazers. 'His sports coats look like there's nobody in them, when he's got them on. He looks like he gets dressed inna morning hoping no one'll notice him all day. Even *see* him; like his ambition's to become transparent. His haircuts make him look like that's what he wants. Boys' regular, short back and sides. He's been going to Harding's ever since his father started going there in Nineteen-fifty-one. He may've never liked the way Russ Harding cuts his hair, but that wouldn't make any difference. He wouldn't have it in him to change barbers over such a little thing as not liking how the guy cut his hair.

'Not that I don't really like him or respect the guy at all; I do. He's the nicest guy the world. It's just that he's perfect. He *looks* like he is what he actually is – and most likely always was, even before he officially became one – a conscientious government worker. You look at him and you just know it. Everything about the guy screams *Government* at you.'

He had gotten his nickname in the course of his government work. His job had obliged him to start 'keeping *exactly* the kind of company,' Merrion said, 'that you'd imagine a guy named "Sammy Paradise" gettin' into on his own, water seekin' lower ground: Hangin' around with the gangsters. Only *I* would've thought they'd be *other* gangsters; his *colleagues*.

'I tell you, it's wonderful. Among hundreds of things that Sammy is not, Sammy isn't a gangster. He's in the world to do good, and nothing wrong with that notion. You and I, that's what we try to do. Don't always succeed, but we try. We're just not as ambitious. Sammy's faith in his fellow man's far greater'n ours: *He tries to do good with the hoods*.

'This is a very big difference. *Knowin*' what they are, *knowin*' that they'll never change, most of the time he can still manage to believe that they *might* reform. That's Sammy's natural mission. He knows his work is hopeless, but he also knows that if he ever lets himself think that, he won't be able to do it anymore. Somehow he convinces himself he doesn't know what he knows.'

For Paradisio it was essential to persuade himself he didn't know what his clients meant when they told him that with his help they now understood where they had gone wrong. They told him they had come to see that the way that they'd been living before they had gotten caught was what had made them move so fast and make mistakes. 'They hadn't taken time enough to think the whole thing out. Quickness's what's really counted in the acts that got them into trouble. It's surprising how big a part that plays in what they have to say to me, about the lives they've lived.'

From listening to them for so many years he believed he had learned to think a little bit like they did. 'Which can be very helpful,' Paradisio told Cavanaugh. 'I'm not knocking it. They often tell me if they'd only taken time enough to stop and think, about whatever got them into the shit, well, they never would've done it.

'They've just *never* had the time. It's the darnedest thing. It always seems to have been they had to act, *right off*, before every guy named Dave and Al, and everybody else as well, found out and started trying, pull the deal off before they could. So things never turned out quite the way that they hoped, and then look what'd happened. I hear those stories all the time, day in and day out. That's how I've spent my life at work, listening to desperate men convicted and then severely punished for very serious crimes tell me the reason was timing. They've had a lot of time to compose their stories. You'd expect that they'd be good, complete, with no loose ends. But they aren't. They always lack something: any admission or recognition that if Dave and Al had in fact managed to go for the loot first, they would've been just as guilty of committing serious crimes, and if caught then convicted and put in jail. The parolees I deal with in that one respect're a lot like the people I work for and with: they all seem to think that what matters is *how good a job you do*, not *whether you should do the job*. Except of course that the people I work for don't usually do felonies. The jobs they pull off may not always be good things to do, but most of the time they are legal.'

He paused. 'I no longer point out to my felons what is missing from their stories. I used to but I gave it up, many years ago. They claimed they didn't understand why the element I mentioned was important to fully understanding what was wrong with what they did. I could not convince them that it was. The smarter ones after a while saw that I wouldn't let them off the hook until I'd made them see the matter my way, so they claimed I'd convinced them. They were lying. I saw that they were never gonna stop lying. So I gave up creating the situations they dealt with by telling me lies I didn't believe. I guess we're partners now.'

He was right. The strategy he'd devised to avoid disbelief of what they said amounted to complicit surrender in their deceit. If he didn't raise the question of repentance, they wouldn't lie to him. 'No one's on parole or probation forever. Sooner or later they either die or we have to release them. The agency can't get much bigger. Process them through, regardless of what they've become. Go along, get along, and go home.'

He was resigned to the collaboration. 'With a name like *Paradisio*, everybody thinks that anyway, you're in the bag with these guys. "Ah, this guy's probably mobbed-up. Fuckin' ghinnies; most of 'em are."'

He was not alleging prejudice. As far as he knew he had never been held back from advancement by suspicion that he might be connected, closer to the men that he was supposed to be supervising than he was letting on, concealing stronger loyalties to them than to the government and the department he was working for. He had found the job to be as it was supposed to be at the time he took it. His nickname was just an insignificant aspect of the acceptable prize that he had wanted, and *gotten* out of his life: a good steady job for himself and his family, Lois and the kids.

Civil Service: that was the kind of job that he'd wanted, the definition of *steady*. He went into Probation because Probation had openings when he dropped out of American International College in Springfield, for the usual three reasons: no money; no great interest in finishing; and lastly, no reason at all. 'I could've dug up the money, I guess, I'd've put my mind to it. Really wanted to try. And the same with the grades. I didn't have to get Cs and Ds; I'm not stupid. But what the hell, I didn't want to, I guess was the main reason. I was young. What the hell do you know when you're young? Nothin': that's the whole of it. Just that you're young, and you'll always *be* young – so half of what you know is shit.

'I see it in my clients. That's how almost all of them got off to their start. Knowing two things for dead-certain sure, and at least one of those things was pure shit. Time they get to me, they've found out which one. Most of them probably were as strong and tough and smart as they knew they were; that part was true. But now they know that the rules *did* apply to them; the idea that they *didn't* was shit.

'The way that they found out was very hard. When it finally dawned on them they were locked up in the can, watching the years of their youth drain away. Like piss hissin' down onna white mint onna strainer, and all they can do now is just stand there holdin' their dick in their hand, watchin'. They've found out their lives've been like something they happened to be *around for*, like a big game and they got tickets, while the years were going by. Their whole youth and middle years; not *lived*, just gotten rid of, discarded by somebody else they don't even recognize, that guy standing next to them. By the time they get to me, all that most of them can do is just continue to stand there and *watch*, while the rest of their lives go away on them. Some day, they know, their life will finally disappear, like something that's never been here at all. All they have to hope for's that the instant when it runs out they'll feel a little better, because at least it'll be ending, whole process of watching it go.

'They look at me like I've got answers, some of them, when they've just gotten out and it's begun to register on them that the years they spent inside're really *gone*. Never get them back. They come in and see me, when they first report, sit there and look at me as though they're thinking – maybe hoping might be more like it – that maybe I can do something important for them. If they're nice to me, I could get their years back for them, all the years they spent inside. Maybe there's a secret way, and I know where it is.

'Those're the most painful cases. These're hard men, very hard men, dangerous and violent and cruel; they've done terrible things. I know it sounds silly to say it, but this's the way I feel. I *hate* having to be the one who disappoints them. It's nothing personal. They happened to draw me, so I'm the guy who has to tell them what they hope for can't be done. Simply can't be done. Randomness's all it is; I'm the guy picked to do it. That's just the way it is. But sometimes I think: "If I could do that for him, maybe he *would* reform now." I often think that a guy with no hope may not see much reason to start behaving himself; he *may decide* he's got nothing much to lose now, if he doesn't – what can he possibly lose? Fear, that's all, that we'll do it to him again, as indeed we will, because that's all we've got left now, to make him obey the law. That's not a good threat; I don't know anyone who'd mind losing fear.

'This I think is what accounts for the successes that the chaplains and lay preachers in the prisons – and on the outside, too – sometimes make of these thugs. No one can get their lives back for them. But the preachers can tell them that if they start playing their cards right for as long as *this* game continues, they'll get a great deal inna *next* one, in the afterlife. Not all those conversions that lots of us laugh at are the fakes we think they are, scams to con the parole board. Some of them are the real thing. Some of the born-agains may've met Jesus, or Muhammed, and some of them may just be too desperate to care if He was out when they called, but many of them really do believe. There's a terrible emptiness to knowing you've pissed your whole life away; you know it when you see how hard it hits these guys, meaner'n vipers themselves.

'There're days when I wish I'd done something else with *my* life, but on the absolute worst day I ever had I've been better off than my clients.'

He had spent almost forty years on the job, ever since he'd seized the opening almost immediately offered to him after he won top grades on the Civil Service exam. 'That, you see, I'm not really stupid, when I put my mind to something. College: I couldn't convince myself that what I was doing had any connection to any life I'd ever lead. The Civil Service exam was the only way I could get to live a life I wanted. So even though I was young, I could see it was important, worth preparing for.'

Merrion knew this about him: he had spent all of his work-days earnestly talking with and about guys who had a sense of crippled-up irony that he'd never gotten, and therefore he had never really understood them. It affected the way he thought about information that he got from Sammy, how he weighed, filtered and interpreted everything Paradise told him, complete with the irony and bitterness the people who had said it to him had come by the dishonest hard way, had had a lot of time to think about, in prison. They had refined it and worked it over in their minds, so that ever afterward it distorted everything they said through a sharpened, crooked smile. The mocking smile that never altogether went away told what they really thought when they saw men and women and their children, the conduct and possessions other people valued and took care of: they saw that they could turn those values into vulnerabilities. Weaknesses they could use to enrich themselves, and demonstrate that they could destroy anything they didn't want – and would, to please themselves.

It was the dialect of real evil, a silent language that they spoke and Sammy didn't. The words were the same in each one but the connotations were different. Not opposite; trickier than that – off-center, skewed and distorted. When they thought a guy who had some power over them was nice enough so that they could be friendly with him – which meant *take liberties with him*; 'you know, like fuck with his mind a little; don't mean the guy any real *harm*' – without really risking anything, it had to mean that he was kind of an asshole, a jerk. Weak, if he wanted to be arms-length friends with them. The kind of guy you'd always have to be putting something over on, kind of laughing at, taking advantage of, to show that you *knew* he was weak. He'd never been one of the boys, and he'd never *be* one of them either.

They would always do it to him because they would always see it as a part of the duty to be cool. Merrion would be several miles and days away in Canterbury, when they saw Sammy down in Springfield, sat down and talked to him, just as earnestly and soberly as he talked to them, but later when Sammy talked about his clients and what they'd said to him, Merrion without ever seeing them would know exactly what had been going through their heads, like lethal gas, while they fucked with Sammy's mind real good – for the Hell of it, for something to do in Hell, to pass away the time: contempt. And Sammy as he talked earnestly to Merrion would still not know what had happened to him. Reciting it to Merrion after the fact, completely unperturbed – Merrion listening to him, hearing what the hard men had been thinking in the discordant music underneath the words that Sammy was repeating – Sammy still didn't know, any more than he had known while the words were being uttered, what evil there was in them.

For Merrion it was like being compelled to attend a delayed broadcast of a sadistic procedure, knowing in advance what had already been done to the victim to degrade him, unable to do anything about it. It was as though he could communicate in his mind with evil men he had never seen and would not recognize on sight, but would know them for what they were, by instinct, if he ever saw them, and know beyond a reasonable doubt the nature, not the details, of what they had done. He understood them. *You did it even though there was nobody else around to see what you were doing; you still had to do it. It was your moral obligation. So in case it did turn out that there had been someone looking, you wouldn't look like you'd been taking him seriously. And the perfect cruelty of it was that you hoped he hadn't gotten it, and wouldn't ever get it.*

Because if Sam ever *had* allowed himself to catch on to what they were doing to him, meanly making fun of him, making a fool of him, that would triple or quadruple the pain they had inflicted on him just for fun. He still would've had to act as though he still didn't know it was going on, *made* himself act as though it never really happened. Because after he got through talking with them and forming his impressions, it was going to be his job to write factual, unbiased reports about them. As he construed it that required never letting his personal feelings influence his judgement of a man, have any bearing, one way or the other, on what he recommended.

'That's my job, part of my job that I'm supposed to do. What I might think of some one particular guy personally; whether I like him or not: never letting that interfere or get in the way, in any way, of what I write down in my reports. What goes in there is what I think of him as a man who's on parole or on probation – he's given his word, after all; he's on a trial; he's not free; he's just been let loose to see if he can, and will, behave, if and when he is fully released. What kind of use I think he's making of this second chance he's getting – or this third or fourth or fifth chance, if that's what it is. If we're all gonna get another chance, after we die, to earn our way in Purgatory up into heaven, like it says in the Bible, then it seems to me that we oughta have something like that for down here. If there's gonna be redemption for us after we're dead, for what we may've done while we were down here, then by rights there oughta be some kind of redemption available on earth.

'And if there's going to be that, well then, getting it shouldn't depend on if I like you or not. What it should depend on is whether I think you've earned it, and deserve it, even if I do think you're not a guy I'd like to see a ballgame with: whether I like you's got nothing to do with whether I think you're doing OK. *That's* what I'm supposed to write down, whether you're *doing* OK. And that's *all* that I therefore write down.' Because he was a US Department of Justice Probation Services Officer, and that had to mean something, didn't it? Or else what did anything mean?

He had told Merrion enough about the genesis of the nickname to enable him to deduce the rest himself. Soon after the beginning of his thirty-four years with the Service, his clients (Merrion seldom heard him refer to them as 'cases') had begun to call him 'Sammy Paradise.' When they reported by phone or came to the office, they asked for him by that name.

'I assumed it must've seemed just as unsuitable for him as a younger man as it did when I ran into him and he was middle-aged,' Merrion told Cavanaugh. 'So naturally it therefore wasn't very long before the filing clerks and secretaries in the office where he worked, and then all other people that he worked with, his colleagues and superiors, began using it as well. It was a *joke*. When someone pins a nickname on a person that's so completely inappropriate for him you can't help but kind of laugh a little, snicker, every time you hear it – laugh at *him*, I mean, not *with* him, just out of general high spirits – it's guaranteed to stick. I think most of us must be cruel, enjoy hurting other people. Most human beings are generously cruel.

'Sammy being Sam, though, he doesn't seem to mind. I mean, as far as anyone could tell. I've never called him that myself, Sammy Paradise, when he was around, but the other guys I've met him with – not his clients, now, his hoods; these're people in his office – they use it around him all the time. Apparently he's never objected. They treat him like shit, do they? It's okay; he doesn't mind.

'One day when he didn't show for lunch I called there, find out where he was. That's when the whole thing first struck me, the way they treat the guy. He'd called in sick, the flu. But the asshole secretary that he talked to, someone that he works with, every day, he asked her specifically to call me? She never bothered.

'I was curious, you know? I asked her why. "Well then, if he asked you to do this, and you work for him, why didn't you do it then? Save me a useless trip to the place where he's supposed to be, like he wanted you to do, knowing he was sick and wasn't gonna make it." And she said: "I dunno. I had something else I hadda do, I guess. I must've forgot."

'I get this stupid broad any time I call up over there and ask for him by name, "Samuel Paradisio." She's the receptionist and she's also assigned to him, to type up his reports. She's the Sammy secretary. When you ask for him she acts like she met him once a few months ago and he didn't impress her much. I say I want to talk to him and she *always* says to me: "Oh you must mean Sammy Paradise. I'm not sure he's in today." When I *know* he's in, because I just had to tell him I'd call him back after hc called me and I had someone in my office.

'One day it got to me, this broad's attitude, and I asked to talk to Sammy's boss. Guy named Anglin, think his name was, seemed like a nice-enough guy. I told him how this typist of theirs acts when I call, and said if she treats me that way she's most likely rude to everybody else. How when I ask for Sam she refers to him as "Sammy Paradise," not "Mister Paradisio," which, I said, can't cause his clients to respect him a lot, much less the general public. And I asked Anglin did he think that was right. He told me Sam'd never objected – which kind of surprised me; it seemed so completely out of keeping with everything else about him. Disrespectful of his dignity or something. And unless he complained about it, Anglin said he didn't see any need to do anything about it. I got the impression I'm the only one who ever griped about that lazy broad, who won't even look around for a guy she works for when someone calls and asks for him. In fact, from the reaction I got to the question over there, it was pretty obvious his boss thought maybe I was some kind of a *nut*. Either that or out of line.'

'Well,' Paradisio said, getting to know Cavanaugh by allowing Cavanaugh to learn what he was like, enabling the judge to evaluate him as though tacitly conceding that the judge outranked him and had a right to size him up, at the same time ate his Italian sub, talking while he chewed. 'Bad enough, when my clients try to do that, get on my good side, as though some day that might get them a break when they really don't deserve one. Wishful thinking but that I can understand.

'But every so often, just now and then, I get one that goes beyond that, acting like we're pals. I'm now his big *brother*, or sometimes maybe even his *father*. Finds out when my birthday is, sends me cards and shit.

'None of them've got any imagination. It's like they're followin' a cookbook. You can almost see 'em, movin' their lips. Here's this repeat-offender, career criminal, moanin' and groanin': he's all alone in the world. He was inside so long he hasn't got nobody left and no place to go. Nobody cares about him. The boo and the hoo and "poor me." So maybe this year you could ask your wife if she would make a little extra stuffing and set one more plate'n usual for Thanksgiving? He'd like to spend the day with you, you're the closest thing to family he's got left, and he's not supposed to see his old friends any more, he used to hang around with, who got him in trouble. As you know; you're the boss now and you're the one who told him that. And you know he wants to do everything exactly how you say, 'cause he's reformed now and he's going to be good.

'He's working on you. Gradually it's all becoming *your* fault, you're to blame, that the holidays're comin' and he's all alone. *He* didn't have nothin' to do with it, or pretty soon he won't've, by the time that he gets through rewriting history around you. This's the pattern with almost all of them. All the bad things you thought he did were somebody *else's* doing. He'll get so he believes the shit while he's slingin' it; just give him some time and he will. It won't be anything *he* did that explains why his family disowned him, and he was inside for so long no one remembers his name – or that he lost track of all of his respectable friends. Always what someone *else* did. That's his way of dealing with the emptiness: fill it up with lies.

'That's what all of that rigamarole is all about. When I wasn't looking, didn't know anything was going on, I *adopted* the guy. God or Fate brought us together. Instead of just having him assigned to me, because I was first in line to get the next bad actor, the day they let him out.

'Well, I can deal with that stuff. I know how to do it. You learn all that early; older guys teach you. What to do when the cons start working on you, trying to muscle in on your life. Let 'em go far enough and pretty soon they'll be in your spare bedroom. He'll take over your personal life on you, be everywhere you look and underfoot. Hoggin' the bathroom, the morning, you're tryin' to shave and get dressed. Askin' you if you'd mind – already asked her and she said it sounds fine to her – if he slept with your wife now and then.

'"Just one night a week now, not askin' too much. Maybe, say, Tuesday, or *Thursday* night, when you're out bowlin' with the boys, give the old lady something to look forward to. Not like I wanna spoil any your weekend plans." Pretty soon he's fucking your wife and you're inna guest room. And these're bad *guys* that're pullin' this mealy-mouth shit, or you never would've even got to *know* them.

'So I think by now, well, I'm pretty well seasoned. I been around quite a while. I must've seen, or at least heard about, most of the flavors of bullshit there are. But now this new guy comes onto my list. Never had one like this one before, Mister Lowell Chappelle. He makes all the others look *tame*, and I've hadda buncha *lulus* in my time, believe me. This is one very bad guy, and he not only thinks that he's my adopted son; he thinks I've adopted his whole *family*. So he tells me anyway.

'I'm not sure this is the honor that Lowell seems to think it is, or that I want it, if it is. Lowell's family doesn't seem to've exactly flourished, deprived as they've been of his affection and fatherly direction while he was unavoidably detained elsewhere, in one prison or another, doing time for all the exciting things he did.

'He believes he has two sons. He believes they both may still be alive, but he's not sure. He hasn't always tried to keep close tabs on the children he's begotten, but if I could locate them he'd like to make amends. Because I have access to sources of information that are closed to him. As usual when it's some nice thing that Lowell would like to see occur, it will require quite a lot of work from someone else, not him. He's helpless. Lowell's *careful* to be helpless – puts a lot of *effort* into it; make sure he stays that way. He'd like me to use "that computer that you're always using there that can do anything, and see if you can find out something about my kids, on it. See where they are these days, what they're doing. That'd be good to know."

'Using information that he's volunteered and that I've obtained by questioning him, like a fool I've tried without success to do this. I have been unable to check or verify any family history that he's given me that's not in his own personal record. He of course is not the sole source of the information in that jacket about *him*; that came from law enforcement officers and public records. That's why it's pretty reliable. And there's a lot of it; he's had a long and eventful career. But that data's only about his military and criminal career; it isn't a complete picture of his background. It doesn't enable us to say with any sort of assurance who his family includes, much less list their current addresses, because he was the source of the entries about them and he's a habitual liar.

'So what I am saying is that the information he's given me about his family members may be true. But I haven't been able to substantiate or verify it. I'm not sure whether he deliberately *falsified* the data that he's given me; or the information that he's given me's the best he has, but simply *wrong*; or because both his sons, and his wife and the woman who bore his second son, have somehow managed, deliberately or otherwise, to disappear from all the data banks that we have access to. It wouldn't be unusual if they did, just decided that Lowell's never going to make their lives better; may in fact cause them more trouble and pain, so they've decided that the safest thing to do is to disappear. The dependents of repeat offenders often do that; the very best they can to divorce themselves from ever having anything to do with their bad boys again. It often works, and I have to say it often seems to me that they're right: it's by far the smartest thing for them to do.

'My guess is some of each factor's probably at work here, not that it matters. Tracking all these people down and making sense out of Lowell Chappelle's family tree would cost a lot more time and money than it could possibly be worth. So, going on the data that Lowell furnished:

'One of his sons, the eldest, is named September. "His mother liked that for a name. She had him in the wintertime but she didn't like *February*." Lowell always called him "Shadow" but he's not sure whether anybody else ever did. He last saw the boy, then two or three, before he went into the service in Nineteen-fifty-nine. That would make "this *kid*" thirty-eight or thirty-nine. Lowell forgets but he thinks that would be about right. From something he heard on the grapevine before he was released the time before this, Lowell believes that he was in maximum security somewhere in the sovereign state of Texas. He isn't sure exactly where, or what for. He thinks the sentence might have been the outgrowth of something to do with a riot that happened at another correctional institution in Texas where he was previously doing time. "For drugs or something, something to do with drugs. Or maybe it was a border thing." He hasn't seen him for many years.

'Lowell lost track of his wife, Norma – this would be September's mother – "years and years ago." He says he didn't go looking for her when he came out of the service and "I guess if she ever went lookin' for me she couldn't've looked too hard, because if she did I never heard nothin' about it and she never found me." He righteously assumes that she and the boy received the allotment checks that he knows were deducted from his army pay, but he doesn't know that.

'The VA computer records consist of entries manually copied

onto magnetic tape from card-files during the changeover from the keypunch system that took place years and years ago. They indicate that allotment checks made out to forty-four military dependents named Chappelle went to a total of seventy-one addresses in the US, Canada and the Dominican Republic during the years that our boy was in the army fighting for his country and the democratic way of life. The only one that seems to have any connection with him at all was a Gloria Chappelle at an address in Atlantic Beach, Florida. "Gloria" was his mother's name, but he has no recollection either of her ever having lived in Atlantic Beach or of himself ever having directed that she be sent any allotment from his pay at that address. Or any other one. He said he hadn't seen her since he was about six years old, and that was in Saint Thomas in the Virgin Islands. So: our first dead end in the pursuit of the history of Lowell Chappelle.

'The last he heard of his wife, Norma, she was living somewhere in Illinois and she was working in a factory "that made things." What *things* he doesn't know. "Could've been pumps." He believes that was about "twenty, thirty years ago," but he's not sure. He thinks she may be dead. He says she had asthma, or maybe it was TB, and it gave her a lot of trouble, so it was hard for her to keep a job.

'The other son's named Rutherford. He'd be about sixteen or seventeen by now. He lived with his mother in the Santurce section of San Juan, Puerto Rico. Lowell's information about him's very old and comes entirely from letters he received some time ago, while he was in prison, first from a social worker and then from a parish priest in Puerto Rico. They seemed to be under the impression Lowell was a wealthy man who owned several restaurants and clubs in New York, and hoped he would see fit to contribute financially to the support of his son and his son's mother.

'This was before the States all started enacting those long-arm Dead-beat-Dad statutes that've become so popular in recent years and just about drive us nuts in the federal system, trying to keep track of all the warrants that're issued under them that we're supposed to enforce. Not that I don't think they're a good idea, but that's a different matter. It seems to me as though the States ought have their own people to do all the work it entails. We're already understaffed and overworked, *before* they started this.

'Anyway, Lowell concedes the possibility that the social worker may've gotten this impression, that he was a wealthy fella, from the boy's mother, who may very well have gotten it from *him*, during his only visit to the island shortly after the four-hundred-thirty-thousand-dollar bank job back in Seventy-eight that was alleged to have been his most recent effort – at least so far as anyone's proven so far. The one that landed him in jail out at FCI McNeil Island before he got out and came here, destined for my attention.

'Lowell of course continues to maintain his innocence of that charge. He does admit that during his visit to Puerto Rico when he knocked up the lady in Santurce he had quite a lot of currency with him, much of which he lost playing blackjack in the casino at the El San Juan Hotel.

'Now, this woman that your Park Rangers surfaced in the woods back on Saturday night, this Linda Shepard: as I understand it, she claims to be Chappelle's daughter. It's possible she is but that detail slipped his mind. Details have a way of slipping where Lowell's mind's concerned. Or perhaps he just kept that fact from me, chose not to tell me for some reason of his own or for no reason at all. I couldn't find Lowell today after you called so I could ask him that. Got no idea where the hell he is, and neither does anybody else I know who knows him. Janet LeClerc's was one of the numbers I called, that you give to me there, Amby. Got no answer from her.'

'She's probably down at the convenience store there,' Merrion said, 'stocking up on butts and scratch tickets.'

'Dunno,' Paradisio said. 'All's I know is that I couldn't get ahold of *her*, either, to even ask, so I don't know if they're still shacked up. Even though you told her she hadda make him leave. But still, pending when we find Lowell and get a chance to ask him a few things about this woman claims to be his daughter: I can't find either from our files or from what Daggett'd tell me – Louella over DSS. You know, there are times when I think I really hate that woman.

'Seriously,' he said, when Merrion laughed. 'I don't know if you'd be familiar with her, with this woman, Judge. But I do know my friend Amby here is, and that's why he's laughing now. He knows how much fun it is when you've got a question that you need an answer to, right away. It'll take you about two or three days to get it through channels, maybe even back and forth with Washington, much more time'n you've got. Louella could answer it for you in about fifteen seconds if she would, but she *won't*. She says she *can't*, but the real reason is she *won't*. She just hates giving out information. I don't know what it is, protecting her clients against us? Doesn't make any sense; we're trying to help them. But if you can get the time of day out of that one, you're doing better'n I am.'

'Sam always speaks very lowly of Louella, Judge,' Merrion said to Cavanaugh. 'I've told him many times he shouldn't do it, but he just won't seem to stop.'

'For the record, Sam,' Cavanaugh said, 'she won't tell me anything either. If instead of dumping the chore on Amby, I pick up the phone and make the call myself, the result is the same. I get the same answer both of you get. The woman was born saying: "No." No wonder she's never been married. She's probably still a virgin.'

'Yeah, well, I guess I'm glad to hear that,' Paradisio said. 'At least now I know it's not just me, not just Feds and all, some grudge she's got against us. Makes me feel a little better, know at least I'm not alone.

'But anyway, Lowell gave us the Shepard woman's address as the place where he'd be living before he got out of jail last March and ended up here, lucky us. He told us she's a niece of his. He definitely did not say she's his daughter. But according to him she'd be thirty-*four* – not thirty-*two*, as she told the Park Rangers. She's a ninth-grade dropout from a school in Lockport, New York. Those three kids she had with her all named after movie stars are by three different fathers.

'"His niece," now?' Cavanaugh said.

'Yeah, "niece,"' Paradisio said. 'Look, I know I don't look too good on this. I didn't do that great a job here. But my guess is she isn't his niece. My guess's that there's some connection between where he was, right before he robbed that last bank with the machine gun after he got out from McNeil Island. He's got some connection out there in New York State that we really don't know all that much about yet. We're not that far along. And then when he got out last spring he came back here and moved in with this Linda Shepard and her three kids, down in Springfield. This Ronald Bennett that you tell me was with her: we don't know where he came from.

'She had a place on State Street way the hell out up beyond the Armory there, up near Winchester Square. Not a bad place at all, pretty roomy; should've been enough for her. Three bedrooms, small dining room, big living room, reasonably good-sized kitchen, not that you'd wanna try and cook a banquet in it, anything; but still, you know, for nothin'? Should've been okay for her. Plus it had a bath-a-half. It's a mostly minority section, African-American and Puerto Rican. That does make it sort of surprising she'd seek that out, want to locate herself up there with them. Lookin' for the trouble, the first place, or else she wouldn't've gone there. But in her circumstances? She's got three kids and she's on welfare: how much choice'd she have? And besides, Lowell's mixed blood himself, half black and white, half Hispanic. He knew he was gettin' out, maybe *he* wanted to live there.

'Anyway, that's where she was when Lowell showed up and moved in. Eight or nine weeks after that, it's June, and now Bennett joins the party here, and then not too long after that, they *all* hadda move out. Which brings us up to the events of this weekend. And that's where you come in here, I guess, Amby.'

'Okay,' Merrion said. 'Putting together what the Rangers and then the cops were able to get out of this woman last Saddy night, plus what I was able on my own before court this morning, managed to pry outta Daggett, everything was hunky-dory with Shepard and the kids until Chappelle showed up. Everyone was doin' fine. Wasn't *workin'*, of course, nothin' quite as dramatic as gettin' a job, maybe *doing* something now and then to earn her keep, but with the Essesseye and the Food Stamps and the AFDC and the rent subsidy, well, they're gettin' along. They're warm and they're eatin' and they've got clothes to wear and the kids seem to've been going to school.

'Bennett may've already been there, against the welfare rules, when Chappelle showed up and made him get out. Then Bennett wasn't there for a while. For about six weeks after Chappelle got there, things were quiet. But that changed. The neighbors start complaining about noise in the Shepard apartment, and then the cops get called. And then Shepard decides one night, fuck the neighbors, and throws a party that turns into a round-robin fistfight, everybody goin' at it, fightin' everybody else. Naturally the night won't be complete until the cops're called. So she gets on the telephone *herself* and invites them to come up.

'Cops arrive and what they find is that there are about a dozen people in the place, and all of them seem to be either drunk or stoned. Some of them're also bleedin'. Except for Mister Chappelle. He's as sober as a judge, begging your Honor's pardon here, and he takes it upon himself to inform the cops that he's been visiting his niece, Miss Shepard, since he got released from jail, and frankly he don't like the way she lives. Doesn't approve of her life-style. Tells the cops confidentially he's got reason to believe she's been supplementing her income by entertaining gentlemen callers and taking money from them. Which is another activity not allowed welfare recipients.

'Naturally the cops are shocked. But feeling that it's only fair to give this woman a chance to defend her good name and reputation, they take her aside and ask her if she'd care to comment on reports that she may be doin' a little light hookin'. She's understandably upset to hear that someone's been saying such things about her, and after telling them that she's a *good* girl and wouldn't think of doing such things, worms the name of the stoolie out of them. Then, *while they are still there*, the cops're still in the apartment, she *flies* into a fucking rage and goes berserk, grabs ahold of a rum jug, and goes after Brother Chappelle, screaming like a fuckin' banshee. Before the cops can grab her she bangs him on the head with the jug, and breaks it. It's not empty. The booze goes all over the place, all over him an' the gas stove. He falls against it. That turns on the stove, which sets the rum on fire. So you've got flames leaping up from the stove and his clothes; cops're beating them out with dishtowels or something. And while that's going on, she's still got the handle and the jagged neck of the jug left, so she goes after him with that and opens up his face before the cops can separate them again.

'This throws a damper on the party, so the cops decide to have some of them arrest Miss Shepard and take her down to the station. And never mind the EMTs, just have some of the other cops who after all're right there on the scene transport Chappelle to the ER and get him repaired. The next day after the judge has heard all about this in Springfield District Court, the upshot of it is that Miss Shepard gets a stern lecture and a year's probation – because she has no money to pay a fine and nobody to stay with the kids if she goes to the cooler, and it seems like that's about the only thing anybody can do to her without going to a hell of a lot of trouble finding foster homes for the kids.

'Mister *Chappelle*, on the other hand, all stitched and bandaged up like he is, is ordered to stay away from her, or the first thing that he knows he'll be back in the federal lockup for violating probation by making a nuisance of himself under State law. Mister Chappelle states his opinion this is a gross miscarriage of justice, him being threatened with going back to jail. He points out that after all, *she's* the one who did all the damage, cut *his* face up with a broken bottle, so *she's* the one should go to jail. The judge is unmoved and tells Mister Chappelle that if he doesn't like getting his face all cut up and Miss Shepard is the one who last did it to him, all he has to do's obey the order, stay away from Miss Shepard, and he should be fine. Oh, and also inna future maybe think twice before he starts going around telling cops any hostess of his is also selling her ass. That isn't exactly what the judge said – just pretty much what he meant.'

'Except that nobody in Springfield then ever gets around to telling me about this,' Paradisio said.

'Or else they did call but you were out, and they got that bitch of a secretary of yours, and she had something else to do, like pick her nose, so she didn't bother telling you,' Merrion said. 'As we know's been known to happen.'

'That could be,' Paradisio said.

'As a further result of all of this brouhaha,' Merrion said, 'at least according to Louella, a week or two later when Miss Shepard's landlord – he lives over in Agawam; owns a number of apartments, all of which are slums – finally gets wind of what went on in the one up in Winchester Square that night, he decides it's *his* turn to get upset. So he orders her to quit and vacate the premises. Says he's trying to run a classy joint there and she's not helping him to do this, so therefore out she goes. This gets the social workers started digging into the whole mess, trying to resettle Miss Shepard.

'They find no sign of Chappelle. He seems to be gone from the scene – probably because he's now taken up with our Janet in apartment fourteen at Sixteen-ninety-two Ike, but this fact hasn't yet reached either Sam's attention or ours. What the social workers *do* find is that Bennett is now keeping Miss Shepard company. Miss Shepard is informed that she can't expect to get another subsidized place for herself as long as Bennett's with her. At least under the statute, he's an able-bodied male. He's supposed to work. She takes offense at this and says what they're planning to do is get married. The case worker says weddings're nice, but that the money she's been getting isn't for supporting unemployed fiancés – or husbands, either, as far as that goes. They put her and the three kids up in a motel temporarily, 'til they can find an apartment for her, but with strict orders to Bennett to stay out, and to her not to let him come in. He ignores his orders and she ignores hers and the case-worker catches them and boots the whole bunch of them out. That's the last that anyone at DSS hears of any of them until the Ranger posse rounds them up on Saturday and dumps them here in our lap.'

'Okay,' Cavanaugh said to Merrion, 'so, where does that leave us all now with Janet? Is the ball in your court here, this afternoon? Or can you kick it back into Sam's?'

Merrion stared at Cavanaugh. He did not say anything. 'I didn't say anything,' he told Hilliard that night, 'because I didn't know what to say. Sam said that Well, as far as he was concerned, he's already looking for Chappelle. Now that the guy is officially missing, or whatever you call it when his probation officer who's supposed to know at all times where he's living, and Sam doesn't, it's his job to find him. As far as *I'm* concerned, I thought once I'd spoken to Louella, gotten her onto the case with the woman and the three kids, that then until the dame comes into court, as she's now going to do tomorrow, the only thing I have to do is sit tight and see what the hell happens. And anyway, where's the judge fit in all this? This's the part I don't like. It seems like Lennie's saying he's got nothing to do; he's just a spectator here. Janet's now completely my responsibility, like the whole thing was my idea. So I didn't answer him.

'And then after that, Sammy's gone, I'm still there in his chambers, I dunno, picking up, something, throwing the sandwich wrappers away, and the bastard does it again. "What plans've you got to handle this damned problem with Janet? Think you can find her today?"

'I looked at him. "Len," I said – when we're by ourselves, we're on a first-name basis – "you're making me nervous, talking like that. Like Janet's now *my* foster child. I've told her what we want done. Had her in Saturday for that. If she doesn't do what I said; keeps on entertaining the guy, then the only thing I can see that we can do is call up her case and get rid of it. It won't cause any stir. It's only attempted larceny and she's been outta trouble almost a year. It'll look okay if we broom it. And there's no way we can try the fuckin' thing now, as both of us very well know. The cops haven't got any witnesses left. So the way that I look at it, that's our only choice."

'So that was when he said to me could I get on that and track her down right this afternoon after work there, mark it up for tomorrow and bring her in right after lunch, "when no one's around. Call it up, blow it out and get rid of it here. Or maybe just lose it, like Chassy and Larry used to do, when they were playing their games."

'Well, I wasn't gonna argue with him. So I just said I couldn't do that or anything else today. I said I hadda see Pooler. And that's when he said to me, outta the blue: "Bob Pooler? Why've you gotta see Pooler? Are you in that too? That federal mess I've been hearing about? I assumed he'd be Hilliard's lawyer."'

23

Robert Pooler in a dark blue suit, medium-blue broadly striped white-collared shirt and red-and-blue geometrically patterned tie had a rural-looking goat-shouldered younger man by the right elbow when Merrion spotted him. The younger man, bald except for an inch-wide fringe of brown hair from ear to ear, wore a narrow maroon knit tie, a homespun-grey shirt, voluminous pleated grey pants, brownish suede shoes and a worried expression. They emerged from a doorway partway down the long corridor leading away from the reception area into the southeasterly corner of the eleventh floor of the office tower in the Bay State West complex on Main Street in Springfield.

'I haven't been in there since they had the time for the governor back in Eighty-eight. Five hundred a head for cocktails and peanuts, not even cashews for Christ sake, and then the bastard's a no-show. No wonder he lost. But they've still got that hush, like a shrine.' Merrion and Hilliard had the bar at Grey Hills to themselves that evening, the honor system operating on weekday nights that attracted few members in the off-season. 'Still very classy. Maybe even a bit deeper, more luxurious, like they had it reupholstered in a heavier fabric. They must have to have somebody come in every year or so to clean it, don't you think? "First of May again, Fleason. Time to call the hush-cleaning people; steam all the wickedness out, freshen up the deception area."'

About half a minute earlier the receptionist, a light-skinned middle-aged black woman with a blunt haircut and a hangdog expression not quite masking undifferentiated hostility had patronizingly taken his name, nodding, 'to see Mister Pooler.'

'Not actually *saying*, but obviously *meaning*,' Merrion told Hilliard, '"Oh, well, then, you must be in one *heavy* peckah shit there, chile, you here to see Mister Pooler."'

She had responded by keying a button on her telephone deskset; when the light glowed steady red, in a tone verging on insolence she said: 'A Mister Merrion to see you, sir.' Then she had said haughtily to Merrion: 'Mister Pooler will see you shortly. If you'll just have a seat.'

Merrion told Hilliard 'the attitude's about the same as ever, too, I'd have to say. Every time I've had any kind of contact with Butler, Corey – no more'n two or three other times in my life; don't see much of their ilk in the lowly district court – I've always kind of wondered what gives with that bunch. They've got more attitude'n the fuckin' IRS. What is it with a law firm that looks down on people who've got problems like they're dirt? They should be glad to see us. Isn't that what they're *for*, for the luvva Mike? Help people with their problems if they've got 'em; help them not to get 'em if so far they've been lucky – isn't that what lawyers do?'

'"Do," yes,' Hilliard said. 'Talk about, no. The good ones're sort of like successful call girls. Truly elegant call girls never took many calls anyway, even before they moved up. They considered themselves "models" or "actresses," sometimes "flight attendants." In Europe a century ago they were "courtesans." Their looks brought them to the attention of refined gentlemen. Their skills prompted the gentlemen to display them to their friends, also gentlemen of taste and breeding. If fate was kind, one of them made a flattering offer of an exclusive arrangement. The working girls became fine ladies, far above their previous calling, so far above it they may never've done it. They live at stylish addresses, two or three of them: city; winter; summer. Their clothes are in *excellent* taste. They have cars and drivers, to carry them to shops and lunch. They arrange formal but intimate dinners for thirty or forty, all without batting an eye. They talk about the theater and the ballet, and what's going on in the art world. What they *do* for what all of this costs still goes for about the same price they charged while they were on a fee-for-service basis, now under exclusive long-term contract to the one refined gentleman, one of marriage. What they *act* as though they do and prefer to talk about are not that sort of thing at all. Your top law firms behave the same way.'

The slope-shouldered younger man had a manila folder thick with yellow papers in his left hand. Pooler was talking as the two of them walked up the corridor toward where Merrion sat in a red leather wing chair next to a reading table with a brass lamp. He could not recall ever having seen Pooler when he had not either been talking or else waiting with poorly concealed impatience for someone else to finish saying whatever was taking so long. Then Pooler would expel '*Yes*,' from his mouth in a whinnying sigh of relief – implying: *regardless of that* – and resume talking.

The younger man, three to five inches taller than Pooler at five-eight or so – like nearly every normal adult male, Merrion thought, with what he recognized as mean pleasure – was stooping slightly, inclining his shiny head so as to hear clearly what Pooler was saying. That made it look as though he was deferring to Pooler.

That was the way Pooler wished it. He deliberately inflicted that discomfort upon everyone he talked to, speaking so softly that anyone taller would have to bow slightly to hear him. He did not look up while talking with anyone, even when he was seated and his listener was standing. He believed that the person inducing another to adopt a posture of deference dominated every situation. He sought dominance at all times, regardless of the apparent absence of any subject in contention or under negotiation.

'That son of a bitch,' Merrion said once to Hilliard, 'you know there has to be something wrong with a guy who makes people uncomfortable on purpose.'

Merrion had first met Pooler on the evening of the first Wednesday in April of 1968 at a small gathering of western Massachusetts Democratic politicians in the private dining room upstairs in a good restaurant in Springfield. The meeting had been called hurriedly by men and women with decades of gritty experience in Democratic state and national politics left puzzled and unsure of what to do in the wake of the shock they had sustained the previous Sunday evening. President Johnson's request for TV time had not been simply to announce, as feared, a further escalation of the war in Vietnam (although he had included that, to widespread disapproval). He had thunderstruck the country by mournfully and reproachfully announcing his irrevocable decision not to seek (or to accept, either, as though there'd been more than an outside chance that someone truly out of touch might call for a convention draft) their party's nomination to be re-elected 'as your prezdun.'

Incorrectly, the party elders imputed their own sad uncertainty to younger regulars like Hilliard and Merrion. They too had been startled when Lyndon Johnson publicly renounced all ambition for a second full term of his own, but Merrion had been relieved and Hilliard had been elated. He had no doubt what to do. He was so sure that he abrogated his policy of saying nothing publicly until he had first tested it aloud on himself by discussing its probable effect with Merrion – Merrion that night had been unavailable, aloft on his way home from a long weekend in New Orleans with Sunny Keller, on leave from her assignment at Lackland Air Force base in Texas. Unrestrained by Merrion's caution, Hilliard jubilantly told the first reporter seeking his reaction that evening that he was backing Bobby Kennedy for the Democratic presidential nomination, 'hammer and tongs.'

Hilliard's commitment was not new. Only his disclosure of it was. Well before Sen. Eugene McCarthy's anti-Vietnam war campaign bucking Johnson in the February New Hampshire primary had yielded a close-second-place finish, Hilliard had said he hoped that Kennedy would challenge the president, but he had not said so for attribution in the media. Rashly doing so that night, he said that LBJ's withdrawal was 'the best news the party's had in years. If he'd wanted the nomination, he would've had it for the asking. Sitting presidents are not to be denied, McCarthy or not. Anyone who thinks otherwise is dreaming. But then he would've lost. Guarantee you, matched-up against Lyndon, Nixon wins.'

'I think that maybe did not play too good,' Merrion told him grimly in the immediate aftermath of the announcement. Hilliard demurred, but after two days of fielding strong reactions, he reluctantly accepted Merrion's assessment: 'You've made a lot of people goddamned mad at you, all at *once*, without doing yourself any damned good at all. No other mistake we've ever made, and we have made some beauts, did so much damage so fast. You've pissed-off people we don't even *know*. They didn't know each *other*, until you lit them off; you're the first thing they've ever had in common.

'First you pissed off the people who've always run the fucking party. Postmasters, Customs collectors, marshals, all the way up to judges and ambassadors: "First our party, then our country, dead right or dead wrong." They think Eugene McCarthy is a rotten, treacherous, party-wreckin' son of a bitch, and anyone who's with him or anybody else, like Bobby, who's against the *President*, is either a traitor or a Republican. Which in their books is much the same thing.

'At the very *same* time you enraged the McCarthy people. They've been scheming and conniving for the past five years to mug the old farts and take the party away from them. Then lo and behold, along comes Gene McCarthy, the answer to their prayers, with the balls to stand up and say "Aw right, if nobody else'll do it, goddamn it, I'll do it *myself*." *Roll* the fuckin' dice, and get the movement underway, even if it does mean the end of his career – they go berserk the guy, the Way, the Truth and the Light. "Peacemakers" they claim to be; *Colt* Peacemakers, maybe. Look like dangerous animals to me; crazy eyes, foam in their scraggliass-beards. So what do you do? Make them as screaming mad at *you*'s they were at LBJ. You ain't got no Secret Service to protect you, and you're *local*; they can get in your face.

'You think you can *reason* with them? Calmly tell them they just have to understand that this's how it's going to be, might as well get used to it? Bobby Kennedy's bringing all his muscle in and he's going to take it away: you got any idea how they're gonna react? They probably won't tear you limb from limb. They'll *want* to do that, but they won't know how. They're from good homes, went to private schools; no seminars in dismemberment. They'll practice self-restraint. Engage you in dialogue. All that passive shit, you know? Non-violent resistance. Pacificism. They'll address you in dulcet tones, probing your *raison d'etre*. They'll say:

'"Hey you fucker, what the *fuck*, the nomination's *his*? Like it was a fucking *tricycle* he now decides *he* wants to play with, and all he's gotta do is just come along and *take* it? This's something that he *owns*, 'cause he's a fucking *Kennedy*? His brother *left* it to him? Whose fuckin' country is this – ours or the Kennedys?"'

Pooler that evening in the spring of '68 was an assistant U.S. attorney in Boston. He was four confident years out of Yale and the Georgetown Law School. Immediately after they'd been introduced by Frank Snodgrass, a State committeeman who owned a lumber yard in Ware, Pooler said: 'Being Hilliard's co-pilot, you're also therefore RFK.'

Merrion, nearing thirty and feeling seasoned, mature and sagacious, failed nonetheless to connect an arrogant young man named Pooler to a powerful political family named Corey at the helm of a powerhouse law firm. He was distracted; Sunny Keller by then was many thousands of miles away from home in Vietnam, and that night like most April nights in the Pioneer Valley was a little chilly. Merrion's mind at that point had been focused on his chances of getting into bed with Mary Pat Sweeney after the meeting – they turned out to be good. Rather absently he said to Pooler: 'I haven't really decided. But Danny's always been a strong Kennedy backer. So I suppose I will be, too.' Levelly, he thought.

Pooler said: 'I suppose that means you won't give the vice president anything more'n lip-service if he gets the nomination.'

'At this point I don't think I'd been in that room more than five minutes,' Merrion said many times after that evening, explaining time and time again, at Hilliard's insistence, to person after person, that he'd never had a beef with Pooler and that as far as he knew Pooler'd never had a reason, that night or any other, to have a beef with him.

Each time word of another such recital reached his ears, Dan Hilliard privately thanked Merrion. 'Since we of course both realize that that soothing declaration isn't one hundred percent *true*, and I know how painful you find it to dissemble, I really appreciate your willingness to repeat it so many, many times.'

The necessity for many repetitions made it clear to them that Pooler had marketed his version at every political gathering he attended, well into the mid-Seventies, long after RFK had been assassinated and Nixon had defeated Hubert Humphrey. He used it to imply that Hilliard and Merrion put personal loyalties before party loyalty, and therefore should not be entrusted with power. Merrion and Hilliard used their sanitized summary of the encounter in Springfield as evidence that Pooler was a saboteur, undermining them to promote his own veiled interests.

Hilliard was the only person who ever heard Merrion's complete and accurate report of his exchange with Pooler. 'I told him I hadn't said that, either that I was gonna be with Kennedy or I'd be sitting out. I said neither one of us ever refused to close ranks and I didn't like him suggesting that we would. I said you hadn't made any threats; you just said you were backing RFK. No dramatics at all.

'Pooler told me he didn't believe me and anyway, I didn't *have* to say a word – it was written all over my face. That sounded to me like he was calling me a liar. I asked him if he'd mind telling me what else he could read on my face, so I'd have some idea of all the stuff I didn't know I knew yet. He called me a typical country wise-ass. I guess that could've been his sophisticated Yale idea of humor.

'If it is, his idea's wrong. He may have a very good barber razor-cut that wavy hair, not to mention an excellent tailor – he probably paid more for his suit than my whole wardrobe cost – but he *doesn't* have a nice way of telling anybody anything. He never will. He's a natural-born prick.

'He gets up too close when he talks to you, and he spits when he says words that have S in them. It's all he can do to keep from poking you in the chest. He's got a couple bad teeth, almost black; you can see them on the upper left side of his mouth when he curls that lip of his. His breath's too sweet; must be really bad before he uses too much mouthwash. He's ugly, too; he's already got jowls, at what, twenty-eight or twenty-nine? That's fuckin' indecent, too young to have jowls. But it figures; he's starting to get heavy all over. His waist's already begun to disappear. Some day pretty soon he won't have one anymore. Wake up some fine morning and find he's dispensed with it. He'll say he got rid of it because he couldn't find any purpose for it. He'll taper: Narrow at the ends, his head and his feet, and thick in the middle, his ass and his belly for ballast, like Tweedledum and Tweedledee.

Thirty years or so from now, he's pushing sixty, he'll have wattles, like a turkey. And those beady little eyes – like a snake, a short, fat snake that spits. A garden adder, green and black. Except I don't think those're poisonous, and he is.'

'Are adders smart?' Hilliard said. 'I don't know that much about reptile IQs.'

'I dunno, why?' Merrion said.

'Because if they're not,' Hilliard said, 'Pooler's no adder. I don't argue with you that the guy's a snake. You know him lots better'n I do, since I don't know him at all, but if he's a snake and adders aren't smart, Pooler's a different breed.'

'Yeah, well,' Merrion said, 'I called him an asshole, which he is, smart or not. I said it politely, of course. Just making an observation: "You're the biggest asshole I've met in a long time."

'He seemed to take it personally, looked shocked and backed away, so that's where I guess we agreed to leave it. Little prick.'

Hilliard said it would be best if no one heard that part. 'Bob Pooler isn't just *trying* to look dangerous – he *is* dangerous. His mother's maiden name was Corey, and his daddy is a partner, along with his granddaddy, Warren, in Butler, Corey. Which means his family's got a major piece of that mammoth law firm, which makes nothing but money. Furthermore, it's *been* a big wealthy firm ever since the first Pynchon, Sam, pulled up a tuffet and sat down by the river to catch his breath, and before you knew it, he'd gone and founded a city.

'And if plain old big money doesn't impress you, you can throw in a herd of state and federal judges, ambassadors, law school deans, and a slew of directors of operas and museums and chairmen of corporate boards. Money buys power, and power brings in more money, which in turn accures more power, even for obnoxious little assholes such as Bobby Pooler who get everything wrong except their choice of ancestors. When poor humble peasants like us go up against powerful rich assholes, the *behoovin'* begins. It *behooves* us to do our best to get along with them.

'It'll be a damned sight better for us if everyone else who meets that kid forms his own opinion of him – which'll probably be the same as yours – *without* any assistance from you. So that when the day finally comes when Junior *doesn't* get what he really wants, at least a federal judgeship, he won't come gunning for us. When he gets it in the teeth, his own people'll have to tell him. "When it's unanimous that you're a little shit; everybody who's dealt with you hates your guts; you're outnumbered. There's too many of 'em to single out one or two like Amby and Danny, and get even."'

Bob Pooler still dressed beautifully but he wasn't aging well, Merrion decided happily, as the younger man with Pooler stopped at the office door nearest the reception desk, clearly eager to go in. Pooler's wavy black hair had thinned out on the top, the remainder growing grey, with a straggly end or two where the comb-over brushed the ears. His waist had all but disappeared. The obtrusive attitude had not. Pooler halted when his captive did, still holding onto him and talking, completing his train of thought.

His conversation was full of minor visible events. He made a chopping motion with his right hand each time he wanted to drive home a point, puffing and deflating his cheeks, furrowing his brows, to vary the intensity of what he said. Merrion could read his lips; he punctuated every third or fourth sentence with 'You see? You see that? You see?'

The younger man, restless, seemed to feel obliged to nod at each gesture, as though believing that there must be some quota of obeisance which when satisfied would enable him to get away.

Then Pooler abruptly released the elbow, frowning, staring after the other man's back, as though considering whether to become annoyed at him for leaving with his folder. He apparently concluded that to do so would be pointless; there was no hope that he would ever understand what Pooler had explained. He shook his head once, irritably, then turned toward the reception area. He saw Merrion sitting in the wing chair; recognizing him incuriously. Giving no sign of having recognition, he proceeded to the reception desk; accepted a thin sheaf of pink messages; riffled through them without evident interest; put them back on the reception desk and looked up again at Merrion.

'He looked at me the same way that you'd look at a school bus blocking an intersection where you want to make a turn. Nothing personal, you know? Just another obstacle in your way interfering with what you want to do. He really is a shabby piece of shit. I think the only reason the bastard finally did acknowledge me was the snooty black receptionist. She said something I couldn't hear, and it was like her knowing I was there to see him made it so he had to see me. That was the only reason he did it. He obviously knew me, but otherwise he would've ignored me. Gone back down to his office, no hello or anything. He must be the rudest fucker inna world. If he isn't, I hope I never meet the champ.'

Merrion uncrossed his legs and stood up as Pooler approached him, taking inventory of Merrion's apparel, head to toe: Ralph Lauren Polo blue blazer; tan twill slacks; light blue Oxford cloth shirt, open at the collar; brown Florsheim loafers. 'Ambrose,' he said drily, extending his hand. 'What can I do for you?'

'The same way I used to say Hello to guys I didn't like when I was at Valley Ford. Gave me some shit about a bill or they did too much complaining. After they did that – just *once*, once was all they hadda do it – whenever they brought their cars in for service, or they had something wrong with them, they hadda wait. That was Pooler's attitude toward me today,' Merrion said to Hilliard.

'You tell me, Bob,' Merrion said to Pooler, shaking his hand once. 'I don't really know why I'm here. Wasn't my idea to come. Danny Hilliard sent me down. He said I should see you.'

'Yes,' Pooler said. 'Looking at me,' Merrion said to Hilliard, 'like now he knows why he thought he smelled catshit in the building. He really hates my guts, but he's got this problem with me.

'His problem is that he can't heave my ass out in the street. He can't get at me. Me getting that assistant-clerk slot almost thirty years ago, couple years before he even met me, much less hated me on sight: that's the only reason that he didn't do his best to stop it from happening. If he'd known me then, he would've, and probably succeeded. But by the time he discovered we despised each other, I was already in. And then four years after that, his grandfather and his father were so busy scheming how they're gonna get their paws on that racetrack, they didn't notice us gettin' into Grey Hills. Otherwise the Big Chief and Little Beaver would've used the blackballs on us.'

'Yes,' Pooler said again. 'Well, I think I know what it's about.' He extended his right hand to usher Merrion away from the chair toward the corridor beyond the reception desk. Merrion held back. Pooler raised his right eyebrow. 'I think it would be better,' he said, 'if we didn't talk about it here, but in my office.'

'Lead on,' Merrion said, smiling, but not very much. 'I'll toddle right along behind.'

Pooler had arranged the framed pictures and testaments on the credenza and the wall behind his desk so it appeared that once he had received his diplomas from Yale and Georgetown Law, his certificates of admission to the State and federal bars and his appointment as an Assistant US Attorney, he'd spent most of his time away from that desk standing behind lecterns, either delivering speeches, shaking hands with other people or assisting them to display laminated plaques, scrolls and certificates now interspersed among the pictures.

'There's one picture of him shooting off his mouth in a white turtleneck under one of those crew-neck sweaters with the big white reindeer marching across his chest,' Merrion told Hilliard. 'Except for that the guy never seems to've gotten within range of anyone holding a camera except when he's had a jacket and tie on. I bet he sleeps in a suit. On weekends he wears his tux to bed instead of pajamas, case a charity dinner breaks out inna middle of the night.'

'He told you what's been bothering him,' Hilliard said.

'He told me what he's been *hearing*,' Merrion said. 'He said what *bothers* him about what he's been hearing is that he's afraid it means the feds're going to come after you in order to go through you to get at somebody else. And the way they're gonna get at you's through me.'

'That's essentially what he told me,' Hilliard said. 'But can you see how he thinks they can do this?'

'Hey,' Merrion said, 'that's your job, to tell me. You and Pooler. You're the fuckin' lawyers. All I am in this fuckin' lash-up's a poor fuckin' clerk of court. I know my part in this comedy, but that doesn't mean I've got any idea what the play is about. Doesn't mean dog-squat to me. I don't know what the feds can do. I assume it's maximum damage, of course, if they can and they want to do anything. You're asking me how they plan to *do* the damage, there I can't help you. I just hope it's not jail they've got in mind. I go into jails in the course of my employment. I don't like 'em. I'm always glad to get out.

'Best I can figure, what Pooler said, it all goes back all the way to Chassy and Larry Lane, Fiddle Barrow and the Carneses; how those guys were doing business around here, thirty, forty years ago, you and me're just gettin' started. I don't really see how they can do this, considering that every statute of limitations *I* ever heard of expires after five or six years. If they haven't bagged you by then, they can't. Except for murder and treason; and I don't *think* they got us on that.

'But according to what Pooler says, they got a way says they can get around it. I don't trust him but I guess I believe him. Still think the bastard'll bear watching, though. He's a shifty mother-fucker and I think he's twenty-to-forty-percent on the side of the enemy here. He told me he hates to lose. Said he goes into every case fully expecting to win. "When I can't expect that, I refuse it." But this time I think if his client loses, he'll be able to take it in his stride.'

Pooler seemed dwarfed by his own lustrous brown leather desk chair. He sat far down in it so that hunched behind the desk he looked like a frog sitting on a rock, partially obscured behind a bigger rock in front that hid his body except for his shoulders and the part of his torso above the base of his sternum. Once he had Merrion seated in the barrel chair he studied him, working his mouth while he used his left index finger to rub his left nostril, hard. Then he picked up large black-framed eye-glasses with visible bifocal lines and used both hands to put them on, spreading the bows and fitting them over his ears as carefully as though he had been preparing to cut a diamond. When he looked up the upper and lower lenses enlarged Merrion's view of his brown irises differently, so that their upper and lower hemispheres did not quite seem to match. Pooler swallowed and said 'Yes.'

Merrion did not say anything. 'I felt like some kind of specimen,' he told Hilliard. 'Something helpless in a lab that this guy was now going to cut up and see if he could learn something. Hard on me, maybe, but useful to him.'

Pooler rested his chin on his left hand and extended his index finger up alongside the corner of his mouth. He licked his lips.

'The gist of it's the club memberships,' he said. 'From all we've been able to gather – naturally not wanting to appear to be *too* interested – but from what we can piece together that's essentially the direction they seem to be taking.' His teeth were even and white.

'Grey Hills?' Merrion said. To Hilliard later he said: 'I wasn't saying that to give the guy a hard time. Playing Mickey-the-dunce with him there. If we're really involved in something here, it isn't all just smoke and mirrors, how the hell could Grey Hills have anything to do with it? Almost twenny-five years after we joined it? It was a legitimate question.

'He thought I was jerkin' his chain. For Pooler that question was all it took. My asking that *really* creased it.'

'Yeah,' Pooler said, glowering at him, '*Grey Hills*. I know, it's a long time ago, but that's the way it is with over-reaching. You may get what you want at the time, but what you have to do to get it, well, those things have a way of coming back to haunt you.

'You probably never heard what I had to say at the time you and Hilliard applied for membership. I knew you by then from meeting you in Sixty-eight, and I didn't like you. And I said then to them, my father and grandad: I didn't like it and I thought it was a *rotten* idea for you and Dan to become members. Quite candidly said so. And not just to them, either; to the membership committee; totally open and aboveboard. I would've said it to you and Dan, if the opportunity'd occurred, said it right to your faces.

'I said it was a very bad idea. That no matter how nice and friendly it might look as though we'd all become, dealing in party and legislative matters, the two of you did *not* belong at Grey Hills.

'My father and the Chief said their concerns were political. They were sorry circumstances had been such that the membership rolls had to be reopened, and very much regretted that had made it possible for people like you and Dan to aspire to membership and apply. They said when they voted to reopen, they assumed that the high price of initiation and membership would be enough to prevent your kind from even trying to get in. If they had ever dreamed that people like you might somehow find the money, they would've blocked the proposal at the outset.

It would've never made it out of the executive committee, much less been approved by the board of governors or voted on by the entire membership. In hindsight they fully agreed it would have been far better if they'd bitten the bullet and submitted to a hefty extraordinary one-time assessment on the membership to meet the club's financial needs.

'But now it was too late. They were afraid that if they kept you out, Dan might retaliate, prevail upon his pals on Beacon Hill to refuse to grant racing days for that damned racetrack the Chief was so obsessed about. They were *obsessed* by that damned track. They virtually *ordered* me not to use my blackball.

'I didn't, but I warned them. I told them no good would ever come out of letting the pair of you in. I said nothing but trouble would ever come out of it. I told my dad that, and I told the Chief, too, it was an awful idea.

'I couldn't know then exactly what form the trouble would take, what repercussions there'd be. I must confess it didn't cross my mind that somehow your joining some day might form the basis for a tax evasion case, which seems to be the way they're heading. But there was no doubt in my mind that some day, sooner or later, something bad was certain to happen. Now my ugly premonition seems to be coming true.

'I want to emphasize that none of this was personal. It was not that I had a thing against you. Even though we'd had that confrontation over the Humphrey candidacy, that was irrelevant. Nor had I anything against Dan Hilliard, or anyone who'd gotten where he is today by means of his own good hard work. More power to him, I say. I just knew that trouble was bound to come out of it some day, if your applications went through. My father and the Chief knew it too. I suspect *you* both knew, regardless of whether you admitted it to yourselves, that the two of you did not *belong* at Grey Hills. You didn't have the *stuff*.

'By rights you didn't have the *means*, the *resources*, to be members. How you came by them, I don't know, and I don't want to. I do know some kind of shady business was involved. Had to be; you had no other way, no *honest* way, to have laid your hands on that amount of money that fast. Sixteen or seventeen thousand dollars? An assistant clerk of courts and a state rep on the lower rungs of power? I'll give you your due: you were cute. No one's ever found out what you did or how you did it. But cleverness purifies nothing: the dirty politician's still like a rotten mackerel in the moonlight: so brilliant, and yet so corrupt, he *shines*, and *stinks*.'

Merrion glared at him. 'You piece of yellow shit,' he said, 'getting me in here to say that to me. The next time we meet where some of my friends're around, so *I'll* have witnesses, I'm gonna call you out, dare you to repeat that. If you don't I'm gonna call you a fuckin' coward, and spit on you. And if you do, you'd better have a friend with you to hold your fancy bridgework or you're gonna swallow it.'

Pooler smiled. 'Sorry, Amby, but there's no other way of putting it, wasn't then and isn't now, and your reaction to the statement of that fact just proves it: you're not Grey Hills material and you never were. Neither of you ought to've been allowed to place yourselves in the position where you'd have to do whatever it is you've done to meet the obligations membership entailed. As the fix you're now in proves conclusively. But back then, no one would listen to me.'

He nodded, pouching his cheeks with air like an industrious squirrel with a cargo of acorns. 'And now the day of reckoning has come, just as I predicted. But now it's too late for my cautions to do any good.'

Merrion said to Hilliard: 'I considered getting up and winding up and letting him have it, popping him one in the chops. Pasting him six or eight good ones, glasses and all, right in his smug little, fat little, face. Hair on the walls and blood on the floor; teeth in the nap of the rug. Change his nose from convex to concave. But I restrained myself. For one thing I don't want his yard-man to wind up behind the wheel of my car, using my house as an equipment shed. Particularly since I'd most likely still be in jail when he won the civil suit turning all of my goods over to him. Besides, my impression is that at least until one of us belts him, he's at least got to pretend he's on our side.'

'Hell, if you think about it,' Hilliard said, 'he may actually manage to get us to agree with him about Grey Hills. He's a third generation member. He's never seemed to *use* his membership much; I've seldom seen him there. But up 'til now I've always assumed it was because he was working all the time. Or else he just didn't like golf. There are people like that, you know. But now you've got me wondering: Maybe it's fear of rubbing elbows with riffraff like *us*, using showers that we've used, that's made him scarce up there. Is he really that petty? If he is, he's right saying we're not fit to be members. What kind of asshole'd pay money to hang out with him? The very idea's disgusting. Fine mess you got us into, Ollie, you and your grandiose ideas.'

'Hey,' Merrion said, 'my intentions were good. I'd had an unexpected bit of good fortune. Shared it with a friend.'

'Yeah,' Hilliard said, 'well, so whaddaya think? Myself I think I'd have to say the two of us by working hard've paved the road to Hell damned well.'

24

'I think the bastard actually *liked* explaining it all to me,' Merrion told Hilliard after dinner in the dim dark-panelled bar at Grey Hills. 'Listening to him . . . I sat there and he talked and I heard what he was saying and it was like I'd stepped outside myself, and what I wanted to do more'n anything in the whole world was stand up and whack him one. It was the same feeling that I had the day I went back with my mother to see the specialist, the "geriatricist" – sounds like a circus act, guy who rides a bike naked onna high-wire, something. Her regular doctor sent us to him, see if he could figure out what was going on with her. "Have him run a few tests." Duck when they say "a few tests"; they're warmin' up to tell you you're doomed.

'The idea was to find out why she was forgetting things, who she was or where she lived; why she mattered in the world and who she mattered *to*. Naturally my dear brother Chris's nowhere to be seen; that's a family tradition. I can tell when the fat's inna fire: Chris's long-gone an' hard to find.

'She went outdoors one cold morning, late November, in her nightgown, barefoot. Went for a stroll down the street. Eight-thirty or so. Lots of people must've seen her, going off to work in their cars, coats on and the heaters going, barefoot lady in her nightgown walking down the street, but nobody stopped and tried to help her, or called the cops, their car-phone. *They* didn't care if something happened to her, nobody they knew; just ignored her and drove right on by. She got about a mile before someone who knew her from the bakery stopped her car and hollered at her, snapped her out of it, thank God; drove her home and called me. She'd only done it that once, but even once gets you worried. Next time she might not be that lucky, wander off and freeze to death, do something else and get hurt.

'And both of us already . . . it wasn't like we didn't have an inkling what was going on. We didn't know the details but we had a pretty good idea. She was gradually losing her buttons. We'd seen it happen to other people. Her mother, Rose; then they called it "hardening of the arteries." "Her brain isn't getting enough blood – she's getting old, and simple, too." Before we'd heard of senile dementia and Alzheimer's. When she was lucid, which she was most of the time – she had a pretty good idea that when she wasn't quite right, that was probably the explanation.

'But we didn't *want* to have that pretty good idea, you know? We didn't *like* having it. And her doctor, Paul Marsh, dead himself now: the reason that he sent us to this baby-faced specialist – looked like he was about fourteen – was because *he* didn't want it to be what we all knew it was. He was the family doctor. He'd been treating her for years, "taking care of all of you," was what he said. She was as much a friend of his as a patient. He didn't want her to have what she had, and for damned sure he didn't want to be the one to tell her. This new guy would do that. Wouldn't bother him; he didn't know Polly from a load of goats. We were seeing him to spare Paul. I suppose it was in a good cause.

'So they did those few tests they had in mind to do on her, and that took quite a while. "A few tests" is quite a lot, you find, when you start taking them. And then they told us to go home until they could "just get all the results back here, take a look at them so we can see what they mean." Give us a few more days or so to make-believe and hope that what we knew was going on was not. Then they had us back again and this time he sees us in his nice office, about sixteen diplomas on his wall and the kind of smooth white face you'd expect to see on your executioner. The vet we took our last dog to, have him put to sleep: he had a kinder face, I swear – he at least *pretended* he felt sorry it hadda be done. But this assassin sits us down and quite pleasantly informs my mother and me that one by one, a few here, few there, she's begun to lose her marbles. And there's nothing he can do.

'For us this was kind of upsetting news, you know? But for him it was all in a day's work, like he's conducting an experiment. "Okay, let's see how these two take it when I hand the sentence down, tell them there's no hope." I suppose in his line of work, has to do this every day, gets to be routine. But my God, it hurts like hell when you're the people it's bein' done *to* – then it's not routine at all.

'I got the same feeling listening to Pooler. I think he was making it sound worse'n it is. I realize this isn't gonna be fun, something we'll really enjoy, fucking romp in a meadow or something, but he sure didn't go out of his way to make it sound better.

'He said they call it the Public Corruption Unit,' Merrion said. 'Said it didn't exist when he was in the US Attorney's office, twenty-odd years ago. I guess this's some new drill they dreamed up recently. Almost smacking his lips, the son of a bitch; I think he envies the bastards. "Gee, that looks like fun; wish *we'd* thought of it." Guys like him're like dogs that've killed once and had that first taste of blood: they never get over it. You know they'll kill again.'

'But then, of course,' Pooler said to Merrion, 'then there were only a dozen or so of us assistants; now there's about seven times that many. And there wasn't any western division of the District of Massachusetts, no federal court or satellite US Attorney's office out here. So things do change. There're more of them now with time on their hands, looking for something to do. They're bound to be more aggressive. To us older hands some of the things they propose to do seem a little far-fetched at first blush, but they've been making them stick.

'Essentially the unit operates on the same principle as the old Organized Crime Strike Forces: target prosecution. They identify subjects they think're corrupt, state and local officials, and then they study their official acts to see if they can find a way to apply federal criminal statutes. They've used the racketeering statutes, which were enacted to go after the Mafia, to go after people paying and accepting kickbacks on state contracts. They've charged mail fraud against people falsely claiming they can't work in order to get state and municipal disability pensions. Hard to argue with; they mail in the false statements of injury and get their checks by mail. The wire fraud statutes've been used to get people who picked up a phone to promise a bribe to a local plumbing inspector, just across town, and nailed the inspector for taking the call and taking the money. And of course they've been using the criminal tax-evasion statutes ever since the Thirties, when some frustrated genius said: "Well damnit all, if we can't prove Capone had people murdered, as he did, let's get him for tax evasion."

'That looks like the approach they're going to take with our friend Hilliard,' Pooler said, his expression a mixture of amusement and contempt. To Hilliard, Merrion said: 'I dunno whether he was sneering at the federal fuckers or at us.'

Pooler shrugged. 'Not that Danny's quite as big a trophy as Al Capone was, but he had a lot of power in his day, and he made himself conspicuous with his not-so-private life, so a lot of people know him. They still recognize his name. Get a grand jury to indict him and you're guaranteed a headline. Drop enough broad hints around before you go for the indictment, which is what they're doing now, you build up suspense; anticipation fed by rumor makes the headlines even bigger.'

'Danny's always paid his taxes,' Merrion said. 'So've I; we both have. Danny never took a bribe. Once when something I said made him think that I might do that, he as much as told me that if I had goin' on-the-take in mind, he wouldn't put me in a job. I eased his mind on that.

'Now, have I ever done a favor for a guy, given breaks to people who'd done things they shouldn't do? Sure, of course I have, and so has Danny: many favors. And gotten many in return. Sometimes a guy's bought me a drink after I've helped him out. Once or twice I've been out somewhere having dinner with a lady friend, and when it's come time for the check I find out I'm not getting one – someone I know but didn't see spotted us when we came in; on his way out told the maitre d', give our check to him. That's happened to Danny too, more times'n me. Not because he's crooked; because he knows more people. Friends of his picking up a check or giving him tickets to the ballgame? Sure, small stuff like that, of course we've done it.

'But never have we taken money, not once. That was always out of the question. Now are you telling me we're guilty of something? A federal offense? I don't believe it.'

Pooler sighed. 'Amby,' he said, 'you and I've always had trouble talking. We just can't seem to communicate. You refuse to hear what I'm trying to tell you, and what you say to me's unresponsive.

'What you choose to believe is *irrelevant*, hear me? Put it aside; it doesn't matter. The feds've picked up on you two. My guess is what got their attention, made them think you might be worth going after, is that you and Danny, especially Danny, have lived very well on your earnings. Danny's real estate holdings for example: a state legislator, lawyer who never practiced, managed to acquire a ten-room house in Bell Woods where his ex lives; a three-bedroom cottage in West Chop; and a three-bedroom townhouse condo in Wisdom House. He drives a Mercedes. All the while living a lavish lifestyle – of which the Grey Hills membership is not the only but certainly a prime example. Quite an accomplishment, considering that until about ten years ago his reported income never exceeded fifty thousand dollars a year.

'They have suspicious minds. When they see a politician who's pulled off something like that, the first thing they think is that he did it by taking kickbacks from state contractors who disguised them as campaign contributions, and converted the campaign funds to pay his personal expenses.

'They realize he and his now-ex-wife had the house in Holyoke, and he inherited his parents' property, their house in Holyoke and the camp on Lake Sunapee, all of which he sold. The feds say if you combine the proceeds of selling off those three properties, that accounts for the big house and land – worth upwards of four hundred thousand by now, all of it debt-free – in Bell Woods.

'Okay, but now what? That exhausts all the capital they concede he came by honestly. Where did he get the twenty-six-thousand-dollar down-payment on the house on the Vineyard? That was over twenty years ago. He was a legislator, making about forty grand a year. As far as the IRS knows, at least; that's all his tax-returns show.

'He's only bought two cars in that period. But they were both Mercedes, very costly automobiles. When he bought the first one he was still in the legislature. It cost him about a year's pay; so what did he live on?

'And that still leaves him to account for the fifteen thousand he somehow found to be put down on the townhouse, *while* he was going through a very costly divorce, buying the second Mercedes, and financing his scandalous high life. The feds maybe can't prove he did any singing, but they've got all the evidence of wine and women they could possibly want.

'They think the only way he could possibly have done all that was by taking payoffs from people who then got big contracts from the state, as several of his biggest contributors did. Contracts to install electrical systems in state buildings: his late generous backer Carl Kuiper's electrical company up in Deerfield did just under sixteen million bucks of that work during the last nine years that Danny was chairman of Ways and Means. During that same period: nine-point-three-million in state printing contracts to Haskell Sanderson's printing plant in Greenfield. An average of nine-hundred-and-eleven-thousand dollars a year in rent for state office space in western Massachusetts: to real estate holding companies owned or controlled by the Carnes family.'

He gazed at Merrion. 'There's probably more, if they look, as of course they are planning to do. But on the basis of what they've told me they already know, and what I can further surmise, I think it's going to be very difficult for Danny and me to come up with convincing evidence to rebut the inferences a jury will draw from those facts. I realize you're not a lawyer, but most jurors aren't either; wouldn't you share my concern?'

Merrion coughed. 'Well,' he said, 'I never handled contributions. I was never involved in finances. I just managed the campaigns, day to day, night to night. Never saw any bills, any checks. Didn't want to. At the beginning Mercy kept the books, and then after he got elected to the House the first time, Roy Carnes's accountants took over the financial end of things, handled it out of his office. That was always Roy Carnes's job.'

'I'm aware of that,' Pooler said, 'but you haven't answered my question. Do you think a jury'll acquit, when they see proof of what I've just said?'

'Look.' Merrion shifted in the chair and crossed his legs. He folded his hands on his right thigh. 'Look,' he said again, 'when you said we never got along, you were right. We agree that we don't like each other; I don't think we're ever gonna. To answer your question: no, I don't think that a jury hearing what you just told me would be very likely to return a Not Guilty. But you *are* a lawyer, and my question for you as a lawyer is this: Why couldn't any halfway-competent attorney for Danny *stop* the prosecutor from proving that case to a jury? Danny's last campaign was in Nineteen-eighty-two. His campaign fund closed a year later. That's over twelve years ago. Have these federal magicians repealed the statute of limitations? Or aren't you competent counsel?'

Pooler shook his head, smiling. 'You must've outsmarted yourself many times during your long career,' he said. 'Always thinking you're one step ahead, when you're generally out of the race.

'They don't *need* to repeal the statute, Amby. They've found a way *around* it. All they need now is you to guide them to their goal. They're aware you won't want to; you're loyal to Danny, and so you'll refuse. But they think they have a way to make you do what they want you to do.

'I omitted an item from that history of Dan's provable spending. I'm surprised you didn't notice it. You can be very sure the feds have. A quarter-century of annual dues and fees for his membership in Grey Hills.'

He gazed at Merrion. 'Which by itself, as you and I both know, has come to a pile of money. The year you two got in you paid close to nine thousand dollars initiation, dues and fees for him. They say that was income to him, as the dues've been too, every year since.'

'*Bullshit*,' Merrion said, 'that was a *gift*. All those dues and things were gifts. Danny and me'd been friends over ten years by the time we joined. He was my best friend inna world. If I hadn't gone to work for Danny I'd probably still be behind the Parts and Service desk up at Valley Ford. No reflection on John Casey; he was a good guy, and he treated the Merrions well, but that was not the kind of life I had in mind. I asked Danny to get me the clerk's job 'cause by then I'd decided I didn't wanna go into teaching and I thought it would be a good job to have. He talked to the Carneses and Judge Spring, and I talked to Larry Lane myself. Nobody had any objections, so I got the job, third assistant clerk.

'It's a good job and I've been very happy with it, but at no time has it ever been what you'd call a major plum. Sure it turned out to be one, after Larry Lane died, but that wasn't the job, it was Larry. By the time he retired, four years after I came in, *we'd* become pretty good friends. Then I find out he's very sick, in addition to drinking too much, and in case he might still feel cheerful while he's dying, his own family threw him out. What can I tell you? He's sick and alone; I did what I could to take care of the guy, not that it was very much. Two years or so later he's dead.

'Until he got sick I assumed all he had was his pension and when he died that'd go to his widow. I never knew he had any other money, much less that he'd leave it to me. And neither did Danny, of course. So I couldn't've done it for that. I was just trying to be a nice guy. So then, what am I supposed to do when I find out about the money? Give it away to strangers? I don't think so. I gave me and my best friend a present, something we both always wanted to have, and never expected to get. Those memberships at Grey Hills you resent us so much for having.

'I always paid taxes on the money, every year, before I spent any of it. You can go ask my accountant. I didn't mind doin' that – well, I *minded*, but no more'n everyone else who pays taxes. But then couldn't I use some of what I had left to give Danny a present? I wouldn't've had it without him.'

'They're not saying you couldn't give it to him, Amby,' Pooler said. 'Quite the opposite: they don't dispute that at all. They're saying that you *did* give it to him, eighty-five hundred or so the first year, and thousands more after that ever since, year after year after year. They don't even really care now that Lane got the money from corruption – death takes the taint off dirty money; they don't see any way to take Lane's loot away from you. But they'll be sure to put the fact in evidence just the same. "See? Graft's a tradition in Massachusetts. Graft over the years if it's wisely invested can go on yielding graft to the next generation. It's like planting a poisonous tree; the booty never stops giving.'

'What they *do* dispute, though, is that it was a *gift*. They say it was payment to him under the corrupt bargain you made: a piece of whatever action you got as a result of him getting you that job. So to him it was income, illegal income, like Capone's bootleg millions, but still taxable, and *he's never paid taxes on it*.'

Pooler lowered his head and leaned across the desk, staring at Merrion. He moistened his lips with his tongue; his eyes glittered. 'He didn't pay taxes on that money last year, Amby. He didn't pay them the year before that, or the year before that one, either, didn't pay in any year they still can reach under the five-year statute limiting criminal prosecutions. And once they prove something *within* the statute, they can go back to the dawn of creation, allege it was all a continuing scheme of corruption that persists to this very day. All they have to do is grant you immunity and you'll have to testify – to what everybody knows you've been doing all these years. That will prove both the source and the income, and Danny's benefit from it.

'They'll try to give you what's called *use immunity*, meaning that they won't be able to use anything you say to prosecute you, except for perjury. But that'd leave them still able to come after you for some crime you committed jointly with Danny they can prove another way, and you do not want that. If you do as I'm suggesting and go to Geoff Cohen, he'll say that's not good enough, make them ante up *transactional immunity*. That would mean nothing that they make you testify about can ever be charged against you.

'They'll do it. They don't want you, they want Danny, and I think they're going to get him good. Unless I can cut a deal for him, the likes of which I've never seen, Dan Hilliard is going to jail.'

'*Ahhhhh*,' Merrion said, closing his eyes, emptying his lungs, and sagging in the chair. 'I do not want to *hear* this.'

'What I'm getting from them is just preliminary,' Pooler said relentlessly, 'but it's bad enough. They figure by the time they get through adding interest and penalties on that club membership item alone, they'll be able to say he's evaded taxes on over two hundred thousand dollars. And more importantly to them, as I say, once they prove that he hasn't paid taxes on those dues and fees for the last *three* years – as of course they can, very easily, then they can allege that that was just one aspect of an elegant scheme. One going all the way back to Seventy-two when he first accepted the payoff from you for the membership, when you got into Grey Hills.

'And *that* then will mean they'll be able to prove all the *other* crooked things he was doing after that, all the kickbacks and bribes they think he started accepting when he really rose to power as the head of Ways and Means – Seventy-three or four, was it? All of those kickbacks on state contracts, calling them "campaign contributions" but treating them as income for his personal use and luxurious enjoyment. Illegal income, to be sure, ill-gotten gains aren't exempt.

'They'll have him in a steamer-trunk, ready to ship. It won't be to maximum security, no, but it'll probably have bars on the windows, and he won't be able to leave. They reckon that with all their multipliers of interest and penalty charges, they'll have him twisting in the wind for taking money and evading federal income taxes on it totalling about two million dollars. And after they've forfeited to the government everything that they can lay their hands on, the state will take what's left.

'So, that's their scenario. First they're going to put the cuffs on him and cart him off to jail, and then they're going pick him clean, take everything he's got. He'll be in all the papers, maybe national TV. "Another crooked Bay State politician went to federal prison today; details at eleven."'

'He's got this look he gives you when he says stuff like that,' Merrion said to Hilliard. '"Local politicians," and "*crooked* state and local politicians," like he's talking about some lower form of life – starfish or something.

'I sat there looking at him,' Merrion said to Hilliard, and what I want to say is: "The *what?* Run that one by me again?" But I don't. I don't think it matters how many times I make him say it, it's not gonna change.'

Hilliard looked grey and stricken. Merrion had not seen him look like that since his first term in the House when he came home from Boston on the afternoon of Friday, November 22, 1963, after JFK was shot in Dallas. 'I called Mercy 'fore I left, and she already knew,' he said to Merrion that day. 'She was crying. So was I. I said "What will happen to us now, what will happen to us now? All I can seem to do is cry." She said: "It's what you should be doing. Eleven John, thirty-five." I looked it up. 'Jesus wept.'

'I can't believe what they're saying,' Merrion said. 'All these years I've been paying you kickbacks for getting me the clerk's job, like Fiddle Barrow paid to Chassy and Larry and Roy Carnes for the courthouse contract, for them lettin' him cheapjack the job, when I thought I was giving you presents. *I* always paid taxes on the money I used for that when Fourmen's Trust made the annual distribution. So therefore I am okay. But they think you *didn't* pay income taxes on the money I paid to Grey Hills for *you*.

'Of course I didn't,' Hilliard said. 'I told my accountant about it, the first year, and he told me it was a gift. You were giving me a present, and as long as it didn't come to ten-grand in any one year or go over thirty-grand in our lifetime, tax laws that we had then, it wasn't taxable. Sam Evans said the same thing, I was going through the divorce and we're making out the statement of my income and expenses. What you were paying for me at Grey Hills wasn't on either one. He said, "Mercy's not entitled to a share of a present you get from Merrion. She's married to you, not to Ambrose. He doesn't have to pay alimony." And now it's even more untaxable'n it was then. Now there's really no limit on gifts. As long as you're not trying to beat the estate tax, you can be as generous as you like.'

'That's what I said to Pooler,' Merrion said. 'I said I wasn't kicking back anything to you. I was giving you a gift. You got me the job which resulted in me getting the money. You did it because you're my friend. As a result of me having the job, I came into some money. Quite a lot of it, in fact. But neither one of us had any idea, going in, that that money even existed. Much less that I would wind up getting it.

'"It was like I hit the lottery," I said to Pooler. "You do that, you naturally want to share it with someone, family and also your friends. All the family I had was my mother, and that fuckin' brother of mine. I paid off the mortgage on my mother's house, which's now mine, and made sure she was well-taken care of. Only reason she stayed workin' at Slade's was because she liked the job. I didn't give Chris a fuckin' thing. I don't like his attitude. Danny's the best friend any man ever had. Why wouldn't I share with him?'

'You know what he said?' Merrion said. 'Pooler said to me: "Very touching. Better hope that the jury believes it."'

'He thinks they probably won't. We been in this club a long time, Danny. We've belonged here almost twenny-five years. By the time they add up everything I paid Grey Hills for you, they've got you evading almost two hundred grand, taxes. They start adding interest and penalties; they're inna millions, no sweat. Pooler says for that you go to jail.'

'In other words,' Hilliard said, 'it's gonna be the end of me, maybe the end of your job as a clerk, but certainly the end of me.'

'That's what he seems to be saying,' Merrion said.

'What the *hell*?' Hilliard said, anguish in his voice. 'Do we know what it was that brought this on? Did Pooler tell you that? Playing golf's not a crime, not the last I heard, anyway, although the way we play it maybe should be. And joining a country club: that isn't, either, even when it's one that costs a lot of money. What made them decide to come after me, and therefore to come after you?

'I asked Pooler that,' Merrion said. '"This smells like revenge to me. Has it got anything to do with anything we actually do in *politics*? Something they can point to and say: 'See? It was a fraud, right from the very beginning'? I don't remember it that way. I don't remember one occasion when Danny and I went off by ourselves and said: 'Okay now, how can we make money from this? Not once in all the years.'" And he shrugged his shoulders and said: "I dunno. Some people think head-hunting's fun."'

'But what brought it on *now*?' Hilliard said. 'I've been out of sight for ten years.'

'Pooler thinks it may go back to when you and Mercy got divorced. He said when he spoke to Sam Evans about it, Sam just shook his head and said it was the pictures inna papers, you and alla blonde babes with big tits and the skirts that just covered their breakfast. Someone, maybe someone in the IRS, maybe someone who's now in the US Attorney's office, painted a target on you, decided you should be punished. Sam told Pooler he told you not to let that juicy stuff happen, to lie low 'til the case was over, and you couldn't even do that. But at the time all he had in mind was keeping down what Mercy'd get in the settlement. He didn't think you'd go to jail for disregarding what he said.'

Hilliard seemed not to have heard him. 'Pooler couldn't explain it to me the other day, either, why they're doing this to me now – scalping me, ripping my hair off.' He shook his head and snuffled.

'It's frightening, Amby. Makes me feel so *exposed*,' Hilliard said 'All these years, and now basically what he's saying is it could be *anything*, anything I might've ever done, or even said, to someone. Some casual remark that pissed someone off, and now they've found a pretext to get even, calling me what amounts to a thief. "You ran for office in order to steal." How the hell do you defend yourself?'

He shook his head again. 'The short answer is that you can't,' he said. Then he began to cry. He sat there at the table in the dim corner of the bar at Grey Hills and his eyes filled up with tears. He shook his head and said: 'It was never that way, Amby. You know that, it wasn't. It was never that way at all.'

25

Shortly after 8:20 on Tuesday morning Merrion raised his right hand to knock on the closed door of Apartment 1 at 1692 Eisenhower Boulevard. He could hear Steve Brody inside, talking at normal conversational level. He remembered Larry Lane: 'Cheap construction guarantees you know your neighbors, whether you want to or not.'

Brody's voice expressed pain. 'Well, but I already told you that, didn't I – that I'd do it? I told you yesterday. The thing is, I can't get to it yet, not 'til I get finished with the pump. I got to get the pump fixed first. I got it all taken apart down there now. A big storm comes along and hits us – and it *could*, a hurricane or something; time of year for that, you know, and we do get 'em through here – dumpa lotta water on us 'fore I get it back together, we'd be in big trouble. And this's something we don't want to happen. Because, you'll remember, we didn't get to it last summer, like we should've done, and we knew it at the time. So it then came back and bit us, served us right, and we both admitted that. You were saying "No, it'll be all right. It'll go another year, make it through another season." And then it didn't, did it.

'And then so as a result, we then had all that trouble it broke down, the end of March.' Brody's voice was becoming louder and his words were coming faster. 'All that snow and then the rain – should've *known* we're gonna get that, soon's we didn't fix the pump – and then we get the thaw and we had a *flood* in here. Basement fulla water. Would've ruined the oil burner, I didn't pull it out and lug it up here in the kitchen by the gas stove to dry out. Tenants screaming bloody murder, two whole days without no heat. I am scared to death myself, 'fraid the pipes're gonna freeze 'nd burst; plaster comin' down around our ears. You remember that, don't you? You yelled at me enough, worse'n any of the tenants, like it's all my fault or something that it hadda go and rain.'

Merrion tapped two fingertips twice on the door.

'So anyway, now I'm fixing that.' There was a note of firm assurance audible in Brody's voice. 'All going to be taken care of, so we won't have to think about that again this year, first time we get snow. I get through with that – plus of course whatever else comes up along the way, something has to, never fails, that can't wait a day or so – *then* I'll paint the third floor hall.'

He hesitated. 'The hallway on the second floor? No, did that one last year, 'chou 'member? That time in April we had the three vacancies up there all at once; I'm practically going out of my mind here, trying to get all of them painted? We both agreed the time it made good sense to do the hallway, get it done at the same time – since it so happened I was working up there anyway.'

Merrion rapped his knuckles three times on the door.

'And then after I get through with that, the one on the third floor, then the *downstairs* hall.' Brody paused again. When he resumed talking his voice was noticeably louder. '*No*, doggone it. Will you just *listen* to me? Just once will you listen what it is I'm trynah tell you? I keep trying to tell you things all the time, and it always seems like I can't get any place, ever make you listen: you can only do one thing at a time, all right? One thing at a time.'

He paused long enough to take a breath. Merrion closed his fist and hit the door. The tone of Brody's voice changed; it took on a conciliatory note. 'Because look here now, all right? I'm not sure you actually realize this, but there's a lot of work to do around this place here all the time, a *helluva* lotta work. Really. Anna people who own the property, you know, that four guys trust? They all live around here. It's not like with Florentine Gardens, say, or Falls Estates, owners're from alla cross the country and never even see the places. Something starts to go those places, you got some time before you really hafta fix it. Owners never see how bad you've let it get, just as long's the checks keep comin'. The four guys on this trust're different, all local. People own *this* place're *here*. We cut too many corners, it starts to look rundown, drivin' by they'll see it. Kick us out and hire new management. You and I're outta jobs, or I at least would be. So consequently what that does, it really keeps me hoppin' all the time around here. Day and night it seems like, sometimes. This's not a well-built building. It needs a lot of maintenance, just to keep it operating. And that's not allowing for any improvements here, either – that's just trying to keep it up, trying to stay even.'

Merrion, now interested, lowered his fist and leaned his left shoulder against the door frame, crossing his arms.

The sound of conciliation in Brody's voice became pleading. 'And sometimes you know, even though I'm doing that, workin' day and night, it just seems as though it's never gonna be enough. I get so that I start in thinkin': "No, it's no use. It's never gonna *be* no use. No matter what I ever do, I cannot keep up." But even though I think that, I still keep on trying. Because I know that no matter what I do, if it's the best I can do then my conscience will be clear. And if it isn't all right, Ginny, that's just gonna be too bad, because it's all that I can do.' He paused.

Merrion looked at his watch, grew impatient and rapped twice again. 'Yeah,' Brody said, adding urgency to his tone, 'I know that. I realize all that; I hear what you're saying – but just listen to me now, all right? There *isn't* anybody else who if you could get them to come in here on short notice, could do it any better – or any faster, either. I'm telling you: It's not just me. It's just the way it is, and that's all there is to it. So if I maybe gave you that impression, thinkin' that, something that I might've said or something, well then, I just didn't meanah, all right? Not what I meant to do. Right. Now, no, now look, all right? There's somebody at the door now and I got to answer it. No I don't know who it is. That's why I got to answer it, so I can find out. I can't talk to you no more right now. I got to get the door. Yeah, Ginny, I know: you're worried about it.'

His tone became plaintively soothing. 'I under*stand* that, I really do, and I'll take care of it for you. No, I can't tell you when, not right now. Because I can't do that. *Look*, there's someone at the door. I can't talk no more. I tell you what: I'll call you back. Later on this afternoon. Yeah, this afternoon, soon's I get a chance, after lunch. Good-bye.'

Merrion heard Brody replace the handset hard on its wall hook and say 'Jesus Christ, now what?' There were two footsteps and the door opened. 'Yeah?' Brody said gruffly. Then he became dismayed and said: 'Oh. Mister Merrion. Diddun know it was you.'

'Morning, Steve,' Merrion said, 'sorry to bother you.'

'Oh that's okay, Mister Merrion,' Brody said, frowning deeply, recomposing himself, 'perfectly all right.' He was average-sized, five-ten or so, big-boned, at one-seventy or so, no more than ten or fifteen pounds heavier than he needed to be, but it looked like more; he seemed to carry all the excess flesh as folds of skin on his face and neck and rolls around his waist. He wore his brownish-grey hair long and combed it back in thick strands from the brow of its recession in the front, arranging them in several sebum-heavy strands over his scalp. He wore a clean white tee-shirt and dark-green chino work pants; heavy black shoes with thick welted petroleum-proof soles. He had a snap-ring of keys hooked to the belt-loop just behind the opening of his right-front pocket. He gestured with his right thumb toward the phone behind him. 'I was just talkin' onna phone. Ginny over management. She called me up again. She's always calling me up all the time. Every morning, got some new thing on her mind, some new project for me to do. Like she wants to drive me *nuts*. And then, in addition, she comes *over* here, two, three, four times a week, see how I'm doin' on something. I don't know what it is with that woman, what she thinks I am.'

'Maybe she's lonely, and hot for your body,' Merrion said. 'Lookin' for love. Just doesn't know how to say it to you, put it into words.'

Brody grinned and reddened. He had clearly envisioned that possibility, perhaps often. 'Nah,' he said, 'isn't that. Can't be that. Guy my age, I'm fifty-one years old, and she's what, thirty-two? Just a kid. Uh uh, I think what it is is that she doesn't understand how long it takes to do a thing. No idea, you know? No comprehension at all.

'You get these kids: it's not their fault, but they never did anything with their hands. Spend all their lives shufflin' papers, workin' with figures. Now the computers: hit a key and what they want to do is done. So as a result they got no idea of how long it actually takes to do something. They think when they say it, they want it done, bingo, that's all there is to it. Now it's time to go on to the next thing onna list. "Can't have you standin' around here alla time, doin' nothin', gettin' paid for it, you know." And then they laugh, "ha ha," like that at you; like they didn't really mean it, they're only fooling with you.

'Well, it just isn't *like* that, as you and I both know, and I try to tell her that sometimes. "You know when I'm working on a thing and it's gonna take a week, all right? Because I told you it was gonna take that, before I even started. I been on it a day and of course it isn't done. So what're you doin' this now for, already; comin' around and actin' like you *still* don't understand a day is not a week? You got me thinkin': how can this be? After I went to all the trouble of explaining it to you, tell you what's involved in a thing, I make sure you understand; you tell me you do; and then, *boom*, like that, you turn around and call me up, *the very next day*, the day after I started, acting like you don't know the first thing about it and I must be finished now. Tell me you now've got something else for me, I got to get started on right away. I mean: How can you keep doing this to me all the time? This doesn't make any sense."

'She always tells me she'll stop,' Brody said. 'Promising me then she won't do it no more; she'll cut it out. She never does, though.' He paused and reflected, 'She's still a good kid, though; we get along all right.'

The anxiety returned to his voice and his face wrinkled up. 'But hey, what's it with you being up here? Something didn't go wrong here or something, I hope? Everything still okay with Mark, up there and everything with him? I didn't hear nothin'. He was doin' okay last I heard. *Sounded* like he was all right. I know I didn't get no call here. Got my machine on all the time here, too, I'm not in the apartment; somewhere else in the building or something. I know they got my number up there and everything 'cause I gave it to them there when he went in. I didn't get no calls. Kid's still all right up there, isn't he? Nothin' wrong there with Mark?'

'If there is, I haven't heard about it,' Merrion said. 'Far's I know, everything's fine.'

Brody's face relaxed. He nodded and smiled. 'Okay then,' he said, 'that makes it easy. Then what can I do for you, here? Anything else is a cinch, long's it's not those fuckin' drugs again. Anything else I can handle, no problem.'

'It's LeClerc I'm here about,' Merrion said. 'I'm here to see Janet LeClerc.'

Brody looked puzzled. 'Yeah,' he said, 'sure. She lives here all right.' He grinned again. 'But hey, you oughta know that. You're the one put her in here. You told me to give her an apartment if I had one vacant and we did, and I did it, which I was glad to, something I could do for *you*. Number fourteen. Third floor. You know the building, right? Sure, you used to come here a lot. Back when Larry Lane's still here; you used to come here and see him, number eleven. Jee-*zuss* he hadda hard time, the poor guy. Anyway, number fourteen: one of our nicer ones. Always gets plenty of sun. Overlookin' the street at the front. All she's gotta do's look out the window, any time she wants, see everything that's going on. She's been here with us almost a year now.

'Not the best tenant we ever had, no, couldn't go that far for her. But she doesn't cause us much trouble. Rent's always paid on time, anyways; that's always the biggest thing. Course it *should* be, town's paying it *for* her; she don't have to pay it herself.

'But just the same, no matter who's payin', I wish they could all be like that. Not to have that to worry about, ever again on my mind: "Well, did so-and-so pay their rent yet, or are we gonna have to go in and throw 'em out onna street?"

'I'm tellin' you: that is one job I really hate. I'd rather eat something that I knew was gonna make me sick and throw up and maybe break out in a rash, everything like that, 'n I would to hear I'm gonna have to go and put somebody out. And it's almost always the same reason. In some buildings I've been in sometimes have to do it on account of someone making too much noise or not being clean or something; that could happen. But in this building it's almost always been because for some reason they didn't have no money, so I have to go and do it. I don't *care* what the reason is. It don't make any difference to me. I got my orders and that's what I hafta do: Out in the street; they haven't paid us their rent. *Cryin'* an' *hollerin'*, weepin' an' wailin', everything like that. Sometimes they wanna fight me. Like this was my idea? *I'm* the one who made the decision that they're gettin' thrown out; this's something *I* like to do?

'I'm tellin' you, sir, and I am not kidding you, one little bit: it's an awful part of the job. It's the worst job in the world. At least it's not gonna be that with her.'

His expression changed, becoming avid. 'But *why* then, what is it? Why is it you want to see *her*? You think she did something wrong? Like that time when she tried to steal all the old lady's money? She in some new kindah trouble? Some kind of a problem we should be concerned about here?'

'I need to talk to her, is all,' Merrion said. 'There's something I need to see her about. But I've been up there. I went up to fourteen and I knocked on her door and she didn't answer. The TV was on in there. Not loud, but I could hear it. I decide maybe she didn't hear me, knocked again. Good and hard, so she would've had to've heard me. But she didn't come to the door that time, either. So that raised another possibility: maybe she *did* hear me; she just doesn't want to see me. Got a guest in her apartment, like I just told her Saturday she was not to do. And so that's when I decided I'd come down here, and see if you knew where she was.'

'She's usually up there, this time of day,' Brody said doubtfully, looking at his watch. 'This's when she's got the news on. Now it's not that I'm watching her alla time now, I wouldn't want you to think that, but this time of day is when I'm getting started, going to work on what I got to do. And so I'm around the place inna morning, upstairs or down. Or on my way down to the basement, all right? Like I was on my way today, when Ginny called up. You move around like that in the building every day, you get so you know where most of the people usually are. And this time of day she's generally in her apartment.'

'Yeah, well, that's what I thought,' Merrion said, 'TV going and so forth. But then when I knocked again, and she still didn't come, I wasn't sure. Does she leave the TV on, if she happens to go out? Because she told me she goes to the store in the morning to get cigarettes.'

Brody nodded vigorously as Merrion talked. 'Uh huh,' he said, 'every day. Faithful as clockwork, you can depend on it. Winter; summer; hot or cold; raining; snowing; I don't care: by ten A.M. she's down the stairs and out the door, on her way down to Dineen's. Raining or something? Doesn't make any difference to her. She's got her little plastic hat on, one of those folding plastic hats they used to give out in banks and dry cleaners – always wears one of those. Inna wintertime, her boots and coat and scarf on, so forth, all bundled up, keep her all nice and warm. Like the mailmen, you know? Whatever it takes. Janet's going out, and that's just all there is to it. She's got her routine she follows, regular rounds every day.'

'But not this early,' Merrion said, 'she doesn't go this early.'

'Nope,' Brody said firmly. 'This'd still be too early for her. Janet by now'd be just about up. Sittin' in her bathrobe in frontah the TV there. Drinkin' her coffee; tellin' everybody off, says something that she doesn't like on the television: "Yah that's what *you* say, always givin' us your *stuff*. Liar, liar, pants on fire. Bullshit." Talks back to it all the time. Oh, she gets *all* upset at them. I've been up there, working on the third floor, and I've heard her inside sayin' all that stuff. Very emotional.

'Assuming of course she got to bed last night; made it in the bedroom and then actually got into bed. Didn't go to sleep there in her chair, front of the TV; wake up still in front of it, still on, same place inna morning.'

'She does that,' Merrion said.

'Now and then, she does,' Brody said. 'She used to, at least. Sometimes I guess she must've been sleeping so heavy she went to the bathroom in her chair, couldn't even get herself up to go in the bathroom and do that. 'Cause there's stains on it. You can see them if you're in there, and she isn't sittin' in it.

'See, the reason I know this stuff is because the people under her and the ones next to her, the next apartment, they complained to me sometimes about the TV bein' too loud and goin' all night. That would mean I would have to go in there and speak to her, and find out what was goin' on. Didn't happen all that much, maybe four, five times, but it did happen. Go up there and knock on her door, and . . . this wasn't something I look forward to, you know? It's not like I enjoy it. But she didn't wanna believe that. She thought this was all my idea, to hassle her and make her feel bad, and it wasn't that at all. I tried to explain that to her, make sure she understood that it was nothing personal, involved.

'See, what I was assuming was that she was probably drinking, passed out in the chair with the television on. There was a lot of bottles I would see that she'd been putting out when she put her rubbish out, you know? That was mostly what her rubbish was – bottles. Newspapers, one or two magazines, cartons from frozen food dinners, which I guess she mostly lives on. Cereal boxes and that kind of stuff. But most of what she was throwing out that you would see when they emptied the barrels was liquor bottles, vodka and rum – sometimes she didn't put the cover back on, and I would see what she put in. But you still would've known; you could hear them empty her barrel because the bottles made a lot of noise, bangin' and crashin' all over the place.

'But I was used to it. It wasn't like this was something new, you know? We've had other tenants here who've had that problem, and it's really not that uncommon. People living alone: they don't have much to do with themselves. Get lonely, start drinking too much. It isn't a good thing for them, but they don't stop; I guess they get accustomed to it.

'Where someone like Janet's concerned, well, Mark was a lot like that. All you can really do when someone's doing that to themselves is say: "Look," and then tell them what you think. And then I don't really know what you do – I guess you just hope for the best. And so I told her quite frankly – I don't mind telling this to you, either, because it kind of worries me, living in the same building with her too, my life's also on the line. She goes up in smoke some night, I could go up with her. So that was also on my mind.

'I went up and I knocked on her door, and I told her that this bothered me and all, her falling asleep like that – I did not say "passing out," even though that's what I really think it was – because I know she smokes. I told her: "What bothers me here is actually a lot more than the noise from the TV anna neighbors complaining a result that they can't sleep. Because you can turn the TV set down, and I know that now you're aware of this problem, you will do that. And then they won't be awake and complain. But what really bothers me about this is the fact you smoke. You fall asleep here inna chair some night, you've got a cigarette going, it could be a real fire hazard here. That could be a dangerous thing."

'And then what I said to her was this: "Now we do allow tenants who smoke to smoke in this building. We don't say that they can't do it. Even though we know that can cost us some business sometimes, people just refuse to rent apartments from us if we allow smoking. But we think ordinarily what you do up here's your business, as long's you're living here. It's your place; you should be able, do what you want in it.

'"As long's you don't disturb nobody else; that's the one major rule. It's your health, not mine that you've got to think of, and if that's the decision you've reached, well then, it's all right by me.

'"But I still have to tell you at the same time if we find there's been some kind of an *incident* up here some night because you fell asleep in that chair there and set the place on fire, smoke detectors in here went off or maybe even the ones out in the *hallway* started to go off, and the *fire* department hasta come, well, God forbid that anything should happen to you – wind up inna hospital, smoke inhalation, something. Because if you haven't thought about that, you should give it some thought – fire inna night is a serious thing. But even if something that bad doesn't happen, I can tell you right this minute what it is *going* to do is make a big change in how we look at things around here. And what we decide then we can let you do in here."

'I think it got through to her. Looked like it penetrated anyway. But like I say, you never know. All I can say's we haven't had any problems with her since then for a while. Nothing I've heard about anyway, and if there is one I generally do.'

'Yeah,' Merrion said. 'Well, what we've been hearing down the courthouse is that she'd been keeping pretty steady company up here recently with a guy we're not all that sure's a wholesome influence. Just the opposite, in fact. You understand: we have to be concerned. So that was what made me decide I ought to come up here today and take a look around.'

'Oh, that would've been right, you heard that,' Brody said. 'She has been. That would be Lowell you mean. Lowell Chappelle. He's been here a few times; seen him around here several times.'

'You'd know what he looks like, then,' Merrion said. 'This's a guy you'd recognize, then, you were to see him again? Does he also have a car, truck or something? See, I couldn't tell just by lookin' around here this morning, by looking at what's parked around in front if the guy's around. And I was, you know, you start thinkin': "Well, what am I gonna run into here, I go up this woman's apartment? Am I gonna find this guy in there, have him to deal with, I go into this woman's apartment?" He's got a reputation of being a pretty violent type of guy.'

'Oh, yeah, I've seen him, good many times,' Brody said. 'But now you ask me, I don't think I've ever seen him driving anything. Seem like he'd almost have to, have something to get around in. Can't you check with the state police? I should think you could do that.'

'I did,' Merrion lied, kicking himself for not having thought of it, 'they report no listing for him.'

'Well,' Brody said, 'if he's got someone else's jalopy I couldn't tell you what it is or if it's here. I guess I must've never seen him in it.

'But now *him*, far as he's concerned: that's a whole other thing here. I've seen him a lot. Fairly big guy, he is, stands out in your mind. Big *face*.' Brody cupped his hands beside his cheeks and puffed, bunching his jaw muscles as well. 'Like this, okay? Only he's like this all the time. The man has a very big face. Sort of dark-skinned. Might be one of those part-Indian people or something; you know how you see those guys in movies. Real black hair, not much grey. Probably about my age or so, at least; maybe a little older. Keeps himself in good shape. Looks like he's always *doing* something, doesn't want you getting in his way.'

'Not a guy you'd pick to mess with,' Merrion said.

'No,' Brody said, 'definitely not. I believe what you said about him being a violent person. The guy definitely looks it. Of course I'm not the kind of guy that likes to go around, you know, picking fights with people. But if I *was* that kind of guy, I wouldn't pick one with this Lowell character. Not if I wanted to *win* it. He looks like he'd be mean, someone got him going.'

'Yeah,' Merrion said. 'Well anyway, basically what I wonder if you'd do for me here is get your passkey and come back to fourteen with me and let me in, so that I can see if my friend Janet's in there – decided she's not coming to the door today, got her curlers in or something.'

Brody looked worried. 'I dunno,' he said. 'I dunno if I should do that. See, you may not know this, but since you trust guys had this whole thing changed around and so forth, eight, ten years ago? Brought the new management in? Well, since they came in here and I hadda start reporting to them, Valley Better, they hadda different way of doing things. They put in different rules. So, you may not know this, but they've gotten very strict about that kind of thing. Lettin' people into the apartments I mean, except vacant ones we're showing. They don't want it done.

'Basically what they're now telling us is: "We don't want this going on, here, anymore, so stop doing it. And don't be calling up alla time and asking is it all right. Because the answer is: 'It's not.'" They're very clear on this. And as you know, this job and all, it means a lot to me and I don't want to lose it. Give them any reason to decide I'm too much trouble so they're getting rid of me.'

Merrion took one step forward so that about eighteen inches of space at the threshold remained between him and Brody. He spoke pleasantly, in a low voice. 'Steve, you work for Valley Better Residences, Inc. And Valley Better works for me, all right? So we understand each other here, I am one of the people who own Fourmen's Realty Trust. Fourmen's Realty owns this building, understand that, Steve? Valley Better just runs it for us, collects the rents, pays the taxes, *and hires you* – to work for *us*.

'Most of the time we are pretty smart people,' Merrion said, 'if I do say so myself. Except sometimes. Sometimes we do something fairly stupid, as even we have to admit. After we've cleaned up the mess we made because we acted stupid instead of smart.

'Steve, this morning's one of those times, for me. This morning I did something stupid and created a minor problem for myself. Now I want you to help me get out of it. That way I won't have to spend the whole rest of the day thinking how stupid I was this morning.'

Brody looked extremely worried. 'What did you do, Mister Merrion?' he said.

Merrion heaved a great sigh. 'I parked my car across the street. Then I waited until all the other cars behind me at the light, all of them went by, and I got out and shut the door and locked it. I looked both ways, and then when I was sure the coast was clear – after maybe I'd let eight, nine cars go by, in both directions – I came across the street and in through the front door. Let it close behind me. Then I climbed the stairs up to the third floor and I knocked on the door of apartment fourteen, where Janet LeClerc lives. As I've already told you, I knocked twice. She didn't answer. So then I came down and knocked on your door, but unlike Janet, you came to your door. And then everything that came after that, all the rest of it you know.'

Brody's rumpled face displayed real pain. 'Mister Merrion,' he said, 'I don't understand. I have to tell you that.'

'Understand what?' Merrion said. 'Tell me what you don't understand. Maybe I can help you out.'

'What you did stupid,' Brody said. 'What did you do that made the big mess you now want me to get you out of?'

'I already told you,' Merrion said. 'I stood beside my car after I parked it. I don't know exactly how *long* I stood there but it was certainly long enough to give Janet time enough to glance out of her window and spot me. She may not recognize my *car*, but she's certainly seen enough of *me* to recognize me on sight. And I stupidly gave her the time to do it before I made it into the building.

'So she probably knows I'm here. And since she doesn't want to see me or talk to me, she didn't come to the door. Instead when I knocked she ignored me. It didn't occur to her to turn off the TV, she isn't very smart, but this morning it looks to me as though I've been a little dumber'n she has. I alerted her to the fact that the next person who banged on her door was going to be me. So that's the mess I want you to get me out of. Come upstairs with me now and use your passkey to let me into her place. So I can do what I came here to do, which is see what the hell's going on.'

'You don't think I'll get in trouble?' Brody said.

'I'm *sure* you won't,' Merrion said. 'I'm an officer of the court acting in the course of official business, my official duties, the supervision of a defendant who has charges pending before the court in which I happen to be the chief magistrate. And in the second place, in addition to that, I am also a beneficial shareholder of a property interest in this building, to a part of which I am directing you as an employee of its management agency to admit me, in order that I may enter upon and inspect the premises. Thereof.

'That satisfy you, Steve? I got at least two heavy-duty rights to get into that apartment. Either one of them oughta do nicely.'

'Okay, then,' Brody said, stepping forward and pulling the door shut behind him, 'but it's purely on your say-so I'm doin' this. I'm still not sure about it.'

'Don't worry,' Merrion said. 'Nothing'll happen to you. I can almost guarantee it. Something may happen to *me*, everything doesn't turn out to be the way I hope, up there . . . but that's nothing that needs to concern you. All you need to do is make sure you got your right key with you now – the one that'll open her door?'

Brody nodded, patting the snap-ring at his belt. 'Gotter right here,' he said 'With me, all times. Never can tell when you'll need to go in. Somebody's locked themselves *out*, or someone *else* locked them out, any hour day or night, and the first they do's come lookin' for you, let them back in. Found that out myself at the very beginning, three or four times all it took. The simplest way's the only way: carry it with you, all times. Save yourself all of that grief.'

Merrion let him by and then followed him up the four flights of stairs leading to the third floor. He remembered Larry Lane denouncing the increasing difficulty of climbing them as his cancer worsened and weakened him. 'Takes me about twenty minutes, make it up this place. Have to stop and rest five times, once on the landing, second floor, and halfway up each flight. And it's all my fault.

'We're building the place,' he said, 'Fiddle told us we should bite the bullet, invest in an elevator. Then we'd get older, quieter tenants, be able, charge higher rent than we could with just the stairs. Four grand more I think he said it would've cost us. I was against it: too much money. Got the others to turn him down. "Nothing doing," I said, "no unnecessary features. If we can get along without it, then it must be we don't need it. Whatever it'd cost would be therefore too much dough." Now here I am, livin' in the place. Wasn't banking on that when I said "no elevator." Don't like that decision at all.'

Ten feet along the landing from the top of the staircase they stopped at the door with the 14 on it. They could hear an announcer promise joyfully that 'Good Morning, America' would 'be *right* back after these few brief announcements from your local stations, so *please*, don't you *dare* go away.'

Brody, unsnapping the key-ring from his belt-loop, used his left hand to knock hard on the door. 'Miss LeClerc?' he spoke in a newly-authoritative voice. 'You in there now, Miss LeClerc? This's me, Mister Brody. You gotta answer me now, if you are. Haven't got any choice in this now. Come to the door now, and let me in. I gotta right to go in there, you know, anytime, make an inspection, during all reasonable times. This's one of those times. Got a passkey right here in my hand.'

There was no response. From the TV a different voice, a woman's, compared the degrees of headache pain relief she claimed to get from Tylenol and 'just plain aspirin, or just plain ibuprofen, either.' Brody pounded on the door four more times. 'Plus which I have got Mister Ambrose Merrion from the courthouse here with me, and I know you know him, and I've got to tell you, he's very concerned about you. He told me how concerned he is now about you, and that's why he's up here today. And all the other people down there at the courthouse with him there, how concerned they also are about you and what might be going on with you in there. So we got to come in, that is, he does, take a look around. So come on now and open the door.'

'Stop talking and open the thing,' Merrion said.

Brody thumped the door three more times. There was no response. He looked down at the bunch of keys in his right hand and began to paw through them with his left forefinger. 'Miss LeClerc, now?' he said. 'Come on, Miss LeClerc. Stop fooling around with us here. We know you're in there. We know you haven't gone out. I always see you, see you and hear you, whenever you go to the store, and I didn't today, yet, so we know that you're still in there.

'So come to the door, please now, willya? Make life a little easier on all of us here. We got to come in, take a look at your premises, and we got to do this today.'

'*Steve*,' Merrion said.

Brody selected the passkey from among the bunch and inserted it into the lock. 'See, Miss LeClerc?' he said. 'You can hear that, can't you? That was me out here in the hall, doing just what I told you I'd have to do, even though I don't wanna; putting the key in the lock. You see what you force me to do here? You won't open the door, when I ask you to in a nice way? You force me to open the door up myself like this, which *I* don't like having to do.'

'Stop talking and unlock the damned *door*,' Merrion said. 'Horsing around with this broad.'

Brody seemed not to hear. He raised his voice. 'And why is that, I'm asking you, that I am doing this? Well, you have left me no choice. Have you? Aren't you the one? Of course you are; and you have to know it, too, I think. Which I by the way have to say that I think is very unfair of you here.'

'Openah fuckin' *door*,' Merrion said, forcing the words through clenched teeth.

The lock snapped open. Brody turned the knob and pushed the door. It was hinged on the left and stopped against something made of wood behind it. 'Bookcases,' Brody said, muttered, allowing Merrion to brush by him and enter the apartment. 'Dunno if you recall how it was back when you were visitin' Larry Lane, but they didn't have 'em then. But alla units got these bookcases in 'em now. Dunno why they bothered.'

To the right of the door there was an oval maple table with four straight chairs grouped around it. There was a *Boston Herald* tabloid folded in half at the corner of the table. The air carried a heavy cargo of stale tobacco smoke, something combining fatty meat and cheese, tomato and beans that had been cooked too long at too high a temperature, human perspiration, stale beer and something else. *Piss is what it is, human fucking piss*. The apartment smelled as though the toilet hadn't been flushed regularly. *Fucking hopeless people, can't even handle indoor plumbing. Fucking hopeless bastards*. In the center of the table there was a beige china bowl with two white envelopes face-down in it. There was a key-ring with four keys splayed out on the table.

Straight ahead there was a small square kitchen alcove lighted by two casement windows over a double stainless-steel sink. The refrigerator flanked the cabinets suspended from the ceiling on the left and the electric stove occupied the space under them on the right. There were a few dishes unevenly stacked on the counter next to the sink; the handles of tableware protruded between them. On the stove there were two matte-grey saucepans, one of them with something brownish-yellow caked on the side of it, along with a frying pan dull with a scalloped rime of greyish grease around its edge. The area was enclosed by a waist-high partition wide enough to double as a snack counter; two wooden stools stood under its overhang. There were four round anodized aluminum ashtrays on it, red, gold, green and blue; all of them had been used. There were four packs of Winston Lights on it, three of them opened, and several lottery scratch tickets scattered along it. There was an uncapped 1.75 litre jug of Old Russia vodka at the furthest end, the one nearest the interior wall at the left of the kitchen area. There was a yellow wall telephone set mounted above the end of the counter.

Next to it there was a white wall with a door opening onto a dim interior hallway leading away toward the southwesterly corner of the front of the building. Visible beyond it was a door ajar on a blue-tiled wall and the shower-curtained end of a bathtub. The rug on the floor of the living-room area was a dark-green swirled-embossed pattern. It was soiled and had not been recently vacuumed. Against the wall there was a bulky two-cushion sofa-bed, the seat cushions high, much thicker than the back-rest. It was upholstered in a nubby maroon fabric with a decorative silver thread. At each end there was a square table made of dark wood. The one at the end of the couch furthest from the door held a lamp with a base made of a foot-tall china model of a pink-dressed and picture-hatted, apple-cheeked country girl; she wore white socks and black mary janes and displayed a white-toothed grin between parted ruby lips. There were four empty Coors beer bottles around her. The table at the end nearest the door held a lamp with a base made of a foot-tall china model of a freckle-cheeked, barefooted farm boy wearing blue bibbed overalls and a straw hat. He was carrying a bamboo fishing pole jagged where the tip had broken off and grinning between parted ruby lips. There were two Coors beer bottles standing next to him and one on its side in front of him.

There was a narrow rectangular coffee table made of chromium and glass in front of the sofa bed. There was a magazine open on it, displaying a two-page color photo of a blonde woman with dramatically black and green eye shadow that made her green eyes look enormous, and bright scarlet lipstick on her tightly puckered lips; she was naked from the waist up, cupping her grotesquely large breasts in her hands with her thumbs and forefingers urging her nipples forward toward the camera, using so much pressure that the pores of the nipples were spread. There were smears of semen on the picture. The surface of the table showed many rings left by wet glasses. There was a small bud vase with one reddish plastic flower in it; next to it there was a one-pint clear glass mug about half full of a brownish liquid. On the rug under the table there was a pair of tan workboots with lug soles, the right one upright and the left one tipped over on its side. A pair of grey socks with red stripes lay over the boots. A pair of jeans with a black belt and a pair of blue-and-white checked shit-soiled boxer shorts inside were heaped open on the floor, still shaped to the lower body of the person who'd removed them and left them there. There was a white tee-shirt bunched up at the further end of the sofa.

Over the sofa-bed there was a three-by-four-foot print of a generic mountain-lake vista shaded by overhanging maple branches on a sunny sky-blue day. Four white vees represented four white birds in flight over the lake.

Merrion remembered first seeing and then gradually growing to dread seeing again another copy of the same picture long before. It had hung over the couch in Larry Lane's apartment. '*Hey*, that's a very good picture,' Larry Lane had said, one day when Merrion sneered at it. 'I want you to cut out that talk now, making smart remarks about my lovely picture. We hadda pay a lotta money for that picture. And there's another one of 'em just like it, or almost just like it anyway, in every single unit here. Got 'em to add a little class to the operation. People come and live here, they then decide they don't like 'em? Fine, they can take 'em down. Perfectly all right with us if they got no taste. But when they first come in to see the place and size it up, that picture tells them that this is a classy joint. They can see it. We took extra trouble make these apartments nice.

'Sure, when they get in they find out you can hear your neighbor two floors down and four doors over if he farts in the bathtub. When it's windy, the walls shake, gets a little drafty, windows rattle. The plumbing ain't that great. The heat comes up it sounds to God like the whole place's gonna blow up with you in it. But they notice those things *later*, *after* they paid the deposit. Before that what they notice is that in the living room we have got this fine scenic picture, so they know that we've got *taste*. Spared no expense on amenities; those pictures cost us three bucks apiece.'

Beyond the couch in the southeasterly corner of the room at the picture window overlooking the boulevard there was a 27-inch Sanyo television set on a TV table with a VCR and a cable-service box under it on the lower shelf. The brief announcement from the local station now concluding was a 30-second ad describing the superior comforts available from a revolutionary new design in mattress coils.

Opposite the TV in front of the bookcased wall next to the window there was a blue and green reclining chair with an end table and a black metal floor lamp next to it. There was a clear glass one-pint mug on the table; it contained about four ounces of a clear liquid. There were two remote control keypads on the table. There was a round purple anodized aluminum ashtray with a coil around the rim to hold cigarettes in place; it was full of stubbed butts. There was a crushproof box of Winstons open next to it.

Janet LeClerc in a white cotton nightgown decorated with small blue and red flowers with little green leaves and some lace around the yoke, under a thin pink chenille robe, sat curled up in the recliner with her weight resting mainly on her right buttock, the footrest up but not in use, her feet and legs tucked up under her, snoring softly and steadily with her mouth gaping open. Her left eye socket was badly bruised, greenish-blue and swollen puffy.

When she exhaled she made the kind of rhythmic, low, rumbling, happy growling sound that came from the television, harmonizing with the large tired golden retriever, first seen playing hard with children on a sunny day, now contented lying down after a nutritious dish of choice cuts of meat and meat by-products in real gravy combined in the dog food advertised in one of the brief announcements from the ABC local-affiliate station in Springfield.

Merrion picked up the VCR remote keypad and punched it twice with no result. Then he picked up the other one and shut the television off. 'Good,' he said. Janet exhaled, making a low whistling sound. Her hair was mussed around her left temple. Her face was flushed and shiny with sweat.

'You aren't gonna wake her up, are you?' Brody said in a soft voice, as though he had been caring for a sick person whose recovery depended on plenty of rest.

Merrion snorted but he kept the noise down too. 'Sooner or later, I'm gonna, yeah,' he said, glancing down at her as he put the remote pad down and then hitched up his pants. 'Before I leave here she's gonna have to wake up and tell me some things I want to know, bet your sweet life on that. But first I wanna find out if Chappelle's in here someplace. Like I told you the guy makes me nervous. He's in here someplace with us, I want to know about it. So the *first* thing I am gonna do is take a look around here.'

Brody remained standing at the door and Merrion crossed the room to the interior hallway. 'Maybe the bedroom,' he said, talking to reassure himself. 'Sleeping it off inna bedroom? Got just as good and drunk as she did last night, but had the sense to go to bed.' Brody did not say anything.

Merrion went through the door and paused at the second door, opening into the bathroom. He pushed it open further and looked in. To his left there was a blue plastic shower curtain drawn around the tub enclosure. Beyond that he could see the front of the flush. All the light came from a high narrow window directly ahead of him. To his right there was a long fluorescent fixture mounted above a large vanity-mirror and a sink enclosed in a countered cabinet below it. There was a long white extension cord plugged into a socket at the bottom of the fluorescent fixture; it dropped down from the fixture to the floor beside the cabinet and led across the blue bathmat up to the edge of the tub, where it disappeared behind the shower curtain.

Merrion stepped back from the bathroom door and went down the hall into the bedroom. The door was ajar. He pushed it open slowly and silently and looked into yellowish window-shaded dimness onto an empty, unmade double bed, a pale-green top sheet and two woolen blankets, one white and one tan, mounded up on a wrinkled and stained pale-green bottom sheet; there were two pillows in pale-green slipcases jumbled together at the head of the bed. There was a small table next to the far side with a clear glass lamp and a small alarm clock on it. There was a four-drawer pine chest of drawers in the far corner of the room. There was a small yellow upholstered chair in the corner to his right; it was filled with a pile of soiled clothing. The room smelled stale and loamy.

Merrion had no desire to go in. He turned around and started back toward the living room. 'Any sign of him?' Brody called softly and hesitantly from the doorway.

'Nothin',' Merrion said. 'Janet isn't what you'd call a great housekeeper, though. 'S pretty rank in here.'

'Because see, I was just thinkin',' Brody said, clearing his throat, 'that unless you really hadda, you know, wake her up and ask her things, maybe what we could do here, we could then just go back *out*, and close the door *behind* us?'

'And then she wouldn't ever know that we were in here; you're tryin' to say that to me, Steve? Nobody else'd know that I made you invade this unit this morning?' Merrion was at the bathroom door again. He paused, smiling, and waited for Brody's reply. He could hear Janet snoring peacefully in the next room. Brody did not answer.

'Steve?' Merrion said. 'You still out there? Haven't gone into a panic here, run out on me here, have you? Certainly hope not. You're my witness here, you know, everything I did was kosher, absolutely by the book, from the minute I stepped in. Can't afford to have you leave me in here now, all by myself.'

'Well,' Brody said, drawing it out, 'no, I didn't do that. I was just thinking here was that if there wasn't any need, you know, to wake her up, well, it does seem as though she's sleeping pretty sound. Doesn't look like she's gonna wake up by herself.'

'Not unless somebody shows up here with a howitzer and shoots it off in the kitchen, no, I don't think she will,' Merrion said. 'But I'm still gonna wake her up, Steve, no matter what you say here, and you might as well deal with it – it's gonna happen.' He pushed the bathroom door all the way open, flipping the light switch outside as he went in. The light did not come on and he hesitated in mid-stride, flipping the switch again. The light did not come on. 'Because this bozo she's been hangin' out with's got a pretty vivid history of being dangerous.

'And therefore what I'm doing here today,' he said, using his left hand to pull the shower curtain back, 'is first seeing if I can find out . . . oh oh. *Uh oh.*

'Yeah,' he said, looking down at the two brown knobby knees protruding from the grey-cloudy soapy water in the middle of the tub, and under the handles and the faucet and the drain shutoff, the white hair-dryer tethered by its own white cord to the white extension cord, half-submerged between the two feet underneath the faucet at the front of the tub. He could make out the shins and calves of the lower legs buckled up behind the ugly feet, and beyond the knees the black-haired swarthy head with brown staring eyes in the gaping face above the milky surface at the back.

'*What?*' Brody said from the other room. 'What's going on in there? Everything all right?'

'Yeah, oh yeah,' Merrion said, making a brief dismissive brushing gesture with his right hand against his pantsleg. 'Yeah, everything's fine here. Well, everything's all right for *me*, I mean, in here, and probably for you.' He heard Brody come into the bathroom behind him. 'But I don't think it is for him. And if what I'm seein's what I think it is I'm seeing, and I'm damned sure that it is, I don't think it's gonna be all right much longer for our friend Miss Janet out there. Not for some time at least. She's probably in for some excitement, and then a nice long rest. Although maybe not; her lawyer'll be glad to see those bruises. This naked gentleman in front of us I suspect is Lowell Chappelle, and also that he's somewhat dead.'

He yanked the curtain back all the way and stood looking down at the shiny-black-haired dark-skinned man in the tub, his eyes staring and mouth frozen open in the head that looked as though it had been impaled on the rigid neck sticking out of the surface of the grey water covering the shoulders and the torso of the submerged body. 'Yes, now I'm sure of it,' he said. 'No longer any question in my mind – he's completely fuckin' *dead*. My guess is that in this very bathtub, Steve, the late Lowell Chappelle, former well-known desperado, learned last night after a few drinks that his electrifying girlfriend didn't like it when he hit her. Just before he became *truly*, *fuckin'*, *dead*.'

He turned aside to let Brody step up to the tub beside him. 'You wanna take a look here, Steve? See you recognize him? After all, you know the guy, seen him around, when he was breathin' and so forth. Before this terrible shock. I'd turn the light on for you but I think the fuse's blown.'

Merrion paused expectantly but Brody did not respond. He continued to stare down into the tub. 'He kind of stinks, a little,' he said. 'I would have to say.' He stepped back and looked up at Merrion. 'You think we should get someone, see if they can, you know, get him out of here maybe, and then maybe do something with him? Undertaker, something? Can't just leave him like this, I don't think, can we? It wouldn't be right to do that. At least not for me, the building and all. We should do something, I think.'

Merrion took Brody's left elbow with his right hand and turned him around to face the bathroom door, propelling him toward it at the same time. 'Indeed we should do something, Steve,' he said. '*You* should do something and *I* should do something, and then after that we should both of us do absolutely nothing. Until the cops get here, and then it'll be all in their hands.'

'The cops?' Brody said, momentarily resisting. 'You really sure we need alla that stuff, get the cops up here? TV cameras and stuff, alla trouble they make?'

'Well, yeah,' Merrion said, getting him going again and steering him toward the doorway onto the landing. Janet snored comfortably in the reclining chair, 'Yeah, I *do* think we should have the cops come up and all, it's traditional, you know? Someone looks like he's been murdered, and you find the body? Well, the cops like it if you give them a call. Invite them to come up and look the place over. See there's anything they might like to take note of and so forth – in case they decide, later on, they'd like to accuse someone of killing whoever it was, and maybe punish them. A little, anyway. That's the sort of thing they *do*. And when you help them to do that, they *appreciate* it. You don't call them, they get mad. My experience's always been that if you can do something that cops appreciate, it makes life a lot easier in the long run to do it; I have always found that.

'So the first thing I think we should do is shut the door and lock it, and have you stand in front of it. We do *not* want Janet to wake up and figure what we're doin' here, and then decide that this'd be a perfect time to take a hike. Then right after that I am gonna pick the phone up – know I saw one, we came in; oh yeah, there it is there, right there by the corner 'frigerator – callah cops an' get 'em up here, tell 'em what we found. It'll be their baby then.'

'You think she murdered him?' Brody said.

Merrion shoved him toward the hallway door. Brody lurched forward. 'Go over there and shut the fuckin' door, Steve,' he said. 'Shut the door and lock it and then lean against it, and don't let nobody out, while I get the cops up here and tell 'em how Janet LeClerc killed her boyfriend in the bathtub by switchin' on her hair-dryer an' throwin' it inna tub with him after he fell asleep inna warm water. He'd had a hard day's work gettin' his belly full of beer and beatin' his meat and givin' his girlfriend a good beatin'. Betcha when that Conair splashed it got his attention. Helluva thing to do to a man, I must say. Jesus, what a surprise. Bops the daffy girlfriend in the eye, just a little innocent fun, and what does she do but electrocute him. I don't know how long he lived after she did it, but I will bet you one thing sure: not long enough to forget it.'

'I can't,' Brody said, after he had shut the door and had shaken himself to regain his composure, watching Merrion punch numbers on the phone while Janet snored efficiently by the window, 'I can't believe she'd do that. She could've done that to him. I never saw a side of her that'd make me think she'd do an awful thing like that, just go and kill a man. Never in a million years.'

'I know it,' Merrion said, hearing the phone begin to ring at the police station. 'I'm the same way too. I can never believe it either. As many times I've seen it happen, I still can't make myself believe it. They always tell you, every time, they *promise* you, that they will be *good* boys and girls. And then something like this happens. It shakes your faith in human nature . . . Hello? Yeah, Amby Merrion. Got a homicide to report. No, I'm not a cop, I'm the clerk of court. Yeah that's me, I am the guy: I know everything.'

26

At 1:45 on the afternoon of the second Friday in November, US District Court Judge Barrie Foote stood up scowling at the end of the table in the library of her chambers. She wadded the bag containing the debris of her lunch and threw it overhand, hard, at the wastebasket in the corner, clanking it off the near edge. 'Bummer,' she said, 'shit.' She walked over to the corner, picked it up and threw it down hard into the basket. Then she returned to the head of the table, sat down and pushed the buzzer on her phone, saying: 'Tell Sandy to send in the clowns.'

She was refolding her *New York Times* when she heard Sandy Robey, talking to someone behind him, open the outer door and come through her office into the library. Geoffrey Cohen, Arnold Bissell and Merrion followed. The judge cast the paper aside and stood up. 'Gentlemen,' she said.

'Lizzie'll be right along with her machine, Judge,' Robey said. 'I assume you want this on the record.' He took his usual chair at the opposite end of the table, near the door.

'Oh, by all means on the record,' the judge said. 'If you'll all be seated gentlemen, we'll be able to get underway on whatever it is we're doing here – I'm not entirely clear on it myself, so you'll have to enlighten me – as soon as she arrives. I'd suggest you, Geoff, here on my left, and your client, next to you. I'm assuming he's Mister Merrion.'

'That's correct, your Honor,' Cohen said. He wore grey flannel trousers, a heather-blue Harris tweed two-button jacket, a blue button-down shirt and a pine-patterned dark blue silk tie. His brown van Dyke was faultlessly groomed.

'Mister Merrion,' the judge said.

'Afternoon, your Honor,' Merrion said, neutrally. He wore a dark blue blazer, grey flannel slacks, a grey shirt and a tie that Cohen had affably described as 'hideous,' red, with gold triangles interlocked kaleidoscopically. His face was taut and although he had nothing in his hands he moved gingerly, as though carrying a possibly explosive parcel.

'And you, Arnie, here, on my right,' the judge said.

Elizabeth Gibson, a stocky black woman in her forties in a tight brownish-grey striped suit with a brown sueded collar, her greying hair bunned tightly back, stomped into the room on her two short heavy legs carrying her stenotype machine by the chrome standard connecting it to stubby tripod legs. She set it down next to Bissell, sat and began to type.

'All *right*,' the judge said, 'we're now in business. If you'd identify the matter for the record here now, Sandy.'

'This'd be *United States of America versus John Doe*, civil docket number Ninety-five-dash-eight-hundred-seventy-four, *In re Ambrose Merrion*,' Robey said.

'And if counsel'd identify yourselves now for the record, please?' Foote said.

'Assistant United States Attorney Arnold Bissell for the government,' Bissell said. He was thirty-four years old, six-two, about a hundred-fifty pounds, his blond hair in a Fifties-retro pompadour upswept in the front. It made his head look disproportionately small. His chin was narrow. Ever since learning from classmates at Cornell Law School why his future as a poker player was not bright, he tried very hard at all times to keep his face expressionless, lest he reveal his trial strategy prematurely and give his opponent time to devise tactics to defeat it. Discerning his effort, opposing counsel misconstrued his apprehensive prudence as slyness, making it plain they distrusted him before he had given them any reason. Perceiving their mistrust as unwarranted hostility, and resenting it as unjust, he often acted precipitously and unpredictably. Those actions created surprises, the situation litigators fear most and therefore loathe as sneaky, thus inadvertently validating their initial suspicions that he was underhanded. Angered, they felt justified retaliating. Judges, most having been trial lawyers, tended to sympathize with them. They exercised their discretion not only to allow Bissell's opponents to get even with him, but to make sure that jurors understood the provocation.

That made Bissell feel persecuted, wounded and friendless, prompting him to become harsh and scornful. In his two years as a federal prosecutor the vicious cycle had happened repeatedly; he acquired the reputation as 'a shifty prick, a sneak, and one rude cocksucker.' He became discouraged; his increasingly perfunctory efforts to deal civilly and pleasantly with opponents he encountered for the first time were usually greeted with disdain.

Mindful that United States Attorneys with hopes of future federal judgeships are ill-advised to discharge troublesome assistants whose families' political contributions have been generous enough to bring them invitations to state dinners at the White House, the Chief Assistant US Attorney in Boston had settled for excluding him from civil matters and minor criminal cases. 'For you this's not a promotion; it's purely damage-control, the only way I can get any use out of you. We now know your only chance of winning is by making sure the defendant's someone the jury'll dislike more'n they've come to dislike you, bite clean through their lower lips and convict him by default. Otherwise they'll ignore the evidence and acquit the bastard, just to give you the finger.'

'Geoffrey Cohen, counsel for Ambrose Merrion,' Cohen said. 'Mister Merrion is also present.'

'And also for the record, before we get started here,' the judge said. 'Several years ago Attorney Cohen was my personal lawyer, providing excellent counsel during my divorce. Mister Bissell, I take it you and your superiors in the US Attorney's office in Boston are aware of this?'

'We were aware of that, your Honor,' Bissell said. 'We perceive no potential problem of prejudice or bias inhering in your past attorney-client relationship with Mister Cohen.'

'And so I take it the US Attorney's office does not wish me to recuse myself from this proceeding, voluntarily, as I am willing to do – is that right?'

'That is correct,' Bissell said.

The judge exhaled. 'Sorry to hear it,' she said.

Bissell frowned. 'Beg pardon, your Honor?'

'Oh, nothing,' she said. 'I'm not in a very good mood today. This morning we had a civil case unexpectedly settle. Ordinarily this'd be a development I'd welcome, parties finally able to come to an agreement without taking up any more of the court's time; too bad they couldn't've done it sooner. But this one was different. Wrongful Death action, but quite unusual. This was the dead parachutist. Remember him? The landscaper from Suffield, Nicholas Hardigrew. Summer before last. Took off from Barnes Airport, one of a party with four other sky divers, planning to jump over Conway. He was experienced; over the course of several years he'd done it a good many times without even spraining an ankle. As far as anyone seems to know, everything went fine, according to the book. He was third in the chain at the door, so two people saw him leave the plane and drop clear of the tailwing. *That's* when you're supposed to pull the ripcord. When he went out his hands were in the proper position. But for some reason his chute didn't open.

'The case was about the reason. His family's theory as the plaintiffs was straight *res ipsa loquitur.* They don't know what went wrong with the parachute, whether it was some defect in the chute itself or the person who packed it didn't do it properly. They do know – and'd proven, at least to my satisfaction – that he was a veteran sport parachutist. People who'd jumped with him considered him highly skilled. He knew all the pre-flight and in-flight precautions, proper safety procedures. He was famous for being meticulous, going through the pre-jump checklist, every item double-checked. They noticed nothing different this time, can't explain why his chute didn't open. Dead men tell no tales, but for his family his death speaks eloquently; somewhere there was a defect. Someone had to've been negligent.

'The defendants are the parachute manufacturer and the technicians at the airport who packed it. They can't account for it any other way than by saying it must've been suicide. The packing's a two-person procedure: one packs and another inspects. Both of the people who prepared his equipment said it passed muster. He was face-down when he hit on a hard-packed clay surface.

His thumb and fingers were still in the D-ring. The chute took the same terminal-velocity impact he did; that probably affected it. Allowing for that, the people who inspected it after the incident said they couldn't find any evidence that it'd been tampered with since it left the packers' custody. They found no indication of pre-impact defect of materials or workmanship; no fatigue-condition of components, wear and tear, before the impact, that prevented it from deploying.

'Obviously it hadn't. The glaring question is Why. The investigators said they found no indication that it hadn't been activated properly, but they couldn't rule that out. He might've had a sudden cramp in his hand so he was unable to pull the ripcord at the precise moment he planned; caused him to panic, and freeze. They can't tell. Maybe the ripcord snagged a little, gave him more resistance than he was used to, and *that* made him panic and freeze. Again, no way to tell. *Maybe*, maybe he didn't pull the cord and never meant to; the fatal defect was the human condition. As far as the defense experts can see, everything else was just fine.

'The defense team put on one eyewitness, another experienced parachutist, fourth in the chain that day. She said she could see him part of the way down, until she pulled her ripcord and her chute opened, but he just kept on free-falling. She doesn't think he ever tried to pop his. She saw no sign he was having a problem or struggling with it. She said it looked to her like he just kept his hands on the pack in front of him, head sort of bowed, "looking down, almost as though he'd been praying." He went by the other divers who'd gone out ahead of him; since their chutes were open and his wasn't, he was now dropping much faster than they were. Their depositions said they didn't have time to see much, and anyway they were too shocked and horrified to've noticed much anyway. He had goggles on and they were too far away to see whether he had his eyes open.

'Nobody on either side ever really addressed the issue that I would have thought to be central to the case. *Why* was he washed out of Jump School? He never told anyone, so far as we know. He always said he didn't know. The Army lost his records in a fire some years ago. Now no one could track down the people in his unit. Did someone there think maybe the kid had a death wish? Or was the reason for washing him out so insignificant, and so long ago, nobody even remembers? Well for sure, no one knows now.

'So there we had it: either it was a mysterious accident and we'll never know what caused it, or else this successful, healthy, well-to-do family-man, real zest for life, movie-star good-looking and very well-liked, *apparently* happy, killed himself for some reason we'll never know.

'This one I wanted to go to the jury. Then at least we would've had a six-person consensus of which explanation's the likeliest. Of course they might not've been able to dope it out either; would've come back reporting a deadlock. But evidently both sides, after hearing each other's case go in and watching how the jury seemed to be taking it, came to the same conclusion: letting the jury decide it was taking more risk than they wanted. The defendants pre-trial offered sixty-five thousand; how they arrived at that figure I do not pretend to know. The family made the customary multi-million-dollar demand. In the pre-trial conferences I had the clear impression that they'd settle only if they got the whole pot in the defendants' liability insurance pool, three million dollars. So the trial accomplished something for both sides. The family gets a million-one that they wouldn't have if they hadn't sued, around eight hundred thousand after they pay their lawyer. And the underwriters, after they pay their experts and lawyers, get to keep about a million and a half they might've lost.

'That leaves us with a *third* mystery: If all of the evidence'd come in, what would the jury've decided? Now we'll never know that answer either. I feel *cheated*. I suppose I'm being childish. I want life to be *neat*, with clearcut answers. Never *mind* about the money: *I* want to *know* why Nick Hardigrew died. But life isn't neat, so I don't.

'Anyway,' she said, 'just what've we got on here this afternoon? Something a bit simpler, perhaps? One of you gentlemen want to tell me what it's about, so I can put my steel-trap mind to work on it?'

'Why don't you kick it off, Arnie?' Cohen said. 'We're sort of coming in here in the middle of things. I'm not sure we've got it all straight.'

'Sure,' Bissell said. 'Back in February, the US Attorney directed the Political Corruption Unit to undertake a very broad-gauged investigation of contracts awarded by the Commonwealth of Massachusetts and its sub-divisions; counties; cities and towns; various and sundry authorities – port, turnpike, state reservations, water and so forth.

'What he had in mind was really a massive undertaking. He told us to develop a data base of every contract, bid and no-bid, that's wound up costing the Commonwealth taxpayers more than one hundred thousand dollars, awarded during the past twenty years. Going back to the middle Seventies; covering not only contracts for projects *expected* to cost more than a hundred thousand, but also contracts originally awarded for lesser amounts – which as a result of cost-overruns exceeded the one-hundred-thousand floor.'

'*Gracious*,' Cohen said. 'That must've been a *huge* project. Who got the contract for *that* work? How much did the taxpayers have to pay *him*? Must've been '*way* over one hundred grand.'

'It was done in-house,' Bissell said, grimly, biting off his words. 'It wasn't contracted out. The capability was already in place. The FBI and the IRS and the GAO have *plenty* of people and *lots* of machinery to gather data and crunch numbers, analyze what they come up with, spit out the files that meet stated criteria. The employees were trained and in place. It didn't cost the taxpayers one extra dime to have them doing this work.'

'Right,' Cohen said. 'Instead of some other work. In the spring of the year with Tax Day coming up, when a civilian'd think the IRS'd probably have enough coming in to keep occupied – but what do civilians know, huh? To the government it was a free play – not just more government waste.'

'Your Honor,' Bissell said, 'I realize this's an informal session and all, but could I ask you to please instruct Attorney Cohen to let me get on the record why we're here? If that's what he wanted me to do, when he requested this session? Because if he's going to sit there baiting me like this and make me spend all my time fending him off, we'll never get anywhere here.'

The judge nodded. 'Put a lid on it, Geoff, would you please? I *do* have the afternoon free, which I certainly didn't expect. But

I bet if I try I can find one or two other pending matters that'd warrant my attention.' Cohen pretended to pout. She chuckled and shook her head. 'Go ahead, Arnie,' she said. 'If he doesn't behave I'll hold *him* in contempt, along with his client.'

Merrion looked at the judge the way a cornered cat measures a large menacing dog, calculating how much damage it can do before the dog mauls it. She saw this and was angered for a moment, but then reconsidered. 'Excuse me for a moment, Arnie,' she said, putting up her right hand as Bissell started to speak. 'Mister Merrion,' she said, 'I think I might've just made a needlessly provocative remark. If it sounded threatening, I apologize; that was not my intention.'

'Thank you, your Honor,' Merrion said, surprise in his eyes.

'Certainly,' the judge said. 'Now, Arnie, if you would.'

'We haven't completed the data collection,' Bissell said. 'It'll probably take another year, at least. But this is a *rolling* program. We're not waiting until we've finished collecting all the data before we start our analysis. We're initiating new grand jury proceedings contemporaneously, each time the data profile another cohering and discrete cell of individuals – we call 'em *hives*, or *nests* – isolating them as it were, picking them off one at a time. Our hope is to keep pace as much as possible between the data-profiling and the field investigations that producing the actual evidence corroborating – or contradicting, also possible but unlikely – what the data tell us to expect. Otherwise we're going to face a terrible backlog down the line. This particular *John Doe* investigation we've got underway both in Boston and out here started during the first week of August.'

Cohen interrupted wearily. 'I know I'm not supposed to interrupt, your Honor, but could we ask Arnie to spare us all the disingenuous *John Doe* make-believe about who's the target here? Dan Hilliard's in the cross-hairs; it's been common knowledge since the day *after* they chose him, which was the day *before* the leaks began.'

'*John Doe*'s a formality,' Bissell said coolly, 'custom and usage. We know rumors and leaks occur. They start the minute we begin serving subpoenas. We know it'll happen, so we don't issue subpoenas until we're pretty sure a given investigation's going to yield a prosecutable case. Usually our expectations turn out to be right; we develop a prosecutable case against the person or persons our subpoenas seemed to point to. Therefore when we complete the investigative phase and enter the formal accusatory phase, the rumors turn out to be true. *Post hoc, propter hoc.*

'That doesn't mean we start the rumors. We don't. The minute some bank treasurer is subpoenaed as the Keeper of the Records, specifying whose records we want, he knows who we're after. The fat goes in the fire and the gossip's in the wind. We can't stop it, so we've done the next best thing: stopped worrying about it.

'So, everyone knows who we're after? Usually. But experienced *criminal* lawyers know we never publicly name any target 'til he's been indicted. We can't, we're not allowed to. Constitution states no citizen shall be held to answer for a capital offense or crime of infamy except upon presentment of grand jury. *Remember*, Geoff? Black-letter law.'

Cohen stared at him thoughtfully, picking at the edge of his lower right front tooth with the nail of his left ring-finger, saying nothing.

'Children, children,' the judge said. 'Get on with it, Arnie.'

'The review of state and state sub-division contracts awarded to private companies and individuals in the Western District showed a striking correlation between people benefiting from them and people who'd been heavy financial supporters of Daniel Hilliard's political career – major campaign contributors. Hilliard is the *queen bee*; his rich pals are his *worker bees*. Or *ants*, as you prefer.'

'I object to this, your Honor,' Cohen said. 'There's no need for Mister Bissell's gratuitous and demeaning insults.'

'I'm sorry,' Bissell said. 'You said *John Doe* offended you. I thought you wanted me to use the same vocabulary here we use among ourselves when we're discussing people like your client here today.'

'I don't want any more of trash-talk out of either one of you,' the judge said. 'Do you want me to make it clearer than that? Get to work.'

'We have a number of individuals under investigation for their dealings with Hilliard, your Honor,' Bissell said. 'I'm going to use Haskell Sanderson, Junior, for an example. He began doing business with the state several years before the opening date we'd arbitrarily chosen for our investigation, but when we saw the pattern emerging in those years, we went back to his first state contracts. The pattern was clear from the start. Sanderson began contributing generously to Hilliard. Very soon he got his first state printing contract. He increased his contributions. He got more state printing contracts. Until the state campaign financing law took effect, he contributed between five and ten thousand dollars to the Hilliard Committee every two-year election cycle, equivalent to thirty or forty thousand today.

'When the statute prohibited corporate donations and limited individual contributions to two thousand dollars per individual per cycle, Sanderson complied. He reduced his contributions to the statutory amount. But his wife, when he had one, gave two thousand dollars, and his son, who claims to be a golf pro but spends half the year tending bar, gave two thousand a cycle. Four of Sanderson's employees gave a thousand each. Hilliard's total receipts from Sanderson were unaffected by the new law.

'In the past twenty-five years or so Sanderson's state printing contracts've totalled several million dollars. He holds three today, long-term agreements worth in excess of nine hundred thousand dollars over the next two years.'

'Dan Hilliard hasn't been in the House since Nineteen-eighty-four,' Cohen said, at the same time gripping Merrion's left forearm to prevent him from speaking.

'Sanderson met his pals in the Procurement branch while Hilliard was still in office,' Bissell said wearily. 'He bought what he needed while the store was open. By the time Hilliard left the legislature, Sanderson was entrenched. Hilliard did such a great job he doesn't need him anymore.

'His company isn't even in the district Hilliard represented. Sanderson never lived in it but he became a heavy Hilliard backer about thirty years ago. His friend Carl Kuiper told him it could be profitable. He introduced them. Kuiper discovered very early there was money to be made by people on good terms with Dan Hilliard. Before he retired and sold his electrical contracting company to GE, it was the largest such company privately owned in western Massachusetts, due in no small part to its robust relationship with the state Department of Procurement and Services.

'Same pattern. Kuiper didn't live in Hilliard's district. His business wasn't in it either. But he jumped on the Hilliard bandwagon right at the beginning, back in Nineteen-sixty-two, when Hilliard was making his big move from Holyoke alderman to state representative. Five thousand a cycle, regular as clockwork, 'til the limits took effect. Then he went to the nominee-dodge too; his wife and his two kids suddenly developed an interest in state politics they'd never shown before: the new program was two thousand from him; a thousand from his wife; and a thousand more each from each of his kids – including his daughter, nurturing her deep interest in the Massachusetts legislature from her home in Santa Barbara.

'Since those five-grand-a-cycle donations began, our figures show Kuiper's company's raked in over nineteen million dollars' worth of state contracts. "And before that?" you ask.' He snickered. 'Before that Kuiper Electric, in business for almost ten years, had had *one* state contract: Eleven thousand dollars' worth of repairs to lighting systems in the barns at the Berkshire County Agricultural Society Fairgrounds and racetrack out in Hancock.

'Those're illustrations,' Bissell said. 'I'm not going to show all the files to you, uncover our whole hand at this point in the game. But I can *assure* you that we've got a dozen more just like them. If you compare the list of Hilliard's major contributors to the list of individuals and companies that got fat while he was in office, what you see is a virtual *template* of political corruption; *rampant* corruption, corruption abounding. If you gave generously to Hilliard's campaigns, your gifts returned to you not a hundred- but a *thousand*-fold, *at a minimum*, in the form of fat state contracts. It's a textbook case of political chicanery and larceny. I know Mister Merrion's Dan Hilliard's close friend and associate, and he won't like hearing me say this, but Dan Hilliard is a common *crook*.'

Merrion inhaled audibly, so that his chest visibly expanded, and he gripped the arms of his chair hard, so that his knuckles whitened. Cohen grabbed Merrion's right forearm with his left hand and said: 'Your Honor, I know you want to move along as rapidly as possible, without a lot of bickering, but could I be heard? This's hard to take in silence.'

'Go ahead, Geoff,' the judge said.

'In the first place,' Cohen said, 'I represent Amby Merrion not Dan Hilliard. Bob Pooler represents Dan. So, when I respond to these attacks, I'm at a disadvantage I assume Bob would not be. But I'm sure Bob'd include among the pieces of his far-better argument the reminder that the period of the Seventies and Eighties covered by' – he deepened his voice – '*this rolling program*' – he resumed his normal baritone – 'were decades of unprecedented prosperity, not just in western Massachusetts but across the entire country. And decades as well of galloping inflation that brought us to the point we're now at, where what was worth a buck when Hilliard first began to run now costs at least three.

'And in the second place, if Dan Hilliard hadn't been attentive to the best interests of the whole region; if instead he'd worked solely within the narrow confines of his own legislative district, he never could've forged the alliances he needed to rise to chairman of Ways and Means, and the influence to channel those state contracts out here.

'The businessmen and manufacturers who supported him all those years weren't acting purely selfishly. Sure, they were in it for themselves, and many of them prospered. But so did their hundreds of employees. And therefore so did the merchants and builders, *and lawyers*, and all the other people who serve our communities. Property values increased, and therefore so did tax revenues. We all depend upon a healthy industrial economy as the foundation of our prosperity.

'Today if we don't have that, we're a heck of a lot closer to having it than we were when Dan Hilliard first ran for office. Those contracts Mister Bissell now finds so sinister were important building blocks, *vital* to this region. Coming from the eastern part of the state – Gloucester, did you tell me, we were chatting outside there?'

Bissell nodded. Cohen continued. 'Yeah, I thought so; growing up there the coastline as he did, Mister Bissell wouldn't know this, but until that state work began coming inland, *out here*, what we had was a predominantly agricultural economy. Our industries, the mills and factories, had first declined, then folded up. The economy was in sad shape. We were in the doldrums. Young people were leaving; they had no choice. Either they went into farming, like it or not, assuming they could *find* farming jobs, or else they moved away. Those state contracts meant they didn't have to; they could stay. Some who had left came back, renewed family connections, once there was work for them here. Those contracts were tickets of admission to a new world of light-manufacturing and skilled blue-collar work, and the new incomes that came with it. A better life for all of us.

'I sound like a candidate myself now. If that record were mine, I might very well be. By rights I ought to do well. A politician with that history to present, I'd deserve to be re-elected by a landslide. But that record isn't mine to brag about. It belongs to Danny Hilliard. It's a *good* one, a wonderful record of accomplishment. Keep in mind that this is coming from the man Dan Hilliard's ex-wife hired to hammer him with everything he could lay his hands on, and we did that. But never once did we attack his fine record in office. No one who knows him ever has. The people who backed his campaigns invested their money wisely and well. Are they and he therefore now to be denounced for what they accomplished, and held up to scorn and disgrace?'

Bissell snorted. Merrion glared at him. Cohen and the judge ignored both of them. 'In the *third* place,' Cohen said, 'and perhaps the one that should most concern this court, Dan Hilliard last stood for office in *Nineteen-eighty-two*. We all know why he didn't seek a twelfth term; as I say, I represented his wife: revelations of his untidy personal life turned many of his constituents against him. It was a very messy and unpleasant time for everyone concerned, but that untidy private life, as scandalous as it may've been, *was not against federal law*.

'The US Attorney now proposes in effect to rewrite history, to impose a new and deeply cynical interpretation on the solid common cause Dan Hilliard made with his constituents, and the people who supported his campaigns. Mister Bissell and his bosses in their wisdom now decree that what we saw as a marvelous alliance bringing great – and greatly needed – benefits to the

Pioneer Valley, we were deluded, just plain *wrong*. They say it was a corrupt bargain.

'The idea's preposterous on its face, but grant it, *arguendo*: Dan Hilliard last sought elective office well over ten years ago. The state Statute of Limitations is six years. The federal one is five. Except for murder or treason, of course – neither of which I've heard my learned friend here mention, at least as yet. So: why in the world is the federal watchdog prowling around out here with his Operation Rolling Blunder, snarling and snapping at Danny Hilliard, and the people who backed him for the office he filled so well?

'If it weren't so scary in terms of the damage he can do with it, you'd think Mister Bissell's mission was a new mega-death computer game for kids; thrills and chills and sound-effects, flashing lights and puffs of smoke, but in the real world, harmless. Too bad it isn't. This game's for much higher stakes; he's playing with *real* people's *lives*. Is the US Attorney really spending all this money; wasting all this manpower; muddying spotless reputations helter-skelter; causing all this *anguish* – when even if he could prove the acts were corrupt he couldn't *prosecute* them? Is that what this is, an exercise here? If it is, this's not law enforcement; this is abuse of authority, power run amok. If not, then what else is it?'

'Good question, Geoff,' the judge said. 'Ball's in your court now, Mister Bissell.'

'Thank you, your Honor,' he said. 'Mister Cohen took umbrage at my description of this project before I finished outlining it. Of course we're quite aware that limitations have expired for prosecution of many if not most of the substantive offenses we believe to've been committed by Mister Hilliard and his co-conspirators – chief among them Mister Merrion, which's why we've immunized him – over the course of the years. But I would point out to the court, and to Mister Cohen as well, that when we can prove that *further* acts, *within the statute*, *have* been committed in the course of that same, *ongoing*, conspiracy that underlay the earlier substantive acts; and that those more recent acts were *also* committed in furtherance of the purpose for which the conspiracy was formed; then by law we are permitted to claim *relation back* to the earlier offenses, *and prove them*, as part of the underlying, continuing scheme. Its fruition.

'In outline what we see here, your Honor, is a convoluted tripartite conspiracy, one branch still thriving, still returning excellent profits.

'The overall conspiracy,' Bissell said, making an arch with his hands over the table, 'involved the campaign contributions. We see that one as the umbrella. It provided the shelter under which at least two more schemes could grow. The fund-raising, state-contract quid-pro-quo scheme's now functionally defunct; there's no further need for it. It's done the job Hilliard and Merrion designed it to do – get Hilliard elected to office; gain access to and influence over the state contracting process; and in return get kickbacks disguised as campaign contributions. Dan Hilliard's retired; the contracts continue; those two set-ups, no longer needed, were allowed to atrophy.

'That's not the case with the other plot under the big umbrella. It survives and we can prove it.

'The first thing Hilliard and Merrion did was to create an organization that would work out of Holyoke in tandem with the voting machine that the Carnes brothers, Roy and Arthur, had put into place for themselves right after World War Two. A few years later they were joined by Roy's son, Roy Junior.

'The Carneses were very methodical. Arthur had come back from the war a wounded veteran and a hero. He had capitalized on that, parlayed the admiration and the sympathy he got into his political career. So Arthur was in charge of getting power. Meanwhile, Roy Senior was doing the day-to-day work of establishing and expanding the family's local real estate empire. Roy was in charge of getting wealth. In time Roy Junior, "Little Roy" or "Young Roy," came along to inherit the aldermanic seat vacated by Arthur when he ran for the House. Then he took Arthur's House seat when Arthur moved up to the Senate. Ultimately he succeeded to his uncle's Senate seat, after Arthur's death, and to much of the wealth his father had accumulated as well. Not exactly what Arthur and Roy had in mind, but still and all, pretty close.

'Their plan'd been that Little Roy would take the Senate seat when Arthur retired to the judgeship the two of them'd created for him, when they carved out the new Canterbury District during the late Fifties. But Arthur died, disrupting their plans. Big Roy wasn't interested in the judgeship. He was too busy making lots of money running the real estate business. Little Roy had further political ambitions; it was too early for him to retire. Charles Spring, a close Carnes family friend, therefore became the first presiding judge.

'The Hilliard-Merrion scheme was conceived as a sort of a Carnes satellite. By necessity it was somewhat less ambitious; Hilliard had no war-wound to display and Merrion had no family cash to work with, but they had some impressive plans. The first was to get Hilliard elected to the board of aldermen. Roy Junior was the only second-generation Carnes with the political bug. If Hilliard could displace the lacklustre boob who'd won Roy's seat on the board of aldermen, he'd be positioned to go after Roy's seat in the House when Roy moved up to Arthur's Senate seat.

'In effect what he and Merrion proposed to the Carneses was that since they were temporarily fresh-out of political horses, Hilliard would serve as a surrogate Carnes. He'd hold down jobs they wanted to relinquish but still control, but lacked homebred manpower to fill. He'd exercise the authority the jobs carried in consultation with Roy and Arthur; they in turn would back him. He even agreed to let them control his financing, in exchange for help in getting it, which in real terms meant they would control not only the power, but him.

'That sounded good to the Carneses. In Nineteen-sixty, with under-the-table help from them, Hilliard and Merrion pulled off their first victory. The Carneses were taking no chances; until Hilliard proved he could actually win, he was their clandestine candidate. That way if he lost they'd be free to dump him and look for a more popular stooge.'

'Your Honor,' Cohen said.

The judge put up her left hand. 'I know, Geoff, I know. If you ever get this case before a jury, Arnie, you can say stuff like that in your closing argument. Until such time as that occurs, restrain yourself.'

Bissell nodded. 'Stand corrected, your Honor,' he said, his expression showing no contrition. 'The second objective was to exploit the leverage and visibility of the aldermanic seat to attract the contributions Hilliard would need to run for state rep, *without* stepping on any Carnes toes. That he and Merrion accomplished by courting the small businessmen and manufacturers who lived in the general vicinity and ran their businesses *around* the Carnes turf. On the perimeter. They did very well at this, so well that one or two years after his first House election, Hilliard commanded enough campaign funds to begin "helping out" candidates from other districts who either didn't like to raise money all the time, the way he did, or didn't get the kind of results he got, because they weren't as slick.'

Merrion came forward in his chair. Cohen grabbed his arm again. The judge shook her head and sighed. 'Arnie, I just cautioned you about provocative language, and now here you go and do it again. Keep in mind that you're in here because you want me to do something Mister Cohen opposes. Goading him and his client is not the best way to persuade me to do it.'

Bissell nodded, his face showing resignation based upon dour foresight. 'That Lord Bountiful ability he had to bestow gifts upon less-affluent reps made Mister Hilliard a popular and respected House figure, far more so than his age or years of service ever would've suggested. Give the devil his due as well: Dapper Dan Hilliard's a likable man. Women, especially, like him,' Judge Foote's face remained impassive, 'which as we know finally got him in trouble, but his charm worked on his male colleagues as well.

'The combination was a potent one. Even as a lowly two-term rep he had considerably more power on the Judicidary and the Ways and Means Committees than many five-and six-termers. He wasn't above using it for private purposes, either. When he and his wife decided she could no longer care for their severely retarded daughter at home, Hilliard threw his weight around to jump the queue and get her into the Walter J. Fernald School – ahead of some thirty other children whose parents had been waiting as much as sixteen months to get their children in. He may be playing the gracious academic these days, but his arrogance then knew no bounds.'

When he paused for breath the room was absolutely still.

Elizabeth Gibson, her fingers poised over the stenotype machine, stared at Bissell with her mouth open. Merrion and Cohen stared. Sandy Robey gaped. Judge Foote inhaled deeply but made no other sound.

Bissell seemed puzzled by the reaction. He frowned, but he was sufficiently unsure of himself so that he did not break the silence. At last Merrion, this time unrestrained by Cohen, said in a strangled low voice: 'Donna Hilliard died in that hospital almost twenty years ago. She was fourteen years old. She'd never said a word, or laughed. She'd never recognized her mother or her father; never fought with her brother and sister. She'd never played with other children; never had an ice cream cone. She'd never been to school. No one ever heard her laugh. No one ever saw her cry.'

Gibson straightened up and typed into the machine what Merrion had just said. Cohen and the judge stirred, blinking. The judge cleared her throat. 'Yes,' she said, dragging it out and exhaling. She shook her head and blinked. She shook her head again. 'I certainly have to hand it to you, Mister Bissell,' she said, 'you're quite a piece of work. Try to get on with what you were telling us. See if we can get out of here before you're challenged to a duel.'

'All I was trying to say,' Bissell said, appearing not to understand any of the reactions, 'is that political power is cumulative, iterative, in anybody's hands. The more Hilliard had of it, the more he found he could get. Because he had that kind of clout, he could make himself extremely useful to Roy Junior, pushing or retarding Senate bills on the House side. Roy in turn was only too pleased to reciprocate, guiding Hilliard's pet measures through the upper body. That improved Hilliard's image on the House side, enabling him to do more for Carnes in the lower body.

'The result was that after a while there was a sort of merger of the Carnes and Hilliard interests. Now it was time for Hilliard and Merrion, in partnership with the Carneses, of course, to start lining their pockets, too. This was the second leg of their conspiratorial stool. Their ultimate goal was to obtain a high-paying lifetime sinecure for each of them in the public sector. Merrion's they wanted fairly soon; Hilliard would put off locating a cushy billet until he got tired of active politics, lost, or decided that he'd gone as far as he could go. But that didn't mean they were ruling out any good opportunities to steal that might crop up along the way to full employment.

'We're not clear whether Hilliard and Merrion expected to find their biggest bonanza in the Canterbury courthouse when Hilliard muscled through Merrion's appointment as third assistant clerk of court in Nineteen-sixty-six. What we do know is that events demonstrated that a bonanza did in fact exist: the Fourmen's Realty Trust. The Carneses, certainly never intending to divulge its existence to Hilliard or Merrion, much less share it with them, had been instrumental in its corrupt creation. But Mister Merrion, resourceful fellow that he is, found it. Six years later, he grabbed hold of a piece of it. From that point on, no matter what else came through or fell through, the Hilliard-Merrion partnership was a success.

'The Carneses – Arthur in the Senate and Roy Junior in the House; Roy Senior still running the real estate business in Holyoke – had made a fairly decent killing for themselves on the contract to build the Canterbury District Courthouse. So had their friends, as the first rule of crooked politics – staying out of jail – requires. Judge Spring was the head of the building committee. An ambitious young fellow named Larry Lane, an assistant clerk in the Chicopee District Court and desperate to get out of there, became Spring's first clerk. Spring knew he could therefore control him. He put him on the building committee, giving the Carnes family two votes out of five. Roy Carnes Senior got a third appointment. After that it was easy; the ballgame began in earnest.

'F.D. Barrows Construction Company rigged the bid and won the contract. Barrows cut the corners on materials and labor; Spring and Lane and Roy Carnes approved each stage of construction and the progress payments therefore due. Spring set up the trust, Fourmen's Realty, to receive the money Barrows skimmed off the construction and kicked back to the other three. It wasn't a great deal of money, by today's standards: just under a hundred-forty grand. But we must keep in mind that they didn't steal it *today*; they took it before Nineteen-sixty. A good annual salary then was less than a tenth of that boodle creamed off the courthouse budget; by the standards of today what they stole would amount to about six-hundred-thousand dollars, a very respectable amount of loot.

'Over the years there were some changes made in the trust. The real estate-insurance man from Hampton Falls, Philip Fox, came in soon after it was formed. The reason was that he'd handled the construction bonds on the courthouse. The Commonwealth was having one of its periodic fits of public outrage about corruption. A state crime commission had been appointed. Fox knew too much to leave him out and maybe make him mad enough to talk. So the first four brought him in, diluting their shares but keeping him quiet – hush money.

'Years went by. Fox died and his grandson Walter took his place. Lane died, leaving his to Merrion, in thanks for befriending him. Shrewdly. The money kept on rolling in. Walter Fox died and his widow, Diane, took his place on the trust. Later on, she agreed to fill the place her husband had expected to serve on the building committee for the new Canterbury Municipal Complex. Mister Merrion was also on that committee. Mrs Fox wasn't originally from around here. She's from Wisconsin. Fairly soon after these developments, she and Mister Merrion entered into a close personal relationship.'

'Is that supposed to mean something?' Merrion said, growling.

'Take it easy, Amby,' Cohen said. 'Take it easy here.'

'Stay away from the personal stuff, Mister Bissell,' the judge said. 'We avoid private matters in this corner of the world.'

'I meant no aspersion on Mrs Fox or Mister Merrion, either, in that regard,' Bissell said. 'The point I was making is that Mrs Fox, being from Wisconsin, probably wasn't familiar with the Massachusetts politics of self-enrichment. So, to enlist her in any later scheme to skim contracts for construction of the Canterbury Municipal Complex, as the make-up of the committee would suggest that he and Hilliard had in mind, Mister Merrion would've had to explain the procedures to her. He perhaps feared she might not like the idea of milking state contracts – might even strongly disapprove. And because they *do* appear to have embarked on what's now a long-standing relationship quite soon after her husband's death, our surmise is that his fear of her disapproval, and what she might do to express it, caused him to abrogate any plans he and Hilliard might have had to plunder the project. Whatever the reason, so far in our review it doesn't appear to have been skimmed.'

'Hurrah, hurrah,' Merrion murmured, before Cohen could silence him.

'Mister Merrion,' the judge said calmly, 'I know this must be very trying for you, very hard to sit through without making some response. But I also know you're a court officer, not only made of good stern stuff but also aware of the rules of decorum we enforce here, even when we're in chambers.

'I'll make an allowance for you this time, because I do think,' shifting her gaze to Bissell, 'that the assistant US attorney has gone about as far as I'm willing to allow without disciplining *him*.' Bissell worked his mouth and swallowed. She returned her gaze to Merrion, stretching her left arm out on the table and lowering her head to sight along it at him. 'But please don't do it again.' She kept her smile very small. 'Do we understand each other, Mister Merrion?'

'Yes, your Honor,' Merrion said, looking chagrined.

She straighted up and nodded. '*Good*,' she said with satisfaction. She turned to look at Bissell. 'And how about *you*, Mister Bissell? We're both on the same page too, I trust?'

'Oh yes, your Honor,' Bissell said without repentance, 'I understand your view. But once again, when I said that, I did not mean . . .'

'*Nooo*,' the judge said, 'the matter's *closed*. Go on now and please finish.'

'For whatever the reason, the Fourmen's Trust thereafter does not appear to have been further enriched by any infusions of capital other than the contributions required to buy out the interests of departing members. Judge Spring was the next to die, after Philip Fox. Then Roy Carnes, Junior, liquidated all his family holdings here in order to relocate down south. F.D. Barrow, Walter Fox and Merrion bought out those two shares. Then Barrow died and his son succeeded him. And as I've said, when Walter Fox died his wife Diane took his place.

'So the Fourmen's Trust as it's now constituted has three named shareholder-beneficiaries, two men and a woman. Otherwise the way it's operated stayed the same for coming up on almost forty years now, still turning a neat profit, close to two hundred grand a year. All through those years, right down to the present day, each and every one of the direct beneficiaries of profits earned on the ill-gotten gains that funded the Fourmen's Trust has scrupulously and faithfully reported, as ordinary income, the annual distributions that the trust has made from earnings, and paid all federal and state taxes due – very substantial sums.

'But during those years there has also been an *indirect* beneficiary, Daniel Hilliard. We find in his tax returns for beginning in Nineteen-seventy-three no evidence, no indication, he ever reported as income the amounts by which he benefited from the Fourmen's Trust, or paid any taxes on them.'

'For the simple *reason*,' Merrion began roughly.

'Shut *up*, Amby,' Cohen said, spinning in his chair and grabbing Merrion's arm again. Then: 'Your Honor, may I have a word with my client?'

'Certainly,' the judge said. 'Do you want a recess so you can take him outside and talk to him privately?'

'I don't think that'll be necessary, your Honor,' Cohen said, 'but I would like this to be off the record.'

'I'll give you that,' the judge said. 'Off the record. You probably don't mind hearing that, do you, Lizzie?'

'Sweetest words I heard today,' the stenographer said, clasping her hands together, palms outward, and stretching her arms out in front of her, then flexing her back against the chair.

'Look, Amby,' Cohen said. 'I warned you you wouldn't like this; sitting through this and having to keep your mouth shut. And I told you you shouldn't come. But you insisted, said you could do it. You wouldn't let him get to you. So do it. Or if you can't do it, get out.'

Merrion nodded, his face like an outcropping rock.

'I think we'll be all right now to go back on the record again, Judge,' Cohen said.

'Very well,' the judge said, 'we are back on the record. Mister Bissell, as you were saying?'

'I mentioned just a few moments ago,' Bissell said, unable or unwilling to avoid looking pleased, 'that when Dan Hilliard and Mister Merrion pooled their resources back in Nineteen-sixty to get Hilliard elected alderman, they had several objectives in mind. The third one was to secure good *lifetime* jobs with the Commonwealth. Hilliard's would turn out to be the presidency of Hampton Pond Community College – which with the help of his cronies in the House he tailor-made for himself. But his sinecure could wait; his political star was still on the rise.

'Merrion's situation was different. After a few years as Hilliard's district aide, he began to feel restless. A secure billet had to be found for him. One was. In Nineteen-sixty-six, Presiding Judge Charles Spring, no doubt at the direction of Roy Carnes, acting in turn at Hilliard's request, appointed Ambrose Merrion third assistant clerk of the Canterbury Court. Merrion and Lane later formed a friendship.

'That was Merrion's shrewd move. By all accounts, Lane'd been a heavy smoker all his life, and he also had a serious drinking problem. Soon after he retired, late in Nineteen-seventy, already diagnosed with cancer, his family gave him an ultimatum: either he would quit drinking and undergo a grueling course of radiation and chemotherapy to arrest the disease, if not cure it, or he would have to leave.

'He chose to leave. He estranged himself from his wife and children and moved into an apartment in the three-story building at Sixteen-ninety-two Eisenhower Boulevard built by the Fourmen's Realty Trust, financed with funds its beneficiaries and trustees had skimmed off the courthouse construction. Lane died in October of Nineteen-seventy-two.

'Early in Nineteen-seventy-three,' Bissell said, 'Mister Merrion used a portion of the first distribution he received from that trust, as Lane's heir and successor, to take advantage of an expansion of membership rolls at Grey Hills Country Club. The Club took this action for the first and only time in order to finance extensive repairs and improvements expected to cost more than a million dollars – *three* million today. That was eight hundred thousand more than the club's officers thought it wise to take out of available capital. The only alternative was to open the rolls to enough new members as would be necessary to offset the rest of the cost.

'Most of the old-money members opposed this. The only way to get their consent was to keep the number of new members admitted as small as possible – a hundred was the absolute ceiling they would stand for. That meant the tariffs had to be extremely high – well over eight thousand dollars a head. The invitation to apply was posted on Groundhog Day.

'If the response left the board of governors chagrined, they had a right to be. Clearly they could've gotten more; the quota was over subscribed before the end of February. The rolls were once again closed, but now Daniel Hilliard and Ambrose Merrion were listed upon them.

'Membership has remained firmly closed ever since, your Honor,' Bissell said. 'For more than twenty years the governors of Grey Hills have been able to run this vast and luxurious resort, really; a famous, groomed-and-pampered, championship golf course on more than three hundred acres of prime real estate, surrounded with every possible amenity; with a seasonal staff of more than two hundred employees, eighty of whom work all the year 'round; entirely on the income generated by their four hundred dues-paying members' fees, and bills they incur at the club. One estimate we have says that the average annual member spends six thousand dollars a year.

'Six thousand dollars a year. One hundred and fifteen dollars a week. At the minimum wage that's what a kid grosses working his way through college at a part-time job flipping burgers at McDonald's twenty-seven hours a week. For most of these people it buys at the most twenty-four weekend-rounds of golf. Six thousand dollars a year – two hundred and fifty dollars a round. Joe Six-pack doesn't tee off at Grey Hills. This is not a watering-hole for the common man. This a club for *rich* men, a closed society of *very* wealthy men. Yet there among their number we find recorded the names of Ambrose Merrion and Daniel Hilliard.

'How on earth did they get in there? What on earth are they doing there? Neither of these men, both of whom we would most likely describe as *liberal populists*, was born into a wealthy family. Neither one of them since the age of twenty-one has ever held any job other than the ones they've had on the public payroll. Yet if we allow for inflation and say the average annual cost of

Grey Hills membership for these past twenty-two years was half of what we understand it is today, Mister Merrion's largesse in Mister Hilliard's behalf would amount to sixty-six thousand dollars. That on top of the eight-thousand-plus initiation fee and dues would be about seventy-five thousand dollars. All of which Merrion got from Lane's treasure chest, money Lane helped steal from *us*.'

'Your Honor,' Cohen said, 'I must ask again to interrupt. Again we have Mister Bissell regaling us with stories that begin: "Once upon a time." We don't for one moment dispute the US Attorney's right to seek out crimes for prosecution – if he thinks, as he seems to, there're too few in plain sight to keep his forces occupied. We don't quarrel with his privilege to go back in time far beyond the statute of limitations and rummage around as much as he likes, to see if he can then find something that will *catapult* him forward into the present tense, still clinging to a trailing string that he can pull on, like Orpheus to his Eurydice, to tow all of those old outrages forward under his cherished *relation back*. It seems like any case you managed to weave out of such flimsy stuff would be a pretty thin one, and a waste of the taxpayer's money, and unless you leave out ego, a personal desire for the limelight, it's mighty hard to see *why* he'd want to do it. But nevertheless, however poor his judgment seems to be, there's no arguing his right to spend his time this way if he wants to.

'Mister Merrion has now known – since the last week in August; he didn't until then – that Mister Bissell the week before had federal marshals serve a subpoena *duces tecum* on Mister Merrion's bank. It demanded the records of his checking and savings accounts much further back than the bank is able to go. They notifed him as they must and then of course turned over to the government everything they had. So, if my client ever had any notion of trying to claim he never paid any club dues, bills or fees in Mister Hilliard's behalf, as he did not, he now knows going in that the US Attorney can prove otherwise, and would certainly reward him for such impudence by indicting him for perjury.

'But even without that, why go through all of it? Why bother to have him before the grand jury? We'll *stipulate* he paid Mister Hilliard's initiation fee, annual dues, and a lot of miscellaneous other stuff at Grey Hills over the years. Thousands and thousands of dollars. We'll even give the US Attorney the explanation for Mister Merrion's strange and remarkable behavior – which despite his formidable powers of data-collection and analysis, seems to have eluded him: Mister Merrion and Mister Hilliard are *friends*.

'It's as simple as that. They've been buddies for thirty-five years. Dan Hilliard's former wife told me she used to tell her husband that if it hadn't been for her, and later on his girlfriends, people would've thought that he and Mister Merrion were gay. Mister Merrion's a bachelor, from a small family. His father died years ago. His mother's terminally ill, in a vegetative state; his brother and he are estranged. Dan Hilliard's the closest thing to "family" my client's ever had, all his adult life.

'Is it really surprising that he's treated Hilliard like an elder brother? Wouldn't you, or even Mister Bissell, as morally demanding as he is, think it appropriate to share a completely unexpected large inheritance – which I assure you this was, no 'shrewd move' on his part, the windfall from the Lane estate – with a family member? Or with someone who had filled, most faithfully, for years, the vacant family place?

'Of course you would. We all would. So our question here becomes: Given the quantity and detail of the evidence that the US Attorney has outlined as already in his hands, what need or purpose except humiliation, can he possibly have for forcing Mister Merrion to testify against Dan Hilliard?'

'Your Honor please?' Bissell said. 'I was getting to that. We don't know where Dan Hilliard got the money to put up the house in Bell Woods that he and his wife occupied until their divorce. We can't figure out where he got the money for the house on Martha's Vineyard. It may've been from innocent sources, bequests we can no longer track down. We doubt it, but it may have been. The Grey Hills money is different. We *know* where that money came from, and we also know he didn't earn it, or pay taxes on it, either.

'We anticipate that if we obtain an indictment alleging Mister Hilliard with criminally evading income taxes due and owing on the monies Mister Merrion paid to Grey Hills in his behalf, Mister Merrion may interpose as one defense for his friend the fact that he himself had paid income taxes on the money, before sending it to Grey Hills in Hilliard's behalf. Countering our allegation that the monies were not annual gifts but a bribe paid in annual installments as a stipend for Merrion's job – and thus, constructively, income to Hilliard when paid to Grey Hills for his benefit – Merrion would be able to tell the jury they were after-tax dollars in his hand, a gift to his pal Hilliard. Exceeding the then-statutory lifetime limit of thirty thousand dollars; perhaps exposing them to civil penalties and interest, but negativing the criminal aspect of intent to evade income taxes.'

'Mister Cohen?' the judge said, 'any comment here?'

'Just that that indeed would be part of the evidence Mister Merrion will give, if Mister Bissell brings about the unhappy event he just described,' Cohen said.

'Secondly, your Honor,' Bissell said smoothly, 'we anticipate that the grand jury may return an indictment alleging Mister Hilliard under color of his official authority sold a state office to, and extorted monies from, its occupant; and further that he conspired with Mister Merrion and others to sell, trade and traffic in a public office, and extort monies from its occupant. And further: alleging that he conspired with Mister Merrion and others to deprive the public of the rightful service and free and unfettered judgment of a public official – in other words, alleging racketeering – that Mister Merrion might interpose in Mister Hilliard's defense the claim that the monies he paid to Grey Hills in Mister Hilliard's behalf were not within the knowledge or the contemplation of the parties when Mister Hilliard arranged the clerkship, and were given of his own free will.'

'Of course he would,' Cohen said. 'It's the same horse under a different rider.'

'Exactly,' Bissell said. 'We have a right to compel Mister Merrion to commit himself to a story before we seek any indictments, to lock him into it before trial. We may never call him at trial, but we have a right to find out what he'll say if we do, and to prevent him from colluding with a clever lawyer to fabricate a *different* story to counter our case-in-chief. Reasonable doubts are counterfeited by such fabrications, to mislead credulous jurors. We want to find out what he'll say, before he finds out what we can prove.

'We know he won't do that voluntarily,' Bissell said. 'That's why we've given him immunity. As Mister Cohen demanded, it's Transactional, not Use. We've told him, through his lawyer, he is not a target. We've told him that nothing that he says will be used in evidence against him, unless he lies to us – if he does, of course, we'll go after him for perjury. Hammer and tongs, to use a Hilliard phrase. We've filed the document declaring all of this with you.'

The judge gazed at Bissell for a long minute. He gazed back without shifting his eyes. 'My,' she said, 'that's *very* ingenious, I must say. You propose to bootstrap all of that stuff forward within the statute and nail Hilliard good, to punish guys who are *dead*? Kill *him* because *they* got away? And make his best friend help with the execution? Is that all you have for us today?'

'It is, your Honor,' Bissell said. 'Frankly, I'm surprised we needed *anything* – that this hearing, if that's what it is, was even held. In my experience the judge doesn't even get involved unless and until the immunized witness refuses to testify. Mister Merrion's not scheduled to come before the grand jury 'til next week. Who knows what he'll do then? He may not know, yet, himself.'

'Yes,' she said. 'Well, I was also somewhat surprised Geoff'd asked to be heard. But then I said: "Geoff wants a hearing, and he's a good guy, so what the hey, give him a hearing." So Geoff, we're all listening.'

'Your Honor,' Cohen said, 'I appreciate the court's kindness. I'll be brief. Congress enacted testimonial immunity to deal with frustrations encountered in prosecuting the Mob. It takes the Fifth Amendment out of play, to prevent underlings from shielding kingpins by claiming, correctly, that if they testify what the godfathers told them to do, they'll hang themselves at the same time, for doing it.

'Congress never meant to enable a prosecutor to do what this one wants to do: transform a man against his will into Judas Iscariot in order to conjure up charges against his friend. Mister Bissell by his own account has abundant evidence of what he calls tax evasion. More than enough to drag Dan Hilliard into court and see if he can persuade a jury to railroad the guy. He doesn't need to involve Ambrose Merrion, the man's very best friend, in this little manhunt of his. This's overkill, and plain meanness, nothing more.'

'Geoff,' the judge said, 'I know how you feel. I know how your client feels, too: that he and Dan Hilliard did nothing wrong; all they did was become politicians and play what some believe is the headiest game in the world. They may be right. Never played the game, myself, but I've watched a lot of it; sure looked like fun to these eyes.

'But fun's irrelevant here. The law gives the US Attorney the power to grant immunity in any case he thinks appropriate. It gives the judge no discretion. If the US Attorney grants immunity, and the witness doesn't talk, I have to order the witness to talk, and if he won't, put him in jail.

'Them's the rules. If I thought that by letting you talk for another hour you'd come up with something to change that, I'd sit here and I'd let you do it. I'm sorry, but I don't.

'So: Mister Merrion, hear what I say to you. If, as and when you appear before the grand jury and are formally advised on the record of the grant of immunity; and asked questions; and you then refuse to answer, for any reason at all or no reason at all, the US Attorney will direct the US marshals to bring you before me. I will then inform you that you have valid privilege to remain silent, and order you to answer.

'You will be taken back before the grand jury, and if you do not answer then, we will meet for a third time. I will then find that by reason of your refusal to testify, you have placed yourself in contempt of this court. I will order the marshals to take you into custody and hold you to some convenient place of confinement until such time as you decide to obey my order to testify.

'Thus endeth the lesson; a hard saying to be sure, but as I told you, those're the rules we have here. Mister Cohen, do you or your client have any questions?'

Cohen sighed. 'No, your Honor.'

'Mister Merrion,' the judge said, 'did your excellent counsel leave anything out that you would like to say now? Within the bounds of civility, of course – don't want to take too many chances here.'

Merrion had the thousand-yard stare of a man who'd stopped

caring what he saw. He spoke off-handedly. 'No,' he said. 'Just, I guess, that I'll see you next week. All of my life I've done what I can to protect people's dignity.' Looking at Bissell: 'I'm not going to give mine to him.'

The judge pursed her lips. She looked at Bissell, already rising from his chair. 'Nothing more from you, Mister Bissell, I take it?'

Bissell shook his head, smiling a parsimonious smile. 'Not today, your Honor,' he said. 'Next week, I guess, unless Mister Merrion changes his mind, I'll have something more to bring before you. But no further business today.'

The judge nodded. 'Very well, then, we're adjourned. Liz, you are through for the day.'

Bissell followed Robey to and through the doorway leading into the judge's office, Elizabeth Gibson with her machine three steps behind; Merrion and Cohen were halfway there when the judge, still in her chair, halted all of them by saying: 'Oh, Geoff, before you go, just one other thing I thought of here.' Then as they all froze in mid-stride, she said: 'No, no, all the rest of you can go. This's another matter that I need to talk about with Geoff. Nothing to do with the rest of you. This's about the *real* headiest game: I want to talk to him about basketball.'

Cohen started back toward the table; the others resumed their departures. She gestured toward the door and nodded at him. He stepped over silently and shut it, returning to the table. He sat down again, looking quizzical.

'If this's about the Sanderson drug case,' he said. She shook her head inquiringly. 'Julian Sanderson? Cocaine? You drew it this week, I think.'

She shrugged. 'I think Sandy might've mentioned something about you diversifying into drugs,' she said.

'Yeah,' he said, 'well, I am, a little, but not with that case. I tried to make it clear to that new clerk in the magistrate session – who doesn't seem awesomely bright, by the way – I was just there for arraignment. Coincidentally, he's the golf pro Bissell mentioned, has to moonlight tending bar but makes thousand-dollar campaign donations? Haskell Sanderson's son. I cut the deal for the two smart-ass kids from Cannonball's who make the case against him. I think I might have a conflict of interest representing the Sanderson kid. Too bad; nice fee in that case.'

'Well, that wasn't what I had on my mind,' the judge said. 'Isn't that Bissell a stinker, though? *Gracious*, what a *son* of a *bitch*. I *hated* to do what I did.'

'Yeah, Barrie, I know,' Cohen said. 'But I couldn't blame you. You had no choice in the matter.' He chuckled. 'When you asked me what I had to say, I had the feeling there was one person in the room who was hoping even more'n my client and I were that I'd be struck with some blinding flash of genius that'd vaporize Brother Bissell, and that was you.'

She laughed. 'Not far wrong,' she said. 'But look, I don't want to have to do next week what it looks like I'm going to have to, if things remain as they are. Put your man in jail.'

'Ahhh,' Cohen said, 'I doubt it'll come to that. I'm going to call Bob Pooler, I get back to my office, tell him what a box that prick Bissell's put us in. See if he'll try to persuade Danny Hilliard to get ahold of Amby and convince him to talk. Pound it into his loyal old head there's no use *both* of them going to jail, and no way Amby can keep him out. And then do everything I can to make *sure* Bissell puts Amby on the stand at trial, so the best old friend an embattled politician ever had can lead that jury straight down the road to a sympathy-Not-Guilty, stick Bissell's case up his ass.'

'I think he could pull it off,' the judge said. 'Let a jury watch Bissell strut around the courtroom for a week, they may acquit on the stairs. But I need more than your *doubt* that what I'm afraid of next week won't happen. I'm going to let Sandy know I'd better not draw Dan Hilliard's case. I'm not going to tell him the actual *reason*, but he'll know I'm depending on him to make sure it doesn't happen.'

'Well,' Cohen said, 'you could always recuse yourself.'

'If I did,' the judge said, 'I'd have to give a reason; we aren't supposed to duck cases. And it couldn't be that once you were my lawyer. You've already heard what Bissell said: the government doesn't mind that. That leaves me with only one reason, which I do *not* care to state publicly.'

'Oh yeah,' Cohen said. 'I forgot.'

'I don't want to be on "Oprah",' the judge said. 'I never told Eric about my fling with Danny. Don't know why, I just never did. I've never known whether you didn't know about Danny and me when you were representing Danny's wife, long before I hired you, or did but kept it quiet because you and Sam Evans're gentlemen. Did Sam protect me on that?'

'I thought you said what you wanted to talk to me about wasn't the matter you just heard,' Cohen said, amused.

'I said I wanted to talk to you about basketball,' she said, 'and that was the truth. This *is* a story about basketball, and I want you to listen carefully, so you'll be able to repeat it to your client before he meets the grand jury.

'This was some years ago now, when Eric and I'd decided we were going to get married, and I took him home to Fairmont, to meet my mom and dad. That's the fancy colony where they lived then, mostly top Ford honchos, outside of Detroit. This was before he retired and they moved to Santa Fe. Then he was still working for the Pistons. It was Christmas-time, and my dad and Eric and I were sitting around in the TV room after dinner and there was a game on, Lakers and Celtics. Bird and Magic; Magic and Bird: world was much younger then.

'Eric, being your normal artist, didn't know much about sports. Isn't really interested in any sport he isn't good at. He'll *play* basketball with me any old time I want, shoot a few hoops in the driveway – which I find I do about every four or five years now, but used to three times a week. He was humoring me; I knew that and I was grateful. Anyway, he's not keen on watching things he doesn't do, reads or leaves the room, but that night he was on his best behavior, and the game was on. It was a good one, and I forget what it was but someone did something that made Dad say: "Look at *that*." I don't remember which player did it or what color he was, but it was impressive – we'll say it was Kevin McHale. And my father said – you know my father's white, don't you? I know I told you that, you were getting me divorced.'

'Maybe,' Cohen said. 'That was also a long time ago. But if you did I wouldn't've seen it had any bearing on the case, so it wouldn't've stuck.'

'Well, *I* thought it did,' she said, 'and that was because *Ray* thought it did. He never believed I was leaving him because he was kissing Whitey's ass all the time and I couldn't stand it any longer. He said *I* was the one who groveled for white folks, and *that* was why I was leaving him for Eric: "because Eric is white." If he'd known about Danny he would've said "Danny." Raymond said I was attracted to white men because my *father's* white, and subconsciously I've been trying to get in bed with him all along. Raymond took his college psych courses much too seriously.'

'Oh yeah,' Cohen said, 'now I remember. That was the time you socked him.'

'Well, it was more like a slap,' she said.

'Made his nose bleed,' Cohen said. 'Cost you, I figure, five or ten thousand dollars, off the top of the property settlement. Have that little item come out in court, that a Butler, Corey partner whacked her poor defenseless husband on the snoot? Warren Corey would've been simply *ecstatic*.'

'It was worth it,' she said. 'Anyway, Ray really needed the dough more'n I did. He lost his shirt on that silly racetrack. The others got fleeced too, but they could afford it. Ray was in over his head.'

'The basketball game,' Cohen said, prompting. 'Come on, I've got a hot desk to slave over up in South Hadley today.'

'Right,' she said. 'Whoever it was and whatever he did, I know it was one of the forwards, made some move and Daddy said: "Now, look at that. That's something I never could do. I just didn't have it in me." And then he started in on how people were always feeling sorry for him, he played before the big money, and he said: "Hell no, I was lucky I played when I did. If I were the right age now to be playing ball, I wouldn't be playing at all. I wouldn't be good enough.

'"When I came into the league, black men weren't allowed to: segregation. It wasn't *right* that I could play, but that was the way it was, and I wasn't the one who'd made it that way. Bird can play today, and so can McHale, and both of those guys're white, but like all of the white guys playing today, they are truly exceptional players. 'Exceptional' 's not what I ever was. 'Pretty good' is what I was.

'"When I retired, I wasn't *all* washed up. I still had a year or so left. But I saw those kids coming along, wonderfully smooth, fluid players, and I knew what I wanted to do. I didn't want to play ball *against* those guys; I wanted to watch *them* play ball, help the team adapt to the times. I'd played in the time that I had to play in, and when it was over, I stopped."'

Judge Foote smiled at Cohen, gnawing on her lower lip, making her eyes twinkle, too. 'Think you can remember that, long enough to tell it to your client?'

'I think so,' Cohen said, smiling back.

'Because I really don't want to have to put your man in jail, Geoff,' she said. 'I don't want to give Mister Bissell the satisfaction, but mostly I just don't want to put Ambrose Merrion in jail for Thanksgiving. It isn't the right thing to do. He's in the same position that my father was, and he has to see it. The game that he and Danny played has changed. It's time for him to stop playing.

'He won't like it. He'll resist. But he looks to me as though he's smart enough to see that, if you push him. They've changed the rules on him; the old code's been repealed. Let the new nasty boys carve their moral arrogance into someone else's tough old hide. I like your idea a lot. Pump him up to testify and help Bissell get himself way out on the limb of his indictment. Then at trial ram it right up his ass. Make him see he can go out with a bang.'

'And that isn't *fighting*?' Cohen said, standing up.

Judge Foote stood up. She extended her hand. 'Well, maybe a little,' she said, 'fighting in a different way.'

Cohen shook her hand. 'Very good,' he said, 'and I'll tell you something too. Sam Evans did *not* know about your frolics with Danny. He said he'd forbidden Danny to come clean with him, give him a list of his girlfriends. He said to me: "He understands that's information I don't want to have, and you're not getting it either, no matter what we have to do."'

For a moment the judge said nothing. Then she said: 'So there're at least four of you left; that's good to hear. Sam is a real gentleman.'